# THE PIRATE LAFFITE

## LEGENDS OF NOLA

### BOOK THREE

## Other Books by the Author

LEGENDS OF NOLA SERIES

*The Lake,* Book One

*Lovers in Stone*, Book Two

Coming Soon
*Enemies and Allies,* Book Four

Published under the name Susan Elliston

*The Wardrobe*

*There's No Explanation*

# THE PIRATE LAFFITE

## LEGENDS OF NOLA

### BOOK THREE

A Historical Time Travel Adventure

BY

# D.S. ELLISTON

Elliston Entertainment • Florida

The Pirate Laffite

ISBN# 978-0-9854801-6-5
Copyright © 2020 D.S. Elliston
Published by Elliston Entertainment

Cover Image: Dylan Daniels
Cover and Book Layout/Design by The Book Team
ISBN 978-0-9854801-6-5  (Original Paperback)
First Paperback Edition: November 2020

Contact the author
On Facebook:
https://www.facebook.com/Author-DS-Elliston-287604241632452/

Book Series on Facebook:
https://www.facebook.com/Legends-of-NOLA-149136808530163/

Twitter: @Ldylstn

NOTE—ADULT CONTENT: Book contains profanities, harsh language, violence, and sexual abuse and is intended for adults.

THIS BOOK IS DEDICATED TO:

DRENA ANN

My Lady,

Time is as fluid as the sea I sailed upon. Its currents like the days washing you along on life's journey. The kindest, most beautiful gift time ever deposited upon my shore was you. The cruelest its waves ever became was the day it swept you from my life. And now it seems, in its grandest moment, I am to be put adrift in the mystery of its depths. Or rather, set free to sail upon heaven's ocean above.

Upon which star I wonder, will I wash ashore? Wherever time and tide take me, I go full of love and in peace. Let me no longer be an anchor to you. Instead, let the memory of us calm your soul, and set you free to sail the most glorious ocean of them all . . . the one called life.

*Jean Laffite*

"He left a Corsair's name to other times,
linked with one virtue, and a thousand
crimes."


~ Lord Byron

# ✑ One ✑

Beyond the strait and as far as the eye could see, lay a secluded bay. The surface of the vast expanse of deep-blue water shimmered in the morning sun, sparkling as if covered in a myriad of small diamonds. This spectacular surface was broken up only in the shallows, where tracks of pampas grasslands grew. Along the bay's distant shoreline, and even closer to where Tori stood on the deck of Laffite's ship, were numerous large swampy areas, each crisscrossed by smaller waterways. Surrounding the bay were oaks and cypress trees, all of which were graced by long grey strands of Spanish moss. Below these trees walked the long-legged grey birds that Tori loved to watch. They were cranes, or possibly, herons; she could not be sure which.

Much of the surrounding area along the Gulf shores was overgrown and formidable looking. To Tori, the tangled greenery looked like an impenetrable wall that had been planted to create a hostile barrier, instead of a natural occurrence. It was a wild environment, filled with dark shadows and unfriendly creatures.

A few open sunny areas, along the shoreline, held narrow strips of sandy beaches that ended, where the thick underbrush began. The sun's rays dimmed in the shadows, nature's colors were muted, and the air stilled among the twisted mangrove roots. Those areas were foreboding to look upon and stood like a warning to any who dare venture ashore.

Laffite had been smart to make this his home base. Tori also knew it was not the only place in this region to which he could lay claim, though. A blacksmith shop, in the city of New Orleans, was also connected to him. This French Quarter cottage remained standing in her time and functioned as a local bar. A bar she had last visited with Dan. Quickly, Tori pushed the images of that night away. Her reason behind this seemed simple enough and valid in her mind. Tori knew if she mentioned any facts about Jean's cottage, the pirate would demand to know how much more his lady knew of his era and him, and she wasn't ready to divulge that yet, if ever. Already the pirate had been told too much by her. Not about himself, or his part in history, but she had talked for hours about things that, looking back, she maybe should have kept to herself. It was too late to change now but not too late to be far more discreet about what she revealed.

As for right then, Tori knew she was about to embark on a new adventure. The female from the future would soon go ashore, and from there, she'd make her way toward the destination that held the key to her returning home. An uncontrollable shudder shook her, and her hands gripped the railing as she took a deep breath. At long last, after enduring so much, the final steps toward going back to her own time were finally within reach.

A surge of excitement filled her as she painstakingly went over the facts as she understood them. Tori knew that the lake held the key to the strange anomaly that had brought her back in time. That time warp was for her, the only way home, and knowing it worked in both directions assured her that there was a way to escape. Her proof of this had been revealed after the truth of the teenager Tommy had come to light. As a three-year-old toddler, the slave had gone forward from this period, just as quickly as she had slipped backward in time. The only difference was Tommy had no memory of the family he lost, or of this era. Tori, on the other hand, remembered everything and everyone from the future. For Kate's son, it had meant freedom; for her, it had meant captivity. Tori had been trapped in a time she did not belong in. She'd been held against her will, then taken further and further away from her only chance of escape. No more though, the time of moving in the wrong direction was over for her. Every step since leaving the island had been with one goal in mind. Tori was going home one way or another and hopefully sooner than later. Her heart skipped a beat, and again, she shuddered.

She squeezed her eyes shut and opened them slowly while allowing her emotions time to calm themselves. The modern-day female felt trapped standing there on Laffite's ship with no way to begin her journey toward Leone's plantation. It was a horrible feeling and one that she tried to overcome. The truth, though, was hard to face. Once on land, did not mean freedom; she'd have no place to run, let alone know in what direction to go or how to navigate her way. Without the pirate, she'd be lost. This thought sobered her, and her uncontrollable excitement began waning, as the actual realization of her exact predicament sank in. What happened to her next was entirely up to Jean and entirely out of her hands. Could she trust the pirate to do as he said he would? "Of course, I can," she mumbled. Knowing the man as she did, he would keep his word to help her, she assured herself. Besides, if he didn't, she had a back-up plan. This consisted of using his second-in-command. Dominique had sworn to assist her in anything she required. If Laffite backed out, Tori would take Dominique into her confidence, and once he believed her story, he'd help her. After all, she'd saved his life and his arm. Ever since then, he'd repeatedly explained how much he owed her. It was a debt that, in his opinion, could never be fully repaid. Tori shrugged her shoulders and softly uttered her response to the old pirate's thoughts on the matter. "Well, you are wrong in that department. I have one way you can repay me if needed."

Thinking of the two men, Tori turned and looked towards the ship's helm and to the man standing by Jean's side. The grey-haired scruffy seadog had become very dear to her in the last few weeks and often teased his much younger captain just for fun. Tori grinned because, as of late, Dominique had taken her side no matter what she said, right or wrong. It was because of this that it had become a challenge to see just how far she could push Laffite before he stormed off. Verbally sparring with the handsome pirate was pure entertainment and had helped pass the time, as they sailed to where they were now anchored in the Gulf. However, the trip was at an end, and no matter what, all entertainment would have to wait; problems would have to be faced and plans carefully thought out. Things were about to get deadly serious.

Maybe it was best that they had not set out for the city so quickly. The lake was not going anyplace, just like her complicated negative thoughts and emotions. This time could be used to make good decisions and sort through all the problems that might arise to prevent her return trip home. Home, the future, her family…she felt the pangs of fear returning. There were just so many problems to deal with. The most complicated problem was Leone. Tori had no doubt he thought of her as a murderous fancy. What choice would the man have had but to believe what he'd been told? She had killed his Kate and the overseer, or so he'd been led to think, by his twisted brother, Edward. Why would Leone ever listen to her, let alone believe what happened, after he rode away from his plantation, on that fateful morning? The only people he'd believe, who knew the truth, were dead. Edward, of course, knew, but would never tell, and knowing this had left her fearing for her life. That fear had made her run and look where that had landed her. A flash of the past few months raced in her mind until she forced the images to stop, telling herself that everything had worked out and now with Jean's aide, the trip back along the river road to the Duval plantation could begin.

A frown crossed her brow. She'd need Leone's permission to visit his plantation because there didn't seem a way to achieve her goal of reaching the cove without it.

Not wanting to think about things she could not change, Tori, who was now full of trepidation, turned to look out over the water. Her gaze fell on the settlement that would soon become her new home, but for how long? She sighed and whispered her thoughts under her breath. "Temporary Home, nothing more or less, and the shorter the visit, the better."

Tori glanced toward the helm and caught sight of the captain.

Laffite had complicated things when he had declared his feelings of love, and even though she told him repeatedly that she could never return his affections, he had continued to hold out hope. Tori saw it in his eyes and in the way, he looked at her sometimes. It was breaking her heart that Jean felt so, but there was nothing she could do to help him. She had to go home to her own time, and the pirate had to remain here, in his.

Watching him standing there on deck, Jean did present the image of a dashing pirate. The way he was dressed, right down to his rugged appearance, oozed sex appeal, and Tori found herself wondering when they went ashore, would he change once again into the so-called 'Gentleman Pirate' she had grown to know in the islands? There, Jean had always been impeccably groomed and dressed in the finest of outfits. Over the past months, she'd witnessed how he morphed easily between two completely different looks and different personalities. The gentleman's side of him was so unlike how he was right then. The man was dressed in his pirate garb as she called it, unshaven, with his hair pulled back and covered by a bandanna. His voice barked out orders, and his eyes flashed as he observed his crew. Tori grinned, knowing there could be no denying, both figures, the gentleman and the pirate, were sexy as hell. At least she could admit that much to herself. So, whichever he chose to be, she did not care, so long as he kept his word and took her to the lake at Leone's plantation. The lake was the key to her returning to her own time, an era where her daughter lived, where Dan waited, and where she belonged. Briefly, she squeezed her eyes closed and tried to keep her emotions under control. 'The lake was the only way home.' There it was again; how many times had she reiterated that thought over the months? How many times today had the words, 'the lake was the only thing that mattered,' filled her head? Sadly, Tori shook her head. If she were going to continue to think about nothing else, it would cloud her judgment and drag her emotions to the point of sheer terror, as it had earlier. So much could go wrong, she understood that, and always at the back of her mind was the nagging thought, 'what if it didn't work? What if there was no going back, what then?'

The worried female looked away from the crew, and their captain, afraid he might catch her staring at him. He knew her pretty darn well by now and would see the worry in her expression. The last thing she needed was for him to begin a barrage of questions, of which she had no intention answering. Far better, she returned to her scrutinizing of the encampments and the secluded bay beyond. It would take her mind off problems that she did not want to face or have answers too, so again she gazed at the sandy beaches and the village beyond.

The sight before her was now viewed calmly and with a fresh point of view. Tori began studying and learning, doing what she should have been doing all along, instead of just amusing herself, to kill time until they disembarked. She'd learned the hard way that every detail could turn out to be essential in this day and era, and nothing should or could be ignored. Knowledge was power, and Tori intended to gain as much of both as possible. With those two items in her possession, she had control, and when she was in control, mistakes were less likely to befall her.

The inquisitive female gazed at the bay and beyond the narrow strait between Grand Isle and Grand Terre. What had she learned, and more importantly, would the information be of any use? Tori scanned the shoreline and beyond. The woman knew here in this period; only a few smaller ships had room to anchor in the bays sheltered waters. The vast expanse inside Barataria, Tori had been told, was far too shallow for large vessels to navigate, and she believed it too, be an accurate evaluation. Dominique had explained the layout of the waters to her, as they had approached Grand Terre, and as far as she knew, the man never lied. The smaller crafts he pointed out, those with one or two sails, needed only nine to ten feet of draft, or less, to maneuver rapidly across the water. These vessels could easily skip over shallows and do so swiftly from island to island, while the larger ships could never travel to such locations, without fear of running aground.

The deck of the ship lifted on a larger swell, and Tori looked at the movement the wave caused between the strait. The tide was coming in, and the sun having passed noon, was lower on the horizon, its light making the white sandy beaches glisten. Unlike the quiet and tranquil interior of the bay beyond, the beaches on both sides of the inlet were a buzz of activity. They had been all day. Two vessels had docked within hours of each other, and men alongside women, worked hard to unload the spoils that the ships had taken. The shouting of orders, from the decks to the shore, often rang out, and Tori wondered how often this same activity occurred? Maybe if it happened often enough, she could use the hustle and bustle to her advantage and slip away, escape the pirate compound via one of the smaller boats and sail across the bay toward New Orleans? It was an idea that could hold some merit and something to consider if Jean did not keep his word.

Just then, the sound of laughter echoed across the sea, and Tori looked toward the place where the noise emanated. It came from where the men on shore unloaded Laffite's goods from the barges that traveled back and forth, from ship to shore. Now and then, one or more of the crew would look toward her. They would wave, before happily returning to their task. No doubt, they were talking about their unusual passenger, who had sailed with them. It was flattering in one way but also a bit unnerving. She'd not spoken to Jean about her fears or how they would handle her arrival back on land, where she was a wanted woman; a woman, she told herself, that had no way of proving the murders were not her fault. Of course, if caught, she'd have to admit to one of them because truth be told, she had killed Jack Kane, but not her friend Kate. A shiver ran up and down her body. Again, the horrid memory had found its way to rear its ugly head.

"Damn and blast it, not again. Just deal with what you cancontrol," Tori hissed quietly to herself. Her hands gripped the railing again as her thoughts continued to race. True, she was safe now, standing on the ship's deck, but after they left, then what? If someone were to mention her by name and that bit of news spread to New Orleans? What if someone remembered her, as the fancy whore who had escaped Roses, or worse still, what if Edward were to learn she was with Laffite? "There I go again, thinking the worse, and worrying over something I have no control over. I have to stop it, and I have to break my habit of talking out loud to no one but myself." She chewed on her lower lip, thinking about how she could stop yapping away like she so often did? In the end, the frustrated female decided the best way to do that was to keep her mind occupied.

Tori slowly scanned the area where the pirates were picking up their captain's contraband. She concentrated on watching where they were carrying all the goods, but once the men left the beach, she could no longer keep track of them. Gauging the direction in which they headed and squinting her eyes, Tori tried to see beyond the trees. Standing on tiptoes for a better view finally paid off. The curious female caught sight of a few small cottages, and just past those were large barn-like buildings that she had not noticed before. These buildings could only be glimpsed when the scrub oaks, all of which leaned and pointed inland, shifted in the afternoon breeze. It was an onshore wind that blew right then, and by looking at the trees odd angle, Tori guessed that it blew most of the time in that direction. This sight was good news for her, for the coastal breeze would keep the island cooler, and lower temperatures were a most welcome gift. Not that she needed the weather to change right then. Tori was pleased with the temperature at present, and the bright blue skies were perfect. No clouds meant no storms, and that was great because she'd had enough of stormy conditions in the last few months to last a lifetime.

IT was the end of September 1810, and the summer heat would soon be slipping away. According to Jim, one of the crew members, this was a fact. Jim talked with her often and had kept her company when Jean or Dominique were otherwise occupied. Without his friendship, her journey would have been far more frightening. They had gone through so much side by side. His words were honest, to the point, and she always knew where she stood with him. When he told her winter on Grand Terre was warmer than in the city of New Orleans itself, she believed him. A smile slipped across her lips. It was, as he put it, the best time of the year to be home. Little did he know, anytime would be the right time for her, but not for Grand Terre, that was not home. Not a permanent one, at least. Thinking of the pirate stronghold as a home was about as foreign as she was to this era. What would it be like living among the notorious group of smugglers? Would she be welcome and more important, could she trust any of them? Laffite and his crew were one thing but mingling with men who had reputations that were far from desirable, that was something else.

Tori stood up on tiptoe and was trying to get a better view again when Jean joined her, slipping his arm around her waist. "I assume by your actions that you are trying to see my home. I can alleviate your curiosity; you can't see the house from this standpoint. It is set back in that direction." He pointed in the opposite direction from where she'd been looking. "And over there, where you were looking, are the largest structures in the village. I know you have spotted those; one can hardly miss them. Those are the warehouses that hold everything one could dream of. Now, they have British sails and goods, to add to the collection."

He was still grinning when Tori frowned and sternly added her thoughts on the subject. "Not slaves, though, right? You can't sell those poor souls into slavery, the blacks taken from the British. It was not their fault they were caught, and you know how I feel."

Jean's expression went serious as his fingers played with his goatee. "We will talk about that later. I told you the Africans would be taken care of, and they will. After all, I agree that selling slaves is not right." His hand dropped to his side as he turned to face the shore. He was not comfortable with the subject of slavery and set about changing the line of conversation, hoping she would not realize what he was up too. "Now, just think about all that I hold in storage that you can inspect. None of it alive, I might add," he chuckled.

Tori could very well imagine what his horde would look like, but it did not change the fact that even with his privateer papers, all of it was contraband, spoils taken from many different ships, whose fate only a few knew. That thought briefly tempered her enthusiasm. The image of the British ship he had crippled in the water did not sit so well, now that they were safely home. Had the crew of the English vessel made it to a safe port? Although she despised them for using the cover of selling slaves to spy, part of her hoped so.

Their captain had been a despicable character, who ruled by fear and brutality, that much had been apparent. At least some of his crew had escaped him and joined them. These men were free of the fate that had faced their former shipmates, who had remained aboard the crippled British vessel. Yet, they now faced another life, just as dangerous. They were pirates and wanted men by the navy they had deserted. What kind of freedom was that?

Jean missed her somber expression as he leaned his head closer to hers and continued to explain his business to her proudly. "I have everything stored in them from flour to fabrics. There are bolts of both cotton and silk. All of it, every inch, excellent material for gowns, I might add, some of which I intend to keep for you." He winked and pulled her closer. "There are barrels of rum, whiskey, and many bottles of liquor, such as brandy and still more bottles of wine." He tossed his head back and laughed. "I have paintings, furniture, fine china, and even some pistols. For those who have no need or desire for such weapons, I have broad- swords, knives, and even a small cannon or two. Indeed, there is quite an assortment of items. I also know that Beluche, one of my trusted captains, brought in a cargo of exquisite carpets from the Far East just before I set sail. India, I assume, was their place of origin. They came off a British ship, that much I do know. 'East India Company' was stamped on crates of tea, a company that I can say in all certainty is English. I was told the crates came off that the very same boat. I think I shall have to give the tea away, not many English here, a few, but lord, I have years' worth of the stuff. Now, the carpets are a different matter and will fetch a handsome price at auction."

As he was telling her all this information, Tori remembered her days touring Louisiana. During those times, she had learned that the pirates would often hold an auction in an area they named 'The Temple.' In her time, there were airboat tour guides that even claimed, Laffite, the pirate, had a treasure buried somewhere around the bayou area, and Tori wondered if she dared ask him if that legend was true?

Airboats and pirate stories were things of the future, though, and she needed to keep her mind on the present. It was imperative that she remain focused. Tori needed to pay attention to what Jean was saying, and not because he was proud of his accomplishments, but because all information, each detail could turn out to be helpful for her plan to succeed. All she wanted was to escape this horrible 1810 and go back, or more precisely, forward into the 1990s.

The pirate broke her train of thought when his lips brushed her cheek close to her ear. She felt his hot breath against her skin as he softly spoke the next bit of information. "We hold auctions regularly, and the people come to sample and buy what is up for sale. They arrive by boat, carriage, and horseback, or by any means they can. Some even walk to the place where we hold our auctions. All come in hopes of purchasing a prize or to simply have a grand time, and maybe meet me." His grin was inscrutable, and his eyes sparkled with mischief. "The day is an entertaining event of illegal shopping for all to enjoy." He laughed aloud at the expression on her face.

Tori did not want Jean thinking he had impressed her, so she changed her tactics and turned the tables on the privateer. "Jean, I knew it, you are a pirate after all. Illegal indeed! All that booty is stolen, and from more than just the Spanish and English. You just admitted as much to me, so see, I am correct…pirate."

"I beg to differ, madame, pirate indeed. I will have you know, I never take from an American ship, and as you have seen, I have my papers, so I can now raid ships listed as a privateer. A privateer, I say. Only a true pirate would raid American ships while living amongst its people, and therefore, it clears me of such a distinction. Besides, what I do, it is only a little illegal. I also assure you, that like myself, many more of my captains also intend, if they have not already done so, to acquire such papers. Soon there will be few if any pirates in our ranks."

Dominique joined them and laughed as he watched Tori's expression. He could see she was both impressed and torn between what was right and what was wrong. Wanting to help his captain impress her more, he added his bit of information. "I shall explain to you, my dear, how Boss gained his power and his wealth. Boss is not one to, how can you say in English? Ah, yes, brag about his power or wealth. Let alone tell how it came to be. I shall explain, no?" He spread his arms, dramatically, while facing the shore and began in a voice that sounded very genuine. "Boss, he took a group of unorganized men, women, and their families, and turned them into a smuggling band of well-disciplined men, women, and children." His arms dropped to his side as he looked toward Jean. "He became their leader, known as 'Boss,' and won their loyalty, a year or so ago. You have no need to worry your pretty head, as Boss here, is not considered by the upstanding people of the city, to be anything like his men. True, many of the citizens in our homeport are coarse, uneducated and would slit their mother's throats for a prize, and no ship sails safely in the waters we have just left behind us, because of Boss's men. Ah, there are many captains who would love to be Boss, but only Jean Laffite holds the title. Maybe a few will challenge him, perhaps not? Wise if not." Dominique thought for a second before continuing. "Here, he lives by a different code than in the city. Ah, but in the city, there, he is accepted and plays the role he is best suited to play. In New Orleans, he is respected and treated as a true gentleman. The ladies of society would have it no other way," he laughed. "Why, the very chance to claim Jean Laffite as a guest in their homes, it is considered quite a coup," he chuckled.

Jean shot Dominique a nasty look at this outburst, one that cut short his belly laugh and sent him scurrying off. Tori, who loved Dominique's sense of humor, jabbed Jean in the ribs with her elbow. "Now, why on earth did you do that? Even in my own time, it's no secret that you were quite a lady's man. Jean, you should be ashamed of yourself."

Laffite did not know how to react to this, or to her having caught him glaring at his second-in-command. His only defense was to try and change the subject. "Ah, my lady, you and I could stand here and discuss this matter for hours. However, that is about how long it will take for me to settle my ship and its men. As I suggested before, you might take this time to go below and rest. Then, when all is completed, I will escort you ashore."

"I don't care what you want," she grinned playfully. "I think I will join Dominique, and his hurt feelings, while you do whatever it is you do. Now, go on with you." She pushed him toward the front of the ship, giggling as she did so. As tired as Tori was, she did not feel anywhere close to needing a rest. Besides, if she went below, she'd miss all the action, something the lady was not willing to do.

Twice after that encounter, Jean asked her to wait below deck until the ship's unloading finished. However, she had remained stubborn as ever, and with her new ally Dominique by her side, Jean lost the argument and gave up trying to persuade her.

THE hour was getting late, and Jean was finally ready to disembark. Slowly he approached Tori, and before she knew he was there at her side, he whispered in her ear. "It is completed. I am ready at last to escort you ashore. You, however, are far from ready, I see."

"I am so. What's wrong? I have been ready for hours."

"Madame, I will not escort you ashore, while you are attired, as you are. My crew and I may have grown accustomed to your breeches," his hand slapped her rear. "Nice as it is, I, however, must insist that you change. This attire is not befitting a lady, and a gown will draw less attention, far less than you in boots and dressed as a man. If you choose to remain as you are, I shall leave without you. After all, you are perfectly safe on my ship, well, almost."

He was grinning, but the expression in his eyes told her a different story. Jean had meant what he said, a dress would be worn, or she was doomed to stay aboard, and realizing this fact, she had no other choice but to give in to his demands.

Without a word, the frustrated woman turned and left to go below to the cabin. The man had won this argument quickly, but not without a quip from Dominique. The older man was about to climb over the railing of the ship when he stopped. "So, the pup has to use blackmail to have his way," he said, laughing heartily. "For me, she does anything. For you, tiz different, no?" He did not stay to listen to his captain's answer. Instead, he joined the last of the men, who were disappearing over the ship's side, all of whom were laughing at the conversation between Boss and Dominique.

"Don't worry," called one of the men to Jean. "We'll see you later." With those final words, the men climbed down the ship's side, which for the most part, was covered by a generous expanse of rope netting. This netting resembled a web and functioned as a large ladder, allowing more than one man at a time to climb on its strands. Using this network of rope facilitated the quick unloading of items that could be carried down to the waiting barges. At any given time, one could see crewmen climbing upward empty-handed, as others passed them with precious cargo, strapped safely to their backs. If any item was small enough, or comfortable enough to manage, this was how it left the ship. More substantial pieces were lowered by a pulley system that supported one of many huge nets, which lifted and hauled the objects over the side. The biggest of crates or barrels moved in this manner were lowered carefully to one of the more massive barges, which to Tori resembled big square boats. These specially crafted vessels had sides, two, sometimes three-foot-high encompassing them. The frame-like structure surrounding the barge stopped water sloshing over the flat bottom. It also kept the cargo from sliding off into the water. Men from the shore crewed these vessels, and they were skilled at their job. Tori witnessed this ingenious method of transporting the goods from ship to shore and supposed they had come up with the system out of necessity, as there were no piers and no docks. Unloading in New Orleans would have been far easier and less dangerous, but that would mean the taxman would be watching. The tradeoff, therefore, seemed to be necessary and well worth the risk.

THE crew had departed, knowing the final joke was on their captain, as Dominique had arranged. Laffite had never rowed himself ashore. It was not that he wasn't capable. It was more of a pride issue. Jean gave commands, and his crew followed. On this note, Dominique had pointed out to the men; he had outsmarted Boss. Laffite had forgotten to give orders about rowing him and his lady ashore. All had laughed as they quickly made their way to the beach, but none would linger on the sandy shoreline, to watch and see what would happen next. They were headed to a tavern for drinks which were on their captain, as custom, when returning home. To remain on the beach, they said, and miss out on free booze was madness. Besides, staying to watch how the Boss managed or not meant someone could be summoned by him, once he discovered their game, and none wanted to be the result of seeing the joke fail.

TORI entered the cabin and realized right away that two of her trunks were already gone. The one she needed, though, had somehow remained. A broad smile filled her face as she stood thinking. 'Oh, you're good, I'll give you that. A girl has to stay one step ahead of you to get her way, doesn't she?' It took her a few more seconds before she saw the dress on the bed, and no matter how angry she was at having to change out of her favorite outfit, a part of her enjoyed that Jean had taken the time to choose what she was to wear. Quickly and without any hesitation, she stripped out of her clothes and changed. Once finished, she packed away her breeches and boots and, last of all, the white shirt she had worn most days over the past few weeks.

The cotton was soft in her hands, and it had an odor of the sea about it. Surprising was the fact that it did not stink of sweat, rather it just a hint of lavender and lemon. With no deodorant to use, Tori had resorted to dousing her armpits with lavender water each day, after she'd rubbed her underarms with lemon. It was not a perfect solution, but it had sufficed.

Due to the number of days she'd worn the shirt, and considering the number of times it too had been washed, she reckoned the top had endured rather well. The garment was no longer white, for now it was dull gray, and yet it didn't matter to her, because it was an item she would cherish right up until the time she left this century. Tears welled up in her eyes, and not wanting to become too sentimental about it, she mumbled aloud, "Shame I can't take you with me as a souvenir, but that's how it is, how it must be. No room for being sentimental or being soft. In you go for now."

Tori folded the shirt and placed it in the trunk and lowered the lid before taking one last look around for any item she might have forgotten. Her eyes had acclimated to the dim interior, and she scanned the small confines without difficulty. Tori understood in her heart that this would be the last time she'd ever see this cabin. The woman would never forget the adventures she'd experienced aboard, most of which had been right there where she was standing. Running her hand along the top of Laffite's desk, she spoke softly. "I can't say I will miss you, and I can't say it was great. It has been memorable and that you can be sure of." Then without looking back, she left the small cabin and slowly closed the door behind her. Her time at sea was at an end. Now, whether she was ready or not, the next chapter of her life was about to begin. This one, on land, at the infamous pirate compound, called Grand Terre.

CORRECTLY dressed, Tori stepped out onto the deck and saw Jean, standing at the ship's side with his back to her. He was looking over the railing while laughing and shaking his head from side-to-side. He had not seen her yet, so Tori assumed that whatever had him in fits of laughter had to be below, on the water.

Without any hesitation, the curious female stepped quietly forward. The only way to find out what was going on was to look for herself. Quickly she joined him and looked down, expecting to see one of the crew, waiting in a rowboat. All she saw, however, was a wooden canoe, bobbing up and down on the waves. The small craft was tethered to the ship by a rope; that was fastened to the bottom of the netting, which hung against the ship's hull. As far as she could tell, that was all there was to see, and it didn't seem amusing at all. Somewhat perplexed, Tori turned to Jean, who was laughing even harder by her puzzled expression.

"Jean, what's so funny, I don't get it?"

"That is my dear," he said, pointing to the canoe. "I should have known better. I knew Dominique was up to something; just didn't know what. He's played jokes on me before, but this one has merit, and unlike many of his others, I never saw this coming."

"The canoe is funny? Forgive me, am I missing something here?"

"He left the pirogue for us, as you can see. It is not a rowboat, just a pirogue. Somewhat seaworthy and easy enough to handle if the water remains calm." He stopped laughing and continued more seriously. "The pirogue is used in the backwaters, not so much upon the waves of the Gulf. They tend to be somewhat precarious when handled by the likes of me. Not that I can't handle it, if I have too, and it seems my love, that if we are to go ashore, I am going to have to use my skills in the art of maneuvering over the waves; hopefully, keeping us dry in the process."

Tori looked back down at the wooden canoe he had referred to as a pirogue. Silently she watched as it continued to bob up and down. Then in almost a whisper, without looking at Jean, she spoke what was on her mind. "Surely, you don't expect me to climb over the side and climb down those ropes and then somehow manage to get into that bobbing cork?"

"I do, my lady," he chuckled.

"But, Jean, that's not fair. I'm in a dress, and besides, I don't think I can or will have the courage to climb down those ropes, even if the net-like mess does cover the whole damn side; so, no, I won't."

Laffite stopped laughing and spoke earnestly while squeezing her hands in his. "Tori, listen to me, you will. I shall go over the side first and help you. If you listen to my directions, both of us can, I assure you, end up in the pirogue and not the water." Then he began to laugh again, and to her surprise, Tori found herself joining him. He would never let her drown if she fell into the water, and if she went in, that meant he'd go in too. That idea amused her, and it helped ease some of the doubts that had swarmed about her.

"Well then, if I have to, let's go before I lose my nerve, and Jean, you leave Dominique, and his joke to me, okay? I will plan something that will make him pay for this, and if I fall, well, he had better be halfway to New Orleans when I step ashore."

Laffite laughed even louder as he swung his body over the side. "Poor Dominique, remind me never to get on your bad side. Come to think of it, I have been, and don't wish to be ever again. Now, it's not that hard; you find the rope with your feet, like so, and then grab hold of the rope and lower yourself down to the next footing, as you see me doing."

"Easy for you to say," she called down to him. "You're not wearing a silly dress and fancy little shoes. Shoes that I am going to drop into that canoe, and you are not going to say I can't. I have a better chance of not falling if I am barefooted. By the way, and for your information," she called down to him, "I hate this." Then she sat on the narrow ledge, with her feet hanging above the deck with her back to the water as she continued. "I have no bloomers on. So, you better keep your eyes on my feet and hands and not go looking up, where a gentleman is not supposed too. Got it?"

His roar of laughter echoed across the water, and Tori found herself grinning at the sound, that and the thought of the rogue pirate trying not to look up her dress. That idea was just hilarious. Knowing him as she did, he was sure to take advantage of her situation. This last thought had her chuckling even more. The man was impossible at times, and she had to admit it was part of his charm.

It was not easy removing her small shoes while keeping her balance on the narrow railing, but she managed. Looking down at the small wooden boat Tori called out, "Look out, incoming." With that, she dropped each shoe toward their intended target. Both landed as she had hoped but not before one had hit Jean's head on its way down. "I told you to look out."

"I was looking out. Out means that way," he pointed toward shore. "You should have said, look up. I would have seen what was coming, looking up."

Tori was enjoying this part of disembarking; so far, it had been a world of fun, but the fun part was over, and the daunting task of joining Jean now lay ahead of her. She had seen how the crew and Jean had placed their bodies across the narrow rail before lowering themselves. So, without hesitation, the extremely nervous woman leaned to the side and slid her hands along the railing. Once her shoulder touched wood, Tori rolled over until her stomach lay flat on top of the narrow surface. Then quickly, she raised her legs and swung them over the side and downward. In seconds, Tori found herself clinging with her hands, while her elbows rested on the top of the smooth wooden rail. Her chin balanced on the wood, while the rest of her body hung below her. Tori's chest was pressed tightly up against the side of the ship, and to her utter horror and surprise, her mind told her she was stuck. Rather than admit that she was frozen in fear at this point, the terrified woman told herself she'd done an excellent job thus far. After all, she had managed to let half of her skirt fall with her legs, and it was just enough to cover her upper thighs, but, if she tried to make any other movement, that situation might not continue, and she'd find herself mooning the shoreline. Mortified by this thought, and the spectacle she would present to anyone watching, well, it was enough to dampen her fears temporally. "You are keeping your eyes on my feet, right? I need to know where to put them; I can't feel the rope. Jean, do be a gentleman, not a randy pirate, got it?"

"Tori, if I had it, whatever it is, my hands would be full, and I would be in the water." He was laughing hysterically, and she was sure it was at her expense. No doubt he was hoping her ass would show any second, without a care of who else was watching.

"Jean, I'm floundering here. If I go in the drink, you will pay, and you better jump in after me, because I doubt I can swim in this getup. I mean it, Jean, and if my ass flashes the shoreline, you can bet I will make sure you don't get any tonight, or for who knows how long?" Tori was now committed to doing what Jean told her, as she did not have the strength to pull herself back up, and try as she could, her bare feet were still floating in the air below her. "Where's the damn rope? Stop your incessant laughing, you bastard and get up here and help me. I mean it. I can't find or feel the blasted line."

"Ah, but I feel you," came his response, sounding rather sexy, and not in the least bit worried. His hand was firmly around one of Tori's ankles, guiding her foot onto the rope's first line. "Nice piece of flesh, and no, I am not looking up your dress. Tempted, but not. I am too busy trying not to get kicked in the head."

"You are impossible; you know that. I have news for you, I can't let go. If I let go with one hand, I know I will slide over and off my perch here. If that happens, I will fall."

"Tori, you won't fall. Come on down here. I know you can do it. You simply have to move…"

"I know, hand-to-foot. God, I hate you right now. I mean it, and you wait until I get my hands, on Dominique. I am going to make him pay." With both feet balanced on the netting, she slowly lifted her head and lowered her body. Then before she could talk herself out of the next step in her climb, first one and then the other hand let go of the railing to grab the top of the net. Her fingers were grasping the first set of ropes so tightly that their tips were tingling. She could feel her feet balancing precariously on a set of rungs lower down, and even though; the net-like web moved around alarmingly, Tori was determined to accomplish the climb without screaming. "Besides, what choice do I have?" she mumbled. Once she moved a step-down, on the grid, as she now thought of it, Tori would wait until she felt Laffite's hand, firmly take hold of her ankle, and guide her foot to the next level. It was the moving of her hands that was the hardest to do.

Thinking about how high she was over the water was not an option; all she had to think about was her grip on the net and let Jean guide her the rest of the way. If Tori allowed panic to enter her mind, she'd freeze in position, until too tired to hold on, and that would result in her falling into the sea. Then another thought came. If climbing down a rope net was difficult, what had to come next terrified her. Climbing into that small wooden boat and doing so without flipping it over seemed impossible without tumbling into the water. Heaven help her if that should happen. Tori pictured trying to climb into a canoe, from out of the sea. Soaking wet, weighed down by her gown, the task would be next to impossible. "Shit! What the hell have you gotten me into this time? I never should have agreed to this." Tori realized she was far more than just a bit nervous; in fact, she was on the verge of pure terror. "Who gives a damn if I talk to myself. If talking out loud helps get me through this, then so what if I mumble out loud. I swear I will never try to stop talking to myself again. God, did you hear me?" Tori had loudly cried out her question, while looking at nothing but the ship's hull, inches away from her face.

Jean heard her panicked question and thought it best to make light of the situation. "God maybe didn't hear you, but I did. Could it be you are thinking of me as a God? Let's discuss that, once you are down here."

"We will not," she snapped, "and I swear if you don't stop your teasing when I do get down to you, I am going to push you into damn Gulf myself."

"Oh? Think about that. If I go into the water, who will row you ashore? And, if I try to climb back in, there is a good chance the pirogue will flip, and you will find yourself in my arms, struggling to stay afloat. Not a bad idea, come to think of it."

"Oh, just give me a break, why don't you?"

"I have no intention of breaking anything, let alone you. Come, let's not fool about as we are. We need you to reach the safety of the, what did you call it? Ah, yes, the bobbing cork."

After that exchange of words, Tori fell silent, and Jean's hand guided her feet each step of the way, carefully placing them into position after position. He'd tell her when to let go of the rope she had a hold of, and twice, he instructed her to reach still lower down, before grabbing hold of the next rung. Then, at last, he was telling her she had only one more step to take, and for Tori, it was a step that was far more terrifying than the climb down itself.

Unsteady on her feet and knowing she'd never been good at balancing, her hands held the rope in a vise-like grip, as she placed her feet on the bottom of the pirogue. It was then that Tori realized, the dumb craft, as she thought of it, would not remain still under her, and as long as it kept wobbling all over the place, she was determined not to let go of the ropes.

Jean had begun trying his best to keep the pirogue close to the hull of his ship and stop it rocking haphazardly, while he continued to coax her gently. However, Tori was not helping him accomplish his goal because she refused to let go of her grip on the netting. As her body leaned backward, her feet would push the pirogue toward the ship's hull; then, as she pulled herself back toward the side of the ship, her feet would push the pirogue in the opposite direction and away from the hull. Once this cycle of events were completed, to Tori's horror, they'd start all over again no matter what the pirate tried or said.

If these actions weren't bad enough, Tori realized the net was not secured in place, as she had thought. This development added to her problems, as the weight of her body pulled on the net when she leaned backward. This action would lift the rope ladder entirely away from the side before Tori could force herself to lean forward and fall back against the hull. Once flat against the ship, her feet would rock the pirogue beneath her and begin to push it away, tugging at her as it moved. All these actions made her act desperately, as she tried her best to keep her feet firmly planted where they were because she understood if she lost her footing, there was no way to hang onto the rope by her hands only. Her body weight was too much, and her strength was not enough to sustain her position of hanging in mid-air.

Jean knew he'd have to move fast, or they both would end up swimming. "Steady on there," he called out. "This pirogue is not as stable as it looks. I need you to let go. Come on, my love." With two steps, he raised himself out of the small bobbing vessel and reached for her with his free hand. He slipped his arm around her waist and pulled her toward him. "Now, move your hands one rung down as I lower us, and when I say, you trust me and let go."

Tori did not utter a word but followed the pirate's instructions. She knew she needed to place her feet back on the bottom of the pirogue again, that, and more. If they both were to remain dry, there was only one way. She'd have to trust the man who had hold of her.

"Tori, I am standing in the pirogue, but I want you safely sitting. I don't think you are too stable on your feet. Come to think of it, neither am I at this point."

"Oh, just shut the hell up. I didn't climb all the way down here, just to have you flip us over. Okay, here I go. I'll let go." Tori released her grip on the rope and quickly allowed Jean to guide her into position. Then to her utter surprise, she found herself sitting in the small craft. Once in place, the pirogue stopped its wild bouncing around, but that didn't make her feel any safer, so she reached out with both her hands and grabbed hold of the small wooden vessel's sides. It was then that Tori saw the water was way too close to the top of the canoe, and she realized if the waves started to slip over, and the sea got inside, they would sink long before reaching the shore. Tori looked up at the ship's side and wished she'd just stayed on board. If the stupid canoe sank, which seemed likely, everything she had just put herself through would have been for nothing.

Laffite sat down, facing her, and began untying the leash that had kept the craft by his ship's side. "Tori, we are stable; you don't have to cling to the sides. I seriously doubt we are going to end up swimming. Why one would think you do not know how to swim, the way you are carrying on, and we both remember, you can." He was smiling as he leaned toward her. "I hope madame, you think of something very befitting for my second-in-command and will allow me to know what it is."

"Oh, you can be assured, I will come up with a doozy, and I might let you in on it if you don't dump us over."

"Doozy? I won't ask, but I will do this." He leaned all the way forward and placed his lips on hers, which were trembling. Seconds after Jean's kiss ensued, Tori's hands left the sides of the pirogue, as he had hoped. Once she let go, he felt her arms wrap around him and cling tightly. He could feel her whole body shaking, and it was only then that he realized how scared she'd been and how brave she'd acted. More than that, he knew how much she trusted him because that was the only way she would have attempted to climb down the side of his ship. He also remembered her telling him once that she had a terrible fear of heights. What he had asked of her was a lot, and knowing she had faced her fears, trusted and followed him, well, he loved her even more.

Laffite let go of the small tie up and kept on kissing her, and by the time they broke their embrace and looked around, they saw that they had already drifted halfway to shore.

Jean chuckled. "Beats rowing for certain. But, as promised, I will take you to the safety of the beach as fast as I can." The pirate picked up the paddle and happily began to make their way to shore. "See, I can handle this kind of craft at sea. This is something that old Dominique was seemingly unaware of; that I could manage easily by myself. That rouge shall have to face you now, and I pity him."

THE encampment was set up very much like a small fishing village. Most of the first houses Tori saw were tiny and shack-like in appearance. These were the minority, though, because the further inland they walked, many more significant and permanent homes came into view. Most of these homes were constructed of ground-up oyster shells, stones, and plaster. Many were raised off the ground and were held steadfast on sturdy wooden stilts. Their roofs were made of wood and had shingles or just overlapping long planks. Some of the larger homes on stilts were built entirely of wood, and all those were raised still higher above the ground and had small verandas. Other dwellings were far more straightforward and made of bits of timber and palm fronds. These huts, which sat on the sandy ground, used fronds for their roof, and Tori knew that a strong storm would blow them entirely away.

"Jean, do men actually choose to live in such structures as those? I see sense in the homes that are raised, but those? One storm surge and they would be washed away" She was pointing to one of the shabbily built shelters with such a puzzled look about her that Jean almost wanted to smile. Her concern about things that should not matter to her amused him.

"Such small shelters are built by men who spend most of their time at sea. When they are ashore, most remain in establishments that you most certainly won't see the inside of."

"But surely if a storm were to hit, a strong wind would blow them away, even if the water did not flood them out and then what?"

"Then Tori, those affected would return to their ship or remain in one of the more permanent buildings, such as one of the taverns. To live as they do is their choice and causes little trouble. Others, as you see, prefer a more established home. On the other side of the strait, you would find it more so. On Grand Isle, many of the men and women intend to remain and make it their home. They can make a good living fishing and trading with those that come to buy what they offer. Fresh seafood for those in the city is always in high demand. Not everyone wants to spend their life taking foreign ships and their cargos. There are quite a few who are making a living for themselves, with occupations other than privateering."

It did seem he was telling the truth on that subject. Many small homes they passed by came with small gardens, and some had fresh coats of paint. They were family homes, not just pirate dwellings, too, for there were obvious signs indicating such. Numerous small children, some white, and still many more of mixed heritage, were happily playing together. To her, it quickly became evident that this place was far more than just a pirate's den as she had thought it would be, and realizing this; her anxiety began to fade.

When they passed by the last of the larger buildings, which were homes to crewmen and their families, Jean's tone changed from lighthearted to sounding more severe. He stopped walking and faced her with a somber expression. "Tori, what you have seen can be deceiving. It true, all you saw around you is quiet at this time. However, one can never know what will happen. This is why I need your word that once we reach our home, you will not venture out on your own. If you should wish to do so," he hesitated and looked directly into her eyes while raising one of his eyebrows, "you will be escorted by either myself or someone I assign." He placed his hand on the side of her face and gently let his fingers trace the outline of her cheek as he spoke. "I know how you can be, always wanting to see things in this time, for yourself, but on this subject, I must insist you listen. It's for your own safety, not to mention my sanity. If I catch you not doing as I have asked, I will take it upon myself to lock you in, and I mean it. This settlement is not a safe place, though

26

it should be, somewhat more stabilized than it used to be."

Assuming she wanted to know the details, he continued. "Not long ago, things around here were getting out of hand. We had too many leaders and not enough leadership. Everyone was working for another captain or themselves. I could see a different way, and that was when I established myself in the leadership role. There were quite a few who were not of the same mind. I was challenged one night in front of two enormously powerful and dangerous men. I have no doubt you will meet them soon yourself. Both are Italian and proud of it. One called Vincent Gambi, the other Chighizola. You'll know him when you see him." Jean grinned as he put his finger to his nose. "He carries the name of Nez Coupe', lost part of his nose in a fight, and he's none too friendly."

Tori was horrified and fascinated at the same time. He was telling her about historical characters, people that she would be meeting, and by the sounds of it, they were not a laughing matter.

"Those two, you have to watch out for, though, I think after I shot and killed the troublemaker in front of them, they will think twice before going up against me."

"You shot and killed a man just because he was a troublemaker?" She couldn't believe he could kill in cold blood. At least the man she knew wouldn't, but then, Tori realized there was much more to Laffite than she knew. He could kill, had killed. The battle at sea had shown her that, but to shoot a man in cold blood, just to make a point. If he did that, it made him a murderer and a bonafide pirate in her estimation. This realization caused her to take a step away from him.

"Ah, Tori, do not look at me like that. It had to be. This rabble of men needed a leader, and with Renato Beluche backing me, along with a few others, I only had the two Italian rebels to bring into line. You see, on this one occasion, they had formed a rather rowdy group and marched to my home to confront me. I had no choice but to take aim and draw blood. That is the only kind of law they understand. It stopped them, caused them to hesitate, and in their hesitation, I knew I had them. I invited a few inside, and before they left, I had formed a council and placed Gambi and old Nez Coupe' on it, along with Renato. Also, I added a gentleman, Jean Baptiste Sauvienet; he handles my finances, and of course, there is Dominique and myself. By forming this council, I was able to gain full control and bed down any contempt that could grow. Don't be fooled, though. There were still quite a few, who even after the event, felt it unfair, to say the least." He took her hand and began again to walk along the narrow dirt path.

Tori looked at Jean. "And they, whoever they are, would want to hurt me?"

"Not so much you, no, they would molest you for two reasons, first because you are a very desirable and beautiful woman. Second, you stand as a prize for their taking. They have no morals where females are concerned. Even if they understand that to so much as touch you will bring about a swift death, there are still those who might try. It would be a way to hurt me, don't you see?"

"I suppose I do. Still, I have not witnessed anyone looking at us other than with pleasant smiles and friendly greetings. Not one has shown any sign of disrespect that I have noticed at all."

"As I said, things are not always what you think." He stopped walking once again. "I shall tell you a story, which happened, shortly after I formed the council that will explain my position and control I have here. When any ship arrives with goods, and after the spoils are offloaded, the dangerous time begins. This is when the crew is paid by their captain. If there is a dispute, they bring it to my attention. That seldom occurs anymore. There is a fine for such action. Not a captain wants to be fined his share of the spoils for being greedy."

"Smart move. So, problem solved, right?"

"Not all problems are easily solved. When a ship arrives with a significant amount of gold, temptation arises; then, greed and anger is fast to take hold. If it is a considerable amount of gold, then that shipment is set out on a table before me, the council, and

28

the crew. I oversee the dividing of such a bounty to keep things equal. Last time I had such a task was when old Chez Nez took a Spanish ship, and the amount of gold was such that the council met, and I Boss, divided the spoils. Gambi had gone along on the successful raid, but the ship was under command by his comrade Chez Nez."

"How did you handle that? I mean, if Gambi is a captain, he should get a captain's share, surely?"

"That is what he thought. He made it clear by kneeling close to the table on which the gold sat. He looked very intense and watched each bit of gold as it was handed out and to whom. Had it been any other captain on that raid with old Nez, there would have been trouble. Nothing I could not have handled, I assure you. Anyway, I saw to it that each man got his pay in gold coin and that Gambi got what was rightfully his. The man got the same amount as the other crew members. He left the gathering full of drink and none too happy, but he made no complaint. I learned later he made his way across the narrow channel and back to his home without incident. The two Italian Captain's prefer to live there; I assume it is because of their wives. Anyway, it took several hours and much to drink to divide the spoils. In the end, there were but two gold coins left in front of me, and that caused a problem. Someone was going to receive more than they should."

"What did you do?"

"I used my head." Laffite laughed. "Old Chez Nez had brought along his wife. She was the only female in the room, and it was most unusual, but no one had a mind to tell the Italian he could not have his wife attend. Most thought, he just wanted her to see how great a spoil he had taken when the chests were opened."

"She's a pirate?"

"She is not. But, for whatever reason, Nez brought her along, and as I said, none questioned. I saw a way out of the dilemma when it came down to the two coins. It gave me great pleasure to offer them to Madame Chighizola herself, thereby keeping the distribution among the men equal."

"Did she take them?"

"Not like you think. Her husband is a greedy man and took them from my hand before she could. He claimed he would look after them for her. A lie if ever there was one."

"Then what did you do?" Tori was enthralled by the story and wanted every detail told.

"I demanded that he hand me back the coins, and seeing my hand on my pistol, he reluctantly agreed. I believe he had it in his head that I would tell his wife, I would look after them for her. If that were the case, the pirate would have found a reason for her to claim them. He would have taken them from her. What I did next sent Dominique into fits of laughter, and it's true, most talk about it now and then. Never in front of Nez Coupe, though."

"Spill it, what did you do?"

"Spill what? I have no mug or bottle from which I can spill." Jean held up his empty hands.

"You know what I mean. Tell me, what happened?"

"Ah, I see, another term I shall have to learn. Well, my lady, I tossed the coins to Dominique and told him to take them to my blacksmith, Thiac. I gave instructions that the coins were to be melted and turned into a thimble for Madame Chighizola."

"You didn't. Oh, I bet Chez Nez was pissed off. Besides, that's a lot of gold for one thimble."

"Tori, please refrain from the use of such language. You must be very careful about how you explain yourself from now on. And, yes, I did that, and she still has the thimble. Not all the gold went into the thimble, as you kindly pointed out. Thiac had to be paid for his work, and that is where one of the coins ended up. One coin was quite enough to fashion a fine a thimble as found anyplace. I ask her whenever I see her, and I assure her, if her husband takes it, he will be made to return it. Something he is aware of, and as such, he allows her to keep it. Besides, he is a proud man, and she is an excellent seamstress. I hear that she has told him, without her new thimble, there would not be such handsome outfits for him."

"So, you got to split up the spoils and make one family happy. I assume they are happy. I would guess the lady of the house is. Bet she remains loyal to you."

"I have many loyal families, but I have many more men, single or married, that are questionable, and I fight each day to remain Boss. It takes skill, cunning, and a steady hand. My weakness was the sea. Leaving here before I was called Boss was always a risk. One mutiny could make life difficult, such as the one that almost occurred. Ah, but that was then, and this is now, and as you see, things are running smoothly."

"You said was. It was your weakness? Are you standing there telling me that I am now your weakness?" Tori was grinning and only kidding around, something that Jean did not understand. He just assumed she had chosen to see the truth of how he felt, and it pleased him.

He smiled and pulled her toward him, close enough to whisper in her ear. "You are my love, and as such, I wish that no harm ever becomes you." Jean stood back a step and added, "In that sense, you are my Achilles heel. I would kill anyone who would dare lay a hand on you. You are, to me, strength also. For you, for us, I intend to build an empire. After all, your history told you that I did, and so I shall." He looked around them and smiled. "Yes, things are far better organized now and will remain so. I can see that. My absence, this time, has proceeded to produce the results I had hoped to obtain. Before we left for the islands, I placed Renato, in my position, as head of the council. Just while I was away, mind you. He, next to Dominique, is the only other captain that I can depend on. As for the others, I have yet not found the need to place them in charge, as I do not fully trust them."

He pulled on his goatee and frowned. Then his serious look evaporated, and he looked toward his left and then back at Tori. This place, on both sides of the channel, runs a lot smoother, and if what your history books say about me is correct, we will profit, no?

I look forward to talking with you about myself and about whatever else it is, you know. More importantly, what it is you have kept from me." He chuckled at the look of surprise in her eyes. "Come, let us walk on."

Tori had been intently listening to Jean and looking at the different places as they walked by that she'd not paid much attention to where they were going. When Jean stopped suddenly and pointed off to one side, she could only stare and smile at what she saw. True, the house was not a grand plantation-style home, but she had not expected to see anything quite like what was facing her. At the end of a small dirt road stood a red brick house of moderate size. It was sturdy looking, with a verandah both upstairs and down, looking out towards the Gulf. The windows had wrought iron bars covering them in ornamental designs, and the red brickwork gave it a European appearance.

"I take it that the lady approves of the living quarters?"

"The lady does indeed. It looks extremely comfortable. You never cease to amaze me. Who would have thought that you would have such a place in the middle of nowhere?"

"This is something that your history books did not speak of?"

"I am sure they did, they would have to. I don't recall reading or hearing about it. I told you, I only know a little bit." A flash of the area in her time and its rubble heap and forgotten fort briefly filled her mind. Among those ruins were those of this village and his home. How could she tell the man all he had built would vanish? Tori could not look at him knowing this, so she stood staring at the house before her instead.

"Well, we shall learn what more you know, as our days pass. There is little else to do here at night, but talk, drink, and other more intimate actions," he laughed. "Now, come, let's go and see what awaits us, shall we?" Jean swung the small gate open, and together they began to walk down the brick pathway across a well-kept garden. In Tori's estimation, someone had a very green thumb, and she was mention this when the sound of a female's laughter filled the air.

The front door had been thrown open before they'd had a chance to reach it. Then bursting outside came a tall Hispanic woman, clapping her hands in delight at the sight of them. Her round face was beaming, and her dark eyes were piercing and held Tori in their gaze. She was wearing a colored blouse that had a neckline, which sat on her shoulders. The sleeves were small and gathered up. This blouse tucked into the long, brightly patterned skirt, and on her feet, she wore leather open-toed sandals. Large gold studs pierced her ears, and on both her wrists, she wore silver bracelets of various sizes. The belt that held her skirt in place also had a large silver buckle and was a work of art all on its own. The woman stood there, all smiles and laughter, and reminded Tori of a grinning cat. Yes, she told herself, she did look like the cat that swallowed the canary.

"So, the Senor brings home, at last, the Senorita?" she laughed. "You have taken my advice and made yourself happy, yes?"

Jean laughed. "Something like that. I see you were told that Miss Victoria speaks only English. You will have plenty of time to practice yours, not that you have too." He looked from the servant and back to Tori while making the introduction. "This is my housekeeper and friend, Carlotta. You will find her English is quite good, even if she does not admit it herself." Then, without hesitating or waiting for Tori to respond, he escorted her over the threshold and into the building's cooler interior.

The front hall into which they entered was decorated with the most exquisite artwork, and as they walked into the living room, Tori was amazed still further. Here was a side of Jean that revealed how different he was from the pirate she had grown to know at sea. This house portrayed a caring man who created a warm and friendly environment in his home. He took pride in his surroundings, and he had style. Her pirate obviously liked beautiful things in his life, and every place she looked, it showed. From stylish furniture to the beautiful oil paintings and other works of art, all were magnificent, and they filled the room. There was a carved bookcase full of wonderfully leather-bound books, but the extravagance and quality didn't stop on those shelves. Tori found herself standing upon a beautifully woven carpet, and like the one at Leone's, it covered a highly polished wooden floor. She looked up from there to the crystal sconces that hung on each wall. The chandelier that hung in the center of the room was, in her estimation, nothing short of magnificent, and for a second, she wondered where it originally came from. The entire room and its contents spoke volumes about the man's wealth and education. He was indeed how history described him. Jean was a gentleman pirate, after all.

"Our quarters await you upstairs, along with a small something," he said, interrupting her thoughts. Jean held his finger to his lips to silence her questions. Then he continued quickly. "One other detail you need to understand, Carlotta. Miss Victoria is called by myself and a few others Tori. The name is a term of endearment. At all other times, unless either of us specifies, she will be referred to as Victoria. Now, ladies, I have to leave. Carlotta will see to it Tori, that you have all you require until dinner. She has been with me from the beginning of this establishment, and should you need anything, she will know just where to find it. Oh, I did not tell you before, but a guest will join us this evening. Please do look ravishing for me tonight." Jean smacked her lightly on her behind, but upon witnessing Tori's reaction and remembering that she didn't like being told what to do, he quickly pulled her into his arms. Softly he placed his lips on hers, hoping to quell any anger.

The spark was instantaneous, and the passion with which she returned his kiss surprised him and caused him to feel aroused. Abruptly his kissing stopped, and he whispered into her ear. "Tori, if you detain me now, I will be late this evening, and that would not do. One thing I am known for is promptness."

Tori simply smiled, then without uttering a word, she turned and walked out of the living room and into the hallway. There, she slowly began climbing the stairs, swaying her hips, and moving in the most seductive way she knew how. In her mind, the temptation would be too much for Laffite, and that would mean she had control over the man and would use it to her advantage.

The response she received, however, was not what she had expected. Female laughter echoed through the entrance hall as Carlotta spoke. "It is not going to do you any good, Señorita, the Señor, he already slipped out, but I can see why he chose you. You are one to stir the blood, like the Spanish. Ah, the passion."

Tori turned and saw that Laffite was indeed gone. It was a disappointment, but that feeling did not linger. A sly smile crossed her face as she thought of how she would tease him later that night at dinner. The conniving female would drive him crazy, wanting her, and yet he would have to play host. After all, the gentleman could not just leave and have his way. The pirate maybe, but the gentleman and host, the answer to that, was never. Yes, tonight was going to be fun to see which one would be sitting by her side, the rogue pirate, or the gentleman privateer? "Carlotta, I think maybe you and I had better get to know one another." Her face was full of mischief, but the expression to the housekeeper was only one of joy. "You and I will have some fun this evening, shake things up a little, maybe?"

Carlotta was not sure what she meant, but she was only too willing to make the woman feel at home. After all, she was the first female that Boss had brought to this house, and that had to mean something. The two women talked, and after a short while, a plan had been set in motion. Tori left Carlotta loving the idea of serving her dinner like the famous cook, Tori, had told her she had seen in the city. The housekeeper knew her food was as good as any, that was served all over New Orleans, and if she could do as Senorita Tori asked, it would be served with such flair and be just as outstanding as anything in town. Besides, if there was one thing she adored, it was dramatics. Toward the end of the hall at the top of the stairs, a door stood slightly ajar, and Tori curiously walked toward it. She saw several other doors, but all of them were closed, so it made sense to her to explore the room that was not shut off. "It is the door that is open, Señorita," called Carlotta, from the bottom of the stairs. "The other rooms are for the occasional guests that stay the night. I shall return to the kitchen, but if you need me, just call out. I have excellent hearing, and like Boss said, anything you need, I will fetch it."

"Thank you, Carlotta. I am sure I will find all I need. You don't have to worry about me. Please, don't let me keep you from your cooking. I have found the bedroom."

The room was large, open, and airy. A massive bed sat opposite two open French doors that led to the veranda she had seen from below. That area was not what held her attention right then; it was the bed that did that. Up until now, all the bed's Tori had seen in this era, were no larger than a double bed back home. This bed, however, came close to a king size in her estimation. Custom made no doubt, and that meant everything to do with it would have been specifically designed to accommodate its dimensions. It was a four-poster bed, which was beautifully hand-carved, and to her delight, Tori could see mosquito netting encompassing the frame. A portion of it was stretched and attached to the top of the frame, while still volumes more of the netting hung by each bedpost. All was neatly tied and held in place around the four posts by golden cords, which matched the tassels on two pillows, propped up against the headboard. The nets were almost touching the floor, and she could see where they would slide into place along a wooden rod. Once drawn, the bed would be completely enclosed, and this pleased her because she guessed that once the sun set, nasty bugs would be swarming all over the place.

Tori looked away from the bed and allowed her gaze to take in the next largest object of interest. There before her sat an ornately carved wooden bathtub. It was full of warm, rose-scented water, and on a small table next to the tub were a variety of oils, soaps, and perfumes. Jean had known she would want this bath more than anything else, and she adored him for supplying it. The man always seemed to think of every detail, no matter the situation. Tori stepped closer, and upon inspection, found several jugs of fresh-water. This water would be used to rinse her hair when she finished washing it. This was the way it had been at Roses,' but unlike that experience, Tori did not have help standing by to aide her. Not that rinsing her hair was going to be a problem, just awkward without Lacy's steady hands. Briefly, she wondered about the dusky colored girl and her child.

Had she escaped Rose's clutches, or had she been dragged back to that gaudy whorehouse to become a new addition to those already working there? Tori hoped she had escaped but figured she would never learn the girl's fate, so there was no use in worrying or specu-lating. Besides, her attention was drawn away from such troubling questions to the opposite side of the bed. There, draped over a chair, was a new silk dress and matching delicate slipper-like shoes. There were undergarments too. On a small stool, a new corset and silk bloomers, trimmed with delicate lace awaited her. This was Jean's surprise then. She smiled, 'you did well, better than I would have guessed.' Tori walked over to inspect the articles. Her hands stroked the silk as she admired the gown. Her friend in the islands, Red, had been with her when she had been measured for gowns, but until right then, this one had been shipped without been seen. 'He must have had it made and kept it for me until now. Sly, you are Jean Laffite, but I am happy and surprised as you hoped no doubt.' Tori held the dress up against her and prayed this it would fit her, unlike Jean's first clumsy attempt at supplying her with clothing. Much had happened since that almost forgotten afternoon. Her smile vanished, and as she put the gown down. Better some memories remained forgotten, she told herself. Turning around, she looked at the inviting tub of water, with a broad smile tugging at her lips. 'I have far more important things to occupy my mind, and oh, how much I need you. A long and luxurious bath, in fresh-water, is just what I want the most right now.' Her hand dipped into the water and swirled the petals around on its surface. With no further hesitation, she closed the bedroom door and then stood next to the tub and stripped.

The tired female left her dress on the floor and stepped into the tub. Without even hesitating, she sat down and then leaned her head back and rested it against the rim of the tub. In seconds, her body was sinking into the water's luxurious silky touch. It was then she realized the bath was far larger than she'd thought, as her feet did not have to stick out at the other end. Jean, it seemed liked having things made for comfort and his size. Tori grinned and slipped a little lower into the water, letting her body relax and her mind wander. "Big bed, big tub, and a bigger house than I ever expected." Laughing, she scolded herself. "Doing it again. Talking to no one, but who cares? I'm going to enjoy this, and nothing more. No more talking to myself, just enjoyment and blissful silence." She closed her eyes, to begin soaking when out of nowhere, and as if a hammer hit her very soul, the painful memory of her child swept into her mind.

Overpowering guilt swelled, consuming her happiness and filling her with sadness and despair that filled her eyes with tears. How could she be enjoying herself like this, when somewhere her family was worried sick? Lord, she did miss them. Heaven knows how many nights she spent thinking of them all and crying out in the dark for her daughter. She longed to see the smile on Linni's small face, to feel her child's arms wrap around her and hug her in a way that no one else could.

Tori sat up, opening her tear-filled eyes, fighting to overcome the emotion of wanting to cry. Once more, she pushed her feelings deep down inside. The pain was so raw that it would consume her if she allowed it, so she squeezed her eyes closed and rubbed the tears away. "Stop thinking about it," she whispered. However, that was hard to do. The thought entered her mind, that never again would she find her own time, and that frightened the hell out of her. This horrible idea was simply unacceptable. So, she repressed it, telling herself that soon Jean would find a way to return her to the lake. One day soon, he would take her to see if the way back was still open and open it would be. Until that time, she had to hang on; she had to be strong. What other choice did she have? Crying or worrying was not about to help matters and to panic, what good was there in that? Either she would return to her family or not. Tori took in a deep breath. 'But if there was no way home, what then'? She'd be stuck in this era with Laffite. This daunting realization began her thinking seriously about her feelings toward Jean in greater depth. What was it she felt for him? Could it be love? Or was this emotion she held for him purely a physical attraction? Tori told herself she did not know. Either way, she simply had to stop analyzing her needs and desires. After all, the fact was quite clear; it was only a matter of time before she returned to the lake and escaped this nightmare. The only trouble was this was no longer a nightmare. It was becoming more like a daydream, a beautiful, fanciful dream, with a very sexy pirate who claimed he loved her.

Tori raised her hands to her ears as if by covering them, she could block out her thoughts and memories. She was mentally being torn apart and had no way to make either Linni's images or the sound of the voices inside her head stop. 'Please…I beg you, shut the hell up! I can't take it.'

At first, Tori did not hear the light knock on the door, followed by the small voice, asking if she needed any help. It was when her hands left her ears and covered her eyes that the stranger's voice filled the room.

As the door slowly opened, the female confidently spoke. "Miss Carlotta told me to come on up and Boss; he said I need to work for you as long as you be staying here. If you need some help with washing your hair, I will be glad to do it. I know how and then I can help you dress and all. Let me close the door, and I be right over to…"

Tori's mouth dropped open, as a gasp escaped her. She could hear her heart beating in her chest as she quickly turned to look toward the girl whose voice she'd instantly recognized. Excitedly she faced the teenage girl in the doorway who was waiting for instructions.

"Well, of all the damnedest things! Of all the people to meet here, I can't believe it. I was thinking about you earlier. Lacy, it's me, don't you recognize me?"

Lacy had not had time to finish her greeting or offer to help. Upon seeing the woman and hearing her voice, the girl was quite simply stunned beyond words and frozen; she could only stare in disbelief.

Tori laughed. "Well, just don't stand there, come on in silly. It really is me."

Gingerly, the girl took a step forward and looked carefully at the female who's voice she recognized. Staring at her, to make sure she was not imagining anything, the young girl took another step closer. The woman sitting in the bath was indeed the same person who had escaped Madame Rose's clutches. There was no doubt in her mind that Boss's lady was one and the same person. This was her friend, who, on the same day, as herself, had escaped the whorehouse. Such a fuss had been put up over Tori's disappearance; it had made Lacy's escape much easier than it otherwise would have been. Tori leaving when she did, had saved both their lives, and Lacy knew that to be so, because Tori was right there, sitting in Laffite's tub. Her friend, who she was not sure until now, had safely escaped after all.

The girl pushed the bedroom door closed and then moved quickly across the room. Her expression was one of sheer joy, and her actions backed her feelings. Dropping to her knees at Tori's bath side, Lacy threw her arms around her friend, getting herself soaked in the process. "I know you had got away. Never heard nothing about you been found and all. But how'd you do it? What are you a doing here?" she asked, looking around the room. Then Lacy was staring at Tori with a puzzled look that soon broke into a grin. "That's stupid of me, ain't it? You be the one they calling Laffite's Lady, the one they say has stolen his heart."

Tori smiled. It had a nice ring to it, Laffite's Lady, even if she kept telling him she was not, nor ever would be his lady. What else were they saying, she wondered? "Slow down, Lacy, and let go of me. You are getting yourself soaked, in case you haven't noticed." Pushing her away gently, Tori continued. "There is much to tell you, and I have a lot of questions myself."

THE two caught up on the past few months, while Lacy helped Tori bathe and dress for the evening. The long warm hours slipped away, and before they realized it, the time for dinner had arrived.

"Lord, you best go down; we been talking too much, and if there is one thing I knows Boss hates, that is being late."

"You don't have to worry about that, Lacy. I'm sure he will understand when I tell him about you, but do me a favor."

"Anything. All you have to do is ask. You need me here when you come up? I'd be happy to wait."

"No, not that. You have your baby to take care of. I only want you to give me your word that you won't tell anyone about me or about Roses. It's vital that no one finds out who I am. Can you understand that? I must not let anyone know."

"You can trust me. Ain't a going to say nothing to no one, not even my man. Don't you fret none. You ain't got to worry like."

"Just as long as the bitch Rose doesn't hear I am here, I guess not."

Missy's serious expression immediately changed at the mention of Rose. "Oh, I plum forgot to tell you the good news. You see, on the day we ran, well, Rose's place burned to the ground."

"It burned? How? Did everyone get out?" Tori was shocked, and it showed on her face. She may not have liked many of the women in that place, but she would never have wished any of them real harm.

"It burned all right, early like. Maybe right after we slipped out. Only a few lived; just them that was in the kitchen got out. They were lucky, all them others, everyone upstairs, they burned. I felt a bit sorry for them, but not her, not Rose. She burned too. So, see, no one is left but me, who knows you was there, and I won't be telling. Look, everyone here in this place be a hiding from something or someone. It don't make much difference like, but you'll see that when you been here a while. I ain't going to say a word. I owe you something. I am free here with my man because of you and your help. I ain't going to say nothing to no one, no way."

"You are sure? The whole house, it burned, and the bitch is dead? I can't believe it."

"That's what I heard tell. Most news gets here some way or the other, and some takes its time, but not that news, no ma'am. We all heard that told fast like. Then, Boss's men who took cargo to sell, they was there on that day, and when they got back, they was telling everyone the news. I was, real lucky, on account, them men, they knew my man, an' I got me an' my son down here real easy. I traveled with them and had a place to stay; on account, I could help with them little one's who's folks is gone. They was real glad of me, and I was happy, on account I had me an' my child a place that was safe. I helped out till my man got home an' he and me, well, we are going to stay here until he makes enough money to buy us a small plot of land on Grand Isle. Then he plans to stay with me an' not sail no more. See Rose's place burning down like it did; it helped me an' you escape, an' we has no need to cry over it. No, we don't. We can laugh an' be happy of it."

"I agree with you on that fact. I do wonder what happened, though. Seems odd, don't you think? No matter, it's one less problem for me. Thank you for letting me know. Oh, and Lacy, I am not going to be telling anyone about you coming from there either. You have my word on that."

Lacy took in a deep breath. She spoke slower, and as she did, her English improved. "Well, I be sorry...I mean to say am grateful and all. My man knows, but he don't care, and he won't be telling on me. It wasn't like I was one of the girls, you know. I only slept with him, and he knows that for sure. No one hereabouts knows where I come from, and I know that be the best for all. None a' their business anyways."

The two hugged each other, and Lacy held Tori back for the last look before sending her down to dinner. "You sure look a lot different than when we were together last. You're lighter. Yes, you are. And it ain't pale from sick like, neither. You ain't a fancy like Rose said, are you? Black, don't fade. You be a white lady. Your hair, it's not only longer, which I know how that happens, but it be a lot smoother now. The color changed some too." Lacy ran her fingers through her own curly mop as she laughed. "You going to have to tell me how you do that one day." The girl shook her head and at the expression on Tori's face. Oh, stop your giggling. I ain't a said nothing stupid; it be the truth. Now, listen to me. I am sounding all sorts of wrong. I need to talk proper like, so my son learns the right way. I have to slow down and try harder." Lacy frowned. "Forgive me asking, but I has…have, to know. You not anything like Rose said, and you ain't stupid either. Way I see it and all, to me, it seems crazy to want to pass yourself off as a fancy nigger and go and gets mixed up with that Aunt Rose LaSalle. Rose was pure evil. She wasn't ever a going to let you go. That madam planned to own you like she did me. Her thinking you was a fancy, and you not telling her different, when the telling might have changed things. It seems plum crazy to me."

Tori's mood turned serious, realizing that the girl had a lot of misconceptions about the way things had happened. "Maybe one day you and I can talk about all that, but for now, please let's just leave it as it is." Tori tried to sound more like Lacy when she spoke again. It was her way of lightening the mood. "You sure I look right and all? Lordy, be! An Mizz Lacy, are you sure my hair be a staying put this way?"

Lacy laughed at her and assured her that everything was fine.

"Well, how do I look, is it right like?" Tori was teasing again. "Lord, you best stop that. You go downstairs talking like me, and I be sure to be sent out and told not to come back. I'll have to watch how I talk around you and do my best not to slip back to the old ways. I do know the right way and all. It just be…is hard. Real hard when I am so happy."

Tori smiled at her and took hold of the girl's hands and squeezing them tightly; she spoke softly. "You can talk any way that you want. When we are alone, I want us to be close and not have to worry about such things. You are my friend, and I hope you will let me be yours. Friends can joke around. I was not making fun of you, just fooling around; that's all."

Were those tears filling Lacy's eyes? Tori guessed they were, and let the girl compose herself while she walked to the bed and picked up a small folded fan. Tori was not used to carrying such an object, so she put it on the bedside table while gathering her thoughts. 'I am not about to use it, and besides, it's not that warm anyway. Now, then, let's get Lacy happily on her way to her man and no more teasing. Poor girl doesn't get it.' Tori turned to look at Lacy and was glad to see her smiling, with no sign of tears.

Lacy couldn't help staring. Standing in front of her was indeed a beautiful and bewitching female. No wonder she held Boss's heart. Miss Tori was a good kind person too. This, she did not doubt. "I thank you much for thinking about my needs, afore yours. It is true, I am a wanting to see my child asleep and my man fed. I have missed him for a while. While it be true, Boss, will pay me good to stay, and I can help save what I make to add to my man's gold. If I dose…did that, well, we will get our land sooner, but tonight I do want to be with him. I know he loves his boy and all. He is with him now, and that be…is good. It's me he needs seeing." She grinned and then stepped forward to the door. "If you are ready, I will take my leave." With a huge smile and a skip in her step, Lacy did not wait for a response. She turned and left, being sure to leave the bedroom door open behind her.

Tori felt strange and a little frightened that a slip of a girl could hold her future in her hands. However, she trusted her not to tell anyone anything, almost anyone that was. Tori reckoned, Lacy had probably never been trusted like this before in her whole life. If Missy were going to tell someone, it would be during pillow talk with her man. 'Pillow talk', a term she had not used in ages. Tori and Jean always spoke in bed before they fell asleep, and it stood to reason that Lacy would be tempted to do so. For now, though, Tori knew that she was safe. It was the 'for how long,' that bothered her?

Laffite's lady stood still for a moment, at the top of the stairs, before making her way down to the front room. She could hear Dominique and Jean talking as the room's door was open. Upon recognizing their voices, the worried look in her eyes vanished, and a smile played on her expression. No need to worry anyone right then; there would be a right time to talk to Jean about Lacy. As for the men, they sounded very earnest, discussing the sale of cargo. The pair were speaking in French, and this made her grin. Her ruse about not knowing French was still intact. Neither of them had an inkling that she was just as fluent as they were, and this amused her. She chewed her lower lip and kept her thoughts on the matter to herself, as she began her descent. 'My best-kept secret, and ace in the hole.'

The sight of Tori caught Jean off guard. He'd forgotten what she looked like in a silk gown with her hair styled instead of pulled back and braided. In his estimation, the woman was a sight to behold, standing there in the doorway. The dark wood surrounding the door was like a frame surrounding a perfect picture. She stood bathed, in the soft golden glow, from the crystal sconces. Their amber light seemed to set her eyes ablaze and reminded him of the stone called Tigers Eye. Jean did not move; he just remained in place, admiring the beauty that stood before him.

Tori had not expected to see Jean dressed as he was. The man must have changed outfits in another part of the house because he stood before her dressed in the finest evening attire. He looked dashingly handsome, and if asked right then which she preferred, the pirate or gentleman, she'd have a hard time choosing. Neither Jean nor Tori uttered a sound; they just stood motionless staring at each other, lost in the moment and joy of seeing each other in outfits not so casual.

It was Dominique who made the first move. He walked forward to escort Tori into the room. "Boss, where are your manners? One would think you are nothing more than a pirate and far from the gentleman you profess to be." Chuckling to himself, the older man took Tori's arm and escorted her into the room, grinning all the way. It was his opinion that Jean was acting more and more like a lovesick puppy, and who could blame him? Dominique had to admit that if he were younger himself, he might very well be acting the same way. Instead, he was, and would continue enjoying his role as a friend and confidant with this ravishing creature. It was a role that gave him dignity, with none of the foolishness or pains that accompanied young love. 'Best I stop with such thoughts and speak up, or be accused of becoming soft in the head, or worse.'

The older man's hand patted Tori's arm. "Is there something I may fetch for you before our guest arrives, something light to drink, maybe?"

"Why, Dominique, such a gentleman as always. Yes, that would be nice. A glass of wine and something to smoke."

Jean choked on his drink, and Dominique laughed out loud, rocking back and forth as he did so. For balance, the man moved his short legs slightly apart. His hands were placed firmly on his hips, and his chin aimed downward. As he bellowed, the toes of his boots raised off the carpet, leaving him balancing on the heels of his boots for a few seconds. Then, he'd lean forward to place his feet back flat on the floor. This rocking motion continued several more times, and Tori thought he looked as if he would tumble right over if he didn't stop. She was about to say something when he ceased both his movements and laughter.

"The drink, I will be obliged to fetch for you. As for the smoke, well now, if I were to comply with that request, Mademoiselle, Boss would run me through, or drown in his drink as he is doing this very second!" He slapped his hand down on the tabletop and turned his head towards Jean, as he continued lightheartedly. "It would be amusing, however, to see the look on our guest's face if he walked in and found her, sitting like an angel, and acting like the devil was in…"

Jean coughed the remainder of what he had swallowed the wrong way, and huskily commanded, "Stop encouraging her, she might just do it." He coughed again, only with a chuckle this time. "Stop this, both of you."

Everyone was laughing as they turned, toward the door, when Carlotta announced the arrival of their guest. It was at that precise moment that the mood in the room turned somewhat somber.

What greeted Tori's eyes as he entered was a rather tall, well-dressed Creole gentleman. He had the blackest eyes that she could ever remember seeing, and the fact that they were small and weasel-like helped make his nose seem too large and out of place on his long pale face.

Jean and the man bowed slightly as they greeted each other. Then in one fluid motion, the guest turned to face Dominique and again bowed politely. Then as the stranger turned toward Tori, his whole demeanor changed. The man's full attention immediately became utterly focused on her. It was in that split second; Tori felt an instant dislike for this so-called gentleman. Her uneasiness grew as he approached, though she hid it well. This guest was nothing more than an overdressed rake if she ever did see one. His beady little eyes looked up and down her entire body as if he was undressing her in his mind. Worse yet, he did nothing to hide his undeniable attraction as he crossed the room towards her.

Tori observed him and decided his hair looked too greasy, and his face was far too flushed. Admittedly, it was not that warm in the house, as to cause him to be over temped? No, Tori told herself, the man was flushed because of his unsettled emotions. He was blushing, maybe even excited, and not at all embarrassed to show it.

(In French) "Madame, it is truly my pleasure to meet such a beauty in such a wild setting. I had no idea that I was to be in the company of such a vision. I look forward to getting more acquainted this evening."

Tori would have liked to tell him where to go, but then she reminded herself, she was not supposed to understand him. Not speaking French perplexed her often but not as much as it did at that very moment. 'Just try and smile and act dumb. Remember, you don't understand the idiot. Keep it together and pray Jean steps in before you give yourself away.' Then as if to add injury to insult, came his next loathsome greeting, as he took her hand in his. His lips were overly wet as they brushed the back of her knuckles, and as disgusting as this action was, leaving saliva on her skin was worse. "Such a beauty indeed, let us become more acquainted." The man was staring at her, proud of himself, and it made her feel like ramming her fist into his pompous, rat-like face, just to watch his reaction and get him to back off. 'You oversexed bastard! Acquainted my ass. Shit, I have to act like I don't get it. Smile, but look like you don't get it. I can do this. You're not going to blow my cover, you, pompous bastard.' It was odd that she had such an instant aversion toward him, and she would have gone on trying to figure the Creole out when thankfully, Jean interrupted.

Laffite had witnessed the odd expression register on Tori's face just before she forced a smile, and he frowned. It was as though his lady understood far more than she was letting on. "You shall have to excuse the lady, Monsieur. She does not understand our language or our customs; I am afraid. We will have to speak English."

"Ah, pardon me, I did not know. You will forgive me, yes, and let me introduce myself to you. I am Bernard Louis Toutant, but please, you must call me Bernard."

Withdrawing her wet hand and trying to smile as sweetly as she could, Tori answered, "I am charmed, I'm sure. Jean, the glass of wine you kindly offered me, is it available?"

The deliberate snub to Bernard seemed to go right over his head. If it was ignored on purpose or not, she could not determine. What she did know was, he was not about to give up on his advances.

"Please allow me, Mademoiselle. It would be my pleasure, I am sure. But, first, you must reveal what lovely name I am to address you. I am certain it will be just as beautiful as the lady herself."

This man was impossible, Tori thought. She looked over his shoulder and saw Dominique shaking his head, rolling his eyes, and smiling to himself. In fact, Tori saw he was doing much more than that. Her friend was trying to keep himself from bursting out in laughter.

Jean's face, however, was blank, and his eyes piercing. His lips were straight and pulled thin, almost in a grimace of sorts. He apparently did not like this Bernard or his unwarranted attention towards his lady. It was a cold, controlled voice he used when he spoke. In French, he addressed his guest in a tone that Tori had never heard come out of Jean's mouth before. It had such an aggressive edge about it that she shivered slightly.

(In French) "Monsieur, the lady's name is Victoria, and she is to be treated as a lady, who is unattainable to both yourself and all others. She is my lady, and I will not stand for any man trying to… ah…shall we say, place certain advances towards her. I would take any such actions as a personal insult and would have to call that gentleman out. Do I make myself clear?"

Jean's words angered Bernard, but like Tori, he hid his emotions well. It would serve him no purpose to make this pirate angry with him. It was only because Jean had spoken in French, thereby saving face, that he could let it be. However, he wanted to see this arrogant Laffite squirm a little.

(In French) "Indeed, you make yourself perfectly clear. Forgive me. I meant no harm. I had no idea that she was your…your…may I be so bold as to inquire as to what position she is exactly?"

(In French) "She, sir, is none of your business. Now, let us speak in English, and dine before we discuss why you came here tonight." Jean walked past Bernard and placed his arm around Tori's waist in a protective, possessive manner, before guiding her toward the dining room. "Forgive us, Victoria, we will speak in English for the rest of the evening, I assure you. Now, let us dine. You may find the wine that I have chosen, more to your liking than the one in here."

So, my name is to be Victoria, she thought. He was quick, her Jean. She may not have told this Bernard anything about her past, but he looked the type that would visit that awful whorehouse and keep up with all the gossip. If introduced as Tori, her identity might have been given away. This thought caused her to shiver, and she thanked God for letting such a careful guardian as Jean come into her life.

CARLOTTA'S dinner was excellent, a mixture of Spanish and Creole, with just a touch of what Tori fun lovingly referred to as 'happy-happy' and kicked up chef style. She even had Carlotta saying, 'wham' when adding her hot spices to the various dishes. The housekeeper acted with such flare that Jean had to hide his amusement behind his napkin.

Carlotta's antics, apparently encouraged by Tori, had his guest in quite a dither. Bernard, he guessed, not only found Carlotta's actions thoroughly improper and distracting but also by the expression on his face, he found the dinner conversation perplexing. The very fact that both he and Tori cleverly avoided divulging any personal information about her, no matter how hard he tried, had to be exasperating. It most certainly had the poor man drinking more wine than he usually would.

Time and time again, their guest would sway the conversation in her direction, and Tori found herself upset by his constant and distinct inquiries. No matter how hard Dominique or Jean tried, the infuriating individual would somehow manage to bring the topic back to her. It was, therefore, a huge relief when Jean made his announcement.

"Gentlemen, I would like to begin to discuss our business at hand. Business that would undoubtedly only bore Victoria. My dear, as you must be tired from our trip, it is acceptable for you to retire for the evening. One could say, I insist on such action."

Typically, Tori would not have given into his suggestion, but she was only too glad to get away from the continued lewd glances Bernard shot her way. His constant scrutiny not only made her feel uncomfortable, but it seemed to be starting to anger his host. She feared that if she did not depart soon, Jean might lose his patience, business deal, or not and then who knew what would happen? Rising slowly from her chair, Tori walked to Jean's side and leaned forward to give him a clear view of her ample cleavage that the low-cut dress revealed. She kissed his cheek lightly and spoke like a genuinely genteel lady. "Thank you for a lovely evening Jean, and you are right, I am feeling a little tired. Your suggestion of an early night is just what I need. Gentlemen, if you will excuse me?"

Bernard, who was sitting on the opposite side of the table, realized if he did not move fast, he'd miss the opportunity to add his farewells in a more personal manner. He would lose his chance to once again, take hold of her hand, to squeeze it suggestively, thereby letting only her understand the meaning of his intentions and interest. It was a necessary move, one that would be discreet, and thus be accomplished without giving anything away to Laffite. If his luck held, the woman would find a way to arrange a meeting at a later date. Of this, he had high hopes.

As he hastily stood up, Bernard's chair fell backward and hit the wooden floor making a loud crashing sound. To everyone there, it seemed that the man had entirely forgotten himself and his manners. His demeanor was undoubtedly a disappointment to himself, too, as he was trying awfully hard to be something he was not while hiding his blunder.

Tori frowned, as Jean and a very embarrassed Bernard assured each other that everything was quite all right. Acting as if she hadn't noticed the incident, she made her way to a very amused

Dominique and placed a light kiss on his unsuspecting cheek. Then speaking loud enough for the others to hear, she spoke seductively. "Good night, Dominique, my dear friend. May you sleep well, and dream the dreams filled with Cupid's delight." With that said, she walked out of the room and turned slowly in the doorway, to look at them once more, before pulling the door closed.

The instant the door handle snapped into place, Tori thought, she would burst out laughing because she had witnessed the dumb-founded expression on Bernard's face. For her, it was a much-needed improvement over the leering face she had seen all night. Fearing the loss of control, the delighted female made her way up the stairs as fast as possible. She held her sides as her giggling was threatening to burst forth into peals of laughter, something that Tori did not want to have happen.

Once inside the bedroom, however, her laughter erupted uncontrollably, and hysterically she fell upon the bed, almost unable to catch her breath. What had just transpired was still vivid in her mind. Dominique had such a look on his face; embarrassment had covered his face for sure. Then there was Jean, smiling to himself and that idiot Bernard, standing there with his mouth hanging open. It had been such a look of disappointment that crossed Bernard's face when he realized he would not have the chance to touch her. His gaping mouth had closed rapidly, followed by the lowering of his bottom lip, which curled out and down. The move-ment of his lip had revealed further development of his disap-pointment and depressed mood. He had in fact displayed a full-on pout. Who knew grown men could act so childish and display such a pouty face? No one in her time, at least no male she knew, had ever acted so infantile.

IT had taken a while before she got herself under control because each time she held her breath and stopped laughing, she would hiccup and begin again. Tori had not laughed this hard in a long time. Maybe, it was needed, she told herself. That, or she'd have to cut back on the amount of wine consumed during dinners. She started to giggle again, like giving up drinking was ever going to happen. The amount may decline but stop, that was unthinkable. One needed a vice to maneuver through each day in this world. Tori sat up and moved to the side of the bed. 'Why was everything darned amusing?' Again, she giggled. "Really? Like I don't know. Could it be that I am more than slightly intoxicated and acting like a minx, throwing caution to the wind? Hell, I am enjoying myself. Nothing wrong with that, is there, Mr. Pirate?" Usually, nothing like this behavior would have taken hold of the levelheaded woman. Tori would always act like a lady, and embarrassing either Jean or Dominique in front of a guest, well that would never cross her mind. Not until tonight, that was.

There was no way around it; Laffite's lady had acted deplorably and loved every second. Even Jean had seemed amused, and as for Dominique, well, tomorrow she would tell him, embarrassing him, was payback for making her climb down the side of a ship and ride in a canoe. "Got you this time. Paybacks are a bitch," she called out happily. "Not that I planned it, but boy, it was sweet revenge. Thank you for the courage, my one too many glasses of vino. You will remain my friend forever."

Smiling at her victory, Tori stood up and walked to the end of the bed, where she could look out the open balcony doors. The evening had left her drained, yet far from sleepy. She looked back at the mattress she had rolled around on and smiled. Carlotta had been busy since Tori had left the bedroom for dinner. Not only were the bed sheets turned down, but she also saw a nightgown and small soft slippers neatly waiting on the bedside chair. Tori walked toward the head of the bed to take a closer look but got distracted by a vase on the opposite bedside table. The display of dried flowers had evidently, been soaked in scented oil because their sweet scent filled the room. On Jean's side table, where she now stood, was a brandy decanter; it was full, and his favorite cigars were displayed in a small, beautifully hand-carved box whose lid was open. She stroked the delicate box with her fingers and then reached inside to touch the long thin rolls of tobacco. Looking around the room, and seeing the bedroom door was closed, her attention slipped back to the small wooden box. "Why the hell not?"

The evening was still young, and the balcony called to her with its evening breeze. It was a perfect ending to a near-perfect day, and no one would be the wiser if she dared to continue. Tori helped herself to the brandy and one of Jean's cigars, which she lit by using the flame from the hurricane lamp. The flame had been turned low, and she had to remove the glass cover to utilize it. The fuel burned cleanly, and for a second, Tori wondered what kind of oil it was? It really didn't matter to her though and after she lit the cigar and replaced the glass, the curious female forgot about the oil and walked outside. As far as Tori could tell, the balcony wrapped around the front of the house, disappearing around the corner. It was to this area she walked, as curiosity drove her to find what was on this part of the veranda. Once there, Tori saw that this area of the balcony faced the large bay, and between Laffite's house and the view beyond, nothing and no one was obstructing the scene. It was a mesmerizing sight, one that could calm the soul.

There were two wicker chairs, which sat facing the bay, but Tori opted to remain standing. She stood sipping the amber liquid that warmed her as it slid smoothly down her throat, and then she inhaled the soft-scented cigar and found that she enjoyed the relaxed feeling that was sweeping over her.

The noise from the bayou came like nature's music to her ears. The atmosphere that surrounded her, with its gentle sounds, was unique. This was the actual sound of mother earth, unpolluted by the noises of the future; no radio waves, no cars or planes, nothing, but the gentle call of the night. Off in the distance, she could hear the waves of the Gulf lapping at the shoreline, and its salty tang filled the air. This woman from the future also knew that the night air was very different from that of her time. It was pure—

unpolluted by chemicals—as of yet. Oh, there was the odd smell of smoke coming from a fire, that someone was burning. Most likely, they were using it for cooking because the odor of smoked fish or meat did waft her way now and then. All these smells were natural, compared to the air she had breathed most of her life. The idea of being surrounded by the pure, unpolluted experience was daunting, and it moved her deeply. Her exuberant mood was softening, but her senses were heightening. It was then that she realized another smell was invading her space, an odor that was not pleasant yet not overly unpleasant.

Tori looked around the balcony trying to locate the fragrance's source in the air and found it by spotting the small whiffs of smoke drifting upward and over the area. It was on closer inspection that she discovered the cause of both the smell and smoke. There were two terra-cotta pots from which the fragrant light-colored smoke rose. It had to be something that Carlotta burned to keep the mosquitoes away, for there couldn't possibly be any other explanation. Why else would they be placed there, she asked herself? Tori had told the woman how much she hated mosquitoes, and Carlotta had responded that she had a way of dealing with the pests. This had to be just that, an old way of dealing with bug problems and who knew, maybe a better way than the aerosol sprays she was used to.

Tori smiled to herself and then looked closer at the jar's contents. Upon inspection, she saw the substances smoldering were coffee beans and what looked like whole silver bay leaves. "Whoever would have guessed smudging with coffee and bay leaves would solve a bug problem? I shall have to remember this, especially if it works. Never know when it might come in handy, and yep, I am talking to myself again," she giggled. Satisfied that she had seen everything, Tori walked back to the front of the house and stood looking in the direction of the Gulf. It was quite something to stand there under the starlit sky and listen to the night's symphony undisturbed.

The sound of the bedroom door softly opening and closing

warned her that she was no longer alone, and instinct told her who the intruder was. Tori did not turn as she spoke. "I thought you had business to discuss?"

"Ah, but I did. And, I must say, never have I put off business… but then, the thought of you up here alone was more than I could stand. Dominique is quite capable of taking over for me tonight, and besides, I think if Bernard is down there, thinking of me up here with you, well, we will come out ahead in the deal."

"You are so bad, Jean Laffite, where is your sense of fairness?"

"And, where, might I add, is yours? Kissing Dominique and making poor old Bernard squirm like you did?"

"Why, I did nothing of the sort." The grinning female turned and faced Jean. "Just come here and show me why you left your meeting."

Jean walked toward her, with an inscrutable expression filling his face. Upon reaching her side, he took the cigar from her hand and placed it to his lips. Slowly and deeply, he inhaled from it once. Then he casually crushed the end on the balcony railing and threw the extinguished butt over the side. The aromatic blue smoke slipped from between his lips as he reached for her glass. This, the pirate emptied in one swig before taking her hand. Without a word, he took her hand and guided her back into the bedroom, toward the bed. Here he placed the glass down on the bedside table, and then before she had a chance to utter a sound, he took her in his arms. Slowly he kissed her, pulling her closer to him as he did so.

Immediately, Tori felt his body pressing against hers, and she shuddered. His hands had found the pins holding her hair in place, and he removed them one by one until he could find no more. Next, his fingers pulled the strands of her hair down over her shoulders. Then, he pushed the few strays away from her face before he moved his body slightly away from hers, but he had no intention of stopping his advances just then. Laffite's lips were traveling down her neck, leaving a tingling sensation wherever they touched her flesh. His breath was warm against her skin, his breathing slow and profound, just as he intended.

Tori thought of her promise not to allow herself to love him. She had to stop him, but it was only her mind that wanted Jean to stop, for once again, her body was telling her something entirely different from her conscience.

Sensing a battle was going on inside her, he advanced more slowly. The pirate had made his mind up to caress her until she called out for his love. No matter what, he would hold back his desire to take her right then. Jean would make her want him, as bad as he wanted her. He would wash away any doubts she was having and help her win this battle she was fighting. He would give her the freedom to love and live with him, here and now, and forever if she would only let him. Slowly he slipped the gown down over her shoulders and exposed the top half of her body. Then gently, using both hands, he pushed the garment down further until it rested on her waist.

"Why Mademoiselle, you are shameless, no undergarments?"

Tori frowned and in a husky voice, whispered against his cheek. "You know that I hate to wear those old-fashioned things. Besides, no one could tell or know that I omitted them this evening. No one, but you, that is. Who else got to take a sly gander down the top of my gown, as I bent to kiss them goodnight?"

His hands slipped around to the front of her shoulders, as a knowing chuckle told her he had understood her intent only too well. He caressed her breasts tenderly, as she felt his lips traveling down her neck to the top of her shoulder. While he was content doing this, Tori's hands had found the small buttons at the back of her gown, and steadily she unbuttoned each. When she had finished with the last of the buttons, her hands reached for Jean's head and lifted it until he was looking into her eyes. He had been aware of her actions, and knowing that his lady had completed unbuttoning the gown, he pulled it with ease over her hips. Once free of her hips, Jean allowed it to fall, and then without warning, he picked her up and gently laid her down on the bed. Not once did he look away from her as he began to remove his attire.

Slipping out of his clothes, in what seemed like only seconds to her, the pirate then lay down by her side. With no touching and no talking, just staring intensely into her eyes, with a look of compassion and understanding, he waited. He would not demand anything of her. If all she wanted, this evening was to be held, then he would give her that.

There was torment on her face, but passion in her eyes. How he wished he could fight her battle for her and release her from her past, which was her future. Her life in the years ahead was what held her at bay against her will. Jean knew she had to win this struggle alone; this was something he could not force, and therefore, he continued to wait.

Tori was trying not to let the guilt of feeling joy drag her down into the depths of despair. She found herself wondering why now, after all the time they had spent together, should she feel that it was wrong? Frustrated, Tori turned her back on him. She could not look into his face, into those eyes, knowing that what he wanted, she might never be able to give him. The tormented female could not allow herself the pleasure of making love with him; it was wrong, and that was that she assured herself.

Jean traced the outline of her body. The light touch of his hand running up and down her skin made her shiver. She could feel herself weakening, knowing the heights that this man could bring her to, the pleasures that he could show her were undeniably exquisite. Did she enjoy making love with him because it was forbidden fruit, she wondered?

Suddenly and with no warning, his mouth was on her back, traveling lower. Without stopping, he moved to her hips. Her flesh burned where his kisses had passed, and now he was moving down her legs. Slowly he turned her onto her back, and then pulling himself up, and covering her with his body; he kissed the top of her forehead. Jean looked again into her eyes, and without delay, he buried his face in between her shoulder and neck. Still, he made no further moves to take her. Instead, he did the unexpected.

Jean began speaking in French to her. His voice, smooth and

seductive, was bombarding her willpower to ignore his advances. Tori was losing her resolve, and she knew it. How could she fight against something so romantic? How could she not want him to make love to her? If it were right or wrong, only time would tell. He had won her body before, but tonight was different because tonight, right at that moment in time, she knew he just might have won a part of her heart as well. There would be no more right or wrong, no more guilt; there would only be him, and whatever time they had to share.

Reaching up, she put her hands on each side of his head and began working her fingers in his hair, until it fell free of its leather cord. Once this happened, she pulled him to her. Her mouth was on his, her kiss deep and probing. Tori pushed her body up towards his, as every inch of her wanted this man to take her, and her actions were indicating such without as much as a spoken word.

Jean's French continued, as he entered her, and moving slowly at first; they clung to each other. At this very moment, Tori was beyond clear thinking, as she was caught up in the passion. It felt as if she were floating. Then, Jean's pace picked up without warning, and his lovemaking sent her soaring to heights that she had never known.

They reached the climax of their union together, and Tori called out his name in her joy. She answered his French with French without realizing her mistake. Swept up in the emotions she was feeling, Tori; spoke words of endearment softly and fluently in the language she had kept hidden from Laffite for so long.

Jean's brow furrowed, and a small twitch tugged at his lips. Finally, he knew that his suspicions were right. He'd found out not only that his lady loved him but that she also fit into his world better than he'd dare hopped possible. She spoke French perfectly, and with an accent that held no trace, other than one spoken as a native Parisian. Jean knew he should be angry at her deceit, but he could not be, for he too was lost in the passion. Now was not the time to confront her; now was the time to enjoy their union.

MORNING found Tori by herself. Jean's side of the bed was still warm, so he could not have been gone long. Remembering the previous night's events, she smiled to herself and had to admit that the feelings she had for him were far more profound than she'd allowed herself to accept.

Until last night, Jean was just an adventure for her, and a chance to live out a fantasy of sorts. Now, things were complicated, and her emotions raced right alongside her thoughts. Her family was real. They would always be loved by her and thought of, but they weren't here and might never be with her again, so feeling guilty about allowing herself to feel love, if that's what it was, well, it could not be so wrong, could it? Tori knew that a big part of her heart would always belong to her family and daughter. That no matter what happened to her now, she would still have them, or a part of what they shared, locked away deep in her soul. Also, she admitted to herself that a part of her would forever hold a place for the romance now shared with Jean. If she did leave him behind one day, nothing and no one could change the fact that she cared deeply for him. Her life would forever be entangled by two completely different worlds, in two completely different times, and would be forever, regardless of where she ended up.

Quickly she slipped into the nightgown and then put on a cotton robe and brushed her hair. Then Tori headed downstairs, feeling very optimistic. There was a new light in her eyes and new hope in her heart. Still, she reminded herself that there was a promise to keep, and that was, to return to the lake one day. She just wasn't going to panic about it, let alone obsess over it anymore. When the time was right, Jean would find a way to take her there, and then and only then, would she learn what her fate was to be.

The dining room was her first choice of destination. Not only was she starving, but she knew that's where she'd find Jean. Long before she got to the door, Tori heard his voice. It was strange to listen to him speaking with Carlotta in her native tongue. To use Spanish was one thing, but to do so with the perfect singsong accent was another. Was it possible that the man's native language was Spanish and not French? There was so very much she did not yet know about him.

"Good morning, Jean. I hope I'm not intruding. You never told me that you could speak Spanish so well."

"Indeed, my lady, I had no need." He took a cup of coffee from Carlotta and took a sip before continuing to talk, "and might I add; you never told me that your understanding of French was, how shall we say, tres bien, (very good)" Without missing a beat, he switched to French. "In fact, I would say you do so beautifully, especially in the heat of the moment."

Tori's mouth dropped open. The shocked woman looked from Jean to Carlotta, who just rolled her eyes and shrugged her shoulders. The poor housekeeper had no idea what either Jean or his lady were discussing. Tori realized she'd just have to face Jean and see what he was implying. She had to know if he was fishing to learn her secret or if by some strange miracle, he'd guessed the truth about her ability.

"But, Jean…"

He switched to English. "No, but about it. Last night, you were not only incredible in bed, but beautiful in your art of conversation as well." He was playing with his mustache, twisting the ends and stroking his chin, and both actions showed her, he was enjoying what he was contemplating. Tori could also see he was watching her reactions closely to his statement.

Thinking back to the night before, it became apparent that he had tricked her into speaking French. Indeed, he must have been planning to do so for quite some time, and she'd played right into his hands. How he had guessed about her secret when she'd been so careful, she did not know, but he had. The now flustered female did not know how to react; she couldn't very well be angry with him, could she? He must have suspected that she was keeping it from him for a reason, but why not just come out and ask her if she spoke French? Maybe it was because he was not one hundred percent sure, and he liked playing games? The pirate continued to study her in silence, with no indication one way or another of how he felt about her secret. In the end, she just chose to find the humor in the situation. At least now it was out in the open. "All right, the cat is out of the bag, so to speak? I admit it; my French is not so bad. Are you very mad at me? I think that you might be, knowing you. Just remember that I have had to listen to you talking about me, and on many occasions, saying things, I might add, that often infuriated me."

"Punishment enough, I would assume." Jean took another sip of his coffee before continuing. "Now, how could I ever stay mad, as you call it? After all, I am quite sane, so remaining mad is impossible. I admit I should be angry, but I have suspected that you might be fluent in French for some time, and in a way, I can understand why you did what you did. You gave yourself away last night when Bernard introduced himself. Your reaction was…how do I say this? I came to realize it was your expression to his introduction; you understood his every word and unwarranted attentions. It was plain to see, yet I needed to be certain. Now, that is out of the way, and we are clear about your talent in French, I see no reason for any more secrets, do you? After all, you can trust me, can you not?"

"No, I mean, yes, I do trust you, and no, there is no need for any more secrets. You have my word that I will keep nothing you need to know, from you again."

Jean frowned. She had a way of saying one thing and meaning another; knowing that, he reminded himself to keep his guard up. "Tell me, do you speak Italian? The truth now?"

"No, Jean, I do not speak Italian or Spanish for that matter. Why?"

"Just making certain. If I should have something that little ears should not hear in the future, then I shall have to speak Spanish or Italian. Or maybe one other language I happen to indulge in, from time to time." He was laughing at the look of thunder on her face, and by the way, she was walking towards him, with her eyes flashing, he knew he'd sparked her temper.

"Why, you arrogant, pretentious, overstuffed pirate! You just said no more secrets."

She would have continued with her verbal attack, but Jean knew she was not really angry. It was just her pride that was a little ruffled, so before Tori reached his side, the cup in his hand was placed on the table, leaving his hands empty and ready to pull the woman he adored close. Jean silenced her with a long, firm kiss that would have continued, if not for the coughing sound behind them, informing them that someone other than Carlotta had indeed entered the room.

Laffite reluctantly broke off his embrace, and Tori turned to see who had interrupted the moment, only to find that Dominique stood in the doorway, looking at them in the most perplexing way. "How do two people who care for each other as you do, fight so much? It must be that you enjoy the making up more, oui?"

Tori blushed and broke free from Jean to greet her dear friend. (In French.) "Some coffee Dominique, or would you care to join us for something to eat?"

Jean laughed and switched to English. He looked only at Tori as he spoke. "You have gone and done it now," he laughed. "That is how you would express the moment. See, I am learning faster than you realize—the grasping of how you speak. But, may I add, now Dominique knows you speak our language, that French is understood, watch out. That and Dominique never turns down good food or the company of a lovely lady. I guess we will have to put up with him for an hour or two and mind our manners." Dominique ignored his younger counterpart as he directed his attention toward the lady, who always made him feel wanted. Not that Jean did not need him or want his friendship. No, this was different; this was the young and beautiful Tori, talking to a foolish old man and listening to what he had to say. He could hardly contain himself and ignoring English, he spoke in French. "Bon! My oh my. The beautiful lady has chosen to surprise us again. French, spoken fluently and with such flair. Boss, it's like she is really one of us, after all. I am pleased as you yourself seem to be." The old man was beaming and would have carried on in his praise but was cut short by the flustered looking female.

It was right then that Tori decided to reveal how she would pay him back for his joke. The kiss on the cheek and the mention of Cupid the night before was not payment enough, as far as she was concerned. No, a far more substantial payment was required for having her almost fall into the Gulf waters. Besides, he was having too much fun and getting away with way more than she could allow. His joy of learning she could converse in French had both surprised and delighted him. He was a happy man who, in her estimation, needed taking down a notch as far as she was concerned. With a somber expression, she began in English. "I suggest you take a seat." Tori pulled a chair from under the table and tapped the high wooden back with her hand. "Here, sit by my side, I have a matter to discuss with you, in English and not French, which seems to delight you so much. As Jean knows, I have been trying to think about a way to make you pay for your horrible prank."

"Me? When? I have done no such thing and especially to you." "How quickly you forget. After all, your dumb idea cost me moments of hell. It is not easy for a woman in a dress to climb down the side of a boat. Let alone jump into a bobbing cork. I had thought, making you embarrassed in front of our guest last night would be payment enough. You did go a lovely shade of red. But more is required to make us, how shall I put this? To make us even."

Dominique spluttered, and Jean roared with laughter. "I tell you my love has the spirit of a real vixen when she wants. Tread easy Dominique, or you shall find her upping her ante. Trust me; she can be downright terrible if she wants."

Tori laughed at Jean's statement. "Yes, I can, and that goes for both of you. Tricking me last night, Jean, well, that won't be forgotten quickly either. So, Mr. Jean Laffite, you too had best join Dominique and tread lightly, get my drift?"

Jean frowned at this statement. Dominique was laughing so hard that he did not seem to have noticed the strange way Tori had of expressing herself. However, he was concerned, and Laffite knew he'd have to remind his love yet again to be careful with her use of words and expressions. Before Jean could suggest Tori follow him into his library, to talk about the importance of keeping up the appearance of being from this era, Dominique spoke up.

"Truce. I declare a truce. I came to see if I might escort Tori around Grand Terre this morning?" He'd questioned Jean while flashing Tori one of his inscrutable grins. "Just while you are working, Boss, that would be proper, no? Call it an apology for my actions, and I promise you, Tori, that will never happen again; you suffering because of a joke aimed at Boss."

Before anyone could say a word, Tori jumped right in and spoke her mind. "Oh Dominique, that would be wonderful! The walk I mean, and yes, I accept your apology. We are even for now. Besides, I was wondering what I would do today." She turned and faced Jean. "That is all right, isn't it? You did say I could go out if I were escorted."

Laffite saw he had no choice in the matter and grudgingly nodded his approval. "Yes, that would be agreeable. The girl Lacy was by earlier. She asked if she could stay home today. Her man sails on one of my ships tonight and will be at sea for a while. I told her, therefore, that she could spend time with him. Even though you have Carlotta to help you, you would have been alone anyway. Carlotta has this house to run and can't spend all her time keeping you out of trouble."

"And just what is that supposed to mean?"

Jean chuckled out loud. He knew that she understood him. It was not that she looked for trouble, it just somehow always managed to find her, and this island was full of situations that could result in far worse scenarios than she had yet experienced.

It was when Jean mentioned Lacy that Tori remembered she must inform him about her and the danger the girl posed. He needed to know who Lacy was, and the quicker she explained, the better. "Dominique, you help yourself to breakfast. I won't be gone long. After all, one can't go out dressed like this. Night garments are for sleeping, not walking," she laughed. "Anyway, I have another small matter to talk over with Jean first. Make yourself at home. Just don't eat everything. Carlotta, you keep an eye on him for me."

"I will watch him, and I will make certain he leaves the fruit well enough alone. More eggs I can cook, but getting more fruit, that would take time."

Dominique frowned and then dramatically reached across the table for the bread. "Since when have I ever had anything but eggs and your bread for breakfast? Tori, the fruit is safe, but you best hurry; I may be tempted," he winked.

Tori smiled and shook her head. "You will not. I happen to love fruit so, eggs it is for you." Excusing herself from Dominique's side, she quickly followed Jean to the library. Once there, and satisfied no one could hear her, she hastily explained her problem to him. Then after several moments of silence, she spoke, her voice clearly sounding anxious. "What do you think we should do? Lacy knows who I am, and that could spell trouble. One slipup could ruin everything. I could be exposed, and then what?"

Jean's brow furrowed in concern. "I am not sure what I can do." He saw Tori's face fill further with worry. "Let me think about it, and remember this; no problem is too big that it can't be solved. One important detail has come from this situation." He placed his hands on her shoulders and looked lovingly into her eyes. "I am glad you trusted me enough to confide in me, and not try to handle this yourself. Now, from what you have told me, I think we can trust the girl, so run along and have a good day." He was smiling, trying to make light of the situation, regardless of how dire he knew it could become. "Tell Dominique I will see him later, and Tori, do try to stay out of trouble," he chuckled. "Also, please do your best to watch how you express your opinions. Your American way of speaking needs to be, how can I say? Yes, it needs to be reined in.

You do understand why?"

"I do, and you know I will do my best. You do understand that. Besides, I am safe with Dominique, and I intend to have a blast today." She giggled and indicated to the man that she was toying with him by wagging her finger in his direction.

Jean said nothing; he just stood a few seconds longer, staring at her with a very perplexed look.

"No, I am not going to blow something up. Having a blast means having a great time. Come on, quit looking at me like that. I was teasing."

Jean could be very exasperating when he wanted, Tori thought, as she watched him turn to leave, without any further conversation. At least he could have admitted that he got her joke. Whatever, it didn't matter because she knew he had her back. She giggled again. Thinking in American was allowed. 'Got her back! Ha, what would he think about that saying? No doubt, he'd turn it into something sexual.' Her smile broadened and then softened. All in all, Tori understood it would be better if she tried exceptionally hard to speak in terms that he and everyone else could grasp. As for Dominique, she had some plans for him. It was time for the real payback for his joke, and this time Tori had him, just where she needed. Better still, there was nothing he could do or say about her request, either. A sly smile crossed her lips. Unlike Jean, she knew she could talk Dominique into anything. To make sure of the outcome, though, she'd add a bit of a guilt trip on him, and then he'd have to cave in to her idea.

REVEALING her intention's over her breakfast nearly caused Dominique to have a heart attack. "All I asked you, Dominique, was to show me how to shoot one of your pistols and teach me how to fence. What's wrong with that?"

"That is just it. I see nothing wrong, but my dear…however, Boss and society most certainly would!"

"I don't give a damn about society, and Jean does not have to know, now does he? It could be our little secret, couldn't it? Just think how surprised he will be when I can show him some of what I have learned. Plus, you owe me. Making me climb down a rope ladder and come ashore in that ridiculous boat. I was quite simply terrified, you know, and, after all, I have done for you, one would think you would have never done such…"

"Enough, enough, please. Enough I tell you." Feeling guilty, and not wanting to be further reminded of his faux pas, Dominique was won over before he had a chance to argue. Besides, he loved the idea of working with her behind Jean's back. Better still, he liked the idea of teaching. After all, he had taught Jean and his brother Pierre, the subtler points of fencing. So why not show the lady who was going to be around from now on? "No more guilt. I am agreed!" He slapped his hand down on the table's wooden surface. "That is, my dear, if you give me your word, which is, that not a breath of this is to reach Jean's ears. If I have your word on that, then I see no reason to delay the first lesson. It could be this very morning…maybe. Don't get your hopes set too high. Due to the circumstances in this matter, it will not be much of a lesson; rather, I shall see how to go about such a delicate matter in the days ahead. We shall need implements."

"Like getting me a sword and a gun of my own?"

"Heavens, no! You shall not have a gun, a pistol, or even a sword, not anytime soon that is." The pirate's face had turned white at the thought of her suggestion, but his cheeks burned red, showing his excitement. We need first to locate a place of discretion and then form a plan. Our walk will reveal how we can obtain both."

Dominique's enthusiasm was infectious, and it ignited excitement inside of her. Tori lost all traces of an appetite, as breakfast now seemed too slow and a total waste of time. She was far too impatient to do anything other than start right away with her lessons. However, Dominique convinced her that a short walk around Grand Terre first would be beneficial to both of them.

He felt that he needed to see for himself, that Jean was indeed busy with the business of the day, and that Tori should observe and learn a little more about her new surroundings. "Never hurts to know the lay of the land. It's one thing to know how to fight if necessary, but far better to know how to avoid it if you can, even if it means leaving, you understand?"

"I think so. What you are trying to tell me, is that if a situation occurred, that called for a fight, that if I know Grand Terre, I could obtain help getting myself out of danger, am I right?"

"You are going to make an excellent student. However, it is important that you know, I am only agreeable to teaching you the art of fencing for the entertainment. Never is it to be for anything, how shall I say? It is not for you to actually fight."

"Oh, of course not, silly. I know that much. It is for fun. Why, Dominique, you don't think this lady would be stupid enough to pit herself against a far more experienced opponent, do you?" She didn't give him a chance to answer. Feeling uncomfortable with the conversation, and fearing Dominique might change his mind, she boldly took him by the arm and walked him out of the house. "Now, let's see the area. I want to see every square inch. After all, it is rather a notorious place you have here, isn't it?"

Tori learned that the settlement had everything a small town would have and more. The place had a population more significant than she imagined. It numbered around several hundred permanent residences at any given time, and that was just on their side of the strait. The population would be more substantial when all the ships were in port, she was told, but not as large as on Grand Isle. That portion of the settlement, which stretched out on the other side of the inlet, was always double and often triple the size of where she now lived.

Everywhere they went, a variety of languages were spoken. Dominique even explained that still, more men arrived every day to join the operation, and from all walks of life and varying in age. Some came alone, while others brought family or female companions. All came to make money, to plunder and pillage. They came seeking captains who would add them to the ship's crew, a task that sometimes took weeks to achieve. Fights were frequent, and more than a few were settled brutally.

As each hour passed, her admiration for Jean as a leader and businessman expanded. They were no small band of pirates like she had thought. The area was like a whole civilization of misfits who had taken up pirating for a living. Looking around, she determined both sides of the large village, comprised of the roughest sorts around. All in all, it was just as Jean had explained, and knowing he had not exaggerated, Tori was glad of Dominique's company.

When she had arrived yesterday on the island with Jean, he'd taken her the quickest way to his house. The man had left much of what she now witnessed with Dominique, safely out of sight. Today, however, not a section was left uncovered in her exploration. The curious woman saw more than one café, a gambling den, and even a bordello. She was to learn that the last, although not one of Dominique or Jean's idea, it kept the men happy and out of New Orleans.

"Boss says it's far better to keep their wagging tongues drunk in our domain, among our people, and out of harm's way. Besides, Boss hates to see them waste their money. He likes to see it come back to the company," he laughed.

Shocked by this piece of news, Tori had to ask. "Jean owns the whorehouse?"

"Oh no, he would never have his reputation tarnished in such a manner. They run their own operation, but purchase all their needs, rum, wine, whiskey, gowns, and so forth, from Jean. See, that is how the place makes the company a profit while keeping everyone happy."

Surprised, Tori gazed back at the building and wondered how the inside looked. She could bet it was nothing like Rose's. It could never be as grand or the madame as gaudy as Rose had been. For example, the female who stood staring their way was far from looking like a harlot, and in no way was she gaudy. Tori interrupted Dominique's laughter with a more serious tone. "It's a company that seems to be doing very well indeed, as is the lady standing over there, waving at us. I would venture to say that by the way she is dressed, her business must be doing well. Such an elegant gown. Oh my…so low cut too, her breasts look almost ready to burst over the top." Tori giggled as she watched him blush. "Oh, don't worry. I am not shocked that a man such as you needs the company of attractive women now and then. She is beautiful, isn't she?"

"Aye, she is. However, I have no desire to make her acquaintance at this time."

"Really? Because she looks like she is more than ready to chat with you?"

"I bet she is. What with myself owing her for her company last night," he grinned. "Now, let me show you this way." He took Tori by the arm and turned her completely around. The old sea-dog deliberately walked in the opposite direction of where the woman stood, making it plainly obvious that he was not about to let Tori anyplace close to her. "A lady of your standing has no need to talk with the likes of her, pretty or not. Jean would have my head if he heard you had been talking with one of the whores. Now, down this way is where I do most of my drinking and socializing; and before you ask me, no, I will not escort you inside. It is a tavern with a reputation. The place is well known on both islands. Those that go there; they are what Boss warned you about; of all the places you have seen today, that one there, that's the one you avoid at all cost. Never go in, trust me. I go in on account they respect me, and one or two of the regulars, keep an eye on me. They know where to take me if I happen to partake of too much drink."

"Bet that would be back into the arms of the lovely thing you just avoided, right?" Tori looked back behind them and saw that the woman was still watching them. She grinned and looked back into the older man's blushing face.

Jean's second-in-command grinned. "I will not incriminate my reputation. There again, as it is you who asks, well, tiz true, my arms are always welcome, as is my money. The lady knows that I'm hers while I am here." Dominique cocked his head to one side and tried to look serious. "Don't go telling Jean now, or I will never hear the end of it."

"I swear never to speak a word about it. Say, you and I are acquiring quite a few secrets from him, aren't we?"

The pirate nodded his head and smiled softly. "Better we slow up some in that department. Here, you best come see something you can talk about, and I have no doubt that you will. Over here is where many of the barges are loaded to make the trip to the city. You might find this interesting. See that load of cargo over there, all stacked nicely too? It is waiting to be loaded on the next barge. A barge that I am sure will arrive soon, or Boss would not have had the items taken out of storage so soon."

"I had no idea that so much cargo was shipped directly from here to New Orleans. I mean, I thought it would go in a boat up the river or across the bay and then by land."

"Some does but most goes the way of the bayous; harder for the revenue men to catch us. We know the way, and they tend to get lost. Fools all of them, I tell you. Still, tizz best, we not cross paths. We avoid them at all costs while they try to find us," he chuckled. "When they have us in their sights, they shoot but hit nothing. Like I said, fools all of them."

While listening to him, Tori gazed at the quiet bayou that he had pointed too. It was leading away from the Barataria Bay's tranquil waters, and just in front of it sat a large vessel that looked relatively new. "That looks ready to be loaded."

"It is, and will be soon. The work was completed on it a few days ago. It was built from raw pieces of cypress found in this area. An abundance of cypress trees grow throughout the swamps and beyond. That barge, along with two others," he said, pointing further down the canal, "will travel, as they do most days, up and down the waterways, with cargo and men. Boss likes to say we take the back door to New Orleans." He was laughing again. Noticing that she didn't share his humor, and most likely did not believe him, he quickly reverted to a more serious attitude. "Our canals, they have been widened by the men, to accommodate such large vessels, and only they know the way through this vast wetland maze." He threw his arms around in a large circle to emphasize the enormity of the area.

"Really? I would never have guessed that," she lied. Of course, she'd learned all about the pirate's operation in her time, so what he was telling her was nothing she didn't already know. Not wanting the old man to see her face and guess that she was lying, Tori changed the subject. "How many men work for Jean now?"

"That I am not sure of, it changes, but I would estimate, between one thousand and twelve hundred, maybe more. Yes, I would estimate more. It varies at any given time. Not all live here, you understand? They come, and they go."

"I had no idea this place was so big. I'm amazed that he handles it all himself."

"Well, not quite by himself." Dominique placed his hands on his hips. "There is his second-in-command, at your service." He bowed dramatically. Then, a little embarrassed at trying to overstate his importance, he quickly added, "and his brother Pierre among others. But 'tiz true, most of the decisions are now made by Boss and myself. Is there more you wish to know? Ask me anything, for I will be most delighted and agreeable to share all with such a beauty as yourself."

She blushed a little at this and decided to continue on as if his compliment had not bothered her. "Then, let us continue, shall we?" I think we should stroll this way, don't you?"

Tori took his arm and continued to walk with him while questioning more and more. In this way, the hours passed, and as time wore on, the older man became more amazed at how intelligent she was. Her mind was like no other female he had ever encountered, and once again, he made a mental note to let Jean know that he would be a fool to let this woman slip away.

Finally, they came to an open area, which stood behind one of three large warehouses. Here, upon closer inspection, it was decided, would be where the two of them would meet every day for their fencing lessons. Only on the days when the other significant buildings lay empty, and these were being utilized, would they find the need for a different location, he explained. Until such a time, it was the perfect location, and both agreed upon that.

"So, my lessons begin. What will you teach me today? Can I try your gun?"

Horrified, Dominique stepped backward and grabbed hold of his pistol, which was tucked in his belt. "You may not. My weapon shall remain here where it belongs; it is no toy. You can be assured that if I am to allow you a chance at firing such, it would be done when there is little chance of us being detected. This is not that time…no lessons today. I have located our place of intention, and our plans are made. That is enough. Come, before I regret ever agreeing to such an arrangement."

Tori realized she had pushed him too far and quickly decided if the idea of firing a gun had to go, so she could keep the fencing, then so be it. One thing was sure; Dominique needed to be assured that she was levelheaded and would listen to him. "If you insist. I won't ask again to fire your weapon, I promise. Silly idea anyway. So, we can begin heading back to the house. Let's just take a more roundabout way, not the shortcut that Jean used yesterday. I want to see all of this and not just what Boss wants me to see."

"I have no problem with that. Let us just hope your man has none," he winked.

On the walk back to the house, Tori noticed an area where something had been taken down. It seemed odd to her because everywhere else, things were being built, not dismantled. "What's going on over there?"

"Ah, that was the barracoon, the area where the blacks were kept until their auction."

"You mean the slaves?"

"Quite so. But upon landing, Boss gave orders for it to be removed. A ridiculous decision if you ask me, a lot of money to be made in slaves?"

"You mean you believe in slavery?"

"No…not as you think I do. Nor does Boss. He respects life, everyone's life, even slaves." Dominique felt uncomfortable with this line of conversation, and so he quickly changed the topic. "He even has a sense of humor that escapes you at first, until you get to know him. Take the name of this area, Barataria. Do you know what it means?"

"Yes, actually, I do. It means deception," she frowned while letting the meaning sink in. "I see what you mean. There is a lot more to the man than one first sees."

"Exactly, everything he does has meaning." He looked at her with surprise in his eyes. "This whole place is built on deception and more." He looked away from her scrutiny. The lady was not easy to fool, and he had a great desire right then, to do so, or his captain would be more than upset. The last thing she needed was to learn that the barracoon was only being moved and not done away with. Out of sight, out of mind, was Jean's idea to satisfy her wishes. Laffite was not going to stop trading in slaves if they came his way, and often they did just that. They stood to make a great deal of money, especially since slavery was outlawed. The buying and selling of blacks had become more lucrative than ever. He did not want to upset Tori by her learning the truth in this matter; therefore, a small lie was needed to keep the peace and everyone happy. 'Lord, I better talk about something else, and quickly, or this intelligent woman will see just what is going on.'

Tori looked directly into the pirate's eyes; the man seemed nervous or worried about something. "Dominique, what happened to those slaves on the ship? I was on deck all day, and I never saw them leave.

Are they still there? Or did Jean sell them after all? He did, didn't he? He lied to me." Her temper was rising, and she didn't care.

Laffite's second-in-command knew he had blundered by allowing her to guess the blacks' outcome, so he quickly sought to calm her down. "It is not like that. Boss cares, look, he is taking down the place where they would have been held until a higher price could and would have been offered. He is listening to you and costing himself a fine profit to do so, I might add. When you get to know Boss better, you will find that Jean is quite an extraordinary individual. Many agree with me on this. I might add, he did this for you and will do far more. You only have to ask. The pup will obey," he chuckled. "Jean Laffite is a fine catch and…"

Tori looked away from him and concentrated on the barracoon area. The old man had changed the subject, and to one that needed nipping in the bud, so she interrupted him. "Are you playing matchmaker by chance, my friend? Or are you trying to avoid the subject of slavery?"

Dominique was surprised that he had become that transparent to his new charge. He would have to be more careful in the future. However, it would be of no harm to let her know that it would not hurt his feelings any if she were to settle down with Jean. As for the subject of slavery, he was going to avoid that at all costs. No need for her to learn the slaves were sold and on their way to a plantation up river.

Tori remained silent while she continued to study Dominique's face. Standing there as he was, with his head turned to one side, with a slightly embarrassed look about him, Tori thought for an instant how very much he resembled Jean at times. The eyes were a different color, but there was something in the mannerisms that bound the two together. Not like father and son, no, it was more like brothers. That they could be brothers was a ridiculous thought though, it could not be, she mused. She recalled there was only one brother, mentioned in the history she had heard, and that was Pierre. True, Tori could not think of ever reading about

Dominique, let alone any mention of him being a relative, but still, the resemblance was remarkable, there was no denying it. Could it be, that for some unknown reason, it had been kept a secret, that he was a part of the family? Had she just stumbled on something that even history had skipped? She'd have to dig carefully to learn the truth behind that question.

Dominique broke the awkward silence. "Which one of us is looking at the other the closest, I wonder? And for what reason do we just stand here, looking, and thinking to ourselves?"

"Oh, no reason, other than I never thought I would see the time when Dominique You would blush twice in one day."

Dominique would have picked up the challenge and tried to deny that he was an old fool caught in Cupid's role, but a shout from Jean spun them both around.

"Here you are. I've been looking all over for you." Turning to Tori, he said, "That little matter we talked about this morning, the one concerning your friend? It has been solved, and quite nicely, if I might add. Come with me and say your fond farewells to the lucky couple."

Shock registered on Tori's face. "Did you say farewells? Jean, how can you ask them to leave, or are you forcing them? Because if you are, it's no way to solve the problem, you know."

"Why, Tori," he pretended to look wounded. "Why would they be forced to leave, and for whatever reason?"

Dominique was entirely at a loss, as far as the conversation was concerned. The fact that Jean seemed to know what was going on did not help him any either. On the other hand, Tori looked as confused as himself and more upset about whatever it was Jean was eluding too. She at least had some understanding as to what his captain was talking about, though, which confused the older man even more. Why did he not know? Had Boss kept a secret from him? If so, how could he be angry when he was also keeping secrets? He had to find out, and the best way was to ask right then. "Am I not understanding something here, Boss? You look too smug, and Tori looks as if she could kill you at any moment. It might be best to clear the air, don't you think? You two fight too much, I tell you. You need no excuse to be romantic. I myself, have found that the times one makes love to his lady, can be the best, only when no anger is in the bed, with them." He put his hands on his hips as was his norm when emphasizing something. The rugged man took a step back while staring at them intently.

It was very evident that Jean was thoroughly enjoying himself, and his humor continued as he baited Dominique. "For whom should I clear the air, Dominique? It seems to me that it is you who wants to know what's going on. Tori is not angry with me, are you my love?"

"I don't know what to think at this moment, but if you are thinking of sending Lacy and her child away, or worse yet, getting rid of her man to force her to go, then you will have a fight on your hands. And, I tell you this, if that happens, anger will be in our bed for a hell of a long time." Her expression and tone of voice made it clear that she meant what she said.

"See why I find this woman irresistible, Dominique? It's the fire in her. When she gets worked up over something she believes in, she is like a storm at sea. It is amazing; is it not?"

Tori could see that he was having fun teasing them and decided that she would say no more for once and just wait and see what would turn up, despite the uneasy feeling creeping up inside her. Besides, Dominique was always on her side, so if this was serious, she could at least count on his help.

LACY spotted them walking towards her, long before Tori saw her. The young mulatto ran towards them, laughing and repeating the word thank you over and over. She was so excited that when she reached Tori's side, she spoke in a jumbled mixture of Creole and English without caring she wrapped her arms around Tori and then bounced up and down, laughing even more.

It took Lacy sometime to stop hugging Tori and remain still enough to calm down and slow up in her rambling. Seeing that her friend could not understand her, she took in a deep breath and spoke slowly in English. "Thank you for this chance. You are an angel, as the men from Boss's ship say. You think of others, and I hope that one day, it all comes back to you and that you find the happiness you deserve."

Bewildered, Tori looked to Jean for an explanation. Stepping in between them, he placed his arms around Tori's waist proudly and spoke for all to hear. "Victoria is quite something, isn't she? Here she does this for you and thinks nothing of it. Asking me to send you and your family to the islands to work for me, free from the bonds of servitude, all because you showed her kindness."

Had she heard him right? Had Jean just said that Lacy was to be free? She looked up into his face, and then at Lacy's nodding head.

Lacy continued, "I know that we have had little time together, Miss Tor…Victoria, and I won't be able to help you none anymore. One day, somehow, I will find a way to thank you both."

"We both will," added a deep masculine voice. A tall young man with a little boy in his arms had joined the group, and he was no stranger. This man was none other than Jim. The crewman who had helped Tori during the long voyage to and from the islands. This familiar figure was Lacy's man, and Tori couldn't be more pleased. She had grown very fond of him in all the weeks at sea and knew him to be an honest and kind person. In his arms was the child she had seen only once before, and by the loving look on his father's face, she now understood that everything Lacy had said about her man, while they were at Rose's house, had been real.

"Oh, Lacy, things are so clear now, and I am happy for you. The whole time I was away, on Jean's ship and all. All that time, Jim was not here, and last night, you stayed and helped me, while all you needed was to be with him. You should have told me."

"I reckon I could have, but how was I to know that my man was knowing you? I needed to help him, and he did not mind on account he had his boy, and I was with you. He reckoned it was a good thing, cause he says you are a real lady and all. Besides, we had our time last night." She giggled and faced her man and child.

Jim carefully handed the child over to Lacy and held out his hand to his captain's lady. "I'm not one for words, Ma'am, best I can do is thank you. Whoever would have thought that you and my Lacy knew each other?" The crewman leaned closer to Tori and spoke softly so no other could hear him. "Your story will remain with us. You helped my Lacy escape Roses', and for that, I am indebted." He stood back then and spoke so all could hear him. "I will see to it that my woman here, and our son will be happy, and you have my word on that." He looked at both Jean and Tori as he continued. "You have both made this possible. You have our word, we will work hard, and you will see profits soon. I always did want the chance to leave the sea and work the land again. Planned on it and thought it would be some time yet before I could stay with my family." He faced Lacy then as he continued. "This here trip will be my last voyage. I'll never have to sail off and leave you and our son again, Lacy."

The two looked at each other as if they could not possibly get any happier. Jean, however, was not finished with surprises. He reached into his jacket pocket and pulled out two envelopes and some papers. "The first paper is to go to the doctor and his wife when you arrive. It is instructions for a friend of mine; the priest will marry you soon after your arrival, in a small church that I know of." He frowned at them, adding, "Jumping over the broom somehow doesn't seem binding enough for a family who is going to work for me." He saw the flash of concern on Lacy's face, one he knew he could erase quickly. "We all know it's against the law for you to marry Jim, as you are technically not a free person with papers to prove it. I took the liberty to have some drawn up. After all, the person that did own you won't come looking for you anymore, will she? You are free to marry. Let's just say this priest owes me a favor and believes that no matter what, two people should stand before

God." He cleared his throat and handed the next envelope to Lacy. "This envelope is a little something from Victoria and myself to help you get started."

Lacy had taken the envelope from Jean with her free hand and tears in her eyes. She didn't hesitate but quickly handed them over to her man without looking at them. Then she cuddled her son close to her chest and softly spoke. "Here, Jim, you best take this and those papers. I'm just too happy to stand still for much longer. Besides, I can't read too well yet."

After opening the envelope and looking inside, Jim just nodded his head in thanks to Jean. He felt too afraid to speak, so he stepped forward and embraced Tori and Jean together. Not wanting to upset Tori too much more, Jean broke free of Jim's hug. "You had best make your way to the ship. The tide won't wait, and long farewells have a way of delaying that which should be hastened."

Tori hugged Lacy and kissed the little boy, crying and laughing all at the same time. It was sad to lose this friend so soon, but she was also happy with the freedom that Lacy was about to gain.

Jim broke the two apart, taking his child back from Lacy. Boss had given an order to board, and Jim intended to obey. "Come, Lacy, it's time."

"I know it is." She smiled brightly at her friend, and without another word, just a nod of her head, she turned and joined Jim.

Lacy and Jim walked toward the rowboat with their son in Jim's arms. The young woman almost skipped her way to the small craft that would take them to the larger ship. Once seated in the small rowboat, she called back to Tori, "I will never forget you, never, and forever my lips will stay sealed!"

A broad smile filled Tori's face. Her secret was safe once again, thanks to Laffite's quick thinking. "Good-bye, my friend. God bless you both," she called out while waving to them. Overcome then, by emotion, Tori just laid her head on Jean's shoulder and silently sunk into his embrace.

He understood her sadness, of how difficult it was to say farewell, just like he knew the joy of knowing her friends would have a good life would soon overcome her sorrow. "Let's go back to the house. It will be some time yet before they sail, and watching them row out to the ship, then climb aboard, well, I think it would be easier on all. Come on," he coaxed.

Tori was glad that Jean had taken control. She stepped away from him and stood proudly by his side, gaining strength in knowing that he and Dominique were with her. For the first time since seeing Lacy, Tori looked at Dominique, who it seemed was not surprised at all, by what had taken place. He was simply carrying on as if this sort of thing happened every day. 'You are such a good actor, aren't you? I shall have to remember that.' "You want to join us, Dominique?"

"Me? No, not right away. Later maybe? Seeing those two has reminded me that I am in need of visiting someone who misses me." He winked knowingly at Tori before turning to leave. They didn't need him around right now, he told himself. He had a feeling that Jean's love was about to thank him for all he had done, and not just with words. Chuckling, he agreed with his thoughts; he knew they would not have a third party called anger, in bed with them this time. It had been obvious that Tori had not known a thing about what had just occurred. Yes, Tori would want to thank Jean all right, and that meant he, Dominique, had best be on his way. "You know where to find me if I am needed, not that I think for one moment you will." With that said, he picked up his pace and did not stop to look back until he was well away from the beach.

Dominique stopped at a safe distance and stood watching Jean and Tori as they began their walk back toward the house. The sight warmed his heart, and he grinned because the old pirate knew that the pup was more than ready to settle down. Just look at all the crazy things the man was doing, he thought. Even if Jean didn't know that his anchor in life was walking by his side, he would very soon, because it was way too obvious. The wind in his captain's sails had changed direction, and Dominique was both happy and sad. As for himself, he was going to the whorehouse to celebrate and drink. The particulars of what had just happened and why would come to light soon enough for him. He had many questions and wondered more about other facts that did not sit right. It was strange how a slip of a girl and Jim had been connected somehow to Tori, strange but not alarming. One way or another, he'd learn the truth about today's turn of events. Dominique You always stayed informed when it came to Jean Laffite's life.

TORI was thrilled. By the time they reached the house, Jean had told her the whole story of his plan for Lacy and Jim, and how he had put it into action so fast. She was amazed that he had arranged so much in such a short time, and it was a comfort to know how capable he was in his role as leader and guardian angel. Laffite was far more than the just the pirate's leader to her, though. Jean was a kind man who cared about more than just himself, as he had just demonstrated.

"We need to celebrate," she laughed.

"That was what I had in mind. You don't think I did all of that just for those two, do you? Now, just how do you plan to show me how grateful you are for my stroke of genius? Not only did I solve our problem, but if I might say, I did it in a way that left everyone happy, did I not?"

Tori laughed and, teasing him, added, "Well, let's see how smart you are. If you genuinely thought this all through, you would have known that champagne was in order, and one of those cigars would not hurt any. And, if you planned ahead, well, they would be upstairs waiting for us. But then, you really could not be that scheming, could you?"

This woman knew him better than she realized, he thought, as he laughed out loud. He was not only happy, but Jean was aware that at that very moment, this was the way he wanted the rest of his life to be. He wanted nothing more than to live his life, making this woman happy. "If you are truly brave, my lady and wish, to see what I have prepared, then may I suggest that we go? But, beware, for if I did scheme, as you put it, then I feel it only fair to warn you that the rest of the day may very well be spent sipping champagne and making love. That is how you plan to show me your gratitude, isn't it?"

"Oh, you rogue, I will go and see, but you best know that I will not remain if the champagne is not there," she teased."

Upon reaching the house, Tori left Jean's side and ran up the stairs ahead of him. He had to be lying, because how could he have known? Yet, when she pushed open the door to their room and saw the champagne, it was clear that he'd won. How did he know her so well? Was it a lucky guess? Had he done all those things for Lacy or more for her? Tori had many questions spinning in her mind. However, before she could utter one-word, Laffite was behind her.

The overwhelmed female experienced many feelings, as the pirate's arms came around her waist, his breath touching her ear. "Never underestimate me, Tori, never," he whispered as he gently pushed her into the room, closing the door behind him.

Carlotta was leaving as she heard the upstairs door close. The housekeeper smiled, for all had been done as he had asked, and knowing that, she left understanding they'd not need her until the next day.

# ⊰ Two ⊱

The weeks had flown by, and before she knew, it another month had begun. It was November 1810, and a chill filled the night air. It had not escaped her thoughts, that for weeks, the subject of the lake had not been mentioned. She had not once asked about or attempted to have Jean return her to the destination she sought. Tori told herself she had good enough reason not to pressure him into taking her right away, seeing how very occupied he was, with running the business. Knowing him as she did, the modern-day lady realized that the man would keep his promise in due time. The lake was not going anyplace, and until they could safely return to that small cove, she would have to be content with filling her time wisely and not concerning herself with the sad thoughts that haunted her dreams.

Her days had become occupied with Dominique's company, and her nights with Jeans'. Most evenings, they dined alone, but there were times that Dominique joined them, along with some merchant or business acquaintance. These nights she found to be enjoyable, as it gave her a chance to brush up on her French. Always she was introduced as Victoria, and if guests wondered what her role was in the house, they never questioned. It seemed to her that the Creole gentlemen were either far too polite to ask such a question, or far too smart. It had become apparent to her that no one dared upset Jean Laffite, for his quick temper was well known to all.

Tori's first fencing lessons had proceeded, a few days after their walk, and they had continued without interruption. Laffite's lady found that not only was Dominique an excellent instructor, but she had somewhat of a natural flair for the sport. Jean's second-in-command had taken her to their hidden spot, and in a serious tone, begun to explain how they would proceed. "I have two weapons with me. It is the best I can do for now. Had them carved yesterday. Told the man I was going to instruct one of the lads. Paid him good, so he'd keep his trap shut. That and the fact it took him the better part of the day and night to finish them on time, cost me extra."

"Carved? You can't mean what I think? Wooden swords?"

"Aye, they are. Such a quick mind, as always. Come here, see." Dominique picked them up from behind a small palmetto where they had lain undetected in the taller grass. He looked at her closely. "Are you certain you have not taken such lessons before now? Maybe you have used such beginning implements before?"

Tori frowned and feeling a tad upset over his idea of using wooden swords; she confronted him. "Stop with the questions and tell me, why can't we begin with a real sword? I am no child, you know, and quite capable of handling such a weapon, I can assure you."

Dominique briefly chuckled and then gained his composure. He had to make her understand his reasoning. "It is for my safety and yours. Also, the blade you talk of is not referred to as a sword. It is a rapier, and though small and thin, it is just as deadly as its big brothers, when used correctly. Not that you will ever use one in such a manner. These lessons are strictly for sport and my entertainment. Should anyone discover us, I think we will be able to talk our way around such teachings. I could say my arm needed practice, and you were the one who suggested it.

"Oh, I see. Blame me."

"No, I am doing no such thing. I am only telling the truth; after all, it was your idea."

Tori grinned. "You have me there, but I still say I can handle the real item." She looked at the wooden blades in the man's hands and lightheartedly questioned him. "So how long do we play with sticks?"

Sounding somewhat stern, he answered her. "Once you have mastered the basic movements, I shall replace the wooden weapons, with the real item. Rapiers with their tips placed in a cork. Until you have shown me skill enough to use the blade without harm. A small cut on my hand or body I can explain, on you, merde, (shit,) that would be challenging, and Boss would quickly learn what we have been up too. Now, if you will kindly allow me to put my pistol over there, we will begin. One can't fence with a weapon sticking in his groin. The art is all about moving and the feet; they dance like this." He moved around while keeping the rapier, steadily pointed in front of him.

THE lessons remained secret, just as they had agreed. On the days that Dominique could not keep their rendezvous, he would send her a message, thereby avoiding her getting caught waiting alone at the arranged spot.

Today had been one of those mornings. A young boy arrived shortly after Jean's departure and waited for Tori at the back door. He'd told Carlotta he had to give his important letter to Boss's lady and no one else. Thinking it a bit strange, the housekeeper had told Tori and who met the child right away. The note stated that Dominique was sorry, he would not be available for a few days, as he had to go to New Orleans on urgent business. He regretted profoundly, disappointing her, and hoped she would understand. Tori tore the note up and asked the housekeeper to burn it and then she turned to talk to the young boy, while the housekeeper returned to her kitchen.

The lad, who was maybe five, stood before her, not knowing if he should leave or stay. His large round eyes looked anywhere but directly at the woman before him. As he waited for his next instructions, the child chewed nervously on his thumb, and Tori could tell it must have taken him an enormous amount of courage to deliver the note to the Boss's woman. This small child impressed her, and she made up her mind that he deserved a reward. "You stay." Not knowing if he understood, Tori motioned with her hands, and once satisfied the child understood what he was to do, she left the area and quickly made her way to the kitchen. She called out to the housekeeper as she hurried along. "Carlotta, do you have any of those small cakes from last night?"

Carlotta looked up from the fire, where she was dutifully burning the note. If seeing Tori burst into the room surprised her, she did not show it. "Si, Senorita. You can have as many as you want."

"No, silly, they're not for me. The cakes are for the little boy at the door. He just delivered a message from Dominique. For the life of me, I don't know why you want me to eat so much lately. I'm beginning to feel like an overstuffed chicken."

Carlotta smiled and shook her head. The housekeeper could not believe that Tori didn't realize that food was not the reason she was feeling bloated. Did the Senorita not want to admit that she was with child? Or could it be that Miss Victoria did not understand her body? Either way, it was not her place to ask, so she ignored the nagging questions filling her mind and gathered together six of the small cakes.

Tori noticed the woman's strange expression when she handed over the small bundle, and fearing she was the cause, she asked her. "Is there something wrong, Carlotta? You're looking at me as if I have upset you."

Carlotta smiled, shaking her head adamantly. "No, nothing. You had best give the cakes to the child. He will leave soon, as he is frightened. It is a wonder the little one has remained so long, as it is. Come, let's both go and see, shall we?"

When they reached the back door, both women could see the young boy slowly backing up. It seemed as if he truly was afraid, and worse still Tori assumed it was herself that the child was scared of. "He is frightened, why is that do you suppose? I have never seen him before; how is it that I scare him?"

Carlotta shook her head. "It is not so much you, as it is this house, I think." She looked at the boy and smiled kindly. "Or maybe he is just timid? Hand him the cakes that might make him happy."

Tori handed the child the cakes which were wrapped in a piece of cloth. At first, confusion filled his little face, but when he saw a nod of approval from Carlotta, he clutched his reward to his chest and smiled. His expression was all the thanks Tori needed, and all she received because her return smile ended their short but sweet moment. The boy turned, and as quickly as he had appeared, he was off, running down the pathway as fast as his little chubby suntanned legs could carry him, and Tori couldn't help but laugh. "Poor little guy. Probably thinks he had best leave before I change my mind and take the cakes back."

The boy was so intent on heading home with his prize that he paid no attention to anything else, and because of this, he didn't see Jean step onto the pathway ahead of him. Before either of the women could call out a warning, he ran right into the pirate's legs, and then things really began to unravel.

The collision caused him to stumble, and his cloth full of goodies was dislodged. The child watched in horror as his cherished cakes rolled out of the small folded bundle, in many directions. Most of the cakes landed right in front of the man who would no doubt think he stole them, and that would not be good.

Almost at once, crying and speaking rapidly, he declared that he did not steal them. The angel at the house had given them to him; he insisted while trying to locate each spilled cake. Then upon seeing Jean holding one of his cakes, he brazenly reached out and snatched it from the man's hand. The lad was so insistent that they were rightfully his, that Jean had no choice but to believe him and admire his spunk. Without a word, Laffite crouched down and spread out the cloth so the boy could place his hand full of cakes on top and wrap them back up. As they worked together doing this, the tears and protests left, and laughter again surrounded the pair.

Jean began talking to the boy softly. He had such a caring smile on his face that even a stranger would have seen his soft spot for children showing its hand. It was Jean's smile that seemed to calm the child as he listened to the pirate's voice. "Now, you take this and hold onto the bundle and don't drop it again. You can do that only if you watch where you are going. You don't see me running around with my hands full, do you?" Seeing the lad's head shake no and then watching him carefully cradle his cloth filled bundle, Jean stood up. The satisfied adult stepped aside to allow the youngster to pass. Slowly, the boy walked ahead, while keeping an eye on the pathway as Boss had instructed. As he cautiously passed by Laffite, he received a playful pat on his rear end, which hastened his pace and sent him on his way. In a flash, once again, he took off running, too fast for Jean to call him back and find out why the boy had been at the house in the first place. He hoped Tori was not making friends with the local children because it would only be harder for her to leave. Jean hoped his lady would be happy about the move when she learned of his plans, but whether she liked it or not, the move was inevitable. The time had come for them to depart Grand Terre, and there was no way he would allow her to remain without him.

Tori's reaction was nothing like he expected. She was elated by the news and not in the least bit upset. The excited woman asked all sorts of questions with great enthusiasm. However, as the implications of what was about to happen sank in, a worried look clouded her radiant face. Tori was experiencing her old, deep-seated fear of being found by Edward and what that could mean. "Jean, if I go with you, then the people, all of your friends, they will meet me. What if one of them should recognize who I am? After all, Tori is not a common name here, and yes, I know you introduce me as Victoria, but some of the crew could have spoken of me, using my preferred name. What if I run into that son of a bitch, Edward? If he should realize just who I am, he could make all kinds of trouble."

Jean only smiled slightly and didn't seem worried. "That is part of the reason why we have to leave now. I have had some of my men asking questions around New Orleans, to learn just where you stand. I think it's time that we found out, don't you? Anyway, looking as you do now, no one will see you as Tori, the runaway fancy, but instead, they will see you as my lady. A woman, I might add, of great beauty and charm. You will be a success; I am certain." His hand took hold of her face by the chin, and he tilted her head up so he could look deeply into her eyes while he continued. "Let us not worry about such matters. We will handle whatever comes our way, together."

His words helped calm her, but then another thought presented itself to the forefront, and it was one she could not ignore. "One other thing, Jean. I have not asked you for some time," she hesitated, then began slowly, "I would not bring it up now... but," she turned her head away from his gaze as she continued, "well...now that we are going into town, does it mean you intend to keep your promise, to take me to the lake?"

Jean froze. This thought had been furthest from his mind. He had almost forgotten that he had indeed agreed to take her to the damned lake. Silently Jean cursed himself for making such a promise, and now he knew she had not forgotten, Jean had to keep his word, for he had no choice. Jean Laffite was a man of his word, and knowing Tori expected no less, what else could he do? The implications of what might occur raced through his mind. When he returned her to that God-forsaken lake, what would happen? He ran his hand over his head, and his mind continued to imagine the consequences of his actions to come. By taking her to there, he ran the real risk of losing the only woman who had stolen his heart. If he did not return her, though, he would still lose her. Tori would not trust him or his word ever again.

Looking at her standing a few feet away, he wondered, did she not know that she was his life? He loved her, even knowing that a part of her was not his. He understood that she should question if there was a way back to her home and that she could not let go of her life in the future until she attempted to return. His mind understood all that, but his heart did not. He looked away from her, taking in a deep breath and exhaling slowly, he tried to come to grips with his emotions. Jean realized he had no right to hold her if she had a chance to return to her home, but he wished right then that he could somehow, this one time, be selfish and find a way to break his word. Sadly, he knew he could not, for his love for her was stronger than his selfish wish. The pirate would give her anything. He'd even make the ultimate sacrifice of letting her go if it made her happy. Such was the depth of his love. Jean looked at her and saw that she couldn't face him, and even though she waited for his answer, there was no way she could look him in the eye. He knew she would not acknowledge him until she heard him agree that he'd keep his word. "You have my word that as soon as it is safe, and a venture can be arranged, I shall see to it that you find your lake. Now, if you will excuse me, I must make ready for the trip. We depart early tomorrow. Carlotta has already started packing your things. You had best see to it that she chooses some good traveling clothes for you, as the journey is long and far from easy."

The man's attitude had turned cold, and without even so much as a goodbye, he'd turned and stormed away, leaving her alone. Tori stood looking at the floor, shaking her head slowly from side to side. How could she have been so stupid? She'd hurt him; that was evident. 'He doesn't want me to go to the lake, but he has to understand that I must,' she thought. Then suddenly, it was too much, and before she knew it, tears began flowing. Standing in the empty doorway, Tori became a complete emotional mess, and not wanting to be seen in such a state, she ran out of the hallway.

In seconds she was upstairs and running into their room, where she threw herself down on the bed. The distraught women did not care if anyone heard her sobbing, but what she could not understand was why she let herself carry on the way she was doing, other than it felt good. It just felt right to give in and sob her heart out at long last. 'Damn the man and what he wants. He promised me, and I promised Linni, and that's all there is to it!'

There was a tap on the door, and before she had a chance to tell whoever it was to go away, it opened all the way, and footsteps sounded on the bedroom floor. Tori looked up and was relieved to see Carlotta entering with a pitcher of juice and a kindly expression in her eyes. The housekeeper she could deal with and welcomed, but if Jean showed his face right then, there would be a fight because she was in no mood to placate the man.

Tori watched as the woman filled a glass with freshly squeezed orange, a drink Tori had come to love in the past few weeks. There was a good side to having the head pirate as your man; she reminded herself. As his lady, she had anything from the island's, and even as upset as she was, a drink of orange sounded good.

"You need a drink to feel better? You have needed to cry for a few days now. I have seen it coming. Now, you can go to New Orleans feeling better. Here…have a sip."

Tori knew she meant well, but it hadn't helped her any to cry and carry on so. She felt no better and didn't think she would ever again. "I don't feel any better at all. I feel awful. I don't understand him or myself. You can't understand Carlotta, but thank you for trying and for caring as you do."

"What is there to understand, I ask?" She was wagging her index finger at Tori. "True, I have never had a child of my own, but I have seen many Senoras in your state, and they all act mixed up in their feelings, in the beginning."

Tori looked at the housekeeper curiously. "And what state would that be, might I ask?" The woman had her attention, and her curiosity was piqued. Slowly she sat up and wiped the tears from her cheeks using the back of her hand. "What do you mean? I don't understand what it is you are trying to tell me."

Carlotta couldn't take it any longer, and with a look of understanding and compassion, she held her ground and spoke softly. "It's because of the baby that you cry. You are going to be a mother; we both know that. I think the reason you cry is because you are not married to Boss, but do not worry, he loves you. I see that with my own eyes. He will do what is right. He will marry you, and you will have a father for your child!"

Tori could not believe what Carlotta had just said. Fear gripped her, as instantly she went into denial. "And just what makes you think that I am going to have a child, may I ask?"

"You do not believe you are? It can be the only answer. Ask yourself." She cocked her head to one side and smiled kindly. "You have been here long enough for us both to realize it. Tori, you have not bled once since you have been here, and you could not have, without me knowing. You would have needed my help. Besides, you have a look on your face, it is softer and the thickening in the middle, the baby is causing your clothes to fit tighter, is it not? Yes, you are going to have a child. It is all too clear."

Tori froze. Now that Carlotta had said it, she knew she could not deny it any longer. She had known deep down but kept trying to talk herself out of it. Now the truth was out. It was going to happen, and there was no running away from the fact. She hadn't had her period, and Tori knew that awful feeling in the mornings was not from too much champagne or wine the night before. You don't get hangovers from one or two glasses, she told herself. Resigned to her condition, at last, Tori begrudgingly admitted it. "You are right, Carlotta. I am with child." Then, grabbing the housekeeper by the hand, she pleaded with her. "Please say nothing to Jean, do you hear me, not a word!"

"Si, I will say nothing, but you will have to tell him. The way you are growing, the whole world will know soon."

"Yes, I know. Carlotta. Trust me; I know only too well how fast I will show. Look, I think I need to be alone. Please leave me for now, and do me a favor, send Jean up when he gets back. We need to talk."

The housekeeper nodded her head. "You have nothing to fear. As I said, Boss loves you. He will marry you, and he will be happy; you wait and see. Carlotta, she knows these things. Now, you rest. I will finish up here later." The woman handed Tori the glass of juice and then left her alone as requested.

Tori drank the juice and then walked to the verandah and sat down to face the truth. How could she have allowed this to happen? What was she going to do now? This pregnancy changed everything! She lowered her head into her hands and closed her eyes. 'Linni, forgive me. What have I done? Worse yet, what in the hell can I do?'

The hours slowly passed, and Tori never left the verandah. She just sat, trying to sort out everything in her mind. She struggled with what would be the right thing to do and what would be wrong.

THE sky was turning dark, as the sun slowly disappeared behind the cypress trees. The sounds of the evening insects and frogs had once again begun their nightly symphony. These were the only sounds that Jean could hear as he entered the front foyer. The lamps were all lit, and the smell of the evening meal filled the air. However, Dinner was the last thing on his mind, as he looked around, half hoping to see Tori's kind face.

He had come home after finishing what he called his rightful duty. That was to spend some time in the canteen, with some of his men. He had been intent on trying to drown his emotions and, most of all, his anger, but to his shock, instead of feeling better and freeing himself of guilt, he'd just drunk his rum and, with each mug full, felt worse. There was no hiding in a bottle this time for him. He had acted like a fool, and he knew it. Tori had every right to want to return to her world, and he understood that she had never meant to hurt him. But damn it; he loved her so much. She had to understand how he was feeling too!

Carlotta's appearance broke his train of thought as she greeted him. It was the look of concern on her face that alerted him to the fact that all was not well. "She has not been out of her room all afternoon. I tell you now, Boss, you had best go and see her. Senorita Victoria, she asked me to send you up as soon as you arrived, and that was hours ago," she finished, shooting him a nasty look of disapproval.

This news worried him, but Carlotta's glare and tone of voice told him she knew more than she was letting on. "Are you telling me everything? Victoria is all right, is she not? She's not ill?"

His housekeeper did not answer him; she acted as if she hadn't heard a word he said and walked away, mumbling to herself, something about men and drinking. Looking at her back as she sauntered off, Jean realized the woman would not be of any assistance. Once her mind was set on something, the female could be very stubborn, and this seemed to be one of those times. There was nothing left to do but make his way upstairs and face whatever was coming. First, though, he was going to have to face Tori and apologize before learning what else was wrong, and something was because never had his love remained in her room for so long. He'd ask for her forgiveness and understanding and promise again to keep his word. If he were lucky, she'd listen and believe him.

Laffite realized right away, upon entering the room, that it was nearly dark. No lamp had a flame, an indication that Carlotta had not exaggerated. Tori had been left entirely undisturbed. Looking around, he could not see her, and then his eyes looked toward the verandah and her favorite chair. She was there, watching him as he walked cautiously toward her.

Jean found himself hoping she would say something first and make it easier for him, something that was wishful thinking though, for she did not.

The full moon had been up for quite a while, its silver rays, adding an eerie luminescence to Tori's sad face. It was November eleventh, and plans had been set for them to arrive in the city no later than the fourteenth. He had chosen to make the trip because of the moonlight, thinking it might add a romantic touch to their travels. Now, seeing his love sitting under its bright light, with such a forlorn expression on her face, the sight moved him deeply, and thoughts of their upcoming trip slipped from his mind.

As he got closer, Jean realized was that she was crying, and this tore at his heart. He could never hurt her, and if staying in this time with him was going to cause her this much agony, he would not hold her back. He would not ask her to remain with him. Kneeling by her side, talking gently, he brushed the tears from her cheeks as he spoke. "Tori, my love, please forgive the actions of a fool. I was wrong this afternoon. It was selfish of me to act so. You have my word that next week we will find this lake of yours, and you will have your chance to go back to your time, to your world and family. If you do manage to find a way home, you have my word; I will let you go. I will settle for the memories we have made together." Jean's voice was trembling with emotion and sounded somehow false, even to his own ears. He would have to do better than this if he were to convince her that he meant what he said. "I know you have a family, who I am sure, loves and misses you. Your little girl, who you need and miss very much; I do understand, believe me, far better than you know."

This was about all Tori could stand. The very mention of her child brought a new flood of tears, and she immediately fell into Jean's arms crying all the more. They stayed like this for a while, each holding onto the other, afraid to let go until she was calm. Finally, she pulled herself up and looked into the eyes of the man she knew loved her, wondering if that was about to change? Somehow, Tori had to get him to understand and agree to what she was about to tell him. She had to trust that he would not turn against her. "Could you light a lamp and get me a glass of wine?"

Jean looked at her and saw that he should give her a few minutes to compose herself. He knew her well enough to know that she was getting her courage up, most likely to tell him farewell. Jean knew he could delay her by remaining at her side, making it difficult for her, but he knew better than to try. To do that would be beyond cruel, and it was not in him to act like a selfish individual.

By the time the simple request of pouring the wine was complete, a calm Tori had entered the room and sat down on the bed. She took the glass from him, took a sip, and then placed the glass on the side table. "Jean, I think you had better have a seat. I have something that you need to know. It's not going to be easy for you to hear, but you have the right."

Jean did not like her tone of voice or the way her hands started to tremble as she spoke. Again, he guessed that he knew what she was about to tell him. It had to be that she could indeed go back to her time, and soon it would be time to say their farewells, so the last thing he wanted to do then was take a seat. "I will remain standing…if you will explain."

Tori spoke softly at first. "I do not want to go to the lake next week or the week after."

Did he hear, right? Dare he hope that she loved him enough to stay? He could hear his heart pounding in his chest; his very soul was shouting, 'let it be true.' His exterior appearance though, remained calm, and his face was guarded.

"Please don't get me wrong. I think the time will come one day when I will have to see for myself if my return can occur. It's just that things have changed, and I don't know how to handle it all."

Tori stood up and slowly paced back and forth. For Jean, it was very evident that something she had to tell him was difficult to say, but what it was, he now had no idea. The only idea that came to mind was to somehow help her to maybe reassure her of his feelings. "If you need to know I want you to stay, you have to believe the answer is yes. I love you more than I could ever love again. You have become my life. Tori, I love you enough to let you go if that is what you desire. I should love you no less if you decided to go or stay. Just tell me the truth, which shall it be?"

"It's not that I don't know how you feel, Jean. I do know, you have made that abundantly clear for some time. A part of me loves you also. We both understand how we feel, of how much passion we share. I don't know how or why all this has happened. God help me for saying this, but it seems that a part of me…that I am in love with you in a way… almost as much as I love my lost family. I am here, caught in two worlds, and in two completely different ways. I'm not making any sense, am I?" She looked at him, knowing that she could not delay any longer. Tori clenched her hands and looked at them as she spoke. "I better just come out with it. Oh, how do you put it? Jean, you say you love me, and you want me to remain here, but would you still feel the same way if I were carrying your child? If I were pregnant?" Jean was so quiet at first that Tori was afraid to look at him and worse, she took his silence to mean that he wasn't happy about the news.

His voice was husky and just above a whisper when he spoke. "Are you telling me that you are going to have a child, our child?"

"Yes, Jean. That is exactly what I'm saying. I'm carrying your child." She still could not bring herself to look at him as she uttered the words, and again she let his silence answer for him.

Afraid, she hastily spoke. "I know I will be an embarrassment to you, and if you don't want me around, well, maybe you could find me a place to stay. Or, perhaps, I could stay here until the baby is born. I will stay out of your way. I will move into the other room." Tori still looked at her hands, which she twisted and turned as she became more and more anxious. 'Say something, just don't stand there. Please tell me I can stay.' Jean's continued silence caused her to panic, and Tori rambled on trying to explain it all to him. "It's just that I don't know what it would do to the child if I tried to cross back to my time. It might hurt the baby, and I can't do that. If I could stay here...?" The sound of the door banging closed stopped her mid-sentence. The shocked woman looked up and saw the empty room. Tori had her answer. The pirate did not want to be a father and had made it clear. Now what?

Carlotta had been wrong, she told herself, and in a way, Tori was glad. She would not have to deal with the romantic part of their relationship anymore, but now that had changed, would he let her stay? Scared, the mother-to-be looked around the room, which was her whole world right then. God help her; she had nowhere else to go. There had to be another way. Maybe Dominique would help. That was the answer. He was always saying how he owed her. He would help, but, hell, she needed Jean. How could he walk out on her like that? If he loved her as he claimed, why would he treat her so? Had he lied all along? That had to be it. The bastard had lied;

how dare he! She was about to go and find out where he was, to have it out with him, when he burst back into the room, carrying a bottle of champagne and two glasses.

Surprised, Tori could barely speak. "You came back. You're not angry?"

In rapid succession, he placed the bottle safely on the small table, and then turned to Tori and picked her up in his arms.

The beaming man swung her around and around. "You silly, beautiful, little fool. Angry? Far from it. How could you think that I would not be anything but thrilled by this news? Father!" he shouted. "I am to become a father! You are beautiful. However, we must set things right. We must marry. No son of mine shall be a bastard!"

"Jean! Put me down, and slowly please." Her expression was puzzled but daring to look somewhat happy. Let me get this right, you mean you are glad? You want this child? I can stay?"

"Of course, I want you and the child! I could not want anything more." He was holding her close and tightly, afraid that if he let her go, he would wake, only to find it all a dream.

Relief and happiness filled the sound of her voice, as she softly answered him, "You left, and I thought… you didn't even say a word. Now, you say you want this. Oh, Jean, that's more than I hoped. I was certain when you left the room that you did not, but now I know how you feel." Suddenly she stopped talking and pulled away from him. "I have to say some things. The first is, I won't marry you. I can't. If I were to do that, it would…might… most likely, could change history. Don't you see? I must not do anything to disturb the timeline." She could see the look of puzzlement on his face. He did not understand or want to. Because of this reaction, Tori realized she had to make it entirely clear. "I have thought it through for hours. Every possible outcome and all have left me with no doubt on this subject."

Jean knew only too well the stubborn streak of hers, but she had to listen to him this time. "Tori, be reasonable. The people will call you such names, and my child, our child, will be labeled for life. I can't have that. Surely you can't do that? In your time, it may be fine to have a child born out of wedlock, I don't know, but here in my time, I can assure you, it is not so. You will marry me as soon as we get to New Orleans." He took her gently in his arms, talking softer now but still very sternly. "It will all be done secretively; no one will ever have to know that it was necessary."

"I will not, and you can't make me! Anyway, I have thought about this all afternoon, like I said. I do have a way around the problem. One that you will have to agree to, because Jean, get this in your thick, stubborn skull, I won't marry you!" His face clouded over, and Tori could see he was fighting hard to control his temper. Knowing him as she did, Tori understood she had to defuse the situation before he exploded. "Besides, who's to say we weren't married in the islands, and I am already your wife. Carlotta calls me Senora now and then, so why can't we pretend, and then we both can have our way."

Jean was quiet. The man needed time to agree to her demands; she realized that, but he had to understand there was no other way around it all. In time Tori knew he'd have to agree because he'd have no choice. For right then, it was best if she held her silence and let him reach the only conclusion that she'd accept.

When the pirate finally spoke, it was a shock to hear his demand. "If I agree to this, then you must tell me now, give me your word, that this child is mine to keep. When you try to go back to your time, and you will try, won't you?" Jean studied her carefully and decided, by her expression, he was correct in his assumption. "When you try, you will do it alone. You will leave the baby."

"I don't know if I can do that. I know the pain of leaving a child behind already. It's because of that pain; I know that I must try one day to return, whether I succeed or not. My family has a right to know what happened to me, Jean. My daughter deserves to know the truth about what happened."

"That might be, but I have the right to keep my child if you feel that you have to go. He will be a child of this time, not yours, will he not? His place will be here with me."

The two of them stared at each other, and Tori could see that Jean was deadly serious. He would have his child no matter what, and maybe it would be the right thing. After all, how could she turn up at home and say, "Well, here I am, and by the way, this is my child." How could she take Jean's child away from him and leave him nothing? At least this child would know what happened to its mother, and Jean would not be left alone. It was a simple solution, not an easy one, but it made sense.

Tori didn't know if history said Jean Laffite had a son or daughter, so all she had to go on was his plea. Sadly, it made sense, and she agreed. "You are right. If I do try to go back and if it works, you have my word; I will go alone. This baby is of this time, not mine like you say. The child will need you as much as you will need…" her voice broke as she struggled to finish, "the child."

Jean looked into her eyes and held them captive with his so she could not look away. Somehow, he had to make her understand that he would take care of her no matter what happened. Reaching out, Laffite took hold of her hand, and softly, he squeezed it as he lovingly spoke. "If, however, you do not try to return, and you fall in love with us enough to stay, I give you my solemn oath, I will live only to make you and our family happy. Be warned; I will do everything in my power to make certain you choose to remain here with me. When that happens, then you must promise me that you will become my wife. That, we will marry within the church. Until then, we will pretend, as you say. Do we have an agreement, my love?"

"We do, but Jean, I will have to try to return as soon as I can after the baby is born." Tears filled her eyes. This was the hardest thing she had ever had to say to anyone, even herself. "I have another promise to keep. You see, I promised both myself, and my Linni, that I would get back to the lake and try to go home. Like you, I intend to keep my word. On the day she was born, I promised my baby girl that I would never leave her like her father had. He wanted no part of her;

she became my life, and I always told her that. I told her that we would have each other until death parted us. I don't know how this time travel thing works. God only knows I could be dead to Linni in my time. Maybe, this is how life works?" She turned from him, angrily wiping her face with the back of her hands, as tears were again running down her cheeks. "All I know is that I have no choice but to try one day." She walked out onto the balcony and looked up at the stars and mumbled softly. "Yet, the longer I stay here, I think I have less and less chance of crossing back."

Jean strode the few steps to join her. He wrapped his arms around her waist and pulled her backward until she was leaning up against him. "Until then, for both our sakes, the child's too, can we put all this time travel into the back of our minds? He will need you to be strong, healthy, and happy if all is to go right over the next few months."

"Ha! What if this he," she said, placing her hand over her stomach, "turns out to be a she?"

"That, my love, would be fine, because she would always remind me of you." His lips gently brushed her cheek, and each felt the other's strength, as they remained embraced.

They would take one day at a time, and the baby would have to be first in their thoughts and actions. This child was very much wanted, and they both knew that.

"Tell me, when is the child due?"

"He or she, by my calculations, is due in June."

"That is not certain?" He looked quite perplexed.

His expression caused her to giggle before answering him. "Jean, you don't have to worry. The child will come in mid-June."

She tried not to laugh at his sudden concern. This man of hers had the potential to be the most concerned husband and father to be of all time, and he proved her right, shortly after that.

It began with Jean delaying the trip to the city. His main worry was making sure Tori was both physically and mentally strong. Carlotta had told him the first few months were the most delicate and that it was her opinion that the trip should wait. Over the following weeks, he became even more attentive and sensitive to her needs and emotions, and there was nothing Tori could do to prevent his undying devotion. At least he listened to her about the holidays, with its modern traditions.

It was Christmas eve, and they had spent the whole day together. Tori watched Jean as he poured himself a brandy, and knowing she had to limit her intake of alcoholic beverages she gazed at the glass container of fruit juice. The idea of not having a nightcap did not sit well, but then drinking more than a few glasses of wine a day was now her limit, and that had been reached with dinner. To take her mind off the idea of asking for a small brandy, Tori decided to engage in conversation about her favorite subject of late. "I can't believe it is Christmas Eve, and you know what?"

"What?"

"For the first time in my life, I don't have a Christmas tree."

"Ah, yes, the tradition that will sweep this land, and oh yes, the purchasing of many gifts. You have told me often these past few weeks. Could it be a hint that you are looking maybe for a gift?" Jean chuckled at the look on her face. "I did listen to all you have mentioned. Not so much about the tree, can't have my people thinking either you or I have, how do you put it, lost our minds. Besides, I could not arrange the transportation of a fir tree. Another reason for not having such a display, but then maybe that is good, we can't do anything to change history, remember?" He was laughing out loud at the exasperation on her face.

"Oh, stop it. I understand, and I agree…what did you mean, could not transport a fir tree? You did try, didn't you? Jean, no, you can't keep on trying to do everything to please me. We can't have a tree, and I would not have allowed it. However, I will admit it is nice to know you thought about it. I will have to tell you all about this holiday and…"

"Not again! Tori, I feel as though I know more about the occasion than you can recall." Her expression changed to a frown, and rather than show him she was feeling like pouting, Tori sat down and shot him one of her famous looks.

"You do not know all about the holiday, and just because you think you do, I am no longer going to describe it, so there."

To her surprise, Jean did not take the bait; he simply reached into his desk and rummaged around before turning to face her with a smug look on his face. He produced a small box that she had never seen before. "This is one tradition that I will keep, though. Here, your gift." He held out the small box and smiled at her squeal of enjoyment.

"Oh, I do love this part of the holiday. It's been years since anyone gave me a gift. My mom did, and Linni, but that was it. Well, not really, a few of my friends exchanged gifts. Now, what is it?" Tori pulled the paper off to find a small wooden box inside. This box she held carefully, as her fingers pulled the top off. "Oh, Jean, it's exquisite and very delicate, but what is it?"

"That my pretend wife is a silver rattle for our son."

"Daughter, maybe," she was laughing. "I do know what it is, just teasing you. Linni had one that was similar from Tiffany's; that's a shop, not a person. Thank you. I know the baby will enjoy it. You, however, will have to wait until the morning for your gift. Oh, did I tell you about Christmas stockings?"

"You did, and no, we are not hanging any such items above the fireplace. Carlotta would think it most strange. Now, before you drive me insane, maybe we should retire for the night. I think maybe all this excitement is too much for myself. How will I be able to wait until morning?"

"You will, and by the way, I know you have been looking around for my gift to you. Don't say you haven't. You won't find it, as I was not silly enough to keep it here." Tori was enjoying herself more than she had in weeks, and for the first time, it looked like she had outsmarted the pirate himself.

"And likewise. I know you have been looking for my gift. A most splendid tradition. Do you suppose our son will act so?"

"I have not been looking, and yes, he or she will. Besides, you just gave me my gift, didn't you? There is more? You are such a tease. I have had enough for this night. Let's take a snack up to our room, and oh, orange juice would be nice. I am going to take your advice for once and go to bed early, or you will talk me into giving you your gift early and what fun is there in that. It's not going to happen." Tori left the living room, giggling.

"Did you not just tell me that my gift is not in this house? Madam, how would you acquire it, to present it to me this night? I am not about to allow you to roam the village or visit Dominique's cottage. I assume that is where you hid it. It is a shame that Dominique is missing all this fun. I shall see to it that next year he joins us. It will be interesting to explain this all to him when he returns from his trip."

Tori was laughing louder and called down to Jean in a mischievous voice. "I swear my talking to myself has rubbed off on you. Jean, I tell you if you don't hurry up here and lay down with me, I will be asleep, and you will have to continue talking to yourself instead of...you know?"

"I do indeed know, and you can count on being awake for a lot longer than you planned. I am on my way, my love. A Merry Christmas, it will be for us all."

NEW Year's Eve day had arrived. Jean had intended to introduce Tori to his brother Pierre but much to their disappointment, Pierre had a change of plans at the last moment. Tori was disappointed but knew she would meet him once they arrived in the city, and until then, they would have to continue their entertainment without him.

The intimate New Year's Eve was attended by Dominique and trusted friend, Renato Beluche. It would be the first time she met the man, and as much as Jean talked about him, Tori found herself looking forward to the introduction and worrying a bit about it too. The mother to be stood before the full-length mirror, looking at her image sideways. The bulge in her midsection was very apparent to her, and she wondered when Jean was going to share the happy news with everyone.

"You look ravishing as always. No, you are not looking fat or even close to that of a woman carrying a child. The only change I see is the size of your breasts, which are in this man's opinion, magnificent."

"Typical man, it seems boobs are always a hit."

"To me, all of you is delightful, and yes, the larger size does give one an idea."

"Jean, you will stop right there. Our company will be arriving at any moment, and we need to be downstairs to greet them. Besides, this will be the first time since I came here that I get to meet your trusted cohort, Renato. Is it true, he has been away at sea all this time?"

"It is. You know I would not lie. The gentleman in question has been a busy man. I have now added to my fleet one Spanish ship and one more British vessel."

"Don't you mean busy pirate?" she laughed.

"I do not. Renato has his papers, and you will like him, of this I am certain. Let us depart this room to greet him before I change my mind and ravish you as I want." Now it was his turn to grin, and he did so as he extended his arm for her to join him. "Shall we?"

LONG before they made it downstairs, Dominique's voice sounded, followed by a deeper voice and laughing. The two men were conversing in French, and Jean switched from English to the familiar language to prepare Tori to do the same. "I see, we are already too late, my love, to greet our friends at the door. It's a good thing they are only dear friends and not clients, who would feel slighted by such an oversight."

"You are to blame, and I will make it known why. After that, I am sure Dominique will agree with me; it was your fault, not mine."

"That is something he always does…agree with you. I have never known him to disagree with anything you do or say." Jean was speaking lightheartedly and sounding confident, he added his intentions. "Now, come, for I wish Renato to meet my wife."

"You can't introduce me as such. Not yet. We agreed to wait until your brother is informed, remember."

They entered the living room, and before anyone had a chance to say a word, Dominique proved he was still one step ahead of his captain. "Remember what? Boss, you have forgotten some important fact? Maybe, because your mind is on other matters such a love? See, Renato. All I have told you is true. Boss is a lovesick pup, who would forget his head, if not for the likes of you and me."

Renato clapped his hands together in delight. "Indeed, I can see for myself that the man has a good reason for his forgetfulness." He stepped forward and held out his hand to Tori. "Victoria, it is my pleasure to meet the woman who has taken Jean from the sea at last, and might I add, I can see why. Such beauty and from what I hear, such charm too." He took her hand and lightly brushed the back with his lips. "Tell me, is it true that you alone saved Dominique from death's door, as everyone has informed me?"

"Renato, all I did was what any woman would have done. I only stitched his arm up and kept him drunk till it healed. Which, by the way, took weeks. He almost drank the ship dry."

Everyone laughed, and then Jean embraced his friend. "It is so, Renato and much more. Victoria is all you have heard. But, let me introduce you the correct way. This is a small fact that we wish to keep a secret, and I know you can be trusted. Those who love her and are close to us, they call her Tori, and it is my wish that you also be included. Only when we are together like this, though…in public or at times when others are present, she will be introduced and known as Victoria."

Tori watched as a puzzled look crossed Renato's face. He was not as handsome as Jean, but he was not bad looking either. His hair had curls, and it was dark brown, not black. He had no facial hair, but his sideburns were long and neatly trimmed. Renato was dressed casually, and he'd removed his jacket before Jean and Tori had arrived. This was a sign that he was obviously comfortable in Jean's home, and this pleased her. Tori went further with her observations, using them to sum the man's character.

The captain's lips, though thin, turned upward in a smile, never downward in a pout. Renato stood just an inch shorter than Laffite and did so with his shoulders back, almost at attention. He was self-assured and used to commanding his surroundings. His demeanor spoke volumes, and his friendly personality was genuine and welcomed by Tori. Instinctively she knew he was a man who could be trusted, and like Jean and Dominique, she knew she would call him a friend.

Renato slapped Jean on the back and then smiled at the lady; his puzzled expression replaced with a warm and friendly look. "Tori, it is then. May I accompany you to the dining room? Carlotta has announced dinner, and I, for one, look forward to her cooking."

"You most certainly may accompany me, and may I also add; it is my honor that you are to be included in our little game."

"Anything for my friend and now his woman."

"Well, if it's anything that you offer, you shall have to tell me all about yourself over dinner. Let those two," Tori looked toward Jean and Dominique, "talk about the cargo and shipments. I am dying to learn more about such a charming gentleman like yourself."

Renato presented his arm and surprised Tori by switching to English. "We shall see how my English stands up to such a task. Dominique has told me you rather the language English; that French is not easy for you. I shall, therefore, endeavor to make our evening a success."

Tori was delighted by his action, and it showed on her face. Switching back to English, she happily added her opinion. "Of that, I am certain. It will be a huge success. Tonight, we speak English, but should you require assistance, my French is improving, I can assure you. I can translate whatever you wish to say into English if you speak it in French. Together we will manage, of that, I am completely confident."

Renato was won over immediately. "Anything you wish to know I will be happy to share." He pulled a chair from under the table and let Tori sit before he took the seat next to her. "Your lady and I have some history to talk over Jean. Like she said, you and Dominique may discuss the cargo I have brought with me. As I know, you want very much to go over, a few business points with Dominique. Please don't let us stop you." He turned to face the woman by his side and smiled brightly. "Now Tori, what is it you would like to know?"

Tori tried to hide her mischievous grin, which, if seen by Jean, would alert him that she was up to something. "Without seeming too rude, I would like to know if what Jean has told me is true?"

"And what is it that he has said, may I inquire?"

"Not too much. Let's see." She looked at Jean, with little luck of concealing her mischievous expression.

Jean recognized the look and steeled himself for whatever it was that his love intended to do. Her eyes left him as she began to answer Renato Beluche's question.

"You were born in New Orleans. Your father, Rene Beluche, came here from France. He is in the wig-making business, which is a front for your smuggling. Oh, and he lives on the family's Chalmette Plantation and owned the cottage that Pierre rents. You are now the owner of the building, I believe. That is about it; I am sorry to say. I do hope you can expand on such a limited amount of information." She was grinning, and her eyes sparkled in the light.

Jean had taken to twisting his mustache and raised one eyebrow, actions that indicated she had indeed pulled a good one on him. He was no doubt wondering what she would say next.

Renato was laughing so hard he almost choked. "Wine, a glass of wine, I say. Jean, she is just as Dominique has said. This woman is a female with her own mind and the courage to express it. Bien!" (good!) Beluche looked at Tori, and even though he tried to sound serious, he was having a hard time doing so. "Ah, but Tori, wig making, it is not a front for smuggling, how could you believe Jean? I am an honest man, unlike others in this room." Their guest was chuckling and enjoying watching Jean and Dominique, who were not sure if they should be worried or not.

Now, it was Jean's turn to add his bit to what was becoming an awkward situation. "Renato, she knows the truth of it all. Including the fact that sometimes you, like myself, move merchandise around the taxman."

Tori burst out laughing. "Some of the time?" Tori took the glass of wine that was to go to Renato and sipped it before going on. "Renato, if I have in any way offended you, I did not intend to do so, and while it is true that I know much, let me assure you that my lips are sealed. I know Jean values your friendship and advice, and because of that, I also will value both, if offered to me.

"You are most welcome of my friendship and, if ever required, my advice. I am in no way offended, just a bit shocked and taken back. You are the first female, maybe the first person, to confront my father's business and mine…to insinuate that we smuggle." He was laughing again. (In French) "Wine, I said Jean if you please, my friend. I think I have just met my match, and now I do agree with Dominique, you are a lovesick pup. I, on the other hand, am just a delighted man, at having made the acquaintance of such a beautiful woman." He held up his glass and returned to speaking English. "A toast to new friendships, and to the New Year. Let us hope 1811 will be profitable and bring much joy."

Jean stood and raised his glass. "I will second that and add, may it be healthy and full of surprises." He winked at Tori, who shot him a look that said, stop now! "Ah, only good surprises, that is." Jean had almost slipped up, and Dominique was looking from him to Tori in the most suspicious way. Jean saw him studying them and thought it wise to add more and deflect his curiosity. "To your health Dominique. No more injuries from the blade of another."

"Especially that," cried out Dominique. "For if I do, then may it be when our dear Tori is close at hand, bonne année (Happy New Year!) May the year of 1811 be all we wish and much more."

Jean sat back in his chair and topped his glass up. "I can't keep the news to myself any longer, and as you gentlemen are trusted comrades and dear friends, I shall impart the best news of this year. This beautiful woman is my wife." Jean looked at Tori's stunned expression, and he quickly continued. "We have endeavored to keep this news secret until Pierre learned it from me. I trust you will contain this information until we have told him, especially, you Dominique. We all know how you keep secrets."

If Dominique was shocked, he did not show it. He looked at his captain and smiled broadly. If ever there was an actor, Dominique was an academy award-winning one, Tori told herself. Springing something like this on him, knowing he would know it to be a lie, well, how did he do it?

"Boss, I have had my suspicions for some time. You two are always acting the part of a married couple. It is my guess in the islands, where you met, that was when you gave your vows. Why you kept it a secret, I now understand. Your brother would be deeply hurt to be the last to hear of such news or hear from gossip. Nay, my lips are also sealed. They are always so when trusted with details that need be. To imply that I would not have kept such to myself is an offense, but one that is forgiven. I shall not utter more till Pierre knows, then I will tell the world."

Renato raised his glass and added, "I also agree. You both have my word, and I am honored that you chose to share such knowledge with me. I toast the happy couple."

DOMINIQUE had been the cause of the latest delay in their departure, insisting that they remain at Grand Terre until certain unsettling matters were resolved. Tori had been packed and ready to depart on their trip when it was stopped. News had reached Grand Terre, and it had caused quite a stir and brought the usually calm Carlotta to tears. However, no one would discuss the contents of this News or explain why it would cause them to delay their plans. Now, downstairs sat a man who supposedly was going to impart all that had taken place, and she would learn what was going on. Tori had insisted that she be allowed to dine with the men and that if whatever news the guest had to tell was shocking, she'd handle it just fine.

She stood outside the living room door, wondering if she had made a wise choice. Jean had tried to convince her not to join them, but she had put her foot down, and so in her mind, there could be no turning back, without feeling like she had lost the battle of wits. Could the news be something to do with her? Had someone reported that the missing whore Tori was living in Grand Terre? Could that be what had everyone upset? Or had word that Laffite had taken a wife, slipped out? Jean had not once hinted at what all the fuss was about, and it had left her guessing. 'There is only one way to find out. Go to the source and learn what's going on. Here goes nothing.' "I can do this," she whispered to herself.

Upon entering the room, the conversation, which had been in Italian, came to a complete halt. The silence surrounding her was deafening, and her nerves, already on edge, began to show visibly. Jean stood up, and with a somber expression and no greeting, he joined Tori and escorted her into the room.

"Gentlemen, while I agree that the information is grim, I also agree with my wife that she, like all of New Orleans, deserves to hear about the tragic news. My wife is of strong character, and maybe if she knows the reason for our delay, Victoria will not keep on with her endless banter. Women can be very persistent."

Dominique chuckled and then looked down into his glass, so he did not have to see the thunderous look on Tori's face. Far better to sip his wine than face her glare, which he was sure she was shooting his way too.

Their other guest put his fist to his mouth and made a sound as if to clear his throat. Jean, who understood the meaning behind the man's action, immediately faced him and ignored Dominique. "Ah, yes. Monsieur, forgive me. Victoria, may I present to you, our guest this evening, Monsieur Captain Louis Chighizola. He has agreed that for the evening, he will grace us with his mastery of English. Speaking his native Italian would, after all, achieve nothing but confusion and many interpretations, of which I could guarantee, you would not trust. Such is the horrific news he's to impart; I am sad to say."

The man stood and nodded his head in her direction. "It is my honor, but let us not be so formal. All here, call me Nez Coupe, and as you see for yourself, it is a fitting name." His finger tapped where his nose should have been and was not. In place of a typical nose, was one that seemed to have had the end sliced entirely off. It was hard to look at and even more challenging to describe. Jean had told her about this man once and failed miserably at the description of the pirate's appearance as far as she was concerned. Raised angry scars covered much of his face. One of the largest ran across his cheek and over the bridge, of what was left of his nose. Tori cringed inside, as she imagined the wound when it was new. The scar, however, did not end there, for it carried on halfway across the other cheek. The only part of his face that seemed to remain untouched was his eyes, forehead, and his lips. He still had both his ears, which sported gold hoops, and his neck was not scared, but that was all she could see, without asking him to remove his shirt, something Tori would never do, no matter how curious she was. He was dressed for the evening, complete with a jacket and clean looking breeches. His boots lacked the shine that Jeans' always sported, but Laffite was a gentleman, and Chez Nez was anything but that.

Tori had seen him walking around Grand Terre several times from a distance and asked Dominique about him. The only answers she had received came as a mixed review. The pirate was one of

Jean's captains, quick to anger, and no one dared ask him about how he lost his nose if they wanted to live. He could be reasonable, and there again, he was known to act totally insane. Remembering that, she smiled and tried hard not to stare at him. Tori had known it would be difficult to look at him without revealing her horror of the image he presented. Still, she intended to prove to Jean that she could handle herself under such awkward circumstances and handle herself with this ugly pirate was her full intent.

Tori looked away, so as not to seem like she was fascinated by his horrific appearance. Then to keep him from thinking she found him too ugly to look upon without fear, she walked to a nearby chair and calmly took a seat before turning his way again.

The pirate had a sorrowful look and spoke in a manner that did not seem to fit his attempt at sounding somber. "I am sorry that we have to meet, on the very day I had to bring such terrible news to your home." He smiled at Tori and then took his seat opposite her. He was looking directly at Laffite as if baiting her. He loved the way his appearance could frighten the fairer sex. Having only seen this lady from a distance, she had both intrigued him and worried him to the point of fascination. Even right then, she seemed either not to notice his looks or chose to ignore the image he presented.

Nez Coupe was not the type of man to be ignored by anyone. Many, however, attempted to discreetly do so, knowing he was like an explosive fuse waiting to ignite. If you ignored him, he got angry, and if you were stupid enough to ask about his face, well, he had been known to kill for that. He was a game player, who often enjoyed pretending his face and lack of nose, was the unjust cause of all remarks and actions. It was whispered that on many occasions, the ferocious individual used his face as an excuse to kill.

Their guest knew that he would never get a rise out of Dominique or Boss, but the evening was far from over. He was there to explain to them, including Laffite's lady, some of the news that he was privy to. The pirate now had a new idea, then just relaying a story as he had initially intended.

As his image wasn't bothering the woman, maybe his news in vivid detail would. Chez Nez was about to launch into the details of what he knew, when Dominique suggested that they go to the dining room, and maybe not discuss such ugly matters until after their meal. Jean wholeheartedly agreed, and so without delay, Tori found herself escorted to her place at the dinner table. Once there, Jean quickly whispered into her ear, to remember not to pay any heed to Nez Coup, and to not remark on any of his news, should he choose to discuss the subject while they were at the table. Tori just had time to nod her head in agreement when the pirate sat down across from her. Once seated, he was again looking directly at her, only this time, he cocked his head to the side, and as a small smile played on his lips.

In Tori's mind, she had never seen such an ugly face, and the sight made her feel sorry for him. However, in no way was she about to make him think she was repulsed by his unfortunate appearance, knowing that could be one big mistake. Laffite's wife, that's how she now felt herself to be, acknowledged him with a slight smile, and thanked God that Carlotta had chosen this moment to place some food on the table. The housekeeper set two full dishes right next to their guest, drawing his unwanted attention away from his hostess.

The housekeeper had placed the dishes down and looked at her mistress with such a worried expression. When Tori witnessed this, she felt her body tense. Whatever it was, this news that their guest had to impart must really be upsetting. Tori had to trust that Jean already knew what it was and that it had nothing to do with her. She smiled at the Italian again and spoke without a trace of her anxiety showing. "Monsieur, you are most welcome to our home, and it is my pleasure to have you dine with us. It is something that should have occurred long before now, I feel. The fact that you have distressing news to share should not have been the only reason for your visit. I do hope you will accept my apology for having not insisted we meet before now."

Tori looked at Jean, and frowned knowingly. She was not

following his instructions, especially the one to pay no heed to the man, and because of that, she'd expected to see a look of thunder on his face. Instead, he was twisting his mustache and smiling ever so slightly.

Laffite was proud of his lady for handling the introduction to his fierce captain, while seemingly indifferent to his scarred face. She was talking to him as if he were nothing more to her than any other guest; they would have visit them. How his captain was going to handle her actions was anyone's guess, though, and he was not willing to play the guessing game when it came to Nez Coupe. Feeling this way, he knew he had to get his lady to stop her polite conversation before she got herself into a situation that would cause the evening's dinner to be over before it began. "Victoria, I am sure our guest would rather deliver his news after the meal, as one can't eat while talking."

She almost laughed at Jean as she responded to his remark. "My dear, I am stronger than you think. I would…no, I need to know what has delayed our departure yet again. Surely the news from the city is not that grim? No matter the content, delaying the telling while eating a meal, will not change the outcome surely?"

Jean's expression softened. "I wish it were so that it could change, but you are correct, my love. I have agreed with Dominique…I am ready to tell you enough so you will understand the horror of it. I will not go into details beyond those which I feel are necessary."

Tori picked up her glass and sipped the wine. "Well, now, you do have my full attention. Please, again, I say, I am not that fragile."

Laffite frowned; there was not going to be any way to delay the inevitable, so he begrudgingly started. "I will tell you what I can, and Nez Coupe here will back me up as he has witnessed some of the events." He reached out and held her hand as he explained to her what he and all of Grand Terre and Grand Isle now knew. "Last week, on January 8th, just three days before we were to depart, a large group of slaves marched toward New Orleans in a bloody revolt. That was the cause of the first delay. This second delay is due to the information that I have become aware of regarding the horrors that occurred."

"A revolt? How large? How many did it involve?"

"It was said that there were over a hundred or more. Facts do tend to get distorted when told by hysterical people, but in this case, my friend here," he looked at their guest, "he has brought the news from a trusted and respected plantation owner, that we all trust and know."

Tori could not believe it. In all her reading and all her visits to New Orleans, she had never heard of such a revolt. A thousand questions formed in her mind, but she remained silent. What she needed was to learn more about the incident and then add her inquiries. Tori just nodded for him to continue.

"By January 10th, it was brought under control. The leaders were quickly apprehended, and those that ran are being rounded up as we talk. The worst was the death of two men."

Chez Nez coughed and gruffly spoke his mind. "Two fine men... white men. Both were murdered by the black bastards."

Jean shot him a look to silence him. "It is true, they were white, as you well know." He turned his attention back toward Tori as he continued. "As I was saying, two men of standing were murdered, during the riot, and those responsible were given a trial and hung."

Nez Coupe had taken a fork full of meat and was chewing it while breathing through the oddly shaped holes that were now his nostrils. It made a strange sound, and Tori looked to Dominique with a questioning look. Nez Coupe was looking at his plate of food, trying to decide what to eat next, so he missed the small interaction.

Jean's wife hoped Dominique would understand her, but all he did was touch his nose and shake his head ever so slightly, indicating that she, do nothing, or say anything more. For Tori, that was enough to tell her to forget about questioning the pirate, who sat across from her.

Tori looked down at her plate and swallowed with difficulty. Between the ugly pirates eating habits, which entailed chewing with his mouth smacking open and closed, and breathing, using what was left of his nose because his mouth was full, well, it was almost too much. The whistling sound of his breath, and occasional snot droplet spraying out toward her, put off her appetite. Questions fled her mind for a few seconds as she struggled to gather herself. No matter the look from Dominique, Tori wanted to know more. So, against all warnings, and feeling more determined, the calmer woman attempted further interaction with their guest but not by asking for more details directly.

"That is sad news. I am glad it is over and thankful you told me."

Nez Coupe looked up from his plate and held his next fork full of food just inches from his mouth. "It is so; they acted swiftly, tiz true, but not with the instigator of the insurgency. With him, they took their time. He went by the name of Charles Deslondes, a mulatto. Light skinned, and a green-eyed mulatto at that. Why, instead of accepting the position and privilege that his mixed blood, and trusting white folk allowed him…"

"And just what position would that be?" Tori asked in an irritated tone, one that seemed lost on their guest.

The pirate was having way too much fun with her, to stop now. He had her full attention, and by the look on Jean's face, Nez Coupe knew he was going to enjoy carrying on. He shoved the fork full of food into his mouth, and as he chewed, he spoke. "That would be a slave driver, an overseer of sorts. I assure you, a most respected position for his kind." He stopped long enough to drink the remaining wine in his glass, and while reaching for the bottle to get a refill, he continued without missing a beat. "Thought that breed had more brains; seems we were wrong."

"If what you say, that he was the instigator, he had brains enough to put together a riot." Tori was angry, as well as shocked, and could not help but voice her opinion. To her amazement, Nez Coupe seemed unbothered by the implications of her words or tone of her voice. Seeing this, Tori surmised, his mind, like many of that era, was made up; blacks were an inferior race. He was more interested in the food he was putting on his plate than debating the intelligence of what he considered to be an animal.

The Italian stuffed his mouth full of food, and before he finished chewing, he spoke. "I am sad to have to admit you may have something there. Never looked at it like that. Still, I think they just got lucky with a simple idea, one that got out of hand. No nigger could carry out such a plot and have a hope in hell of success. They can't think how to do things; they have to be told."

Tori looked back at Jean. "How could someone, a slave, get so many others to join in a revolt as significant if they were not intelligent? Tori was determined to make a point regardless of the warning looks Jean and Dominique were shooting her way.

Nez Coupe interrupted before Jean had a chance. "Niggers talk, my dear. Talking ain't a sign of intelligence, even I know that much. Hell, half my men talk better than niggers, and they are dumber than drunken whores. Look, this is what happened, far as we know. News often gets from plantation to plantation, faster than we can spread it ourselves. Fact that is. It's said that many joined in from other plantations, and it seems likely, that they heard of this nigger's plans and decided to join him. I heard myself that they had been planning the revolt for over a year. That there tells you how stupid they are. A whole year for a simple plan, something that would take the likes of me, to arrange in an hour."

Jean interrupted and hastily added, "As I was saying, my love, those who were a part of this nasty happening, have been dealt with."

Nez Coupe grunted. "As well they should Boss. Our dear friend Manuel Andry, owner of the sugar plantation Woodland, will be happy to hear it. His son Gilbert, who you knew, was ferociously hacked to death. The savages took anything they wanted, all eighty of his slaves, guns, and all other items that could be used to fight. They joined and marched cheering, and beating drums like they were going to win. I was told that those in the front were African warriors. Yes, savages they are, called Asante. Been out of Africa just going on five years. I got some off a ship I took once. Nasty black bastards they be. Sold the lot for a good price. Not top price, mind you, on account they could not speak anything, much more than their own garbled mess. It is rumored they can't be controlled. Murdering bastards proved that right. Goes to show you, my dear, you can't trust 'um. Not when they are that black and new." He turned to face Jean, and before anyone had a chance to interrupt, he continued. "Why, Manuel barely escaped with his life. He made his way right across the river. He was madder than a hornets' nest, and strong-willed because he raised up all sorts of good white folk, to go back and teach them niggers, a thing or two."

Dominique, who had been silent until now, thought it best to add his bit. "I heard it was Claiborne, who called out the militia, which put a stop to their march. Stopped them at Jacques Fortier's plantation."

"Good job, he did," added Nez Coupe. "They nearly got themselves into the city. Not that me and a few of my men would have allowed that to happen."

Jean wanted the subject stopped and coldly, but firmly spoke. "They did not get into the city, and for that, we can be thankful. Now, can we continue our evening of fine food and wine, without further discussion on the subject?"

His captain had no notion of dropping the issue. Nez Coupe would not let the matter end because he had more to impart and intended to do so. He'd see how far he could push the story, and how well Laffite's woman would take the description of what he was about to reveal.

"That is the truth of it. Still, the bastards were made an excellent example of what will happen should another nigger decide to gather up such a group. Why, they tell that Charles Deslondes had both his hands cut off, then they shot him in both legs." He sipped his wine, and while looking right into Tori's eyes, he went on with the morbid details. Shot his body too, and then my dear, they wrapped him in straw, and while he was still alive, they roasted the bugger. Word of how he was dealt with will travel fast among the slaves. Doubt any of them will join in another such event. You have no need to fear them if they are kept in their place. The animals are quite harmless if dealt with proper like."

"Chighizola! I demand that you apologize to the lady and discuss the details of this matter no more. Such gruesome facts are not for delicate ears, don't you agree?"

The man looked across the table at them both, and upon seeing the thunderous glare on Laffite's face and the shocked look on his lady's, he hardly knew what to say. He was enjoying toying with the female, but he was not so stupid as to stir things too far. To do that would bring down the wrath of Laffite for sure.

"Forgive me for my blunder, madame. Monsieur Laffite, Boss, you are, of course, right. Let us put this nasty topic away and enjoy this splendid meal Carlotta has prepared. I always enjoy her dishes." He looked down at his food and added still another piece of fish to his already filled plate.

Jean looked at Tori and could not discern what her emotions were. She was sat stone-faced and looking toward their guest with what he thought could be rage in her eyes. After several more seconds, she turned her attention away from the Italian and looked at Laffite while he spoke to her.

"So you see, my dear, until I am confident that our trip will be both safe and an uneventful one, you can understand now why we have remained here?"

Tori wanted to answer but took a sip of wine instead while she tried hard to control her anger. Jean sat silent, and Chez Nez sat watching and waiting to see what would happen next. It was plain as could be that Laffite had one angry woman on his hands.

Without looking away from Jean, Tori spoke with an edge to her tone of voice, one that indicated her anger. "I do understand why we remained here, that's true enough. You should have told me yourself about this awful affair, and maybe together, we could have decided not to delay. How much longer do you feel we will need to remain here?" She didn't know what else to ask him right then. Her eyes looked from Jeans' face to the Italians'. The man was now enjoying his meal. It was as if none of what he had spoken about bothered him in the slightest.

Laffite tapped her hand and allowed a small but brief smile to cross his expression. "I think we can assume we can continue in a few days. I will wait until I hear from my men, that the way is clear."

"Wise choice Boss, if I say so myself. It's not a pleasant thing to come upon a view such as I did, on my way back here. Met a couple I did, heading toward the city. The gentleman was agitated. I stopped them to ask what was going on. He explained his wife had fainted dead away at the sight of some nigger's heads on spikes. Good thing she stayed fainted if you ask me. Waking up and seeing this mug of mine would have caused her to think she was in hell." He laughed hard and held his napkin up to his face, and then lowered it and said, "Boo! See, my face can come in quite handy. I told the man to go on, but to keep something over his wife's eyes, as they were going to pass by a few more heads before they reached the city."

"Dear God!" Tori wanted to scream at the man. He had just sat there and told her people's heads were on spikes. It seemed worse than the news about the one who'd been mutilated and then burned alive. Making matters harder to grasp, the horrible story had been relayed, in a most deliberate way, and again, the ugly pirate continued to eat as if it meant nothing. Had he expected her to do the same? Maybe not, maybe he was trying to see if he could upset her, and if that was his intention, he had succeeded. Tori felt ill and placed her glass down. She pushed her plate away and glared at the insensitive Italian.

Jean had to put a stop to the situation that was spinning out of his control fast. "Victoria, look at me, it is finished. The revolt is over, and I am confident that what the authorities did, no matter how barbaric, was done to warn others. I assure you we will not be passing by any such a horror for your eyes to witness, and I am sorry you had to hear about it. If I had had my way, you would never have had to hear of such an atrocity."

The ugly pirate looked her way again, with what she was sure was a fake look of concern. "I beg your pardon for my part in such. I did not realize that you had not heard yourself of such goings-on. Please forgive my discretions." His eyes looked from her to Jeans' and then to Dominiques', and his demeanor completely changed.

The man looked most uncomfortable to Tori and rightfully so. Dominique looked as if he could strangle the man, and Jean's eyes had turned a darker shade, but his tone of voice was caring as he addressed her. "Under the circumstances, I think it better if Carlotta brought you up a tray and you finish your meal there. We shall conclude our business without you. Tori, are you listening? Do you agree?"

Tori was more than willing to accept his suggestion. She couldn't stand the sight of the ugly man, eating and acting as if his news was nothing more than a slight inconvenience. "I entirely agree with you, Jean. No food though; I am sick to my stomach. Please excuse me, gentlemen." Abruptly she stood, and before Jean could stand, Tori was at his side. "Don't bother; you stay here." She kissed him on the cheek and quietly whispered, "You and I have a lot to talk about when you come up. I'm fine, but make it quick." With that, she glared at the other two men and left the room without uttering another word.

As the door closed, Jean faced Nez Coupe and angrily spoke. "I did not invite you to bring a storm into my house, and if you were anyone else, you should know I would see to it that they weathered no more storms themselves...ever!"

"Well, I am me, and I do have one small bit of news that you should know before I depart." He finished his drink and then put down the empty glass slowly. "I heard that the trials of some of the niggers were held in part, by your friend, a one Jean Destrehan. I also heard on good authority, another fact also. Some of those heads on stakes were put up in front of his plantation. Such friends should be kept a close watch on, don't you think? That is all I have to tell; if you excuse me, I will take my leave and go to my ship. You may be glad to know I sail on the morning tide."

"Smooth sailing then," said Dominique, a blank look on his face.

Jean was frowning, and his tone was deadly serious as he spoke. "Do try to remember that there are certain ships we do not take, and you are not to lay a hand on ever. You do remember our last meeting on the subject?"

Chez Nez said nothing more. He only laughed as he left the room. The cocksure pirate walked out of the house slamming, the front door behind him.

Dominique had a scowling look about him as he spoke. "So much for our meeting. Boss, you know very well that man takes any ship he comes on. He and Gambi are alike, and you can't stop them. It's best, I think, if we keep a close watch on them until they overstep in a way as to threaten us here. Pierre feels it best to steer clear. Those two are like powder kegs and one spark, well, you understand."

"My brother does not have to deal with them as we do. I agree, though, for now, I shall avoid another confrontation. But, so help me, if that man steps out of line around Tori again, I shall shoot the bastard. Now, let us talk about what it is we best do. I am needed in the city, and Tori will be more than ready to depart, despite the horrors she has heard tonight. You know her as well as I, and keeping her here is no longer an option. She has begun to look at her stay here as if kept in prison, I fear."

"Boss, you are mistaken on that fact. The lady is enjoying her visit and has stated such to me."

"Maybe she has said so, but there is far more to my Tori than you know."

"In what regard, may I inquire?"

"I wish I were at liberty to explain; it is a strange matter, that for now, I feel should remain between Tori and myself."

"You are talking of the sham of a marriage, maybe? I feel that you delay only because you have yet to realize that she is the one you love and the only one. Matters of the heart can cause any man to act irrationally."

"It has nothing to do with that. I admit that I love Tori, and I intend to marry her as soon as circumstances allow. Never could fool you..."

"What pray tell, can the other matters be? I see for myself how she feels about you. No, again, I say it is you who holds back. I will also tell you that if you let this beautiful woman slip away, I shall never let you forget it."

"Oh, Dominique, I have no doubt about that, and I can tell you I have no intention of letting her slip away." Jean rubbed his brow. "No other man will steal her; of that, I am certain. Time, however, time could take her."

"Now you speak sense. It is like I say, if you wait too long, Tori may not wait for the question..."

"Dominique, stop! You don't understand, and I can't talk about it."

"Well, then I shall have to ask Tori myself."

"No. You can't do that; it would upset her."

Dominique frowned. "After watching her come to grips with the horrors she listened to over dinner, I doubt she is the kind of female who would become despondent over a few questions of the matter of the heart."

"That is where you are wrong."

"Then trust me and help me understand, or I promise you, I shall ask the woman."

"I know you will. Even if I beg your discretion and demand you don't, you will. That is so... you." Jean was pacing the floor and seeing he was struggling with his decision, his second-in-command just waited.

"Dominique, if I were to disclose to you, here and now, a secret of great importance, like the one we hold between us, well, I will need your word that it remains between us. Tori is not to learn I have spoken of it, and you are not allowed to hint or even ask questions at any time. Do I have your word?"

"As always."

"Then we shall have one last drink this night, and I will try to explain to you why our Tori is the way she is. It is simple, and a fact that you will have to come to grips with." Jean took a bottle of brandy and filled two glasses. He picked them up and handed one to Dominique.

"I thank you for the brandy Boss, but you were saying? Delaying the subject will only make the night long, for I will not cease until you explain."

Jean downed the entire contents of his glass and looked directly at his second-in-command. "She is not of our time. Tori hails from the future, and so you see, time can steal her away. Not in the way you thought but in a real sense of the description. It can steal her away, as sure as you sit there, and I stand here, telling you this fact. Now, let's have another drink."

"I think maybe that is a good idea." The older man wanted to laugh, but the look on Jean's face was grave.

"Dominique, you look like I felt when I realized this truth about her. It is the truth. You see, it is why she acts like no lady of this era, why she has a different way of talking, and, most of all, why she knows things about me...about Grand Terre. There you have it. That is all I am willing to engage on the matter now, or in the days ahead. You have given your word. I know you will be a man of discretion and reveal nothing about our conversation. At least until I have had time to explain to Tori why I saw fit to disclose our secret. You shall remain silent?" Jean handed the older man the bottle of brandy.

"You have my word." Dominique stood up and placed the bottle down without refilling his glass. "I will leave now and walk down to the beach. I have some thinking to do. One item is evident that makes me know what you have spoken to be so. It is my arm. She saved my life and had the knowledge to do so. Her inquisitive mind and yes, her strange language can now be explained. I will wait until you can talk more. One thing you have done is to clear my head of wondering. Too often of late, I have found myself questioning about her and who she is. Then the announcement of marriage, when there is none. All is coming clear. You have no need to concern yourself. I will not treat her any different; at least I shall do my best if you do yours to keep her with you. You must keep her with you. Find a way to do that…at least try."

"You have my word; I shall. There is much I could share, but until Tori feels she can talk to you, or anyone else, about what I know, what she knows, and who she is, it remains as is."

"If I did not know you, as I do, it could be said; the drink is talking. However, I do know and trust you, so I shall wait. Let us not discuss this matter again until you or she brings it to light. Now, about your trip to New Orleans, when shall you depart?"

Jean was thankful for Dominique's understanding, and knowing the older man was brimming with questions, he admired his restraint. What Tori would think about him revealing her secret, he could not imagine and hoped he didn't have to explain it, at least for some time.

In less than an hour, Jean entered their bedroom and sat by Tori's side. She looked at him and spoke with a concerned tone in her voice. "I had no idea, none. God forgive me if coming to this time has done something to change history." She shook her head. "I mean, if I was not here, you would have gone to New Orleans, and maybe, you could have stopped, would have stopped it. I can't believe that, though. I won't because if that were true, I'd go off the deep end."

"Tori, listen to me. I don't understand this deep end you worry over, but I do know history. I think that it is highly unlikely you had anything to do with what has occurred. You can't know everything that goes on in this time. Think about it. Do you honestly think your generation would want to remember such a gruesome and tragic event? You have told me repeatedly that the history of slavery caused considerable racial tensions in your time. That said, it stands to reason that this event would not be a subject to remember, let alone discussed. Don't you see my love? This is why I wanted to keep it from you. I knew it would upset you. I did not guess you would think it was your fault."

"Do they know how many died?"

"I have heard. Nez Coupe has said, two white men died, as you already know, and more than a hundred slaves. That could be wrong. We do know, of forty-five slaves for certain. They were brought to justice and tried in a three-day hearing. All were found guilty and shot."

"Just shot? Tell me then, what he said about the heads, did they really do that?"

"Yes."

"Before or after they were dead?"

"I don't know. It is likely that a few were killed in such a manner. It was…un grand carnage (a great carnage.")

Tori's voice trembled, and her eyes filled with tears. "I don't think I want to know anything more about it. Can we not talk about it anymore, please?"

"I agree. Let us go to bed and in the morning. I will see when we will be making our trip. You can trust me, my love; nothing will harm you or the baby, and you will enjoy the venture. Now, come here, my brave and beautiful love."

"Not till you promise me that Nez Coupe, never eats dinner with me again. He is just as awful on the inside as he is on the outside."

"You have my word that he will not bother you. I agree he got carried away tonight. The man had drunk enough to place most unable to talk, let alone remain upright. He is complicated, and he is a pirate. Even with papers, he will always have a fierce aura about him. Sometimes I think he is one angry and hurt man who puts on a show of power. Inside, he suffers, of that I am sure. He enjoys making others suffer, but not his family, I am told. When it comes to family, he stands tall and takes care of his own. It is others he toys with, who he takes out his anger on, like he did to you tonight."

Tori tried to smile. "Misery loves company. It's a saying from my time. I suppose if I was ugly like Nez Coupe, I would be angry too."

"Now you understand why I gave such warnings, of never walking around here without Dominique or myself? There are a few others just as threatening as he. As for Nez Coupe, he sails tomorrow, on the morning tide, and my bet is, when he returns, he will have many goods and slaves to sell. His scruples are such, and making money guides his conscience."

"But selling slaves is illegal for now."

"It is, and it means nothing to a man such as him. He sees a chance to make some gold, and he will take it. Under our law here, at Grand Terre, I can't stop him, nor will I try."

"You know how I feel, so why tell me?"

"Because we have no secrets, and you might hear that we still deal in slaves. It is common knowledge in the city. Well, knowledge among those that have dealings with us. I promise you that it is I who will try my best, never to take a ship with slaves again. As for Nez Coupe, I am sure he will be gone for quite a while. You can forget about him, oui? (yes?) Now, let us put this evening and the evil spirited man behind us, shall we?"

"I can try, but come to think of it, now that I have met the man, I don't think he is evil at all. I think he is just angry about what happened to him, and in a way, I don't blame him. I just wish he could see that it does not help him to act like a barbarian."

"I think he would disagree with you on that point. Acting like a barbarian gets him just what he wants when he wants it. Enough, about the man, he is gone, and it is my desire that you two never cross paths again.

THE goodbyes at the house had been tearful, with Carlotta making Jean promise that she would be allowed to visit them once the baby came. Tori had wanted her to go along, but Carlotta had explained that she had to stay and look after the house, as no one else, it seemed to her, could do it as well as she.

Though, the final farewells had almost made the housekeeper change her mind, for she had grown very fond of Tori, even if she was hard to understand sometimes. Carlotta had found it even harder to comprehend the news that Jean and Victoria were man and wife. The reason they gave for keeping it a secret was that Jean wanted to tell his brother Pierre himself. He wanted it that way because to hear it from a stranger or friend was not right. They had decided they could tell her their secret because she was one to be trusted. Yet, the more Carlotta thought about it, the more she knew that there had to be another reason why they had kept the marriage a secret, and she would bet her life; it had something to do with the married woman that Jean had seen before his trip. Oh yes, she knew about that rumor. Nothing happened in the city, with either Laffite's that did not find its way to the island. True, it was only a rumor to most, nothing confirmed, and yes, Boss was a lady's man, but now things would change. The rumors would stop. They would end, as fast as Jean's love affair with that woman had.

It seemed to the housekeeper that she was the only one that knew the rumor was a truth. Lacy had confirmed the whole sordid story to her when she escaped Rose's. It would have been nice to talk to the girl more about it, but she was gone to the islands. Strange how Lacy was said to have known Boss's wife, when there was no possible way, she could have met her. Then, to be sent away to the islands because Tori wanted her free. No, there was far more to the stories that Laffite and his lady spun, and in time, Carlotta figured she would learn the truth of it all.

One fact was clear, and for that, she thanked the Lord. Jean belonged to Tori now. There wasn't a shadow of doubt in her mind. However, a woman scorned is one to fear, and there was going to be trouble. The housekeeper could smell it coming, and if she knew it, then Jean would surely understand what he was up against when they arrived in town. Yes, she was right on this one. Jean had kept the marriage quiet until he could calm the waters ahead. If only Carlotta had known how wrong she was. Calming the waters ahead was the last thing on Jean's mind.

LAFFITE had seen to it that the very best of care was taken to make it an easy trip for Tori, both emotionally and physically. He had chosen to travel by barge for several reasons; the prime reason was simple. Jean did not want anyone to see his love before he was ready. Sailing into port with her was not dramatic enough for his ego. Besides, if they sailed up the Mississippi, his love would stand on the deck and watch the banks. It was suggested by Dominique that some of what she may see would unsettle her, and he mentioned Chez Nez's warning of the spiked heads to strengthen his opinion. Traveling the bayous, therefore, was a far more acceptable choice and had sealed the deal.

"JEAN, you are telling me I have to travel through the bayous on a barge? You are serious, aren't you? I mean, we are walking to where the barges dock and not toward the beach." Tori tried looking into his eyes, but the man just kept staring straight ahead. His face held no expression, and she couldn't imagine what he was up to. Not wanting to give up, she tried again to engage him. "I thought you were joking, but you are deadly serious, aren't you? Explain to me why can't we just go on your ship?" She grinned and poked him in his ribs as she added her next remark. "I rather like that idea, and I do miss that cabin. Come on, you know I am right; you would enjoy it as much as me."

He looked her way, frowning. "Tori, might I remind you, what it would take to get on board. You don't think for one second that I would allow you to climb the side of my ship again. Especially now, because you carry my, forgive me, our child. I take my son's side on this. He would not enjoy the sounds of his mother crying out to God to help her when she could not find her footing." He was laughing, and Tori had to admit the very idea of climbing the rope ladder to get on board was a bit much.

"Well, you could have Dominique build a hoist, and I could be pulled up. That would not be too awful, and I trust him to make certain that I would not fall."

Jean stopped laughing and turned very stern. "I forbid it. No wife of mine will be treated in such a manner. You will travel the way I have planned, and that madame is the end of any further discussion of the matter." Jean had a broad smile, and he rubbed his chin with pleasure. He had won this battle, with an excuse that made common sense, but heaven help him if she ever learned the truth behind him insisting, they travel by barge.

THE air was crisp, and the sounds of men talking carried on the wind. Jean's hand had hold of hers, and even though she had a pair of deerskin gloves on, she could feel the heat of his palm. His fingers were rubbing her knuckles, almost as if he were worried about something. They did not stroll, nor did they walk at a fast pace, and once or twice, Tori saw him look back at the way they had come. "Are you looking for someone? You seem worried. Jean, is something wrong? Look, I really don't mind us not going on the ship, if you are thinking about reconsidering, please don't."

"No, I am not changing my mind, and nothing is wrong; I can assure you of that. I had hoped that we would have a chance to say farewell to Dominique. He was supposed to stop in before we left the house, and now, we are almost ready to depart Grand Terre, and still, there is no sign of him. I am sure he has his reasons. Maybe saying goodbye to you is one of them. The man is quite taken with you and…"

"And perhaps because you decided to confide my origins to him, it has him thinking I or we are both nuts. I told you not to speak to him."

"Nuts, as you say, are for squirrels, and you know I had no choice in the matter. The man was asking questions, implying all sorts of idiotic notions. It's true, Dominique took my explanation far better than I did. He also had time to talk with you, and there seemed to be no problem with his grasp of your situation or stories." Laffite looked around, and concern filled his eyes. "I was certain he would be here to wish us well. The man has had plenty of time to come to grips with what he knows. At least I had thought so."

The voices of the men ahead echoed off the still waters of the bay, and as she looked forward, Tori could make out the silhouettes of several large pirates carrying large bundles. At this precise second, one of the shadowy images stepped closer, and as it did so, she recognized his gait.

"Jean, look ahead, not behind, you idiot. It's Dominique; I'd bet my life on it. He has come to wish us well, after all. Now, will you stop worrying and please stop rubbing the back of my hand, or you will wear a hole in it."

Jean looked ahead into the thick gray mist and smiled. His love was correct; there was only one man with such stature and walk. His second-in-command had come ahead of them, no doubt to make sure everything was as ordered.

"Boss, you have arrived at last. The men and I were beginning to think the trip had again been delayed. Tori, it is nice to see you, and may I add the cloak looks good on you. I knew it would."

Tori happily stepped up and hugged him while chatting away. "I can't thank you enough. It is lovely, and it does keep the chill off. I can't imagine how you ever acquired it. Even Jean could not find one around these parts."

Laffite laughed and looked at the two people he loved. "Tori, my dear lady, I can assure you that our Dominique won such a fine garment as it is, in a game of chance and nothing more. Lucky for you that he did so, or I would have surely purchased it."

"I most certainly did nothing of the sort," snapped a frustrated Dominique. "I borrowed the item from a friend and assured her that the cloak would be returned promptly."

This statement had Jean laughing even more. "Well then, Tori and I will make your word stand true. It will be on its way back to your lady's possession tomorrow. Is that soon enough?"

Tori was confused. "What lady are you two talking about? This cloak is nothing like I would imagine any lady here wearing. It is an expensive item for sure."

"Aye that it is. I had it made and brought it as a gift to one of my acquaintances." Dominique was blushing and looking most uncomfortable.

Seeing his reaction, Tori realized that the woman in question had to be the whore that she had often seen waving their way. The same woman who she had seen on a few occasions, the one that spent all her time with Dominique, and he, it seemed, had quite a soft spot for her. To purchase such an item had to mean that his companionship went a tad bit further than him being just a client, as he had sworn to her. Jean's wife also recalled how Dominique didn't want to make a huge issue of his friendship, especially in front of Laffite. "Well, please thank your lady friend for the loan, and I thank you for thinking of asking to use it. It's Jean here, who should have known I would need such an item. He, on the other hand, always has me dress in the most, shall we say, provocative gowns and of material that is way too thin for such a trip."

Now it was Dominique who laughed. "Boss, she has you there. Don't worry; I have taken steps to see that all our dear Tori may need for comfort and warmth has been loaded. Now, I must be off—duty calls. I am, as of today, in charge of this place. That is until Beluche returns from his trip. That should not take long. I swear, Boss, the man is happier onshore these days. Once he is home and takes over, I shall make use of my papers. It is good that I acquired them when I got yours. The Pandoure, she is back in port, and as her true captain, I intend to make full use of her." He chuckled as he pushed his broad shoulders back and stood as tall as he could. His dark eyes seemed to twinkle, and Tori thought that the rouge pirate looked like a man with mischief on his mind. "The British, they may try to block our way and our ports, but they are no match for me." This time he laughed out loud. "Take care of her, Jean, and Tori, you best keep him out of trouble. I think maybe, this match between you has happened by the hands of the Gods. The two of you need each other, more than you know. I despise farewells, so I am off." He hugged Tori and kissed both her cheeks and stepped back with a massive grin on his face. "New Orleans is in for a shock. Wish I could be there to witness it." Dominique turned and walked past Laffite, and without a word, he slapped him on the back and then quickly picked up his pace, disappearing into the morning fog.

Tori took Jean's hand and squeezed it to reinforce what she had to say. "He does care about us both, you know; a great deal, I can tell you that."

Jean smiled. "I have never known him to be so attached to anyone or anything but himself. When it comes to matters of such bonds between us, it seems he is indeed quite moved by our union. Something I shall have to discuss with him when next we meet; his attachment to you, that is.

"Don't worry. He is dedicated to you and you know it. It stands to reason that he would feel the same way about us as a couple."

"I suppose, but I will still have to talk with him, after all, I am Boss in name and deed." Jean laughed at Tori's frustrated expression, and knowing that he needed to end the discussion, he spoke to her in a softer tone. "Come along; it's time to board and be on our way." He dropped her left hand and took hold of her right hand, and without rubbing the back of it with his fingers, he walked toward the sound of the men's voices.

"Jean, one thing bothers me."

"And what is that, may I ask." He stopped walking and looked at Tori's puzzled expression.

"It's Dominique; he never mentioned he took out his ship to do what pirates do. I just assumed he sailed with you all the time. That his ship was under the command of someone else."

"Ah, I see. You are worried the old sea dog will come to harm if he is not with me." Jean was grinning and once again teasing her.

"You know that's not it. I am quite certain that Dominique can be just as good, if not a better commander." Tori was teasing, and she loved the look on Jean's face. "Look, all kidding aside. He never once told me details about his ship or the fact that he sails as its captain. This ship of his, is it safe, can he protect himself and his crew?"

"You have no need to worry. No kids or women on board, all are seasoned adult males," he laughed. I understand you and I am sorry, just had to make fun. Look, the Pandoure is a fine schooner. He pointed her out when we arrived, remember? She is large and swift. If it makes you feel better, I will try to describe her to you in detail using the measurement terms you are familiar with. Let's see, she is seventy-five feet long from stem to stern, and at her widest point, she is maybe twenty-two feet. The vessel has one large cannon and six twelve-pounders, two eight-pounders, and more, all stored in the hold. I know you have no understanding of their size by what I have said. Let me assure you, their size and range are spectacular. My second-in-command is the best at using such weapons; I am proud to say such. He does love his cannons, and he should. Dominique learned the ways of such weapons when in France. He mastered the art years ago, and his skill has saved his life more than once. The powder burns on his face tell some of the story. But that is for him to tell, not me. I tell you this, my love, Captain You is quite a formidable opponent and has not lost one battle to date. Now, let us depart and worry less about our dear old friend." He was grinning when he said this, and Tori knew he was trying to be funny and alleviate some of her concerns.

"If you say." 'Seems I have no choice or say in what anyone does around here. At least I am getting better at keeping my thoughts to myself. Got you there, Mr.'

Tori had agreed with him, yet she still looked worried, and Laffite wanted this trip he had planned to be one of enjoyment, not concern over his second's sailing abilities. "I am surprised Dominique has taken this long to return to the sea, but glad he was here to help me keep you out of trouble." Jean was chuckling as they began to walk again toward the barge.

'Huh! If only you knew what we have been up too. You wait.' Tori decided that she would remain silent for the moment, but that didn't mean she'd stop worrying about her dear friend. Knowing that he loved the sea and had chosen to stay onshore meant a great deal to her, and she made a mental note to tell him one day, just how she felt. For now, she was going to miss him and their lessons; however, in time, they would pick them back up, she'd make sure of that too.

THE bayous were cold this time of the year, and as usual, for this time of year, a dense fog hung above the waterways. It was typical to do so well into the late morning hours, and because of this, extra blankets were loaded for Tori to use until the sun warmed the air. There were two baskets of food and quite a few juice containers, along with one large barrel of what Tori correctly assumed was water. These were the items that she first became aware of after stepping on board but watching the crew occupied her after she was comfortably seated.

The entire group had been polite when Tori and Jean arrived. She even recognized more than half of them from her voyage aboard Laffite's ship. At first, she was surprised to see so many of his men and happily greeted them. After that, Jean's lady made sure to say a kind word or two to welcome the few men she did not know. It was a safe feeling, having so many friendly crew members around her. There were ten of them, all ranging in age and skill. Looking at each one, she found herself wondering why Jean required so many men to go along; she could only guess. It had to be for her security if nothing else, and once again, she realized how much the man loved her.

As the barge pulled away from the shore and began its trip, she saw the female for the first time. Tori had been so absorbed by watching the men that she had not noticed her. The woman sat quietly, leaning against the pile of camping goods, happily knitting away. Seeing Tori looking at her, she smiled, showing off her stained tobacco teeth; then she nodded her head, and without so much as a word spoken, went back to her knitting. Tori continued to wonder about her role on this trip and observed her carefully. The female was older than anyone else judging by her hair color, which was solid silver. It was pulled back in a bun and held in place by what appeared to be a stick. Her dress was simple, with long sleeves and a blue slip was showing itself, where her dark leather boots propped up against a bale of cotton. She had a weathered face, dark brown in color, which was either a tan or her natural color, Tori could not tell which. The lines that crisscrossed her face spoke of a lifestyle that had been hard and spent mostly outside. To Tori, it was like looking at an old crone from one of Linni's storybooks. Whoever she was, and whatever her role was on the trip, the woman seemed far more interested in her knitting than her surroundings.

"Jean, who is that, and why is she here? I understand, everyone here knows we are married, so that means I no longer need a chaperone and don't look at me like that. You know that the word has spread and is whispered, even the children know. I told you it was not a good idea to tell Dominique, but it's done. Anyway, I am right; as a married lady, I no longer require a chaperone when I go anyplace with you."

"That fact may be true to a certain extent, but not entirely so. You do require Agnes and her assistance, I assure you. It is a long trip, and I wanted to make certain that every mile of it is made easier by having her aboard with us. I think you will see how much you need her, as the day progresses," he winked. "As for now, I shall help my men, so sit and enjoy, and if you require anything, ask me. Are you warm enough? Maybe one more of the blankets would help?"

"Jean, I am fine, please don't let me keep you from whatever it is you need to do. The faster we get to New Orleans, the better. I have waited long enough to return to the city."

"Let's begin, men. You heard the lady; she is most anxious to reach the city. Let me see how good you are at moving this craft. You there," he pointed at a young lad of maybe sixteen, "give the pole to me and watch upfront for any obstruction that could block our way. I will hand you your pole once we are well into the bayous. After all, I am Boss, and as such, I wish to accompany my wife and not do your job for you." He smiled as the boy handed him the pole, and then without further delay, all the men began the task of pushing off. Once free of the shore and out into the middle of a massive bayou, they steadily headed toward an opening in the undergrowth. As the barge picked up speed, they entered a gap in the dense foliage, and soon, the craft was under the canopy of mangroves and tall Cypress. Once there, it took only minutes traveling along the waterway before Tori could no longer see any sign of Grand Terre or its shoreline, and she realized at last how concealed their location was when approached from land or the bayous.

ONCE underway, Tori sat back and witnessed the terrain, while Jean sat by her side and explained his plans. "I hope you can accept the reasons why I choose to stay overnight in what may seem to you to be a very hostile terrain."

"Do try because I have not seen one place that is not underwater. I do hope we are not remaining on the barge. I mean, you said, camping and camping means just that. If I wanted to sleep on a vessel, I would rather it had been the ship."

"I keep my word, my love. We will camp and not sleep where you now sit," he chuckled. "It is true that a bit further North of where we will be staying, there are a few plantations. All of which would have gladly had overnight guests, but I have no intention of venturing anyplace that my scouts have not visited. A few cabins I know about in the swamplands are inhabited by people I could trust, but I have no intention of exposing my wife to such unpleasant characters. They are a rough breed who make a living out of fishing and acting as guides to those who want to travel along the maze of waterways. For me and my men, we have no need for guides, but we keep those who live in the swamps friendly. It is far better to keep most in the vast swamplands, on our side. After all, it is this massive area that has kept Grand Terre and Grand Isle safe from those who would seek to destroy them. Sit back and enjoy the view. Ask anything, and I will explain and Tori, trust me, we may not have a bed in a sturdy building, but we will sleep on dry land when we camp."

By the middle of the morning, the sky was clearing, and the air, now warmed by the sun, blew the gray mist into swirling curtains of wispy clouds kissing the water. It reminded her of that fateful swim that brought her to this time, and the memory unnerved her.

Jean's wife looked around the immediate area surrounding the barge. She was determined to enjoy the trip rather than have it become a nightmare. Mist or not, memories or not, Tori reasoned she better forget about the lake and her swim for now. Instead, she concentrated on the unfolding view before her as they slipped across the still waters.

Beyond the deep, clear water, they traveled upon lay marshlands, dense with foliage, and it was ominous looking. The shallow water was stained a reddish-brown, and sometimes in the shadows, that color looked inky black. Jean explained that the hue came from the cypress trees, along with the red dirt, which flooded into the shallows during the rainy season. In some of these swampy areas, she could see the remaining stumps of large trees. These remaining trunks, Tori reasoned, were what was left after Laffite's men cut the giant trees down. They did so to use the wood to build their barges, like the one they were on. She also remembered seeing the pirogues the pirates used, all constructed by hollowing out logs. If Dominique hadn't explained the trees' use, Tori reasoned she would never have known why there were so many stumps sticking out of the shallow waters. To her, they stood silent, like sentinels guarding the waterways. Maybe those who tried to find the pirates looked upon them as a warning, for how could they not? So many downed trees meant a hell of a lot of workers, and those workers were all Laffite's men and enemies of the government.

No matter which way she looked, the area was utterly inhospitable, an almost impossible terrain to make one's way through. It had snakes, gators, and who knew what else lurking just below the surface? There again, on dry land when there was some, it was not much nicer either—bobcats, wild hogs, and creepy crawling things, like black widows. The very idea of spiders terrified her, and judging by the number of webs that clung to the brush; there had to be thousands of the nasty things both large and small. It was better to look away and not worry about the nasty critters. Instead, she chose to concentrate on how the large barge moved along the bayou, with such ease, always avoiding the dense foliage and shallow waters that surrounded them. She smiled at the friendly critters she witnessed, such as the odd deer and raccoon. The turtles sunning themselves on downed logs would slip into the water, and now and then, she swore an otter or two popped their heads up to look at the strange craft floating by.

Tori marveled at how Jean's men had been able to carve out such complicated mazes of open waterways. Many of the canals were large enough for the enormous barges to transverse easily like they were doing at that very moment. Even now, as they made their way effortlessly along, two men would stand each side of the vessel using their machetes. They hacked at the branches that had grown too far over their waterway, and on occasion, they'd pull half-sunken branches into deeper water so they'd float off.

As the day progressed, Tori found that Jean often would order his men to find a place to stop so their passengers could stretch their legs, while the crew ate and drank. On these stops, each of the men would jump to the little shoreline first and disappear into the dense foliage, making sure to leave a more open pathway into the brush, for the ladies to walk if they needed. Laffite's wife took these breaks to be the equivalent of potty stops, as her daughter would have called them. Funny, she thought, even out here in the bayous, she'd found a way to link the journey to her baby girl. Not wanting to recall past memories, she moved her mind away from Linnie and concentrated on her surroundings and the experience.

Seeing that Tori was enjoying, herself Jean relaxed. He wanted to explain his plans to her and felt he could do so without trepidation. He placed his arm around her shoulder and pulled her closer. "I think it is time I told you all I have planned. It is my hope you will enjoy each step of this journey and remember how proud I am to be taking my wife to New Orleans."

Tori began to say something, but Jean placed his finger up against her lips to silence her. "We will go some of the way on the water. Then travel by coach, as I should have explained to you before now. Madame Jean Laffite, she must enter the city in style," he said, laughing, watching the expression on her face. "Look at it this way, no one will ever dare mention you are Tori from Roses' now," he whispered into her ear. "How could they? Besides the Duval bastard, Rose, and her girls, no one else saw you in that place."

"The kitchen staff did. They all saw me when I arrived, and Lacy told me they lived."

"They did, and then each one ran, and I would bet left the area. Their freedom is more important to them than talking about one of Rose's dead girls. Think about it; you should have been upstairs, and, like everyone else, burned alive. Tori, they all perished in the fire but not Duval, much to my disappointment. Wish he could have been there in the house when it caught fire. Shame, he was not. Not to worry. Trust me, you are more than safe as my wife. A woman who hails from the islands and all my crew will swear to it. I dare say that even the bastard Edward will never recognize you once your new identity takes hold.

Tori smiled at him. He would always look after her, but then he did not know the devious Edward Duval as she did. She shivered a little just thinking of him and hoped they would never have to cross paths. Maybe they never would, Tori assured herself. After all, the city of New Orleans was a large place. "I do hope Jean, that you have not overdone things, but knowing you, I can't stop you from showing off. I just wish it was not me you were putting on display."

"You have nothing to fear. I know what I am doing. Just trust me and now, sit back and look at the beauty that surrounds us."

Tori did not respond because there was nothing; she could say to change his mind. Instead, she turned her head and looked at the view slipping slowly by. Twice they passed by larger deeper canals like the one they traveled on, but where they went too, she could not guess, and so she asked. "Where does that go? I know that is not natural, right?"

"True, it heads another way, and you are indeed correct. That one is a man-made canal; it has been built with my barges in mind, but not specifically for my private use. It only worked out that way," he explained with a sly smile. "You will meet the builder of that particular canal; he is a close and dear friend. His whole family is very dear to me."

"Then, I look forward to it. Just remind me about this when we do meet. I want to see who else is crazy enough to build in these swamps," she laughed.

THAT night they camped in a cleared spot. Jean had arranged for some of his men to prepare it ahead of their arrival, so once they pulled ashore, there was nothing to do but enjoy the evening. It was as if they were camped inside a dark bubble because the whole surrounding swamp was cloaked in inky blackness. Even the moonlight was not bright enough to penetrate the wilderness.

In fact, beyond the campfire, one could hardly see anything and many, including some of his men, always felt on edge after the sun went down.

Jean had seen too it that Tori did not need to fear the dark of the night. Lanterns hung everywhere, and the fire pit burned brightly, also producing plenty of heat. A mosquito netting had been draped over where they were to sleep, and Tori found sleeping in Jean's arms, in the fresh air, brought about a most relaxing break. When she woke up, Laffite's wife could not even remember if she had dreamed and not for one single moment had she been afraid.

TORI sat up and began watching Jean giving instructions about breakfast, which made her giggle. He was trying hard to explain why her meal needed to be on a china plate and her tea, in a cup, and not a mug.

Wrapping herself in a blanket, Tori climbed out from under the netting and joined the group around the fire. "I think I would drink anything warm out of a mug or cup, and Jean, we are camping, so I think that eating off a tin or pewter plate is just fine, thank you very much."

Several of the men chuckled, and Agnes smiled brightly. "Boss, this here wife of yours is quite something. I myself, being a lady, recognize truth when I hear it. She knows what she wants, and I would listen to her. You still have quite a journey ahead, and making it with a wife that is happy, is far better than not. Here you go, Miss Victoria; you take this mug, it's full of hot fresh coffee. Somehow, I reckon it is better than the so-called tea; I tried to make. Them bits of leaves just keep on floating about, while my coffee grinds, they ain't' found in one cup."

"Thank you, Agnes; it is perfect, and I do like coffee, as Jean well knows. Don't you worry yourself about not having me a cup of tea. Now, move over and let me sit by this fire and enjoy my morning meal with everyone. It smells wonderful."

AFTER a hearty breakfast, they had once again taken to the waterways. However, this time, Jean had them wait until the layer of fog had lifted several feet off the water. His reason was two-fold. It gave Tori a chance to continue to view the area, and it gave his men from New Orleans time to have the next part of the journey ready for them when they arrived.

Tori was stunned when they emerged from the bayous onto the Mississippi river itself. She watched in amazement as effortlessly, the crew switched from poles to paddles, and in no time, they were crossing the slow-moving water. It had never occurred to her that they traveled on the wrong side of the river, something that when she pictured a modern-day map in her mind, Tori found she should have realized this fact. New Orleans was on the far side of the river, and the settlements she'd just left were on the other. She and Linni had, after all, made the drive down to Grand Isle once, just to see the Gulf. Again, Tori pushed the memory of her daughter from her mind. She had to concentrate on her surroundings to do that. Putting Linni out of her thoughts was never an easy task but often, like then, a necessary one. Tori decided to see if she could guess where they were in relation to the city. It was difficult to guess where they were in relation to the French Quarter area, and looking up, and down the river, Tori couldn't even tell where any of the bridges would cross in her time. In the end, she just allowed herself to enjoy the now and not worry so much.

Finally, the barge pulled closer to the opposite shore, where Tori was able to see a carriage waiting on the higher ground just beyond the small levee. "Is that for us?"

"That it is, and I must say, that had I known the weather was to be this cold, I would have had a larger, closed-in carriage awaiting you."

"Oh, don't be so silly. I'm not ill, you know. Besides, it's not that cold once you're in the sun, and having an open one will give me the chance to see the countryside, and all of New Orleans far better."

Laffite hugged her. "And, might I add, an opportunity for all New Orleans to steal a glance of you, oui?"

"Really, you are impossible, you know that?" She did not wait for his response but hurried on talking. "Anyway, I was thinking now that we are to leave the barge and they will be going back to Grand Terre, maybe Agnes could take the cloak back to Dominique?"

Jean raised an eyebrow in recognition of his surprise. "You are extraordinary. You would expose yourself to the chill of the day, so you can return the cloak to Dominique. I dare say; he is not in such a great hurry to acquire the item."

"You don't know that, and I am quite sure the lady in question, is one of the women, you know, one of the whores, and if she is the one I have seen, who is always with him, I think the cloak needs to go. I want it returned as soon as possible. Besides, I think your arms around me can keep me warm enough. This dress is nothing like an evening gown. It's got long sleeves made of thick cotton. Not to mention, I have on winter bloomers and two, not one, stupid petticoat. I assure you I will be warm enough. So please, return this now." Tori gave him the look of you better listen, and to her surprise, the man listened.

As soon as they stepped ashore, Jean looked back at the older woman on the barge, who was watching Tori remove her cloak. Jean held out his hand and to receive the garment from Tori as he spoke to Agnes. "Will you see that Dominique gets this as soon as you return. My wife demands it so, and I am taking heed of what you said this morning. I would much prefer to travel with a happy wife than not. Oh, but don't tell Dominique it was her idea."

One of the men laughed out loud, as Agnes took the garment. "Boss, the old dog will know the truth behind it, told or not. He will claim the pup has been tamed, by the most beautiful woman." The rest of the crew began to chuckle, and rather than give them more to laugh at, Jean turned and began to escort his lady toward the waiting carriage. He had to admit to himself, they were right, but he did not have to tell them or show any sign of that fact.

The day was crisp and clear; the sky was a blue that seemed to border on silver. Tori could not remember ever seeing such vivid colors. Maybe, she thought, it was because she'd never actually taken the time to look before. Or, more likely, it was because the heavens were minus modern-day pollutions. Looking up, Tori saw only white puffy clouds here or there and not one chemtrail. There were no planes flying, only birds riding the air currents, and the beauty of such a pristine moment caused her to hesitate in her walk. 'I want to etch this into my memory, every detail, every shade so I can remember it for eternity. After all, memories might be all that will remain of this time one day.'

Jean watched her as they walked toward the grass-covered bank. He could see how she was taking everything in, and he loved how her face would light up over the simplest of things. The man was a lover of nature, and to find someone else that took joy in exploring; it was an overwhelming feeling. Her face was full of wonder, as any child would be, and her questions were many. It even shocked him when Tori was able to tell him something that was, up until then, unknown to him. Each step along the way, they surprised each other, and, in the end, what should have taken a short time; the walk to the waiting carriage, took over a half-hour, and he didn't mind the delay at all.

Once they reached their waiting transport, the transfer to the carriage only took a few minutes. The pair had watched as the large barge slipped slowly and effortlessly back out into the river, and the woman who had accompanied them waved. It was Tori who responded and enthusiastically, waving her hand until the barge was several feet from shore.

The men were pushing hard on the long poles to ease the barge over to where a slow, steady current ran. This was a simpler time, but so much harder in many ways. The men had to work very aggressively at moving the massive vessel, even with the help of natural elements. "You must remind me to tell you about outboard motors some time."

Jean looked at her with a quizzical expression. "Outboard what?"

"Oh nothing, just a little something that would sure make things simple for your men, that's all."

Jean knew he dare not carry on with the conversation, not with the blacks around. They were trusted, but why talk about things that they undoubtedly would find outrageous and be sure to spread among themselves and beyond. Word would soon spread of their arrival, and inquiries would arise, with questions that were sure to be of the ordinary kind and easy to answer. He and his lady did not need to add to the speculations that her appearance was going to cause. Knowing this, Jean made a mental note to talk about the 'outboards' another time, so he placed his finger to his lips and shook his head. He had no need for words as Tori realized her slip up. She nodded her agreement, fell silent, and went back to watching the river.

Jean knew she'd have to watch what she said and to whom. The pirate frowned as he recalled how Dominique had picked up on some of the things Tori mentioned, without her realizing it. It had been because of her blunders, that in the end, he had wound up having no choice but to bring Dominique in on their secret or have him think her crazy. Laffite knew their secret was safe, that the man would die before letting anything slip. His loyalty went well beyond friendship. After all, Dominique was far more than just his second and trusted friend; he was family. Besides himself, only his brother Pierre knew that Dominique was, none other than Alexander, their oldest brother. A secret they intended to keep hidden always. He glanced toward Tori, and for a second considered telling her but decided against it. Maybe in time, he would divulge the whole story if there was a need too. Until such a time, he would remain silent on the subject as per Dominique and Pierre's wishes.

TORI could see that they were approaching the outskirts of the town. Buildings and side roads were becoming far more frequent as were the inhabitants, all of whom watched as they drove by. For her, it was like going on to a detailed movie set. The very air of the place looked and sounded foreign. Nowhere was there a sign that this town was linked in any way to America, at least the one she knew, and once again, Tori had to remind herself that she was a part of it all. Everything around her was genuine and not a dream or a figment of her imagination. As a time-traveler, she was now fully emerged, in 1811 New Orleans, with no foreseeable way out and realizing this; she told herself there was only one option on how to handle herself and her precarious situation. Live each second, each hour, and day to the fullest, and try to survive without going insane with the what if's or other negative thoughts.

Once in the city itself, Tori took a deep breath and allowed herself the luxury of openly observing and enjoying the moment. The streets, while busy, were not overwhelmed with horses or carriages. Even those on the sidewalks, where there were such structures, had plenty of room to maneuver along. Now and then, another form of transportation like she was riding in would pass them. When this occurred, it seemed to her, that always, the occupants would acknowledge Jean first. The men dipped their heads and touched their hats, while the ladies nodded slightly. The wild curiosity of the males and females that followed did not escape Tori, though. Jean's lady could see the occupant's strain to get a better glimpse of her. It was obvious they were trying to discern who she was. Even the people on the sidewalks, and those sitting in the cafés, would wave at Jean. Then all would stare at her, before turning to talk amongst themselves.

Jean was thoroughly enjoying himself. His soft chuckle accompanied a protective embrace as he spoke proudly. "It is as if all of New Orleans wants to know you. See how you've already caused a stir, my love. Why I bet, we will have callers at the townhouse before the afternoon is over."

"I had no idea that you were so well known. I mean, I'd read, but this," Tori looked on both sides, "is more than I imagined."

"You don't know the half of it yet. At least now, I have you to accompany me in this madness; they call civilization."

Tori felt as if he were enjoying it all too much, and knowing him as she did, she feared he might continue to drive around and around, just for the sheer fun of it. It was then that fear snuck up on her. With everyone looking at them, there could always be the chance that one of the people could be Edward Duval, or maybe even Leone, and no matter what, Jean said she was not stupid enough to think that they would not recognize her. Tori was far from ready to face what would happen if the wrong person saw her, and because of this, Laffite's wife determined she had to find some way to get Jean to speed things up. Slowly sauntering down one street and another was inviting the scrutiny they were under, and it was stupid and dangerous as far as she was concerned.

With an edge of fear in her voice, Tori faced Jean. "How much longer before we reach the house?"

Concern crossed his face. Jean had been so engrossed in the spectacle of the moment that he'd forgotten about his wife's condition. "You will see it around the very next corner. Forgive me; you must be tired. How do you feel? Have I put you through too much?"

Once again, Tori became exasperated with his numerous questions pertaining to her condition, and as if those weren't enough, his continued insinuations that she had become frail because she was pregnant infuriated her. The mother-to-be realized that she had to set him straight, once and for all or suffer the consequences of being treated as the weaker sex for the duration of her pregnancy.

"Jean, if you don't stop treating me like I might break, I will be forced to do something to show you that I am not fragile. I only asked when we would arrive, because the thought of a glass of something to drink, and the chance to get out of this ridiculous outfit, and into something a little more to my liking..."

Jean chuckled. "I'm afraid, my dear, that you will have to become accustomed to dressing like a true lady now that you are in town. As my wife, I require such. Besides, it's expected." He raised one eyebrow in a questioning manner. "Do I have your word that you will save your favorite outfit, for when we are alone? Better still, for when we are at Grand Terre?"

Tori could see that Jean was trying to be very serious, and even though concern filled his face, surely the man had to know; that as his wife, she would do nothing to embarrass him in front of society. She took his hand and lifted it to her lips. "An outfit that no longer fits, I might add. You have nothing to worry about, Jean. I will be the perfect lady but get me alone, and I promise it will not be a lady you have on your hands."

Jean's head fell backward as he roared with laughter toward the heavens. "I shall hold you to that bargain."

The carriage pulled off the cobblestone road and onto a narrow flagstone drive, which was more of a tunnel than an open driveway. The entrance to the courtyard they approached was between the walls of a two-story building. The tunnel-like entry was created because the second story formed the roof over the space between the road and the courtyard beyond. Tori had seen such entrance ways into buildings in the French Quarter in her own time but never had the chance to see beyond the closed gates.

Once they emerged, she found herself in a small open space, which was sparse but well kept, and before the carriage came to a complete stop, a black man was at their side, opening her door.

Jean glanced at Tori and frowned. He understood how much she hated slavery, yet it was the way things were, and his love had to come to an understanding of it, no matter how upset it made her. "You will find that I have a small staff here. I keep a cook and three girls to help maintain the place. Oh, and four men, whose job is to keep the horses, gardens, and help as needed. I have one gateman who doubles as a guard. Before you ask, I will tell you, yes; they are slaves. Well treated, I may add and trusted. They like their work and their home, and have been with me for some time. That is the way it is, and knowing how you feel about the situation, I will now remind you that this is how it will be. You had better understand that it is only when we are alone together that you may comment negatively on such. You must learn to keep your feelings about slavery to yourself, if you are to be accepted, in New Orleans society." Jean smiled kindly and lovingly added, "that is the way it will have to be. Do you understand me?" Tori just nodded. She knew he was right, but that didn't mean she had to like it.

"Come see your new home." He stepped down from the carriage and took her hand to steady her. "This is the courtyard that most who visit will see. I have another courtyard that is for us alone. That, I shall keep for last. As you see, the house expands over the entry drive, that is where my slaves, sorry, our help live. Below as you see, on the left are the stables. On the right side, behind those doors, is where the covered carriage is stored, along with other items I require. Over here on both sides actually, are small gardens that I let Bessy have. Our home is separate from the building you just passed through. Now, let me escort you inside for that drink you are so desiring."

The door into the townhouse was open, and once inside, she could see she was going to love the place. Jean guided her through the hall and turned to the right, and stepped into a large formal room, where the doors opened out onto a small but lovely sun-drenched garden. This area was completely enclosed from the outside world by a high brick wall and two sides of the house they now stood in. Once again, she found herself thinking of a movie set and 90's New Orleans. What she saw before her looked very much like one or two of the courtyards she and Dan had tried to look at through locked gates.

Tori pictured her friend as he had held her up to get a better view at one such courtyard. They had laughed and would have continued searching out others, but the hour had been late. Dan had acted like such a gentleman and good sport, and they had connected. She'd had instant feelings toward him, something that was most unusual and stranger still, the man had shown he also had felt deeply attracted to her right away. What would have happened to them if the swim had not occurred? The French Quarter, its history, and charm had brought Dan and her together, then time had swept them apart. 'Stop it!' screamed a voice in her head. Tori knew she did not want to think of Dan. Not even the future or anything she'd seen, on their walk around the Quarter. If she allowed herself to do so, it would only serve to make her miserable, and Jean was acting so proud of his creation, as well he should be. Taking a deep breath, Tori stepped into the warm sunlight, determined to put all thoughts of her era out of her mind.

Outside in the shade of a small fiscus tree, there was a table and some very comfortable looking chairs. The flagstone, covered space was surrounded by pots of ferns, and hanging baskets, which over-flowed with the bright green foliage. Climbing the red brick house walls was a vine she recognized as jasmine. It even covered the one wall that blocked the street beyond, and against this wall, nestled in a corner, was a small pond. Tori was so surprised by the view that greeted her that she stopped walking to stare and take it all in. Jean allowed her to remain still for a few seconds before contin-uing his tour. The more than pleased pirate guided his wife further into the garden and toward the comfortable chairs.

"This is one of my favorite spots. The peaceful feeling one gets here seems to make a person forget that they are in the city. Even on a day like today, the sun warms it, and the wind is held at bay. As this house sits on the edge of the city, we tend to remain free of any noise or foul odor, all year long. And, when the wind does blow this way from the center of town or the river, the jasmine manages to infuse the air, rather than the..."

"It's beautiful, Jean; it really is, and I think it will become one of my favorite spots too. It's like a dream. Though...at this time of the year, jasmine is not in bloom, and yet I swear I can smell it. That is impossible, so how? I know my imagination is not that great."

"That my love is Bessy, my...no, our cook and housekeeper. The woman buys the scent, and when she knows and somehow, she always knows ahead of time when the garden is to be used, she hangs the small baskets you see around the area. Each is filled with dried moss that has been drenched, in the concoction she declares, is the very best to be found. Right up there," he pointed to a balcony, "is where our room is. To sit there in the morning, overlooking this garden is a delight and one I think you will enjoy as much as I do. Bessy hangs the scented baskets up there also as you can see."

"I have to agree with this, Bessy of yours. It is a marvelous idea, and it works incredibly well. The smell is just as strong as if the vine is in bloom. I do admire the time someone takes out here to create such a sanctuary. The ferns are so lush, and I would bet that come spring, flowers bloom among them, am I right?"

"I can confirm that, and once Bessy learns your favorite, if she can't obtain them, I shall. That woman has a unique touch with plants of all kinds."

Tori held up her thumb. "In my time, we call it having a green thumb. Sorry to admit I don't have one. I seem to kill all plants inside and out. Not even orchids grow for me. I am glad we have someone who can plant a garden and keep it. Oh, and look, I see lanterns hidden here and there, how romantic."

The two of them were acting like young children. One was delighting in discovering a new place, the other, in showing off his very own secret hideaway. Jean was about to show her the fish pond when they were briefly interrupted by a young slave girl, who Jean introduced as Leona. She had brought two glasses and a bottle outside with her and smiled brightly before departing. The slave had not so much as uttered one-word, and Tori didn't ask why. To talk about the subject of slavery was not what she wanted to do right then. She wanted only to make the most of the tranquil moment.

Jean and Tori sat down to enjoy a glass of wine. After pulling off her shoes, she started to remove the hat that she'd worn all day, and Jean leaned forward to help untangle her hair from the silk ribbon. The two were so involved with each other that they did not notice someone staring at them from the doorway. Laffite took her hat and kissed her lightly while softly saying, "I think my wife feels very much at home."

"So, the mystery lady is none other than your wife." It was a male voice, and it had spoken in English, with a thick French accent.

Jean turned to look into his older brother Pierre's face, and his expression lit up with pride as he did so. The two of them stared at each other with broad grins before they turned their attention towards Tori. "Pierre, may I present to you, my wife. Tori, my brother Pierre."

Pierre walked towards the pair as he spoke. "A brother who is just a little upset at not being told of this arrangement before now. I can, however, see why Jean would want to keep you a secret, and all to himself, for as long as he could. Such a find, my brother, she is a true beauty." Placing a hand on each shoulder, Pierre raised Tori gently to stand before him, and then he welcomed her into the family with a kiss to each cheek.

Jean's wife immediately felt such warmth towards this man, who, in many ways, was very much like his younger brother. He was a tad shorter and much thinner in build, and his eyes were not as dark as Jeans', but they were no less intense. One of the eyes seemed slightly crossed, and the side of his face had a palsy look about it. It was then she recalled how Jean had told her his brother had suffered a stroke but was still determined not to let the side effects deter him in life. Pierre wanted to continue living as if his health was as normal as anyone else, he had explained. Watching him right then, she could tell that Jean had spoken the truth about his brother's attitude, and Tori admired the man and his determination.

Unlike Jean, Pierre was clean-shaven, and his hair was shorter, also a few shades lighter in color. His nose was more prominent, but all in all, like his brother, he was a handsome man. Also, like his brother, when he smiled, his eyes seemed to sparkle. They had a touch of mischief in their depths too. That was the dead giveaway, as far as she was concerned, the eyes were identical to the way they expressed their delight or anger. Right then, both Pierre's and Jean's eyes were lit up with pure pleasure, but when Pierre glanced her way, his expression changed ever so slightly.

'Oh no, you can't be angry, that would kill Jean. I have to make this right; I must speak up now, and give him an explanation of some kind if he is mad.' "You are not too upset with Jean, are you? After all, everything happened so fast that we did not have time to tell everyone about the marriage."

Jean's brother smiled, and something in his expression softened, giving her a clue as to what mood he was in. Tori thought it was better not to let on that she could read Pierre's expressions like a book. After all, she'd had months of practice with Jean. Still, she had to make certain that he understood what she was explaining. "Jean wanted to wait until he could tell you himself. He said you would be upset if you learned any other way. You're not upset; please say you aren't."

"Upset with him, no. I learned a long time ago that my younger brother does as he pleases. I am only happy to see that he has finally settled down. I must warn you though Madame Laffite, in so doing, he will have broken more than one heart in this fair city."

Jean and Pierre laughed as Tori sat back down, observing them. It had not occurred to her that Jean would have had anyone else. Yet, that was silly, wasn't it, she told herself. He must have had quite a few ladies. She then recalled what her friend Red had told her while they were on the island. A slight smile tugged at her lips as she looked towards Jean, who was now her handsome rogue of a pirate and her husband for all practical purposes. She would have to talk to him later about his other ladies. Right then, however, she wanted to get to know his brother.

As time wore on, Tori got to practice her French and dodge the odd question that could not be easily answered. Jean did most of the talking, and in the end, she got to sit back and listen to them and witness how close they were. The strange thing was, the more Laffite's wife observed Pierre, the more she had a feeling they had met before. There was something familiar about him, and yet she couldn't quite put her finger on it. Then it hit her; he reminded her of someone else, someone who was very dear to her. Pierre's expressions were very much like Jean's, and those same expressions were identical to Dominique's. Again, she wondered if she had stumbled onto a family secret. Could it be, that in fact, the three were indeed related? And if so, why were they keeping their relationship secret? For now, Tori decided to keep her observations to herself; there would be plenty of time to confront Jean in the months ahead if she desired too.

As the hours passed, it became clear to Tori that Pierre had accepted her into the family. Because of this, Jean's brother was comfortable enough to explain his situation when it came to the matter of his own marriage. The older brother turned toward her and added information about his life. Information that was on a more personal level and most likely only discussed with family. This action made her feel even more welcome and very much a part of their lives. "Tori, you will have the occasion to meet Adelaide, but it is more likely that you will find me with the love I adore. She resides not far from here, and Marie will be so happy that Jean has chosen such a kind and amazing woman."

Jean had explained to Tori about his brother and his marital situation long before they even reached Grand Terre. He had laughed when she looked shocked upon learning that he spent most of his time with his mistress and not his wife. Also, he added that Pierre had a son by his first lover, who he no longer saw. Jean's last words on the subject, though, had stuck in her mind. "He is a lucky man to have such an understanding wife." That was how Jean saw the situation—understanding indeed! If she were married to Jean, there would never be an understanding of him taking a mistress. However, they were not married, and for a second, she worried about what that could mean to him and their so-called arrangement?

Pierre laughed at something Jean had said, and the interruption caught her attention. She'd worry about her so-called married status later, because right then, Tori understood she needed to pay attention to the conversation. Jean's brother was very polite, asking only simple questions, which she could quickly answer. Earlier, he had even agreed to speak in English instead of French, knowing it was her language of choice, making it easier for Tori to converse, and so it was that things went along smoothly until after dinner. When they returned to the living room, the conversation became more involved, and Pierre started asking her questions, which she could not answer. The look on his face when she stumbled was all-telling. He turned to look at his brother, and without a spoken word, he raised his brows and glared. It was as if he knew his brother was instinctively keeping something from him, and that something had to do with the woman, who seemed lost for words. More than that, his expression was one that demanded he be told, whatever the pair were hiding from him. During the uncomfortable silence and glaring stares, Jean decided his brother was also going to have to know the truth, just like Dominique.

It had not been easy to get Pierre to listen to what he called a fantastic tale, but upon seeing that the two of them believed in what they were saying, he had to take it a little more seriously. He stood, shaking his head from side to side with the inscrutable Laffite grin tugging at his lips when all was said and done. "I have to understand that what you have spoken of is something you both believe to be true. I, therefore, will abide by your wishes and hold this secret close to my heart. Not a soul shall hear of this matter from me. Besides, if I were to talk about such an outrageous idea, who would not call me crazy, and I have no wish to be thought of as someone who has lost his mind. It is all I can do to bare the innuendos that are hurled my way as is. In your matter, I will admit I have my doubts about the whole idea. However, you two must have reasons, beyond my comprehension, for wanting to believe in this time travel."

Jean looked at his wife to see how she felt about his brother's reaction and was surprised to see her seeming unbothered. However, witnessing how tired Tori was and knowing she would not rest until he suggested it, Jean took her hand in his and softly spoke. "Tori, it has been a long day, maybe you should go on up to bed. I still have a few matters to discuss with my brother, and I am quite certain he will not mind you leaving us so soon."

"Of course, I don't mind."

"Leona," called out Jean, and before he could help Tori stand, the door opened, and the young slave stood to wait for instructions. "Will you please take my wife up and see that she has everything she requires?"

Leona, smiling brightly, nodded her head. "I will see to it, and should she require me to stay with her until you come up, I will."

Tori frowned. "Leona, that is sweet of you to offer, but I think I will be quite able to await my husband by myself. Gentlemen, if you will excuse me, I shall take Jean's advice." Tori allowed Pierre to hug her once more. It was a warm embrace, and regardless of what he thought about her time travel, Tori knew that Jean's brother accepted her as a part of the family. The pleased and happy female smiled and spoke to her brother in law using French. "I am so glad we finally met, and I do so hope to see more of you soon."

"I can assure you that is something that will happen."

Jean was now standing at her side, and Pierre took a step back to allow them to say their parting words. He also took the time to closely observe them. He was searching for a hint of falsehood on either part but saw only love surrounding the couple.

Jean took Tori's hand and lifted it to his lips. "I will not be long." He then kissed her cheek and turned her to face the open doorway and the waiting slave. "Now, go on and do not worry if you cannot stay awake. I will be up soon." Not waiting for a response, he hurried her out of the room, and then closed the door and turned to face Pierre.

(In French) "There is something else that I must inform you of, and on this matter, I must have your help." Pierre started to

160

interrupt, but Jean silenced him with a look and continued. "Wait until I finish, and then we will talk." Jean opened the door and looked back into the hallway, making sure there was no one there. "Can't afford to have one of them listening to matters that I have to discuss. Before, when I called for help, Leona came too quickly. Standing outside the door, listening, no doubt. Anyway, we are alone now and so let me begin. From here on out, my wife Tori will be known as Victoria. The reason for this is simple enough, as you will soon understand. It should not be for long, but I feel it is necessary until we can prove she is safe."

AFTER hearing how Jean had come to meet Tori, and how she was wanted for murder by her own admission, the room fell silent. Pierre stood looking at the fireplace, with his back to his brother.

"You are certain of all of these facts, brother? You have had this lady, your wife…ah…how shall we say…investigated? She is somewhat of a mystery, is she not? Could it be she is lying? That this time travel she has you believing, is just a story to hide her past?"

"No, Pierre. She is what she claims. Of this I am convinced. Will you help me? Inquire around and find out all you can about this so-called dandy, Edward Duval. This despicable bastard, who set her up at Rose's! Will you do it for me? I ask only this of you, for if I were to do it, I feel that I would not control myself, and should I be the one to find him, I would call him out the minute I set eyes on him." Jean stood up and walked a few steps away, then turned and faced his brother grinning. "That would be on a good day. Otherwise, I would just run him through or shoot him."

Pierre wanted to laugh, but knowing his brother and his temper, he felt it better that he concealed his amusement. "I suppose you have attempted to learn more about this situation?"

"I had tried a few months ago to acquire more detailed facts… nothing came of it. Seems this Duval is not always an easy bastard to locate. When he is, it is in the company of women or at a card table.

This is where you, my dear brother, can be of help. I need to know much more, and discreetly so. My men do not attend the same circle of friends this man has, you do. Or someone you know does. Either way, I want to know the dandy's every move, and all else about the matter of Tori's standing." Jean's mood had darkened, and his eyes flashed as he spoke the next thoughts on his mind. "I know I would gladly end his miserable life and enjoy every moment of it."

"To do that would be stupid, and completely out of character for you," said Pierre. "There would be questions, far too many questions, I feel. No, you had best steer clear. I will learn all I can. Fear, not brother, for if there is anything that needs to be known, then I will hear of it. You did say that this Edward, kept her at Rose's?"

"I did."

"Well, on that front, you have no need to fear. The place burned to the ground, killed all inside. Only a few escaped the flames that day."

"I had learned of this. A piece of news that was most welcome, and might I add, it was fortunate for Madame LaSalle that she died. I would not have been so kind should she have survived. The bottom of the river would have greeted her one way or another, had she lived. Holding Tori prisoner for the dandy was a despicable act, and may God forgive me, but the bitch got what she deserved. I just thank God that Tori was not inside when the fire broke out."

Pierre decided a change of subject was needed to lighten the atmosphere. The two of them talked of Pierre's mistress, the young woman from Santo Domingo, who lived in a dwelling on the corner of Saint Philip and Bourbon Street. "You know, my dear brother, you are not the only one that has a surprise this evening," chuckled Pierre. "My Adelaide has given me a daughter while you were away. She was born on October 6th. We have named her Marie Josephine. She was baptized a few weeks ago on January 16th to be exact. I had hoped you would be with us."

Jean embraced his brother. "Why, you should have told us right away! Forgive me for not asking. I quite forgot that she was with child when I left. Tori will be thrilled for both of you. Tell me, how did your Marie take to the news? As your mistress, I am sure she had feelings about the matter."

"She does. I told her myself, and if she was unhappy with the news, she did not let on. She is resigned to the fact that Adelaide will always be a part of my life, and as long as I am discreet in matters concerning my life, all parties involved agree it is acceptable."

Jean rolled his eyes, and jokingly spoke as he handed a glass of brandy to his brother. "You are fortunate to have such a wife that understands your life and your love affairs. Something tells me that my Tori would not be so...shall we say, willing in such matters. Now, how is young Pierre and the Sauvients, how are they? They are looking after him as they said they would."

"They are, and I would rather not talk about that subject, while we have much more to catch up on this night. If I begin to explain all aspects of my life, we shall be here the entire night and that my brother will not happen. Marie has a temper when she wants, and I intend to see to it that this evening ends early enough for me to join her as promised."

Jean saw that he meant what he said and let the subject go. He would learn more about his nephew on his own. The lad may not have much of his father's interest, but he most certainly had his uncles. The conversation switched to the business and the upcoming social season. This time of the year would bring dinner parties that they would undoubtedly be invited to attend, and it had become apparent to both of them that Tori had best be ready to answer questions about who she was, and from where she came. In Pierre's mind, she had failed when he had questioned her, and if she could do no better, they would be in trouble. Knowing this, Jean realized it was going to be harder to present her to society as his wife than he thought. She was smart, though, and with his help, they would give her an identity that would satisfy even the most curious. Besides, Jean knew they had no choice, for already they had received several social invitations, invitations that could not be turned down.

Tori took one last look in the mirror. The emerald necklace around her throat sparkled in the lamplight. Her earrings twinkled like shooting stars. Each consisted of two inches of small cut brilliant diamonds, attached to a thin gold cord. Because of the artful way her hair had been styled, each chain swung freely and glittered when the light caught them. Tori knew if she had been the one to do her hair, the earrings would never have worked out. With no handheld dryer, brushes, or electric curling iron to smooth out the tangled mess, it would be impossible to achieve any sort of style like she now sported. Maybe, knowing the vision he wanted was the reason why Jean had sent for the best in the city at styling and aiding the women of prominent families prepare for special occasions.

Marie Leveau was his choice, and as surprised as Tori was upon meeting her, she didn't so much as give the slightest hint to either Jean or Marie that the woman's history was known to her. Instead, she acted shy and spoke little, while thinking about all she had read or learned about this historic voodoo queen.

Tori let her thoughts wander as she began to recall as many facts as she could. The young woman was a free mulatto, who began her career by working with prominent families. She recalled reading that the girl gained a deep understanding of her clients and their lives by picking up inside information on the job. It was speculated that in this way, she knew who was an alcoholic or impotent, who was feeble-minded or crazy. Most important, though, was her knowledge of who was cheating on whom. She was a practical sorceress who mixed black magic with blackmail. Her spies consisted of slaves, the city's free men and women of color, and her associations with prominent families. All this enabled her to gather further knowledge in greater detail. In the end, her wisdom had allowed her to successfully practice her black art for years and teach her daughter the trade. A daughter, who would also go by the name of Marie. Thus, in later years, this would cause considerable confusion. It was whispered the Voodoo Queen could be seen in two places at once, and her powers were something to be reckoned with always. No doubt that was because mother and daughter worked in cahoots and conspired to work their so-called magic in the same manner, thus maintaining their hold over the populace of New Orleans.

All smoke and mirrors, all tricks of the trade, Tori told herself. Voodoo was nothing to fear, and if one kept their mouths shut around the girl, Marie could not gain insight or any information she could use against you. Understanding her source of power was not magic, gave Tori a sense of calm, and allowed her not to fear the young woman. As of right then, Tori, not the voodoo queen, held the advantage, and it was going to remain that way. She also understood it would be wise to keep all her knowledge about the young woman to herself. To expose the girl and her ways would most likely end her career and thus change history.

Tori took her time in front of the mirror, admiring the vision Marie had created, and as she turned this way and that, she continued to recall more pertinent details. At this moment in time, the so-called voodoo queen was followed and respected by all, both black and white, rich or poor; it did not matter. The mulatto was destined to hold sway over many, and her influence would only grow as each year passed. Even in modern times, those years from which Tori herself came from, many people still paid a visit to her grave. They would perform a ritual of knocks on her vault, followed by the verse that each would repeat. This was all done; in the hopes that Marie would grant them their wishes from beyond the grave. If they did get their wishes, they would return and leave three X's marked on her tomb. At least, that's the way Tori thought it went. The details were close enough in her estimation, so she would not bother herself with their accuracy one way or the other. Besides, who was she going to tell anyway? She had not even mentioned what she knew about the girl to Jean when they had taken a short break. Her gut instinct was telling her to talk less of what she knew, even to him. Tori blinked and looked back at her image. Then she turned her head side to side to admire the outcome of the carefully crafted work.

Marie had gathered up her hair in soft swirls, and Tori had marveled when she saw the girl pin in some extra hairpieces. These fell loosely down her back, creating the illusion of having far longer, straighter hair than she did. The weaving in of some delicately placed dried flowers and strands of seed pearls, added to the stunning effect. Still not completely happy with her masterpiece, Marie expanded her handiwork. The finishing touches were expertly applied makeup. Marie did not use the garish techniques of the day. This woman used her own style and insisted on using her powders and lip stains that she'd brought with her. The teenager applied them like a true artist with just enough color here and shadow there. In the end, all efforts enhanced Tori's beauty.

Stepping away from the mirror, Tori took a quick glance at the mulatto. Just how did a girl of around sixteen become so good at what she did? Maybe Marie was older and just looked like a young teen? It was hard to tell, and the way she dressed did not help much either. She wore a headscarf called a Tignon, constructed of the same material as her dress. The way it was artfully wrapped around her head and knotted framed her face, allowing the girl's features to stand out. Her cheekbones were high, and her face was almost a heart shape; her nose was simply perfect in size. Hoops of gold hung in her ears; they were not too large but thicker than most Tori had seen. Her lips were full, and they had been stained with a color that bordered on purple. The girl's eyes were the darkest color of brown, and only when the light hit them did they offer up a hint of a golden hue. The young mulatto was not tall, and her frame was thin. Not that she looked like she needed to eat, just small-boned and delicate would be how Tori would describe her. Marie was well educated and spoke in a way, as to indicate, she was not only a free woman of color but also a woman you needed to take seriously. So again, as far as her age, Tori could not guess. One thing was sure, though; she did not come by her all her talents without a teacher.

Someone in this city was helping and guiding her, and just who that someone was, Tori thought she would like to find out one day.

With the job completed, the girl smiled and told Tori that she thought Madame Laffite was a beautiful woman, and in a hearty high-pitched laugh, added, one who had caught the biggest catch in the city.

Tori smiled as she turned to face Marie and asked her what she meant by that comment, but before she had a chance to question her, Tori saw Jean standing in the doorway. He did not acknowledge overhearing what Marie had said. He simply extended his arm and held out his other hand for his love to take. He'd come to escort her to the waiting carriage, as well as to satisfy his curiosity. Jean had to see if his lady was going to look as beautiful as he imagined. He was not disappointed. The pirate stood like someone in a trance, mesmerized by what he beheld. So deep in thought was he that he did not even notice Marie Laveau, as she quietly slipped past him, leaving the two by themselves.

Jean's lady was a vision of beauty, dressed in a gown that he'd had commissioned especially for her, and he found he could not talk, for his emotions were beyond him. All he could manage for the moment was to stand and wait, as she slowly walked toward him. How was it, he wondered, that she could render him speechless?

Tori was far from calm now that the moment of departure was upon them. Her nerves were on edge, and she feared she would not be able to carry out the charade required of her. More so, she told herself that she did not want any part of what lay ahead. "Are you sure I have to go? I mean, couldn't you make some sort of excuse for me, blame my condition? I'm sure they would understand."

"Come now, Madame, where is your sense of adventure? We have been all over this. You can do it. Tori, my love, you may hide in this house if you choose, but my friends will take the liberty to come in if you do not come out. They will pay you a call. One way or the other, the fair citizens of this town will make the acquaint-ance of my wife. As to using your condition as an excuse to remain sequestered, that is out of the question. I have yet to determine the when and where our announcement about the baby will be made. I almost told my brother the first night but decided that I should wait just a bit longer. This upsets you?"

"No, that's not it. It's just that someone could recognize me, and I could get you into trouble. You have not yet heard anything about my situation, not even from Pierre. Besides, I am…what I am. What do I know of being a Southern belle?" She was rambling, and Tori knew it.

"You are right; you are no Southern belle," he said jokingly. "That is why we are telling everyone you come from Europe." He could see the doubt in her eyes. "You can do this easily. You don't have to be anything else, except the beautiful creature you are, and anyway, I will be right by your side to help you. I have let it be known that your language of choice is English and that you have a fair understanding of French but choose not to converse in that way. Tonight, most, if not all, will undoubtedly speak French, so your lack of fluency will be hidden by the fact you choose not to use the language, and it will allow hesitation in answering questions. Stroke of genius, if you ask me, because it will even allow you to make mistakes and cover such errors; if there are any, that is. You will manage this evening by my side with no trouble, I assure you. Many of my friends will be there, and not one of them wishes to bring you upset, only acceptance. Now hurry up, or we shall be late, and I am not known to be late, punctuality is my usual manner. Also, I look forward to seeing my close friend. You will like Noel and his wife; I am certain of it. I spoke of him on our way here, remember? You said you wanted to meet the builder of the waterway that was man-made; well, tonight is your chance. The owner of the Destrehan canal will be most honored to meet you, I am certain. As will his wife, Marie."

THE evening was colder than it had been up until now. It was evident that the crisp winter air had finally arrived. The wrap he placed around her helped ward off some of the chilling touches, but Tori was still glad when they arrived at their destination that offered a warm interior.

The enclosed carriage rocked slightly as the driver pulled the horses to a halt, and it seemed to Tori's dismay that her stomach tightened almost immediately into a knot, and her palms began to sweat. The female hated being nervous and calmed herself somewhat by the knowledge she held within. The frightened woman knew deep down; she could carry off this charade if she really wanted to; acting was not that difficult. More importantly, she knew she had no choice at this point. Besides, having Jean at her side would ensure her success. He would always explain that English was her native tongue; thus, if she made errors in her French, which Tori felt she was sure to do, she'd not make a complete ass of herself.

In what seemed like a few seconds, they were inside the grand home and entering a large overcrowded formal room. As everyone turned to look at them, a silence fell over the place, and had it not been for Jean holding onto her; Tori was sure she would have tried to turn and leave. Just don't start talking to yourself, she thought. Then, rather than look at anyone in the room, she looked up into Jean's proud face for support.

A friendly male voice broke the silence, as its owner quickly walked up and warmly welcomed them. He slapped Jean on his back, and then hugged him in the French tradition of greeting, as he spoke. (French) "So, we finally get a chance to meet the woman who has stolen your heart, and broken many others, I am sure."

Again, Tori wished people would stop saying that. It made her feel uncomfortable, especially when all eyes were on her. That and the fact that everyone would pay attention to every word she spoke, and by the looks of it, French was indeed going to be the only language spoken. As the stately gentleman talked, Tori concentrated hard so she could understand him.

"Madame, may I present myself to you. I am Jean Noel Destrehan and your host for this evening, along with my dear wife Marie, who I have no doubt will be making her way to greet you momentarily." The distinguished man glanced around himself as if wishing for his wife to appear and join them, and as he did not see her, he turned back toward his friend. "Jean, you old rogue, you should not have kept this beautiful vision all to yourself for so long. Still, upon seeing her for myself, I can quite understand why." Then without warning, Destrehan took Tori in a warm embrace and kissed her lightly on both cheeks before stepping back. He laughed in a kindly manner, and Jean chuckled along with him.

So this is Jean Destrehan, Tori mused. The close friend Jean has told me so much about, and he is as Laffite described him. Tall, gracious, well dressed, and yes, stately looking. The touch of grey in his hair suits him, and his soft-spoken way impresses, far more than that of a boisterous voice. The way he looks at Jean and me, it's almost with a proud fatherly gaze. Jean is right this time; I do like him very much.

Laffite let go of Tori's hand to place it on Destrehan's shoulder. "You are correct, my dear friend, and please forgive me for my bad manners, but as you will soon see, I had my reasons for acting so." Then, right before he could go on with his explanation and planned announcement, a female voice from across the room broke into their conversation, causing Jean's body to stiffen slightly at its sound.

It was a sultry Latin accent that filled the air; a female voice speaking perfect French. "Why you must tell us, Jean darling. I am sure we are all dying to hear the reason. Could it be that you wished to keep the woman from the almost certain advances of other possible suitors?" Laughter filled the room, only to stop as she continued. "Shame on you. I'm sure that the gentlemen would love to meet your new friend, wouldn't you gentlemen?" There was more good-hearted laughter around the room, as a few of the men stepped forward, eager to be introduced to the lady in question.

Tori looked at Jean carefully to confirm her assessment of the situation and Jean's strange reaction, only to see his top lip twitch ever so slightly, an indication of his anger. Her assessment had been right. He was upset by this woman's actions and remarks, but why? Tori continued to stare at him, as he forced a smile to camouflage his unresolved feelings. His upset was even more evident to her, with his sudden grip on her arm. His hold was firm and had a slight tremble to it.

As difficult as it was, Jean tried to relax. He had to gain control. In all their preparations for this evening, Laffite had never anticipated that 'she' would be here, and yet he should have known. The female in question was always at these dinners; that was how they'd first met, and he recalled that not long after that first dinner engagement, their secret affair had begun.

Tori knew something was wrong; Jean had let go of her arm and taken hold of her hand and tightened his grip ever so slightly; then, he would relax his grasp only to squeeze once more. These actions may have been subtle, but they were enough to indicate that his sudden mood change was real, and it was not for the better. Laffite's wife could sense the uncomfortable feelings this woman stirred in him and witnessed his eyes narrowing and the dark scowl that turned his lips slightly downward. All of these actions spelled trouble; she was sure of it. But why, that was the question of the hour?

Slowly Tori's eyes left Jean's face, and she turned to appraise the woman in question. Whoever the female was, she was standing there fanning her face and looking demure, a look which contradicted the calculating glare that flashed now and then, from behind her carefully placed fan. She had long jet-black hair, which had been pulled away from her face and held at the back of her head by a large ornate comb. The beauty had a flawless pale porcelain-like complexion. There was not a blemish to be seen anyplace on her skin, and accentuating her face were full, dark red lips. If she had applied any lip stain, she had done so most expertly. Her dark eyelashes framed the most exotic green eyes Tori had ever seen, and those had to be natural, as colored contacts were years from being invented. Briefly, Mama Kate's image flashed in Tori's mind. Tori saw her friend at Leone's plantation in the vision, holding Tori's two small blue contacts and grinning. Tori blinked and pushed that memory to the back of her mind and looked again into the sarcastic woman's green eyes. They were fierce eyes that bore into her, and not once did they look away. It was almost as if the Spanish beauty was daring Tori to look elsewhere first, something that Jean's wife had no intention of doing. The two were locked in a stare-down, and while it lasted, the sarcastic female's eyes reminded Tori of snake eyes, sly, cold, and calculating.

Then the Latin beauties tactic changed as she spoke in Spanish to the few women close by. Her slight Southern drawl vanished as her voice took on more of a Latin accent. This explained a few things to Tori, first of which was the large ornate comb in her hair. Tori knew ladies of Hispanic heritage, which she was certain that this woman was, wore them in this era. The tortoiseshell objects were used as a sign of wealth and standing, something that this stranger seemed to have. Her elegant clothes and expensive jewelry, along with the way she conducted herself, demanded attention. Everything about her was blatant, almost as if she were screaming, look at me. It was plainly obvious this female wanted the attention of all who were gathered there and was used to having her way. Whoever she was, she was clever and cunning, allowing only Tori to catch her vicious glare and odd sly smile. Altogether these observations led Tori to quickly surmise that this woman was the spoiled belle of the ball.

It was Jean who was talking now sounding calm. He spoke like he did when he was in command on board his ship. Yet, no one could see what Tori could feel. His hand, which she still held, squeezed hers. It was as if he tried to indicate all would be okay. His free arm slipped around her waist, and he pulled her a little closer. For Tori, it felt as if he was embracing her in a very protective sort of way, and this action gave her the courage to continue to hold her gaze with the stranger.

"Well, my dear," said the beautiful woman, switching back to

French, "are you going to introduce your friend or not?" Tori could see the female was almost laughing behind the stupid fan, which she artfully used to conceal her amusement. This woman was intent on making a scene, and so far, she was succeeding beautifully.

Before Tori had time to think further, all pandemonium broke loose, as quite a few gentlemen pushed forward, to be among the first to make her acquaintance, while others whispered a translation of what had just transpired.

Then, Jean held up his free hand amongst all this action, somewhat like a modern-day policeman would do to stop traffic. "Gentlemen, gentlemen, please do not be in such a hurry. You will all be introduced to my wife in due time, I assure you!"

The stunned look on the simpering woman's face was quickly hidden from view, as she was obliterated from Tori's line of sight by the sudden crush of well-wishers. From all around, congratulations started as soon as the rumor of Jean's marriage had been confirmed and done so, from none other than his own lips.

There was not a single person in the room, it seemed, who was not intent on meeting her, and all surged forward at the same moment. It was then that Tori realized English was understood by more than she had been led to believe. Many were trying to engage her in her native language. Done to impress her, she thought, more than to congratulate. It was just too much. In seconds, Tori was overwhelmed by the multitude of people who rushed to greet her. The almost instantaneous crowd surrounding her and Jean brought on a surge of claustrophobia and panic. Visibly she was flushed, her cheeks burned, and her breathing was shallow. The pace of her heart had picked up, and if something or someone didn't get her out of there quickly, Tori felt like she would scream. Jean, it seemed, was oblivious to her predicament but not so Destrehan's wife. Thankfully, the hostess came to her rescue out of nowhere and whisked Tori away from the crowd, using the excuse that the new bride needed a few minutes to gather herself.

"My dear Victoria," she said in perfect French without a Southern drawl. "After traveling on such a chilly night, let me escort you to my parlor for a few minutes to warm yourself. Coming from the tropics, you must find our winter terribly harsh. As for Jean, that man can handle himself. I declare I have never seen him so exhilarated. He is in such a state as to have quite forgotten himself, and his manners." She giggled like a schoolgirl. "I am Marie Destrehan, and you, my dear, may call me Marie. It is my honor to meet you."

Mrs. Destrehan was so happy for Tori and Jean that at first, she did not seem to notice her guest was in a state of panic, but when she did, she took pity on the young woman and just took over, as was her nature. She ushered everyone out of the small parlor and promptly mothered her way into Tori's heart. She fussed and "pooh-poohed" about the crowd, and their actions in the other room, telling Tori not to worry, then clucked on and on like a mother hen in the barnyard, protecting her young chick.

In the short time that followed, the two females became instant friends, and Tori knew she had nothing to fear from her, unlike the other woman in the main room, the one whose looks could kill.

Mrs. Destrehan was everything Jean had told her and more. As for that Spanish female, the one who had put Jean on edge, now that was someone to keep an eye on. Instinctively, Tori knew that the attractive Latin was her enemy, and she had a bit of an inkling as to why. Red's words came to her mind. 'He has many females who would love to take him as their husband. Be warned, more than one will not be happy when you show up.'

The hostess touched Tori's arm and smiled kindly. (French) "My dear Victoria, is there anything I may fetch you, a drink, maybe? Or is sitting here for a little bit longer all that you require. I have to tell you; I understand just how you feel. Being the new bride, among so many, is not always what one wants." Marie frowned before continuing in English. "Forgive me, my dear, for speaking in French; my English is I fear, not so good as yours." She smiled and then continued in her native tongue before Tori could respond. "Being new to our city on top of everything else, well now, it seems you are in need of a few close friends to guide you through the transition. I have no doubt that you will come to enjoy the city almost as much as I."

Tori had taken a seat by the fire and was glad of its warmth. Her nerves were settling down, and she did love the way the older woman fussed. Marie Destrehan spoke with a thick French accent, just as her husband had, and so far, both were easy to understand. Feeling slightly calmer, Tori decided to try her hand at French and hopefully explain away any mistakes she'd make when using the language. (French) "A small drink would be nice; thank you. I don't know what came over me; really, I don't. I suppose that I panicked, having to talk in French, which is not so easy for me. English is what I am used to speaking. So please forgive any mistakes when I do try French."

"Ah, but my dear, one would never think so. Mistakes, never. You speak our language very well and with such flair. To speak so, one must have spent time in France, maybe? We shall have lots to talk about you in the days ahead."

As Mrs. Destrehan set about pouring a small glass of what could only be sherry, Tori took the time to study her. The woman was shorter than her husband and on the heavier side. Not that she was fat; she just had a rounder face and fuller frame than many of the other females gathered in the other room. Her dress was styled to hide what Tori would have called a few too many extra pounds in the tummy area. Her breasts were not overly large, but she did have an ample bust line. Again, the garment seemed sewn to hold body parts in place. Tori thought about how uncomfortable her hostess must be in the corset she had on. At least Jean has given up, trying to get her to wear them so tight, if at all. Tori's hand went to her stomach where the baby bulge was growing. She'd only worn a corset tonight to try and conceal the fact that she was with child. Why Jean had chosen to keep their news a secret and not tell Pierre or anyone else for that matter, had her worrying. He'd have to announce it soon.

Marie turned around and walked toward her with a glass more

than half full of sherry. Madame Destrehan's hair had been styled in what Tori would call an up-do. Two long curls, on each side of her face, hung freely and bounced as she moved. In her hair, Marie wore an ostrich feather, which waved about as if it had a mind of its own. It was not large as feathers went, but Tori was sure she'd never attempt to have such an adornment tugging at her scalp. Marie had two strands of large pearls around her neck, and in each ear was a pearl stud. The woman wore no rings or bracelets, something a person of her status could show off. Her expression was one of caring, and her voice was soothing. This hostess had the most endearing motherly attitude about her, and at that very moment, it was just what Tori needed. Jean's wife realized that she wanted to be mothered and taken care of, more than ever, right then. This realization was almost overwhelming to admit, as Tori had never felt such a need before.

Marie handed her the small glass. (French) "There is no need to worry about any mistakes you may make in conversing with anyone this evening. I will explain to all, and they will understand. Noel has already passed the news along to most that you prefer to speak in English. I am sure, my dear, as time goes by, your command of our native tongue will improve, and may I be so bold as to say, my English may also improve." Then to Tori's joy, Marie continued in broken English. "My husband and I, we try to make talking English better. He is far along than me. I understand much and talk little. It shall be good, no?" She was smiling brightly.

This was more than Tori could have hoped for, and she responded speaking slowly in English, emphasizing each word carefully. "It will be good, Marie, and I will help you learn English if you help me improve my French."

(French) I will do just that. But please, we will do so when we are alone. My husband does not wish anyone to guess that he understands English. That my dear is another story, for another time, maybe." Marie was about to explain when that time might be when there came a light tapping on the door. Thinking it might be the new groom who would undoubtedly be worried, Marie left Tori's side and opened the door. "Kristen, my dear girl, just the person I need. Do come in, quickly now, before someone spies you."

Tori took a small sip of her drink, put the glass down on the side table, and looked up when she heard Kristen. Fearing it might be the woman who had been sarcastic in her remarks, and very rude with her glaring looks, she braced herself for more of the same.

The female voice spoke using French but did so with a strong English accent. "I thank you kindly, Aunt Marie. Father had told me to remain out of your way, but you know me. I said I would, and at the first chance, I just had to slip away. I came right here. He is such a darling, but he is not my husband, and I do have a mind of my own. You know, being his daughter can be quite exasperating. It's no wonder I get upset."

Laughing, Marie replied. "My dear girl, you have always had a mind of your own. Now come in here, and please speak in English, it is Victoria's native language. I want you to meet…"

"You speak English? How grand. My French is not so good as Aunt Marie will attest too. Mrs. Victoria Laffite," Kristen held out her hand in greeting, "It is my pleasure to meet you." Tori took the girl's hand, surprised by the familiar greeting of using a handshake. They briefly shook, then Kristen burst on with her introduction. "As you can gather, I am more English than American or Creole." She laughed softly and sat down in the chair opposite Tori. "The French are too touchy-feely for me. Most of them, that is. Aunt Marie isn't, but then she is not my real aunt. Now, your husband can greet me with a light kiss on both cheeks and embrace me in a firm hug, and I would never complain. He is so dashingly handsome. Please don't misunderstand me; I do not have any unwarranted feelings toward him. I am very much in love with my own beau. I just simply had to meet the woman who Jean Laffite married. It's been the gossip around town for weeks that he had taken a bride, and well, here you are. How very splendid."

Marie saw that Kristen and Tori were entirely safe for the

moment, and on the pretense of carrying out her hostess duties, she walked to the parlor door. "See to it that no one else enters. Kristen, are you listening to me?"

The young girl turned to face her and spoke in French, "Yes, ma'am, I am. You can count on me, to keep Mrs. Laffite entertained and only me until you return." She looked at Tori and switching to English; she asked, "that is if it is all right with you, Mrs. Laffite? Maybe you wish to be with your husband. I can take you to his side if you want. Or I can bring him here."

Tori shook her head. "No, thank you, Kristen, if you don't mind, I would rather sit a spell and Madame Destrehan…"

The hostess understood the conversation between the two younger females was going well and smiled. Maybe her English comprehension was not that bad, after all. As to speaking the language, she would wait a bit before trying to engage Laffite's wife further in anything but French. "My dear, that is far too formal, Madame Destrehan indeed. Please, Marie will do nicely, I assure you. Now, let me leave for just a short time, and when I return, we will see to it that Jean has his bride by his side." The older female smiled brightly and left the younger ladies to chat, confident that Victoria would be herself and ready to face the entourage and their greetings by the time she returned.

Once the door closed, Kristen stood looking at the door and spoke in earnest. "Aunt Marie really amazes me. I think sometimes she can read minds; honestly, I do. She always seems to know just what to do and say. Most times, she is in such command that no one dares do anything other than what she tells them."

Tori studied the girl, who didn't seem much older than her mid-teens at best. Her pale skin denoted that she was not of any Creole descent, and her accent, while British, had a slight Southern drawl. Kristen had walked to the table where a few glasses and bottles had been placed. She pulled a small glass toward her and reached for a decanter filled with a golden colored liquor. Without asking, she began filling her glass while dutifully paying close attention to her actions. For Kristen, at that moment, her duties as hostess were far more important than staring at Laffite's wife, and this gave the now much calmer Tori more time to observe her closer without seeming rude.

The young English girl had thick brown hair that was nearly waist length. It had just a hint of auburn about it and a wavy appearance. Unlike many of the females attending tonight's affair, her style was simple. Kristen's hair was pulled back from her delicate face, and each side had been artfully braided. These two braids met at the base of her neck, and there they entwined, leaving a full five inches of hair to fall loose. This decorative way of keeping her long tresses in place was graceful and suited her. Her young face was like that of a modern-day model. Kristen had the longest thickest eyelashes and full lips that needed no stain to enhance them. Her brown eyes were like large orbs, that once you looked deeply into them, you knew you could trust her. The girl had been excited to come into the room and meet the bride, disobeyed her father's request to do so, and now she sat sipping her drink quietly. To Tori's mind, it was as though the girl was at a loss for words, or maybe just a small bit shy, now that she found herself alone and having to act like an adult.

Jean's wife decided to break the silence. "I don't know Mrs. Destrehan at all, so I can't comment. She is very friendly. I will say that. Come, I think maybe you and I can chat for a while. Please do call me Victoria, I will call you Kristen, and as we are on a first name basis, let's pass some time, shall we? Do tell me about yourself."

"There is not much to tell, I am afraid."

"Oh, I am sure there is Kristen. Let me see…ah yes, you mentioned a husband, or that your father was not your husband, thank goodness for that." They both laughed, and when Kristen stopped, Tori asked, "Are you married?"

"Not yet. I wish I were, but it has taken me longer to convince my father that I am ready and that the man I wish to marry is the one for me. You see, I have no intention of allowing my parents to pick who they think is best suited for me. Did your parents choose your husband, or did you marry for love? I bet it was for love. He swept you off your feet, right?"

Tori grinned. "I would say it was a bit more complicated than being swept off my feet, or simply marrying for love. But we are not talking about me; we are talking about you. So, you have chosen your man. How exciting."

"It is very. I have been trying to talk father into announcing our betrothal for over a year. My beau is not like your dashing husband, but he is rather good looking. He lives just South of us and maybe an hour outside of Baton Rouge more in the direction of North of the city. I guess what I am trying to say is, he lives between my home and Baton Rouge. The whole area is quite simply settled by the English, you know. Of course, you don't, but it is. Do you know where that is? Baton Rouge, that is? Silly me, I should have explained myself better and thought before speaking. Father has told me to do so for years. I am quite a good listener, you under-stand, or so I have been told."

Tori smiled. Kristen was refreshing to chat with. For one thing, the girl didn't seem in the least bit interested in learning more about the new bride. She was more excited to talk about her own life and love, and Tori wanted to keep it that way. "I am aware of Baton Rouge. May I ask what your young man's occupation is?"

"You may. He works in an office for a company that he holds shares in. He helps coordinate the shipping between here and Europe, as well as up and down the river. He even handles father's books. All his friends seem to be involved in shipping. Either they go overseas or up and down the river. One of father's acquaintances talks about the steamships that are soon to be on the river in many numbers. If that happens, father will own one or more, maybe even many more. I find it all terribly boring. My husband to be, well, he agrees with me. He thinks that I will be most happy helping build our home and decorating it. That is to say; I will never find that task dull. That is if it does not interrupt my helping the nuns. They have a small hospital, nothing like here, but they do let me help, and I adore helping, especially with the children. Not to change the subject, but those emeralds, they are emeralds, right? They are beautiful."

"Yes, they are."

"Green is one of my favorite colors. Just not my very favorite, which is pink, by the way. I just adore that color. This gown," she smoothed out the skirt with her hands, "it was supposed to have been dark green, like your emeralds, but father chose the lighter shade. I think he is maybe remembering me as a child, not a woman about to marry. I do so wish David, that's my love, was here tonight. He arrives tomorrow or the next day if the weather has been good. He had to sail to an island called Martinique. Have you heard of it?"

"I think so, and for what it is worth, the color of your gown is just right. It quite becomes you. Your father has good taste."

"Yes, he does." Kristen giggled, and then she totally surprised Tori with her next subject. "You know, I have not been in town for two years, and I had forgotten how some of these so-called ladies carry on. Why, didn't you just want to scream at the one who was so rude? I would have. I feel sorry for her husband. He loves her very much. I don't think she loves him back. I think she loves his money more. Oh, dear, I am gossiping, and I shouldn't do so. It's true, though. When I was younger, my father would have meetings, and my mother she would let me go with father, especially to his favorite business partners. The rude woman's husband is one of my father's favorite partners. Anyway, when their meetings were finished, I would stay a few hours longer and read to him. He can't walk anymore without help. Father said he fell ill, and when he woke up, his legs no longer worked like they should. He can't read too easy either, and I know he loved to read, by all the books he has in his library. Anyway, whenever I could, I stopped by, and we would have tea, and I read to him. Father is most proud that I take the time to do so, and spend less time shopping, as my older sister does. She has been married for three years and still shops more than ever. You would think it would be time for her to begin a family, but not Elizabeth. I like to read to her husband's niece and nephew, and insist I do so, even when they are both sick."

"That is exceedingly kind of you, and I must agree with your father, doing for others is a thoughtful act, and I admire that. It would be nice if more adults acted like you."

"That is nice of you to say so. We British have standards and manners, but I shall tell you here, and now, not many of those out there act so. It seems to me that they thrive on drama and who knows what. Oh, I am so happy I got to talk with you like this. I feel as if we can call ourselves friends, which, if you listen to these Creoles, is one step closer than acquaintances. We do have a friendship, don't we?"

Tori laughed. This young lady was the epitome of innocence, with just a hint of mischief about her. She was charming, adorable, and maybe quite a handful. It would be intriguing to get to know her better and meet her father, a man who seemed by all accounts to dote on his headstrong daughter. Watching and listening to her, Tori guessed that if the young man she had chosen arrived in New Orleans, in the next few days, Kristen would twist her father's views, around and marriage would be sure to follow, sooner than not.

Thinking of marriage made Tori think of Jean, and she realized that she was more than ready to rejoin him and the crowd of people who waited to greet her. Laffite's wife stood up and smiled brightly at Kristen. "I believe you are my first friend here in New Orleans, and I do hope we have the chance to see each other again. Right now, however, I feel it is my duty to face the masses and join my husband, who, I am certain, is looking for me. Shall we return to the party? If you slip in and join your father, he will never know you disobeyed him surely?"

"Oh, that would be something, but Aunt Marie would have told him by now. He won't mind once I explain I stayed here with you because she asked me too. I won't exactly tell when it was, she asked, and in that way, father won't feel like I had my way once again. We will, though, won't we?" She giggled louder and then stifled her mirth by covering her mouth with her hand.

Her laughter was infectious, and her impish ways had Tori smiling and then giggling herself. "Oh dear, I think maybe I am a bad influence on you."

"Try telling father that. He will never agree. Trouble, it seems, always finds me, that's what he will say to you. I don't go looking for it, but I do admit, I do find myself making a nuisance of myself sometimes. I might be forgiven for my disobedient ways if I escort you back to the party, though. Only because it seems that Aunt Marie's duties are keeping her from returning anytime soon. She does so love to organize each detail. You wait and see. Aunt Marie is a dear, but sometimes she is too much so. Oh, don't make me laugh again. That look on your face is quite unbecoming, you know. Let's depart now, shall we? I promise to behave for the rest of the night if we do."

AFTER Tori had returned to the gathering, it became apparent that Jean knew the woman Kristen had spoken about. For once, back in the middle of the mayhem, Jean made it a point to break free of the small crowd surrounding them and escort Tori to a quiet corner of the room where a small gathering were talking to a man sitting in a wheelchair. Jean's intention was to introduce her to the lady in question and her invalid husband.

Laffite seemed determined and yet cautious as he spoke. (In French) "Madame Simone Claudette La Combe, I would like to present to you, my lovely wife, Victoria."

The attractive woman looked from Tori to Jean, and without showing any real interest, gave her answer in a nonchalant manner. "A pleasure, I'm sure, as well I might add, as somewhat of a shock. Ah, but let us continue in English. Simone faced Tori as she continued. "That is your preferred language, I have been told. Shame on you, Jean, using French. You are so unpredictable these days, it seems." Again, she turned away from Tori and addressed Jean. "There are those of us who would have bet that Jean, here," she patted his arm, "would never settle down with just one woman. Especially in matrimony; isn't that so my dear?" The woman looked lovingly at her husband for a few seconds. Turning back to Tori, she added, "Why I do declare, where are my manners? May I present to you, my darling, and most devoted husband, Monsieur Adrian Philippe Le Combe, and please, do call me Simone."

"And my dear, do feel free to call me Adrian," added the grey-haired old man in English. "I wish that I was not confined to this chair, for if I were not, I would most defiantly have to kiss the bride." He laughed, which caused him to cough, and Tori waited until he had gained his composure before smiling brightly and returning a compliment.

"How very kind of you, Adrian. You are a true gentleman, here let me give you a kiss instead." Tori leaned down and brushed the old man's cheek with a light kiss. "Kristen has been telling me how very much you enjoy her visits and her reading. It is so gracious of you to allow her to visit."

"Now you have this old fool feeling like he was young again. Such attention I have not had in quite some time. That is attention from other beautiful females other than my wife." He looked lovingly into the face of Simone, who smiled and stroked his cheek.

Simone spoke lovingly while rubbing the back of her husband's hand. "I would read to you if you would allow, but always you tell me to visit or shop. I shall have to make a point to stay home a bit more and read some poems of love. That, or you may find Madame Laffite here knocking at our door, at the request of the dear child Kristen. Where is she, by the way? I must say hello before her father takes his leave. He does not allow his daughter to remain so late at these gatherings. No child should remain too late, don't you agree, Jean?"

"That is not for me to say. But, if the Kristen we are talking about was the one I saw talking with Adrian earlier, she is far from a child.

A stunning young lady is how I would describe her, wouldn't you, Victoria?"

"I most certainly agree with that observation."

Simone flashed her eyes in a disapproving way before once again turning her undivided attention toward her husband. Most of the conversation that followed was between Jean and Adrian, while Simone fussed continually over her aging husband as if nothing else mattered. Had it not been for the way she would turn ever so slightly and look at Tori with dagger stares, Jean's wife might very well have fallen for her stupid act. Kristen might have been closer to the mark when talking about this woman, Tori thought, and she made a mental note to listen more attentively to whatever the girl had to say, for it seemed that her gossiping was entirely accurate.

Thank goodness Mrs. Destrehan had come and whisked her away again, or she was sure she would have shot Simone a go drop-dead look of her own. It was clear to her their dislike of each other had been established, and if that fact wasn't strange enough, the knowledge that no one else seemed to notice or care was mind-blowing. The Spanish beauty had fooled everyone around them but not Tori.

Marie Destrehan made Tori feel at home while introducing the bride to those who had not had the pleasure yet greeting her. Within a half-hour, Tori knew a great deal about this remarkable lady and her family. She discovered that they were on excellent terms with more than half of New Orleans, including a few Americans, who Marie explained, were not your average run of the mill upstarts. She also told Tori how she and her beloved husband held Jean in high esteem, and for quite a while, she went on and on about their relationship with him. The Destrehans, it seemed, considered him family, and always included him in the social events they held, such as the one they were attending right then.

While they were talking to another very distinguished couple, who explained how lucky it was that they had the pleasure of meeting Laffite's wife, Marie began thinking of an idea. She observed the new bride while planning her next announcement.

The conversation between the couple and Tori had been in French, and Tori was proud of the fact that she pulled it off without a hint of nerves or one major mistake. It had impressed all those around them, and many smiled, thinking there was far more to Laffite's wife than not. Jean's wife may speak English, but her French was perfect, and her accent gave them a hint of where she might have lived before her marriage. Marie was proud of Tori and her ability to converse in their native tongue and could see that her friends had immediately accepted her into their circle of preferred acquaintances. It was then that her idea solidified, and without hesitating, she announced her intentions.

"You must visit and spend some time with us. I insist that you and your husband, I do so enjoy saying those words; well, we would love to have you join us for our winter ball. I won't take no for an answer. There is more than enough room at the plantation. I will talk to my husband Jean, and your husband…dear me, we have a slight problem, don't we? What with both our husbands having the same name? We often call my husband, Noel. That's his second name, you understand, and the one he prefers." She was babbling on, and happily planning the big event, while Tori half-heartedly listened. "Anyway, I will see to it that you come to us, for it will give me a chance to formally introduce you, as Jean's wife at the ball. I adore being the first to hold such an affair. It's the start of the season. We do so love to party before Lent. This year's affair will be on February 15th, a week from now. Ash Wednesday is the 27th, and we plan to return for Palm Sunday on April 7th. The dates fall perfectly, and that leaves us plenty of time for you and Jean to make plans to join us both here and at the plantation. At the ball, you will, of course, be our honored guests. That will ruffle someone's feathers for sure." Marie giggled like a schoolgirl again. It was like she was playing a dirty trick on someone and getting much joy out of doing so. "Oh my, yes. It's going to be wonderful, and such fun. Now, I must return you to your husband's side. I am sure he wishes to be with you to show you off." As she guided Tori towards

Jean, she kept up the conversation, hardly giving Tori a chance to get a word in edgeways. "You really must tell me more about yourself, and your family, my dear. Not tonight, though; we will have plenty of time to chat in the days ahead. Come on now, or Jean will not be too pleased with me."

Tori loved the way she seemed to go on and on about so little and how she took control of everything and everyone around her. Twice, she had caught Kristen smiling her way, and one of those times, the young lady was trying hard not to laugh out loud. Tori knew what had a hold of her funny bone, too. Poor Kristen was watching how Mrs. Destrehan had taken over the whole evening instructing this person and that, along with keeping Tori by her side at all times. It was entirely up to Marie, who and to whom she was presented, and in what order. The hostess was a controller for sure, and though more than once, Tori had tried to break free to rejoin Jean, Marie had not given her a chance.

When Kristen and her father came to say goodnight and to offer their help in the upcoming events, the young, headstrong female leaned and whispered in Tori's ear, using English, so Marie would not understand if she overheard. "You see what I mean. You can't say I didn't warn you. She is hard to say no, to, isn't she?" The girl smiled brightly and then stepped forward and gave her hostess a big hug. In her best French, she addressed the hostess. "Aunt Marie, I shall be staying just down the road from you as always. Just send word, and I will be more than happy to help. Father would have it no other way, what with mother, not joining us on this trip. I mean, that puts me in her place, and father knows how important it is, that I begin to learn all I can in the running of a house as grand as yours."

Kristen's father coughed uneasily. "You must forgive my daughter, Mrs. Laffite. Using her knowledge of French to impress us all to try and wiggle her way to an invite." He gave his daughter a knowing look that silenced her. "She is headstrong and tends to overstep her bounds, and may I add it has been a pleasure meeting you this evening. You must excuse me, though; I gave my word to my wife that our daughter would not remain out later than required."

"Of course, and it was my pleasure to meet you both. You have a lot to be proud of. Your daughter has been quite a help to me this evening, and I thank her for it. Talking in English is a delight for me, and Kristen fully understands that. You, yourself, have obliged me by using English, and I thank you, sir."

"Most kind of you to say. Now, I bid you goodnight." The man offered his hand, and Tori accepted. They shook briefly before his attentions turned to his hostess. Switching to French and bowing slightly, he addressed her. "Marie, thank you again for your hospitality, and we look forward to seeing you again soon."

"You will indeed. I am certain that we will be seeing your daughter long before you, but be assured it is our pleasure to have her pay a call. The children love her company."

Kristen's father was not so convinced about his daughter's intentions. "Marie, please do not allow Kristen to overstep her welcome. I would rather that she do as she declares and helps you in your preparations. In fact, I insist." With that said, he again bowed slightly and left their company.

Kristen was mortified and called after the man before facing Marie. "Father! I never overstep my welcome. Aunt Marie, I meant what I said. I offer you my help. Besides, who else does Mrs. Laffite have to talk with using English? I am sure she will enjoy my company and take a break from using French all the time. I know I do."

Marie knew the girl had a good point and smiled. "I will accept your offer, and as soon as we are settled, you will hear from me, my dear. By the way, your French has improved much since last we met. Such a sweet girl you are. You do have a good point, though. In such that English is beyond me. You will be most welcome in our home. Until then, do try to listen to your father. I see, he has your cloak and is waiting, so you best hurry. I will escort Victoria back into the lion's den to find Jean. Run along now. Come, Victoria, if we linger, Kristen will talk your head off, and her father will be left standing at the entrance for who knows how long. I am certain you will have plenty of time to converse with both Kristen and her father during the ball. Have no doubt, Kristen will see to it." The hostess was in high spirits and laughed at her observation as she took Tori's arm and began to walk toward the main room, where most of the guests had gathered. "It is rather like entering the lion's den, is it not? Do not worry yourself; I will see that you are not left to face them alone. Now, where do you suppose that husband of yours is?"

Jean saw them enter the room. He had not worried about Tori while she was with Marie, but seeing she might need his support, at last, he made his move. Excusing himself from those gathered around Adrian and Simone, Jean began to make his way to Tori's side. Laffite remembered he had given his word to help answer questions about her identity and where they met, but by the looks of how things were going, his talented lady had only faltered once and was now doing just fine. There she was, winning everyone's hearts, just as she had his. His beautiful wife was talking and laughing, as if she had done this a thousand times before, making friends with everyone, everyone, except Simone, that was. Jean had seen the animosity pass between the pair and decided it would be best to explain things to Tori once they got home. His wife deserved to know why his ex-lover was acting the way she was.

Simone had always laid claim to being the attractive young belle of the ball. That was until tonight. The sensual female was always the center of such events, flirting and laughing her way around the room. This evening, however, she did not stand a chance. Tori had stolen the spotlight, and to Jean, it seemed Simone's eyes were a deeper shade of green, with utter envy.

Laffite knew Simone was going to be trouble. Just how much, he wasn't sure, but then you could never predict what the woman would do or say. That was one of the things he had liked about her. The other reason was the fact that she was a vixen in bed.

Married to a man old enough to be her grandfather, she had been without sexual encounters until their affair, or so she had told him, and Jean now doubted that statement very much. His desires had blinded him and more than clouded his judgment of their situation.

It had suited him well enough; their times together, and there had been many. The meetings were always discreet and carefully arranged. Her love of her husband's fortune kept it that way. Never would she run the risk of losing that. Whenever her husband was present, she was devoted entirely to him, the poor fool. He had no idea that his money was her only attraction. Jean recalled how Simone often told him, that when he died, and that could not be very far away, she would be a very wealthy widow, one who would be free at last to be observed in public with the well-respected and much-admired Jean Laffite.

He could see now that she'd had more in mind than just continuing the way they had been. It had become apparent to him this night that Simone had wanted to become Madame Laffite. Why else would the envious looks have flooded Tori's way as they were still doing? Watching his ex-lover across the room, as she stared at his wife, Jean could not help feeling somewhat sorry for her. The woman would have to accept his marriage to Tori, he told himself. After all, there was little else she could do, and in time he had no doubt that she would find herself another lover to console her loss. Strange how things worked out, he thought. If he and Simone had not had that disagreement, on that fateful night, he never would have gone to Roses'. He would never have met Tori. Well, they would have met on his ship, but he would not have known where Tori was running away from and maybe acted differently, who knew. Jean looked at Simone, who was once again fussing over her husband. Perhaps, in a peculiar, sort of way, Simone got just what she deserved, and somehow, by some miracle, he had been blessed by God. Only time would tell, and time, for now, was on his side.

Marie had let it be known, in a not so quiet a tone, that the newlywed couple had accepted the Destrehan's invitation to spend time with them and would be departing the city soon. When this statement was announced for all to hear, Tori watched in utter amazement at the events that unfolded. It shocked her to see the speed with which the women flocked toward Marie, ignoring Tori at last. Each lady wanted to offer help, in any way possible, for the preparation of the upcoming event and declared their intentions loudly. As if that wasn't blatant enough, some physically shoved their husbands to the side, in their haste to make their voices heard. They would do anything it seemed, to obtain an invite to the ball. Taking a few steps away from those who surrounded Marie, Tori overheard it said that the ball was sure to be the season's event, a statement that quickly became common knowledge and spread like wildfire.

Laffite's wife was forgotten for the moment, which was a relief to her, because of all the sudden excitement that filled the room. Seizing the opportunity to escape Marie and the women, Tori looked around for Jean. It took only seconds to spot him, and when he looked her way, he mouthed the words 'meet me outside.'

Nodding her head in agreement, Tori stepped quickly to the double doors he had pointed to and slipped outside into the chilly evening air. Once there, she looked back into the room and smiled. Marie was still surrounded by many women, and yet still somehow remained in charge. At least Simone was not among those sucking up to the Destrehans, and Tori was glad of that. Maybe having an invalid husband kept them from making such a trip? Whatever the reason was, she was thankful, because she knew she had formed an intense dislike for the vile female.

It felt good to be outside of the stuffy house. The large number of people gathered inside had made it quite warm and overbearing. Add the two fireplaces that were continuously burning logs and the lamps that burned oil, plus, with all the candles spread around, it felt more like a sauna than a comfortable party, which it could have been if air conditioning were invented. Tori had become quite over heated, and knowing her condition; she was not surprised. Standing there in the fresh night air at that moment was a most welcome relief. A chill touched her, but rather than return inside, she allowed the cold night to continue to surround her. Parts of her body, mostly her armpits, were radiating heat and wishing to cool down faster; Tori raised her arms to allow the air to circulate better.

It was then that she acknowledged a good stick of deodorant was another invention she was missing. The kind that stopped you from sweating altogether. Both her armpits were soaked from perspiration, and she could feel that was not the only area to claim such a distinction. How could they all do it, she wondered? Not a single person seemed to feel the heat, let alone show their discomfort. The men in their jackets, shirts, woolen pants, and high boots, had not even hinted that the rooms were stuffy. Oh, and their necks wrapped with lavish cravats, was another item trapping their body heat. How could they even breathe, she wondered? As for the women in their corsets, pantaloons, and long gowns, they also had not shown one indication of discomfort. Each one of them had to feel miserable and have sweat running down their bodies, surely? No amount of fanning could help bring much comfort, so why didn't more step outside to cool down like she had? Tori walked to the edge of the patio area, and at last, began to feel the heat that was emanating from her body begin to subside.

The verandah was peaceful and quiet. Looking briefly back into the house, Tori couldn't help but wonder how lovely the home was furnished. It was splendid with many marvelous antiques. This thought made her uncomfortable as Marie would not appreciate her new furniture, being referred to as antiques. A flash of her telling Kate, Leone's housekeeper, the same about the plantation's furniture brought a wave of anxiety. Better that she turned and looked out into the dark gardens beyond, while she waited for Jean to join her. At least the gardens could take her mind off things she was not ready to face, such as confronting Leone.

Deep in thought about her friend, she was suddenly interrupted by the sound of the verandah door opening behind her. Turning, she assumed she would find Jean joining her, but Tori was wrong; it was Simone who stood there. Laffite's wife was even more stunned when the woman spoke to her using perfect English with just a slight hint of sarcasm about it. "Well, it seems we both had the same idea. Or did Jean ask you to meet him out here as well?"

Tori could hardly believe her ears. This woman had it in for her; she was sure of that. The tone of her voice and the way she was acting made it clear at last, as to what her problem was.

Simone walked up to her and continued coyly, "Why, don't look so shocked, my dear. Of course, we always meet on balconies such as this one, and in the gardens such as those, I might add," she cooed, fanning herself. "He is such a romantic. Ah, but do forgive me." She closed her fan and leaned slightly forward. "I completely forgot you are his wife now, aren't you?" She tapped Tori's arm with the closed fan and continued. "I should have remembered that, silly me. You would not want to hear about such dalliances, would you?"

Tori was fuming but didn't want to give the bitch the pleasure of knowing she had gotten to her. Therefore, in a calm and casual tone of voice, as if she didn't have a care in the world, Tori set out to cut Simone down to size. "It does not bother me one way or another. Not what he used to do, and with whom, that is. As for him asking you to meet him out here, I think you are gravely mistaken. Jean only has eyes for me, or can't you tell?"

Simone had not expected such a reaction, a shocked look of horror maybe, or running back inside crying, but never this! Victoria was supposed to feel anger toward her new husband, or better yet, fall to pieces. She never expected her to be filled with such selfconfidence. The vixen was thrown entirely off guard. This Victoria was so confident of Jean's love, a love that the bitch had stolen, that she had dared, to answer back, in a manner unbefitting a lady. This female of Jeans' was not your typical woman of standing, and Simone was confident of that fact. Then, more anger filled her as she realized that Jean would be meeting 'her' out here if it were not for this conniving hussy standing before her.

Jean would, or should be making plans to meet later, to make love, and not doing so, was more than Simone could bear. "You must be very sure of his love. Oh, my poor dear. Do take this observation from someone that knows him well. I feel it only right that I warn you he won't stay yours for long. I know far better than you can imagine, this is true. I understand what will happen in the days to come. I know what he likes, and what he needs," she said, almost spitting her words at Tori. "Why, for now, marriage might seem right to Jean, but it will bore him soon enough. Then you will bore him, and I can assure you that I can wait. I will never bore him, nor would I have been so stupid as to marry him. To try and tie him down; oh no, it will never work."

Tori could not believe this woman's audacity, to talk to her as she was, and so brazenly too. No woman was going to talk to her like that and get away with it. Simone could dish it out, but could she take it? Tori would soon know. "Poor, poor Simone. Not marry him, you say? It seems to me if you get any greener with jealousy, you will match that dress you have on. Lovely shade of green, I must admit. No, better still, you will match the emeralds around my neck that Jean gave to me as a symbol of his love. You are green with envy. It is the term from where I come from, my dear, in case you didn't know. You are so very transparent, it's sad. Yes, I would say you are positively jealous. It is so obvious you do not know how to handle the loss of the gentleman pirate Jean Laffite. Nor can you handle having lost the chance to snare him for yourself. I am right, aren't I?"

Simone was stunned for a second time, as Tori had spoken the truth of how she was feeling, and it infuriated her. She fired back quickly, with a venom-laced voice. "I do not need to stand here and listen to you. I did not need to miss my chance at snaring him, as you so crudely put it. I had him many nights. Does that shock you? I know how he makes love, and I will have him again in my bed. He will soon miss our nights of hot passion together. Maybe he already does. Maybe that's why he asked me out here." She saw her words had some effect, but not quite enough. So, she decided to continue with her onslaught. "He had not told you of our love, had he?" She laughed, enjoying the upper hand and the cruelty of the moment. "No? I did not think so. He kept it from you."

Tori laughed. This conversation was ridiculous, and this female was even more ridiculous. "Oh, just shut up before you make a bigger fool of yourself. You are living in a dream world. I don't doubt that he slept with you. A man will sleep with anyone he can to satisfy his needs. That does not, however, mean he loves her. I'm sure he kept you from me, as you put it, for a most excellent reason. Out of respect, for your husband, maybe? You are a married woman, are you not? I do feel sorry for you. Your bed will have to do without Jean, tonight, and all the lonely nights to come. Definitely for the rest of your pitiful life." Now, it was Tori's turn to enjoy herself. She was on a roll and not yet finished. "If you had meant anything other than a quick fuck, he never would have married me, now would he? I suggest that you get your ass back to your husband before you are missed, and I have to explain what it is we are arguing over. I'm sure you have not told him about your little, and I stress little tryst; have you?"

Simone's color drained, and she knew that for the moment she had met her match. The woman needed to lash out and would have continued with still further onslaughts, but the sound of the doors opening behind her stopped any new retort.

Jean walked outside, his face carefully concealing his worry over stumbling into a situation that looked about ready to explode. He looked closer at Tori, who winked at him, and then he glanced at Simone and smiled. It was plain to see who had the upper hand. All Jean had to do now was wait to see what had been said, and by whom?

"Everything all right, ladies?"

"Everything is fine. Simone and I had a little misunderstanding, but I think that we have cleared that up, haven't we? As a matter of fact, Simone was just leaving. She knows how newlyweds like to be alone. So, come here and show me how much you have missed me." Tori stretched out her arm and opened her hand towards him.

Simone was furious. The laughter on Jean's face not only hurt her, but it also made her even more determined to seek revenge. Oh, how she would see to it that one day Victoria Laffite paid for this humiliation. Until then, she would play this silly game of theirs. A silky-smooth voice slipped from between her pouting lips as she spoke to Jean. "I will see you both again soon, no doubt. Victoria do be sure to keep an eye on him; he does seem to roam day and night. Do try to enjoy the evening, Jean. It might prove more difficult than you think." Gathering up her long gown in one hand, she left them. Simone's laughter could be heard as she closed the doors behind her.

Jean leaned his head close to Tori and whispered. "Dare I ask?"

"No, Jean, you should not. But next time, let me know when one of your ex-lovers is going to be around, will you?" Tori laughed at the roguish grin that slipped across his lips, making his mustache on one side twitch. His eyebrow lifted, in a playful sort of way, as he took her in his arms.

"I am amazed you are not more upset."

"Listen to me, Monsieur playboy."

"Playboy?"

"Yes, you heard me. Look, in my time, we are a little more open-minded about such matters. What you did before we met is your business. What you do now is up to you. I have no real hold on you. Just please, be discreet if you have to have an affair, and not with her, all right?

He nodded his head but did not speak, as he was trying hard not to let his emotions get the better of him. To do so would cause him to burst into fits of laughter, and laughing right then would mean trouble.

"Stop grinning," she slapped at his arm. "To have an affair... it's not all right. What I am trying to say is, if our marriage were real, then to have an affair, even in my time, well, it is wrong. Then again, our marriage is not real, so what can I say?"

"Come here, you beautiful woman. I could never have an affair now that I have you. I need only you. You know that I love you. You are carrying our child," he placed his hand lovingly on her middle. "You need not fear anyone, least of all Simone. She is of my past, and a huge mistake. I can see that error now. I should have told you about her, but I did not think it that important." He grinned as he continued. "I can tell you safely; there are no others…none that you will meet anyway. Now, how about us going home so I can show you in more ways than mere words, how I feel about you?"

"You are something, Jean Laffite. I would love to go home with you, but let's stay just a little while longer. I need something to drink to warm me up. It's freezing out here. Not to mention that if I leave now, it could be misunderstood. I don't want Simone thinking she has chased me off, do I?" she winked.

# ꗞꗞ Three ꗞꗞ

In the week that followed, it seemed to Tori that she was either in her room being fitted for a new gown or attending some dinner given in their honor. Only once had they entertained at home, and that was when Jean had Pierre over for dinner. He had invited his brother to learn what news he had about Edward Duval, which turned out to be very little. Pierre explained that the dandy was out of town, staying at his family's plantation, something the man was known to do quite frequently. The only other detail he could reveal was that a woman, a friend of Leone Duvals, was missing and that the Duval brothers were searching for her. As for Kate and Kane's deaths, he had nothing to report, and the conversation turned to matters of family, Pierre's new daughter, and Marie, his true love.

The Laffite's were wined and dined by the elite of New Orleans, and it did not take Tori long to see that the same people were always on the guest list, with maybe one or two exceptions. In this way she experienced, what she lovingly referred to as the life of the rich and famous of old New Orleans.

Jean and Tori were the hit of society, and nothing changed their popularity. Even the fact that Tori revealed nothing about herself, during multiple conversations, was not interpreted as a negative quality or an issue that should cause concern or suspicion. Instead, the intrigue about her identity and from where she came from worked more to their advantage than against them. The mystery that surrounded her served only to increase both interest and speculation and was, for the moment, the hot topic of conversation around town. However, not one soul among the citizens they congregated with would dare ask Laffite or his bride to confirm any rumors.

Tori quickly realized intrigue and romance were two subjects that the Creoles thrived on. They loved spreading gossip, which was a Creole forte, primarily if the scandal was juicy and involved the dashing Laffite.

It was clear that the Cajuns often believed all whispered innuendos, even when it came to second or third-hand information. Only if they learned something from outside their community would they maybe question the validity of the information. Tori was told that Americans were among those who could never be trusted, and Tori, who, upon hearing this, wondered what the Creoles would do if they ever learned Laffite's wife was not what they fantasized frowned. Knowing she needed to remain on the good side of New Orleans society, not only for herself but also for Jean's sake, Tori determined her identity was one secret she intended to keep, no matter the cost.

To be accepted into the society of this city was the goal of any new arrival. So it was that Tori began to realize the power of two influences, mystery and romance. She summarized that in no small degree, these two entities had been more than half the reason the Laffite brothers had risen to fame and glory in such a short period.

Jean had arrived in New Orleans a year before her crossover from her own time. His brother Pierre had come to the city sometime before, and with ease, he had been accepted. His marriage into a respected family brought him standing, and his overall appeal opened many doors. It was when Jean joined him, and the two were seen in public, that the tongues started wagging, and the women started to talk about the dashing younger brother Jean. Now, with Tori on Jean's arm as his blushing bride, the gossip increased.

The rumors swirled, and many thought Victoria had connections to royalty. The way she carried herself and her gracious actions spoke for themselves, they said. It was whispered from behind fluttering fans that personal reasons, connected to France, were the key to her silence, and her continued wish not to converse in French. Those who had heard her use the language reported that her accent was Parisian. It was not Creole or from the islands, all agreed. For many, this notion established that Victoria's native language had to be French and not English, as she claimed. Why she chose to conceal her identity and where she came from must have reasons linked to only the highest places and people, they reported among themselves. That Victoria stumbled in her French at times had to have been done so deliberately. It was a ruse, to through anyone off, who saw past her deceit. Once this rumor had taken root, it was said, whatever reasons the Laffites had for their secrecy, would at some point be revealed. That until such a time, their privacy should be respected, and to pry further would be considered nothing less than an insult.

All these speculations and goings-on helped to amuse Jean's wife. She enjoyed the fact that she held the limelight everywhere they went. It was something she did with ease, especially since Simone had not been seen at any subsequent parties to annoy her or raise questions about her heritage. Tori's mastery of French was improving rapidly, and this gave her the confidence to inquire discreetly about Madam La Combe and her husband. By the so-called rules of etiquette of the day, Tori's inquiries slipped by unnoticed. After all, as far as the other guests were concerned, she was merely making polite conversation by inquiring about the La Combes' welfare.

Tori found out that Simone's husband was ill and that his wife was by his side, day and night. The older man's wife was perceived as a dedicated and caring young partner. Not once did anyone even hint that the woman was a cold-hearted, money digging bitch, that Tori knew her to be, and little else was ever mentioned about the family. Soon, the couple was forgotten altogether because there were far more interesting subjects to discuss, and of those topics, other than the Laffites, which remained at the top of the list, was the upcoming ball, and who was to attend?

THE day came at last when Jean and Tori headed out for the

Destrehan's plantation. Tori looked forward to seeing the couple again, and the idea of spending time at their home was intensely exciting. She had enjoyed Leone's plantation lifestyle, and knowing that the Duval plantation was miles away from the Destrehans gave her confidence that she would not be seen by anyone who knew her. Jean had assured her that he had been informed Leone Duval was residing at his country home. It was well known that these days he never ventured far from his plantation, let alone into the city and surrounding areas. The man had become a bit of a recluse, they whispered, and it was lucky for him that his younger brother kept a close eye on him. The knowledge that Edward was known to be staying with his brother at this time was also an added bonus. Tori could relax and enjoy herself knowing she was safe and among friends.

The ride was slow and damp, and the sky had a gray overcast to it. The countryside had taken on a soggy new coat for the season. In a few locations, the roads were still covered with standing water and were nearly impassable. According to Jean, they had flooded after the last heavy rains and would often do so in many places. Tori knew that having the levees break rarely occurred in her own time, and she wondered how long it would be before the constant threat of flooding would subside for these people? Neither their driver nor Jean seemed too worried about the road's poor conditions, and knowing this, Tori deduced she could relax. So it was that Laffite's wife was left with nothing to do but sit and watch with utter amazement, as they were able to navigate the problematic areas and push on without too much of an effort.

Once they were well out of the city, the going smoothed out, the remainder of their trip passed with ease. Often Tori sat in silence, contemplating the view and recalling the last time she had traveled this road. The idea of talking about the river road was something she had not considered until they were well on their way. It had been down this very route that Edward had brought her, when he had kidnapped her, and that memory was one she did not want to recall. It was better to forget that episode of her life and not bring it up right then or ever. Tori looked into her husband's smiling face and returned a happy expression before again looking out the window. If Jean ever heard the whole story of how Edward had kidnapped her, there would be no stopping him from killing the man. Some things were better forgotten; she assured herself. Now was the time to enjoy the view and think of the days ahead, not about the horrors of what she'd endured at the hands of the dandy.

AFTER many hours of what she would describe as grueling travel, Tori caught her first glimpse of Destrehan Plantation. Looking at it as they approached, she wondered if it would ever become an antebellum mansion that would be restored and set up as a historic site? She hoped the house would never fall to ruin or be torn down, as many would be. How many in the area had burned to the ground during the civil war? Did the war reach this far? These were questions she did not have a clue as to the answers. She'd read once that quite a few plantation homes had succumbed to the unfortunate fate of being destroyed. Undoubtedly a plantation this far away from the fighting would stay safe, though. A home so grand deserved to be shared and admired in the generations to come, and if she ever returned to her own time, Tori made her mind up that she would go and see if it had survived the ravages of time and remained standing.

Jean started to explain what it was she was looking at and smiled when he saw the look of surprise lighten up her eyes. He explained to her it was the back of the house that faced the river. The magnificent gardens that framed the entire building were Marie's doing, as her husband had little interest in such matters, he laughed. Noel Destrehan was a busy man with many interests, of which gardening was not one.

Tori nodded her head as she listened. She was thinking more along the lines of what the gardens would look like in her time. The open grass areas were dotted here and there, with small trees. Many were still oak saplings, and one day in the future, they would be grand, majestic old trees, draped in Spanish moss. As to the flowerbeds, she knew those would likely vanish. As to the lawns, they were not like the gardens of her time. Even though all were trimmed, they looked rough and seemed to be filled with more weeds than grass. How she wished Marie could see what St. Augustine grass looked like, especially after weed and feed fertilizer. What a difference a proper lawn would make. Tori told herself she had to stop thinking about things that could not be and begin to pay attention to what was and especially what was being said right then.

Jean was enjoying himself and kept right on with his explanations and descriptions about the place "This plantation was a place that harvested indigo at one time, but now it is a sugar plantation. A large and powerful place since Destrehan and Villere found a way to crystallize the sugar. They did not invent the process, you understand, but once they learned and applied the method, then cane became the crop of choice. This place keeps him quite busy when he is not playing politics. His home life is always first and foremost, though. Look for yourself; there is proof before you. Noel has added two wings on each side of the building, to accommodate his ever-expanding family in comfort." He laughed and hugged her playfully. "They have many children of their own, you know," he said tenderly, patting her stomach. Jokingly, he added, "and here I worry with just one on the way. To me, it is still a dream. To look at you, one can hardly tell. The baby you carry has barely made himself known."

"Or herself, remember? For your info, I mean information, I will begin to show, not actually show my belly to anyone, mind you. What I mean is, I will get large, very soon. So far, we have managed to conceal our little one, thanks to the clothes of today.

"It is true; they do have a way of hiding the bump as you call him, and the loss of your small waist, not to mention the ever-expanding size of your breasts."

Tori laughed at him before jabbing her elbow into his side. "You're terrible, you know. But, speaking of children, we will have to tell everyone our secret soon. I'm afraid that I have begun to show more than you guess, and I can't hide it much longer. There is no way I will squeeze myself into another corset to hide my condition. It's not healthy for either the baby or me."

"Well then, we had best let it be known this evening at dinner," he said, beaming. "I look forward to announcing our news. I want to share with everyone the joy that I feel. The Destrehans will be thrilled. The fact that we have chosen to inform them first will mean a great deal. You think I spoil you? Watch out, my lady. There is nothing more they like to do than spoil a mother-to-be, something they do very well, I might add. After all, they have had enough practice at it. At last count, they have spoiled Marie over fourteen times."

"Fourteen!"

Jean laughed, and Tori turned and looked out toward the house again. 'Fourteen times indeed! Like anyone had that many children. Well, poor families maybe, but Marie was neither poor nor did she look like she was a mother of fourteen. My how Jean loved to tease her.' She glanced his way still thinking to herself. 'How happy he looked and sounded. This was the home of his best friends, people who seemed like family to him. Yes, she knew he was going to enjoy sharing their secret with them.'

"Noel is home, a rare occurrence these days. I believe Marie has demanded he be here for us. Under normal circumstances, he would remain in town until the day before such an event. We are truly honored; he has chosen to arrive ahead of us." Jean continued talking about his friend, and Tori sat and listened intently.

She had learned much about the man since arriving in the French Quarter. Noel was quite accomplished. He was one of the authors of the Louisiana Constitution and was present at the signing."

"Did I explain that Noel hopes to hold the position of President of the Legislative Council. His political connections, it is said, reach all the way to the White House, not to mention royalty back in France. The Destrehans are very proud of that connection, and they make it evidently clear at every opportunity. It is no wonder that the man spends more and more time in the city. He is important and has grand ambitions for not only New Orleans but for himself too. Tori, I am happy he is here, and we will have this time with him and his family. It means so much."

'I know it does. Talk about pressure.' She had to let him know how she was feeling, after all the man was not a mind reader. "I will try my best to fit in, but..."

"You have nothing to worry over. They love you, and the children will too." Jean looked out the carriage window as it left the road and began its slow drive up toward the house. He was so caught up in the joy of the moment that he had not picked up on how anxious Tori was.

Laffite's wife was worried about spending quality time alone with both Noel and Marie. At the final few dinners they attended, before leaving for the countryside, it had become apparent to Tori that the Creoles held no love for the Americans, who they saw as barbaric in their actions and manners. Tori had found herself feeling lucky that none even suspected she was one hundred percent American. That fact could have caused quite a problem for them. It might have cost them their friendship with Destrehan, regardless of his close ties with Jean, and she would never want that. Keeping up the ruse was going to be work; one slip-up could undo all she had accomplished so far.

The Destrehans could understand and accept Americans; she knew that and had witnessed it firsthand. Noel had introduced her to the then much-disliked governor of the Territory of Mississippi and Louisiana. The American's name was William Claiborne. He spoke no French, and that was probably a blessing, considering what the Creoles said about him behind his back and sometimes to his face. It had been Noel's acceptance of the man that amazed Tori. Destrehan was a wise man indeed, for he could see that things in New Orleans were not destined to remain as they were. She'd overheard him telling Jean that it would be far better to have

Claiborne as governor of this new state, other than some unknown American. Tori had smiled, knowing that Noel would have his way. What she had almost done was tell him he was right, and that Claiborne would be governor, a slip-up that could have been costly. Tori shuddered; how could she have explained away her knowledge on the subject? Jean's friend would have thought she favored the American to declare such an outcome when Creoles like himself, also sought the position. Noel might have even put two and two together and guessed the secret about her heritage. Thoughts such as these were racing in her mind. This visit was not going to be so easy as she had hoped, but with Jean by her side, Tori told herself she stood a good chance of not letting anything slip.

The sounds of shouting children running up to greet them caught Tori's attention breaking into her daydream. A few of the younger Destrehan clan were making their way toward the slow-moving carriage. They were followed closely by many other children, who could only be plantation slaves. Tori determined this, judging by their color and the way they were dressed. All were barefooted, and their squeals of delight added to the mayhem that swarmed toward them. Tori laughed, as did Jean, who leaned out the carriage door and waved. The moment he did this, their excitement increased, as all the children recognized who was in the carriage.

(In French) "Uncle Jean! He is here, Mama! Oh, do come see. Uncle Jean is here!"

The youngsters surrounded the carriage as it came to a halt, and they did not seem to notice Tori at all. All their attention was on Laffite and for good reasons. The man was always known to have sweets in his pockets or the odd coin that he could slip into their eager hands. Tori watched as the pirate spoke to those right in front of the open door. "Take a step back, give me some room, and I shall see what I have in my pockets for you." He smiled toward Tori and took hold of her hand. "Shall we?" Jean helped his love down as he continued to greet each of the screaming youngsters. "Just wait a second. Give me time to help the lady, and then, if you are willing for a race, we shall have one." As soon as Tori was standing beside him, he turned to face the children and reached into his pocket. "I have here three coins, and the fastest today will win. Ready?" He raised his arm, and before the children could turn, he tossed the coins well into the distance. "Off you go then." In seconds, the couple were left standing by themselves watching the children run in all directions, searching the ground for their prize. "It will take them a while to locate those coins and a good thing. I quite forgot to put sweets in my pockets and that my love is nothing to laugh about."

Tori looked away from them and concentrated on her new surroundings. Now that the small crowd of squealing children had run off, her view of the house was unobstructed. The building was a grand one, with eight white columns evenly spaced along what looked like the front of the building, but according to Jean, it was the back. The top and lower verandahs were deep-set and ran the entire length of the structure and along each side. Standing between the verandahs and the main building, were the extensions, called 'garconnieres', which Jean had previously pointed out. These two buildings were as long as the main house's side and in no way detracted from the home's appeal. While neither of the expansions had verandahs of their own, each wing had large windows on the outer walls; Tori assumed the doorways were on the wall between the verandahs and the main building. That was not all she saw, either, because judging from the number of chimneys, many cozy fireplaces were also to be found in the extra rooms. This made perfect sense to her, as heating could only come from fireplaces, and during the winter, people would appreciate having a warm bedroom, especially the children. The additions, as Tori referred to them, were as large as some of the small homes in the city, and they contained two floors, which meant quite a few rooms were inside. With so many bedrooms, it was no wonder that the Destrehans could accommodate more than just a few guests.

Mrs. Destrehan was the first to appear, and as always, she took charge of the moment. Orders were given for the guest's belongings to be taken up to the large bedroom; it had been put aside just for them. Tori and Jean were to stay in the main house. An honor seldom offered to anyone, and once word spread among the other guests, it was a given that there would be a few ruffled feathers. Jean had explained that those who were not staying with the Destrehans had either a long dark trip home after the ball or were staying at other houses nearby. Either way, their lodgings were sure to make many envious.

(In French) "It is so good to see you again, Victoria. I have looked forward so very much to your visit. It will be so nice to have another woman to talk with when I can. True, the girls are growing up, but they are still my daughters, and talking to them is, well…like talking to my daughters." She rolled her eyes and laughed aloud at her statement.

"Marie, if you don't stop rambling on, Jean's wife will never get a word in," boomed a male voice. "Let her have a moment to gather herself, my dear, don't you agree, Jean?" Destrehan was laughing and enjoying the moment. He knew his wife would take no offense and smiling broadly with his arms extended; he walked ahead of her. In three large strides, Destrehan stood in front of Tori, and immediately, he took her in his embrace and kissed her on both cheeks like he did every time they met. "How are you, my dear? You look as lovely as I remember. No, more beautiful. Doesn't she, dear?"

Touched by the man's greeting, Tori found herself blushing, and in her best French, she responded. "That is very kind, but before we go any further, there is a small matter that I have to clear up."

"Anything, my dear. Please, ask."

"It's just that I know Marie calls you Noel and that still others call you Jean. Now, please tell me, is it Jean or Noel? I am never sure which."

"You may call me whatever you desire, I'm sure. Now, go on in out of the cold, while I greet one of our other children. I see they are about to arrive and will expect me. They never seem to leave home for long, always dropping in for a visit with their family, isn't that so, Marie? Especially Justine. You will get to meet our latest grandchild Victoria. She was born only a few months ago. Nothing stops our daughter from visiting, nothing at all, and it pleases her mother that it's so." He was laughing as he walked toward the approaching carriage.

ONCE inside the house, it was the size of the place that struck Tori first, the furnishings second. The Destrehan house reminded her a little of Leone's plantation, even though it was not so grand or as large. Also, unlike Leone's, this house was filled with reminders that young children lived there.

Marie took them into the dining room, located on the ground floor. It was quite a large room and had the largest extended table Tori had ever seen. A fire burned brightly, and the hefty logs crackled and snapped at the amber flames. The floor was blue and white tile, none of which were covered by carpets of any size.

The long table sat dead center, and already a few food plates had been placed, while still more were being brought in. Tori and Jean were guided through the dining room and then quickly ushered to an adjoining room and finally out to an area where two staircases, one on each end, led upstairs. They had entered the home from the back instead of the front. Standing there, Tori now saw what Jean had been describing to her. Most carriages pulled around to this side of the house, and the guests would enter the room behind where they now stood or take either staircase to the upper story. She and Jean followed Marie to the right and then upstairs, where they all followed the verandah around and between the extension and main building. Once at the end of this walkway, they again turned right, and Tori found herself walking down a covered area facing the river. It was about halfway along when they stopped and entered the front parlor, as Marie called it. This space was a real family room to Tori, and for a split second, she felt a pang of loneliness. The thought of her daughter, enjoying the children, and this place pulled on her heartstrings. Strange, how the memories of Linni continued to pop up for no reason. These days, Tori tried to avoid thinking of her daughter, and when she did, she worked hard not to dwell on what was or could be. In the last few weeks, she had finally reached the point where she was able to reassure herself that her daughter was in good, loving hands.

Her family would see to it that the child was well taken care of. Linni would have everything except a mother, and like always, she quickly pushed that horrible thought to the back of her mind, telling herself she had to remain happy and not spoil the day. Right after they entered the room, Noel caught up with them, and Tori took the opportunity to announce that she had decided what she would call him. To her surprise, she realized, it quite simply never occurred to anyone, he could be called by his initials. It was an idea he was fond of the moment she told him and from that day on, a few close friends and sometimes, even his wife, would lovingly refer to him as J.D.

JEAN and J.D. had left the room and were standing outside on the balcony, and seeing Tori was looking their way, Marie took her by the arm and opened the door, so they could join them. The second story gave Tori a clear view of the river and clear across to the opposite bank. The gardens directly below were empty of children, and the roadway in front of the plantation showed no sign of any traffic.

(In French) "May I ask Marie, what are those small carriages and wagons are for? The ones off to the far side of where we arrived. I think they are for supplies or maybe guests, but I have not seen any. Oh, I do hope my French is correct; you will have to forgive any mistakes until I am better at speaking it."

"Your French, it is very good, no need to apologize.

You will forgive my English when I misuse it, I know. As to those pesky, wagons. They bring the luggage and items that the guests want to contribute to the festivity. Their owners will begin to arrive the day after tomorrow for the ball," she giggled, "I thought you and Jean would like a day by yourselves before all the hustle and bustle; pray tell, I was right in my assumption?"

Jean smiled brightly and placed his arm around his wife's waist. "You were indeed, Marie. My lovely wife and I appreciate your kind thought, and if you don't mind, I think maybe a small rest is in order before we eat."

"Just as I had planned. Now, you go with Jean, my dear. He knows just where your room is. My husband and I shall pop down and see that the younger children are behaving themselves, and then we will hold our newest grandchild. That is if I can get her away from my Nelly. Nelly has been with me so long that I swear I quite forget myself where she is concerned. You will understand once you meet. You know, I told my husband, even if we gave the woman her papers of freedom, she would never leave me."

THE evening meal was to be served in the large dining room, with everyone sitting around the long, highly polished wooden table. Marie told Tori that she had the table made for just such occasions. "You see, my dear, I always knew I would have a large family, and so after the second child, I had my husband searching for a table such as you see now. I must say it did keep him busy." She smiled brightly, and for a second, Tori wondered if she also might need to think long term. Would she need large tables, more bedrooms, and a nanny? In the end, her mind was racing with questions and speculations. Panicked, she tried to put a halt to such thoughts. 'One baby at a time. No thinking beyond that for now,' the voice in her head whispered. 'Pay attention to Marie, she is so proud, and if you keep on, the way you are, you will spoil Jean's surprise. Pull yourself together,' she sternly told herself.

Jean noticed his wife's brief frown and took hold of her hand. He smiled at her, and she, in return, lightly squeezed his back. It was her way of letting him know she was doing all right. Marie had been rambling on and was so caught up in the moment that she missed this small detail. J.D., however, had seen the exchange and stepped closer to his wife.

Tori was impressed by how orderly everything seemed and was still more amazed by the Destrehan children, who stood waiting to meet her. She watched silently as their mother, who was joined by her husband, turned to face her, before stepping forward toward the children, who she lovingly called her brood.

"Before we sit for dinner, I would like you to meet the children. I will begin with Antoinette, the oldest at twenty-four years, and a newlywed, like yourself. She married Rene last February. Then, there is Justine, who is twenty, and a young mother. Mathilda was born last year. I am sure you two will have much to talk over. Next to her is Nicholas, who is just eighteen and feels like he is a man."

"I am one," spoke up the tall young man. "It is a pleasure to make your acquaintance and Uncle Jean, you and I shall hunt this visit, shall we not?"

"That remains to be seen, Nicholas. If my wife agrees, I may find some time to join you."

Tori smiled and spoke in French to the boy. "I am sure I will not need my husband by my side all the time, and as I will need time to spend with each of you, then you will do me an honor by keeping him busy."

"Nicholas, you will wait to be invited. In no way interrupt Jean and his wife's visit," added his mother. "Marie, step up, child, don't be shy. This is Marie Elizabeth; she is 16, and the one who has been so looking forward to your visit. She is the best at English here, and I know she wants very much to talk and use what she has learned."

Tori liked the young teen immediately and spoke to her in a kind voice using English. "I look forward to spending time with you."

J.D.'s wife clapped her hands in delight. Then in a teasing sort of tone, she added, "That is if Nicholas, yes, another Nicholas I am afraid. I do so love that name. If he leaves her alone long enough, you will have plenty of time. Nicholas is incorrigible. Always teasing the girls." Marie looked directly at the lad and added. "Don't think I did not see you poke your finger in Elenore's side. You had best behave." She smiled brightly at J.D., and he shook his head.

The man was chuckling under his breath but stopped long enough to add his lighthearted statement. "My wife has a hard time with trying to remain stern, I fear. Don't you, my dear?"

Marie ignored him and continued. "I was about to add, if he and his sister Elenore leave our Marie alone, I can continue. As I said, they do so love to tease her, and now they know I see what they are up too, they will behave. Tori, you will have plenty of time to sit and get to know each other."

"Oh mama, that's not true, called out a young boy who was standing next to his younger sister. Elenore was only eleven but smart for her age. Elenore, unlike her brother, wanted no trouble. She just nodded her head in Tori's direction and remained silent, while her brother continued his rant until he caught the look his papa was sending. One look was enough to silence him, and Tori was impressed.

Now it was J.D.'s time to shine and take the spotlight from his wife. "Let's speed this up, shall we? I am hungry, and at this pace, the food will be cold. Step up, you five, front, and center. I present to you our youngest children. Louise, who is nine, Bienaime, who is seven, Leonie is five, Rene is four, Marie is three, and over in the cradle is Amelie, who is eight months. See my dear wife, introductions made and in record time I might add." J.D. was laughing and hugged his wife close before kissing her lightly on the cheek.

Tori was delighted. "Oh, my goodness, what a beautiful family, and Marie, I had no idea you had such a young baby. It bothers me you didn't mention her before. I would never have known. I have to say you look gorgeous and in such great shape after such a short time. Oh, please, I forgot, I should not talk about such delicate matters."

"Nonsense, Tori, you are family. "

"That is kind of you, Marie, but let me change the subject before I embarrass myself further." Tori turned and spoke to the children in French. "I do so look forward to getting to know you all." Laffite's wife meant each word as she looked at all the smiling faces. Jean had not lied after all. Marie and J.D. did have a large family.

"Now children," announced Marie in a tone that said, listen and obey. "Take your places, and Jean, show Tori to her seat next to mine." She began to ramble on again, about how she felt that it was so important that her entire family could fit at the table when Jean interrupted her.

Picking up a glass of wine from his place at the table, he raised it. "Speaking of important, before we sit, I would like to take this opportunity to make a rather special announcement."

Jean raised his glass higher and turned to Marie and J.D. with such a grin on his face that Tori was sure everyone would guess what he was about to say before he got the words out.

"You are the closest I have to a family here in New Orleans, and you have always treated me as such. It gives me...no us," he turned and faced Tori as he continued, "great pleasure to announce that we too will need a larger table this year. We are to become parents. I am to be a father."

The room was instantly filled with happiness and excitement. Everyone was hugging and laughing, and congratulations came from all. Even the young ones, who did not fully comprehend the announcement, found themselves caught up in the excitement.

Tori was entirely unprepared for such a response. To her thinking, they were acting as if it was the most wonderful news in the world and more. It was almost as if this child would be adding to their ever-expanding brood and not just the child of a friend, who would visit sometimes. Watching Jean enthusiastically hug J.D. was the last thing she could stand. Overcome with raw emotion; she burst into tears.

Jean was immediately at her side, wondering what to do and what could have caused his wife such grief. The room quickly fell into a deadly hush, as one by one, they noticed her tears. "Is anything wrong? Are you all right?" asked Jean in a nervous tone.

"I'm fine, Jean. Just a little, oh, I don't know. A little overwhelmed, that's all."

J.D. half laughed as he spoke to Jean in English. "Of course, Victoria is, how shall I say...ah, yes, overcome. That is the word, is it not? What more could it be, with all this noise and dancing around? It is just we are happy, no?" He continued in French. "Take my word for it, Jean; all women seem to do is laugh too much, or cry for no reason, when they are pregnant. If that's not enough, they have you getting up at all hours of the night for some of the silliest foods. You wait, my friend, and if that's not enough..."

"Oh, stop it, J.D., you do go on so. All Victoria needs is some rest. It's been a long day for you, my dear." No one else was included in her conversation, as her full attention was on the woman standing beside her. "I am sure you will feel a lot better after a warm bath and a good night's sleep. Jean, you will remain here, and enjoy your dinner. Victoria and I will excuse ourselves and see you later."

There was no arguing with her, and Jean gladly gave in, as seeing his love cry was not something he cared to witness and even less able to handle just then. Tori, feeling somewhat foolish of her emotional display, followed Marie back upstairs, glad to be away from the gathering, to have some time by herself and maybe, gain her composure.

"Tori, I will send Nelly to help you. That's short for Penelope, you know. Of course, you don't know. She's been a part of our family and helped me bring each and every child into the world. Fourteen to be exact, lost two when they were young, and Nelly helped me then too. Honestly, I don't know what I would do without her. Enough about me, we need to take care of you." Marie sat Tori down on the edge of the bed. "Now, don't you worry, the men will be busy, the children soon off to their beds. My oldest, Justine Marie, will see to it. I know you wanted to see her newborn and that little one of mine, not to worry, though. My daughter has all the help she needs. She may be disappointed that your evening was cut short, but she understands. There is always tomorrow for you to get to know each other. When you are ready, I will have Nelly bring you into my upstairs parlor so there won't be anyone around to bother you." Marie took a robe out of the wardrobe and placed it over Tori's arm. "Anyway, dressed in a robe, it will be perfectly acceptable for us to sit and chat. You are like a sister to me, so don't fret yourself about getting dressed again. Now then, I knew that you would like a bath, so you will find it waiting for you. Just say I have a mother's instinct. Besides, you showing as you are, I was wondering when you were going to announce the news." She was looking very pleased with herself at having been right. "I think I will pop into my parlor and spend a bit of time with the baby."

Tori hugged Marie, and as her eyes started to mist up again, the overwhelmed female struggled to maintain her composure. Jean's wife just wanted to let her friend know how grateful she was. However, the words just sobbed out in a blur, making no sense to her or anyone else as far as she was concerned.

"Hush now, none of that. Off to the tub with you, and you will feel better. You will see. Lord, I have been through it enough myself, I should know. Now you walk down there, right to the end, then pop through my room, and you will find what you need waiting for you. Take your time, no hurry."

TORI entered the bathroom, and her mouth dropped open. She could hardly believe what was in front of her. There, up against the wall, was a large marble tub, one that made Leones seem small. Right away, she realized it must have been this tub that Leone's wife had seen and then asked him to get her one like it. Kate had said something about it but never mentioned whose tub it was her mistress had envied, not that the woman would have remembered. Now though, she knew, and for a split second, she wished she could tell Kate that she'd seen it too.

Ever since leaving Leone's plantation house, Tori had taken baths in all sorts of tubs. Some were metal or wood. Most were moved in and out of rooms when needed. Those had been built to be carried, but this one, never. Even in her own time, she had never seen anything quite as magnificent. Before her stood, a solid marble tub that was quite something in any era. Tori was wondering how in the hell they got the thing upstairs, as it was likely to weigh a ton. Then just as she began to picture in her mind the way the slaves would have moved the tub, she was interrupted by a knock at the door.

"I be Nelly, Miss Victoria, and I kin help you just like Mistress Marie done said. You just let ole Nelly take care o' you. Nelly dun take care ob da Misses, an' know'd how ta make you feel like you don't a knows you has a babe a comin.'"

"You speak English?"

"Yes, Miss Victoria, I sure enough does. Not fancy like you, but I kin talk it just fine like. Mistress Marie, she done tol me you speaks English better, on account you has not had time to practice much French. I speak me that too, has done most my days. My Mama, she be da one done spoke English and da Master, he tol me ta make sure I kept talking it good like. I can listen fo him somedays and peoples don't know I be understanding. Then I tell da Master what dey be yapping about. So, you just tell old Nelly, which you want me ta use and I kin do it. If it be English, no worries der, as I will, learn me ta do better. See, I already doing better." She smiled so big that the deep lines each side of her lips vanished.

"That is so kind of you, Nelly. English would be nice if you don't mind. I am so emotional that trying to understand anything else at this moment might cause a problem."

Nelly laughed as she rolled up her sleeves. "Miss Victoria, I be thinkin' some of my words might be a problem, but we will manage. I don't get ta...to practice much. Only time be when I go down the quarters, on account that a few of da blacks, dey... they speak English and not much else. Now, you relax and let me do my job. I be, real proud to do so and all, I tell you that."

It wasn't long before Tori felt like a new woman. She was bathed and then massaged from the top of her head to the bottom of her legs. Even her feet had been rubbed, right down to the little toes. By the time Nelly had finished and dressed Tori in the soft robe, the mother-to-be felt like she was ready for anything. To her surprise, instead of relaxing her to the point of sleep, she felt invigorated.

"Now, you let me brush your hair some, and we will let it just be down like. No need to go pulling it up or tying it back. No way. We just has to git it untangled and smoothed out."

As Nelly brushed Tori's hair, Tori had a chance to watch the slave and size her up. The woman was old, most likely in her late seventies, and she had short gray hair. She wore a clean cotton dress with a bright yellow apron over it. Her sleeves were rolled up, and the tops were wet. If Nelly had let Tori bathe herself instead of insisting she wash her, the slave would have stayed dry.

Nelly's face was kind and wise, and her small build hid the strength that she possessed. Her hands were soft but strong, and the deep massage she had given Tori took strong hands as well as skill. If she were in Tori's time, there would be no doubt that she would be in high demand as a skilled massage therapist. The black woman hummed a tune while brushing the tangles out of the guest's hair, and if she found it strange to see such unnatural spiral-like curls, she never once hinted so. Once she was satisfied that the hair was to her liking, Nelly placed the brush on the dresser and stood back happily observing Tori.

"Nelly, if you ever need a job, you come to me. You are a lifesaver."

"Oh, Mistress Victoria, you be teasin' me some. Dis ol' woman don't save no lives." Nelly chuckled. "Sides, I be happy here an all. Dis here be my home. Sure'n will thank you kindly for da offer. You done gone an made me feel all special like."

Chuckling again to herself, the old lady walked with Tori back toward the parlor. Once there, after knocking once, and not waiting for an answer, Nelly opened the door. Smiling, she stepped aside and waited for the houseguest to enter the room.

The slave was not going to join the women or be of any more help to them right then. All she had left to do, was get the young ones to help her clean up the bathroom and set it right for her mistress, should she be needing it.

"I be right, nearby, Mizz Marie. You enjoy your visit." With that, the door closed, and the women were alone.

Marie was waiting by the roaring fire with a plate of cold cuts and freshly baked bread. Two large chairs faced the fireplace, and she motioned for Tori to join her. The older woman used French as she welcomed her guest. "She is a dream, isn't she? I doubt that I would have had fourteen children without her. There again, maybe it's because I like the way she pampers me so much that I had fourteen children."

The two of them laughed. At last, Tori thought, I have a family in this time, one that can fill in for my own, until I know what will be. "I have to agree with you. She is a dream and what hands. I feel so much better."

Tori and Marie sat by the open fire talking for several hours. Marie spoke the entire time in both French and English and declared it was a good way for her to practice. No one came near the room to disturb them, not even Jean and so, uninterrupted as they were, Tori was able to ask questions and to listen, as she learned more about the history of the Destrehan family and their plantation.

"You know, Victoria, as much as I adore the countryside, my favorite place will always have to be New Orleans. I remember the day that Noel purchased this place. Its crop back then was indigo. The plant that is used to make the blue dye."

"I do know that. Now, it's a sugar cane plantation, correct?"

"It is, and we have our brother-in-law Etienne to thank for that. He introduced the way to turn the sugar into a granulated form, easier to ship, and it has proved to be most profitable. Back when Noel told me we were not only to buy this place, but we were going to plant cane, I thought he was in the wrong. We had young children and one on the way. The plantation was nothing like you see today, far from it. He added to this building and continues to purchase land, but the cane, yes he was correct, it did exceptionally well."

"I have been told. Jean does talk to me about some matters that involve those he cares about. This plantation and your family are among those you know."

Marie smiled. "Tori, you know if not for politics, I think my husband would have remained a planter and expanded way more to our land. Still, life it has a bright side. If not for his involvement in governing, he would never have purchased the house in the city. I am lucky in that fact. I adore that place, as well, you know. You and Jean are so lucky to be living in town. I shall be back in time for Lent. Not that I need an excuse to visit my own home. I am expected and glad of it."

Tori reached out and grasped Marie's hand in hers. She squeezed it lightly when she spoke as if adding, 'I understand' without using the words. "You utterly amaze me, you know? Here you sit surrounded by a beautiful family, in a magnificent home, and no one knows how much you long to be in town, do they?"

"No one but you, my dear. Now, don't get me wrong. As you will see, it is a blessing to be out here at certain times of the year and not in that hot and airless city. We always have a breeze here, you know. It comes right off the river. Then there is the running of the place. We simply can't stay away for long when the cane has to be tended. Noel, I mean J.D.," she giggled again, "has taken it upon himself and built the plantation to quite an impressive size. It's nearly a thousand acres now and stretches from the Mississippi to Lake Pontchartrain. That's on this side of the river. I am told he has purchased more land across the river, also, to add to our holdings. It takes so much of his time." Laughing, she added, "Why, between this place and his playing politics with Jean, it's any wonder that I had one child. You know, my dear, sometimes I do wish I had him all to myself like you have your Jean. That man of yours always surprises me. He was so very busy introducing us to all sorts of visitors from the East coast, the islands, and France; then he turns up with you after a single trip away! Not only that, he kept you to himself down at that place he likes to stay…the house by the sea. I understand it is quite lovely, not that I shall ever see it for myself. Oh no, but I do know about it. Everyone in New Orleans knows of it."

It was a simple statement and not said in a wanting to know more way, just spoken in a matter of fact sort of way, and it unnerved Tori. She needed to change the subject. After all, Jean's wife had no idea if Marie knew just what Jean Laffite did for a living. True, all of New Orleans called him the Gentleman Pirate, but that did not mean that Marie believed him to be a real pirate, and Tori hoped to keep it that way. "I think maybe it was more his business than keeping me to himself, that kept us away. I assure you, he tried to return to the city several times, but circumstances did not allow. I know how much he enjoys talking to your husband about matters of state."

"Ah, but unlike J.D. who continues to work at his politics every single day, be it here or in the city, your Jean has made you his life. J.D. has told me that Jean has not attended as many meetings as he would like, since his return last year."

"I can't deny that. Jean has spent most of his time, since returning to the city, with me, that's true enough."

"As newlyweds, that is understandable. The results have proven to be a delight, have they not?" Marie lightly touched Tori's stomach and giggled again softly before shifting in her seat and regaining her composure. "Our husbands work together rather well, and Jean guides mine on matters that have helped him tremendously. Not many know that my husband understands more English than he lets on, let alone speaks it quite well. That was Jean's idea, you know. People tend to talk about things more candidly when they think you don't understand. Jean acts as his go-between during meetings. He translates, and thus, those who don't speak French, believe my husband has no understanding of English." She grinned again. "Keep Jean at your side as long as you can, Victoria...enjoy your time together."

"I can try, but like your husband, mine is just as stubborn."

"That may be so. I feel I need to offer you words of wisdom. In the days ahead, Jean will be drawn into politics and the meetings that the men will attend before the ball. Fear not; you will have plenty to entertain you. I myself will have much to do. As my husband is set to serve on the council for Orleans Territory, his time will be taken up with matters of government; it's to be expected. He will be the president of the council and trust me; he is looking forward to his duty. I stay clear of all matters pertaining to such tedious goings-on, as should you. Your Jean, and my husband, are bound by them. Most men are."

Marie gazed at the fire and spoke as if she saw the events unfolding in the flames. "A few years back, when I was heavy with child, two years running, 1804 and 1806, when Noel was speaker of, 'The Territorial House of Representatives' I tried my best to show interest. It was during those years; I learned it is wise not to interfere and to allow them their time; in this way, you will have a stronger hold on your husband. Newlyweds can demand much of each other, and with a child on the way, well, should you ever have a need, turn to me as your friend. I had no such friend when my husband began to show such interest in matters other than the heart."

Marie continued staring into the dying fire, and for the first time that evening, she seemed to be in a world filled with her memories. Tori did not disturb her, for she too was in a deep, thoughtful state. Just who was Jean Laffite, and where did he come from? They had never talked about his past, and somehow Tori knew they never would. If he wanted her to know more, he would tell her; she understood that. Until then, she would have to respect his need for privacy. Tori just wished she had read more about him, studied history, and paid better attention in class. She'd been a good student, but like most, she quickly forgot many of the facts she'd learned once out of school. Her knowledge of New Orleans history did not even come from her schooling in Texas; it came from her trips sightseeing the area as an adult and going to the museum next to Jackson Square's cathedral.

Tori looked at Marie, who seemed to be nodding off to sleep. To have a friend as dear as her meant the world to Tori. It wasn't any wonder why Jean loved them all. Hell, he even seemed to care genuinely about a few friends in the city as well, something one would not think a man like him would do. To think that many only saw Laffite as a pirate made her chuckle. He was highly educated and had friends in high places, both in America and France. If Marie had told the truth and Tori didn't doubt that, then some of those friends in France were of a royal connection. J.D.'s wife had even gone so far as to mention Napoleon was a close acquaintance and that the marble tub, she had bathed in had been a gift from him. Jean's wife frowned; if her husband was connected to Bonaparte, it wasn't any wonder that he kept his past secret. Tori had also learned that J.D. had spent his childhood in France and did not return to New Orleans until he was a young man. He had known the man, who was to be his brother in law while growing up, and that brother in law was very well connected. It stood to reason that if Laffite came from France; if all the Laffite brothers came from there; then they were all connected, the Destrehans and other men of prominence. Tonight, Tori had glimpsed what a tangled web of history she walked in and with so many people who had a huge role to play in the outcome that was her future.

One thing was sure, J.D. and Jean went back a long way, but she knew something about them that they didn't. Her dashing rogue of a pirate, who was always one step ahead of the law, together with the sensible and upright statesman, J.D., would make history together. These two men would have a great deal to do with the City of New Orleans's future. Sure, it would be in different ways that they would accomplish what they had too, but the results would be the same. They would not only affect the history of New Orleans, but all of America as well.

"My it is late," Marie whispered. "Forgive me for keeping you up. You must be tired. It has been a delight, though, hasn't it, dear? I do hope we will have many more evenings together. Somehow, I feel as if I can talk to you. I trust you and love you as if you were of my own blood. I have said that, often, tonight, haven't I? Well, I hope by now, you believe me?"

They hugged briefly before departing, and it did not surprise Tori, when she opened the door, that Nelly was waiting with a lamp just outside the parlor. As Marie had said, the woman was entirely devoted to her, and yes, Tori could see, slave or not, Nelly was loved.

"Good night Nelly, and thank you again, Marie. I will leave you in Nelly's capable hands. I shall see you in the morning." Tori left them and strolled toward the bedroom that she and Jean were staying in. She was reflecting on her first impressions of Marie Destrehan to those of now. Tori recalled thinking the woman was on the plump side. No wonder she was. After giving birth to so many children and the last only months ago, her body had no time to get back into shape. Not that she was out of shape; she was fit as a fiddle as far as Tori could tell. The woman was amazing, running around like a girl, not a middle-aged lady. If Marie could do so, then Tori assured herself, she could do the same. Having one child in this era was going to be a piece of cake, a walk in the park. After all, it was not like this was her first child, was it?

Tori stood just outside the bedroom door and hesitated. "This is not the time to think about things. Now is the time to find Jean and cuddle up. To worry over something that is months away and something that is out of my control is not going to rule me. I am stronger, I am, and I will be more like Marie, a woman in full control of herself and her surroundings. I just need to stop mumbling. One of these days, talking to myself is going to get me into trouble." She stood straight and nodded her head in affirmation of what she'd just uttered. Having declared that statement firmly, Tori opened the bedroom door, with a smile, on her lips. Laffite's wife confidently walked toward the bed, where Jean sat waiting for her.

COUPLES began arriving for the ball three days before the grand event, and with these changes, the house took on a whole new atmosphere. If Tori thought it chaotic before, she hadn't known what chaos was. The plantation was full of activity no matter where she looked, and each person, black or white, played a role. Marie was the expert, though. She was every place at once and never seemed to tire. J.D.'s wife was in her glory, and Tori could now see why the home's mistress would find regular plantation life dull. The woman seemed to glow with the challenges that arose. One purpose filled her time, and that was to make this ball the success she knew it could be.

It was just after lunch on the second day that Tori found herself at odds with what to do. She had seen both kitchens, the inside one, and the small freestanding building with its burning ovens and busy cooks. Tori had toured the house with the older children and shown every detail they could think of. Even the youngest took her by the hand until they were told to leave Miss Victoria alone.

With no Destrehan children of any age to keep her company and not wanting to risk spending time alone with any one of the early guests, Tori was left to wonder what would be the best way to spend her time until the men's meeting was finished. In a way, she was glad that Jean was occupied and even more delighted that she was not required to join in, with whatever it was they were planning behind closed doors. Tori was taking Marie's words of advice to heart. The ordinarily inquisitive Tori was leaving the men to themselves.

The few other female guests that had arrived that morning were doing as was custom and had taken to their rooms for an afternoon rest. Unbeknownst to them, their absence was most welcome, however, because when Tori was around them, she always had to be careful about how she talked and acted. It was difficult and often exhausting to keep up appearances, and the less time she had to place herself in such difficulties, the better.

THE day was bright, and the sun was shining. The chill that had accompanied them on their drive from the city had lifted. With no one to stop her, and preferring to be left alone, Tori picked a book of poems from Marie's collection and set out to find a spot on the grounds where she could enjoy the fresh air and practice reading her French.

Once downstairs, it was easy to make her way to the back entrance, and as she was on the side of the house, where the men had sequestered themselves, there was no other person around to disrupt her thoughts.

Sauntering past the wing, where upstairs the ladies rested, and below the men were meeting, Tori let her mind wander. There were six males inside the downstairs room, which she had seen the day before. It was the bedroom of the oldest son who had just returned home. Nicholas, who was twenty-two, had spent time in France finishing his studies and would remain home after his younger, also called Nicholas, left. From what Tori could gather, it was a regular occurrence for those families who could afford such to send their sons overseas to educate them. The idea of sending a young boy so far away did not feel right to Tori, just like calling more than one child by the same name did not feel right.

Marie had joked that it made things easier for her when one was away because having two sons with the same first name could be difficult. "I declare, those boys had me using their full names when I called for them. It was either Nicholas Guy Noel or Nicholas Noel," she laughed. "Take my word Victoria, do not name your children the same, no matter how much you like the name."

Tori was laughing to herself when she stepped outside onto the driveway before realizing she'd not gone in the direction she had intended, and her laughter stopped. The thought of going back inside, to find the shorter way to where she planned to go, crossed her mind. It was all just so confusing. The back of the house was front, and the front was back. Naming children the same and always playing second place to the men in their lives had her feeling like she was in wonderland. Alice had a hard time in her story, and only now did Tori appreciate how simple things could confuse one so. Things were not as easily understood as they appeared, and Lord did these Creoles love to complicate matters. They were a breed unto their own and very easily offended too.

Jean's wife was flipping through the pages of the book, while deep in thought and did not see the man walking toward her. It was not until he was right in front of her that she realized he was there. The sound of his greeting stopped her progress and caused her to look up with a shocked expression.

Embarrassed by his blunder, the man spoke rapidly in French. "Pardon me, Madame Laffite. I did not mean to startle you in any way. I am late for the meeting, as you see. That is why I am in such a hurry." He bowed and then looked concerned at the surprised expression still on the woman's face. "Pardon, in English, yes? Finding you here by yourself, must imply that your husband, was, as always punctual?"

"That he was Monsieur…I am sorry I have quite forgotten your name. I apologize and offer only that I have met so many people of late, as my excuse."

"Ah, that is a very reasonable explanation and one that I understand. I am Jacques Villere, a friend of Jean and his brother Pierre, who I understand will not be joining us this year."

"That is so. Pierre has chosen to remain in the city. Monsieur Villere, I do remember you, and Jean speaks highly of you. Please do not let me delay you further, as the meeting has only just begun. I shall take my walk, and you gentlemen may proceed with whatever it is you are about. Politics, plantation news, and such, all subjects that are too much for me to bother with," she lied. "Incredibly boring, for females and pure entertainment for gentlemen, it seems." She smiled brightly.

Jacques laughed and bowed slightly. "You are a wise lady; we do find such matters as very entertaining and challenging, which means we are not bored in the least. Please excuse me. I look forward to talking more with you later."

"I also. Good day." Tori watched as the man hastily made his way to the room on the corner of the wing. Without hesitating, he opened the door and stepped inside to join the meeting. Tori made a mental note to ask Jean just what it was all about. Meeting Mr. Villere indicated to her that there was more going on than she'd been led to think. For right then, though, she looked forward to a few quiet hours alone reading.

AFTER about half an hour, reading French poems was not going to fill the afternoon, and she knew it. The very idea of sitting there for who knew, how long, before she saw Jean, was not very inviting. Maybe if she were to take a walk, that might speed things up a bit, she told herself, and so Tori stood up and was brushing her skirt free of leaves when she saw a carriage arriving. It immediately brightened her mood, as Tori recognized the female who was waving her hand and calling out to her. It was the young girl Kristen, who had promised to visit and keep her company. It was delightful to see her and gave Tori hope that the afternoon would not be such a loss after all. In her joy, Tori waved back and started to walk toward the occupants of the slow-moving open carriage.

Kristen's voice rang out in the afternoon air. Her father was being instructed in a loud voice, to stop right where they were, and that same female voice had quite a demanding tone about it. "I am not a child father," she snapped at him, "and if you don't listen to me, I will most certainly jump out right here and right now."

"You, my daughter, will act like a young lady if you wish to be treated as one. If you jump, I shall insist on you returning to our hostess's care, and you will remain there for the duration of our stay."

"I will do no such thing. You, father, are so infuriating. You better stop this carriage now, and I mean it."

"Very well, you have your way; we shall stop, I will leave, and you will remain seated and return to the Butlers. Halt the carriage, driver. I shall leave you here." Just as they came to a stop, Tori reached their side and looked up at an angry young lady and a furious looking father. The fact that Kristen was acting like a spoiled brat did not seem like her at all. However, Tori had to admit that she did not know the girl that well to make such a judgment. As to her father, his lips were drawn thin and were twitching. Tori did not know if he was trying to control his temper or doing his best not to smile?

"Miss Victoria, will you please explain to my father that I gave my word, that we would meet, and I would keep you company, while father and the other men have their silly meeting. I would have come sooner, but father insisted I would only get in the way, which is not what I would do, right?"

Tori wanted to laugh, but she hid her amusement. The way that the girl was fabricating the truth was making it hard to keep a straight face. Kristen's father's expression showed Tori that he understood only too clearly that his daughter was not being entirely honest, and Tori felt it best to step in before things got out of control. "I assure you, Mr. Kirkwood, that Kristen will be no bother to me. I rather looked forward to her visit, and as you see, I am in need of some company."

"See father. Now, please excuse me. I promise to behave and act like a young lady. Miss Victoria will be my chaperone; it is all perfectly proper."

Her father looked from his daughter to Tori and then smiled slightly. "If that is all right with you, Mrs. Laffite? My daughter always seems to manage to manipulate me."

"It is, Sir, and it will be my delight to accompany her and keep an eye on her for you."

Kristen didn't wait for her father's answer. She wrapped her arms around his neck and kissed him on the cheek. "You are the best father a girl could want, and I forgive you for not understanding." With that, she climbed down and stood beside her new friend.

"You had best leave, or you will be more than fashionably late. Miss Victoria and I will return to her spot under the tree to sit and visit."

Mr. Kirkwood could only agree with his daughter and nodded his head before instructing his driver to move on. "You may proceed, driver, and Kristen, I will send for you when we are finished. Also, may I suggest that you might take this opportunity to practice your French. Mrs. Laffite will oblige; I am quite sure."

"But father…"

"I will send for you, and that is that. Mrs. Butler has agreed to help you with your fitting, and you will not be so rude as to not allow her help." He turned away from them and tapped his driver on the shoulder. "I said to proceed, boy, I am late."

Once her father was out of hearing range, Kristen burst out giggling. Father, really thinks I am going to sit under the tree and practice French? Come, I will show you what we do with our afternoons." The girl took hold of Tori's hand and began to walk toward the house. "I have it all planned, come along, we both are expected in Aunt Marie's parlor."

"Who expects us? All, or most of the guests are resting, and I know Marie is."

Kristen rolled her eyes. "I know that poor dear; she has to rest each afternoon and does so for a few hours, at least. That is why we can play cards. You do know, how don't you? If not, I will show you. I learned not long ago, and now I am rather good at it. I almost always win. The game I used to play is called Brag, but now I have learned the new game that is all the rage, you will see." Suddenly she stood still with a perplexed look on her face. "Well, maybe not. I don't think Aunt Marie has those cards yet. We shall just have to play Brag, and you will enjoy it, I know you will. Come on," she tugged Tori's hand as she began to walk. "I taught Marie Elizabeth. That's Eulalie; she loves that nickname. Anyway, I taught her how to play in one afternoon. I was surprised because I did not think a sixteen-year-old child would be able to grasp the game."

Tori almost burst out laughing. Kristen was calling a girl a few years younger than her a mere child. For the Destrehans to call Eulalie, a child was right, but having what Tori considered to be a contemporary do so was plain amusing. Kristen didn't seem to notice or care that she looked at Eulalie as a child, and herself as an adult. As for Tori, something told her that the afternoon was about to become far more interesting than she could have ever guessed.

True to her word, Kristen had thought of everything. When they entered the parlor, besides Eulalie, three other women were sitting around a table, all of whom Tori had met before. If they were shocked to see her, they did not show it, and before long, everyone had nothing else on their mind but taking turns at beating Kristen, who, like she had said, always seemed to win.

"I tell you, Jean, the child is a wiz at the game. I never won a single."

"Wiz? Another term I am not familiar with. I think I shall keep a small book and write down these phrases. Wiz?"

"It means, wizard. Magic, top of the line."

Jean rolled his eyes.

"She knows more than others and is excellent at it." Tori had to add that bit of knowledge.

"That must have been frustrating, having a child as you call her, win all the time."

"Will you stop teasing me and okay, she is not a child exactly and not a woman either, I might add."

"I think maybe the term you are looking for is a young lady?"

"Dinner was nice tonight, wasn't it? And the children were great."

"Changing the subject already, Tori?"

"Maybe and no, just saying. I love all the children, that's all. How Marie has had so many in such a short time is amazing."

"One could say so."

"Do you know that not all of them lived?"

"I do."

"It worries me. Our child, he or she will be all right."

"Come here," he hugged her and held her close for a few seconds before letting her go. "Now, you know you and the baby will be healthy, and nothing will happen to either. So, let me help you out of your..."

"Only if you will do as you promised. You said you would explain what the big secret meeting was about, remember?"

"If you come to bed, I shall do so. Just slip out of your clothes and join me."

"You, sir, are amazing. Always thinking about... well, never mind. If you go and get me one more slice of pie, I will agree to your terms. If you hurry, maybe I will agree to more than listening to what you have to say."

"Agreed. I shall be right back."

Tori giggled as Jean took off to go and snag her another slice of pie, but in the time it took to undress and slip into a nightdress, and for Jean to return from the kitchen, Tori had to admit defeat. She was too tired to sit up and listen to what she could easily learn in the days ahead. Laffite's wife was also too tired to think about making love with the man she adored. The bed was warm, and as she waited, her eyes began to droop; then, before she realized what happened, sleep overtook her."

At long last, it was the day of the ball, and even though most of the men still found a few things to entertain themselves, it was the women who were now the center of attention and wanted nothing to do with, let alone see, one of their husbands. Slaves were everywhere; some were the regular house slaves, and others had either been brought in from the slave quarters or had arrived with their owners.

Nelly oversaw what had to be accomplished with each of them. Doing this allowed her mistress the time to rest and prepare for the night's gathering without a worry. Rooms in both wings of the grand home were full. All but one had guests occupying them. Only one room upstairs near Marie and J.D. had been set aside for the children. That room had every available space used and turned into makeshift beds. Though crowded, they all had a place to sleep, and not one complained.

The women's gowns were being fitted, and last second alterations were made. The competition among the females, to outshine the other, was fierce, and it did not stop there. Makeup and hair were also a priority. For some lucky enough or wealthy enough, they would only be attended by the best, but not the most talented. That position belonged to Marie Laveau. The woman had been sent for by the Destrehans, and she had arrived the night before. The mulatto would remain until the day after the ball, and thus, she had many hours to spend on her two clients.

Tori learned from Nelly that Marie Laveau was staying in a cabin in the slave quarters, which seemed a bit out of place for a free woman of color to be, but the black nanny had explained to her, it was the right and proper place, even if she were free. Being free, she said, gave her no right to think she would sleep anyplace else. Tori, remembering what Jean had told her when they first arrived, decided it would be better to let things alone. Besides, she did not have long to dwell on the talented woman's housing, because excitement overtook her. Nelly had also informed her that Marie Laveau was to help only Tori and her own Mistress Marie until they were both satisfied. Only then could the girl acquire other jobs that required her talent, and it would be just for those few who were willing to pay her price. Tori had grinned upon learning this little bit of information. She knew only too well how all the other ladies would be envying them, and for the first time, she adored her position in the upper echelon. It was a far cry from being one of Rose's girls or even a friend of Leones'. Tori went so far as to tell herself that she felt a bit like royalty, and enjoying the moment was her top priority.

<br>

234

FINALLY, the hour arrived, and standing out on the large balcony, Tori watched with Jean, as one by one, the carriages began to arrive. At one point, there was quite a line waiting to turn off the river road, to start their procession up the driveway. Knowing that many of the guests had traveled for miles to join the Destrehans, to welcome Jean's new wife, made Tori feel both excited and embarrassed. Having made the trip herself, a few days ago, Tori understood that each passenger in the carriages suffered a considerable amount of discomfort, to attend the ball and that quite a few would endure the return trip to the city that same night. Hours spent in a cold and dark carriage, just to be able to say that they had attended and met the Laffites, seemed a bit much. Suddenly she trembled, at the anticipation of meeting so many strangers and prayed that not one of them would be let down.

Jean felt her tremble and guessed correctly; it was because of nerves and not the air's slight chill. "You know, of course, that they are all coming to meet my lovely wife, the one woman who has stolen my heart."

"Jean, stop it! We both know that is not true. Besides, I have already met most of them, I'm sure. It's absurd to think otherwise?"

"My wife doubts me. You have wounded me deeply." Jean placed his hand on his heart and looked at her. "I would never say anything that was not true. Exaggerated maybe, but not true..."

"Oh, stop teasing, you scoundrel, and do come inside. What will people think?"

"I don't know what they think, how could I? That is for them to know and maybe for us to learn from their lips, later?" Jean placed his hand in hers and escorted her back into their room. "I know what I am thinking, and that is, you should have a glass of wine to help calm you a little before we go down. I also think this is one time that I believe we should arrive a little late and make a grand entrance."

"You are terrible; you know that. I promised Marie that I would help, and here you are asking me to stay up here and drink."

"Well, I could think of a few other delightful activities that I would ask of you, but you do look as if you would run me through if I tried to get you out of that gown."

"You're, damned right I would. It took forever to get into this thing. Never again will I think it romantic to have to wear such outrages contraptions," Tori pulled at the top of the delicate corset. "Day and night, one has to squeeze into them, and really Jean, I feel as if I am going to fall out of the top of this. Look, do you see what I mean?" She leaned forward and at a slight angle, then bounced up and down, making sure that there would be no wardrobe malfunction.

"Indeed, I do madame, and it will be driving me mad with wanting you all night, along with all the other male guests, I'm sure; however, you will not be leaning downward and acting like a monkey on a string, jumping around bouncing your breasts for all to witness." He laughed out loud at the look of horror on her face. "Maybe, I should have your gowns made to conceal a little more in the future? You do have a way of continually reminding me of the discomfort of such items as undergarments, which would, maybe not be necessary if we had the gowns not styled so..." he traced his finger along the top of her breasts, "low." He chuckled as he turned and picked up a bottle of wine and filled two glasses.

She took her glass of wine from Jean and toasted him. "Here's to the one glass of the day then. I would rather enjoy it here with you now, in the quiet, than not."

With a puzzled look on his face, he quizzed her. "Explain to me again, why it is that you insist on only one glass a day? You are certain it has nothing to do with the fact that wine seems to agree with you and your passion. Which, I am convinced, I do not have to remind you, climbs higher as you drink?"

"Jean, stop it! I know you think I am overly passionate when I'm loaded, but that has nothing to do with it, and you know it. I've explained to you that one or two glasses of wine a day won't hurt the child, but more than that could. Same goes for coffee and smoking. Do I really have to go over it again?"

236

"No, not again." He laughed, holding up his hand. "I believe you and love you all the more for taking such care of him." He saw her look of disapproval and quickly added, "Or her. Let us not discuss the child now. Let's just sit and enjoy this time alone, as I am sure it will be the last, for hours to come."

They had waited another hour and checked to see that the line of carriages had ended before Jean decided it was time to join the party. He was going to be quite the showman this evening and planned on making the most of their grand entrance. This would be followed by the moment he longed for the most introducing his wife to those who had not yet had the pleasure—then announcing the happy news about the baby.

THE pirate still had a difficult time convincing himself his wife was going to make him a father. Looking at her now, standing at the top of the staircase, he knew she would be the night's belle. Tori did not show her condition in the gown she wore unless you knew what you were looking for. His eyes looked at her midriff, and he told himself, this would be the last time he would see her dressed in such a form-fitting gown, until after the baby was born. He had to agree with Tori that strapping a corset firmly, to continue to keep one's shape was not healthy, but part of him was glad she had done so this night. The woman looked like a temptress, instead of a mother-to-be. Heads would turn, and tongues would start wagging when their news slipped out, and he relished it.

Most of the guests were already in the dining room, which had been cleared of all furnishings. The adjoining room doors were opened to create one ample space, thus accommodating one large ballroom instead of two separate ground floor rooms. When they had first arrived, the dining room had been significant, but Tori had no idea that it could be expanded by removing the center paneling. When she had seen this done and watched as some chairs and sideboards were re-arranged, it all made perfect sense. This was how the Destrehans were going to accommodate the crowd of people in one place at the same time. Until that moment, she had assumed the ball would be held in two or more small areas and nothing quite so spacious as it was now.

At one end, a small stage was waiting for those who would play the music, and even then, with that room taken up, there was plenty of open space to waltz around and dance the night away. Refreshments were to be found on the sideboards along the edge of the ballroom. While, outside, under the covered veranda, awaited tables of both hot and cold foods. Chairs and tables had been placed all along the spacious area. At comfortable intervals and out on the grass, a few feet away from these place settings were fire pits, in which logs would burn to help keep the chill of the night at bay. Three small slaves consisting of boys and girls, attended these fires, and all were overseen by several adult field workers, who constantly walked from one site to another. Everything had been thought of, even the prospect of an accidental fire igniting the house. Tori was amazed to see that cleverly hidden close to each pit were buckets of water in case of just such an accident.

JEAN and Tori gradually descended the stairs that wound down and around toward the lower floor and main entrance hall. Laffite had hoped to get Tori to the door of the ballroom before being seen. By doing so, they'd make a grand entrance as planned. That plan failed quickly, as a few of the guests spotted the two descending and alerted the rest of the crowd within the ballroom. Instantaneously, it was clear that everyone was quickly pressing toward the entrance hall, for a better view.

Tori had hoped not to be seen until downstairs but for a different reason. Maneuvering about in all the material that made up both the gown and petticoat was extremely difficult. The layers seemed to wrap themselves around her legs with each step, threatening to trip her, and for a split second, she began to panic, causing her to grip Jean's hand tightly and standstill. "I can't do this. If I move one more step, I'm going to land on my ass," she whispered to Jean through her smile, like a ventriloquist.

"And, if you whisper any louder, everyone will hear you and your choice of colorful words. Some angel!" he retorted softly using the same tactic.

Tori continued to smile and, speaking through her smile, answered, "If that's what you want, the choice is yours. Help me, or by God, I swear..."

Laffite was more amused than upset. "I am well aware that you swear madame, and if we stand here smiling and talking through our teeth much longer, everyone will think we've gone quite insane. Here, allow me the honor, and thank me later." Jean removed Tori's hand from his arm, and then with a more attentive action, he wrapped his arm around her waist. "Feel better? Just trust me. Shall we continue?" Without waiting for a response, Laffite stepped forward and down a step, helping his wife maneuver carefully.

With her hand no longer on Jean's arm, she found that it was quite easy to gather up the front of her gown and raise it an inch or so, allowing her the freedom to walk without fear of treading on the gown's hem. "This is much better, thank you."

"Anything for you, my love. Shall we? It would seem that if we do not hurry, all the guests will exit the interior of the house and step outside..."

Jean would have continued to talk, but he was interrupted by a woman's voice. She spoke loud enough for all to hear, and in no way did she mind that she had rudely interrupted. "My, my, my, it would seem that you are not accustomed to wearing such elegant garments. Or could it be that they don't have such fashions where you are from, wherever that is? No one seems to know, do they? How positively intriguing."

The boisterous and somewhat noisy crowd calmed down, and all eyes were moving between looking at the stunning Simone and Jean Laffite's beautiful wife. Those closest to the stairs had only seconds more to admire the spectacle the couple of the night made because Simone had not finished her retort. As she continued, heads turned, and all attention fell precisely where the Spanish beauty intended, on her.

"Or is the ability to maneuver gracefully, beyond you, my dear? Jean, you darling, you are such a good husband. Wouldn't you say, everyone? He is all but carrying her down the stairs. Now, that's what I call dedication."

"And that's what I call a class A bitch," Tori hissed softly so only Jean could hear. Simone was standing there, brazenly tossing rude remarks and getting away with it. The Latin bitch had returned, it seemed, to do nothing more than claim the spotlight and have another go at her. Why, in hell, did she think that she'd seen the last of her? Tori knew people like Simone didn't give up. Bitches like her bide their time and then strike when they can accomplish the most damage, she reminded herself. Making Laffite's wife look incapable of social graces seemed to be working too because several women were shaking their heads ever so slightly, as if in agreement with their Latin friend.

It had never occurred to Tori that this despicable female would be invited to this event. She had quite put her out of her memory until now, but like it or not, here she was once again, turning up like a rotten apple in a crate of good. If she kept up her selfish act, the woman could end up spoiling the Destrehan's event, and Tori was not about to let her get away with it. Laffite's wife was seething but smart enough not to show a sign of her dislike or anger. She was, however, determined to stop Simone in her tracks.

Jean was furious and had he not had his arms full; he would have marched down to Simone and escorted her away from the entrance to tell her a thing or two, regardless of the spectacle it caused. Laffite knew that he would have to put her in her place very soon, and the sooner, the better he told himself. If he did not, tongues were going to start wagging, and their short affair might become common knowledge. For him, that was one bit of information he intended would never become public, for Tori and Adrian's sake. No, better, he began placing Simone in her place and right then. He smiled brightly. "Simone, a pleasure to see you again. Does this mean that we also have the honor of Adrian's company? My wife and I would enjoy seeing him."

The woman nodded, and to everyone close by, it was a warm greeting. What they did not witness, and Tori did, were Simone's eyes, which remained ice-cold, and locked on Jeans' as she spoke. "You do indeed. Adrian is attending the party in the parlor upstairs. He has been ill, you know. It has been hard for him to get around. Maybe Victoria would like to visit with him. The two of them do seem to have the same difficulty, getting around unassisted."

Everyone was shocked by Simone's behavior. The whispering ladies could be heard in the background, while a few of the men coughed uneasily. This awkward moment continued, as everyone waited to see what would happen next because whatever it was, would surely be entertaining and talked about for days. Adrian's wife had insulted both her hosts, Laffite and his wife, something that no lady or gentleman of standing should ever do, and once again, all eyes fell on the Spanish beauty.

None of what was happening seemed to bother Simone. She proudly stood her ground with the same demure look on her face. She even had the audacity to look around her and smile softly, as if she had said nothing wrong.

Tori would have loved nothing better than to walk up to her and wipe the stupid expression off her face with a good slap, but she knew Simone was hoping for just such a reaction. It would give her great satisfaction to prove Tori was not quite the lady she portrayed. Besides, Jean was acting calmly, so she would continue to do so. Tori would follow his lead. After all, there was more than one way to skin a cat.

Smiling brightly, Tori beat Jean with a retort of her own, and nothing could have made him prouder. "Simone, you are too kind. Between Jean looking out for my well-being and you, offering your kind observations, to alert my dear husband to take care. Well, now, I do feel so fortunate and blessed. It is hard for me to walk down these stairs safely, as you have observed. Let me assure you that it is not because of my gown that I am cautious, it's just that a woman in my delicate condition," she placed her free hand over her stomach, "would not want to fall, and neither would my husband want me to." By the time Tori's statement had been made, and before it could cause a stir, Jacques Villere stepped forward.

"Does this mean that Jean is going to join us in fatherhood? That the rumor is true?" He chuckled while looking at the crowd. "One of the younger Destrehans let it slip this afternoon, and you know how these females are. They have been talking about it ever since." Jacques climbed the stairs quickly and slapped Jean on the back in a friendly gesture. "Well, come on then, tell us, is it so? Is what Madame Laffite is implying just and true?"

"It is indeed," Jean announced loudly.

"Well, congratulations, and let me be among the first to offer my family's help in any way."

Here they go again, Tori thought. This southern hospitality was more about who could outdo the other than it was in helping. Now, more than before, Tori and Jean would be wined and dined. It would be a never-ending party of sorts, for the next five months, as everyone would want to claim they had the friendship of the Laffites and the inside gossip. All of them would profess to be the closest, and each would undoubtedly try to outdo the other.

Tori had to smile at that. At least she was smiling. Simone's face was an emotionless mask. The woman's only indication of her upset was how she clenched and unclenched her left hand that hung at her side. Tori took satisfaction in knowing that the bitch had been rendered speechless, and before Simone had time to gather her thoughts with a witty reprisal, the moment had passed. The Laffites had become the center of attention, and the sulking Simone had been pushed aside and forgotten.

Left standing alone, the fuming female stormed off to find a drink and to try to figure out what to do next. Once again, she had lost face, and it was all that Victoria's fault. Now Jean's wife had gone and gotten herself pregnant, no doubt to hang on to him, and gather sympathy for herself with the city's citizens. Probably wasn't even Jean's child, she told herself. Now, that would be poetic justice, she thought. Different ideas of revenge simmered in her head as she sipped on her wine and scanned the room for a willing and gullible accomplice to whatever she could come up with next.

TORI was glad that Jean remained by her side, the very idea of having his ex-lover in the same room had unnerved her. Because of that situation and nothing more, she was trying to think of a way to return to their room without looking like she was ditching the awkward situation. This problem and possible solution soon escaped her, though, as a familiar and welcome voice called out across the room.

Kristen had arrived with her father and another couple, which Tori rightfully assumed were the people who were hosting them. The young woman looked radiant, dressed in pale pink, with her hair arranged in a far more mature fashion than the style Tori had witnessed at their first meeting. Gone was the image of a young girl, because walking toward her was a confident, young lady.

Jean grinned and leaned his head closer to Tori's and added softly, "This looks interesting. If you don't mind, I shall take this moment to leave your side and acquire a drink. Don't worry; I shall return long before Mademoiselle Kristen stops talking. By the look on her face, she is teaming with excitement. Forgive me, but I am going to allow you to handle this on your own. She is, after all, just a child, right?" Jean was grinning as he walked away.

"Coward," whispered Tori as she turned to face the young couple, who were only a few feet away from her, and before she could prepare a greeting or utter one word, Kristen had a hold of her in a tight embrace.

"Oh, I could not wait to arrive. Father was delayed, and we had to wait for him. This is the most exciting night. I heard your news about the baby. Congratulations. Now, if you allow me, I have to share my... no, excuse me, our news." Kristen turned to look at the man standing by her side. He smiled and nodded his head in agreement with what she had declared and spoke up before Kristen could continue.

"Mrs. Laffite." He held out his hand, which Tori took hold of and began to shake. "Please do call me Victoria. Any friend of Kristen's is a friend of mine."

Kristen burst out laughing. "That's just it, Victoria. David is not just a friend anymore. Father has given his permission at long last. We are to be married. Is that not the most romantic notion?" David grinned and removed his hand from Tori's grip.

"Mrs. Laffite, Victoria, it is a pleasure to meet you. Kristen has not stopped talking about you. May I present to you, Colonel Richard Butler and his charming wife. They are the proud owners of the plantation just down the road. The Ormond plantation is hosting my darling Kristen and her father. Without their aid, I fear I would never have received the honor of gaining her hand."

The gentleman stepped forward. "A pleasure to meet you, Victoria, and it is our hope you will pay us a call before you return to the city. This lovely lady on my arm is my wife, and like me, extends our offer of hospitality." His wife shook Tori's hand but uttered nothing. She seemed the shy type, and for a few seconds, the atmosphere seemed strained. Lightening the moment, the Colonel looked at Kristen's fiancé and added, "As to us being the sole reason for gaining the hand of Kristen, that is nonsense. It was your dealings with my business partner that secured your place. Captain Samuel McCutchen speaks highly of you."

Kristen burst out giggling. "I told you David was brilliant, didn't I? Even my father had to admit defeat finally, and accept him, and his dealings."

Tori smiled brightly. "Congratulations to you both. I know you wanted this for some time. I am happy your endeavors changed your father's mind. I seem to recall he was most insistent that you were too young when last I spoke with him."

"It was all David, and Captain McCutchen helped, by offering him a position of high ranking with his shipping company. Plus, David has purchased a parcel of land close to my family home. That is where we will build our home. Father could not say no after hearing that. You see, I will be close enough to help mother with the twins, and as my older sister is moving upriver, it was a prime factor in his decision. Isn't it all so perfect…look," she spun around, "father even allowed me to wear a gown that I wanted and, he allowed me to arrange my hair, in a more mature style, as befitting; at last, I think maybe he sees me as a woman and not a child at last.

Colonel Butler and his wife thought I looked very mature for my age, and father had to agree. After all, he could not afford to offend our hosts. Especially, I might add, if he ever intended to revisit the Ormond Plantation. Oh, I do so hope you will call on us there. We could talk about my plans for the wedding, and I could show you around. Colonel Butler re-named the plantation after he purchased it, you know. Named it after his ancestral home in Ireland. He has some drawings of the place. Really it looks nothing like the plantation. I have strong ideas as to what our home will look like, you know. David has plans drawn up already."

Tori could only smile. The girl had much to learn. She was acting like a teenager who just got permission to date, not marry. Her excitement infused all around her, though, as she excitedly talked on and on. It was a complete wonder to Tori that everyone around them just allowed her to dominate the moment. David was most certainly going to have his hands full. Kristen was no shrinking violet and far from a simpering belle.

"Mrs. Laffite, sorry, Victoria," David interrupted, "would you please excuse us. I would very much like to dance with my future wife, and I see your husband is returning to join you. I have had the pleasure of making his acquaintance before, and so I know he will understand my rather unorthodox actions."

"You may. Also, Colonel, please do not let me detain you, and I am certain Jean understands. Enjoy the evening, Kristen. I am sure we will talk again in a little while."

Kristen laughed out loud. "If I dare drag myself away from my love, I have no doubt we will. Bye for now."

The Colonel chuckled. "Young love, it warms the heart and stirs old memories. Madame Laffite, we shall look forward to your visit." Smiling broadly, the Colonel faced his wife. "My darling, let us show the young lovers how to dance and remind them that romantic love is far from theirs alone. Victoria, I see your husband approaching; till we meet again." He nodded his head and escorted his blushing wife onto the dance floor.

Jean reached Tori's side and slipped his arm around her waist. "I take it the news was good?"

"You can, and it was. Kristen has had her way. Her father agreed to their marriage. Jean, she is so young; they both are. I do wish them well, but lord, they are children."

"I am confident that the young lady will not let it be any other way. Besides, they have a lot of support around them. The Destrehans are close to the Butlers, and when you meet Captain McCutchen, you will see how all three families support each other. It was only a matter of time before Kristen had her way. All has been arranged after all. You don't think a man of her fathers' standing would allow her to marry just anyone, did you?"

"Are you telling me, this marriage was…is arranged?"

Jean chuckled and whispered into her ear. "You still have much to learn about this time. Come now, if you would join me, I have someone I very much would like you to meet."

"If I must. I thought I had met everyone, but still, people do seem to be turning up."

"Many will arrive and depart as the evening progresses. It is like I told you," he winked. "All have come to meet the belle of the ball. One such gentleman slowly approaches us as I speak. He is very well connected, and I might add, has links to the upper echelon in France. A few years back, before I came to New Orleans, Lois-Philippe, Duke of Orleans, came for a visit with his two brothers. The royal family were guests at the Marigny Plantation, and I have heard such tails of that visit. You think I am extravagant," Jean chuckled. "It is told they ate from gold plates, and after the stay, all the plates were tossed into the river. Seems that Bernard thought no one else was worthy of eating off them. He is, as, how do you say? Ah, yes, impulsive and spoiled, but good to have as an acquaintance, better still a friend. I have known him for some time and just a hint here; he may be called a French-Creole American nobleman, but the man detests all Americans. Just because he was born here, does not in his mind, make him anything but first and foremost, French. Not that it should be a problem for you. Your French accent is perfect, and he speaks English only when he chooses, and that is seldom."

Tori turned and watched as the distinguished gentleman walked toward them. By his side walked J.D., and he seemed pleased with himself. (In French) "Ah, Victoria, may I present to you, Monsieur Jean-Bernard Xavier Philippe de Marigny de Mandeville."

The dashing gentleman bowed, and Tori dipped in a slight curtsy. "Madame, it is my pleasure." He took her hand and kissed the back quickly before letting go. "Jean," he nodded his head Laffite's way. "I have missed you at the tables." He laughed and embraced Laffite in a traditional greeting before turning his attention back to Tori. "That Jean has been absent, Madame, is good for me, as your husband has all the luck with the cards and dice. Since he has had you in his life, my game has improved." Again, he laughed.

J.D. smiled and added his bit of information, hoping to make clear in Tori's mind that the man before her was not a dandy; instead, he was a serious contender in New Orleans's future. "Come now, Bernard, the way you present yourself; one may think you nothing more than a rake. Victoria, he is more than just a player of cards, I can attest to that fact. He is also more than a mere friend his maternal grandfather was my father. So, you see, I know his character, which stands fast. He holds the fate of our fair city seriously and intends to be elected to the city council. A position, I can assure all, he will acquire easily." J.D. looked at Bernard and smiled. "Then, my friend, you and I will work together often, shall we not?"

"Of that fact, I am certain." Bernard turned back toward Laffite, paying little attention to Tori. "Jean, you will undoubtedly be of great help in all matters pertaining to my upcoming position."

Jean placed his arm around Tori's waist and nodded affirmatively. "It would be my pleasure, as always. More so after the birth of our child."

"Ah, yes. Congratulations, and you Madame, you will honor me by visiting my home soon, I hope?"

Tori smiled brightly. A genuine member of the upper echelon from Paris itself had invited them to visit. "It would be my honor to do so, I can assure you. Jean and I will look forward to such an event."

"It is set then. If you both will excuse me, duty calls, my presence is required across the way. I look forward to getting to know you, Madame Laffite."

"Please, do call me Victoria."

"Very well, Victoria, I am honored to do so; if you will do me the honor of calling me, Bernard?"

"I most certainly will. Thank you, Bernard."

"The pleasure is all mine. Why, having such a beautiful French noblewoman as you around my home, will be my delight. Jean, you have acquired a real beauty and one that I most heartedly approve of my friend. I shall no longer worry about the dashing Jean Laffite falling prey to an uncouth American upstart." With that said, he bowed again and walked away.

Tori did not quite know what to say. The man had assumed she was a French noblewoman. His statement had been overheard too because looking around them, Tori watched as people began spreading the news. "Does he actually think I am a noblewoman?" Tori whispered into Jean's ear, so as not to be overheard.

Laffite grinned and answered her, speaking softly so as not to be overheard. "It seems so. I told you your accent was perfect, and the fact that Bernard and I know some of the same families in France, his conclusion, you are of noble blood was what I expected."

"You knew?"

He leaned in and whispered in her ear. "I assumed as much, that is maybe close to knowing. This could be fun, all of the city will believe him, and your identity is sealed. My friendship with Bernard is secure, no matter what. Why, Madame after this, may I be so bold as to say our friendship is beyond reproach. The fact you are my wife, and he heartedly approves, well now, I am most certain he will welcome my investment in purchasing a piece of his land. The man has such gambling debts that he is selling sections of his land. Only to the Creoles, you understand. Those with French ties, too if, they are in good standing, will have an opportunity to purchase parcels of his plantation. Until now, I was not sure he would allow me the option to obtain one, now I believe that is no longer a problem."

"He is selling his land?"

"That is so. The man gambles on anything; horses, cards, and dice top his list. He is, as he says, not to good at the games of chance. That and he does not overly care if he wins or loses it seems. I have had my eye on a strip of land, well several actually. I think I shall allow you to choose. The names of the streets are quite fascinating. The Avenue to his home is called Elysian Fields. Many of the Americans translate it as Parisian Avenue des Champs-Elysees."

Tori giggled. "I think I like our home right where it is. You may want to purchase a bit of land, but I don't know if that is what you did or didn't do? I can't help you there, I am afraid."

"Then we shall make history together; it seems," Jean chuckled. "Let us not talk about such matters now. Let us dance; I am anxious to place you in my arms."

As the evening progressed, things went along smoothly enough. Simone and her friends stayed clear of Jean and his wife. For Tori, this was both a blessing and a curse. The mother-to-be observed the Latin beauty and began to understand what she was up too. It was obvious that the small entourage the former belle of the ball, had gathered, followed her around the room. They were being manipulated by her blatant whispered remarks, after which the females would look Tori's way in aghast. There was nothing Tori could do to stop the gossiping, but it also would not prevent her from undoing the damage.

'Well now, two can play your game Simone, and unlike you, none will suspect I have ulterior a motive.'

"Jean, I think we should mingle a bit more. I need to greet a few of the ladies that have been held at bay by a certain, former belle of the ball." Letting the bitch get the upper hand was not going to happen, as two could play at her game, she told herself. Jean had only chuckled and was more than willing to aide her in whatever it was she had planned.

Upon being introduced to new visitors, and sensing the feelings of slight animosity, Tori would immediately go to work undoing anything Simone had, until that moment, accomplished. "I do hope that I can look as lovely as you do after the baby comes," she said to one woman. "You did say you have four children, did you not? But, my, you look so…so, wonderful." Tori leaned in and whispered into the woman's ear, so her next statement would cause no embarrassment. It would, however, be a huge compliment and well-received, she was certain. "I declare, in my estimation, it is as if you haven't even carried a baby! I shall pray; I am so blessed."

With constant positive remarks made to each female Tori was introduced too, the results were overwhelmingly positive. Swept away were any doubts as to Laffite's wife's gracious actions and reputation. By the end of the night, all at the affair would decide that Victoria Laffite was a genuine person, regardless of what Simone implied.

The only one who did not believe Tori's act was Simone. She had watched from across the room, ignored and entirely out of the limelight. Her efforts to darken the reputation of Jean's wife were failing. Worse still, she again had been pushed aside and neglected. Not giving up, the frustrated female began drinking continually, to bolster her next move. One way or another, she intended to obtain the upper hand once more. If Victoria could act the part of a lady, then she could also. Instead of acting like a scorned lover, she planned to turn the tables and use her circumstances to outmaneuver the new bride.

The Spanish beauty walked up to Jean, just as he was about to escort Tori to the dance floor. The crowd around the pair fell silent, not knowing what to expect, and all were incredibly surprised by what happened. Known for her sarcastic remarks and sultry manner, the small group waited for a showdown. Sadly, they were to be disappointed.

Simone began by lowering her eyes and speaking softly; she began to explain herself and her actions, while sounding genuine, even to her own ears. "I must apologize for my actions earlier. I honestly did not mean any harm. It's just that I have been under such a strain of late. I do not know what came over me." She forced a tear to fall from her eye and made no attempt to remove it. "Believe me; I don't. Could you find it in your heart to possibly forgive me and maybe even understand?" Her Latin accent was laced with a thick southern drawl and filled with self-pity. Simone's latest move was almost more than Tori could stand. However, she decided it was best to play the woman's game and give her what she wanted. Tori looked at Simone and smiled slightly.

"Of course, we all understand. It must be hard for you, tending to your husband and worrying day by day. I took no offense, neither did my husband, I assure you. Now, if you could be so kind as to excuse us?" Tori turned to look at Laffite's face. "Jean, I think a little fresh air would do me good. I am feeling a little warm, the baby, you understand…shall we?" Tori did not wait for a response; instead, she took Jean's arm and began to escort him across the room.

When Jean and Tori left the crowd, a few women, who had been close by, turned their attention to poor Simone as she had hoped they would. The sly female was milking the moment for all it was worth and was back at the center of attention. It was not the way she preferred, but it was a start, and the scheming beauty intended to keep it going.

"Victoria is so understanding, isn't she?" Simone wiped the tear from her cheek before continuing. "Why I do declare, Jean is so lucky to have her. They were made for each other, were they not? It's so hard when you don't have a husband to take care of you. I mean, I'm the one who has the burden of taking care, you understand? Not that I'm complaining, it's just so challenging, and I love my husband so..."

Once outside, Tori and Jean laughed and shook their heads. To Tori, it was quite amusing how Simone poured on her charms to all who would listen, and she was amazed by how many were sucked into believing her act. "You mean to tell me that they believe her? How can they?"

"They will for now, but the time will arrive when her true colors will show and that my dear is when we should be as far away from her as possible."

Tori was shivering as she stood looking out over the dark garden. The night air was cooler than expected, not to mention Jean's last remark about his ex-lover upset her.

"Come here; you are cold." He pulled her into his arms and kissed her slowly. "That should chase the chill away for a second or two. Follow me." Jean turned and walked to another set of doors and escorted her inside. It was one of the rooms on the left-wing. Only this was not a child's room; rather, she found herself standing in a small study. "If I don't have a few moments alone with you, I think maybe it's very possible that I shall go crazy."

"I know how you feel. I have never seen so many people all wanting to talk to us. It's not so much fun when you're the hot couple of the night."

"Hot? Is that what they say in your time, hot? Seems strange, some of the things they have done with the English language."

"No stranger than what they have done with French." She was teasing him and loved the puzzled look that played about his eyes. "Do we have to go back in there right away, or can we just slip upstairs and not be missed?"

"What an intriguing idea, but an impossible one, I am sorry to say. If you think that we would not be missed, you are greatly mistaken. I'm afraid we are, as you say, 'the hot couple.' Besides, there are still people who have not yet had the pleasure of your company."

"There are? How can that be possible?"

Jean stroked the side of his wife's face with his finger and then lightly kissed her cheek. "They would feel insulted if they did not have the chance to greet you. Duty calls, my dear." He presented his arm, and she slipped her hand around it.

"If we must, but you will have to secret me away soon."

"That I will, you have my word. Now, shall we? I can offer you one small delight. Before any further introductions, I shall take you in my arms and dance with the most beautiful woman in the house."

"You are a smooth talker, Mr. Jean Laffite, and I accept your invitation to dance and your estimation that I am the most beautiful," she laughed. "I accept that too, even if I don't think it so."

Back inside and feeling confident again, Tori asked Jean to get her something to drink before they danced. It was J.D. who, upon hearing her request, insisted that Jean go to Nelly and ask her for a glass of her tonic. He swore it tasted good and was most excellent for both mother and child. Jean did not hesitate after hearing this and left his wife's side, confident that she was safe in Destrehan's company.

Tori watched Jean hurry from the room and smiled. The man would do anything for her, even if it meant hunting down Nelly for an obscure tonic. "Thank you, J.D., you and Marie both take such care of me."

"It is our pleasure, I am sure," J.D. whispered into her ear in English. He had just hugged Tori when a voice from behind her asked to have the honor of been introduced to the lovely Madame Laffite. However, upon hearing the voice, Tori's blood instantly ran cold, and she paled as she swayed slightly.

(In French) "Is something wrong, my dear?" asked a concerned J.D. taking her by the arm. Fearing she was too upset to understand his French, he switched to English and gently whispered against her cheek, so only she could hear, "Do you feel all right? Can I fetch you something? Perhaps a chair?"

Tori still had enough wits about her to answer him in French, thus not giving away the fact that J.D. had spoken in English. "No, no. I'm fine. It's just all the excitement. The baby... this is a new condition for me. I am just not used to it, I suppose. If you would excuse me, maybe I should go up and rest a little. Would you go and find Jean for me and let him know?"

The voice behind her spoke full of concern. Unaware that the lady spoke English, he addressed the situation using French. "Very sensible idea, I'm sure. Monsieur Destrehan, you go and find her husband. As I have yet to make his acquaintance, it seems only right that you and not a stranger, such as myself, should inform him of his wife's request. Madame Laffite, it would be an honor to be of assistance, I'm sure." He stepped closer and lightly touched her arm. "I shall stay by her side until Monsieur Laffite is located," he added.

"That is most kind of you, Sir. You remain here, my dear, and I will be right back with Jean. I thank you for your assistance, Monsieur. I shall return momentarily."

As Tori watched J.D. turn to depart, the man behind her spoke up. "May I present myself to you, Madame Laffite?"

Without any way to excuse herself from the terrifying situation, and not wanting to draw more attention, Tori began to turn slowly, while her mind raced wildly. Her hate for this man behind her must not show, no matter what. Tori told herself she had to act calm, somehow. There was a good chance he would not recognize her if she did so. When she finally faced him, he was bowing, as was the custom. Tori realized she only had seconds before he would raise and look directly into her eyes, and to her horror, there was absolutely nothing she could do to prevent it. Her only option was to make their encounter a very brief one. As these thoughts raced through her mind, Edward straightened up and looked right at her.

"Monsieur Edward Duval, at your service."

Tori was already turning away from him as he spoke. Her hand was shielding the side of her face closest to him, as this encounter happened, and she prayed it was enough to conceal her identity. With an expression of dread, she uttered her excuse to exit the room, being very careful to use French with her best accent. "Sir, please excuse me. I'm afraid that I am not feeling well." Her back was now entirely turned toward Edward, and Tori had no intention of facing the man and his scrutiny again. Had he recognized her? She couldn't tell and was not about to wait and see. Everything had happened so fast, and her mind raced with the thought that maybe, the bastard only got a glance of her face, and that was not enough for him to realize who she was. Either way, she had to get out of there.

J.D., who had overheard Tori's exclamation, was looking more than concerned when she excused herself and all but ran out of the room. He quickly recovered his wits, though, as pregnant women's actions were never explained and always odd. He understood this, but did the fine gentleman? J.D. returned to Edward, who was standing with a puzzled expression, to assure him that his actions had in no way led to the departure of Laffite's wife. "If you will excuse me, Monsieur. I must go and locate her husband, to let him know that his wife has become faint. I assure you it is most unlike her to be so ill-disposed, and I do hope you take no offense. Pregnant women are a puzzle, are they not?"

"Indeed, Monsieur Destrehan, please do not let me delay you. I fully understand."

J.D. nodded his head and left to look for Jean. The gentleman had been very understanding, and he made a mental note to learn just who the stranger was and who had escorted him. Right then, though, finding Jean was his utmost priority.

For Tori, the stairs were a lot easier going up than down, and it was only minutes before she found her room and rushed inside, locking the door behind her. Edward Duval was here at their party! How long had he been watching her? Damn him! Did he know who she was? How could he not? She had panicked and run, but what choice did she have? Anytime now, they could come for her to take her away. Would Jean be able to prevent it? Would it be his friend Jacques Villere, who would come to escort her to prison? After all, Jean had explained that Jacques had begun a group very much like Tori's modern-day police force. He had done this after the horrible slave revolt. He thought it to be a grand idea, and Jean had agreed. Bet he wouldn't feel quite the same when those same men came to collect her. Lord, such an embarrassment it would be for J.D. and Marie, not to mention, for Jean himself. How could she deny anything, with Edward accusing her? He was the brother of one of the most influential plantation owners along the river, and they would listen to every word the bastard Edward had to say. It was a nightmare, and Tori knew she was in deep trouble, with no way out!

With her back leaning against the door, she stood waiting to see what would happen. Tears of terror slipped down her face as she covered her eyes with trembling hands. The terrified woman hardly noticed that she was shaking violently. One thing she did notice after a few minutes was that her hands were resting on her stomach, as the thought of protecting her child was overtaking her own need for self-preservation. What was taking Jean so long? Why was he not with her, helping her to escape? She had to get to safety and protect the baby. Sitting in jail, pregnant, would not be good. Did they hang women who were carrying a child? Shit, they chopped off heads for far less than murder. Heaven help her, the baby, and Jean; they did not deserve this.

Tori turned her head to the side and placed her ear on the wooden door to see if she could hear anything. Too much time was slipping by, and nothing was happening. Had Edward approached Jean already, and was he in the process of telling the pirate that his so-called wife was wanted for murder? Maybe the dandy was explaining everything he knew to J.D. and Marie. If so, was he doing so discreetly, or was he creating a scene like that Simone bitch? Oh, that bitch, she was going to relish this piece of news, there was no doubt in her mind on that.

SIMONE had been sitting with her husband when she witnessed the strange confrontation that had just taken place. Just who was that man, and why had Victoria acted so oddly? She had seen the panic written all too clearly on her face as she fled the room. It was very unlike Laffite's wife to act so, and again, she asked herself, why had the woman acted so rash? Could it be that Jean's wife was ill and feared making a spectacle of herself, or was it something more? She would have to leave her husband's side to investigate, for instinctively, the conniving Simone knew it was imperative she learn all the details before jumping to any conclusion. "You will excuse me, my love? I have just seen someone who I really should not ignore. To do so would be most impolite." She patted his hand and then leaned down and kissed him lightly on his forehead. "Just remain here, and I will return shortly, my dearest."

"You go ahead, my darling. I believe coming down here from the parlor has taken its toll. You are young and should enjoy the evening. I shall sit a spell and enjoy watching you dance."

Simone's husband smiled up into his beautiful young wife's face. He was so proud of her; how could he possibly deny her mixing with the guests? After all, it was him that she always came back to; it was him she loved, and always, she was so devoted to his needs. Nodding his approval, he let her leave.

Quickly Simone made her way over to the punch bowl, where the stranger was helping himself to another glass of champagne. "Excuse me, Monsieur, but could I possibly impose on such a fine gentleman as yourself, to come to a lady's aid? It seems as though my glass was misplaced, and I am in desperate need to quench my thirst."

Edward turned to look at the woman who had made the request, and he was not disappointed. Standing before him was the most desirable female he had seen in quite some time. If he played his cards right, the evening would not be so dull after all, he told himself. "The pleasure is mine, I assure you. May I present myself. Monsieur Edward Duval, your humble servant, Madame. You will, I hope, call me Edward?" He had turned on all his charm, and why not? She was a ravishing creature, who it seemed was extremely interested in him.

Simone laughed inside. Men, even this one, were so easily manipulated when their attentions were not averted, by the likes of Laffite's wife. "Why certainly, Edward. I would be delighted to call you by your given name. That is if you will consent to call me, Simone?" She was pouring on all the charm she could, and it was working. The vixen was using her eyes seductively and touching his hand, stroking it lightly as she spoke. With her husband sitting directly behind her, all he could discern from his point of view, was his wife having a polite conversation. She was free to continue her provocative actions without fear of Adrian realizing what she was up to.

Not a single detail of her forward and brazen attention went unnoticed by Edward, who was now glad that he had come to the party. Indeed, he was delighted, as it seemed the evening was going to be far from a loss, as he had thought it would be just seconds ago. Of course, he had come to meet the lady, who all of New Orleans was talking about and calling the most beautiful, and he had to agree she was that. Even pregnant. Edward had found her extremely enchanting. Pregnant was not a condition he would ever have thought could draw his attention, let alone be agreeable, but then she was not yet so heavy with child as to look revolting. No, he had found her far from that, and it puzzled him. Ah, but even more, she had seemed awfully familiar. That's why he had approached her, to be introduced and to see her up close. There was something about her that kept pulling at the recesses of his inebriated brain. She resembled someone he knew, but who?

It was exasperating, and had he been sober, he was confident he would have recalled that which puzzled him. If only he'd had the opportunity to spend time conversing with her, the woman's identity most assuredly would have come to mind. Right then, however, what did it matter? Here, he was talking with a woman in need of attention. Besides, Laffite's wife was off-limits to him. Edward, like everyone, knew better than to be on the wrong side of either of the Laffite brothers. However, this extraordinary creature, standing next to him, was not off-limits and making matters better; she was all but throwing herself at him. It was true; she had an invalid husband, sitting not too far behind them, invalid, being the optimum word. Edward smiled in the old man's direction and bowed his head slightly in recognition. The frail old fool did the same, a clear indication that he did not worry about his young wife conversing with him. Edward smirked inwardly. An aged man like him would present no challenge. The husband merely had to be treated like a gentleman and manipulated into thinking that his wife's friendship with him was nothing more than platonic. The dandy's intentions, however, were far from platonic. Simone was fascinating, very desirable, and all but asking him to pay more attention to her. He would think about Victoria Laffite another time. Right now, he had to allow himself the time and concentration to get to know this Simone better because if he was reading her correctly and he was seldom wrong, he would soon get to know her intimately.

JEAN could hear Tori crying and had tried several times to get her to unlock the door and let him in. With no response coming from within the room, he was getting more worried as time slipped by. Not knowing what else to do, Jean raised his fist and beat on the door, demanding that she let him enter. He added, if she did not, he would be forced to break it down.

Upon this demand, Tori, in a daze, opened the door, fully expecting to find the rest of the guests standing behind him, just waiting to bring her to justice. It was when she saw he was standing alone that she allowed herself to fall into his arms sobbing.

Jean was horrified by her lack of composure and the terror in her eyes. "My God! Look at you. What in God's name is wrong? J.D. said you ran from the room and that you were not feeling well. Is it the baby? Are you ill? Are you in need of the doctor?" He put his arms around his wife and held her close. As he did so, she collapsed further into his embrace, sobbing, while trying to tell him all at once what had happened.

Jean could not understand much of what she was saying and knew that he had better calm her down if he were going too. Whatever had upset her must be severe, and he needed to know what it was, to help her. "Tori, listen to me. This is not doing you or the baby any good. Calm down, please, for both of your sakes. I am here, and I won't let anything happen to you. Listen to me. You have to help me understand, just what it is that has you so upset." He held her at arm's length and softly added, "You have to gain control of yourself." Then he pulled her back into his embrace and waited.

Tori took in long, ragged breaths and slowly stopped crying. He was with her now, and he'd save her. It was true; her Jean would not let anything happen. 'I have to tell him now.' "Edward...Edward." That was the only word she could trust herself to say clearly, and even then, she had stammered over it.

Had he heard her correctly? He knew that name and what it meant, but he needed to find out more. Jean continued to hold her, not saying a word. He understood that when she was ready, she would tell him what he needed to know.

"Edward Duval is downstairs, and I'm sure he recognized me." She had spoken just above a whisper. Then feeling stronger with Jean holding her, she spoke louder. "Jean, do you understand what

I'm telling you? He is here!" She pulled away from his embrace and took a step backward. "He will tell everyone who I am, and then they will have no choice but to come and get me. We must get out of here. You have to get me away fast." Tori had almost screamed this last statement at him, and before he could say anything in response, his wife threw her arms around his neck, pleading with him. "Jean, I did not kill Kate; you know that. I admit I killed the bastard Kane, but I had no choice. It was self-defense, and I had to help Kate. No one else will believe me. Edward will make sure his story is the one told and believed. Oh, God. You do trust me, don't you? You believe me, right?"

Jean was stunned. The fact that this Edward character was here, let alone had gotten so close to her, frightened even him. He had been so stupid letting the deadly situation go on as it had. Not dealing with the bastard before now was proving to be a huge mistake. Right at this moment, however, he had to keep his wife calm and find out just what the swine was up too. "Of course, I believe you and let me put your mind at ease. I doubt that the bastard knows who you are, or he would have done something by now. He has not, and that indicates he maybe did not recognize you. Did you speak with him?"

"Shit no. Are you crazy? No, I ran."

"Then I am sure he is not certain who you are or who he thinks you might be. If he does send for you, he will have a hard time proving his story against yours. You are my wife and among friends here, remember? You look nothing like the Tori I found hidden on my ship. You are of noble blood, from France, remember?" He raised her face to look into his. "Look, I shall go downstairs and see what I can learn. You stay here and rest. Try not to worry; no one is taking you anywhere. When I come back up, it should be with good news."

Tori only nodded her head. She had the awful feeling that the good life was over. That from now on, she would have to fight for her survival. The distraught woman watched as her husband left

261

and did not miss the worried expression on his face, or the fact that he had picked up a small derringer and slipped it into his coat pocket. Again, she placed her hands over her stomach as she sat down to wait because there was nothing more she could do at that moment.

Time seemed to drag by very slowly. Tori had no idea what was happening downstairs. The only sound she could hear when she cracked the door open was people having a grand time, laughing, and carrying on as if nothing was wrong. When at last Jean walked in, she ran to him, demanding to know every detail.

"There is not much to tell. I went down and looked everywhere. It appears our guest left sometime after you came up here. He either did not know who you were or he left knowing. If it is the latter, he may be trying to decide what to do with the knowledge. I even inquired about him to J.D. as I wished to thank the man for aiding you. Seemed like a logical idea and a good excuse that would not raise suspicion. Not that it mattered much. J.D. has not had the pleasure of being introduced to our Edward. He had no idea who he came with even. My guess is he arrived uninvited, why, we can only guess."

Tori was very worried. "Well, I guess it was to meet me. If that's the reason, then all we can do now is play the waiting game. Wait to see what he does next, that is. What can I do other than that? Running away tonight is one option, but you won't do that, will you?"

"My love, trust me. I won't let that bastard near you again. Let us forget him for now. He is gone, and you are here, safe with me. I do have some good news to cheer you up." The twinkle in his sparkling eyes told her that it must be something she was going to like, and lord knew she needed something to cheer her up.

"Seems that Simone got tired of the party, and she and her husband have left for home."

"Weren't they to stay over? With Adrian's fragile health and the long drive back to the city, I thought surely they would be..."

"Not such a long drive. Adrian has a place not far from here."

"But I don't get it; she told everyone she was staying over."

"That's what I thought." His face held a puzzled appearance for a few seconds. "It seems that the lady changed her mind. Anyway, you won't have to face her sharp tongue in the morning. I think she lost her courage to remain here with you."

Tori frowned, and then, seeing the concern on Jean's face, she forced a more quizzical expression into her eyes. "I don't understand why she was invited in the first place. Marie knows how uncomfortable that woman makes me."

"Marie, in most likelihood, was not the one who offered the invite. It would have been J.D. who asked Adrian. He has remained a friend, even after the fool married Simone. I, however, think Simone has met her match, you little minx. She could no longer stay under the same roof as you, let alone remain as a guest. The woman can't compete with you, and she knows it."

Tori was glad that the bitch had been chased off. If being the center of attention was not hers, it made sense that she would have snuck away. This image made her smile. Feeling a bit more secure, Tori also decided to try and not worry about Edward because there was nothing she could do about him. It stood to reason; he had not put two and two together. If he had, Jean would handle it, but it was how he would do that exactly that worried her, though. "You know, it's a hell of a way to start off our child's life, isn't it? I mean, this should be a good year for you. It's 1811, the year you become a father. I'm sorry Jean, I have messed it all up, haven't I?"

"You have done nothing but bring me joy. Did we not have a wonderful Christmas together at Grand Terre? Then, New Year's night, it was the first I have celebrated in years. The celebration of the New Year was symbolic of the beginning of our new life together. Of the joy that awaits us in the birth of our child. This will be a great year. If it makes you feel any better, I have a man already checking into this Duval character and the whole damn mess that happened at the Duval plantation. I did not push him hard enough. When we get back to the city, we should have some answers waiting, and if not, I know who can acquire what we need—enough talk for now. You need your rest, and I will go down and let Marie and J.D. know that you are doing better. They will only worry if I don't. Everyone will understand why my wife is indisposed."

Tori lay in bed for a while, wondering what was going to happen in the months ahead, and just before she fell asleep, her last thoughts were not of Edward or Jean, but of a lake, home, and safety.

# ❧ Four ❧

L ess than a week later, Tori found herself situated safely back in the townhouse. Afraid of running into Edward, however she refused to go out. Jean had not forced her to leave their home and agreed that they should remain secluded until they learned more about the dandy and his intentions. Then one morning, Jean announced that he had someone he wanted her to meet, and he insisted she do so, regardless of her fears.

"He's a close friend of mine, even if he is an American," Jean laughed. Then more seriously, he continued, "He is also my attorney, a small fact that very few people in this fair city are aware of at this time, and I prefer to keep it as such."

By his tone, Tori knew this information was to be kept confidential, and she wondered just who this American man was?

"He is here with some rather interesting news for us. I would say, mostly for you."

By the smile on his face, the news obviously was going to be good, so Tori took his arm without any hesitation and let him escort her into his study, where the mystery man was seated, waiting for them.

Jean proudly spoke before the man even had time to stand. "John, let me introduce you to my lovely wife, Victoria."

Instantly a very well-dressed man rose to his feet and held out his hand. He was about the same height as Jean, and his hair was just a slight shade lighter. It was trimmed shorter, and he had no facial hair. His sideburns were long but not overdone, and like Jean, his boots shone like brand new. His brown eyes locked with hers, and his gaze had a sincere expression about it. Then the American smiled as he spoke. "Madame, Mr. John Grymes, at your service, and, I must say, it is a great pleasure to have the opportunity to make your acquaintance finally. Please do call me John. Mr. Grymes sounds too formal for friends, does it not?"

Tori took his hand and shook it. His grip was firm but gentle, and his accent was one that she recognized. There was no hint of French, no southern drawl. This unexpected circumstance had her smiling broadly. Standing before her was the first all-American to visit them in their home, and Tori was pleased he had.

Grymes let go of her hand but hastily continued, not allowing her a moment to get a word in edgeways. "I am of the understanding that you have had a certain, ah, shall we say, misunderstanding hanging over your head?"

Tori's eyes flashed in Jean's direction. It was a questioning expression that he saw, with just a hint of fear. "It's safe, Tori. I trust John, and so should you. He is aware of all the details behind Kate and Kane's murders and Edward's involvement."

"I seriously doubt that Jean, and do you realize you just called me Tori?"

John interrupted. "Begging your pardon Tori, but I can assure you, I most certainly am fully aware of all the sordid details, along with details as to your preferred name, which I have to agree, is most unusual and could pose a problem if used in public. Now then, as we have cleared the issue pertaining to your name, let me begin. In my humble opinion, the actions taken by Edward were most deplorable. The outcome of which created a set of circumstances, both utterly appalling and beyond reproach. Furthermore, if I might be allowed to say, it has been a very trying and arduous matter to investigate. I can tell you both; I offer my sincere apology that it has taken so long, but one has to be certain of all the facts before presenting them. Now, if we can take a seat, I will attempt to put the whole ugly matter to rest."

Gradually they began to piece the puzzle together as to what happened after Kate's death. John had been able to quietly investigate the murders, and what he learned was fascinating in his opinion. In the first place, Tori learned she was not wanted for murder, nor had she ever been.

"It would seem that this Mr. Duval, that's Edward of course, not his brother Leone, kept you both ignorant and misinformed about the charges. We can only assume that he had selfish reasons for carrying out such a despicable act. Now, this is how I see it. You may have to answer some questions as to what happened that day, and it could get a little uncomfortable. I mean, it would become your word against this fellow Edward's, especially if he chose to continue with his vile concoctions. Therefore, my dear, it is our consensus," he nodded his head in Jean's direction, indicating that he was the other person he referred to when he used 'our'. "To avoid any further incriminations, that you meet with one Mr. Leone Duval first." He mumbled the next statement to no one in particular. "Damn decent chap Leone, known him for years." Then John looked directly toward Tori. "Such a damn shame, pardon my language, Ma'am. This ugly situation just sits wrong with me. I can assure you Edward is nothing like his upstanding brother. Edward is the black sheep of the family, in more ways than one, as I am certain you are aware."

The room was quiet, and to Tori, it seemed as if they were waiting for her answer. The men were waiting for her to decide, and to Laffite's wife, it seemed she needed to do so right then. Should she face the bastard Edward and tell her version or not? Or should she meet with Leone first? Her head was swimming with questions, and things were moving too fast. In her mind, there was only one thing to do; she needed to slow the process down. "You are correct; to my friends, it's Tori, my name that is. Just thought I would clear that up first. It is short for Victoria. Please, do continue to call me Tori or should he call me Victoria?" She looked at Jean, who cocked his head to one side, thinking.

John did not wait for him to express his thoughts on the matter and continued with his statement. "As I was saying, about that brother of Leone's, he is an embarrassment to their family name. Anyway, back to the point. You would discuss with Leone the matter of what happened that fateful day. It should shed some light on one or two rather troubling questions. Once that is accomplished, then, if this Edward decides to pursue the matter, one visit from me should put a stop to any inclinations the swine, beg your pardon, might have of blackmail or the like."

Tori had listened carefully to this last bit of information. She knew that Jean would not have chosen just anyone to defend her. He would only have the best that there was. This man standing before her was more than just an employee of Jean's; John Grymes was a trusted friend. Jean had introduced him as a friend first, and he chose his friends carefully. Her fate sat firmly in the hands of these two, and apparently, they had discussed it thoroughly. Tori just wanted to hear it from Jean before giving them the go-ahead.

"Do you think it's a good idea, Jean? I mean, he could ask a lot of questions that I will have some difficulty answering if you understand me? Do I tell him everything?"

"My love, it seems to me the question is, how do you feel about him? You know this man, and I do not. All I know is what John here has told me. John holds him in high standing, something that puts him in a trusted light." His top lip twitched as he half-smiled. "What do we have to lose? As I see it, we have no choice, do we?"

Grymes slapped his knee and stood up. "It's settled then. You will meet with him, correct?"

Tori looked at John and spoke affirmatively. "Yes, John, I guess I must, for more reasons than just trying to protect myself. I have always felt that I owed Leone an explanation about what happened. Meeting him will give me the chance to do just that. I guess the only thing left to do now is to tell me where and when this meeting will take place."

"That is the easy part, my dear. The man is, at this very moment, outside this very establishment. Leone is sitting in my carriage. He is waiting for me to finish up a small piece of urgent business before we attend a luncheon together. You see, my dear, he, like Jean, is also a client of mine, as well as a dear friend. Has been for years, come to think of it. That is how I was able to arrange these circumstances. I was able to explain that while we were on our way to lunch, I had to stop here. Rather convenient, don't you think? It seemed to me that you would concur with my findings, and so, Ma'am, I mean Tori, if you would like, we might get this meeting over with. Shall I send for him?"

Tori looked at Jean and then down at the floor. Things were moving so fast. What would she say to Leone, and how? One thing was evident, though; putting off the inevitable would not make it any easier, something that Jean and Mr. Grymes must have known she might do if given the opportunity. Why else would they have arranged it this way? She took a deep breath. "Might as well get it over with then," she said, looking toward Jean. "You will stay with me, won't you?"

"Now, where else would I go? I intend to be right by your side, so don't worry. John here seems to feel that this fellow is of a decent sort, much like you do. I think we will find an ally in Leone Duval."

Grymes broke into their conversation while walking toward the door, "My thoughts exactly." He stopped and looked back at them both. "The only way I see it is that to beat this Edward at his own game, we have to stay a step ahead. Take the wind out of his sails before he even gets going." He was all but laughing. "Fancy me trying to tell you how to navigate a plan. I think it better if I stay with land-locked terms." He left the room in good humor, still mumbling. Mr. John Grymes, it seemed, was enjoying himself and not in the least bit worried.

THE room fell silent as the two of them waited for his return. Tori was trying desperately to make up a speech, explaining to Leone what had happened and why she had not attempted to reach him until now.

Jean paced the floor. He was going over every possible conse-quences of what they were about to do. Once Leone saw Tori, she would lose her identity as Victoria. They would be at Leone's mercy, as well as that of his brother. His only hope lay in John and Tori's judgment of the man's character.

The men's voices sounded as they approached, and both Jean and Tori heard Grymes before they saw him. "Just thought it would be nice if you could step in and meet them both. Such good friends of mine; the least I can do. Sort of make amends for delaying our luncheon so long."

Jean turned and faced the open door as he walked back and forth. He usually never showed his emotions, but this was different, and he was concerned. So much could go wrong, and he did not like not being in control. It was too late to prevent the meeting, but he could stand between his wife and the man who would hold her future in his hands.

"Here we are, Mr. Laffite, may I present to you, my trusted friend, Monsieur Leone Duval."

Jean's pacing around the room had placed him between Leone and Tori. So, Leone stepped forward until he stood a few feet in front of Laffite, rather than approach the female first, who he had not seen. The Creole bowed from the waist as did Jean, and ever vigilant, Laffite observed the man carefully trying to sum him up. Leone had looked him directly in the eyes, a positive trait as far as he was concerned. If first impressions counted, and for him they did, then he knew he liked what he saw.

"A pleasure to meet you." Jean had spoken in English, and if this surprised Leone, he did not show it. "John has spoken highly of you and your friendship. Now, if you will allow me." Jean escorted him to where Tori was standing, and as the two came face to face, his arm slipped protectively around his wife's waist. "Monsieur Duval, may I introduce my wife, Victoria."

Leone took her hand and lightly kissed the back, all the time looking strangely at her face.

"Is something wrong?" Tori had spoken the words slowly and directly. She did not avoid his scrutiny because to try to avoid him now would be senseless. Still, she did not want to alarm him by saying something stupid like 'Hi there, remember me?'

Leone could not be sure; he rubbed his temples as if to clear the images he had in his mind. "Please forgive a foolish man his manners. I do not generally stare at someone in such a blatant way, as to cause them embarrassment."

"Especially when their husbands are so close at hand," added Jean. He was trying to make light of the situation, something that John picked up on.

"I would say not! Especially when that husband is Jean Laffite, the notorious pirate. It would most certainly not be a wise move?" He laughed and looked at Jean's stern face. "It is what some of the honest citizens of the city are calling you, you know? Your reputation is that of a gentleman pirate if that helps any. As if such could exist, I ask you? The two are complete opposites of each other. gentleman and pirate, that is. You are either one or the other. I shall, therefore, cover all my options and choose to remain on your good terms by not choosing." Everyone laughed, and the room took on a less stressful atmosphere.

It was Leone, however, who interrupted the light-hearted moment. "I feel I should explain my behavior before your husband calls me out. It is just that you remind me of someone who was once very dear to me. Madame Laffite, you look so very much like her, sound like her. It is as if I stand before the very woman, I had thought lost to me. The resemblance is, to say the least, quite remarkable."

The sadness in his eyes hurt her, and she could not delay telling him who she was any longer; it was too cruel. But how was she to tell him, she wondered? Then before Tori knew what was happening, the words started flowing. "I am known as Victoria to most, but to a few, I am Tori. You are right, Leone. Your eyes do not deceive you. It is me."

Leone froze. The stunned look on his face remained, as he turned toward John. "John, I think you had best explain what's going on here. This is not just a chance meeting, is it?"

Tori could hear the anger in his tone of voice. They should

271

have told him whom he was to meet, not spring it on him as they had. Still, what was done was done. She would have to make him realize that John was not the only one responsible for this blunder. "Forgive me, Leone. It's not how it looks. Our actions are not a cruel joke played for our amusement. John is our friend, and we have asked for this meeting for a particularly good reason. Please, give us...allow me a chance to explain. Join us for lunch, and we will tell you everything?"

Tori had reached out her hand to Leone, and when she touched him, he thought he would die. His Tori was alive! Very much alive, and nothing else mattered. His anger was quickly overshadowed, by the sheer joy of this knowledge, followed immediately by curiosity.

OVER the next few hours, Jean and Tori decided to take Leone and Jean's attorney, Grymes, into their full confidence. They could see no other way around the problem of answering all the questions that arose. In order to be protected, she had to be believed and to do that; the truth had to come out, all of it. So it was, after many hours of discussion, the room was still, and the four of them sat silently looking at one another.

It was Tori who finally broke the silence. "Leone, do you see now why I had to keep the truth from you about where I came from? You're having a hard time believing me this very minute. If I had told you the whole story back then, you would never have believed me, would you?"

"Tori, you should have trusted me. I wish you had. Never would I have let anything happen to you. I admit that I might not have believed you at first, but you seem to have won over quite a few intelligent people with your account. You would have convinced me in time...your physical appearance alone, the change would have accomplished that by itself in due course. One just can't go from, forgive me, my dear, black to white. Here, you sit before me, with proof my eyes cannot deny. Your skin color, it is many, shades lighter and your hair, it too has changed. I would have had no choice but to believe you." Leone rubbed his brow and spoke softly. "I had strong feelings toward you. You knew that. I still do, I must admit. But, seeing you here with Jean, as his wife, even a blind old fool, can see you are happy, not to mention carrying his child. It would never have been the same for us, would it?" He stood and walked towards the French doors, his back toward them. "Please forgive me for rambling on and on. It's just been a shock seeing you again and finally learning what occurred on the plantation. Not knowing what happened to you, that was the hardest, you know? But now, finding out that my brother had a big hand in the whole damnable mess, well, it is unforgivable. I shall give you all assistance you might ask of me. But never will I find it in my heart to forgive Edward for what he has done!"

"I take it then that you believe me?" Tori's face expressed relief and joy, as she felt she already knew his answer.

He turned to face them. "You know that I believe you, but I have to tell you on this matter of time travel, I'm having some difficulty. It does take some getting used too, regardless of the undeniable proof. We will have so much to discuss. There is so much I would like to know. Ah, I have jumped ahead of myself yet again. If I am allowed to pay you and your husband, visits in the future, as a friend to both of you, that is, then maybe we can talk."

"Of course, you may," Tori said, smiling. She knew that Jean would not mind, as he had taken her hand in his and nodded his approval. "But, be warned, I may not answer all your questions. Some things should remain untold. I don't want to have the responsibility of having changed anything. Just coming here to your time, I have done enough of that already, I fear. If not for me, Missy, Kate, and Kane would still be alive."

"Who is to say? You may well have been destined to come here, my dear. I just wish I had known. I could have helped you. I feel it's my fault that you had to suffer so. I have always felt Edward knew more than he let on about Kate's death and your disappearance.

Now, I know for certain. I can't say that I am sorry that the beast I had working for me is dead. Beast is the only way I will ever refer to that nasty piece of work after what I learned about him and his actions." He walked over to Tori and sat next to her, looking directly into her eyes. "However, it does seem clear to me that the only one who could have killed Kate would have been Kane. You were close to my Kate, and that fact was undeniable. What you did to the overseer is forgivable and understandable. You are not to blame. What my brother did was despicable. Even if he thought you had a hand in Kate's death, it did not give him the right to act so. I greatly fear, knowing him as I do, he felt no lasting remorse over Kate's demise. He thought only to hurt me, and to do that, he tried to manipulate your life through lies and intimidation. That, my dear, is the lowest; and for his actions, I apologize. I give you my word that he will harm you no more. Indeed, he will pay for his actions!"

Leone was angry and hurt, and it was evident to all, he was far too emotional to think rationally. John had to act quickly for all their sakes. "Now, the way I see it, we have to proceed carefully. The law would be on Edward's side at the moment. It would be his word against Tori's and forgive me, my dear, but your story would not hold up too well in a court of law. Many in town would also see this situation as a golden opportunity, a chance to strike at Jean. That Claiborne, for one, dying to get on the merchant's good list. Using you would be a way to blacken Jean's reputation, and we simply can't have a client of mine lose his hard-earned standing, now can we? Not good for business or New Orleans. No, I think it best, Leone, if none of us says or does anything for the moment. Just sit and wait a while. See what young Edwards going to do next. We are not even certain he recognized Tori. You, Jean, had doubts about that. No, we wait, hold our information and let him make the next move. Rather like a good game of cards, wouldn't you say?"

Leone shook his head. He knew his brother too well and knew that the time to strike was now, or he might very well harm the

274

one woman that still meant so much to him. Even if Tori could never be his, Leone would see to it that she stayed happy and free. He could always admire her from a distance and be there for her and her husband. He intended to remain a part of her life of both their lives, and no one, was going to prevent that, especially not his brother.

He spun around and looked at the men. "No, I firmly disagree! Let me face him as soon as possible. He must be stopped!" He then looked directly at Tori, speaking softly but firmly. "I am confident he knows just who you are my dear, and knowing him as I do, he will try to use the information for his own gain. This emotional blackmail has to stop and stop now! He slammed one fist into the other. "I will put the fear of God into him, along with the law." He looked at John, and turning his attention to Jean, said, "Not to mention Jean here. Your reputation is well known and feared, as much as it is respected. Together, this matter can be handled discreetly and admirably, which is far from what I am feeling or wanting to do to Edward at this very moment."

Tori smiled as the three men nodded their heads in agreement. She did not doubt that it was Edward who was in trouble now and not her.

Grymes looked at Jean and grinned. "May I suggest a bottle of your finest. I always work best under pressure and with a good drink."

"I would never have guessed," laughed Jean. "I shall see to it immediately."

"Very thoughtful of you. I have to let you know that I don't have another meeting, that as of now, requires my attention, but I do have time to sample your best."

"You always have done," chuckled Jean.

As the four of them began to make a plan of action, across town in another grand townhouse, two figures frolicked in bed, enjoying each other and the pleasures that they shared. Edward had found a dream come true. His luck, it seemed, was about to change. Indeed, in his mind right then, it had already begun to do so, for in his arms, was what he considered the ultimate catch. She was going to be the answer to all his financial problems. Simone was not too young, a few years younger than himself, and that suited him. The Latin beauty was stunning to look at, and she was married to a dying old fool. A rich sick old fool and far more affluent than Leone would ever be. Looking at the woman he now held, Edward knew he would tell her anything to keep her. The dandy would even tell her he loved her when the truth was; he did not. She never had to know his feelings; no one did, and he liked it that way. Keeping secrets had always worked in his favor, and to change that now would be stupid, he thought. If this female knew him, really understood his intentions, he'd run the risk of her slipping through his grasp.

Duval understood just what kind of a female she was; Simone was a cunning manipulator who was self-centered and vengeful. She was very much like him in many of those aspects. That, however, was just where the similarities stopped. Unlike him, she needed and desired attention, to feel loved and wanted by all. Slyly he grinned to himself. He was excellent at knowing what to say and saying it persuasively.

Edward realized that no matter what, he was not about to let this new golden opportunity escape. Besides, the way her husband was failing, she would undoubtedly be a very wealthy widow in the foreseeable future, and he, Edward Duval, would be there to console her. He would, of course, have to give her time to grieve. Not too long, though, just a long enough period, to be considered respectable. Then he would make her Madame Duval. By doing that, they both stood to gain what they wanted. Simone would gain respectability and the attention she craved, and he would want for nothing. Her money would be more than ample enough to live on, to gamble, and enjoy the lifestyle of the grand plantation owner. It would be his, all of it without any tedious work or an overpowering big brother telling him what to do.

Edward looked at her lying beside him. Ah, to have a woman such as this to come home to every night. She was a vixen in bed and a woman whose station in life was admired and respected. The soon-to-be-widow was also just weak enough that he knew he could keep her in place if needed, unlike that Tori bitch. He frowned as he thought of his brother's lost lover.

Yes, he had remembered who Victoria Laffite was. There was no doubt in his mind. How she had managed to get where she was, married to Jean Laffite and loved by all of New Orleans society, was beyond him though? Then there was that other puzzling matter, the color of her skin; she almost looked white. There could only be one explanation for that. It was said that Marie Laveau had dressed her hair for the ball, and no doubt she'd given the fancy's hair its longer and straighter appearance. The talented woman had to have found a way to bleach her darker complexion too. Yes, Marie was well known for her voodoo magic, and no doubt it was voodoo that had something to do with the fancy's new persona. For a moment, he shivered at the very idea of such mysterious powers, but powers could be worked around, and Tori's defeat would most certainly be his victory.

The dandy understood that he would have to move slowly and very carefully for his plan to work. He also knew in time, and with Simone's help, he would succeed. Just as he had succeeded in his plans to destroy any happiness, his brother had hoped to have.

Edward was proud of how he had manipulated Leone, who was still grieving the loss of his fancy wench. It had given him great pleasure to keep the man's grief alive. Not only did his brother suffer, but because he felt obligated to his younger sibling for helping him search for Tori, he often, and without hesitation, gave him hefty advances on his monthly allowance. Stupid fool that he was, how easy it had been to convince him that he, Edward Duval, was searching for the whore, to return her to Leone's waiting bed.

A smirk tugged at his lips as he recalled that his brother thought his constant visits to the plantation were merely to see how he was fairing, to give him updates and support him in his time of need; stupid idiot. He went only to gloat, to witness his brother's misery, and collect his much-needed funds, money that he shortly would no longer need.

Edward reached over and let his hand lightly rub the woman's back as he continued to make plans. Once he got hold of that bitch, Tori, he would kill her if things got messy. Then Simone, the woman who had slept with the pirate, and lost him to the whore, would be happy. She would be so thankful to him for helping her achieve her revenge that she would show her gratitude. Edward grit his teeth and smirked. He understood only too well that the higher society knew of Simone's dislike of Laffite's wife. It was also evident that what they couldn't understand was why? He was the only person who could, and it was going to remain that way. He'd keep her secret, and she'd keep his. They were the perfect match. Smiling at her now, he reached up and pushed back the woman's long dark hair. She was beautiful. How the fool Laffite could let her go was beyond him, but Laffite's mistake was his gain, and anyway, Laffite already had enough power and money. Now, it was his turn to have both.

"What are you thinking about, Edward?" Simone slowly opened her eyes to look at him. "You seem to be miles away from here. Do I bore you?"

"How could you think such a thing? Your beauty takes my breath away. I was thinking, without you, it would be the end of my life. I love you so, my dear Simone, and I know you were meant for me from the first moment my eyes beheld the vision that you are. For me, you are a goddess. I can bring you such joy, if only you let me. Such a small price to pay for happiness." His mouth covered hers before she could answer him, and the passion with which he kissed was no act. It was a real passion, driven by his lust for wealth and power but not from undying love as he led her to think.

Simone moaned and artfully went through their lovemaking as

if the man were everything she desired. "You can't mean what you say, I can't believe you," she softly spoke as he placed one kiss after another down her side. He was so wrapped up in his own pleasure that he did not notice her coolness. "You declare you love me? Then show me. I mean, really show me."

True, when his mind was not elsewhere, and he paid more attention to her needs instead of his own, he was most excellent in bed, but his mind had drifted to other matters. This was a situation that Simone wanted changed, so seizing the opportunity, she had spoken up. A perverted sexual hunger drove her, and for the moment, the dandy could satisfy her needs if he paid attention.

"I will," he spoke, making sure she felt his hot breath was against her hip. "I speak the truth; I love every part of you."

Simone looked away from him. The stupid fool had declared his love for her like she didn't know it was her wealth he was chasing after. How easy he was to see through; how easy to control. The Spanish beauty dug her nails into his back, and in return, he bit her hard on her thigh.

Simone had found Edward was a perfect lover, but he was not Jean. No one could ever be Jean or take his place. The one person she wanted more than any other in her life had been stolen from her. Victoria! What a lie. Edward had told her everything that first night when they had been together at her husband's plantation house. While her husband slept upstairs drugged by his medication and brandy, she had let her new conquest in. They had made such love that night, and in the heat of his passion, Edward had talked, the fool. The dandy had spilled it all before he passed out. Ever since then, Simone had been obsessed with just how she was going to use the information. Even right then, she did not know yet how to go about implementing such powerful knowledge. What she did know however, was that she would keep using this fool. Edward helped fill her lonely nights and feed her sexual hunger as he was doing right then. More than that, he could help her to either get Jean back or destroy him. If she could not have the pirate, then no one would. Simone wanted Jean, and Edward wanted that Tori bitch. If she was careful, they both might get what they wanted.

A sharp pain raced up her thigh, bringing her attention back to her lover. He always instinctively seemed to know what she wanted. The sadistic side of her enjoyed it when a little bit of pain was added to their lovemaking. No one, not even Jean, had known this about her. This dandy had found out, though, and he applied his skill in the pain department with such finesse. She would miss Edward when she had to end their relationship, and Simone also had no doubt; she would finish it when the time suited her and not the other way around. As for now, she would enjoy herself and hope that her husband would die soon, because she was going to need more freedom to come and go, along with the use of his money. Yes, it was clear she was going to need quite an amount of money if she was going to succeed in her plans. With her husband dead, she'd not have to explain to him where such funds were spent. The old bastard always kept track of his funds. Not for much longer though, Simone told herself, and that thought aroused her.

"Edward, if you bite me one more time, I will have to slap you, and if I do that, you will get angry with me, and then you will have to show me what a naughty girl I have been. Only this time, Edward darling, slap me harder."

A mischievous smile spread across his face as he put his head down and placed his mouth again on her thigh. This afternoon was going to be a lot more fun than he had imagined. Maybe, he would not ignore her after they were married. Perhaps, once she was his, he would start to show her who was in charge of the relationship and use her to his liking whenever he deemed it.

Outside the bedroom door, a man stood silently listening to them, his face was sad, and his heart was broken. He turned and ambled back to his room, using his cane for balance. By the time he had reached his bed, Adrian was beyond hurt; he was consumed with a hateful rage.

Simone's husband sent immediately for his attorney and then

asked to be left alone until the man arrived. He made it clear that he was not to be disturbed, even by his wife. Adrian had told his loyal butler that he was to be kept up to date on his wife's comings and goings. She was not to know that he was spying on her and her lover, so care was needed to not arouse her suspicions. He wanted to discover the identity of the man in her bed and if there were others. The butler happily agreed, as his dislike for the old man's wife had grown over the years. Simone had made his life hell, and now he would do the same to her.

After his butler left him, Adrian had time to sit and think. Simone had made a fatal mistake, Adrian thought. She had threatened his faithful servants to keep her secrets, never thinking he would learn of her real character or evil attentions. He had never wavered in his admiration or his love and never questioned her life or her explanations about where she went or whom she visited. Like today he had been informed, Simone did not want to be disturbed as she was resting. Typically, he would have abided by her wishes, but he had wanted to surprise her with a small token of his love. Looking at the jewels in his hand, the old man dropped them onto the table and slowly walked toward his bed. Their life together had been lies; all lies, he thought angrily.

How many lovers had she taken to her bed as she was doing right then? Adrian looked back at the jewels and spoke allowed. "Why, Simone? Why did you do this to me? I had thought all along that you loved me, that you were actually mine." He sat down heavenly on the side of the bed and looked to the heavens and called out. "By God, you were not mine alone; you never were!" Simone's husband looked at the floor, his eyes brimming with tears. "You lied to me, and now you are in your room, spreading your legs like a common whore." He looked up and talked toward the closed bedroom door. "You are bedding some young man, who no doubt thinks that once I am gone, he will have you and my money." Adrian hit the mattress with his fist. "Hell no! That will never come to pass." He hit the bed several more times with his cane before he tossed it across the room. "It won't happen!" he shouted in a determined voice as a searing pain shot down his arm.

Adrian grabbed at his chest and stood, determined not to let the pain stop him. He stumbled across the room to his small desk and sat in the chair. Slowly his trembling hand reached into the drawer, and he took out a document, which he tore into small pieces. Sheer willpower would keep him alive now, and he knew it. Adrian realized he was close to death, but death would not visit him until he had made a new will. Only then would he allow himself the pleasure of dying.

He was aware that Monsieur Grymes would come as soon as he received word that he had been summoned. The man was reliable, which was a Godsend. He should have listened to his advice years ago when he had drawn up his first will.

Simone's husband looked at the scattered paper about him and frowned. Why had he been so stubborn and not listened to his dear friends? He had been made a fool. They all had to have known what he now knew. All of New Orleans must have been laughing at him and his undying devotion to the bitch he called his devoted wife. His anger was causing considerable pains in his chest, and he cared not. He would show them he was no fool. He knew what had to be done, and by God, he'd do it. Simone was damn lucky he was a God-fearing man, or she'd have found herself destitute upon his demise, and heaven knew the bitch deserved it. Tears of despair rolled down the old man's cheeks as the pain in his chest grew. His young wife was about to learn the hard way, how to pay for her sins. God would reward him for not making the wrong choice. What he was about to do was well within the church's teachings. He was not the one that would be going to hell for his actions, but his so-called wife would be living in a hell she made, long before the real one allowed her entry.

TORI lay in bed, watching Jean as he poured her a cup of black coffee, topping it off with thick whipped cream. This was a treat, one that she felt could be allowed, even if caffeine was not supposed to be consumed by a woman in her condition. One cup, Tori told Jean, would not harm her or the child. Sipping her coffee, she allowed herself to reflect on all that had transpired. Tori was glad that they had invited Leone to dinner last night. It happened when Grymes had been called away on urgent business. Tori had wanted to spend some time with Edward's brother, so she could explain how she felt. It had been very evident to everyone in the room that the man was still in love with her, and she never wanted to hurt him. If not for Grymes leaving, she might not have had the chance to set things right, and then there was the pirate. Jean was so understanding about how Leone was feeling. He had realized the two of them needed time alone and explained to them he'd offered to accompany Pierre to a business meeting. Tori knew, of course, that it was a lie, and she loved him for it. Leone had no clue that Jean was giving them time alone to talk, and that was a good thing because if he had, the plantation owner never would have agreed to remain; he was such a man of principles.

Leone and Tori had spent hours talking and healing. For Leone, it was an extraordinary time, one he would always hold dear. He learned how Kate knew about Tommy before her death, and that pleased him. His housekeeper had died knowing her son had not drowned after all. Leone had not had to explain that he was the boy's father because Tori had also revealed how Kate had confided in her.

Tori's eyes began to tear up as she remembered their night of truths as she'd come to think of it. Talking about Tommy with Leone was difficult, as he had not actually allowed himself to admit that his grief over the boy's loss had been a hard blow. Discussing Kate and Tommy had brought all the sadness back, and the agony filled his face like it threatened to do to hers right then. Still, she had helped Leone in the end, hadn't she?

Tori had decided to reveal what she suspected was true about his son. For Leone, it was both a blessing and again a grave feeling of loss. He understood that his son would forever be beyond his reach. The greatest comfort he had, though, was the knowledge that in Tori's time, his son was a free man.

Laffite's wife remembered what she had done to help ease his pain. In her mind, she recalled each detail again, sure that she had done the right thing and yet wondering and second-guessing her decision. "You see, Leone before I can allow myself to love freely here in this time, I have to know, beyond a shadow of a doubt, that I can never reach my own time again. Only then will I be able to love and live here, free of guilt."

"What guilt can there be? As I see it, you have no need to feel that way, my dear."

"Oh, but I do. My life is not really meant for here. I still have a family who must be so worried. I owe it to them, to try at least once, to get back. Don't you see? I not only let myself down but my family also, if I don't try?"

"So, you will try after the baby is born? You will come to the plantation and the lake?"

"Yes, I will. I have to, and now that you know, I hope you will help me when the time comes."

"You only have to ask. Anything I can do for you, no matter how hard it will be for me, I will do it. You will, of course, be my guest at the plantation, along with Jean and the child. I would have it no other way, and if you should succeed and return to your time, then you have my word as a gentleman and friend that Jean and your child will become my family. Forgive me, but I assume you will be leaving the child here. I am correct, am I not?"

"You are. I have no choice." Her eyes were filling with tears when she had told him her answer.

Quickly, before Jean saw her, she dabbed at them with the end of the bedsheet and forced herself to smile at the next memory that sprang to mind. Leone had responded as only Leone could. He had replied and meant each word of that she was sure. "It is the logical assumption, and knowing you, the only conclusion I could come too. Please, Tori, know I shall stand by them always."

"And, you have my promise that I will talk to Tommy, and he will know about you and Kate."

Jean was dressing, and as was his way, he gazed upon the woman who was his life. Seeing she was deep in thought, he decided to leave her to whatever she was contemplating.

Tori replayed the last part of the conversation she had with Leone, repeatedly in her mind. Jean would not be alone; should she make it back. He would have friends, and he would have their child. Leone would always look after them. There again, if she never went back, her Linni would never know what happened to her. Tori would go on suffering from the knowledge for the rest of her life. She would have to live with the pain of knowing the mystery of her disappearance in the future would never be solved.

A knock on the door caught them both by surprise, and they were even more shocked when Bessy informed them, they had a visitor downstairs, one who urgently requested their appearance. Upon hearing it was none other than Monsieur John Grymes, both knew right away that he must have important news, as the man never came calling so early.

The attorney was sitting calmly in a chair, drinking a cup of coffee and looking fatigued. Other than his state of exhaustion, he did not seem too worried or upset, so whatever his reason for the visit could not be of any real concern, Tori told herself.

"Good morning to the both of you. I apologize dropping in like this, but some developments have arisen pertaining to our case. I thought you both needed to know about it right away."

Tori was far more worried about their attorney's haggard look than by any news he might have acquired. He looked as if he was about to have a stroke, and one could not just dial 911 for help, could they? "John, you look as if you have not had a moment's sleep," she said gently. "Does this have anything to do with your client, the one that sent for you last night? Or is it Edward?"

"Oh, dear, please forgive the way I look." He ran his hand through his hair and then smoothed out his jacket sleeves. "Tori, I have been up the entire night, and yes, it was with a client. The gentleman, he wanted his will rewritten. Seems he found out that his wife was not as faithful as he had thought. He died shortly after the completion of the new document. I had to go from there to my office to complete and verify the document. It had to be stamped and made official. By the time I got home, it was late or very early. Depends on how one looks at it…I suppose. Anyway, not to bother, either is correct. As my client was also a dear friend of many years, so you can imagine, I was in no frame of mind to sleep."

"Oh, I am sorry. What can we do to help" Tori looked from Grymes to Jean and back again?

"There is nothing you or Jean can possibly do to help. It is I who needs to help you." Tori looked back at Grymes and his drawn face. It was evident that there was a more to Grymes story, and it seemed, whatever it was, this new problem was causing a significant amount of upset, as his expression had changed. He seemed genuinely worried about something.

Jean's brow furrowed, and witnessing that caused a small wave of fear to sweep over Tori. She seldom witnessed her husband look so puzzled "What I don't understand is what this has to do with us? The death of your client, that is, did Jean know him? Is it someone we both know? There's more, isn't there? That's why you are here and not at home. I am right, aren't I?"

"Very perceptive of you, and yes, there is more." John turned to face Laffite. "The problem is, my client was someone we knew Jean. Your wife is right about that, and I see by your expression, you are wondering who I am talking about." Grymes was now staring at Jean with a solemn expression, one that remained as he continued. "It was Adrian La Combe…I have full instructions to read the document directly after Adrian's funeral."

Tori gasped and looked at her husband. This news was sad and frightening. Worse, the expression on her husband's face, was now blank, he revealed nothing of what he was thinking, and that indicated trouble to her.

Jean stood there for a moment, staring at John. Was he telling him that Adrian had found out about his affair with his wife? Had Simone told him? He had liked Adrian, and it had never been his intention to hurt the old man. If Simone had told her husband, it stood to reason; she would not stop there. He'd thought she would keep their affair secret, safe from public knowledge, but now, he wondered.

"The thing is Jean, that before he died, he learned the identity of his wife's lover and wanted to make certain that the man got not one penny of his money." John saw the shocked look on Laffite's face and quickly raised his hand as if trying to stop his obvious conclusion. "It's Edward Duval," he hastily added. "You could have knocked me over with a feather. I did not even know that the two of them were acquainted. Anyway, the will is quite clear. All I can tell you is that Simone is to be left little." He hesitated before going on. "The only reason I am here now is because of Edward. One of the servants, a decent butler, been with Adrian for as long as I can remember, confided in me. He had heard your name, Jean, along with Tori's several times. The servant seems to think that the two of them, Edward and Simone that is, were planning something 'no good,' as he put it. What do you make of all this?"

Jean stood there, rubbing his chin unconsciously. He was not sure what to think, but one thing was certain: Simone had become dangerous. To be left without the fortune she thought she was to inherit and to have an affair made public would be intolerable. Her humiliation and resentment would get the better of her. She could very easily make her past relationship with him public knowledge. After all, she'd stand to lose nothing in so doing, and if she thought she knew the truth about Tori, that would put his lady in a perilous position. He looked at his wife as his mind filled with further thoughts.

Laffite reasoned that if Simone had to fall, she would not go down alone. Edward, on the other hand, was obviously a fortune hunter.

He must have set his sights on her forthcoming inheritance. Why else would he have begun a relationship with the now widow? It had to be her fortune he sought. Now both were about to lose, and that multiplied the danger. For himself, Jean did not care, but he would not allow Edward or Simone to hurt Tori in any way. Having her publicly embarrassed, or worse, was something he had to avert. In the most serious of tones, he spoke to Grymes as if Tori wasn't even in the room. "Seems to me we have until the reading of the will to silence Edward. Time is no longer on our side. We must act and act fast. I am involved in this now, John. It won't be Tori alone; they will want to discredit her. No, they will want more. They will want to destroy us both! Simone's involvement makes that certain."

Grymes' expression did not waver, and clearly, he did not seem shocked.

A deeper puzzled look, clouded Jean's eyes. "You don't seem shocked, my friend."

John frowned. "I am not. Do I have your permission to continue this here and now, or would you rather we spoke in private?"

"You may divulge all you need; Tori and I have no secrets."

"If you are sure then. First, forgive me. It may not be common knowledge; I am referring to your past activities pertaining to a certain married lady that is. You do know, of whom I refer too? You still wish me to continue?"

"You may." Jean placed his arm around Tori's waist and pulled her closer.

Grymes nodded his head. "I do my own investigating, you know. I do so to help ready myself to protect my client's interests, you understand? Especially if that client is a good friend like Adrian. Once again, forgive me if I overstepped my bounds, but I have known about you and Simone for some time." Then, realizing what he had just said in front of Jean's wife, he turned to her.

"Tori, I assure you that Jean is dedicated to you and you alone.

This unfortunate affair of his took place long before you entered his life. This fact, I swear, on a gentlemen's honor, it is the truth."

"Calm yourself, John. I have also known for some time about Simone. Let's not worry about what is past. What I want to know is, what do we do now?"

Jean answered first. "We send for Leone, and we make our move on Edward today. That, my lady, is what we do. Edward will be easy; the hard part will be Simone. She will be wild with rage at first, and so abundantly vicious when she strikes." He spoke this last word in such a deadly tone that it caused Tori to inhale audibly. With her gasp, he could see he had alarmed her and set out to make amends quickly. "Don't worry. This old sea captain has weathered many storms, and I will never allow any storm, man-made or natural, to get the better of me. John, I believe it is time to send for Leone and for us to act."

Leone, who had been staying in his townhouse rather than returning to his plantation, was quickly summoned. It took him no time at all to arrive at the Laffites, and before the hour was up, the small group had told him why he would have to confront his brother that very day and what they had planned. He readily agreed and left with Grymes shortly after.

LEONE and John found themselves standing outside of Mr. John Davis's establishment. It was the best hotel in all New Orleans, and many said, in the entire South. Edward had rented a small set of rooms upstairs, around the back of the hotel and would most likely still be there at this time of day. Just what Leone was going to say to his sibling was somewhat of a problem. He knew that he had to reach his brother for Tori's sake and make it quite clear that she and Jean were off-limits, all while getting him to admit to the crimes he had committed. It was a surmountable task indeed. "I'll go up first, John. We best do it as planned. Let us just pray that it works."

"I see no reason why it shouldn't." Grymes put his arm over

Leone's shoulders and pulled him closer. In a lowered voice, he told Leone the facts as he knew them. "It has been my experience that despicable men like your brother can be dealt with if you handle them right." He grinned at his old friend and gave him a hearty slap on the back. Grymes did not like the fact that Edward had to be handled in this manner, but what choice did they have? Leone was their only hope of reaching the dandy to gain power over him and stop any attention he may have to harm Laffite and his wife. If they took care of Edward, they also took care of his lover, Simone. Disarmed before they could put Edward's false facts to use was the only sure way to prevent certain disaster.

LEONE knocked at the door and waited calmly for Edward to answer. However, the longer he remained standing there, the more impatient he became, and against his better judgment, his temper began slowly rising. If he allowed it to take over, he knew he would do far more than just reason with his evil brother.

After what seemed an eternity, Edward finally opened his door and was surprised to see his older brother standing there. It was easy to see that the man was very agitated, a sight that caused Edward's surprise to transform into suspicion quickly. "To what do I owe the pleasure of this visit, and at such a damnable hour, I might add?"

"This is no time to become insolent, and if you know what's best, you will allow me to enter," Leone took a step forward while continuing in a firm and controlled voice, "that is, if you don't want the whole of New Orleans to hear what it is, I have to say and believe me, dear brother, you don't." Before the dandy could respond, Leone pushed his way into the small room.

"Please, by all means, enter and make yourself at home, brother," Edward slurred. "I am afraid I can't offer you anything to drink unless you would like some brandy." The disgusted look on Leone's face made him laugh, as he bitterly continued. "At this hour? I thought not. You're such an upstanding gentleman, aren't you? You don't touch the stuff before sunset, how could I forget?"

"Edward, if you don't shut up, I just might take it upon myself to beat the living daylights out of you and believe you me, I have wanted to do just that for a very long time."

"My, my, aren't we in a testy mood today? What has got you so riled up, or do I want to know? If you are here to give me another one of your so-called lectures about my conduct and the family name, you can quite simply go to hell," he spat. "I soon will have no need of you, the family name, or your money."

That was the final stroke. Leone was beyond holding his temper. This brother of his had pushed him too far. Not only had he brought out Leone's anger but his contempt as well. Before Edward could duck out of the way, Leone delivered a full-force blow to his chin, followed by another to his stomach, which made him buckle over. Then the older brother quickly used an undercut; the strength behind his fist struck his brother's chin full force. It was such a powerful blow that it sent Edward flying across the small room, where his brother's head slammed up against the wall. After that, with his back against the wall, his body slid down to the floor; the dandy was unconscious before he ended up lying out cold on the dingy dust-covered wood.

Leone looked at him for a moment. All he could see was a person that he despised. How they could have come from the same womb, be raised by the same parents, and turn out so different was beyond him? He had loved his younger brother once, but that seemed a lifetime ago. Looking at him lying there on the floor, half-naked, bleeding from the corner of his mouth, Leone could not help but feel disgusted at what Edward had become.

He looked around for some water and finding none; he walked into the small bedroom beyond the living area, only to find it too was a mess. There was no drinkable water in sight, no bottle of spirits, and that posed a problem. He was about to give up when he spied a pitcher on a small table by the window. It was almost hidden from view by the pile of dirty clothes, but it was clearly available if one knew where and how to look. The washbasin it sat in did not look like it had been used, which was a good thing as Leone needed as much water as he could obtain. Carefully he picked his way around the obstacle course of shoes and clothes and retrieved the half-full pitcher. He returned to the front room and then very slowly and deliberately poured the contents onto his brother's head. Edward's reaction was instantaneous. Swearing and spitting blood from his mouth, he regained consciousness, then painstakingly, he pushed his body to a sitting position and watched his older brother through half-closed eyes.

Leone walked over to the far side of the room and, swearing out loud, pulled back the curtains, and opened the window shutters. "God damn it, man! This hellhole smells like old whiskey and dirty women. How can you live like a pig? To be surrounded…worse yet, immersed in such filth, and still portray yourself as a gentleman…I cannot, for the life of me, fathom how you do it. What did you do, gamble all your allowance away? I see to it that you have more than enough to live comfortably. Plus, I have been paying you to help me learn what happened to my…to, the young lady, Tori. Even without that extra, there should be an ample amount left over after your expenses, to at least hire someone to come and clean. Or do you enjoy living in such squalor?"

"If you are referring to that measly amount of money you allow me each month as enough, well, I would like to see you live on it. If you don't like what you see, then may I suggest increasing my allowance? Or do you enjoy forcing me, your own brother to live, how did you say, like a pig?"

"I did not come here to talk to you about your lifestyle. What you get is far more than you deserve. If you continue to push me, Edward," he shot him a cold look full of warning, "I might very well stop the allowance altogether. Considering what I have learned in the past few hours, it would not take much to get me to do just that. I think it best you close that sarcastic mouth of yours and pay attention to what I have to say!"

Edward could tell by the way his brother was talking that he had better stay quiet and let him have his say; besides, he'd heard it all before, a thousand times, so there was no need to pay attention. Another lecture on the evils of gambling was a small price to pay to get what he wanted. He would put up with Leone and his high and mighty ways, just so long as he could collect his allowance. He had to have it this week. He had to get himself cleaned up and get Simone to think of him as a Duval. Indeed, he might very well use this meeting to his advantage and win over Leone as well. If Edward admitted he had a problem, which he did not, and asked his forgiveness, his brother would be taken back and maybe be more reasonable. Better still, he could ask the one question he knew Leone had always hoped for, and that was, 'could he come home to be a respectable Duval again?' If that were to happen, it would ensure winning Simone's hand, when her husband died and die, he would, probably sooner than later.

All that lovely money for the taking would mean no more groveling before his big brother. Suddenly another idea jumped into his rapid-moving thoughts. He could not leave town now. No, he quickly rationalized, he had better remain. The plantation was too far away. Someone else might pay attention to Simone, and he could never allow that to occur. Once he married her and was in control of her wealth, then he could tell Leone to get out of his life. Yes, all would be perfect if appropriately handled. Then he'd have no need to speak or see his miserable excuse of a brother again.

"You see Edward, I have talked with Tori, and I now know the whole sorry story. If you were not my brother, I would indeed turn you in to the authorities myself, for holding the murders over her, of trying to place the blame all on her, to hurt me; and might I add, there is the matter of kidnapping her and taking her to Rose's whorehouse no less."

Edward could not believe he had heard right. He had not been listening until the bitch's name came up and caught his attention. His face drained of all color, and his breathing became short and

293

fast, causing sharp pains in his side as he struggled to gain his composure. He had to think quickly. What had Leone said, damn it? He wished he had paid better attention. Better, he learned what was going on slowly. "You mean to tell me that black bitch has contacted you after all this time? She has told you a pack of lies. You know, that, right? What does she really want? You back in her bed or your money perhaps? It's her word against mine, you know." Panic and lack of control over the situation made him desperate. "I might be the one to go to the authorities myself. Have you thought of that?"

Leone's expression hardened, but he remained silent.

"I see you have. Why else would you be here? Yes, I can do that, and they would believe me before her, and even if they did not convict her, her life would be ruined. After all, I have little left to lose because I am sure as hell certain, you are about to cut me off for good. I must, therefore, come forward, because duty dictates, I tell what I know and will do..."

Leone's eyes narrowed as he interrupted his brother. "You mean to tell me besides everything else you are guilty of, you would lower yourself to commit perjury? You would deliberately try and get someone who is innocent to take all the blame, knowing full well that Kane killed our Kate and Tori fought for her life?"

"Why not? I might even come out a hero if I play my cards right on this, and dear brother, I have many cards to play. Didn't you yourself tell others that Kane had spelled out, in his own blood no less, the name of Tori? That and a large sum of money was stolen, and her bloody gown was found hidden under her bed. That, the only horse missing, was the overseers, and no one, not one of the niggers saw a damn thing. All very compelling evidence, but the writing in blood seals it. Seems to me, the man was writing the name of his killer. Nice touch, I thought. That is indisputable evidence that even you can't deny. I, however, will feel no compulsion to reveal, or ever admit, it was myself who wrote the name, using his long-dead finger. You can now guess rightly, who took the money, and the overseer's horse." The room fell silent for a second, as Edward let the facts sink into his brother's mind.

"There are many people who have wanted to get something on the Laffites for some time and to hide an escaped black whore who is wanted for murder, well now, that is something," he chuckled.

"How quickly you forget, Edward. She is not wanted for murder, only for questioning!"

"I have not forgotten anything brother. Besides, that would change rather fast if I came forward, would it not?" He cocked his head to one side as he continued. "I would say I had held my knowledge of the ugly incident to protect you. Now, however, I can't stand by and watch a murdering nigger get away with it."

"You would do that, wouldn't you?"

"Maybe, maybe not. The way I see it, you want your precious little Tori to remain free, and I need more, how do I say it? It would be nice to have a larger allowance for a short time. Do we understand each other?"

"So now it's blackmail, is it, on top of lying, kidnapping and perjury. You are despicable. You are filth, worse than the dirt beneath my feet."

"Careful, Leone. I don't see that you have much choice in the matter, do you? And, if you know what is good for you, I suggest not making me angry."

"That is where you are very wrong. Making you angry means nothing to me. Indeed, I think you don't know how angry you are about to become. See, it is you who has no choice in what you will do or not do. I have not come empty-handed to this meeting. I am the one who will offer you a deal, my baby brother, one that you will accept; I am quite certain of that. You will not go anywhere or tell anyone of this abominable matter. In exchange, I will not report to the authorities, as I would like to, that it was you who is on the wrong side of the law."

"You make me laugh, Leone. Do you not understand? Only you and Tori know the truth. No court will take a white gentleman's word, over that of a nigger, and a whore, at that. If you ask me, I did you a favor. If you do speak up, people will only think you want to protect your former mistress and destroy me. It's no secret in this town that our relationship borders on hate. Now, once again, I ask you, who will listen to you? I fear you not, and had best be paid well."

"No! I will not give you one penny, and that's final. You have hung yourself this time, Edward. As I said before, I did not come empty-handed to this meeting. What would you say if I were to inform you that there was another witness to your admitted crime? To not only your blackmailing me, but to your hand in all the despicable plans you admitted to carrying out? A witness, who is not only white but highly respected? Yes, even by the authorities."

"I would call you a goddamned liar!" He shouted. "You are only grabbing at straws. No one was around to see what I did. No one knows, or they would have come forward long ago. I win, and you lose."

"No, I don't, you do!" exclaimed Leone, and with that, he walked over to the door and opened it. "You can come in now, John. Let's see if we can't come to a little understanding, shall we?" Leone stepped aside to let Grymes pass. When the attorney was standing a few feet away from Edward, Leone closed the door and pulled the open window shutter closed. "You may proceed, John, please explain to this individual just how this ugly matter will be solved."

"John Grymes, attorney at law and the about-to-be-appointed U.S. District Attorney for Louisiana, at your service," he announced to Edward, as he stepped a bit closer. "I must say, however, due to what I overheard just now, I am sorry to admit that I cannot represent you, no matter what you claim. However, I can watch you pay for your crimes, all of which you so kindly have outlined."

"You bastard," whispered Edward under his breath, looking at his brother.

"Then there is this nasty issue, about accusing Mrs. Laffite, of being the black wench, you believe committed the murders. Why it is quite impossible to believe that she and Leone's missing individual are the same person. Mrs. Laffite is far from being black as anyone will attest too, and Leone here will swear she is not the young lost soul who stayed with him. He has already given me his sworn word on that matter. Then there is Mr. Laffite, who claims Victoria was married to him in the islands, and his whole crew will swear to that. Also, a one, Monsieur Bernard Xavier Philippe Marigny de Mandeville, will swear that Madame Laffite is of royal connections in France, as denotes her mastery of French, spoken with a perfect Parisian accent. This is a fact that already circulates the population of New Orleans and is readily accepted. I, for one, would never dare declare Monsieur Mandeville a liar! I hear he is most excellent in the art of dueling. I can go on and on and present you with a list of upstanding citizens of this city and beyond, who would be only too happy to step forward and swear under oath pertaining to Madame Laffite's standing. With that said, may I be so bold as to remind you that the incident on the plantation has long been forgotten and will remain thus, that is if you abide by what I have to say. If not, the tables can and will be turned quickly and convincingly against you."

Edward realized that he had been outmaneuvered. He was trapped, and there was nothing he could do but listen to what they had to say and then abide by their wishes until he could solve this unwanted dilemma. The dandy looked at his brother with pure hatred in his eyes but could not utter a single word because he was beyond simple agitation; he was on the brink of rage. The man seethed and swore to himself he would get even with Leone for this. He would see to it that the bitch Tori suffered. Oh yes, they would pay for this humiliation, and he would find a way, no matter how long it took.

LATER that afternoon, Jean, Tori, and Leone sat laughing and drinking champagne. Tori felt safe from Edward's clutches at last. He would not talk now, or ever about what happened, for if he did, the man ran the risk of paying for his crimes and possibly paying for one he did not, the murder of Jack Kane. That last idea had been Leone's, and he swore he'd use it if he had to.

Jean, on the other hand, was not convinced they had won. True, this round was theirs, but unlike Leone and Tori, he knew better than to let his guard down. He would continue to have both Edward and Simone followed. Besides, after tomorrow's reading of Adrian's will, Simone was going to become dangerous, if not more so than Edward.

UPON hearing about Simone's husband's death, Edward wasted no time in rushing to her side. He played the perfect gentleman, trying only to comfort her in her so-called time of need. This support was mostly given in bed, as the two of them lay side-by-side drinking and celebrating her newly found freedom and wealth.

Edward started laughing as he watched her. He could see that she cared not a damn about the sad news. All that mattered to her were the facts; she was now very wealthy and free to do as she pleased. "You will have to excuse me for smiling." Edward stroked her arm and let his fingers trail their way across her breasts. "It's just that you look so pleased with yourself, and it strikes me funny."

"What does?"

"That all New Orleans is sad and wondering how the devoted wife, I mean widow, is holding up, and here you are, looking more ravishing than ever. I dare say that you are the happiest I have ever seen you. My, how you would shock all your female acquaintances, if not the entire city. What would they say if they saw you right now? They would positively swoon at your behavior, Madame."

"You had best be careful, Edward. I am not all that cold-hearted, you know. I mean, I do feel sorry for Adrian. After all, he was good to me, but it goes deeper than that. Way deeper. I think that's why you and I understand each other. A common bond of sorts if that's what you would like to call it. My family disinherited me. Threw me out without a care, and never did they expect anyone, let alone someone like Adrian, to marry me."

Duval sat up and looked at Simone with a perplexed expression. "I'm sorry I don't follow you. You did just say your family disowned you? Are you not exaggerating, my dear? I mean, for what reason would they do such a thing? You must have been a very naughty girl," he said, kissing her cheek. "Do tell." He rubbed her shoulders and caressed her body, paying careful attention to how she responded, while at the same time encouraging her to talk. Edward was interested in these new facts about her past. It was common knowledge her family did not seem to care what she was doing or where she was. Also, it was rumored that she had been snubbed by her father and mother at the last Destrehan ball. Maybe, it had not been a mere rumor but the truth, and he was about to learn why.

"You see, Edward, I knew that father would leave all he had, the land and the title, to my younger brother. All I would get out of life was an ample dowry and then be married off to some fop who would most likely be less than desirable to my needs. So, at one of father's gatherings, I set out to find my own beau. Adrian was what I needed. He was older and very wealthy. The problem was, he was also one of father's dearest friends, who considered me a little girl, and nothing more. What was I to do? All those young idiots, falling all over me. I knew the truth about why they wished for my hand in marriage. All they really wanted was my dowry, and to be in good standing, once a member of my family. It sickened me to the point that I could never allow myself to be packed off with the likes of one of them. So, I seduced Adrian, making sure that we were caught of course."

"Why, you, brilliant little vixen. By getting caught, you knew that your father would demand that Adrian marry you?"

"Well, yes. That was what I had planned, but my plans got lost, so to speak. Father was so upset that he went quite out of his head. He said things to me that were very cruel, and not true, to say the least. Anyway, in the end, father had said far too much, and I simply could not tolerate any of it. Then he literally threw me out.

I was banned from anyone in the family and the house for good. It was as if, and still is…that I am no daughter of theirs. Adrian felt that it was his fault, and we were married quietly and quickly, leaving right after the ceremony on an extended honeymoon. It was on that honeymoon that I realized I had to get him to fall in love with me, to think of me as a devoted wife. I knew I would end up very wealthy if I managed that. I would not need my family or their money, now would I? I would have all my dearly departed husband's estate. Not just a sample of it, to live on, as he promised. No, if I had to suffer the indignity of being the black sheep of my family, then I was going to make sure I ended up with far more than they could ever dream of having. I intend to have all of Adrian's estate and money. The total of which is far more significant than my fathers and other relatives combined."

Edward felt a new bond with Simone. He did know what it was like to be denied family and, more so, money. Taking her in his arms, he told her she would never have to be alone, that he understood, and he would always be there for her.

"Edward, if I can only get that Tori bitch out of the picture, then Jean would be free to return to me." She twisted around and looked at him, smiling. The dandy was very handsome, and he did understand her; she could see it in his eyes and hear it in his voice. Simone reached up and stroked the side of his face gently. "Then, you know what? I would teach him a thing or two. I would ruin Jean Laffite. I would bring him to his knees and make him beg me to remain his. Then, my dear Edward, I would leave him, as he did me. After all, I have you now, don't I?"

She'd a look of genuine hatred in her eyes when talking of Laffite. Her whole body had gone rigid as she went on about getting even with both the Laffite men, husband and wife. For Duval, there was no doubt the woman meant every word of what she was saying. It was then Edward saw the first kink in his plans surface. He had to keep Simone on his side and convince her that to expose what they knew would be foolish, not to mention dangerous for him.

"Simone, there is something I had best explain to you before you go on. I did not want to bother you with the sordid details, what with all you have on your mind, during this time of grief. However, I think it only right and necessary that you be made aware that Tori's situation has changed."

"Changed? How can being wanted for murder be changed, pray tell?"

"We have to do this a different way than we planned. You see, my dear, Tori is not wanted for murder as I had thought she was, as I had planned for her to be. Truth is, she is not wanted at all. If we go to the authorities, there is a good chance that I will be blamed for the scandal, through false incriminations and lies by my brother, who you know hates me," he said, coughing nervously. "It seems that my brother wants me ruined, so the family fortune does not fall into my hands, should something happen to him. He can do it. Trust me. He has Laffite's help on this, I dare say. I do know he has one John Grymes, on his side, and that was made clear indeed. At any time, he could make advances to ruin me, using his standing in society, and the trumped-up lies with the bastard pirate backing them up."

Simone looked into his face and could see that he was terrified, and she believed he was telling the truth. Her Edward stood the chance of having to suffer like she had, of having the humiliation of losing what was rightfully his and worse, having all New Orleans against him. All because of that bitch, who no doubt got Edward's brother to believe her lies.

She turned on her side and pondered what her lover had just told her. How could she get that nigger Tori out of Jean's life? That was the one thing that would hurt him, losing his beloved. With her gone, Edward would no longer be at the mercy of his brother. She would have to rethink it all. One thing became evident; Simone did not want Jean or his money for herself any longer; after all, she had all the money she wanted. No, what the widow wanted now, was respectability and power, that and revenge against her family by becoming something her father never thought was possible. If she helped Edward, she could end up Madame Simone Duval, Mistress of one of the largest and most respected plantations along the Mississippi. With Edward's estate merged with Adrian's, they would probably, be the wealthiest and most powerful couple in the South, certainly in New Orleans. Duval's name was well known and highly regarded. Edward and his family name were the solutions, but how to go about it, that was the question? She would have to get Edward to tell her in detail all he knew. Simone would listen and learn. Until then, she had to keep the dandy thinking he was the stronger one in their relationship.

Simone turned to face him, "What do you suggest we do? I want to teach Jean a lesson, and you want his wench. How do we do it? We have nothing to use against them, or do we?"

"I am not sure, but we will find a way, of that I am certain. Let us bide our time. After all, we have all the time in the world, don't we? And tomorrow, you will have all the money you need and me, to help you through your sorrow."

The two of them grinned. Edward and Simone were becoming more than cold, calculating lovers; they were becoming close friends, who needed each other and thought they knew just where the other stood.

EDWARD watched as Simone dressed for the funeral. He had not left her side once since arriving several days before, and he was not so sure that he should let her attend the service by herself. "Are you sure you don't want me to join you, to support you in your hour of grief?"

"I'm quite sure. Let us not start people talking before Adrian's body is even laid to rest. If you escorted me, it would not look good. Let us just do this, as it should be. Some of Adrian's friends are coming by for me, the doctor also. I have asked him to accompany me, as I feel too weak and distraught to go alone. Nice touch, don't you think?"

Edward smiled at her. "You are quite an actress. Tell me, how will you play out your role at the reading of his will?"

"Well, I am not going to attend and clap my hands, that's for sure. It will be hard not to smile, though; guess I will have to swoon." She dramatically raised her hand to her forehead and demonstrated for him the little scene she had in mind. "Oh my," she placed her hand over her heart. "I never realized he was so wealthy. After all, I married him because I loved him so. Married him, against my family's wishes, giving up all claim to them, for the love of my dear husband."

"Now, do not overdo it. You have to be believed. I mean, we don't want people to get the wrong idea. You go over the top with this, and they may think that you're acting. After all, you have to stay in good graces with society here, because that my love is the only way we will keep track of Laffite and his bitch."

"Yes, yes, I know all that and don't worry your head about it." She kissed his lips softly. "You do understand, after the funeral, I will have to decline all invitations for a while, out of respect, and I will have a period of mourning. What a way to mourn, here in bed with you." She wrapped her arms around him. "Maybe I shall have to mourn for quite some time."

He untangled himself from her embrace and pushed her away, frowning. "You had best finish dressing, or you will be late. I will run a few errands that I need too. You can count on me being here tonight, though," he said, winking at her. "We will celebrate together, and you can tell me in great detail all that happens today." Edward stood to leave, then stopped. "You know that Jean will most likely be there at the funeral? He did know Adrian, did he not?"

"He did. I had not thought of that. I do have something to look forward too then. If I can convince him that I truly am in mourning, then the rest will be easy."

"How you do love challenges, my beautiful, wonderful lover. Such an actress, such a face," he said, holding her cheeks between his two hands and looking at her carefully. "No one would guess you to be anything other than a sorrowful widow. Hiding your real emotions is not easy to do, but let me be the one to inform you; you are an expert at it. Let me teach you the game of cards some time. I feel that you would do very well." Picking her up, he swung her around.

Playfully, Simone pushed him away, and smiling coyly, asked him to leave so she might finish getting ready. He kissed her long and hard and then departed, careful to use the back way. Soon, he would enter via the front entrance, and no one would care. It would be his right to do so, but for now, they had to keep their affair a secret.

Simone placed white powder on her face, just enough to make her look as if she were genuinely ill with sorrow. Then remembering how that girl Marie Laveau had shown her, she rubbed in the darker powder under her eyes, just enough to create the no-sleep look. The widow had sent for the girl the same day as her husband's death. It had cost her all that she had hidden away, for both the spells, the make-up, and special drops. This voodoo stuff came with a high price but worth it. Besides, what did she care anyway? She would soon have all the money she could ever need.

The drops were the hardest. The girl had told her only two for each eye. They would burn and make her eyes red, causing them to water for at least four hours. Simone would look as if she had been crying for a long time, and that was something that she required if she were to pull off this act of hers. She had not asked what the drops were, just that they were safe and would not do any permanent harm. Marie told her that if she followed her directions, she would be perfectly safe.

The widow looked at the small bottle in her hands. The drops had been such a stroke of genius. She was so clever. She'd thought of everything. Even if Marie were to tell anyone that her tears had been purchased, it would be too late. They were going to produce the effect she needed. Simone doubted the girl would tell but had thought of an excuse just in case. She would say that she could not cry. Try as she might, she had not been able to grieve. Then fearing for her health, she had sought out Marie in the hope of obtaining a potion that could help her. Marie, she would tell them, had helped her, and the tears they saw were real. Once she'd started to cry: she would tell them, she simply could not stop.

ADRIAN'S attorney had made all the arrangements. That had been her husband's wish, and Simone had not protested. It was a bit unusual to have such a quick funeral service, but then her husband had planned everything years ago. The faster he was in his crypt, the faster she would inherit his estate, and that was the important outcome to consider. If she had asked for the funeral to happen so quickly, people might have asked the reason why? As it was not her idea, then Simone felt confident that no one would ever know of her true reason behind marrying such a decrepit old fool. In no manner or form did she look like the money-hungry widow. It was all so very convenient. The pleased woman was glad that someone else had to perform the mundane task and deal with the church, even if that person was John Grymes. She didn't have to lift a finger, not even go to make certain the family crypt was ready.

The spot where his remains were to be placed was in a massive white marble mausoleum. Its upkeep had been seen to over the years, and all of her husband's family was laid to rest inside. Simone made a mental note that she would have her own crypt built long before her death. No way was she going in there with his family. Nor would her body go in with the Duvall's come to think of it. No, she would have her crypt, complete with great marble angels looking over it. Depending on how good her new husband was, Simone might allow him to lay at rest alongside her, but time would tell, she thought.

THE Catholic bishop held the service instead of the parish priest, not unusual for someone like Adrian, who, through the years, had been so generous to the church. Simone sat thinking about this while waiting for the service to begin. The greedy woman told herself she would have to remember to see to it that the annual allowance be cut back, and then stopped altogether. What right did the church have to any of her money?

The choir had stopped singing, and the service began in earnest, and so then did her act. For all purposes, she was the young, grieving widow, who could not be consoled. Many women of society came to her side before and during the ceremony, but try as they might, they could not seem to comfort her. Even the doctor was concerned about the way she appeared. He had told several people around him of his worry and made it clear that he would accompany her to the cemetery, which he had not planned on earlier.

Simone knew she was good at acting, and the people were unwittingly playing their parts as well. Strangely, she found herself liking all the unasked-for attention. With so much fuss going on around her, the widow hardly had to do anything at all. It was like she had explained to Edward; for her, it was easy to fool the masses. Then out of the corner of her eye, she saw Laffite watching her. To convince him she was in mourning would be the final coup de gras. The church service may have ended, but that had signaled the next stage of her plan.

Jean had been observing her secretly, not wanting her to know she was under scrutiny. He knew that he would have to pay his respects to the widow before he left the church but delayed doing so until the last moment. His reasoning was sound; the longer he waited to talk to her, the more time he had to see if she would reveal her real emotions because he doubted, she was the grief-stricken widow at all. Knowing this, Laffite was glad he had taken Grymes's advice and talked Tori into not attending.

At first, he could not believe the performance Simone was putting on or how everyone seemed to think that she was very sad. How could they be so gullible, he had asked himself? Then it was time, and Jean had no other choice but to make his way toward her and did so with all eyes on them.

Once at her side, he could see the tears streaming down her face. The woman looked as if she had been crying all night. Even through the widow's black veil, he could see the dark circles under her eyes. Then, there was the way she stood, bent and shaken. Could it be that he was wrong about her? Could the cold-hearted Simone really have cared about Adrian? If so, then why had she sought out the arms of a pirate? Had she used him merely for sex? If Simone were acting, she would not be able to maintain the level of grief she was displaying for long. He would hold off judgment till after the internment.

THE spring sky was gray, with a darker overcast moving in. A light wind blew, making it unusually bitter for this time of year, and the weather seemed to befit such a somber occasion as a funeral. Even the typically shining white marble crypts had lost their beauty and sat cold and dimmed by the drizzling rain. Standing looking at her dead husband's mausoleum, she shuddered. The gray granite blocks were a foreboding image and hardly a place that looked restful. The door to the crypt had been opened, and the darkness beyond the entrance was terrifying to her. The whole graveyard somehow seemed steeped in a grim and ugly undertone. It was a sad place and one that was for all purposes aiding her in the ruse she was attempting.

Simone could not believe how everything was working her way. If she were fortunate enough, it would start to rain during the service. How positively perfect it was that man's God himself was on her side. God, she thought, huh! He had nothing to do with it at all. She did not believe in God or praying. She only believed in making things happen. Adrian had believed in God and look at him now. Where had his beliefs gotten him?

Then before she realized it, the graveside service was over, and the rain that had held off began to fall lightly. People were quickly departing, with many of the women saying how they'd pay a call to Simone soon, to see how she was doing. Some of Adrian's older friends were telling her that she was not alone in her hour of grief, and they too would stop by. Jean overheard a conversation between two upstanding gentlemen, and they were saying that it was a crime that Simone's family still had not forgiven her for marrying Adrian. Worse, they had not even attended the funeral. Their actions were a sin before God, and they promised each other that Simone would not be alone. They would see to it that the women of New Orleans took the place of her family. It was the least they could do for Adrian and his grieving widow.

Jean reached her side at last. The doctor was telling her that it was time to leave. He thought it best if she went home instead of to the reading of the will. He was genuinely concerned about her health at this point. It was his opinion she was too overwrought, he told her. Simone only shook her head and told him that it would not be any easier to go later. She'd prefer to get it over with and then be left alone to grieve her loss.

Jean stood before her with concern on his face. Simone looked up into his eyes and then lowered her tear-soaked lashes as she spoke. "Thank you for coming, Jean, I did not expect it. Adrian would have liked to know that you considered him your friend. He was very fond of you." She looked back at him and tried to smile through her tears, which continued to fall slowly down her cheeks. The dark drape of beautiful lace could not hide the fact that she was still crying, and it moved Jean deeply. He reached out and touched her arm. "I am sorry, Simone, for everything."

"Me too, Jean. I am going to miss him. I will be all alone now. Maybe that is the price I am to pay for all my evils." She started to sob aloud, and instead of going to Jean, she fell into the old doctor's concerned arms. This action caused the doctor to insist that he accompany her to the attorney's office if she was determined to go.

Jean watched them as they left and felt terrible for thinking the worst of her. He felt sorry for Simone, because as upset as she was, and he believed now, that she was deeply saddened, then what she was about to find out would devastate her even more.

Once in the carriage, Simone turned her head away from the doctor and smiled. She had succeeded. Jean had bought her act. Falling into the doctor's arms, instead of Jean's, had been pure inspiration. What a touch. That had been the crowning glory. God, how she hoped Jean felt awful and went home to his nigger wife and told her how sorry he felt for her. If she had been alone in the carriage at that point, she might have laughed aloud at the thought of Laffite's bitch of a wife having to listen to Jean's concerns about the widow. Right then, however, she just hoped her eyes would clear up soon. The burning was easing some, but the watering was still causing her to wipe her cheeks continually. The tears were quite annoying and of no further use to her. Simone chewed on her bottom lip as she prepared herself for what lay ahead. This stage of the game was going to be the best part of all. The payoff was almost hers for all the time she had spent married to a decrepit old fool.

SIMONE was shown into the attorney's private office on the arm of her doctor and offered a seat. She did not like John Grymes at all, as she had an excellent memory, where he was concerned. Sure, he had been polite to her whenever they met, but she knew that he did not like her one bit. The widow had not forgotten he had almost talked Adrian out of marrying her in the first place. The thing was, he had not, and that cheered her up, knowing that under the present circumstances, it must be killing him to know that in just a short while, she would become the sole heir to Adrian's entire estate, and there was not a damn thing he could do about it. 'Serve the upstart American right.' Once she had more power and money, Simone planned on making Gryme's life a living hell. So as to not give her feelings away just yet, she turned her head away from his stern eyes and grinned with pure joy. Making the man suffer, that was for later, for right then, she had to continue her charade. Taking a deep, ragged breath, she turned back to face the attorney.

John looked at Simone and saw an incredibly sad woman. However, unlike Jean, he was convinced that it was an act. Looking at her made him feel physically ill. He would go along with her little charade for a bit longer, and then it would be over. It was going to be quite something to witness how the so-called grieving widow would react to the news. John almost smiled. The attorney was going to enjoy the moment thoroughly and hoped Adrian was watching and feeling vindicated. His friend had insisted that his funeral be held quickly, thus allowing no hint of what he planned to be revealed to his unexpecting widow. Simone had bought the idea his burial had been arranged years ago, a fact that showed her greed to Grymes. Adrian deserved a grand funeral as he had orig-inally planned, but he was wise in his last hours. Simone's husband wanted his wife's life destroyed. He intended her to be utterly shocked, and with no forewarning, she would have no recourse but to accept his last act.

John shuffled some papers and then looked around the room. "We are all here, I see, and so, without further delay, I shall begin. The circumstances of Adrian's will, are shall we say, a little out of the ordinary. He requested a few stipulations be met before the reading. First, was that a doctor be here with us, which I see, we already have." He nodded his head in the doctor's direction. "I thank you, sir, for your concern. The other request was that the Mother Supe-rior also be present. Therefore, if you would excuse me, I will go to the outer office and escort her in."

Simone still had no idea of what was about to happen. She imagined that Adrian, being a God-fearing man his whole life, had left the church some money, the fool. It was her money he was giving away now, but then as long as it was not too much, it didn't matter. It might even help her position if she insisted that a modest sum, of course, in her dearly departed husband's name, be added to the amount for the convent. It could never hurt, to have the church on your side, and word would spread of her good deed, winning over the doubting few. She also remembered how earlier at the church, she had decided to cancel Adrian's annual donation, something that she now decided would have to wait. No use in upsetting too many fair citizens, until after she was Madame Duval. Yes, that was a perfect idea. The scheming woman felt as if everything was going very well if only her eyes would stop their infernal watering because they were indeed beginning to infuriate her.

The doctor stood off to one side, and Mother Superior sat in the chair next to Simone. Although the nun was short in stature, her presence was strong, and this made her appear much taller. The Mother Superior always had the ability to create an atmosphere where she could make one feel tiny. The nun also had a way of making one feel as if they had best confess their sins before her, and right away, or face God's consequences.

Simone found it difficult to look her in the eyes, for fear the woman would see the deception that lay hidden within her. Of all the people that could make her quake, it was this self-righteous nun. To hell with her, for making her feel inadequate and uncomfortable and for doing so, Simone decided right then that no more money would be added to whatever the church was about to receive. She concentrated on Grymes's face and ignored the old nun completely.

"Now that we are all present, the time has come for me to do Adrian's bidding. Before I start, I would like to take this opportunity to tell all of you that he was a dear friend of mine for many years and one who will be sorely missed. I would like to think that I was more than just his attorney, that he considered me his friend also." John fell silent for a few seconds. He seemed to be reflecting on something before continuing. "I think maybe he did. Now, down to matters. Simone, your husband, asked me to inquire if you would care to read the will yourself or if you would prefer me to do it for you? I know it is somewhat unorthodox, but he felt it might be easier for you."

311

Shaking her head, Simone spoke with a tremble in her voice. "Monsieur Grymes, my husband always tried to do what was best for me. However, I feel that in this case, it would be best if you would read it. I don't think that I can manage at this time."

"If that is what you wish Madame, I will oblige you. It is concise, simple, and straightforward."

Of course, it would be simple and straightforward, she thought. Bet it reads a small amount to go to the church, and the rest to me."

"I shall begin then…I, Adrian Philippe La Combe…"

Simone found her stomach in a knot. The moment was here, what she had waited for all these years. What she had planned for, from the very beginning, and now here it was happening. It was going to be hard not to show her immense satisfaction, but then did she have to hide it? Once it was hers, Simone could do or act any way she wanted.

"It is my wish, that the following be administered to the last detail and complied with, before a period of no more than six weeks, after the reading of this, my last will and testament. To Simone, my wife, for everything she has done and only she knows what I am referring to by that; I do hereby leave her the following: One, the townhouse on Royal Street, with a staff of two slaves, an allowance of…"

Simone wished he would hurry up with the reading. The attorney seemed to be enjoying himself as if reading it slowly, gave him more self-importance. Of course, she would get the townhouse and an allowance to run it. It was only one of many investment buildings her husband had purchased over the years. True, it wasn't large or in a part of town that she would ever consider to her standards, but it could be sold for a profit if she so chose.

"She is to be allowed to furnish her home with any articles from the Manor House in town. All and any personal items, such as clothing and jewelry, are to be included. It will be up to her sole discretion as to what she wishes to take. The remainder of the contents, the house, the household servants, the carriages, and all other slaves and articles therein are to be sold at public auction.

My attorney, John Grymes, will oversee this project for me. He will see to it that all the proceeds are given to Mother Superior and the Sisters of the St. Ursula Convent. This is in addition to a sum of money to be determined by Mr. Grymes after the settlement of my last wishes are abided by." John looked up at Simone, who, by all signs, was still blissfully unaware of what was happening.

"To my butler, Mr. Patrick Jones, for his honesty and service. I leave a sum of two thousand dollars, my gold watch, and one hundred acres of land of his choosing from my plantation. If he chooses to take any member of the staff from the Manor house, he may do so at no charge. Rather, he will be given their papers to do with as he sees fit. I wish him well and thank him for his assistance in my last hours. The remainder of my estate, land, plantation house, slaves, and all therein are bequeathed to my second cousin and his family, whom I contacted by letter and are at this present time, on-route to assume their rightful inheritance."

Grymes paused briefly to look at Simone again. He wanted to see if any of what he was reading was registering yet. He continued slowly.

"The running of such a large estate would have been far too severe for such a delicate woman as my wife, and I am sure she knows why I have chosen to do what I have. If indeed, should she have any questions, I feel obliged to tell her to remain and have my attorney explain in greater detail, pertaining to the arrangements, that are about to be activated on my bequest."

Simone was paralyzed, because if she understood correctly, then she was not the wealthy widow she had expected to be. There had to be some mistake; there just had to be! Her blood was boiling. If she had not been in the presence of witnesses, her temper would have shown itself. She would have jumped across the table and destroyed all evidence of any such will. She had been a fool. Somehow, it had all gone dreadfully wrong, but now was not the time to make a scene and do something she might regret. No, she had to think. She had to calm down, and she had to get out of there before losing control!

Grymes coughed. "That is it then, like I said before. It's simple and straightforward. Are there any questions?"

No one spoke, and John had difficulty keeping a somber expression as he observed Simone. The widow had gained a reddish color about her face, due to her rising temper, no doubt. He was observing her, wondering what her next move would be, for surely, she was far from in agreement with what had transpired. Grymes had to admire her, though. For someone who had just lost a fortune, she was controlling her emotions very well. It amazed him further as the so-called grieving widow stood calmly and quietly, without a word, turned and walked out of his office.

How could her husband have done such a thing? The will had to be wrong! There had to be a later will, one leaving everything to her like he always told her he would. Adrian would never have humiliated her so. He had loved her! Why would he have taken such a cruel and bitter action? Stamping her foot and letting her real emotions show, she made up her mind to correct the wrong. Simone was determined to fight. Somehow, she would get what was rightfully hers. As his rightful heir, she would not let all that wealth and money she had worked so hard for slip away.

The doctor came to her side. He was very concerned about his patient's well being. The reading had been extraordinary. It was apparent to him that such an elegant woman had no way of living in the style she was accustomed to with the circumstances described. It hurt him to see such a devoted wife as she was, cut out of so much. What had Adrian had in his mind when he wrote such a will? It made no sense to him. The man had loved his wife and had been so proud of her; it seemed utter madness that he'd taken such horrendous steps.

"Doctor, I feel as if I have been hit with much more grief than that of my dear husband's death. My poor Adrian, he must have been out of his mind when he wrote that will. Never would he have done such a thing otherwise." She grabbed the doctor's arm, desperately continuing. "You must tell them he was sick, so sick he did not know what he was doing. Please, he was not well, was he? Surely, he did not know what he was doing and hadn't for some time."

"Quite the opposite, Simone," came the sound of a voice behind them. John was standing there on the steps with the Mother Superior. "He knew exactly what he was doing when he drew up the will. If you would step into my office, I will be happy to explain it to you, as best I can. Doctor, would you please be so kind as to escort Mother Superior back to the convent? I will see to it that Madame La Combe gets home safely after our little chat." John took Simone by her arm and forcibly escorted her back toward the door. "If you will excuse us, please, Madame La Combe needs to be out of this weather, as we all do. Good day to you."

Once inside and out of view of anyone on the street, Simone let go of her pent-up rage. The widow did not care, what this idiot of an attorney thought of her, and with no other witnesses to her temper tantrum, she unleashed her verbal tirade. The widow ripped the black lace veil from her head and threw it to the ground while screaming. Then she allowed Grymes to see her glaring eyes, eyes that clawed at him like talons. "You had something to do with all this; I know you did! Adrian would never have cut me off like this, never!"

John walked away from her and toward his private office. He stopped at his open doorway and looked at her with a slight smile. Simone's rage increased as she took his grin to be an affirmative answer to his part in what had been done. Her lips were drawn thin across her mouth in anger, and her nostrils flared with fury as she inhaled. The slight flush that had graced her up until then grew; white cheeks, increased in color, as her eyes bulged.

Jean's words from the night before came to the attorney's mind then. This female was indeed like a storm, and from what he could assess, she was just getting started. Simone reached for the closest

315

thing, picked it up, and screeching, hurled it toward him. John ducked just in time to avoid the vase, which smashed against the wall behind him. Calmly but not without the contempt he felt for her, John spoke. "If you are quite finished with your childish antics, and Madame, I highly suggest that you are, I will clarify why your husband saw fit to call me to his bed-chamber on the night of his death. He held on, you know, so that he could have me draw up this new arrangement.

There was silence for a few seconds as she stared back at him coldly. Could that be so? It was impossible. No one visited the house unless she was told, and Simone was always informed when a caller came. Every damn nigger in the house knew better than not report to her. They feared her; she'd had total control over them for years, so what changed? The butler had betrayed her, maybe? After all this time, he had turned against her orders. Most likely bribed to do so by Grymes, for the promise of land and money. "Why, should I listen to you, you swine? You had the will changed long before, and you know it. You will pay for what you have done to me. Trust me; I have not even started yet."

John lowered his voice as he spoke to her calmly. "I have done nothing that you should hold against me. Simone, this was all your doing. Adrian called me to his deathbed. That's right, his deathbed, to change his will. Up until he found out about your, shall we call it, your 'little indiscretion' with a particular young man, you were indeed to inherit his entire estate. You, Simone, in your stupidity, brought this on yourself."

"Lies, all lies, and I will fight this so-called will to the end. You have no proof of what he thought he knew. He was very sick, out of his mind. I loved my husband very much; anyone will tell you that. I left my own family because of my love for him. It's you. You changed his mind on the night you came to the house. You told him a pack of lies. Lies that most likely killed him! I shall see you hang for murder." Breathless with rage, the woman gasped for air, then spoke in a low, calculating voice that hissed across the room.

"If you do not see to it that I get all I am entitled to, I swear to you that I will bring you down. I will see you and your career ruined. I, too, have friends in high places, so don't underestimate me."

John's eyes bore right into hers, and his next words would ring in her ears for days. "But I have seen to it; that you got what you deserve, my dear, and I intend to see to it that it stays as it is. You had best let me take you home so that you can tell Edward Duval that you will be meeting him in your new place of residence in the future and not in your room down the hall from your late husband. It is also my hope that you do not want any detail of this sordid affair to come to public attention. That, you leave well enough alone. New Orleans would not forgive you, or would they be as generous as your husband was. Adrian was admired by all, as well you know."

The mention of Edward visibly shook her. Upon hearing his name, Simone realized that all John had disclosed was true. Somehow, Adrian had found out about Edward. Damn it; she had been a fool to meet Duval in the house. For the first time that day, the widow understood that she had been so close, so very close, and now she had nothing, well almost nothing. Ever the survivor, the conniving female, started thinking. At least she had Edward, and there were always her New Orleans society friends, who would feel sorry for her. They would not cast her out. Simone knew she could not let them find out the reason behind Adrian's wishes, for if they did, that would indeed be the end. Grymes was right on that point. The fury of seconds ago was gone, smothered with the knowledge that she had well and truly lost. In a hushed tone of voice, Simone spoke as real tears tumbled down her cheeks. "What am I to tell people? How can I explain the will...my status?"

How pitiful she looked. The beautiful widow was a woman facing the harsh realities of having lost all she had hoped for, and losing was not something she handled well. For a fleeting second, he felt sorry for her, but then Grymes remembered his old friend, who had died, with a broken heart. "I must say that I am sure you will come up with some story that people will believe. You usually do.

It was my agreement with Adrian that as long as you do not hurt anyone, with whatever you say to explain your situation, I was to leave well enough alone. Now, I can see Adrian's wisdom. You will pay enough for your actions, and I have no reason to add blight to his memory, by revealing all. Oh, and one more bit of advice, my dear. If I were you, I would leave the Laffites alone."

The mere mention of the Laffites was more than she could handle. Rather than let this vile man see her sink any lower, she stormed from his office and ran out into the rain toward a waiting carriage.

THAT night Jean had his guilty feelings put to rest, as Grymes felt it his duty to inform Jean and Tori about the reading of the will and Simone's outburst. Tori felt sorry for her but was quickly convinced by the men that a scheming woman like Simone would soon find a way back into the social group to which she was accustomed.

# ᘓᘓᑫ Five ᕼᕼᕼ

In order to stay close to Tori, Jean turned the running of Barataria over to his brother Pierre. The dread he was feeling was nothing he could put his finger on, but it was always there. The pirate had learned a long time ago to listen to his intuition. This time, however, he was listening to his gut instincts for something far more critical than the business. It was for family that he worried. He would never let any harm come to Tori and the baby, on this, he had sworn to God, and to both his brothers.

Pierre and Dominique supported him in his request, merely stating that they would run Grand Terre, as long as they could count on Jean's help in town now and then. He was sure to get bored soon enough, they had confided between themselves, so letting him find his way, was the fastest path to having him back at the helm. A pregnant woman was known to be difficult at best, they had laughed, and so they determined Jean's absence would be short-lived, something the man adamantly denied. Laffite insisted, he enjoyed spending more time alone with Tori, something he had sorely missed since their return from the islands. What he did not divulge to them was his real reason behind his actions.

As Grymes had predicted, it did not take Simone long to land back on her feet. Even after moving to her new home on Dauphine Street, the sly actress had won the hearts and sympathy of all who heard her story. Playing the ever-grieving widow, who was bound and determined to abide by her late husband's wishes, was all a part of her plan. To all who knew her, she maintained a position of dignity. This, despite the hardships that she now had to endure. It was true, the small house she now inhabited was nothing close to Adrian's grand home, but it was far from where she would have found herself had he not made allowances. Simone had taken only the absolute best furniture, and she still had all her jewels and clothes. The mighty may have fallen, but this woman was bound and determined not to remain in her current circumstances for any longer than necessary.

At dinner parties and other gatherings, the widow would explain to anyone willing to listen, why she continued to live as she did. "I intend to mourn my dear late husband and will refuse any help offered, no matter the consequences," she told everyone. Lies fell easily from her lips as she continued to reinforce her position and standing. "Adrian was very generous in regard to my financial needs, and God bless him for knowing that I could in no way run his plantation, let alone manage the upkeep. The same, I am sad to admit, applied to our large home here in the city. The grand residence we had before his untimely death was run entirely by him. Adrian spoiled me so in life, and his kind actions have seen to it, that I remain unburdened by matters that simply are way beyond me." The cunning actress would dab her eyes at this point and receive all the praise and offers to help her, should she need it. "The only matter that can help me now is that my dear friends do not forget me and continue to include me in their thoughts and prayers."

Everyone who heard this vowed they would never disregard her, and many offered to have her visit them, so she would never feel lonely. In this way, Simone wormed her way higher up the social ladder. Adrian's widow gained the respect of the older generation and the younger's loyalty, who thought it to be the most romantic and courageous act of love that they had ever seen. Her act was so convincing that one prominent family even gifted her a second housekeeper, who also served as a cook. It was a well-received gift, as Simone had wondered how she could afford to hire more help, let alone purchase a nigger so well qualified. The greedy woman needed every penny she had to maintain a certain standard of living, to remain socializing, in the circles, she'd become accustomed, without them fully knowing of her dire situation.

Jean and Tori were somewhat taken back by Simone's lies and trickery, but they did nothing to discredit her on Grymes' advice. So it was that the months slipped quietly by with what seemed to be an unwritten truce between Edward, his lover Simone, and the Laffites.

THE long hot days of summer, which should have come later in the year, suddenly arrived. June felt like August, with its high humidity and soaring temperatures. Day and night, the sweltering, sticky heat continued with no escape for anyone. Tempers were short, and many altercations, seen on the streets during the day, were uncalled for. Tori soon came to know the truth in what Marie Destrehan had told her. There was no way to avoid the smothering wet blanket of stifling air that had descended upon the city. Many inhabitants were taking trips up or downriver. Wisely, they were seeking out the cooler refuges of the mighty plantation homes. Many, she was told, would not return until there was a break in the weather or better yet, until the summer's end.

The Destrehan family had invited Tori and Jean to join them for the summer, in their far cooler and more relaxed location. This had seemed like the perfect solution to Tori, but due to her delicate condition, as Jean called it, he insisted they remain in the city until after the child was born. As far as he was concerned, the deciding factor was simple and could not be argued; her doctor practiced only in town. For Jean, going any place else was merely out of the question. His wife was to have the absolute best, including a knowledgeable and highly educated doctor at the birth.

Even heavily pregnant, Tori radiated beauty. Charm seemed to flow from her as naturally as breathing. The few dinners that she and Jean attended were made particularly special, it was said, by the presence of Madame Laffite.

William Claiborne was even enticed by her looks and seductive charm but not enough to give up his dream of catching the Laffite brothers and their gang of cutthroats as he referred to them. He might have let a lot slide, even turned a blind eye, given enough time, but the truth was that Edward was by his side most days, always fueling his insecurities and misgivings about the public's opinion of him.

CLAIBORNE'S residence sat on the corner of Levee Street and Toulouse. The large home had lavish gardens that extended to Chartres Street and was a showplace used for many political gatherings. When Claiborne first arrived in New Orleans, he had brought with him his wife and daughter, both of whom died in a yellow fever outbreak in 1804. Heartbroken and needing companionship, he married for a second time, in 1806. This marriage produced a son, but once again, he suffered the loss of a wife. She passed away in November 1809. Since then, Claiborne had become deeply engrossed with his political aspirations and, more importantly, with trying to gain the trust of the Creole population. Without the votes of the Spanish and French-speaking people of the city, Claiborne knew his chances of becoming the first state's governor, when Louisiana gained statehood, would not happen. That distinction would fall to Jacques Villere or Jean Destrehan, who were both admired and respected in the Creole society. The American could see no way around his situation, and it frustrated him tremendously. Knowing his predicament, Edward and Simone saw a chance to seal their friendship with the American, and slowly but steadily, they begin to play a more significant role in Claiborne's life.

FROM a very early age, a young girl named Cayetana Susana Bosque Y Fangui, who lived across the street from Claiborne's mansion, had watched the American and was deeply moved by his loss. Cayetana, herself, in the year 1810, at the tender age of 14, had felt the pain of losing someone close. Her father, Bartolome Bosque, a wealthy merchant and shipowner, died, leaving his wife Felicitad to raise their children. Now, nearly two years later, Simone, a longtime friend of the Bosque family, set to work on a plan she and Edward had concocted. They needed Claiborne to win the upcoming election, and Felicitads' young daughter, now sixteen, was at last eligible for marriage. If Claiborne married into the family, it would almost assuredly win him the position he sought. Then with Claiborne as governor, on their side, and owing them, it would only be a matter of time before he acted and turned on the Laffites.

William Claiborne knew that the Creole society of New Orleans did not like him, and if he were to be elected when the time came, he would have to win them over. The very idea to many of the Creoles that their beloved New Orleans would become an American State horrified them, and because of this, their intense dislike of Claiborne was well known to him. It was a long-standing problem for the Territorial Governor and one that seemed to be solvable, by the advice of his friend Edward Duval. The man had suggested that the American look for a suitable Creole wife of standing, which made sense to Claiborne, so he began to seek out the perfect match. Many introductions were made, and yet none were deemed suitable, as far as the influential and high standing Duval was concerned.

Having bided her time and knowing the governor was getting desperate, Simone very subtly convinced Felicitad to invite her dear friend, William Claiborne, to accompany them for dinner. Once the woman agreed, Simone made certain that among the guests joining the dinner party was her young daughter, Cayetana.

Edward made sure that he explained to Claiborne before attending the party, that Cayetana was the sixteen-year-old daughter who had watched and admired him while growing up. He made sure that the lonely widower felt more and more excited about the introduction and even coached him on how to approach the very protective mother.

From the time they were introduced, Claiborne was smitten,

but hesitant because of their age difference; after all, he was thirty-nine. However, both Edward and Simone assured him that even though Cayetana was young, she was precisely what he needed and came from a family with diverse connections among the populace. The Bosque friendship, they explained, would boost his chances of winning the state election, but having Cayetana as his wife, would most certainly, see him succeed.

After that, he was continuously seen at the young beauty's side, declaring his undying love to win her hand. Simone helped in her own influential way by manipulating the younger female every chance she had. Always, she would praise the dashing American and his attentions toward her young friend. This task was easy, compared with convincing Felicitad, that a marriage between her daughter and the American would be very advantageous and not a step-down, as the older widow thought.

Simone would often visit the Bosque home, under the guise of genuine concern for Cayetana. As the weeks passed, both Simone and Edward saw to it that the blossoming romance was the talk of the town. After all, Claiborne and Cayetana were often seen strolling the gardens of the governor's mansion. Their efforts paid off because soon, the budding romance became a hot topic in both the Creole and American societies, boosting Claiborne's resolve to gain the young woman's hand. Many whispered the American wanted her because of her standing with the Spanish and Creoles. That he wanted only to connect with the Creoles of French descendants, others hinted, he desired a younger wife, as he had lost both his older wives. Younger would be stronger in childbirth and also easy to bend to his will. So, the gossip went, and as it did, Edward played down the negative comments to his now close friend William, and Simone worked tirelessly at changing the populace's thoughts about the romance.

While Simone was carrying out her end of their plan, Edward concentrated on William. His greatest achievement as far as he was concerned came when he explained to a doubting state governor-to-be a few facts that the man could understand, thus allowing him to be persuaded to make his move. "You don't have to love her. Besides, it's not like you're deceiving her. You do have strong feelings towards her. In time you may even expand those feelings. As for the lady in question, if you do not ask for her hand soon, someone else surely will." He had added his final touch, not knowing if it were true or not. "Besides," he continued, sounding very sure of himself, "it is evident that Cayetana is very much in love with you. I assure you, though, she will do as any dutiful daughter would and listen to her mother, even if that means marriage to another. I suggest, therefore, before Felicitad has a chance to change her mind about you and your attentions that you make your move."

Once again, taking Edward's advice, Claiborne made his attention known to both Cayetana and her mother, and soon after, knowledge of a wedding arrangement between William and Cayetana became news all around town. It was disclosed that the pair were betrothed and would marry in November the following year. William had hoped for a wedding much sooner, but due to the girl's family, wanting relatives from Europe to attend the affair, he had no choice but to agree to the mother's terms. Once the betrothal was official, though, the Creole society began to warm toward the American. Realizing that Edward had been right, Claiborne decided to listen to Duval more closely, and thus, his casual friend became a part of Claiborne's trusted inner circle.

Once seated firmly by William's side, it was an easier task to manipulate the ambitious Claiborne. Edward made sure that Laffite was becoming an ever-increasing thorn in William's side and an even more significant source of embarrassment. Following Simone's advice, Edward never allowed his remarks to be overheard by anyone outside of Claiborne's inner circle, and most times, they were only whispered into the man's ears in private. In this way, Edward was able to gain still more respect, trust, and, better yet, a stronger bond to the ever-clueless Territorial Governor.

Simone and Edward did nothing that would openly make their

hostilities towards the Laffite circle known. They would work slow and bide their time, picking their opportunity carefully, as to when to destroy those they hated with a vengeance. It was vengeance that had become an obsession with both of them, and their hatred continued to grow with each passing day.

During different gatherings, Tori often caught a glimpse of Simone or Edward, mostly Edward, staring at her. He would always look away and act as if he had not even noticed her, yet her instinct warned her that the only reason they attended specific functions was to follow her or Jean.

Generally, the Laffites found themselves surrounded by close friends, who did not invite Edward and Simone for one reason or another. Then there were times that Jean and herself could not avoid crossing paths with the pair. Events, like the large garden gala they had been present at the night before, was one among these. "Did you see Edward at Claiborne's side last night? I don't know how he has become so close to him. Or what he's up to, but I'm sure it has something to do with us. You don't think he has told the man about me, do you?"

Jean rolled over and took her in his arms. The cooler air of the morning was the only time the two could lay close together. The days and nights' oppressive heat made being close uncomfortable, even with the balcony doors wide open.

Jean was recalling their conversation from the night before, of how she'd explained to him about an invention called air-conditioning. He could only imagine how comfortable it would make the long summer days that still lay ahead of them if they had such a contraption.

"Cat got your tongue?" Tori laughed as she poked his side to get him to answer her.

"Sorry, I was thinking of something else, but I admit I too watched Edward and Simone. It's easy to locate the two of them these days, always hovering around Claiborne or his entourage. I agree with you. It did seem as if the two of them were spying on us. I shall have to learn what is going on." He stroked her brow gently, pushing a strand of damp hair off her face. "The past few months with you have been so wonderful; still, I fear I might have become too lax in my observance of that dandy and the black widow." He chuckled at the name Tori had chosen to call Simone. Seeing her frown right then, he told himself, it was best to continue the conversation without referring to Simone in such a derogatory way, even if it was his lady's idea. "Edward spells trouble; I am certain of it, even if nothing has happened yet. I have not wanted to say anything to you, but I do not trust him or Simone, for that matter."

Tori's eyes widened at Jean's admittance. 'I knew it! You and I are on the same page with those two.' Then her mind was filled with another more unsettling revelation. "Did you see her last night? I mean, really watch her. Her husband's not cold in his grave, and she is out on the town as if nothing happened and getting away with it."

"Indeed. It was amusing, to say the least. Even the old widows, who would typically be shocked and horrified at such goings-on, are condoning her actions. She should still be in mourning, I agree. It is the custom to have up to a year or longer to mourn but not her. Simone has rewritten what is accepted, it seems. I overheard a couple of ladies, and they think that it was just what Simone needed. To attend the social event, that is. Said it was acceptable. Can you imagine? The 'poor child,' they called her. I can tell you, my love, that when I heard that, I all but choked on my wine!"

Their close proximity was causing him to respond with a desire he knew he would have difficulty controlling if he continued to remain. Jean moved away from Tori's side and smiled. "He sure is active this morning, isn't he?" He touched her midsection, caressing it gently with his caring hand.

"You amaze me. How many times do I have to tell you, it could be a girl? You know, you just don't seem to get that through your head, do you?"

Jean smiled and continued to stroke her swollen abdomen, his every touch driving sparks of electricity up and down her spine. It had been weeks since they had made love, all because he insisted on doing what was right. The stupid doctor had said that there was to be no loving of any physical kind. No intimacy at all, due to the heat and how far along she was. Tori knew better but could not convince Jean or the doctor that continuing to have a physical relationship was nothing to worry about.

That's when the physician had dug his heels in. "Surely they would not want to jeopardize the baby or its mother," he had questioned? His retort and concern had swayed Laffite.

Jean could be so stubborn and bullheaded at times, she told herself. He would follow what the doctor said to the letter, and nothing was going to change his mind. Tori had begged him just the other morning, pleaded with him, telling him it was not dangerous, and that the doctor's concerns were silly. After all, she should know, shouldn't she? This was not her first child, and in her time, they had proved lovemaking was perfectly healthy for pregnant women; in fact, it was recommended! However, all her pleading had fallen on deaf ears. "You know, we can be closer, it is alright." Tori took his hand and raised it toward her breast, but Jean reacted instantly and pulled back before she could place it on her chest.

"I will not be swayed and you know that to be so. I suggest you refrain, or I shall have to depart."

Angrily, Tori responded. "Run far away from what you want, what I want, what we need? I don't understand why you won't listen to me on this. I do have needs and feelings, you know? It's not all about what you want or think is best."

"Enough, I see that you will continue to discuss that which can't be." Jean rolled on his side away from her and climbed out of bed to begin dressing without saying one word. In the foul mood he was now in, Jean told himself, what he needed was a good long horse ride and someone who could explain it all to him. Just what in the hell was happening? He had never seen Tori act like she was. She was demanding and tempting him to do what he believed was detrimental to her health. Not even caring about the child it seemed, or worse still, what she was putting him through. It was cruel. He would never understand women, especially pregnant.

It was then that an idea came to him; his friend J.D. might be able to shed some light on the matter. After all, he'd been through this with Marie, so many times. It was time for a long talk with his friend. "I will leave you alone for now. Maybe some sense will come to you, and you will see that I am right." With that said, he turned and stormed from the room, closing the bedroom door none too gently.

Tori was left alone with nothing but her angry mood for company. Just what in the hell did he know about her feelings? For weeks, she had been waging a battle against herself, always managing to hold on somehow. It was not easy dealing with the guilt of loving one man in one century and having a family and a child in another. She squeezed her eyes shut and screamed at the ceiling. "I miss Linni, and I love you, but God help me, I love that dumb, pig-headed pirate more than he knows." There, she had finally said it out loud and with a depth of feeling that was stronger than ever. She had finally admitted how she felt out loud. Oh, she had said the three words often. I love you, were easily spoken, and she had meant it but not like this. Tori had loved him as a dear friend, and as a lover, but now? In her own words, she'd admitted the truth. She was 'in love' in every sense of the word and could no longer deny it.

The mother to be began to face the truth she'd put off for so long. Her love for Laffite was paralleled by his love for her. It had been, ever since that day on the island beach. Oh sure, she'd felt a part of her heart go to him back on Grand Terre, even admitted it somewhat; however, what she'd done since then, was skirt around the depth of her feelings and even held back. Now, she'd burst the dam. She'd gone and told herself the truth once and for all. Angry at this acknowledgment and not wanting to face its repercussions, she tried forcing her thoughts of love to the back of her mind and focused on her upset mood instead.

It was all she could do to push down the wave of raw emotion that threatened to overtake her and drown her in a pit of despair. Love hurt, it hurt to miss her daughter, and it hurt to admit she loved Jean. It hurt all the way around. Worse yet, he hurt her. A cold knot seemed to fill her heart and squeeze. If this was going to be Jean's attitude, blaming her for everything, she was not about to go running after him, no matter how bad she wanted. "I can be just a stubborn as you, and you know what, you are not right, so there," she shouted toward the door, knowing it was useless. The infuriating pirate was already downstairs and well out of hearing range. Still, it felt good to let off some steam.

The tension between the two of them had been building the past few weeks. Why didn't Jean get it? It was not her fault that she could not reach out to him and satisfy his sexual hunger, as she wanted, it was his. He was the one who always pulled away. He was the one who did not accept that her condition was not an illness! Damn him, she thought. Everything was his fault, every bit of it, and what did he do? The ignorant pirate did nothing more than accuse her and then leave.

Tori's whole body seemed to tense at the very thought of him and his childish way of dealing with the situation. Gone was any form of reasoning she might have had. Jean's wife was past tolerating or understanding; she no longer cared why she felt as she did. It was just far easier to blame Jean than admit she was letting her guilt and emotions run away with themselves. Tori flatly refused to acknowledge the small voice in the back of her mind, telling her that she was the one who was being difficult this time.

THE lonely woman felt awful. The day was hotter than usual, and the air that hung in the room was stifling. Tori had to get out, maybe sit downstairs in the cool of the courtyard. Once outside, however, she found it no better. Even under the tree, Tori could find no relief. The atmosphere was so thick and stagnant that she swore she could physically drown on each breath she took. If only the humidity would drop, she might feel more comfortable, she reasoned, knowing full well that it was like asking for a miracle to happen. Such miracles, though, did not occur for her. There was one thing that might help her cool down, and though not a miracle, she would demand it right away. "Bessy, anyone, someone? I want my bath filled now, not later, and I mean it. Now, or I will have Boss sell you."

Realizing she had never spoken in such a hostile manner to any of the household help, guilt flooded over her and brought with it a sense of great embarrassment and shame. What was wrong with her? 'One thing is clear; I'm mad as hell, and I'm miserable.' This and other such negative thoughts filled her mind as she climbed the stairs.

God only knew how she hated New Orleans, its weather, and its people right then. Most of all, she hated being stuck in this time. Hated being with a stupid man who did not want to understand her or her feelings. Dealing with being pregnant was a good reason to be frustrated as all get out, and now to top that off, she had to put up with everything alone. Add the heat, and trying to get by without the aid and comfort of simple things, like an air conditioner, ice cold soda, or a decent massage, was torture. 'Hell, I would even go in a pool, but they don't have those yet, do they? Stupid people. What do they do, just sit inside fanning away all day? Hell no, they run out of town, just like he's done. I bet he's gone to some secret place to sit in the shade and sulk.'

Upon hearing footsteps, Laffite's wife turned to see two young slaves standing in the hallway. Each carried buckets of water. Without waiting to be told, they entered and began to empty the water into the wooden tub. Tori stood watching impatiently while the tub was filled.

Instead of feeling pleased by their actions, she felt a surge of anger. They were new servants, who had been brought to the house by Jean, and she didn't know them. If he kept changing things, how could she ever hope to feel comfortable with those who worked for her?

Jean had changed the household without even asking her, said something about her becoming too attached to them, that he was merely remaining cautious about little ears and big mouths. Like she would go and tell one of them her secret so that they could spread it all over town. Did he think her a complete idiot? At least he had kept the cook Bessy, and only then because she had insisted over the past few weeks, that anyone else's cooking would make her ill.

Tori continued to pace the bedroom. Her mind and her whole body cried out for relief from the infernal heat that surrounded her. She knew the last weeks of carrying the child were making her act and feel so at odds, but that did not matter. Right then, the only thing that mattered was feeling cooler.

It took nearly a half an hour to fill the tub to Tori's liking, but finally, the chore was finished. As the young girls were leaving, their Mistress told them that she was not to be disturbed. Then she pushed them from the room and slammed the door behind them. God, it felt good to be awful and lash out, she told herself. If she had to feel miserable, then so did everyone else, she reasoned, and she prayed Laffite was feeling the same. 'How could I ever have thought I loved him,' she thought with tears springing to her eyes. Angrily, she wiped them away, deciding that she would not let him have the upper hand.

Slipping down into the fresh, flower-scented water was like opening the refrigerator door on a hot summer day. The instant relief felt so wonderful that Tori knew she could relish it for hours. The frustrated woman sunk down further until only her head was above the waterline. True, her toes were left sticking out at the other end of the tub, but who cared about toes being hot. All she knew was that she had been foolish trying to stand the heat when she could have been in the cool tub all the damn time.

Off in the distance, she heard the rumble of thunder. It had done this for several days. Nothing had ever come of the display. It was just a big show of forked lightning on the horizon, teasing the city's citizens, with the possibility of rain. Laffite's wife closed her eyes and prayed that this time, it would pour down and cool things off. Touching her stomach, she talked to the baby. "You would like that, wouldn't you?" Tori could not feel the baby moving and realized it had stopped kicking after Jean had stormed out. For a child who loved to toss and turn, giving her little time to rest, this was a blessing. Laying her head back on the tub's rim, with her eyes closed, a very emotional and physically drained Tori drifted off into a blissful sleep.

TORI wasn't sure how long she'd slept. Nor was she fully aware of what had caused her to wake up so suddenly, from such a deep state of slumber. The still sleepy woman yawned, taking in a deep breath of the muggy air. Disappointed, she realized nothing had changed. Just like earlier, she could feel the hot, stagnant atmosphere around her; it was just as still and as heavy as ever. The room, however, was different. It was bathed in an eerie greenish light. It was the kind of light that appeared when a big storm rolled in at her parents' home in Texas.

A sudden flash of lightning lit up the room, followed closely by nothing short of an explosion. This bombardment brought her sharply out of her drowsy state. Its crackling, blue charge caused her to sit up and grab onto the tub's sides out of sheer terror. Never had she been so close to a lightning strike. The bolt that had just flashed had in, her estimation been damn near on top of her. Sitting there, Tori winced in pain as she tried turning her head to look outside. "Wonderful now, I have a stiff neck to add to my discomfort, and if that's not enough, there's stupid lightning flashing and hitting God knows where." Tori listened as the next clap of thunder rolled. The sound seemed to go on and on, as one continuous low rumble before fading away, and Tori found herself wondering if they got tornadoes often or at all in the area? They sound like a train she'd been told, but that rumble had stopped, and so it had to have been nothing more than maybe two or more flashes of lightning close together. Thoughts like this bombarded her mind as she stepped out of the bathtub. The main storm, she figured, must still be some distance off. The one thunderbolt that had scared her so bad was just the front approaching, she assured herself. "Nothing but static, but let's hope not, hey little one? Rain would be nice for a change." She was talking to the baby and herself and didn't even realize she was doing so, to remain calm and not panic.

Everything was so still, and looking around the large room, she could not help thinking how eerie and quiet the place was when the rumbling thunder stopped. There was not a sound in the house; only the approaching storm, with its bolts of lightning and crashing roar, kept her company. The nervous female knew that it was her fault she was alone. After all, she'd told everyone not to disturb her, hadn't she? An act she now regretted. The nervous female looked from the closed bedroom door to the open French doors that led outside. 'This is silly. It's only a thunderstorm, and you don't need to act like a child. Pull yourself together. Let's take a look, then decide if we need to go downstairs or not.'

Not bothering to dry off, she walked over to the verandah and pulled back the thin lace curtains that hung lifelessly over the opening. Tori had hung them in hopes of keeping out some mosquitoes, but they had not helped much. Looking at the delicate fabric hanging limply, Tori was confident that the only thing they were doing at that moment was keeping the cooler air out and nothing more.

Pulling hard, she tore first one and then the other down, tossing them to the side, where they fell in a heap upon the wooden floor. Then, as if to answer her hostile actions, the threatening storm swept forward, with its first strong gust of wind. Like magic, it came out of nowhere and not slowly or gently, like a caressing breeze, but hard and forceful, with gale-force strength. It blew in on her, almost taking her breath away and caused her to take a step backward but not in fear. Unafraid of the sudden onslaught, she stood there, loving how the wind cooled off her wet body.

The pregnant woman felt glorious and stepped forward onto the balcony, where she stood looking toward the darkening sky. The clouds, like great ocean waves tossing on a raging sea, came racing towards her. They were purple and black, rolling and boiling as they blew overhead. Tori observed these ominous clouds and instinctively realized they were not your typical storm clouds. They were not high up and flat on the bottom. These were low and angry and swirled around each other. The churning sky was so close that she thought had the house been three more stories high, the furious mass would have undoubtedly enveloped her.

Watching them hurl by, Tori felt as if their very power surged throughout her body. Then without warning, a mighty bolt of electricity shot across the heavens, its fury tearing open the abyss above, with a tremendous explosion. The crack vibrated the floor beneath her. So loud was the noise that it shook the windows, and from somewhere outside, she heard the scream of a terrified child.

Then the rain started, slowly one drop, then another. Large and heavy, they began to tumble towards the earth. Tori looked away from the clouds above, to the courtyard, surrounded by the high brick walls. She witnessed each drop spitting down, watched as they landed upon the parched ground, bouncing and dancing about before the dry soil sucked them up.

Mesmerized, Tori continued to stand where she was, watching the rain as it rapidly increased. It was as if each drop were trying to penetrate an invincible surface. Some of the more massive drops splashed and bounced so high that she thought they might be hail instead of raindrops, but she ruled that out with no sign of ice. Laffite's wife looked out over the wall and watched as low gray clouds swept toward her. Another brilliant flash of forked lightning lit up the sky, this time striking the ground not far away, and was quickly followed by another tremendous blast of thunder. The proximity of both indicated that the storm had to be almost on top of her, but to her surprise, Tori no longer stood in fear of the raging weather surrounding her.

This latest roar, it seemed, was nature's signal for the whole onslaught to begin. The heavens responded to its call by opening the floodgates and allowed the real deluge to begin. It came toward her like a sheet of solid water. The kind that when driving a car, you would have to pull over. Standing there looking at the sky, Tori could no longer determine where the clouds were and where the rain began, because both, had in her mind, become one and the same. She just stood and watched, captivated by the sight and the cold shower's feeling against her body. One second, she was nearly dry; the next, her skin was soaking wet. Unabated, Tori thrilled in the lovely refreshing shower, as if she'd never seen or felt a rainstorm in her life. Standing naked on the balcony, Jean's wife had no fear of its fury; instead, she enjoyed letting the raindrops sting her body, not caring because she was cooler at last.

The wind whipped around her, adding the final sensation of shivering. Exhilarated and caught up in the glory of the moment, nothing else mattered. Her hair was soaking wet, dripping cool liquid down her back. Little rivers of water ran down her skin, slipping and sliding to the wooden decking. She could feel each stream of water on her back, like ice-cold fingers, they traveled along her skin. They tickled her, and it seemed to Tori that every pore on her body was responding in delight. Slowly she turned, slipping her hands up under her hair, as if she were in the shower, letting the onslaught continue to bombard her. Tori allowed the sheets of rainfall to pound down upon her, and then like a child, she leaned back her head, opened her mouth, and tried to catch some of the cold water.

Then without warning, the pleasant sensation vanished as a pain grabbed her midsection, and like the storm that raged around her, it was powerful. The first contraction left no doubt in her mind about what was happening. Another crack of thunder drowned out her screams as she buckled over, grabbing her stomach. With the pain came the realization that it had not been the storm that had awakened her. It had been the beginning of labor. Tori had just not wanted to face it. For hours she had been in the beginning stages and chosen to ignore the signs. It was instantly apparent to her then why she had been so moody and upset, so why hadn't she admitted it to herself or Jean? "Because I'm scared, that's why!" she shouted, as the contraction eased. Tori knew she was about to have a baby with no modern hospital, no doctor, and God knows, no help. If something went wrong, and things could go wrong, she understood that there would be little anyone could do. Marie Destrehan had told her of how things had gone wrong, for no reason, with two of her pregnancies and how for no reason, the Almighty had chosen to take her newborn children to heaven.

Slowly Tori straightened up and placed her hands on her stomach. How far along in labor was she, she wondered? Undoubtedly there was time yet to send for the doctor and get word to Jean, but then to her utter surprise, she felt her stomach begin to harden under her hands, and with it came the next contraction. This second labor pain was hard and long. It seemed to go on and on, and all she could do was bend over and grit her teeth and groan. Her mind raced as she tried to remember back to how things had been, the first time she gave birth. The contractions hadn't come on so strong at the beginning of labor with Linni, but there again, she remembered hearing how second babies often came a lot faster.

Slowly she uncurled her body and let go of her stomach while taking in deep gulps of air. Tori reached for the balcony railing to steady herself as the contraction had left her shaken up. Determined to calm down, Tori took some deep breaths and gave herself a few minutes to gather her emotions and thoughts. She was preparing to walk back into the bedroom when before she knew what was happening, another labor pain hit, and before a step was taken, she found herself down on her knees. Tori had no time to call out; there was just enough time to grab a deep breath and try to gain control over the wave of agony that now held her in its grasp. She bit her lip, trying desperately to keep from screaming, and just when she felt she couldn't stand it any longer, the pain began easing.

Panic overtook her; how could this be? The baby was not due for another couple of weeks, and here she was, all alone and about to give birth early. Not only that, but the contractions were coming way too close together, and she realized that the doctor had to be sent for immediately because things were progressing rapidly. Besides, she told herself, his medieval help was better than nothing at all, and if they did not send for him right away, judging by the spacing of the contractions, he would not get there on time. Hell, even Jean might not make it, because this child was coming faster than she wanted to admit.

With the storm right overhead, Tori knew calling out for help would be useless. Nature's deluge and howling winds would only drown out any noise she made. Laffite's wife had to think and act smart. 'First things, first,' she thought. 'I have to get inside. I can grab my robe and go and find help downstairs. One of the household servants will run and fetch the doctor, while someone will stay with me, and Bessy can send for Jean.' "Come on, up you get, hang in there, baby. I'm not ready yet."

Once again, she rose to her feet; then, while holding her hands over her stomach, the frightened woman walked into the bedroom as quickly as she could. She grabbed her robe, slipping into it quickly, as she felt the next contraction begin to build. The labor pains were coming way too fast, which meant she needed to hurry because they were only going to increase in duration and frequency. How long in between had they been? It seemed like they were on top of each other, and that did not bode well. This knowledge spurred her on and gave her the courage to act before the next set rendered her helpless. Tori made her way to the door and opened it.

The hallway was dark and empty without a sign of life. The whole house seemed to be like a tomb, dark and foreboding. The next labor pain began, and it seared through her, like a knife. Again, she found herself buckling over and not in control of the contraction.

Tori knew either something was very wrong, or this child was indeed about to be born.

It had been so easy with her daughter. She had breathed her Lamaze, and her sister had coached her. The pain had been manageable. However, what she just experienced was like nothing she had ever gone through. Tori stood frozen in the doorway, too afraid to move. It was more than the pain that held her in its grip, much more. She was terrified that she might have to deliver the child all alone. "No, I won't let that happen," she swore, through clenched teeth and waited. As the contraction eased, she again caught her breath. Then truly terrified, she screamed for help, a call that echoed throughout the empty house. Tori cried out again and again for help and did so with all the strength she could summon.

The only response so far had been flashes of lightning and rolls of thunder. At least those had been intermittent, unlike the pounding rain and howling wind that was constant. Surely, the sound could not possibly drown out her cries for help. Someone would hear, and they would come any time now, she assured herself. Closing her eyes, Tori waited. To her, the seconds passed like hours, and the waiting was agonizing.

Tori knew that she did not have long before the next contraction would erupt and that just standing there would not help her any. After thinking over her options, the mother to be surmised that she might have to make her way to the top of the landing. From there, she could call down for someone, because surely, they would have to hear her, over the storm then. Her eyes looked out at the hallway before her, and she hesitated because the image of giving birth at the top of the stairs filled her tortured mind. Going out of the bedroom would be stupid and most likely futile. The wind was howling, and the thunder seemed to rock the home too frequently. The slaves were most likely huddled in their rooms and would never hear her cries for help. There was no one close enough to come to her help, and she knew it.

Tori was now resigned to facing what lay ahead. "God, help us, little one," were the words she mumbled through her tears. She was about to make her way back to the bed when she heard footsteps pounding up the stairs. Relief filled her mind, as Tori knew without a doubt, someone had finally heard her cries for help.

A relieved Tori saw the dark shadowy shape of Bessy May, their cook, reach the top stairs. The slave just stood on the second landing looking her way, hesitant to do anything unless told. After all, she'd never in her life ever visited the upper floor, and never needed to do so, until now. Hearing her Mistress's calls for help, she'd come immediately, but now finding herself facing the most extraordinary sight, Bessy froze.

Out of relief and searing pain of another contraction, Tori allowed her body to slip to the floor, and as she did so, the words "Lordy be child!" rang in her ears. Then like a miracle, the slave's hands took hold of her shoulders. "It be real, good, I stayed in the kitchen to has me a nap, cause if I had gone, what would you have done? I be here now. What is it you be needing? There be no need to fear the storm none. It's loud for sure, and the wind howls like a dog, but it won't hurt you none. Might gits them that's making their way home from the market and Congo Square, wet and scared, something bad like, but that be them, not you."

It had utterly slipped Tori's mind that today was market day when the help was given the afternoon off. Ever the anti-slave female, Tori had insisted that if she and Jean were to have slaves, they would at least be treated the way she thought they deserved. Along with Sunday, they should have one afternoon a week to themselves, she had explained in no uncertain terms, and Jean had agreed, saying if that's what it took to keep her happy, then it would become the house's rule.

Looking at her Master's wife, Bessy thought it had been a stroke of luck that she'd decided she did not like the sky's look earlier. Bessy had stayed home instead of joining the others to go to Congo Square and was glad she had done so because the woman on the floor was in real need of help. Miss Tori had herself all worked up over the storm, and in her condition, well, that was not right like.

Kneeling by Tori's side it only took the cook a few seconds to realize what was happening, fear of the storm had nothing to do with her young Mistress state of distress, and instantly the slave began to do what she instinctively knew was needed.

Reaching down, she lifted Tori to her feet while talking to her in a calm and soothing tone. "Come on now; you don't want this childs ta be born on the floor, now do you? We's best gits you into that there, bed, and settled down all comfortable like. Then we's a goin' ta send for that doctor. You don't a worry any, Bessy's be here, and everythin' be fine. The first child, they take their time a-comin', and we's has lots a time to gits ourselves ready. That be a real good thin', us having the time. Cause it be just the two of us here in this here house. Don't you worry none. No sir. You be just fine. Bessy, she sees ta that. There be a plenty a time and them others, well, with this here storm, they be home sooner, then not. That be, when I tell first one I see's, ta go fetch the doctor."

How could Tori tell this woman that she did not think there would be plenty of time? That this was not her first child? God help her, deep down, she had a sinking feeling that she would indeed, have to deliver the baby without a doctor.

Before they got her back to the bed, Tori stopped walking as another contraction hit, confirming her suspicions. Then as if to back up what she was thinking, her water broke, something that she knew to be the last thing to happen before the need to push. Before she had time to reflect much on that thought, the pain again took her breath away.

The wave of nausea that flooded over her meant transition had begun. The baby was entering the birth canal, and with the next contraction, Tori understood she would want to push. At least, she was not so afraid anymore. Somehow having another person by her side helped give her the strength she needed. This time Tori did not lose control of the labor pain because, at last, she knew just what to do and how. Instead of fighting the contraction, she

341

automatically started to do her Lamaze exercises and use the breathing techniques she had learned to deliver Linni.

Bessy looked at her strangely. This white woman was not only brave, but she had apparently been around someone who had given birth before. She knew'd how ta breathe, ta ease the pain. Somethin' that few, if any proper white women like Miss Tori, practiced. She'd been told most of them, just screamed and carried on somethin' fearsome, makin' the labor harder on both themselves and those present at the birth. Bessy knew that the white doctor would give them ladies somethin' for the pains, and most time, that made it all the worse, cause then they be too weak ta push the baby out. Maybe it was best the doctor was not there, cause the way things looked, Miss Tori had everything she needed, and she didn't need no white man powders to stop the pain.

With the contraction easing, Tori looked up into the kind, black face and realized that her Lamaze breathing must have shocked the housekeeper. "It's all right. Really, Bessy, it is. I learned this breathing from someone who used to deliver a lot of babies. I have even seen it work. Don't look so worried. I assure you I'm not going to swoon or scream. I'm just going to have a baby, and that's a natural thing. Just hard work, right?" She took hold of Bessy's large hand and squeezed it reassuringly. "My water broke, and that means that this child is coming sooner than later, so I think we better get me onto that bed."

Bessy broke out into a broad grin. Her smile seemed to fill her face as she shook her head from side to side while thinking. 'Ahh, huh. This here was a-goin' ta be somethin' ta tell about. It would be the talk of the household for some time. Imagine a white lady of her standing, so strong and brave and not fearin' the pain o' birthin.' She herself would not have believed it, if'n she hadn't seen it with her own eyes.'

"I best try an goes ta git help. You a-goin' ta be wantin' the doctor here. What with the baby comin' early like."

Tori weakly smiled at the woman. Oh, how she wished with all her heart that they could reach the doctor, but she doubted it in this storm. She shook her head slowly. With no one else in the house, Tori knew Bessy would have to leave to go for help, and that idea frightened her. Somehow the cook had to be stopped from leaving. Jean was sure to be worried about her in this storm. He would be here soon, and then he could go for help or stay with her and send Bessy. Either way, she needed someone to remain with her. "I think I'm going to need your help. You can't leave me now and go out there in this storm." Tori grabbed Bessy's arm, holding her tight. "There is not going to be enough time!" Then before Tori could stop, she snapped angrily at the woman. "You will not go! I forbid it. You will stay here. Do you understand me?"

With a shocked look on her face, the slave answered her Mistress quickly. "Yes, Miss Tori. I sure does."

Knowing that the cook would never disobey an order, Tori softened her tone. "I'm sorry. I did not mean to shout at you. Bessy, have you ever seen a child born?" These last words escaped through clenched teeth as another contraction began to build and, once again, the soon to be mother started her breathing, but faster now, as she held tightly to the slave's hand for added support.

"Lord child, I seen um come, yes sur. I seen um easy, an I seen um hard. It ain't nothin' new ta me. An, I think you be right, for sure. We's best git's you ready. Cause I a guessin' this little'un ain't a goin' ta waits for no doctor ta git here."

Bessy reached up and pushed the wet hair away from Tori's face, and with the corner of her apron, she mopped away the beads of sweat that had formed on the laboring woman's forehead as she struggled to breathe.

For Tori, the pain seemed to reach deep inside her and twist its way all through her body. Her midsection rose in a tight ball and became as hard as a giant marble, and she watched as Bessy's large black hands rested on her stomach and began to stroke and rub the abdomen, while her contraction peaked.

"It's a easin' now. You kin take you some slow breaths in through your nose. Blow um out your mouth, slow like and try's ta think o lettin' your body rest. That be the way."

Tori listened to her voice as she concentrated on relaxing. There had been no time for Bessy to prepare anything, for it seemed to her that as soon as she got over one contraction, another took its place, and as they hit, the urge to push took over.

Time swept by, as the two of them worked to bring the child into the world. The wind howled outside, blowing the rain inside the room, soaking everything in its path. The thunder rolled, and the storm raged with its full fury. The height of the storm was upon them, and neither noticed nor cared. So, it was between the violent flashes of lightning, wind-driven rain, and thunder that Tori pushed a new life into her cook's loving hands.

Jean would be pleased; it was a boy. He was small, but strong and cried out in protest at having to leave the warm sanctuary of his mother's womb. The infant was handed to Tori, who placed him next to her skin, in between her breasts, where he nuzzled into an instant state of calmness, oblivious to the cataclysmic violence raging around his new home. His mother studied the child as if this were the first time on earth; a small baby had been born, and then she looked at the woman who had helped her. The look on Bessy's face told Laffite's wife, the child was nothing short of a miracle. Without the slave's help, Tori wondered if the end result would have been so. She smiled at the housekeeper and spoke proudly. "He looks just like his father...do you see, Bessy? Look."

The black woman just placed her hands on her hips and laughed. "In more ways, than just looks, if 'n you, ask's me. His papa, don't have the patience ta wait for nothin' either. Always got ta do thin's in a hurry. Yep, his son, weren't a goin' ta wait none, ta be born. Ah, huh, he like his papa." Bessy wiped at her eyes with the back of her hand because tears of joy were rolling down her round face. She was so happy. There was nothing like the successful birth of a child to make a person joyful.

A soft lullaby left Tori's lips as Bessy cut the umbilical cord, setting the child free of his mother's body, to start his life. 'Tommy's song' had long ago put other children to sleep during a storm. Now, it would do the same for her son. Tori hummed the tune as the thunder and wind gradually eased off, but the rain kept falling. The new mother found herself wishing it would ease up a little, to give Jean a chance to come home. Looking down into the sleeping face of her son, she smiled. "Your mother can't seem to make up her mind up on what she wants, little one. First, I beg for it to rain, and then I want it to stop. I'm sure it's the weather that's keeping your father away. At least I hope it's that. I was such a fool; we both were."

Tori thought Jean would have been home hours ago. Night had come, and even though the rest of the slaves had returned home, their Master had not. Surely, Jean would not have stayed away from her this long, without good reason. He had to be worried about her. Then again, maybe he was still upset with her and her crazy moods. If that was true, she could not blame him, and if it was the reason, it had cost him witnessing the birth of his child.

Bessy came into the room, lit a few more lamps, and mopped up where the rain had washed inside. With the wind all but gone, the remaining rain that fell would do so without blowing into the bedroom. It was safe now to leave the French doors open, allowing the evening's cooler fresh air to circulate. The bed was changed, with a fresh mattress brought in from one of the guest rooms. Her Mistress had sat and watched from the overstuffed chair that Bessy had brought up from the library. Then Bessy had stood proudly by Tori's side, as Madame Laffite showed each household slave her son. This action was remarkable, and as news spread of it, the white population would say that Madame Laffite had to have been overcome after giving birth and not realized what she was doing. The black community would scoff at this because they all knew that Tori Laffite had known exactly what she was doing, and as far as they were concerned, she was nothing short of an angle and quite possibly the only white person they would ever trust with their lives. Lucky were those who worked for the Laffites, it was said, and many prayed that their situations would become more like those under Jean Laffite's roof.

Bessy left and came back with a small tray of food. The cook was in her glory fussing about and taking care of Tori and the baby, a baby she would tell everyone that she alone had helped bring safely into this world. Generally, her duties kept her confined to the kitchen, but now the slave knew her situation would change. She was going to become important. She might even have a chance of being the child's nanny. The cook smiled brightly as she talked. "Now it be just a bowl of broth and some cool juice ta drink. A few tasty bits ta, bite on. You gotta, eat, and git strong. That, there baby, he might be small now, but the way's I see's, it, he's a goin' ta eat a lot, ta catch up like. Once the Massa gits the wet nurse, one who be full of milk, he be fine."

Tori chuckled. "There will be no need for any such thing, wet nurse indeed. Why would I want that when I can feed him myself? No, Bessy, I will do fine. You keep on bringing me food as good as you make, and this little one will grow big and strong."

Bessy broke into a broad grin. I suren will be doin' so. So's you best rest up like. A tired, underfed Mama, she, don't make good milk." She looked at Tori and shook her head negatively. "Still don't understand you any. You kin git a nanny ta feed him an all. If 'n I had any milk left, I be glad and proud like, ta feed him myself."

"Oh, Bessy, you're a dream for thinking about us, but as I told you, I want to feed the baby myself." Tori watched as the smiling expression left the cooks face, and a crestfallen appearance took hold of her. "Look, I understand other women of high standing, might want to hand over their children to be raised by a nanny, but I'm not like other women."

"That you ain't, ta be sure, like them other white women. You ain't like no ones I ever met, that be white like." Then she lightened up some. "I be very proud ta know's you, Miss and the Massa. An he's goin' ta be a proud of you too when he git's here that is. You see if 'n he ain't."

Tori just nodded her head. Where in the hell was he? Why was he staying away so long, she wondered? Later that night, she held her son close and shed a few tears. She had prayed that it was only the weather that kept Jean away and nothing else. For what else could it be? Bessy had sent word to Pierre, for surely, he would know how to reach his brother? She had even sent word to Grymes. The doctor had stopped in and was pleased that both mother and child were doing good. He had left orders for her to rest in bed, and he would return the next day. She overheard him giving instructions to Bessy, things like two weeks in bed, and no lifting. The part of remain in bed was a laugh. What was not funny was Jean's continued absence. That was her last thought before slumber claimed mother and child.

JEAN had not made it as far as the Destrehan residence. Ever the sailor who watched the horizon, he had scanned the sky as he rode. Knowing that stormy weather was out in the Gulf, and not yet threatening inland set his nerves on edge. The clouds above him moved at a good pace and swept inland by winds that he could not feel. The air was too dense and far too still for his liking, something he had experienced many times at sea. This calm, known to him as the doldrums, happened when not a breath of wind was to be had. He looked at the trees and could see that nothing stirred, not one leaf moved. The air was stagnant and threatening. In the distance, thunder rolled, and on the horizon, he could see the forked lightning lighting up the dark sky. This was the calm before the storm, a time when one would prepare if they were smart.

In his mind, there was no other choice to be made. He decided not to go forward. Destrehan and their talk could wait for another time because the pirate's gut instinct told him that what was heading their way was going to be one hell of a storm front, and he needed to be at home. Once that thought settled in his mind, he turned his horse around and headed back. What the man had not counted on was the incredible speed with which this weather traveled. It blew in off the Gulf, catching him and several other travelers, off guard, and he, like them, had to seek shelter from its onslaught to wait it out.

A small tavern under two hours ride from home became his sanctuary as the storm howled outside. Hour after hour, he waited for a break, his anxiety building, as he sat helplessly waiting for Mother Nature to play out her drama. Summer storms could last a few hours or linger far longer, and there was just no way of knowing which kind of storm surrounded them right then. The winds were high, but it was no hurricane, and for that, the pirate was grateful. That was, however, the only good he could find in his situation.

JEAN could not sleep. He wouldn't allow himself that luxury, for fear of missing his chance to make a dash for home as soon as there was a break in the weather. Late afternoon had turned into night, and as it did, so did his chance of reaching his love before early the next day. To ride in the inky blackness on roads that would be nothing short of muddy waterways would be insane and Jean never pushed his luck. For Laffite, the long night dragged by, with each hour feeling like an eternity. Then finally, with dawn's early light only a half hour off, and the worst of the storm gone, he weighed his options and decided he could wait no longer. While most thought him crazy to depart before full daylight, they knew better than to try and talk him out of what he was determined to do.

Jean was no fool, as many thought him to be, that morning. Instead, he was a realist who knew in his heart that although the first part of the ride would be slow going, he could be well on his way home, before full sunrise.

The rain came in short heavy showers for the first hour of his ride, and several times, he'd had to halt his animal, waiting for the visibility to clear. There were moments; he could only see a few feet in front of him, as the wind-driven squalls pounded down on both rider and horse. Besides these treacherous conditions, the road was a quagmire in spots and lay deeply covered by flooding water in others. This made his ride both exhausting and risky. In several places, the water was deep enough that it brushed the animal's belly, but still, he slowly pushed on, continually seeking the higher ground to avoid the muddy pitfalls. It was well after dawn's gray light filled the heavens that Jean stopped and dismounted his weary mud-covered beast.

The rain had ceased, and the sky was partially clear at last. The storm had blown itself out, leaving the ravaged landscape in its wake, and despite the debris, Jean knew that the ride home would be far more manageable from there. The desperate man was so close to reaching the city, but he was worn out like his horse. He did not regret his choice in stopping, only angry that he had to do so. He was a lover of animals and respected the horse's needs before his own. To push the horse harder, under the still treacherous circumstances, would be cruel, as well as dangerous. One misstep could send them both tumbling, which could result in broken limbs. For him, a broken bone could be mended, but not for his horse.

Laffite slipped from his mare begrudgingly and sat with his head between his knees, listening to the Mississippi's raging waters. In his estimation, half an hour would be long enough for them to catch their breath before moving on, and in that time, the light by which they traveled would be far better. Jean looked up at his horse, who stood with its head hung down, breathing heavily. He had pushed the animal hard, over the last hour, and judging from the mare's breathing; if he were to try to push onward any sooner, it would end the animal's life. Should that happen, his journey on foot would take much longer, and the guilt over killing his mare would never leave him.

He sat back against the tree trunk and looked longingly at the road in front of him. Soon he would begin the last leg of his journey. He just had to have patience and faith that his decision to wait a bit longer was the right one. It occurred to him then that he would not have had to stop at all if he had what Tori called cars. He grinned at the image in his mind. Carriages that moved by something she had called gasoline and horsepower. Horsepower! What a contradiction that was when horses had nothing to do with making them work. She had explained how an engine-turned, what was it called? He closed his eyes to think, but so many thoughts raced around his weary mind that he gave up trying to recall the name of what moved the wheels. Many inventions from Tori's time could help him right then, and somehow thinking about them and imagining them helped relax the anxiety he'd felt while riding. Exhaustion was overcoming the pirate who had not slept, and his chin dipped down to rest on his chest. Jean was just drifting off to sleep when a voice rang out in the morning air, jolting him upright.

"So, you just a going to sit there like that! Last thing I heard about you was that you were no quitter. The horse has rested well, for her sides show no sign of labored breathing. Should you choose to open your eyes and see for yourself, you will know I speak the truth."

Jean had not heard her approach, whoever she was, and turned to see where the voice had sounded. It was the voice of a young woman, so that was what he looked for among the early morning shadows. It took him only seconds before he saw her standing motionless on the edge of the clearing. The female was wearing a hooded cloak, and she showed no fear. Intrigued, Jean spoke. "May I ask who addresses me?"

"You may, but idle talk wastes precious time when you could be home with Victoria, where you should be."

He was shocked but did not show it. Laffite stood up slowly and looked even harder toward this mysterious character. The stranger stood her ground, just outside the range of his vision, her face hidden in the shadows and by her cloak, yet he felt sure he knew her.

She called out to him again. "I passed by your home earlier. Carried on the wind, came the sound of a woman, about to bring life into this world. The river's water runs free of the road in this, the last few miles to home. You can safely travel to her side if you leave now. The river, she will not stay low too long, for many waters up North, flow downstream, and will cover this land again soon. I suggest you make haste."

Jean didn't hesitate; he mounted his horse as she finished speaking and quickly turned the animal around toward her. Promptly he coaxed his animal ahead a few steps, intent on finding out more, but all he found was an empty road. Whoever she was, the female had vanished, and Laffite knew that if he searched, it would be a waste of time. The underbrush was so dense in the area that a person could easily take cover and hide with no fear of being located.

He coaxed his horse slowly forward while scouring the underbrush when a sobering thought hit him. If what the stranger had said about Tori was true, then his wife needed him. In that second, he no longer cared who the mystery woman was, or how she came about her information because something far more pressing had taken hold. The man wanted to reach his house and wife, as fast as he could. Jean spurred his horse forward and raced for home, revitalized with the thought, and the possibility of a child's birth—their child. With the sounds of nature and a female laughing, echoing across the land, he rode harder still.

Marie Laveau smiled to herself. Jean Laffite would not stop for anyone or anything now, she had seen to that. When he rode past her, the look on his face as she crouched only feet away had sent her into fits of laughter. The young woman loved the power she had, the power of scaring people or creating a feeling of awe. Laffite would tell his story and wonder who had called to him in the middle of nowhere, and she would see to it that word leaked out among the slaves about their encounter. Yes, soon, it would be common knowledge that it had been none other than Marie

Laveau, the voodoo queen, that Laffite had talked with. Everyone would say that Marie always knew all that was happening and always helped those she chose too. No one would have to know the truth, that it had all come about by sheer chance.

It was early morning when at last, he approached his home. It had taken him many hours of hard riding to reach the house. There had been a lot of damage from the storm, and even though the strange woman had said his way was clear, she had not mentioned that it would be a grueling task to navigate the debris-strewn roads.

No one met him as he rode up to the front entrance, and the interior of his home was dark and silent when he opened the door. The pirate tried to remain calm as he made his way inside, telling himself everything was normal because, as far as he could tell, they had weathered the storm just fine. As for his household slaves not being seen anyplace, he would get to the bottom of that quandary later. The quietness about the place could be a good sign, yet it was the continued silence as he reached the stairs that began to unnerve him. By now, someone should have welcomed him. Even Bessy would typically leave the kitchen to see him. Something was not right, and his heart skipped a beat as he began to climb the stairs two at a time rapidly.

Quickly, with his heart pounding and praying that everything was as it should be, he made his way to the second landing and then down the hallway toward their bedroom. He hesitated momentarily outside the door to their room, listening for any sound to indicate what was going on. When he heard nothing, Jean cautiously pushed the door open and looked inside.

Sitting by the side of the bed was their cook, Bessy. She had been sleeping, but like a good guard dog, she woke up at the sound of the door handle clicking. Turning to see who it was that had disturbed her and ready to chastise them for not listening to her orders, the cook stood up and was stunned to see a man's outline standing in the doorway. She was about to speak but stopped upon recognizing the man was Laffite. Quickly the slave put her finger to her lips to silence him, and without looking at Tori, she stood up and quietly made her way out of the room.

Once by his side, and not thinking about what she was doing, the cook physically pushed him back into the hallway, closing the bedroom door behind her. "Now don't you go wakin' her up any. She, be needin' her sleep and that son of yours, he's a-goin' ta keep you both up many nights ta come on account of her wantin' ta nurse him and all."

Disbelief filled Jean's face. "Son? Did you say, son?"

"Yes, Massa. I sure'n uff did. Miss Tori, she, do it all herself and all; the birthin' and all. Weren't no time, for no doctor, no Sir, no time at all. I just helped her some, and you best be proud of her. Miss Tori be one special lady. Like I said, she didn't have no doctor nor nothin'. She just, work herself birthin' that child, till she plumb worn out. You best be good ta her." Bessy lowered her eyes, as she realized that she had over-stepped her bounds, telling the Master of the house what he should do, and Lordy, by actually pushing him out of the bedroom and baring his way, what was she thinking? Heaven help her; she had really gone beyond herself. He'd have every right to become angry or worse, but he had to see that she'd done everything out of caring for the Mistress and his child.

Jean didn't care about any of her actions. All he could hear was the word 'son' echoing in his head, and before the cook could raise her eyes to look at him, Jean hugged her in an embrace, which surprised them both.

The girl in the bayou had been right after all, and the how or why of it mattered not. He pushed the cook away from him and stood to look into her large brown eyes. "How will I ever be able to thank you for what you've done?" Joyfully, he added, "No way will I ever be able to live without you after this." He was softly chuckling as he continued. "Your standing in my household has taken a leap in its placement. We will have to talk about that later." Jean's eyes were alive with happiness as he took Bessy by the shoulders and said in a more serious tone, "You do not have to worry now, Bessy. I will not wake her. You can leave and get yourself some rest." Seeing her expression turn sad, he added with a soft but firm tone. "Now, don't you look at me like that; it's natural. Who else do you think should have more right to sit by her side than me? I might add, to cheer you up, when I am working, that will be your task, you know."

Bessy's expression immediately changed hearing this, and she broke out in a huge grin. Her Massa was acting more like a child on his birthday, who had received every toy he wanted. He most certainly was not acting like a responsible adult, hugging her and all. Lord, above, he did not have a clue as how to handle a newborn; neither of them did, so he'd be calling her back soon enough. She could leave him rightfully enough, but just for now, and not long either. Bessy found herself thinking that it was useless to tell Laffite that he looked like he needed to sleep, just as much, if not more than his wife did. That he also needed a good bath and maybe some of her homemade bread and ham. No, he was going to be stubborn and headstrong like always, but yes, um, they would be needing old Bessy real soon like, and that meant she'd have plenty of time to see to the needs of the baby for them. She smiled and mumbled to herself as she headed downstairs to start breakfast and heat some water for his bath.

Jean stood for a few seconds outside the door. He felt as if he could shout from the rooftops. Never in his life had the man felt such joy. The woman he loved had given him a son, and nothing could compare to that. Carefully he opened the door and stepped inside, all the time watching the bed and his wife's sleeping face. Seeing that she was undisturbed, he closed the bedroom door softly behind him and tiptoed his way toward her, careful of his every step.

Tori lay there sleeping. Her breathing was deep and rhythmic, her face peaceful and calm. He thought he saw a hint of a smile on her lips, and then he saw the baby nestled close to his mother's side. His blue eyes were open and looking right into his fathers. To Jean's amazement, the child did not move or make a sound, so carefully, he knelt by the side of the bed and held his breath as he reached out slowly to stroke his son's cheek.

How small he was. How perfect. It was almost too good to believe, and yet there he was, his son. The infant had taken a firm grip on his father's finger and didn't let go, and at this point, Jean was quite simply overcome with emotion. If ever he felt joy before, it came nothing close to this, and the man honestly felt as if he might explode. The strong pirate's eyes filled with tears of love, as he slowly reached forward to pick the child up gently. Once in his embrace, Jean marveled at how big his own hands seemed compared to the baby's size. Gently, he handled this small human, in fear of hurting him and cradled him close to his chest. The child made no sound; he just continued staring back at the man, who now held him.

This small human was his son, his flesh, and blood. This child was the result of his love for the woman, whom he had no claim too. Looking at Tori, Jean felt that the hardest thing he could ever do would be to lose her. But surely, he had hope also? After all, he realized, Tori now had something more to anchor her to this time and keep her with him.

As if sensing someone was looking at her, Tori opened her eyes. Seeing Jean by the side of the bed holding his son so lovingly, she knew there was no need for words. The two adults looked deeply into each other's eyes and spoke volumes without uttering a sound. Gently, Jean placed the baby in his mother's arms and then slowly joined his wife, by her side.

The child nuzzled closer to Tori and finding her nipple, started to suck hungrily, and the gentleman pirate placed his arms around them both. Jean tried to say something, but his throat was too constricted; it was as if he had a large lump blocking any sound, so he just smiled, and for the first time in his life, he let tears fall freely.

"I take it you are pleased it's a boy?"

"My lady, I am far more than pleased. My state of mind is filled with more emotions than you can grasp. That you have given me a child, us a child, is beyond mere words. True, I am thrilled it is a boy, but more, I am happy that you are well, that is, according to Bessy's word, and I have no doubt she is correct. Oh, my love, you have given me something that I can't find the words to describe. Just know that I love you both, beyond all reason, for now, and forever." Tori smiled.

"You look tired, and I know I am. Let's rest, and then we will discuss what has happened to both of us."

They would talk later about what had taken him so long to return because all that mattered right, then, was he had returned, and they were a family.

## ⸎ Six ⸎

One day quickly and happily, followed another. The weeks flew past in a blur to both Tori and Jean. They were so involved with their newborn son and each other that they had become oblivious to the world around them. Jean's small family became the center of his life, and every hour spent with them was etched in his memory for all time.

A brilliant idea emerged one morning, as Tori sat on the balcony, nursing the baby. Quietly he walked to where they sat and kneeled beside them; he had decided to share his thoughts immediately and see how responsive his wife would be to his idea. Tenderly stroking his son's cheek, he marveled at the image. There in Tori's arms lay a child who seemed far too intent on his breakfast to allow anything or anyone to distract him. Hoping to keep it that way, Jean spoke softly, so as not to disturb him. "You know, as much as I adore keeping you both to myself, the time has come..." hesitating, the pirate looked into Tori's eyes as he continued, "I wish to share my son with the city of New Orleans. I shall show him off with great joy and pride to the people of this town. They will meet the newest and by far, the most handsome, Laffite." The child seemed to smile as if he understood his father's words and finally let his little mouth relax. Grinning, Jean went on to explain. "The idea has come to me that we shall have a grand party. No! Better still, a ball, in celebration of his Christening. What do you say? Are you and my young son here, up to such an event?"

She could see how pleased he was with himself and how it would mean so much to him, but Tori could not resist having a little fun. With a straight face and stern voice, she answered, "Oh Jean, you are such an exhibitionist, but if that is what you want, then, by all means, go ahead." The new mother laughed at his pleased yet perplexed expression. "It is your right to show him off. I'll agree with this idea of yours, only because he does need to be Christened." She put the baby over her shoulder and began patting his back gently. "Which brings me to another significant question." The baby burped and was returned to his original position in her arms. Once comfortable, the child again latched onto her nipple. Tori looked into her husband's eyes and continued. "Something, I might add, that you can't put off any longer needs attending. We need to come up with his full name, and there is another thing to consider. There is the small matter of whom you want for Godparents. Jean, are you listening to me, or are you just going to sit and stare at him for the rest of your life?" She was grinning. How could she be angry? It was fine by her if all Jean wanted was to gaze in wonder at the bundle of joy, who had fallen asleep in her arms for now.

Their son was still refusing to let go of her breast, even in his sleep. The child's little mouth anchored him firmly to his mother, and his tiny hand gripped the edge of her gown. It was as if he were defying anyone to separate him from her or his breakfast. Tori smiled at her son. He was already showing some of his father's traits, one of them being his stubbornness.

Jean's voice was filled with a mixture of disbelief and joy. "You mean that you would not mind if I were to have such an affair? You really do feel up to it?"

Slightly annoyed now, she reached out and pulled Jean's face up with a firm grip on his chin. If she could get him to look her in the eyes and listen, maybe he would believe her once and for all. "Jean, how many times must I continue to tell you? I am not sick or weak. I am not a frail female, who has to be waited on, all the time, nor do I want it." His face showed a trace of disappointment at her last statement. Realizing she had hurt his feelings, Tori tried quickly to make it up to him. "Well, some of the time is all right. You have to get it in that thick skull of yours, though; all I did was have a child. It is nothing new, you know? Women have been accomplishing this feat for quite some time, I hear. Now, you go ahead and plan whatever it is you have in mind. I know you too well. That expression on your face tells me that to try and get you to do otherwise is useless, am I right?"

"Quite right, but..."

"No, but's," she laughed. "There is one small favor I want in return for all this hullabaloo, though. Just one little condition." She looked at him with a coy expression on her face. "I get a new gown." Then she began laughing again at the beaming expression on his face. Of course, she had been teasing him; she had not meant it. It was just that he was taking this all so seriously. Besides, knowing him, he'd already thought of this idea.

"That is something I anticipated. Already, I gave the seamstress your old measurements. She expressed her concern about the gown fitting. After all, hadn't Madame Laffite, just had a child, she asked? I assured her it would fit, as my wife's having a baby had in no way changed her size. The woman reluctantly agreed to make the gown but insisted if it did not fit, I would still be charged the full amount, and an added cost would be charged for any alterations. I informed her that none would be needed." Jean was in high spirits. "After all, who better knows your body and its size, better than me?"

"Jean, you are intolerable at times. The woman very well may be right. My boobs, for instance, are far larger than before and may not squeeze into whatever you have commissioned."

"I have no doubt they will, as long as my son can let go." Jean couldn't help it. He laughed as Tori shot him a frustrated look.

TOGETHER they agreed on the ball's idea, but it was to be Jean's affair, as she put it, and all the arrangements were to be made by him, to which he readily agreed. What she did not share with him was her reasoning behind this decision. Tori was going to sit back, and enjoy the baby and the precious time she had left with her son. For always hanging at the back of her mind was the thought that she would eventually have to try to return to her own time. Her promise to find a way back to the future after the child's birth had to be kept, regardless of how difficult or painful.

It would soon be time to leave her son and his father; she could not put it off forever. However, lately, whenever she was faced with deciding when to go, she'd hastily tell herself she'd deal with it later. Sadly, for her, Tori knew the day was just about upon her when delaying could no longer be her choice. Sooner or later, there would be no more excuses, no more important events to stop her.

The invitations were sought by all and anxiously awaited. The Laffite christening was to be one of the top events of the year. Everyone who received an invitation was held in high esteem, and all spread the word once they had obtained their invite or were certain they'd be receiving one. That was, everyone except Edward and Simone.

The two had not been invited. Not that the pair expected to be, but that did not stop Simone from fuming about it. After all, nothing was preventing her from attending such an event. The widow had come out of full mourning, telling the women of society that Adrian had requested that she not mourn his death; instead, she was to celebrate his life. Being the ever-devoted wife to his memory and wishes, she was going to abide by what he wanted. In the old quarter, it was whispered that following her late husband's wishes was indeed the reason she had broken with tradition. What other explanation could there be, they asked? Simone was a dutiful dedicated widow, following her late husband's wishes, and by doing so, she was admired. Such a short period spent in mourning would never have been so readily accepted otherwise. In the end, Simone's deceitful tale had blindly fooled them.

The ladies and a great many of the gentlemen had not turned their backs on the lowered-in-status Simone. The fair citizens had kept their promises, never to forget her, regardless of other not so friendly rumors. True, she was merely the widow of a once prominent and wealthy gentleman, and was greatly impoverished, but was that her doing, they'd asked? And did they really care or understand why

Adrian had left her so? Adultery, some had said, was the cause of her demise, but if she had been unfaithful to him, there had never been a scandal, and she had undoubtedly been faithful to his memory so far. Many just pushed the ugly rumors away, dismissing them as just that, vicious rumors, spread by jealous rivals. Besides, they would counter, one only had to spend a few minutes with the grief-stricken widow, to know what a true Christian woman she was.

Then, there was the matter of the dashing Edward Duval, and how she had changed his wild ways. He was the talk of the parlors and more so. Many at John Davis's gaming establishment were shocked by the lack of his frivolous spending and change in life-style, something they never imagined would occur.

Simone knew only too well that New Orleans society loved scandal and gossip. They held their heroes high and quickly cast out the fallen. Emotions and opinions changed rapidly, and one's whole life in the city could be ruined or made, depending on the people's hysteria. The conniving female had no intention of having anyone turn against her or Edward. Her ambition to destroy the Laffites and marry the dandy depended heavily on both of them remaining accepted in all the right homes and gatherings.

The young widow had held her status because the people had blindly allowed her to do so. In their romantic view of what happened, they no longer concerned themselves with why Adrian had chosen to do what he did. That trivial matter was far less impressive than the fact that the same beautiful Simone had taken the fallen Edward and changed him. It seemed to them all that he was now trying hard to gain back the respect of his brother and live up to Duval's highly regarded name, a name that he had tarnished for years. It was whispered, behind women's fans and gentlemen's smirks, that Edward Duval loved the young widow and would do anything to raise himself to higher standards, to obtain her hand. So it was, he had become the handsome young hero, trying to win the eligible and vulnerable young widow, who, in her beauty and wisdom, had managed to bring respectability, once again, to one of their own.

People would have been shocked if they had realized the ugly truth going on right under their noses. Con-artists to the hilt, Simone and Edward, were linked together for two reasons: greed and revenge. Simone had laid down all the rules, first of which was for Edward's gambling to stop. She assured him it was the only way to succeed in their plans to gain control of Leone's plantation. When that was accomplished, they'd have the power to ultimately bring down Victoria, or Tori as she was now called, and her pirate husband. Second, his public drinking and wild nights on the town had to end. Not that he minded that too much, because, behind her closed doors, his nights were filled with all the pleasures her body could give him.

After the most significant changes in Edward's behavior had been established, it was easy for them to wangle their way deeper into Claiborne's inner circle. This much sought after situation was accomplished through Simone's connections and the Duval name. Once accepted, the two were invited to many affairs that otherwise would have remained out of their reach.

Claiborne and Cayetana were only too happy to be among the first to help the young couple establish themselves, as they liked to put it, and were proud to call themselves close friends. So it was, that many nights would find the four of them attending one function or another, amicably enjoying each other's company. Simone and Edward slowly and gently continued poisoning Laffite's good name at these gatherings, something made easier, as William Claiborne already had a healthy mistrust of the Laffite brothers and their business practices.

THE widow had worked hard to gain the standing she now held. She felt that she and Edward should have received an invite to the Laffite ball as upstanding citizens regardless of the unrest between them. To not have an official invitation could raise many awkward questions, and she had not come this far to let anything go wrong.

"It is imperative that you obtain an invitation to that event and escort me there. To not show could undo all that we have fought for, the past months. To show up will seal the beginning of the end for those two," she shouted into the dandy's face. "Can't you see that?"

"Madame, how do you expect me to obtain one?" Edward spit back at her in an angry tone of voice. "Am I supposed to walk up to Laffite, and say, I would love to attend the christening of your nigger, son. How about inviting me?"

Simone fumed; her anger was simmering almost to the boiling point. "Don't be so stupid. Of course, I know we can't get one simply by asking." She sat down as if giving up, but the cat-like grin Edward had come to know so well slipped across her lips. Her eyes became mere slits as she made a little humming sound while she thought her idea out. Once satisfied, she had solved the problem; Simone spoke in a low voice, laced with contempt. "We don't need an invitation at all. We will just accompany the Territorial Governor, and his betrothed to the church and then ride with them to the evening ball. Who in their right mind would dare to ask to see our invitations? I mean, can you think of any time that anyone has asked to see Monsieur William Claiborne's invitation? As for the stupid American, he will assume you and I have been invited. We will walk in with them, and once there, I am positive that Jean will not want a scene. Of course, he will have to be the gentleman and let us remain, no?"

For a moment, Edward stared at this woman who sat smugly before him. His beady little eyes were open in astonishment. Her solution was simple and so perfect. "You are truly brilliant, as well as beautiful. It will be a sheer delight to be able to make this happen. Think of it, the challenge. I can imagine the look on both the Laffite's faces as we enter with Claiborne. It's marvelous! Nothing and no one can stop us. If we keep this up, very soon, we will end up with everything we have ever wanted."

The two shot evil smirks toward each other. Simone's eyes flashed like a feline on the prowl, and Edward's cold and calculating eyes squinted slightly in recognition of her unspoken message. The conniving woman watched him warily as he walked toward her, his face handsome and determined, his desire, passionate and hungry. There was no mistaking his expression. Her body went rigid with anticipation of what he intended to do.

THE cathedral was filled to capacity with every seat taken. Even the aisles of the church were occupied with those not lucky enough to obtain a pew. For an August turn out, it was highly unusual. The summer heat alone would have normally kept parishioners away. What had surprised Tori the most as she entered the church was that the date had not stopped quite a few of their friends returning early from their summer homes, the Destrehans among them.

Tori knew that most people had not been invited to the affair. They were in church merely to be able to say they had attended the Laffite christening, and the sheer number of people who fell into this category astounded her.

Tori handed the baby to one of his godmothers, Marie Destrehan, before looking at the congregation. No one seemed to notice or mind that the child had far more godfathers than godmothers. Glancing back at the godparents, Laffite's wife smiled at Marie. She'd had no difficulty choosing the two women that stood by her son's side. Marie and Pierre's wife were the only two women whom she trusted enough to watch over her child once she was gone. As for the godfathers, their son was named after each of them, something that pleased both parents.

"I christen you, Christopher, Pierre, Dominique, Leone, Laffite, in the name of the Father, the Son, and the Holy Ghost. Amen."

Smiling, Dominique turned and took the child from Marie and then handed him to Tori. The proud mother could see by the older man's broad grin, how much it meant to him to be one of their child's godfathers. For Tori, this meant the world. The man, who loved the sea as much as Jean, Dominique, was making every effort to remain a huge part of her life, and now the childs. Her love and respect for the older pirate showed, and when he had suggested the baby be called Christopher, instead of Jean or Pierre, that the child should have his own name, she had agreed. Even Jean had liked this idea, and now it was official.

The boy now had the names and protection of all those who loved him. He would be well looked after; she knew that arrangements were slowly falling into place, and soon the last event would be put into motion.

THEIR home was filled with friends and well-wishers from all over. All afternoon, people came in and presented the young Christopher with lavish gifts and compliments on what a perfect child he was. People commented on how beautiful he was and how much he looked like his father. But it was his eyes that drew the most attention. They were pools of dark blue, like an ocean at night, on a full moon. They were dark orbs, but when the light hit them just so, one could glimpse a tinge of a light blue. Then, there was the expression the infant had on his cherub face. This look affected everyone who gazed at the little lad, even the uptight gentlemen.

All day, he continued to win hearts and, even briefly, won the heart of Simone. If Tori was shocked when Simone and Cayetana walked up to see the child, she did not show it. Instead, a sort of sadness filled her as she looked at Simone. How lonely the widow must be, not to mention desperate to cling to a man like Edward. Tori had heard how he was a new man but doubted that the leopard had changed his spots. He had to be up to something she'd often told Jean. Even then, that notion remained because while watching Simone, she had the overwhelming feeling that both she and Edward were up to no good. Backing up her unease was the fact that the pair were as thick as thieves and even had the audacity to enter the house as if invited, which they were not. For now, though, she was not about to create a scene and was determined only to enjoy showing off her son and not worry about the unwelcome pair.

Cayetana asked if she might hold the child for a moment, and Tori agreed. The fact that her Christopher was getting fussy was a sure sign the girl would only hold him for a moment. The female did not seem the type who would like a fussy baby, let alone know how to handle one. Within seconds of handing him over, Christopher began to cry, and his instant tears gave Tori the perfect excuse to reclaim him. However, just before she took the child from Cayetana's arms, Simone stepped closer.

Casually, she observed the baby's face, and her heart seemed to soften as she looked at the boy. What she'd expected to see, Simone was not sure? According to Edward, the child was of mixed blood, so the telltale sign, such as a darker complexion or some negro facial features, should have been evident, but they were not. He was small and perfect in every detail. The baby had a mass of dark hair, framing his chubby face, and even at his tender age, the resemblance to his father was striking. This recognition caused an instant icy wedge of jealousy, which immediately pushed Simone's contempt of the child's mother to the surface. So intense was the feeling that it completely smothered any tenderness she'd initially felt towards the baby. This could have been her child if Tori had not come along when she did. She should have been the one to give Jean his son, not the half-cast bitch who was reaching for the squalling infant. The scorned woman stared at Cayetana, who was fussing over the brat, as if he were her own, for God's sake and, in so doing, was drawing unwarranted attention to Tori and her child.

Realizing that she was beginning to lose control, Simone bit down on the inside of her lip, tightly closing her lips together as she controlled her anger. The fuming woman masked her emotions and moved in closer to study the child's face more. Surely there would be something that would reveal the secret behind his heritage. A small detail that if not looked for, would go by unsuspected, or noticed. There had to be proof of the boy's tarnished bloodline, but try as she might, she could not distinguish a single indicator, as to the child being anything but pure and innocent.

How was it possible? The disappointed woman shook her head slightly. How stupid of her. If his black heritage wasn't evident now, it would most likely come out in his children, would it not? But hell, Simone did not want to wait for generations, to bring down the bitch that had birthed him. He was pale to be sure, but that side had come from Jean. What a shame he had not inherited his mother's real color, not the shade she was now, but the far darker complexion Edward had described. No doubt, Tori's new appearance was a shade made considerably lighter by some sort of cream or potion. She'd heard that Marie Laveau had a lotion that could, over time, lighten a nigger's complexion, especially those whose skin was already the cafe au lait shade.

Tori had taken the crying child into her arms and smiled lovingly at him when he stopped his fussing. It was as if he knew right away that the embrace which now held him was his mother's, and it was the place he wished to be.

"Do not feel upset, Cayetana, the child knows his mother and wishes to be in my arms, that is all. You will understand the bond between mother and child one day. William's son has taken to you already, I hear, and I am sure will look upon you as his mother as time passes. It is harder to win over a child of two or three years old than a baby of a few months, I assure you. I give you and your skill full credit. I would say you already have a mother's touch."

"That is most kind of you. I do understand a bit about children, it is true, and in time, as you say, I look forward to having my own." Simone looked away from Tori and her child, so as not to arouse suspicions and start any gossip. After all, it was common knowledge that the two were far from friends. Edward's woman had done what was expected of her, and nothing more. There had been no fawning, over the bitch's child, no complements one way or the other, and she had concealed the fact that she was scrutinizing the child for signs of his nigger bloodline. Cayetana had done all the talking and kept the child's mother distracted, as she had hoped, allowing her to discreetly complete her mission.

Simone saw Edward watching her, and she smiled while thinking about the dashing young Duval that fawned over her. He shared everything with her; every detail about his life was known by her. Including all the details he'd revealed about Tori, the darker Tori who had been at Leone's side in the beginning.

Edward had sworn to her that there had been no mistaking her true heritage when he had first laid eyes on his brother's mistress. He'd insisted that Tori had been so much darker than she was today, and Simone had no reason to doubt him then or now.

Again, she wondered how the Laffites had managed to lighten her complexion and keep it so. Simone heard how the women discussed the new mother's olive complexion. They all had agreed it was due to Victoria's European bloodlines. That, and the fact that Tori, as her friends called her, did not stay out of the sun as much as she should. That was another factor that caused her darker hue, they said. After all, it was known Laffite's wife was often seen taking a carriage ride, without even wearing a hat! Simone frowned. She knew better than to believe in their stupid assumptions. It was bloodlines all right but African, not European ones, and she intended to expose it to all of them one day.

Tori had watched Simone studying her and her son and rightly guessed that she was hoping to find a hint of colored features upon her son's cherub-like face. No doubt, Simone had expected that the baby would look like a slave spin-off as some called it, thereby confirming what Edward had believed from the first moment he'd laid eyes on her. Tori would always be nothing more than a fancy nigger's offspring to him. Knowing that the pair were now a couple, almost assured that Edward must have confided his assumptions to his lady, and that meant Simone must feel the same way about her; how could she not? It made her sick to see that the widow had not changed after all. She was still the spiteful bitch she knew her to be.

Tori felt angry for feeling sorry for Simone earlier. The woman was here at her son's celebration, in the hopes of exposing the shocking news she believed to be true, to all those around them, she was sure of it. Well, Simone was the one who would receive a shock. She decided two could play at this game, and it was time to put an end once and for all to Edward's stupid assumptions.

Edward was smiling their way, and Simone was no longer paying any attention to the new mother and child. It had to be a stalling tactic, Tori thought. For if she were no longer interested in them, she would have joined Edward and his small group, instead of hovering around.

The new mother chuckled inside as she made her mind up to carry out her next step. "My, you do look well, Simone. It must have been so difficult for you these past months. Your loss of your husband and the chance to have a child." Simone turned her attention back to Tori with a blank expression. "Yet, you seem to have managed quite nicely, and I admire your strength." Laffite's wife touched Simone's arm gently and spoke with concern in her voice as she proceeded. "I see a hint of sadness in your face. You study the child so closely. Maybe it would cheer you to hold him for a while. You could carry him upstairs for me if you would like. It's time for his feeding, and we would love the company."

Simone could hardly believe she'd heard right. Oh yes, she would love to carry this brat up to his room. Once there, Simone would be alone with his mother and would enjoy telling her a thing or two. The widow smiled at the new mother, who to Simone, was being way too agreeable. Edward's cohort knew she would have to be careful and stay on guard because something was not right. Simone knew Laffites wife did not trust her. Why then, would she act so friendly, she wondered? What was she up too? There again, it could be that Victoria had dropped her animosity toward Edward and herself, thinking they had done the same. A foolish mistake on her part and lucky on mine, she told herself. Simone smiled and held her hands out to take the child. "Why I would be honored, I'm sure. That is if you really mean it?"

"Simone dear, I never say anything I don't mean, do I, Cayetana?"

Cayetana did not have a clue as to what was going on. Neither did she sense the hostility that now encompassed the child's surroundings. The gesture was just such a lovely thing for Jean's wife to do. Victoria was such a thoughtful woman. Her William might have reasons to dislike her husband, but she would tell him that his wife was nothing but a compassionate woman. It was strange though, that a female of her standing chose to speak English most of the time instead of French. Maybe she did so to make others feel comfortable, like the American's who had been invited today. This was another fact she intended to point out to her American beau. William, after all, was trying so hard to bridge the gap between the Creoles and Americans, just like Victoria.

As the Territorial Governor, he went so far as to suggest that all politics be discussed in both English and Creole, and all juries had to be represented by more than just one language. By doing this, justice could be served evenly, he had explained. Making sure his decree was carried out was often tricky, but Cayetana knew that once he had more power and support, things would change, and all the citizens of the city would unite. Yes, if her William would give Victoria Laffite a chance, listen to her, and see how good she was, they might all become friends. Cayetana watched her friend Simone depart with Victoria and nodded her head. She would find William and tell him about what she had just experienced.

Tori and Simone headed up to the baby's room, and once there, she took possession of her son. She walked calmly over to a large chair as if nothing was wrong and positioned herself in full view of Simone's curious gaze. "I have to sit while I nurse him. Would you like to stay? If so, please close the door behind you."

Simone nodded her head, turned, and closed the nursery door gently. Finally, they were by themselves, and no one would hear or see anything, things were going to get interesting. After all this time of wanting to be alone with the so-called 'wonderful Victoria Laffite,' it was happening. Simone turned and faced Tori, trying to keep her expression as blank as possible, but failed to do so in the end. It was just too good a position she found herself in, and her delight showed if delight was the right description.

Tori recognized her expression for what it was and decided to wipe it away once and for all. The smug bitch was about to be put in her place. "You do seem to have something on your mind." She looked Simone in the eye as she continued. "Is anything wrong with Christopher? You study him so closely. Almost as if you are looking for something."

That was about as much as Simone could stand. Whatever Tori was up to, was of no importance to her anymore. She was the one that would say what she wanted and not the other way around. The seething woman decided to tell the fancy, just what she thought, right there and then. "You know why I study him. Don't pretend with me. The child may look white, but we both know that he's as black as you are, is he not? Tell me, does Jean know, or have you somehow neglected to inform him that your blood is tainted?"

"Why I don't know what it is you are talking about, I'm sure. Could you help me? I need to pull this sleeve down lower?" Tori had a plan, and she could hardly wait to see the look on Simone's face as the realization hit her. The sun had been hot the past few weeks, and Tori had been sitting outside. This time, however, she had been more careful. This time, she had made sure that parts of her stayed covered, and as she slipped her gown down to expose her breast for the baby, she was also exposing her very white flesh. Her face, arms, and neck were lightly tanned, but there was no denying the fact that white was her actual color. Once and for all, she'd reveal that the darker skin came from the sun and nothing more. Thank God for tan lines, she told herself, while trying not to smile.

Simone saw it immediately. Her face blanched at the realization. How could this be? Edward had told her that the bitch was black, but she could see for herself that he was mistaken.

"What's wrong, Simone? Have you never seen a child nurse from its mother before?" The room remained silent after that, and Tori waited, knowing the bitch was still trying to come to terms with the truth.

Simone's mind was spinning with the undeniable proof before her. It all fit. The woman's hair was long and wavy, but not kinky as Edward had told her it used to be. Laffite's wife had white skin, where the sun had not touched it. No voodoo spell, no creams or magic could explain away what was obvious. There was no room for any doubt. Edward was mistaken in his assumption, and the how and the why didn't matter right then. The fact that Victoria was not a fancy did. Laffite's woman was as white as herself, and she hated her for it even more. Tossing her head and putting her nose in the air, she spoke, sounding disgusted by the sight of Tori nursing the child. "I am not accustomed to a lady of your stature nursing her child, that is true. Why, my family, any decent family of good breeding that is, always has a nanny, a black nanny to do that loathsome chore. The husbands I know care about the mother's weakened condition and want to help them regain their health and figures of before. If that is possible, that is. In some, I am told the lady's figure never seems to go back, though, does it? Take Marie Destrehan, for example." Spurred on by the disappointment of learning the truth, she continued. "I must say I am shocked that Jean makes you do this bothersome task. It does not seem right, even for you."

"On the contrary, my dear Simone. It was not his idea to have me do this loathsome task, as you put it. I told him that I wanted to do it. You see, I love this child and wish to do the best for him, and Jean agreed with me. Besides, it is common knowledge where I come from, that if you nurse your child, your shape returns faster and even better than before. After all, my breasts were not as ample as they are nowadays, and if I am right, they will remain so long after Christopher stops nursing."

Simone had to get out of there. The widow knew if she stayed, she would expose her plans of ruining the Laffites by letting something slip. Oh, how she wanted to tell this self-assured bitch, to enjoy what little time she had left with her son and husband. Simone wanted nothing more at that moment than to wipe that smile from the mother's face. Her blood pounded hard in her temples, and her breathing was so shallow that the angry female was beginning to feel dizzy. The explosion she was fighting to keep under control was fast approaching the eruption stage. Both of her hands were gripped in vice-like fists at her side, as she slowly turned toward the door. Not looking back, the incensed woman let free, her last remark, hoping it would hit hard. "Well, we shall see about that tonight at the ball, won't we? I do hope you have a gown that fits you around your middle, my dear. And I hope Jean's eyes are on you only, that they don't stray, to…shall we say, shapelier ladies. He does seem to be drawn to those whose waists are defined." Simone swept out of the room, slamming the door, and left Tori laughing softly.

"Oh Christopher, will she ever learn? Will she ever give up? I hope so, my son because if she does not, Simone will end up a lonely and bitter old woman, waist or no waist."

Tori spent the next hour holding her son close to her and thinking about him and his future. What would it be like for him, without her? What was it like for her daughter now? She had to face facts. When she finally did get to the lake, she might very well accomplish crossing back to her time. That meant she needed to make sure Christopher's life, without her, was set up, so he never felt she had abandoned him or that he was not loved. A stupid thought indeed, for she knew that the people who cared about him would surround him with love, and when he was old enough, unlike her daughter, he would be told what happened to his mother.

The problem was, when would it be the time to leave? When should she try the crossover? Just how was she going to pick the day to say goodbye? Her eyes misted with tears as she looked into the gentle sleeping face that nuzzled close to her bare skin. The mother could feel the moisture of his warm breath on her body and the pulse of his tiny heart that beat so fast beneath his little gown. Slowly, as she sat in silence, a plan began to form. It would be Christopher, who would be the one to seal her fate. He would be the one who would let her go, not the other way around. Tori would not worry about when that would be or rush the day; instead, she would wait, content in knowing the decision was out of her hands. The day her son stopped wanting his mother's milk, the day he pushed her away, no longer needing that part of her, would be the day to say goodbye. Even though the decision brought sadness, the relief of having a solution gave her a new lease on life. She could be content, at least for a little while longer.

THAT evening, people started arriving for the anticipated ball at Leone Duval's grand townhome. Their friend had insisted that he be allowed to host the event. He'd won his case by stating the simple fact that his home had the space and resources for such a gala.

By the time Tori and Jean arrived, the evening was well underway, and everyone attending was eagerly awaiting the honored couple. Their late arrival was not a mere coincidence, but rather a planned maneuver by Jean and Leone. Their grand entrance, as planned, was spectacular. The proud couple stood in the open doorway, while Leone announced to the crowd that his honored guests had arrived at last.

Many who turned to greet them let out soft exclamations of praise. Whispers spread rapidly around the room, followed by soft clapping. Then the applause grew, and loud cheers filled the room, completely smothering all other sounds. The festive mood surrounding the Laffites enveloped the couple with such pride and joy that their happiness radiated back into the room.

Jean could not ever remember feeling so overwhelmed by such a reception. Finally, he had a deep feeling of home, of having found what he'd been searching for. His happiness and pride set a glow about him that shone and danced from his sparkling eyes.

Like his eyes, a diamond attached to his cravat twinkled and reflected sparks of light from its perfect prisms. It was a diamond of blue-white color, which seemed to draw its shade, from his dark blue coat. His white cravat was of the purest silk; chosen because its color enhanced his already bronze tan. His boots were of the softest black leather, their highly polished surface, acting like dark mirrors beneath him. His breeches fit his legs snugly and were of the same dark blue material as his jacket. His shirt, with ruffled cuffs peeking out of the sleeves, had a soft hint of blue. So subtle was the hue that if one did not look closely, they would assume the shirt to be white.

Jean stood there looking every bit a gentleman and as far from a pirate as one could be. As his gaze fell on one guest and then another, his dark eyes seemed to change hue as they captivated each person, leaving each of them with a sense of awe. Laffite was every bit the dashing new father and proud husband of the vision that stood next to him.

Tori's gown was a work of art, far surpassing all the others in her wardrobe. It was of the same soft silk that his cravat was made from, which gave it a luminous quality. Unlike his cravat, though, Tori's dress was not white; it was the purest shade of indigo blue one could imagine. The lamplight on the material made it shimmer like moonlight on the sea. Tori's waist was small, and the garment seemed to cling and mold to her body. The gown fit each curve like a glove, and the low-cut bust line, tastefully presented and outlined her more than ample breasts, but it was to her neck that all eyes fell, for around it hung a gift from Jean.

Flashing in the lamplight, the necklace of diamonds and sapphires lay against her soft skin, framing a picture-perfect face above. The jewelry had been a token of thanks for the wonderful gift of a son.

To Tori, it was far more than just a thank you; it was a bitter-sweet gift; she knew she would not get to keep. For her, the weight of the necklace hung around her throat like a hangman's noose. Still, Laffite's wife had accepted it and worn it to please him, while hiding the sadness it brought her. Anyone looking at Tori standing by Jean's side would never have guessed that she was anything but ecstatically happy.

Jean turned from the crowd and looked at his lovely wife, admiring her appearance. Like the stones around her neck, she was exquisite and unique. Instead of having her hair placed up, as was the fashion of the day, Marie Laveau had artfully swept it to one side and held it in place with a pearl and diamond-encrusted comb. Tori's hair fell in soft swirls around her shoulder and glistened with red highlights in the candlelight. The pirate's wife was stunning, transformed from the morning vision of a new mother to the evening vision of the goddess Venus and he could not have been prouder of her. Jean leaned over and kissed her lightly on her cheek, and then they took a step forward to join in the night's gala.

Edward had openly gasped when he saw Tori, a fact that did not escape Simone's ears. She watched him admire the bitch, and even if she did agree that Tori was beautiful, she did not have to stand by the dandy while he drooled over her. With her nails digging into his arm like claws, she very quietly pulled him off to the side.

"So, your nigger grows more beautiful each day, and you can't wait to have her, can you? After all, she is just a nigger, high class, of course! A real fancy, I give you that. Your brother had good taste; wouldn't you say? You can't wait to abuse her and use her like the black whores down on the riverfront, right?"

He nodded his head but kept on looking to where the Laffites stood to converse with many of the guests. He was not paying attention to the dribble Simone was spurting, and then everything changed.

"Well, what would you do, if I were to tell you, she is out of your reach, my dear Edward? Not only out of your reach, but out of your league, now and forever!"

Simone had his full attention then, and he looked at her and her smug grin. "Just what do you mean by that? And, for God's sake, keep your voice down, someone might hear you." He pushed her further into the corner of the room as he spoke, smiling the whole time as if nothing were wrong.

"I mean, my dear love," she continued, "that you cannot abuse her without having all of New Orleans come after you. They would never stand for it."

Simone was making no sense whatsoever, rambling on like she was. Edward guessed that she might feel some jealousy, and well she should as Tori was beyond stunning, but this was ridiculous. The widow knew he only wanted to bed the bitch out of revenge, so why this reaction?

"My dear Edward, you are listening to me." She cocked her head to one side, and coyly smiled. "Good, because I have something to tell you. If you were to abuse a nigger, you might have a chance but to harm a white woman and get caught, never!" She watched her statement register on his face. "Yes, that's right, my dear, I thought that would gain your attention. You were wrong. At first, I thought you were not telling me the truth, but then you had no reason to do otherwise. At least none that I could determine. You did not lie to me about her. You really do think she is of mixed blood, don't you? You think she's a fancy nigger, right? Quadroon or better still maybe Octro…?"

"Shut up before someone hears you, I say. You are acting entirely irrational, and I won't have it. Not here, and especially not now."

"Irrational, you say," she hissed. Well, let me tell you, Edward, it's just not so. I am very rational, and I have learned something you are not going to like. I wanted to tell you when we left Laffite's house today; then, I thought not. I wanted to see her here tonight to confirm what I already knw. I wanted you to see her, and now that you have, I can divulge to you the truth. She is white, as white as I am, as you are."

Edwards' face grew dark, and he was about to question her when Simone continued. "Don't you dare question me on this. I know what I am talking about because I have seen the proof for myself. That bitch made sure of it and Edward; it was no mistake. I saw a part of her skin that only Jean and their child see, and it was skin that was so pale that the sun-kissed flesh next to it stood out. Her dark color is from the sun and nothing more. So, pray tell, what do you plan to do now? How will you get your hands on her, tell me that? You do still intend to have her, don't you? A difficult task, knowing what we do."

Edward hated Simone at that moment, but he also loved her when she hissed like a she-cat, clawing and spitting. That's what he had imagined it would be like with Tori. All fight, until submission. The man shuddered as he realized precisely what he liked about them both; it was the fighting side to their personalities. Now, however, he'd have no chance of blackmailing Tori into submission. That had been his final hold over her. His leverage was gone, and it left him where? Did he still want Laffite's wife? Yes, indeed, he did. He would have her by merely taking her. When she turned up missing, Jean would search for her, but that didn't worry him. He had plans for Laffite that would get him out of the way and stop any such actions he may take to locate his beloved wife. As for Tori, the fact that she was a real lady, one that all New Orleans would look for, it just upped the stakes. For him, it made her even more desirable. Plus, as a lady, what he had planned for her made it a given she'd fight him harder.

Edward blinked his daydream away. For now, he had Simone and her cruel ways to deal with. She had enjoyed keeping this bit of information from him until it could be thrown in his face. The woman was green with envy, that was plain to see, and a jealous woman needed to be satisfied. This one, however, also required to be taught a lesson and kept in line. He took hold of her face in one hand and squeezed her jaw tightly, pinching her skin as he pulled her towards him. Once he knew he had her undivided attention, Edward released his grip on her face and grabbed hold of her arm. His fingers then dug slowly and painfully into her skin, pulsing with each word he uttered. "I don't know how, but I will indeed have her, my dear. I will abuse her, and by me doing that, you will get even with Jean and I with my brother. That is our purpose and goal. To have our revenge on all of them, need I remind you of that? Then my dear, when I have finished with her, she will be disposed of, and we will end up with each other. We will be together because you and

I know and understand each other. That is a simple fact of life, and that's the way it will be. Now, let's leave this damned gala and let me show you just how little I think of that bitch and how much more appealing you are to me."

The Spanish beauty turned her back to the crowd and smiled at Edward, licking her lips seductively, nodding her head in approval of his idea. Edward had aroused her, and it sounded like it would be one of those special nights with him. The widow knew she had angered him, and because of it, the evening ahead would be long and beautifully painful.

They could not leave without making the necessary excuses to Claiborne and Cayetana, of course. Neither wished to offend their newfound allies and if presented correctly, they could turn the early departure to their advantage. While Simone was talking with Cayetana, Edward took Claiborne off to one side, apologizing to him for interrupting his campaigning. The man always did that, no matter where they went, and Edward typically would support his efforts. He would remain at his side and continue to help him, for hours if that's what was needed, but this night was going to be different.

Edward began by lowering his voice and leaning toward the American; he spoke in a low tone. "You are already the respected governor of the territory of Mississippi. I should, therefore, think you have both the experience and integrity to win in the upcoming election. Why not, simply enjoy yourself this evening; you can more than afford to do so. To openly campaign here, it might be taken as an offense and undo all the hard work you have accomplished. In my opinion, you are way ahead of the competition; so again, I say relax. May I suggest you take this opportunity to get to know more about the people whose votes you will seek in the coming months. Accomplished discreetly and with your charm and Cayetana's backing, you will succeed tonight, without anyone being the wiser or anyone unduly offended." He continued to boost the man's spirits and then skillfully steered the conversation in another direction, explaining why he and Simone were departing early. Edward made it clear to William that he was sure it was no headache that was causing Simone to act so rashly. Instead, he sensed that she was missing her dearly departed husband and was too upset to stay.

Claiborne observed Simone, as Edward talked on about how lonely she had been lately. He felt sorry for the young widow and had a certain amount of admiration for her also. There had to be something he could do to help his friends. "Edward, why don't you bring Simone by for dinner, just the four of us. Maybe to be out and about, with only a few close friends, will help her overcome her melancholy mood. I shall inform you how the rest of this evening turns out. It is smart advice you have given, and I do intend to put it to use. Now, escort your lady home and wish her well for me. I will see to it that Cayetana sends an invite tomorrow. Give Simone something to look forward too." He shook Edward's hand and then watched as the young Duval made his way back to the sad widow's side.

William knew he'd been correct to confide in Edward, when he told him that becoming the first governor of the state, was his ultimate goal. In return for sharing this goal of his, both Duval and Simone had offered their support and aide. Quite an extraordinary offer, considering that Edward was a Creole, and Creoles never supported the Americans, no matter who they were.

William was determined to use Edward's friendship to his advantage, and he also needed Simone to keep things between him and Cayetana on track. Until they were wed, Claiborne could not relax. As for right now, he had another matter to handle. Where was his betrothed? He had to get closer to this Laffite character and learn what he could. He may have been told how Christian his wife was, but if Edward and the rumors were right, he had more to fear from this so-called gentleman pirate than he thought. After all, he was close to Destrehan and Villere, both of whom were planning on running for governor's position.

Tori had a wonderful time, and the evening was a great success. Shortly after her arrival, she noticed Simone's departure and breathed a sigh of relief when the spiteful female and her lover quietly slipped out. To Tori's way of thinking, it seemed that the woman did have a bit of diplomacy within her after all. Or maybe her exit had been out of a growing sense of shame, having come with no formal invitation. Most likely, the pair feared being exposed to all attending for doing so. Whatever the reason, Jean's wife was glad the couple were gone. The evening's big surprise had been when Claiborne and Cayetana offered their best regards and openly chatted with their host and hostess in the friendliest manner. After their encounter, the evening continued with no further incident, and all enjoyed themselves well into the early hours of the morning. By noon the following day, the event became the talk of the town, and those few who missed it because of the long trip back to the city wished they'd made an effort to attend.

September 1811 was long and hot, and Tori found herself wishing for winter. Even the gulf breezes that usually stirred this time of year were stagnant. The oppressive heat hung over the city and its populace, slowly baking not only the land but also the tempers of all who lived there. Night and day, there was no escape from the sticky humid bath. It clung to everyone and everything. Clothes already damp to the touch, were soon wringing wet from sweat, and because of this, it was common to find one's self changing several times a day.

To make matters worse, bugs, swarms of them, both large and small, biting and stinging, never seemed to rest. During the daylight, clouds of them could be seen, but at night, it was the sound their wings made that filled the darkness. Having never experienced anything like it, Tori told everyone in the house, New Orleans was in the grip of what she called a living hell and gave instructions to keep the sage burning. If anyone saw a mosquito, it was to be squashed. The baby's room was assigned two slaves whose sole job was to keep it bug-free.

Jean tried to reason with his wife, telling her that nothing could be more horrible than being foolish enough to remain in the city and endure the worst that summer could bring, especially when escape was possible. Going upriver was something he tried to get Tori to agree to each night before bed, explaining if not for her comfort, then she should do it for their son's. The pirate assured her repeatedly that as soon as the business would allow him to get away, he would join them, but stubborn as she was, Jean could not make her budge. Tori told him if he had to stay, then his family would remain with him. What Jean did not know was that his wife wanted to cherish each day with him and their son because each day brought her closer to when she would return to the lake and possibly to her own time from there.

So far, she had avoided being packed off, as she put it, by one delay or another. After the hellish day she had just had, her excuses were beginning to look like foolish decisions indeed. The few friends who remained in town no longer came to visit, as the heat was too much. For Tori, the unbearable temperature had turned every task into a major effort. Every joyful activity had vanished overnight, as one struggled only to be comfortable. Even Christopher, generally a placid, happy child, was crying out of misery. As much as she wanted to remain with Jean, she finally had to confess that remaining stubborn about leaving did not gain her anything other than feeling miserable. Therefore, Tori decided she'd admit defeat to Jean during the evening meal, and agree to take his advice and leave the city as soon as it could be arranged. Spending time with the Destrehans along the Mississippi's cooler banks had won out over her wifely duties, or continuing to make memories with her small family. Remaining by Jean's side was no longer an option for her and her son when comfort beckoned and was within reach.

# ❧ Seven ❧

The first reports of something wrong came by way of the slave grapevine. It had begun slowly as the slaves and household help talked among themselves of the gossip that came their way. Then, like wildfire, news, not rumors, spread rapidly through their intricate network, jumping from one place to another. On city sidewalks, in the market, and over walls, the urgent news was quickly reported from one home to another. Before word reached Tori, from any of their friends, the housekeeper Bessy was able to warn her of the illness, and this was many hours before it became official.

Tori had heard the day before that a couple of sailors on the docks had died of a fever in the past week. The stable hand at one dockside inn had insisted to Bessy that it was not just an ugly rumor. It was something to take notice of and prepare. Laffite's wife had wondered if it was true and mentioned it to a few neighbors. Their reaction was nonchalant. It was nothing to worry about; they had assured her. After all, if the story was true, the ship the sailors came in on had left port, taking with it any further chance of contamination. Seeing them so nonchalant about her household's gossip, Tori relaxed and went back to planning when to take the trip upriver.

It was Bessy, a day later, who told her of the newest update. It was said that one of the families who had arrived on the ship had sent for the doctor. Their daughter, only a few years older than Christopher, was very ill, and even though they insisted it was not the same fever that had killed the sailors, their household help knew better. The gossip was ripe, and it spread quickly. Within hours Laffite's household slaves received the news and, in turn, began talking about the fever. They said the child had died, and that was enough for Bessy to believe the devil was in town.

"It's a startin' Miss Tori. Lord, have mercy on our souls. Yes 'um, it sure be a startin'. I, seen it afore. It spread so fast; like the fire in them cane fields. If 'n you ain't out of the city in time, you be as good as dead. I neber stayed afore. The Massa, he always see's ta it, that we be long gone, an, I'm a tellin' you, it be time to git!"

Tori looked at Bessy. She'd never seen her so upset and scared. Sure, Tori had read about the fever outbreaks that had hit New Orleans and of the terrible death toll, but this could not be what she'd learned surely? First of all, Tori remembered the fever outbreaks took place in the middle of the summer. If that was right, it was far too late in the season to seriously concern herself with such an occurrence; and what's more, she seemed to recall that the significant outbreaks happened later in the century. Tori wasn't entirely confident, but she trusted her memory on the subject rather than panicked slave gossip and refused to worry. Besides, she had nothing to fear, having been vaccinated against yellow fever and other illnesses, so catching anything was highly unlikely. Hell, she'd had shots for cholera and typhoid also. Going to Africa, with her father on safari, had required them. It had been a trip meant to cheer her up and give her a break from single motherhood, with all its burdens. Tori shook her head. It was the vaccinations that she needed to remember, not the trip. The shots were good for at least ten years, so she was sure she was still immune. It would be the baby and Jean; along with their slaves and friends, she should be frightened for.

Right now, she had to calm Bessy down and reassure her that her worries were needless. "Bessy, look. I'm sure you are getting all worked up over nothing. If it was the fever, yellow fever that is, then I am sure we would have been officially informed. I can't imagine something like that could be kept quiet, and for what reason would anyone want to anyway? Look, you trust the Master, and I'm sure he would have heard something, and if he did, do you think he would allow Christopher and me to stay in town? Now do you?"

Bessy could not make her understand. How could she? But,

Lord, if she didn't make her, it would be too late; they'd catch it, and they'd die. The cook had to get her to listen. Putting her hands on her hips and lowering her voice to her most serious tone, she spoke with such sincerity that Tori found herself reconsidering. "Miss Tori, you ain't goin' ta listen, But, listen here, you must. It be right, what my peoples say. They know the truth. Ain't got no reason ta lie, more ta tell the truth though. I ain't a carin' what the white folk say or don't say. I just know that if we stay here, then someone is goin' ta git sick. True, it might not happen." She shook her head slowly. "I know crazy thin' this fever be like. It, be the devil's work for sure. Some peoples neber gits it. Even after they be right close, ta it. That white doctor, he neber gits it. Then there's them that thinks they be safe and don't go out. Don't get anyplace close ta it an' Lord, next thin' they know'd, they be dead." She rolled her eyes upward and sighed because she had to get Miss Tori to listen one way or another. Lowering her gaze, Bessy began pleading. The black woman looked directly at her Mistress as she continued. Her eyes filled with unspent tears of frustration and fear as her voice trembled. "I just a fearin' for the little un. He and the rest of my family. You, an' the Massa be my family. An I ain't got the heart ta see no one's git sick. You just ain't seen it like me, that's all. It's be horrible, an' you can't run none once it git's you!"

Tori listened to her, and a small voice in the back of her mind told her to think this through carefully. If this was indeed the beginning of an epidemic, she wanted no part of it. The now nervous woman had no desire to witness such a horrific historical event, let alone put those she loved in danger. That was the very last thing she wanted. What did it matter if they left a little sooner than planned? After all, she had already made her mind up to leave the city for Destrehan's cooler riverfront home. She would ask Jean as soon as he came in, about departing first thing in the morning. They would all go, and he'd have no choice in the matter. Looking at the slaves beaming face, Tori knew Bessy guessed what she was about to say. Still, it had to be handled in such a way that left Tori in control. "Bessy, I want you to know that I still do not think there is any yellow fever, but the heat is so unbearable, and Christopher is so miserable. I'm going to take Jean's advice and go upriver until it cools off. Please see that things are ready to go by morning. All our things and that includes Jeans too; if he thinks we are going without him, he can think again." Bessy was on her way out the door as Tori added, "and Bessy, we might as well close up the house until we get back. Everyone could use a break, don't you think? Maybe the others could go downriver or wherever it is Jean sends you, when he closes house."

Instant relief flooded Bessy's round face. She did not care what reason Miss Tori used for their leaving. The fact that they were going was plenty good enough for her. She would pack and work all night if necessary, for only then could she rest. Once they were safe and away from the Black Death, she would relax, and not a second before because she knew in her bones, she was right; demon death was in town.

Before Jean arrived home that evening, plans had taken another drastic turn and with no time to stop and think of the consequences of her actions, Tori found herself hurrying to Leone's townhome. She had left Christopher in Bessy's care and told everyone to keep on packing. Then just in case, Jean got home before she did, Tori left word for him to meet her at Leone's townhome. It was a message that he would not receive until later that night.

Tori had been busy with plans for their trip to Destrehan when the doctor interrupted her. He had been making his way to another patient when he received word that Leone was ill and needed his attention. Knowing it would be some time before he would be able to stop by the Duval home and that the man lived alone, with only his servants to keep him company, he thought of a solution when he saw the Laffite house. It just took him a short visit to explain his concern to Tori and ask that she send a request to the convent, asking for one of the sisters to stop in and see if there was anything Leone needed. The doctor never thought that it would occur to Jean's wife to take it upon herself to attend to the sick man herself. No sooner had the doctor left, Tori had ordered the carriage brought round, and against Bessy's advice, she left for their friend's home. Could it be true that Leone had been ill for days, Tori questioned, as she rode toward his home? It was his stable boy that had reported the news to the doctor. He could have gotten it wrong, surely? What was Leone thinking of, not sending for the doctor earlier if he was ill? What if he had the fever? Her mind reacted violently to that thought, and her stomach churned with a sickening feeling.

Leone was just sick, a mild something or other, that was all, she assured herself. There was nothing to worry about; the fever was down by the docks. Leone's home was miles from there. She'd see that some chicken soup was made, and that would do the trick. Then she'd tell him to leave the city and go to his plantation until the possible outbreak was over, and the heat, gone. When that was done, Tori would return home to help finish packing and make ready for their trip.

Her mind kept racing on and on as the carriage slowly moved forward. It's not the fever; it can't be, she assured herself repeatedly when in reality, she knew that it could very well be just that. The doctor had confided in her, that yes, he was treating many cases of an illness, and it was spreading. He'd advised her that she and her family should leave town as soon as possible because, in his opinion, it was going to be quite an outbreak. True, he had not said it was yellow fever or cholera, but she had not asked him to name the illness either. That was something she was regretting now, as it would have been better to know than not.

SITTING in the carriage, Tori looked at the buildings they were passing by, and something seemed quite odd. Was it her imagination, or were there fewer people outside than usual? The sidewalks were empty, and as they drove by some of the larger homes, they looked eerily dark and vacant. The usual activities one would see, such as slaves working in the beautiful gardens, children playing, or adults sitting on the verandahs, were nowhere to be seen. Oh, the odd household showed signs of life, but still more were seen loading carriages with belongings as they prepared for a hurried departure. Tori realized that this all meant one thing: word of the impending plague must have spread further and more rapidly once confirmed. Bessy and her household may not have received the formal confirmation, but by the looks of it, others had.

The carriage took a turn onto a less traveled street, and it was then that an echo of cannon fire suddenly filled the heavens. Surprised by the sound, Tori let out a cry of shock, and the carriage came to a sudden halt. The driver turned his head while pulling on the on reins to control the horse; he tried his best to calm his Mistress. "It ain't nothin' to a fear none. Them soldiers, they be scarin' the evil plumb aways. They a-goin' to set off them cannons now an' then. They goin' to see to it, yes Ma'am, they sure is. Then, they be goin' to light the barrels of oil an send the smokes up, to carry the sickness off. You see, it always works, nothin' to be fearin' now they be doin' it. The evil that makes them sick like it be leavin' soon enough."

Tori settled her racing heart and tried to smile at the driver. She knew it was hogwash, old superstition, and such, but she'd let him have his peace of mind, thinking that burning oil and loud noises would do the trick. Her thoughts were like quicksand, though, pulling her optimism down deeper and deeper every moment. If they had begun acting like this, to drive the outbreak away, then it had to be very bad, maybe even out of control and spreading. One thing Tori did know was that regardless of how she felt, she had to try and remain calm. Looking at her driver, she spoke as calmly as she could. "Let's just get to Mr. Duval's before they set another blast-off. The animal is worse off than I am, I can tell you that."

"Yez, Mistress, I be tellin' her to git up now. I sure enough will, just as soon as they load that there wagon up ahead, an moves it on. Don't want to spook her anymore. Horses don't care none for death." He pointed up ahead with a trembling hand. "Mizz Tori, I's don't want to go to near that there cart. We best wait a bit. The Massa, he be real glad we did."

Tori trusted her driver's judgment and looked ahead to see what had him so worried and why he refused to move. At first, she was confused and could not understand what it was she was seeing. Then it became only too apparent. Two black men were carrying a body out of a house, and behind them, she could see a woman holding what looked like a dead child. The horror of what she was witnessing caused her to gasp audibly. Unable to look away, she continued to watch as the man's body was tossed in the back of the wagon, which already contained quite a few bodies. Then one of the men went back and took the child from the wailing mother's arms. The child's mother did not stand on the porch, to witness her toddler's body, joining what must have been its father; she just turned away and walked inside, closing the door behind her. Once the child's small frame was deposited on top of the man, the two black men led the horse-drawn wagon away. The individual driving the cart was calling out something, but Tori was not clear on what it was, and so she could only imagine it was something like 'bring out your dead.' That's what they did in London during the great plagues; she'd read that and knew it to be true. Through tear-filled eyes, Tori watched as the wagon turned onto another street and disappeared.

"Sorry, you had to see such sadness, Mizz Tori. We will be goin' another way now. Good thin' we ain't' got to go by the river none, cause, that be somethin' the Massa be sure you do not want to see."

"And why is that?"

"Cause, that be where they be goin' to take them, the bodies that be. They has to git them gone so they don't get anyone else sick. That, an' they a goin' to smell, bad, fast like. No, they goin' to let the deep-water carry them off. I seen it once myself, all them bodies floatin' down the river. No, Massa, he not want you to see that. He not want you to go to Massa Duval's an all. You sure'n you still be a wantin' to go? I kin turn this here rig around an' has you home real fast."

She looked into the black man's concerned face and understood his worry, and for the first time, Tori was not so sure she wanted to go on either. The thing was, she really didn't have a choice in the matter. She was safe against the fever; it was Leone who might not be. This made her mind up, and once again, she was dead set on seeing her mission through. "I'm sure. Now, let's go and no more stopping if you can avoid it. We need to get there, and once we are, you wait with the horse until I know what I need, if anything."

He looked away from her determined face. The Mistress was crazy for wanting to help; he knew that. Still, she had told him to go, an' he had to listen, she was his Mistress after all. "Yez 'um. I hear what you wants. Don't got to like it none. I be doin' my job. We be there real soon. Then you does what you needs to, an after, I be takin' you home right quick like."

The sound of leather straps hitting the horse on its back was all that was needed to move the animal reluctantly forward. Death was in the air, and even the horse knew better than to get to close to it. As they made their way, Tori held out hope of finding Leone just slightly ill. After all, he had not been near the river or the docks that she was aware of. His life and dealings kept him far away from those parts of town. He socialized with the same friends as they did, and none of them were sick. It was true that most had already left town, but the few who had remained had not sent word of sickness. Thoughts such as these continued to accompany her all the way to their destination.

Upon arrival, she faced the truth about how far the disease had spread. The big home next door was void of any sign of life, except for one old black gardener. He called out to them that the sickness had taken three of those inside, and he was all that was left of the household slaves. Then he stepped a few paces closer and added, "That there place be in trouble too. Aint seen nobodies for days, ands the helps, they all staying aways. They be out back in them quarters. You best be takin your mistress away from there if 'n you knows what's right."

Tori snapped at her driver. "You will do nothing of the sort. I intend to go inside and find out what's going on."

Her driver just looked toward Leone's home front entrance, with fear clearly showing on his face. His grim expression made Tori tremble, and she almost changed her mind. Leone's house was miles away from where they were lighting the tar barrels. It was at least a mile from the home where the father and toddler had been taken away, but Tori knew it didn't matter; the distance or the location had nothing to do with how it spread. It was very evident to her right then that yellow fever now held all regions of New Orleans firmly in its grip no matter the distance between those infected or not.

Leone Duval's home was quiet. No one was in the garden, and no one came out to meet the carriage, as was the custom. The slave quarters were in the back, over the stables, and knowing what the black man next door had said, Tori sent her driver to fetch them and have them wait in the kitchen for instructions.

The nervous woman stood looking at the home's front, and instinctively knew that something was terribly wrong. All the upstairs windows were closed, and the curtains were pulled shut. The verandah doors, which at this time of the day, were usually wide open, to let in the late afternoon air, were also closed tight. Had there been a mistake? Could the house be locked up because Leone had already gone to his plantation? Somehow Tori knew that was not so. Leone would never leave without sending word or stopping by to say farewell. Then there was the doctor himself. He would never lie or mistake a message, and he had told her he'd been sent for.

Tori's hand reached for the brass knocker, and as she listened to the sound of the loud thump echo inside, she began to pray. "Don't let it be. Please, he has to be all right."

The door opened, and stepping aside was a gaunt, sickly looking black man that she didn't recognize at first. It was when the man spoke in a whisper-like fashion that Tori realized who he was. He was Leone's trusted servant and valet; that is, what was left of him. Too stunned to speak, Tori stared in horror at the individual. Could this be her first direct contact with yellow fever? If so, what was she supposed to do?

"I's sure pleased that you come by, Mizz Tori. I be, so tired. No one else here to take care of the Master. He told them to stay away. Told me too, but I just can't be a doing that. He needed my help. He's real sick, Mizz Tori. I sent for the doctor when I knowd it's the fever. Master said he didn't need him none, but he do, sure'n enough he, do. This mornin', I knew it was time for help no matter what he ordered. The doctor has not been here yet but bless you, bless you, you're here now. You kin keep me company till the doctor gits here. I sure'n could use some company, yes um, I could."

On these last words, he began slipping to the floor. Tori could see that the man was too weak to carry on the conversation or even stand any longer. She reached out and took his frail arm, guiding him to a chair in the front hall, where he thankfully sat his shaking body down. "This is not right, Mizz Tori. I'm not supposed to…" he hung his head down, "Master Leone, he is the one that needs help. He needs the doctor."

Tori pushed the servant back into the chair as he struggled to get up. "I don't care what is right or wrong; you are worn out, and if you don't get some rest, you'll be the next sick person in this house. Now, you listen to me. I'm telling you to stay here until I need you.

I know my way around. I'm sure I can find Leone's room by myself. I will go and see what he needs and be right back."

The poor old man did not fight her. He was on his last leg of endurance, for sheer exhaustion was written all over his face. Who knew how many hours he had kept going in the past few days, and without little rest, let alone sleep? Tori guessed he had not rested or slept in all that time.

"Mizz Tori, I ain't able to git sick, cause I done had it once afore.

The doctor, he said, I never goin' to git it again. You knows, you can't go up to Master Leone. He goin' to git you sick, if 'n you does."

Jean's wife frowned. "You, let me worry about that. I like you, can't get sick, so you just sit and wait till I tell you what I need."

"Yez 'um, Mizz Tori. I do that cause truth be told, my old bones is plum wore out."

She took the old man's hand in hers and squeezed it. "I can see how tired you are, and I don't need to be worrying my head over you too, so sit here until I know what to do. I have told my driver to fetch the others and put them in the kitchen. None of them are sick, are they?"

"No, Mizz. Not a one, on account, I kept them away."

"Well, they might have to help me, so you see to it that they are ready. Tell my driver when he comes in to follow your instructions. Tell him I said to. Now, I won't be long." Tori left the servant's side and turned to face the uncertainty of what lay ahead.

Frightened but determined, she made her way upstairs and onto the landing. It was gloomy and stifling hot. All the doors along the hall in each direction were closed. To her right, there was one long window; it reached from the ceiling to the floor, and even though it was at the far end of the hall, the glass allowed enough light shining in to see her way. It was a magnificent stained glass, a twelve-foot oblong, that when the sun hit it in the morning, it would gleam and sparkle. In the afternoon sun, as it was right then, the glass was still pretty, but admiring the magnificent scene depicted upon its surface, was not why she was there.

Tori was thankful for the light, as dim as it was. The window should have been more than ample to supply light, but a large magnolia that had been planted for shade worked against her. Its thick foliage blocked most of the sun's rays through the glass and what little did manage to filter in, cast dusty beams of light throughout the already gloomy hallway.

Knowing Leone's location had to be behind one of the doors toward the same end as the glass window, Tori started to walk slowly in that direction. She listened for any sound that might guide her quickly to the right bedroom, a cough, or call for help, but there was nothing. In the end, it was not sound that guided her. Instead, it was the odor of the sick-room itself that alerted her. Even with the door closed, the stench permeated the air in the hall. There was no mistaking the stink of urine and vomit, but it was mixed with another vile, sickening smell, one that assaulted her senses, halting her in her footsteps.

Tori stood outside the door, terrified of what she would find on the other side. Lord knew she wanted to turn and run, but she also understood she had to go in and help; there was no other choice. There was no one left to help Leone, but her, and she knew it. The trouble right then was, Tori was frozen to the spot, unable to move because the stench was like a physical barrier, holding her back.

Laffite's wife closed her eyes and asked herself, had she come this far only to turn and run, leaving a sick friend waiting for a doctor that might not arrive for hours? Knowing this, she'd have to enter and fight the nausea that was threatening to overtake her, no matter what. With determination ruling, slowly, the frightened woman placed her hand over her nose and turned away from the door and inhaled deeply through her mouth. Then, before she could change her mind, Tori opened the door and entered the room while holding her breath.

Standing just inside the doorway, Tori understood that her first task was to let her eyes grow accustomed to the darkness. Once her vision was adapted, the panicked female looked frantically for the curtains, so she could open the room up and let out some of the stench and heat. If Tori had thought it was unbearably hot in the hallway, she realized the bedroom was worse. No way had she been prepared for the overwhelming temperature, which assailed her inside Leone's room. It was nothing short of an oven, well into the high eighties or more, she reasoned.

Rapidly she went to the first set of curtains and pulled them back to reveal a large window. Her fingers fought with the brass knobs,

394

and in seconds she was unlatching the frame and throwing the window open. Once opened, she leaned out as far as she could, to take in a much-needed breath of fresh air, which turned out to not be enough to ward off what was coming next. Her mouth filled with saliva, a sure giveaway that she was about to throw up. The urge was so close to overpowering her that she remained looking down into the empty gardens for a few seconds. Knowing she had to do more, Tori fought back the nausea and swallowed hard. Holding her breath again, she hastily went to the next set of drapes and pulled them back. Behind these floor-length drapes, she found a set of French doors, which she opened wide and, taking several uneven steps, she stumbled out of the room just before falling to her knees.

Quickly the sickened woman picked herself up and made her way to the railing. While doing this, she was trying to gulp in the fresh air, but this time the stench had somehow followed her, and she could not get rid of it. Leaning over the balcony, Tori heaved for all she was worth. She did not attempt to stem the flow of the contents from her stomach and doubted she could have if she'd wanted to.

For several minutes, after the last of the retching ceased, she stood, waiting for the urge to puke more, to pass. Tori had never felt so awful or so afraid. She feared what was in the room behind her. Was it a dead Leone that she had found? Could that be what smelled so bad? She had no idea what a dead person smelled like, just that it was awful and one that you would never forget. All she had to go on was the fact that the stench permeating Leone's room was like nothing she had ever encountered, nor could she compare it to any odor she knew of. "God help me, is it death I smell? Please, God, don't let it be that." Tori was trembling and almost ready to cry. Was she prepared to look at a dead man? Could she stand it if she had too? Looking up at the sky, Tori pleaded, "God, please help me." Almost immediately, an answer to her questions and prayer sounded from within the room's confines. It was a pitiful sound, agonizing and pleading at the same time, but regardless of how he sounded or smelled, at least she now knew without looking, that Leone was alive, and he was desperately in need of help. Without another thought, she turned and went back inside.

Tori was horrified when she finally saw him and the condition of the room. Someone had left soiled sheets and towels piled on the floor against the far wall. A bucket, half-filled, with what one quick look told her was vomit, sat by the bed's side. Flies greedily buzzed around the rim, and still, others hovered over the bed in a small swarm, landing on the excrement that surrounded Leone's lower half. He was lying on the bed, covered in his own vomit and filth. How long he had been like this, Tori could not guess. For several days, the household help had been told not to come near him so it could be, he'd been there that long unattended. Their fear of the illness, or of what some of the whites called 'bronze John,' was upon them, and no matter how much they cared for Leone, they would gratefully have listened to his orders to stay away. Only one of his slaves had tried to help, but this was too much for one old black man. This was almost too much for her. Tori began to cry because this was Leone, a human, and not some foul animal. He did not deserve this. No one did.

Pulling herself together quickly, she turned and ran to the top of the stairs, where she yelled for help. Tori snapped her orders, leaving no doubt that the whip would fly if they were not carried out. Satisfied that things were rapidly moving along as she wanted, Laffite's wife could now turn her attention back to the man inside the stinking bedroom.

It took several hours to clean up the mess. The room was cleared of everything that had been touched by the foul mess. The sick man was bathed, and his bed changed. A new mattress from one of the other rooms was exchanged with his. Bowls of scented water were set around the room, along with onions cut in half. These were placed on the bedside tables in small china bowls. The old footman had told Tori it was what they always did when the Master got ill. If Tori had not heard of such a practice in her own time, she would have thought them crazy, but it was an old home cure that her grandmother used. If it worked or not, she did not care. It most certainly could not hurt, they needed all the help they could get.

Tori's anger and determination had allowed her the power to get all this done and more. She had the soiled sheets burned, along with the drapes. The mosquito netting around Leone's bed and other items were tossed over the balcony, to where the waiting bonfire blazed.

Everyone who entered Leone's room did so with rags tied around their faces, making sure that their noses and mouths were covered, and they scrubbed their hands with soap and water before and after they left his room. They especially had to wash when they touched anything that was soiled. They did this under the watchful eye of the valet, who remained seated at the bottom of the stairs by a large water tub. It was his job to see that this water was changed often and that the rags around the slave's faces were discarded into a bin, to be burned later. He sat tearing new strips of linen and handed them fresh pieces, each time they headed upstairs. The old man never questioned these strange instructions; he just obeyed and prayed that Mizz Tori knew what she was doing. As for Tori, she was not sure how yellow fever spread and tried to remember. It seemed to her that mosquitoes had something to do with it, but she was not certain. One thing was sure, she knew it was highly contagious, and that meant that maybe it was in the air that they breathed. So washing and sterilizing could not do any harm, and keeping the slave's mouths and noses covered could prevent further contamination.

The windows stayed wide open, and out on the balcony, the stable hand stood with a large piece of linen that he had attached to a hastily made wooden frame. It was odd-looking and awkward to handle, but it served its purpose. It was his job to keep the air moving from the outside to the room's interior using the home-made fan. He would sway it back and forward, up and down, and continue to do so until sundown when God willing; the air would stir on the evening breeze. Only then would he switch position and have another of the household slaves take over.

The twilight was not strong enough to hurt Leone's fevered eyes, and Tori kept the oil lamp turned down low. A gentle breeze finally crept inside the room, now and then, helping to cool off the interior, but not Leone. His fever raged unabated, burning into his mind, as well as his body. Time and time again, Tori sponged him down, calling for freshwater after each effort. She desperately tried to get him to sip small amounts of fluid. First lemon-scented water, then mint-flavored, but nothing worked. He was too far gone to be induced into taking anything, and as the hours slipped by, he grew steadily weaker.

The educated woman knew she had to do something for him until the doctor came. She could not just sit by his side and allow him to slip away. Using her knowledge, Tori carefully went over all she knew from her era to try and save her friend. If she could not break his fever, then she could keep trying to force water between his parched lips, because at this point, he was severely dehydrated. A person didn't have to be a doctor to diagnose that. If he'd been in a modern hospital, an IV would supply his body with the necessary fluids. In this day and age, she had only one way to administer the life-giving liquid. Yet, each time she tried to get him to drink, precious little, if any, slipped down his parched throat. "Leone, it's Tori. Do you hear me? I'm here. Come on now. Let's try again. You must drink. Please, Leone, I know what I'm talking about." She held his head up with one hand and tried to force the rim of a china cup between his cracked and bleeding lips. "Come on, my friend, you have to drink to get stronger, and you have to fight to live."

The water was once again spilling and running down his chin onto the pillow. His panicked glazed eyes searched for her face but were unable to locate it. For Tori, the fact he had understood her was a sign that maybe he was going to have a chance at recovery. However, that small voice in her mind had her look at the man and truthfully assess his condition. His complexion was gray, and his eyes were sunken, set back in black holes that encircled them. Leone's appearance resembled that of a living skull, not the man who she called a friend. She hardly recognized him anymore and knew deep down inside, that only a miracle could save him.

Then, for a brief instant, she thought that perhaps a miracle was about to happen. Leone seemed to know her and realize what she wanted him to do. He was attempting to drink something at long last. Gently, she held his head up off the pillow and placed the glass to his lips. She was coaxing him softly, when suddenly and without warning, he retched. His whole body rose off the bed as his head fell backward and then reared forward, knocking the glass from her hand. He heaved with such a force that within seconds everything in range of three feet was showered with a bloody black scum.

Instantly Jean's wife realized what was happening. Her brain registered the horror, and she reacted without hesitation. A terrified scream escaped her as she released his limp body and hysterically backed away. Her hands and the front of her gown were covered with the thick black ooze he had thrown up, and it began to seep through the material and end up warm against her skin. On her neck, the black blood trickled down in gooey rivulets of stench, immediately, coagulating as it cooled. The odor of it assaulted her nose, and the fear of the dreadful substance gripped her mind. Knowing it was on her skin hit her hard, driving all sanity into the recesses of her soul.

Tori could hear a woman repeatedly screaming, not realizing that the sound was her own hysterics until she stopped. What she was now looking at had quite literally stunned her into silence. She was frozen, paralyzed by the horror and the sight of Leone lying dead upon his pillow. No matter how much she wanted to escape this image, she could not. Tori wanted to leave, but God help her, she could not abandon her friend, and yet if she remained in that room, Jean's wife knew she was going to lose her mind. Beyond acting rational, she did the only thing left to her; she began to scream again.

DOWNSTAIRS, the doctor had just arrived, and as tired as he was, he hastily made his way up to the room, pushing his weary bones and aching muscles to their limit. He could not understand a word of what the old black man was trying to tell him as he followed closely behind. The only sound that vibrated in the doctor's head was that of a woman's terrified screams. Bursting into the room, the old physician realized at once what must have happened and was shocked when he recognized the woman standing by Leone's bedside. Making his way to her side, he glanced around the large room. Where was the sister, from the convent, and why was Madame Laffite here? With no time for questions, or answers, the doctor reached for her hands. "Now calm down, Madame. Do you hear me? It's not going to do you any good to carry on like this." He pulled her away, moving her to the other side of the room, where he sat her down on a wooden stool. Tori had stopped screaming as soon as he had taken hold of her arm. To him, this was a good sign, but was he reaching her? A person in shock could be tough to reach, and for such a delicate lady as herself, well, there was no doubt as to her condition. "Here, let me wipe your face." His hand reached into his pocket and pulled out the last of his clean handkerchiefs. "Madame, can you look at me?"

She only shook her head and softly uttered, "Leone."

His initial diagnosis was correct. This woman was suffering from shock, but judging from what he could discern, she was strong and would be alright in due time. His first concern now was to get her out of the room and cleaned up. He turned and spoke to a wide-eyed young boy who was carrying a fresh bowl of water toward the bedside table. "Boy, you there. Don't just stand there gaping, put that down; go and fetch two of the girls. Tell them to get in here and take Madame Laffite to another bedroom, to strip her and bathe her immediately. Move boy, now!"

The doctor turned back to Tori with a look of concern on his face. She was pale and still visibly shaken, but she was calmer, and her breathing was now slower and more rhythmic. After a bath and some laudanum, she would sleep because, Lord, she looked as if she could use it. In sleep, the female would have time to escape the horror of what she had witnessed and gain back some strength. Then he prayed that exhaustion and shock would be the only ailments she would have to deal with. Madame Laffite had placed herself in grave danger by coming to this man's side today. She could very well catch the fever. Most likely would if he had to bet on it. He looked away from her and glanced toward the gruesome image on the bed. There was no doubt that was what Leone Duval had after all.

There was nothing else he could do now for Madam Laffite, so his attention turned toward the quiet bed, where the unmoving body lay. As he approached the bedside, the doctor knew before he reached Leone, that his assumption was correct, the man was already gone. The lifeless eyes stared up toward nowhere. His lips remained pulled back in agony, frozen in a hideous sort of snarl, as the last racking painful spasm had left him. How many more eyes would he have to close with his gentle touch, before this plague ended, he wondered? How long would this outbreak go on? How much longer could he stay on his feet before he collapsed from exhaustion? The doctor had no answers to these questions, and so he took some time to sit his weary body down in the chair that Tori had occupied for hours, trying to save Leone's life.

Turning toward Tori, he caught the anguished look in her eyes as she accepted the knowledge of her friend's death. Behind her, he saw a young black woman enter, followed closely by another. They had come as ordered to escort Madame Laffite to another room, and he was glad of that. He looked again at the brave female, and fear filled him. The color was draining from her face, and she was swaying from side to side. It was his guess that at any moment should he not reach her in time, she'd fall to the floor.

Suddenly the stress and sadness were just too overpowering for her. She had suffered too many shocks to her system, in too short a time. Tori couldn't take anymore; Jean's wife had to escape all this horror and grief. She wanted to forget and let the blanket of darkness cover her with its blissful oblivion. Closing her eyes, the blackness came, and it swept over her painlessly. Fainting brought a wonderful peaceful sleep, safe and secure, where no one and no agony could touch her.

AT first, Tori thought it had all been a terrible nightmare, and she was glad to wake up to find herself safe and sound in her own bed.

A movement off to the side caught her eye, and she saw Jean walking toward her. "I have been so worried about you…it has been hours," he said softly, taking her hand in his as he sat down on the side of the bed. "Do you remember anything?" He had to know; the doctor told him that in cases where the mind had been given too much to handle, it could wipe all memory of the ordeal away. After hearing what she had been through, it would not shock him if that were to be the case with Tori, and maybe that would be for the best.

"Jean, was it only a nightmare?" Her voice was shaky at best. "Tell me it was? Please tell me that I have been dreaming. Leone is not… he's all right, isn't he?" Tori felt his hand stiffen and deep down inside; she felt a great fear rising on a wave of sadness. "Jean, answer me?"

God, how he wished she had not gone through it. That Leone's death had been only that, just a bad dream. He took her in his arms and rocked her slowly back and forth. "It was no dream, my love. Leone is at peace and will suffer no longer."

Tori let her body go limp against his chest. She would have to face the fact that it had all been horribly real, that their friend was gone. Slowly and quietly, Laffite's wife started talking as if somehow, she could help make some sense of it all. Through her tears and clinging tightly to Jean, she spoke. "I'm glad I was there to help make his last hours more comfortable, really I am. No one should have to die alone, especially as he did. I never want to see anyone die such a horrible death again, never!" A shudder shook her body as she continued. "I had read of these plagues in my time and the horrors of it all. It just never seemed, well, it never seemed so…they were just words, in a book. How could I have known the truth or imagine how terrible it is? I know. I will never forget it."

Tori shuddered, and the pirate held her tighter, trying to give her all his strength. There were no words needed to express what he felt or how he so desperately wanted to help her overcome her harrowing experience.

Jean's wife instinctively felt his anguish and worry. "Oh, my love, do not fear. I know in time, it will all dim. The memory of it will ease somewhat, along with the pain. Time heals everything, or it deadens it enough, that in the end, it is a shadow of its true self."

Did she believe that? Or was she just trying to make herself believe it, so the image would somehow stop repeating so vividly in her mind? Then another thought pushed her sorrow to the side. "Jean, we have to get out of town before you or the baby get sick. Promise me that we will leave right away, promise me." She knew she sounded desperate and far from rational, but he had to realize the danger they faced. They had to get out right away. "I am fine; I can travel. Don't worry about me; we have to go, don't you see?"

"We can't, Tori. There is nowhere we can go. You have been too close to the sickness. Already, what you did today has been talked about from one house to the next. You know how these things can't be kept quiet." He stroked her face and brushed the hair off her forehead. "Even if we could, I would not ask our friends to take us in, only to have them turn us away, because that is what they must do. Don't you see? In their minds, you could be bringing the fever with you. They would have no choice but to deny us entry, and I won't ask them."

"Jean, you have to listen to me," she said, pushing him away from her and holding him at arm's length. "Look at me. I cannot get the fever. In my time, they have medication to stop you from ever getting it. I had that medicine. It is you and the baby who are in danger. You must believe me."

"My love, I do. I believe anything you tell me, but how can any of our friends believe that you cannot get sick? They simply will not, and we cannot convince them. This sickness drives people to do desperate things. They will only think you are desperate and lying to get away from the city. Now that you have been with me, they will think not only you but our whole household is contaminated."

Frantically, she tried to make him see her point of view. "Jean, we cannot stay. We must go! Somewhere, somehow, there must be a place. We could go to Barataria, to Grand Terre. Can't we go there? It is your home. We would be asking nothing of anyone. We would stay at the house. Not see anyone until they knew for sure we are free of this horror."

Now it was Jean's turn to make her understand. Firmly he replied, "No! We would not be safe even there. I do not trust some of my men under the best of conditions, and we would most assuredly not be welcome under these circumstances. Desperate times call for desperate acts like I have said. They are men who have killed for far less reason. No, I am sorry. You have to understand. We have to stay put for a while. In a few weeks, we will leave. When people see you don't have it, we will be safe. Until then, we will stay in the house and see no one. We will have no contact with the outside. I have sent everyone but Bessy away. She would not hear of leaving us, and I am thankful for her loyalty."

Finally, Tori saw there was no other way out of the situation she had gotten them into. She knew he was right and only prayed that it was not too late for her family's sake. With that settled, her mind drifted back once again to Leone. "Jean, does this mean that we will have to miss Leone's funeral? Surely, he will not be tossed into the river? He will be buried, right? If we are going to have to stay, just to prove that I am not contagious, well, I don't see the point in not attending his burial. I doubt anyone will want to be there. What harm could there be in going? I want to be there, and we can keep our distance from others who might attend."

"I have already made inquiries, and John stopped by earlier to let me know that he has seen to all the details. He was Leone's lawyer, remember? The funeral is to be first thing in the morning, and as you said, I doubt it will make that much difference if we keep our distance. I'm sure the gathering will be tiny, and the service short." Nodding his head, he continued, "Yes, he was a good friend, and we owe him our respects. You and I will stand apart from others, as I fear exposing us any further to this sickness…it would be dangerous to stand with them, but we can be there, yes, I agree. We will attend if you are up to it. Now rest. I will go and see Christopher, then return, to join you once I know Bessy has all he needs.

John Grymes arrived at the house early that morning to accompany them to the funeral. He had no desire to leave town and no fear of catching the fever. He had been exposed to the sickness many times in the past and never caught it; therefore, he doubted he would catch it now. Besides, coming down with the bronze John, as he called it, was the least of his worries.

The sadness of losing a close friend had been tempered early on that morning, by a very unsettling discovery, one that had left him in a high state of agitation. His mood was foul, as he paced the parlor's floor, slapping the side of his leg with his cane as he did so. His face was dark and brooding; his eyes seemed drawn together, making narrow slits, out of which came a look that could frighten anyone.

He had been greeted at the door by Bessy, who, upon seeing the look of thunder instead of grief, upon his face, quickly left the room. Besides, she did not want to expose herself to anyone outside of the house, no matter who they were, regardless of if they claimed they could never catch the fever or not. Now that she knew they would be staying awhile, she intended to do everything in her power to keep the sickness away from herself and the baby.

John's face softened when he saw Tori enter the room with Jean. She was pale, a condition made more evident by the black outfit she was wearing. Sadness hung on her face and in her voice, and for an instant, Grymes debated whether he should add to her grief; but if he were to replace the burden of her misery with that of anger, might it be a far better emotion to bear, he asked himself. Sadness could eat at your insides, leaving a hollow, helpless feeling. Anger could bring life and determination. Yes, his fast thinking, determined, it was far better she be angry.

Tori did not seem to notice John's dark mood. She walked up to him, and the two hugged without saying a word. The grief-stricken woman knew that he, like herself, had lost a good friend, and she was glad that he would be with them today and not alone.

John had grown close to Tori and admired her strength and spirit. To see her crushed as she was now hurt him. He heard how Leone had spent his last hours, tended too by her, and how Tori had gone into shock when he died. The attorney felt a great deal of admiration for the woman's heroic actions and doubted that most men could have experienced any of what she had and walked away unscathed. "Here, Tori, sit down for a while and have some coffee. Maybe something light to eat? You must keep up your strength, you know. There is still time yet before we have to depart. Besides, my dear, after I tell you my news, I think that you will need to have a lot of strength to avoid physically killing someone."

Tori searched Jean's perplexed face for answers. It was apparent that he had no idea what John was talking about either. His brow was wrinkled, and his fingers were twisting one side of his mustache repeatedly. Jean looked away from his wife and turned his attention to Grymes, with a grave look of concern filling his expression. Tori also looked back toward John, wondering how much more could go wrong?

"Look, there is no way to tell you this except to come right out with it. I went to the office this morning to pick up Leone's papers. He had changed a few things in the last weeks…ironic if you think about it...the provisions of his will and a few other wishes he had wanted to be revised were handled. I had helped him work out a lot of the details and was in full agreement with what he did. You must understand that as his lawyer, I could not, nor would I, break his trust by revealing anything till after his death, even if it involved you both, which it does. Neither did I think that he would be taken from us so soon. Leone was a good man and a better friend than you could ever have known." Grymes paced the floor twice, and no one said a word. It was as if he was struggling with himself, as how to proceed. He stopped and turned to face Tori and nodded his head. "You see, my dear; he did not expect to die so soon. However, he was smart enough to know that in case the unexpected did occur, that it was better to be prepared. With his death and with what happened, well, I feel I can divulge all without breaking my word or the law. Indeed, I feel it is imperative that I do so."

Grymes sat down by Tori's side and took her hand in his. "You see, my dear; he did not want his estate to fall into the hands of his so-called brother. Despicable as Edward is, rotten to the core and deserving nothing, that's how Leone felt. I can't blame the man for how he felt toward his brother. Nor do I blame him for his actions, as they were not unwarranted in my estimation. He was a decent man. Far better than myself, I tell you, for I would have left the swine nothing. However, I digress. Sorry about that. Anyway, Leone made an allowance to see Edward received a small inheritance. What I am trying to say is this. The bulk of the estate was to have gone to Christopher on his twenty-first birthday. Jean was to oversee the running of the plantation, and I was to be executor. I use the word was because, as of right now, I have no proof of any of this!"

"Just what are you getting at?" Jean asked.

"Jean, Tori...this morning when I arrived at my office, I knew something was wrong...I just felt it. Nothing seemed out of place at first, but the more I looked around, the more I knew someone had been there. The door was locked when I arrived, so I checked the windows. They, too, were secure, so why did I have an uneasy feeling? Then it hit me. Papers were not where I had placed them; I was certain of it. Little things had been moved around. Then, my friends, my fears were confirmed. The file that held Leone's will had been gone through. Everything, all the deeds and such were still in place. That is, almost everything...everything except his will, which was missing! No matter how many times I went paper by paper searching, thinking, it had slipped in between them somehow; it was not there. The fact of the matter is someone has taken it. Without that document, I'm afraid that there is nothing I or anyone of us can do. What I'm telling you is this. Christopher will not inherit what Leone had hoped. Everything, as I see it right now, goes to Edward and there is not a damn thing we can do about it."

John's fist hit the table, and the temper he had fought to keep under control, came boiling to the surface. Physically shaking, he faced the two of them. His head shook from side to side. "It's all my fault. It is always my professional practice to have a copy of such an important document drawn up. I just never got around to having a copy made right away. Never expected anything to happen. God, how can you forgive me for making such a stupid blunder? It was my responsibility and mine alone. I not only let Leone down but you also!" He sat down so hard that his breath escaped his mouth, making a whistling sound before falling silent. He was beyond himself at this point. Never could he accept anything, but perfection, when it came to his law dealings, and now he had not only let himself down but also his two closest friends. To John, it was unforgivable.

Tori was the first to act. She went to Gryme's side to speak to him. The softness of her manner and the expression of genuine concern took away some of his self-loathing. Her hand held onto his with a kind of firmness. It was the way his mother used to hold his small hand, when he was a child, after having caught him doing something wrong, but not unforgivable. "John, don't be so hard on yourself. Besides, it might be a good thing that it has been taken. My mother always told me that things often happen for a reason. I was with Leone in the end, and that meant more to me than anything he might have left to us. He died with someone taking care of him. Now, I know he might not have realized that, but I believe he would have wanted it. Don't you see? I love him for wanting to make our son his heir but think of all the problems it would have given us. Edward would never have given up trying to take back what he believes is his. Our son would never have been safe, no matter what you did to guard his wellbeing. I think it is far better that we leave things alone. It will work out in the end, I'm sure of it."

Jean quickly added to his wife's statement. "It is clear that she is right about the matter of Edward. And might I add, that he, and he alone, had the most to gain from stealing Leone's will. I assure you that if you find Edward, you will find the will."

Tori shook her head no. "I don't think you will ever see a copy of that document again. I agree it had to be Edward's doing, but think for a second. He is not going to be so stupid as to keep the evidence around, especially when that evidence can take away all that he now has. Gentlemen, I think Edward has the upper hand. He and Simone have won this round. I'm sure that she is in on this with him somehow. Look what happened to her after her husband's death. Think about it; they would have received word about Leone and fearing the same may happen to Edward; they made a bold move to prevent it. Yes, indeed, they have outmaneuvered us. At least we can let them think so."

John spoke now, intrigued by where Tori's thoughts might be leading. "Just what do you mean by that?"

"Simply this. Edward and Simone, I'm sure, will be so thrilled with what they have acquired that they will most likely not think of my family at all and leave us alone once and for all. They have everything that they wanted after all, and if they leave us alone, then we have what we want. We win."

"Yes, I do see your point, but it is just so damn maddening," added Grymes. "It is inexcusable as far as I am concerned, to just let him get away with it. I don't know if I can do it. Damn it to hell, Tori, that bastard has no right; none at all!"

Jean was seething with anger, yet he had to agree with his wife. "Look, John, she has a point. We could make it work to our advantage for a while. If we do nothing, that will put him off guard, and he will think he's won. Edward will be confident that we do not suspect him or anyone working for him. He is going to expect that you will fight him on this. So why not do the unexpected? That will take some of his joy away, at least. You do nothing because you can bet, he is looking forward to us challenging him and nothing less."

Tori smiled at the thought of Edward's anticipation being blown apart. Jean nodded his head in her direction. "Then in a while, we will rethink this whole situation, and John, my friend, I assure you that we will find a way to make that weasel pay. Don't you agree?"

"I do, my love. You are right, and John, may I add, we will take back in time all that belongs to Christopher, not because he needs it. No! But because it was Leone's wish." Tori smiled at the men. It was not much of a smile, but it was a start. The small ignition of anger had sparked, and once it caught on, the fury smoldered. It was not a helpless feeling that she now felt, and not an overcome feeling of sadness either; this was different; this was an energy that brought with it, life.

"Look, already I feel that this news has helped each of us here. I, for one, was dreading going to the funeral this morning. Now, Leone's burial will not be as difficult for me, and I assume, nor will it be so for either of you. I have something other than sadness hanging over my shoulder. I have a spirit in me, and like the two of you, it is fighting mad. I am no longer overcome with grief. Don't you see, Edward, has helped us? He has given us a purpose." Tori was smiling even more as she continued. "I hate Edward Duval, and it will give me the greatest of pleasure to know that we will take it all away from him one day. That, we will hurt him, where it counts, and do so because, like you said, John, it was Leone's intention, to keep the inheritance out of that bastard's hands. Yes, it will hurt him more so than if we took it today. This is going to be one battle that we will not lose if we play our cards right. Think of it like a good game of cards, and we all know that Edward is a lousy card player, don't we?"

John and Jean both chuckled. It was good to see some color return to Tori's face again; she had indeed needed something to help get her through the loss of her friend and now had it. The fact that the fighting Tori was back with them convinced John that he had been right in his judgment call. Telling her had been a positive move, but with or without his friend's help, he would see to it one way or another that the child would inherit all. He did not have a clue how he would accomplish it, but he was damned and determined too. On this, he made a silent oath. No matter the time it took, years if need be, John Grymes swore that Edward Duval would never keep that which Leone had bequeathed to Christopher.

ACROSS town, a pleased Simone sat with a smug look on her face. In her hand, she held Leone's will, and as Edward handed her a glass of wine, she waved the papers in the air triumphantly and gloated. "I told you, if you followed my directions, you would be all right, and you would win." She frowned, and her voice trembled as she went on. "That old fool Grymes, he took away what was supposed to be mine when he had Adrian change his will. But not this time," she said, finishing her drink in one large gulp. "If I had gotten Adrian's will and destroyed it, I would have had it all. Unfortunately, I was too stupid and trusting. Grymes outsmarted me, but not you, my dear. Not you!" Simone walked over to the half-empty bottle and refilled her glass. "I learned my lesson well and now look at the results! We beat him to it, my dear wonderful Edward. I just wish we could have seen his face as he entered his office. He was so sure of himself, that pompous idiot." She again emptied the contents of her glass before adding to her tirade. "You know that incompetent bastard of a lawyer, now knows he has met his match. He must have gone into quite a rage, to see that he had been outsmarted." She placed her empty glass down and spun around, waving the papers in the air once more. "You have won! You, Edward Duval, are the sole owner and Master of one of the grandest and most powerful plantations in the entire South, and you know what? There's not a damn thing anyone can do about it."

Edward felt proud of himself. He was as ecstatic as Simone. For once in his life, it seemed that everything was the way it should have always been. He, not his brother, was the plantation's owner, and he held the revered family name. Oh, he understood only too well that the outcome could have been very different if it had not been for this ravishing creature that spun around the room before him. Edward realized that he would have been left with nothing more than a pittance of an income, while that bitch and Laffite had it all. It hurt when he read the copy of the will in Grymes's office and learned that he was to get next to nothing. The place that was his rightful home and a Duval heritage would have been Tori's and that bastard child of hers. It had hurt less, as his crestfallen feelings turned to pure anger. If he had despised Tori before, he really hated her now. In his blind rage, his warped mind blamed her for turning his brother against him. She had turned Leone against his own flesh and blood, he assured himself. Leone had loved him until she had meddled in their lives; of that fact, he was now most certain.

How glad he was that he had gone to the office and found the will. Happy that he knew Leone would not be made a fool. His brother would have wanted him to destroy the will if he had known the truth of how the whore had played them both. The bitch's seductive ways had blinded his dear brother, and Edward did not blame him. After all, had he not also almost fallen into her trap? Hadn't he found himself fantasizing and wanting her in the past? She was clever, all right, but not intelligent enough to win. Tori might have expected to have it all, and now, she would have to look him in the face and know she could never get her greedy little hands on anything with the Duval name attached to it.

"Edward, are you listening to me? Are you sure there was no other copy of this will? If there is one, we could still lose, you know."

Edward came out of his happy daydream world with a crash. Simone had a frightening point. Could there be a chance of another document? Sounding nervous, he responded. "I'm not certain. There was only this copy in Grymes's office. I went over the file twice, just like you said." He rubbed his worried brow as he thought over that morning's activities carefully. "I have gone over all Leone's papers in his townhouse, and there was nothing. That's why I went to Grymes's office. I suppose he could have sent a copy to the plantation for safekeeping. That would be the only other place he would have put it. Not to worry, after this morning's ceremony, I will ride to the plantation and see for myself that my dear brother's papers contain nothing more than the books and deeds pertaining to the working of the land. I had planned on leaving anyway. Too much fever around for my liking."

Opening a new bottle, he topped his glass up with the deep red liquid and relaxed his worried look. As far as he was concerned, everything was under control. He had paid off the wharf rat that had picked the lock to the lawyer's office. The man would not divulge his part in the break-in, and knowing him, he'd wait to be useful again. The lowlife was always on the lookout for certain activities that paid handsomely and took little effort. Locating him had been easy enough, and Simone had once again proved herself to be most inventive. She had, after all, suggested he carefully have someone break into Grymes establishment. The dandy grinned, locking the door after he had obtained his brother's will, was a stroke of genius too. Edward could picture the American as he stood empty-handed in his office, wondering just how in the hell he had lost the will? Yes, his love was very smart, and he was so glad he'd listened to her. Her more devious manner had proved to be most delightful in its outcome.

Simone looked at her lover. This was a different Edward that she saw before her. He was more in command of himself and his surroundings. He had an air of confidence that he'd not had before, and she realized it would not be so easy to control him from this

413

point on. After all, he no longer needed her. He could buy anything and anyone. What could she offer him other than sex and support? Edward was truly independent for the first time in his life.

Smiling, the dandy added a thought that had just occurred to him. "If you want, Simone, you may accompany me to the funeral. Leone was your friend too, you know, but do as you choose. I have no choice in the matter, as he was my beloved brother. You may stay here if you wish."

Was he already dismissing her? Didn't the fool realize he still needed her? She'd gotten him this far, hadn't she? Without her guidance, he'd not be in the position he was. No, the man would be standing there before her, with nothing more than a pittance of an allowance. Instead, he was free to do as he pleased. She'd lost Adrian's fortune, and now, it seemed she stood to lose becoming the Mistress of the Duval plantation and all its wealth as well. Edward was not acting the way the widow had imagined he would. He was not fawning over her, thanking her for her wisdom and help. He was instead full of himself and his fortuitous position. She'd lost one wealthy man, lost all that she'd been promised because she'd been blind and stupid, and the desperate woman was not about to make the same mistake twice. Simone had to make the dandy want her, and it had to be now and forever.

Edward's love walked over to him and reached for his brow with her hand; she pushed back his hair, that carelessly hung over one eye. Then gently, she traced his face longingly. Tenderly, the scheming female let her hand wander slowly down the front of his shirt to feel his heart thumping against his chest. Holding his attention with her misty eyes, she looked into the depths of his, while a solitary tear slipped down her cheek. When Simone was sure Edward had witnessed the tear, she looked away, dropping her head in sorrow and dejection. "You sound as if you no longer want or need me by your side, now that you have what should have rightfully been yours anyway…that, dare I say…you no longer care for me. Maybe, you never did. I feel lost, Edward. I have come to

414

care about you so much," she hesitated, "to love you. Was I wrong to think you felt the same way? Everything I have done was to show you how I honestly feel. I have helped you in every way I could. Now, it seems, I am to lose you."

At this point, rather than breaking down and crying, making her look as if she was begging him to stay, she turned the tables. After all, Simone had to make him want to keep her and think it was his idea. She did not need him to put two and two together and realize he was being manipulated. The cunning woman went to the door and opened it to let him out. Standing there ready to let him go, the actress didn't look directly at him; instead, she turned her head slightly. With half her face visible, she said softly, "I will not keep you here, go. Maybe, in a while, you may come to think of me as a close friend. I will always be here."

Edward had meant nothing of the sort. To toss her aside, as she was implying, had been the last thing on his mind. He had grown very fond of her, maybe even loved her, if such a thing were possible. To see and hear now, hear how much she cared for him, and then to see how she could just let him go baffled him. He studied her carefully. The dandy understood this woman was just as conniving as he. Yes, she was his match in that department, but by studying both her expression and statement, he was convinced that this was no act. She would find someone to take his place if he left her because someone like Simone could not be on their own for long. That's how she could let him go because she could replace him easily. Being both beautiful and talented, the widow would get whomever she wanted, and he wanted that man to be him. With her and the power of his fortune and family name, what more could a man want? A small voice seemed to whisper the name 'Tori' in the back of his mind, but he pushed it away as he walked forward to take her in his arms. Edward knew he could control her and have the beauty for his own and would. Simone was one woman, who for some strange reason or another he could not let go.

This was Tori's first visit inside a New Orleans graveyard in this era. She had driven by them many times in the future, marveling at the sight of the stone and marble crypts. The cemeteries had seemed so foreign, with all the standing tombs and beautifully carved statues. The somber female recalled how each old cemetery was so compact, with hardly any available space's left, especially in those graveyards located in the French Quarter. On one trip, Tori had learned that Cemetery number one had been an elite graveyard and kept for only those of the Catholic faith. Concerning that requirement, Tori remembered another small piece of history. Claiborne, had been buried there, only to later be reinterred in Metairie Cemetery, because he was not Catholic.

Walking with Jean and Grymes, Tori continued to reminisce. In her time, cemetery number one and two had become a part of the tourist attractions. There were many people who would never leave the city without saying they had seen the crypt of Marie Laveau. What a horrible thought that was. The young girl would grow old and someday be buried in a tomb to rest in peace. The trouble was, there would be no peace, just hundreds of strangers, laughing and taking photos. Hell, even Hollywood would come here to film movies, like they had in 'Easy Rider.' No, this would not become the peaceful resting place those buried here thought it would be. The beautiful crypts would remain, a few would be maintained, but still, more would decay and fall to ruin.

Tori trembled; most everyone she had come to know in this time, maybe even herself, would end up being a tourist attraction, buried here for all the future citizens to visit. She felt more out of place than ever and hesitated in her walk. Tori did not want to think about the future, yet she could not help it. Curiously she continued looking around, trying to see if there was anything that she might have seen in her own time but quickly knew it was futile. The graveyard they were in was nothing like what it would become. It was still a long way from full, and for now, it was beautifully kept up. It sat on the edge of town, and there was no noisy freeway passing close by. Tori looked up, and beyond where they were walking, and for a second in her minds-eye, she pictured Hwy 10 and its many cars speeding by.

The image faded as Laffite's wife reached for Jean's hand. He took hold of it and looked at her, concern in his eyes. Rather than explain why her emotions were so torn, she looked away from his gaze and continued her observations. There were no high walls to keep out the graffiti artists and vandals. No paved road between one cemetery and the other. No iron gates to close at sunset.

The City of the Dead had trees, and small gardens filled with plants and flowers, making for a peaceful 'bury garden,' a term her daughter had used for graveyards. Sadly, Tori wondered when it would begin to transform from this tranquil state to end up how she remembered? The cemeteries would, in her time, become areas where one had to be careful for fear of foul play. For now, though, it was clean, and oddly it felt peaceful and deeply spiritual, and it was not a place to fear for one's safety when visiting.

As they walked further into the graveyard, Tori soon realized that they were not the only people on that sad day with a funeral to attend. She counted six other small groups in the area, and all were there to bury a loved one who had died of the fever. Most held a cloth over their noses and mouths, while others stood further back, fearful that they might catch the deadly sickness that had brought them there to pay their final farewells.

Jean looked again at his lovely wife. If it had been up to him, Laffite would have insisted that she stay home with the baby, rather than face this sad gathering. Yet, looking at her now, determined to survive the ordeal, he was proud of his wife. The pirate knew that nothing short of death itself would have kept her from his side today and that knowledge comforted him.

They reached the Duval's family tomb, where a few friends had already gathered. It was going to be a small turnout for such a fine man, who deserved so much more. Many of his friends would not know for days or weeks that he had passed away. Many of those in town who had heard, would not attend out of fear, and Tori did not blame them.

Jean acknowledged the few people who stood there. They spoke softly and briefly while moving away from him and his lady. Tori wanted to offer her words of condolence but could not find a way to talk. She had words that would be appropriate, yet they could not be uttered, and she understood why. It was because if she spoke one word, all the sadness bottled up would come to the surface, and tears would flow. In the end, Tori just nodded slightly to acknowledge whoever looked her way and allowed them to ascertain the meaning behind her silence.

The priest joined the small group almost immediately. He had just finished a service not more than fifty yards away, and Tori could hear someone crying as the tomb was being sealed shut.

Everybody watched the weary man as he stood looking around at the few people gathered before him. It did not go unnoticed by Tori how very worn out the old priest appeared. She also witnessed and admired his determination to remain steadfast enough to face this sad service. He and Leone had been friends for many years, and she had met the priest on many occasions. Leone was a very well-known man and a good friend of the church, so in Tori's mind, it was only right that his friend performed the service, and maybe the church would hold a memorial, later, after all the sickness was gone. That would be the proper action to take, and if that happened, they would attend that too. How could they not, knowing, how much he had come to care for them?

The priest began, sadly shaking his head as he fumbled through his prayer book. It was as if he was reluctant to start. Maybe he was hoping that delaying would allow more people time to attend? Whatever the reason, he seemed quite perplexed. "Is something the matter, Father?" asked Jean. "Can I be of any assistance to you?" Jean was worried that the old man might be ill and in need, so he took a step forward.

"No, my son." The priest held up his hand to stop Laffite. "It is just that I have so many services to attend today, so many dead. There are still others sick and in need of me at their side. I have to give what little comfort I can on their deathbed, you understand." The tired man rubbed his sweaty brow, smudging dirt across his skin as he did so. He squeezed his aching eyes tight against the bright light reflecting into them. Impatiently, his voice echoed as he spoke. "You would think that Leone's brother would be on time for once in his life. This is, after all, the last of his flesh and blood that we bury here today. Two brothers. So different. I have known them both since birth, you know. Just a sad affair it is. Makes one question why God would choose to take the more righteous brother? Forgive, my thoughts it is not for me or anyone to judge." The priest opened his eyes and squinted. "All in all, it's unfortunate, and here, I thought that he had begun to mend his ways of late. Edward that is. Shame it is. Well, we shall just have to proceed without him. Let us begin."

His words seemed far away to Tori, who still could not put the horrific images out of her mind. Looking at the casket and knowing Leone lay inside, brought back the events of the day before. She would never forget his death, how could she?

It was the sudden sound of silence that took her attention back to what was going on around her. The service had stopped, and everyone was looking behind her, and some with pure shock on their faces. Tori turned to see what it was that had distracted them all and instantly understood. There, off in the distance, walking toward them were Edward and Simone. They did not hurry, and to most, it seemed, that the pair deliberately took their time, as they sauntered toward the small gathering.

They walked right past Jean and Tori, as if they were not there, to stand with the priest. Once close by his side, they stood without acknowledging anyone. Edward's head lowered closer to the priest's ear briefly as he quietly spoke, and Simone looked only at the coffin. Clearing his throat, and profoundly moved by whatever it was, that he had been told, the priest started the service over. As the words droned on and the morning heat intensified, the small group all stood listening and thinking about the friend they were saying farewell too. That is, nearly all of them.

Edward's gaze traveled from his brother's coffin to Tori. His hatred was evident, and the feelings he silently exuded caused her to take a step back. Duval had the crazed look of a demented man, one which held Tori's gaze paralyzed and frozen to his.

Jean did not miss the looks that passed between the two of them. Hopefully, his squeezing of her hand added a little bit of comfort that she could hang onto, and he prayed she understood that. Feeling his wife needed a little more than him holding her hand, he placed his arm around her waist and pulled her closer.

Feeling his touch, Tori knew that she was safe. Jean had not missed Edward's hateful glares. His tight hold of her was a reminder that he stood between her and this twisted individual. The pirate would never allow anything to happen to his wife, and she was thankful he was by her side. Tori looked away from the new deadly stare the dandy shot her and gazed upon Leone's casket. She would not give Leone's brother the satisfaction of seeing he was upsetting her.

ALL too soon, they were placing the coffin inside the tomb, to lie next to the other family members. The end of the service was on hand, and like all those there, Jean and Tori turned to walk away.

"Just a minute, Madame Laffite. I would like to say something to you if I may?" Edward's voice was laced with sweetness and his face a mask of sadness, as he joined them. Jean's arm again slipped quickly around Tori's waist, an act that did not escape Edward. "I simply wish to ask you why you did not send for me when Leone was so close to the end? You must have known, or was it your hope to get him to leave his once Mistress, more than just memories?" His tone of voice and expression changed, as anger tinged both. "You, tried my dear, to come between my dearly departed brother and I, for an exceedingly long time, didn't you? Even on his deathbed, you did not give up, did you? But I won, after all. God blesses those who are worthy. Leone loved me, and he left you nothing. Everything we have stays with the Duval name. But don't be too sad. He did leave you with one small thing." His lips curled up into a cruel smile as he continued, "he left you, Edward Duval, to deal with. I will never forgive you or forget how you drove him from me. You turned him against me, with your lies, keeping him away so we could not communicate. Even in his final hours, you kept him from me."

The few people left standing around, let out a gasp. Had the grief of his brother's death made Edward insane or was it the heat that had gone to his head? Surely, he did not know what he was talking about. After all, everything the man was saying was pure fantasy; everyone knew that Leone had always felt his younger brother was not worthy of the family name. He'd felt like that, long before Victoria Laffite arrived in town. To have the audacity to claim she had once been Leone's mistress, it was crazy talk. Surely the man was ill; maybe he was coming down with the same fever that had claimed his brother? What other explanation could there be for his exaggerated lies they asked each other?

They might not have understood, but Jean most certainly did. Before John had a chance to stop him, Jean released his hold on Tori, and with the swift movement of a trained athlete, he moved between Edward and Tori. The next thing people witnessed was Edward lying on the ground, his face down in the dirt.

Simone was quickly by Edward's side, wiping the blood from his nose. "How could you? How could you hit a man in his hour of grief? Is it not enough that he is suffering already? Have some compassion, some understanding! If the truth hurts, then may I suggest that you take your wife and leave us alone? Go on, get out of here!" She was spitting the words out, directing them right at the pair, and had she not felt Edward's hand on her arm at that moment; she would have said more.

Jean looked away from the despicable pair and acted as if they no longer existed. Taking Tori by her hand, he turned and walked calmly away. Grymes, who had witnessed everything, joined them and spoke his mind. "The man is evil, and to speak of such dreadful accusations at such a time is unforgivable. No one will listen, and I, for one, will make certain that my friend's memory is not blackened, nor will your standing, my dear. Let us ignore him and depart before I lose my temper and do more than just hit him."

Edward was not finished. He could not allow Jean to saunter off like he was and with Grymes too. He had one last thing to say to them, in front of witnesses. Shouting at them through tears, he had to fight from breaking down completely. "On my dead brother's soul, I promise you that God will help me seek out just revenge for all your sins. You think that you are above the law, above us all. Well, your time is coming, Laffite! And may I also add that if I ever catch either you or your wife on my land, I will see to it that justice comes swift; by God, I will. Do you hear me? You will pay for all you have done. Leone will be proud of me yet! You had best advise them, Grymes. Explain to them I have the right to keep them off my plantation. The right to kill them should I catch them there. Tell them..." Edward could not go on. His voice broke as he lost his composure, and tears of frustration streamed down his face. The dandy cried in Simone's arms as the small crowd walked away, shaking their heads in disbelief.

A few of those who had witnessed the scene came as close as they dare to Tori, offering their apologies and condolences, telling her how brave she had been to be with Leone at the end, risking her very life as she had. They were sure it was guilt that made Edward carry on as he did. They knew that it should have been him, not her, nursing Leone, but he had not dared. Didn't she know he had chosen to stay away out of fear of catching the illness, they explained? All his anger would pass in time when this horrible plague left, and things would turn once again to normal, they assured her. One of the ladies went so far as to add that not one of them would ever believe such preposterous accusations as Edward had spoken. All knew Leone to be a fine upstanding gentleman. Not only would he never have had a mistress, but to blacken Leone, by insinuating such an action, was unforgivable.

With that said, the small group departed. The priest walked up to Tori and added his own brief words, before heading in the direction of still another service needing his attention. He told Tori that Edward would have to live with his actions and grief and learn not to blame others like he always had. In time, he thought he might even apologize for his outburst. After all, that would be the gentlemanly thing to do, and Edward was a Duval, which denoted he should act like one.

Tori was not so sure. She knew in her heart that today Edward had declared war. He was going to try everything he could, to destroy her and those she loved. The question was, could he? One thing was certain; Edward had made an excellent start.

SINCE the funeral, the only people Tori and Jean had seen were Grymes and Jean's brother Pierre, who stopped by to keep Jean up-to-date with the city's news. After his second visit, Pierre had left town, taking his Mistress upriver to a small establishment he rented in Donaldsonville. His wife and child had left weeks ago, with her family, and as long as Grymes agreed to keep an eye on Jean and Tori, he felt it just that he departed to protect himself as well as those he loved. Shortly after his departure, the lawyer told Jean that already the days claimed fewer casualties and that no one feared Tori being sick any longer. Laffite's wife had stayed healthy and was now considered safe and free of the dreaded fever. So it was that finally, after many long worry-filled days, the morning came when at last, they would head to Destrehan and leave for a much-needed break in the cooler countryside.

Tori had been up for some time. Christopher had fussed most of the night, and the final time she'd gone to see him, she had picked him up and rocked the little lad until daybreak. She and Bessy decided it was his teeth that kept the poor boy fussing hour after hour, and as he had no sign of fever, the worry of him coming down with any sickness was ruled out. By the time the sun was up, her little man, as she often called him, was fast asleep and did not even wake when she placed him back in his crib. Slowly Tori backed out of the room and closed the door. It would be better for him to sleep a bit longer before their trip, and she would be sure to tell Bessy that.

It had seemed like such a good idea to make breakfast for Jean and take it up to him. She quietly opened the bedroom door and imagined his face when she told him that his wife, not Bessy, had made the whole meal. As tired as she was, the fact that she could surprise him had her walking lightly toward the sleeping man, while trying to contain a giggle.

Slowly Tori placed the tray on the side table and stepped toward Jean, with the intention of jumping back into bed, but she got no closer than the bedside when the baby started up with his morning hunger cry. Knowing that if she ignored the child, he would merely get louder and wake his father, she decided to take the baby to Bessy herself. Tori was determined not to let Christopher break the sexy mood she was in and ruin her little rendezvous with her husband. Quickly Jean's wife tiptoed out of the room and entered the nursery, where she picked the fussing child up and carried him down to the kitchen. "Here you go, young man. I think it's more than mother's milk that has you fussing. You're ready for some real food, aren't you?"

Bessy, who was busy in the kitchen, with the clutter Tori had left, started laughing. She reached out and took the child from his mother's arms, happy at last that she would have a chance to feed him. Christopher was going to have whatever he wanted to eat if Bessy had anything to say about it. The cook had been waiting for weeks for this day. Though no one in the house knew it, the house-keeper had prepared a bowl of baby food every morning, but today it would not go to waste. Today, Bessy would finally get to spoon the mashed-up food into his chubby little face.

Tori had intended to leave the two alone and return upstairs, a thought which escaped her for thirty minutes as she watched and laughed with Bessy. The baby spilled and slurped his way through his first sloppy solid food, getting more on him than in him, it seemed. Tori had worried at first that her son was maybe too young to attempt solid food, but like his father, he was damned and determined to succeed at anything sent his way. Bessy assured Tori that the lad was more than ready, and together, they enjoyed his first attempts. The Mistress of the house had finally left the two alone when it was cleanup time. "I will leave him in your hands, Bessy. The Master and I need a little alone time, so I will see you in a while."

Bessy was only too proud and happy to comply with the Mistress's instructions; after all, her dreams of becoming the child's nanny were coming true.

TORI was surprised to find Jean still asleep. It was not like him to be so lazy, and she knew it. He had to be playing a game with her. Knowing that was more his style, to play opossum and then spring into action, Tori decided on her own tactic. Smiling to herself, the grinning female picked up a pillow from her side of the bed. A shiver of excitement crossed her body as she anticipated how the pillow fight of theirs would end. Trying to disguise her enthusiasm, she spoke in a serious tone. "Jean…oh, Jean, you lazy good-for-nothing pirate. You had best protect yourself because you are about to pay the penalty for playing opossum." He did not move, nor did he chuckle, trying to bait her. Tori stood over him, pillow poised and ready, awaiting his expected reaction, but nothing happened. He was playing with her; she told herself because instead of jumping up to grab her, he slowly turned his head her way. This was an improvement of sorts, on his regular course of action and not knowing what to expect next, Tori held her breath as he rolled the rest of his body toward her. This was it; her moment to strike was at hand, and she raised the pillow higher to begin the fun, but it was his weak voice that halted her action.

"Tori, Tori, my head hurts so bad. The light hurts: I don't wish to open my eyes. I thought I would feel better. Don't want to disappoint you; we must go today." His voice was raspy, and the feel of his skin was burning to her touch. Horror filled her mind as both sent a screaming message to her brain, as he continued to try and talk. "Better send for the doctor. Too sick to go today, sorry." His apologetic look came from behind two fevered eyes that he tried to shield from the morning light, with his trembling hand. A weak smile left his lips as he turned away, burying his face in his pillow and pulling at the sheet to cover his shaking body.

Tori dropped the pillow and quickly ran to the door shouting for someone to fetch the doctor. "I want him dragged here if they have to. When they find him, they must make it clear that he is to come straight away, if not sooner!" Tori did not wait for confirmation that her orders would be followed. She didn't have to. The sound of the front door slamming shut let her know Bessy had seen that someone left immediately. Turning, the panicked woman went back toward Jean's side, realizing that what she was looking at, once again, was a clear case of yellow fever.

As time passed, she kept herself busy waiting for the doctor by wetting a sponge with fresh water and wiping Jean's fevered brow. She refused to believe that her efforts were futile or that Jean's outcome would be like that of Leone's. Tori would keep a positive attitude and keep Jean fighting. As for the doctor, surely, he had learned something in this last outbreak that would help. After all, she reasoned, the man had spent more time with the disease than anyone. The doctor had even told her, had he known Leone was sick right away; he might have saved him. Jean had not been ill when they went to bed, so undoubtedly there was a chance that they had caught it early enough. One thing was sure in history, Laffite didn't meet his end like this, but if he did, it would be because of her.

Tori knew he had to keep on track. Jean Laffite had to fight in the battle of New Orleans, not die here in bed. He did not die of yellow fever in her history books, did he? Had she read once that he died of yellow fever? Maybe she had, but it seemed to her, it was in another country and long after the battle. He was destined to help Andrew Jackson and supply the man with guns. He was the reason that they could fight the British and win against all the odds. Now he lay in bed with an illness that could kill him and, worse yet, prevent him from keeping his date with his historical role. Could she have caused this by bringing the fever home after leaving Leones? After all, her attempts to keep things on track, had she finally changed the outcome of history, as she knew it?

Jean's wife sponged him down again. He was going to live; he had too. Jean had to have been exposed at Leone's funeral. That was the answer. It was not her fault. Then that thought vanished because she realized the truth in the matter. She had been at Leone's death bed. If not, Laffite would maybe never have known about his demise, let alone attended the man's funeral. He only knew Leone because of her. There was no way around the facts, everything pointed to her being the culprit, and now history and its outcome could be in grave jeopardy.

Jean would wake now and then, to take a sip of the water. Tori remembering the dehydrated last hours of Leone's life, insisted he drink, and after doing so, the fevered man would go back to sleep. The last time he tried to drink was difficult for him, and it was even harder for him to talk. Having guessed he had the fever, the pirate wanted to make one thing clear to the woman he loved. "Tori, you must keep Christopher away from me, do you hear? No one else, but you are to come in." He struggled to continue. "It is the fever. I know it is." Weakly he took hold of her hand and tried to sound reassuring as he spoke. "My love, do not fear. I will not leave you. I love you and my son too much. I shall fight, and I shall be, as always, victorious."

It broke her heart to hear his raspy voice struggle through the pain and seeing the weakness that already raked his body almost made her cry. He was getting worse as each hour passed, and she had no control and no way to help stop it. Twice she went to the door to call for Bessy. "How come the doctor is taking so long? Didn't those you sent for him understand how sick the Master is? His fever is climbing, and the rising temperature outside does not help matters. Find the doctor and find him fast, Bessy."

There was the sound of more doors slamming as Tori walked back to their bed. She sat looking at the man who was the love of her life and father to the sweetest baby boy. Jean was strong, but no matter how many times she wiped him down or fanned him, it was not going to help. Her thoughts swirled, mixed with both hopes and doubts. The facts about this fever were grim no matter how strong Jean was, it could take him from her, faster than the doctor reaching them. Fear gripped her. She did not know which way this could go or what she could do. Only one thing was clear; Tori had no choice but to wait and see what the doctor had to say.

THE doctor had done nothing more than confirm what she already knew and told her he would be back the next day to see how Jean was doing and that maybe he would bleed him. Until then, she was to keep on doing what she was and try to get him to take more water. He did not want to give him any medication such as he had, due to the incredibly high fever, and the man left feeling less hopeful than he let on.

Tori knew of the old bleeding practice and how it did more harm than good by weakening the patient. She would never allow it. What her husband needed was all his strength if he was going to win the battle. Tori wanted help from someone who could give him medication to fight the fever, someone who had drugs that worked! The only problem with that idea was that what she needed was years away. She had to think. Where and how in the world could she get drugs that could help? Both modern medicines and doctors were out of reach, but maybe not everyone with such knowledge was. Marie Laveau; that's who would have the medication Jean needed.

She knew the young girl was doing much more than fixing hair and handing out her strange love potions and gris-gris. Laffite's wife knew that the girl was also a herbalist. Tori recalled reading that Marie always had a lot of remedies for sale, some of which would cure all sorts of ailments. They would work because they had the base of many modern drugs. Marie would know how to draw from herbs and plants, the ingredients that Jean needed. If Jean was to have a chance, she had to get this girl to come and help. That was her answer, and his only hope. As Tori went to the door to call for Bessy, Laffite's wife prayed that Marie had already started her career of mixing her medications, besides strange, useless potions for attraction, warding off evil and other such nonsense. Without thinking further on the subject, she departed the bedroom to tell Bessy that Marie, the voodoo queen, was who she wanted to come to the house. They met on the stairs, and before the housekeeper could say a word, Tori gave her instructions. "Bessy, tell her I'll pay whatever she wants. Anything…anything at all. She just has to come and see him. It's his only chance!"

If Bessy had been surprised by Tori's request, she had not shown it. She just listened and then left to do her Mistress's bidding. How could the slave explain to Miss Tori that she was plain scared to death of that voodoo? That no matter what the church told her, she knew it to be plenty powerful and nothing to mess around with. The housekeeper would take the message to Marie because she dearly loved Jean, and Tori and that was a good enough reason to do so. Besides, she also knew that if her Master was going to get better, it would have to be with the help of some mighty powerful gris-gris and God's will.

LATER that night, when a light knock came on the bedroom door, Tori let in the young black girl who had up until now, only been her hairstylist. Upon entering the room, Marie stood looking toward the bed in which Jean lay, not saying a word. Her gaze then fell on Tori's face, and Marie could see the hope and desperation written on its worried lines. What if she tried to help this man, who all New Orleans loved? What if she failed? What then? Ah, but if she were to succeed? If he were to live, then this family of power would be indebted to her for life. Marie was not stupid. She would only take on this challenge if she thought the odds were on her side. It would not take long for her to decide what should be done, and much depended on the strength of the woman, who stood before her.

Jean was burning with fever, and twice, he had made such a mess that Tori felt she could not handle the situation without going out of her mind. Still, she had managed to keep control of her emotions, and now that help had arrived, she was able to calmly tell Marie everything she could about Jean and his condition.

Marie listened in silence as if she were not sure yet of what she was going to do. She stood so still, her eyes questioning and seeking the truth. To Tori's mind, it was as if Marie was in a trance, and she found herself doubting the girl and her abilities. Tori stood thinking, 'could I have been wrong about her?'

Then, as if in answer to her doubts, the girl pushed past her and walked toward Jean. She removed her dark wrap and placed the cloth bag she carried by the foot of the bed. Without a word yet spoken, she started to work.

There was no fear in her actions as she examined her patient. Watching her, Tori had the odd feeling that she was watching a nurse from her own time, but knew that was impossible. The girl took his pulse, looked into his eyes, and felt the glands around his neck. She touched his forehead with the back of her hand and mumbled something close to his ear. Putting her head on his chest, she listened to his heart as it raced beneath his burning skin. Satisfied with what she found, she turned toward Tori and smiled for the first time. Then Marie gave orders of things to be done and things that she would need in the next twenty-four hours. Carefully she lay out the small bags of herbs and powders that she'd brought with her. A cross was placed on the table, and a small candle was lit. Incense burned, and a large white feather was used to fan the smoke from burning sage bundle while prayers were said. As Marie waited for all that she'd asked for to be brought to her, she continued to smudge the room.

"We have a good chance of healing him. He is a strong man with a will to live. You have done well. Everything you did so far was what I would have done, but now the real work begins. You will help me, for a while, and then you will leave. You must believe in him and me. Then you will pray. You must do as I ask if we are to drive the devils away. No questions. Just obey." She was determined as she spoke. Seeing that Tori was not going to oppose her, Marie softened and smiled at her. She realized fear would not have to be used here, to have her way.

Between them, Jean was stripped naked, with only a cloth laid across his groin. This, Marie told Tori, was so she would not have to feel embarrassed or uncomfortable.

"But he is my husband. I won't be embarrassed. Should I be? I mean, if it will help him in any way, to lay completely naked, then let him be that way. He's past the point of realizing what is going on."

"I'm sure it would not embarrass you, but how about me?" The girl laughed and wagged her finger in Tori's face. "I'm just a young girl. Not supposed to look at any man that way," she said, grinning ear to ear, revealing that it had all been said in jest. Marie wanted to lighten the moment, to help Tori relax a bit. She needed her to cope with trusting her, and yet there was doubt in the woman's face. "Something bothers you?"

"You seem to be so young, and yet so wise. How old are you, Marie? How have you come to know and learn so much?"

"I am as old as you want me to be. Years, days, they really don't mean much, do they? It's what a person is and knows that counts, don't you think? Now, let us wipe this man of yours down; he's still getting hotter, and the worst is yet to come. I must see that he drinks my potions and keeps them in him. If some come back up, I must see how much, because that's how much more I have to get him to take. Too much is not good; too little is no help. Now, let's start."

Repeatedly the women worked on cooling their patient down. The only time Tori left Jean's side was to check on their son, and by the second day, she was so exhausted that Marie insisted that she sleep for a few hours. "The fever should break soon. One way or another, we will have our answer today. I will call you if there is any change. You are the one that concerns me now. Please go. You need your rest. You must prepare for that which lays ahead."

Marie looked saddened for a fleeting moment as if she knew of some horrible fate, yet, how could she, Tori wondered? Surely, she meant that even when his fever broke, there would be many long hours of care needed. Jean's wife felt her heart skip a beat as this strange girl looked at her. Just how much of this Voodoo-Queen-to-be, was a legend and how much was fact, she did not know? One thing was sure, though: the girl did seem to have a sixth sense. Afraid to stay and ask questions about what she meant a very tired Tori welcomed the few hours of rest. After all, she knew it would be days yet before Jean would need less attention. With her son in her arms for company, the mother slept deeply for the rest of the afternoon.

Marie worked with Jean. He was strong, and he had the will to live. That would help, but he needed more. Mixing more of the herbs she had with her, she forced his parched lips apart and slowly let the vile liquid trickle into his mouth. Every few minutes, she would force him to sip the concoction, knowing it was his only chance to beat the fever.

Jean called out often for his love. Tori's name was the only one on his lips. Over and over, the man went on about his wife, about her staying with him, and Marie sat and listened to him, taking in his jumbled ravings, which at first sounded like nothing important. A few hours later, a sly smile crept across her lips as she put the pieces of his delirium into a story that made a whole lot of sense.

IN the late afternoon, she stood and looked contentedly down on Jean, speaking to him softly. "You will live, Jean Laffite. The fever has broken, and the sleep you have now will be deep and silent. I have learned much from you about you and your lady. Much that will come in use, in the future…maybe, for you, and maybe for me. It will be a secret for the two of us to hold until I know what to do about this knowledge you have let fall my way." She was pleased with herself. Jean Laffite would owe her his life. Marie looked at her slumbering patient and let her happiness slip away, as a grim expression caused her lips to tighten. She bent down to speak to the pirate, whispering in his ear. "Sleep, my friend, for soon you will carry a far heavier burden. Your life is about to change once again, and you will have to be far stronger than ever before."

No sooner than she finished talking to Jean, a piercing scream sounded from the other room. It could be heard throughout the house, and she turned knowingly, looking toward the adjoining room where the terrified cry emitted. Behind the closed door, she could also hear a female slave's wailing join in with Tori's desperate call for help. A sadness clouded Marie's eyes, her lids closing as if wishing to deny that she had hoped could have been delayed. The hours of no sleep and the worry that fell on Leveau now aged her far beyond her years. "It begins Laffite. I had hoped that you would have had longer to recover my friend, but it is not to be. You will rest this night. My drugs will see to that, and then you must be strong. I cannot help this time, for this time, I already fear the specter of death approaches. God help this home and the people here. They will need all the help they can to bare what comes their way."

Jean slept on blissfully, unaware of the girl who stood talking at the end of his bed. He was totally unaware of the panic that had gripped his home as Marie walked toward the door that separated the rooms.

Tori was racing toward her, holding their child in her arms. Tears streamed across her face, and fear filled her eyes as she stood before Marie. "He has it! You knew, didn't you? That's what you meant earlier. My son has the fever! Dear God, Marie, do something! Help him, please!"

Marie's heart twisted in agony as she knew there was nothing she could do to save him. Children of this age did not last long with this devil's curse. The fever would go too high, too quickly, and her potions would not help, not this time. All she could do was try and make the child more comfortable, something that Tori, his mother, could do far better than herself. How she hated the feeling of not being able to do anything more, and Marie hated that she had to explain it to the desperate woman. How could she tell his mother that it was hopeless?

The young girl reached out to take the baby from Tori's arms. "See to your husband. His fever has broken, and he will live, but let him rest. Do not wake him this night with such sad news. He is still so weak. I will do what I can for the child." She took Christopher from his mother's arms and left the room.

Jean's wife walked toward the pirate, with a mixture of happiness and hellish worry. Tori was so relieved he was going to be all right... but now her son...their son was fighting for his life. The baby was so sick. How would she tell him that when he woke up? She could maybe give him hope, though. After all, Marie had saved him with her potions, so the baby had a chance; they just had to believe that and remain strong.

THAT night became a living nightmare for Tori. It was one that seemed endless in its horror. Jean slept, and Marie worked with her child. Tori would go from one bedside to the other, praying that one would continue to sleep, and the other would stay awake and fight. By early light, it was obvious to her that the stronger Jean got, the weaker Christopher became. Looking at Marie, who had not stopped her endless work trying to win against all the odds, Tori dropped all hopes of her child's recovery. Marie did not need to tell her that which she could see for herself. Jean would live. Christopher was going to die.

Tori had to touch the girl's arm to let her know she was standing alongside her because she was so intent on trying to cool down the baby's fever that nothing else mattered. "Marie, I know he is very ill, too ill for you or anyone to help. I understand, really, I do. It's not your fault; you have done all you can."

Marie looked into Tori's agonized face and found something she had not expected. Along with Tori's pain, she encountered compassion, understanding, and acceptance. Seeing this, the young girl nodded her head and stood up. "If I were to tell you that I thought he would survive, I would be lying. You are right. I did not know how to tell you. I had to try, you understand?"

Tori could see Marie was not only exhausted but also, she was deeply sad. The young face that looked at her was like that of a lonely child, not a wise woman. "I know you did all you could, and I thank you for that." Tori's voice sounded calm, but her eyes showed the agony of defeat and the torment it was causing.

Marie raised her hands toward the ceiling and spoke in frustration to both the heavens and to Tori. "It is beyond me why such a babe has to leave so soon. Beyond my reasoning and my herbs." She lowered her hands and looked Tori directly in the eyes. "You can hold him and try to keep him cool, but the little one, he only gets hotter and hotter. If we had a way to break the fever, but there is nothing. Not for him and those like him. The child is just too young. I have done all I can! Forgive me. I can do no more."

"Oh Marie, you have done so much already, don't you see? Without you, I would have lost them both. At least I am to keep Jean. The baby's life is out of our hands now; we both know that. Christopher's life is in God's hands." She picked her son up and rocked him gently as she spoke to herself. "Maybe he was not meant to be. I guess I should have known. Never did I read of Jean having a son."

Tori was making no sense to Bessy, who stood wringing her hands and sobbing quietly, but it made sense to Marie, and she secretly agreed with Tori that it was as it should be.

Marie knew she might not be able to help the child, but a few words of wisdom might help comfort the mother. Taking Tori aside and out of earshot of Bessy, she talked softly and knowingly to her. "The little one will not have to grow up wondering where his mother is. I think it is, as it is, written. All has passed as it should, and still much will happen. Have strength in the time to come, Tori. Your love for this child, and for Jean, it will get you through." She smiled a knowing sort of smile, one filled with such a depth of understanding that it helped calm the baby's mother. Once again, the wisdom of years filled her face.

Had Tori heard her, right? How could she know? Could it be that Marie knew the truth, or was this voodoo queen guessing? Had Jean spoken out loud in those hours that she had left him in Marie's care or was it that power, that ESP she had?

Marie saw Tori's shocked expression and decided to avoid further questions that might give away her hand. She quickly changed the subject. "Your man has a right to see his son, I think. The time grows short. You must go to him now. I will leave. There is nothing left here for me. Be assured that I will stop on my way and tell Laffite's brother that he will be needed. He will be the only one I tell, fear not."

Tori could barely see Marie through the tears that clouded her eyes as she held her dying son. The young woman was right. Jean, as weak as he was, had a right to see his son before the end. Tori could not talk or explain to Bessy what she needed to do. All she could do was walk slowly toward the other bedroom.

Marie closed the door and told Bessy to leave them alone until they called for her. Then she swiftly collected her things and left without another word. It was not until she entered her home where her closest friend and lover waited, that Marie broke down and cried. It seemed to her that life was nothing more than a cruel trick, played upon all, by the devil himself.

TORI sat by Jean's side of the bed. Laffite looked so extremely weak. He was pale and drawn, but his breathing was steady and clear of any rasping sound. His forehead was covered with a film of glistening perspiration, which was a good sign. He might still have a fever, but not one that was raging out of control. Jean was on the mend. He would live, but how would he ever heal from the loss of his son?

The baby was so hot. His little hands just lay wherever Tori placed them. He was already so weak and dehydrated that even crying was too much of an effort for him.

His mother looked lovingly at him through tear-filled eyes. Christopher looked as though he was sleeping. If only that was the case. If only he were just sleeping, instead of near death she thought. The broken-hearted parent knew she had to wake Jean soon because the end was coming. The baby's breathing was labored, and his small heart pounded so fast that it felt as if it would jump right out of his little chest.

Tori touched Jean's arm gently. Twice she felt as if her voice would break when she tried to speak. Then drawing on a strength that the woman knew she had within her, she spoke to Jean in a calm tone. "Jean, you need to wake up, my love. Come on, please...wake up."

Finally he awoke, forcing his eyes to open in response to her gentle coaxing. His tired face looked at her, as a weak smile acknowledged the fact that he knew he had won his battle. "I told you that I would not leave you, did I not? You and the baby can rest easy now. It's going to be all right. Had the damnedest dreams. Thought I saw a young girl here with me. Seen her before…the night the baby was born. I think it was her, not sure, something about her voice. She was the same one who told me about the baby coming." His speech stopped as he seemed to gather his strength to go on. He wanted so much to make her realize that he was going to be fine. "I see you have Christopher there. Let me see him." Jean lifted his head slowly, struggling as if this small effort would be too much for him. The already pale color of his skin blanched further, as the room started to spin before his eyes, so Tori waited a few seconds to give him time to adjust.

"Jean, the baby is sick. He has the fever." How she had said those horrible words, she did not know, but she watched as they registered on Jean's face. Instead of sinking into despair, as she had thought he would, she watched as a look of determination filled him and caused him to pull his body up higher in the bed. He was fighting the waves of nausea and weakness that flooded over him because nothing mattered except what she just said to him.

"We must do something. Send for the doctor. He must come at once. He saved me. He can do it again and save our son." His head fell back against the pillow. "What can I do?"

Tori became frightened by Jean's overwrought reaction. She knew he would kill himself, trying to save the child if she let him, and that was not going to happen. "Jean, listen to me. The doctor has not been here for days. Marie Laveau saved your life. She was the young girl that you saw. If it had not been for her, you would not have made it. She has looked after the baby for hours, but Jean, oh my love, he is just so small, and he is so very weak now." Gently she went on. "Jean, our son, is dying, and there is nothing we or anyone can do."

Jean shook his head. He would not accept it; the fact that he had lived, only to lose his son? The child's father tried to get out of bed, only to fall back, too weak to go anywhere or attempt anything. How he hated himself, his child needed him, and he could not do a damn thing.

Tori watched him as he struggled. Laffite's wife wanted to hold him, to try to take away his pain, but all she could do was sit and look on, as she rocked the child in her arms.

It was as if Christopher knew he was needed. He opened his eyes and let out a small whimper, so weak and yet so powerful. His little cry stilled the room, and Jean leaned back, looking at his son in Tori's arms.

"Are you sure it's the fever? That there is no chance, he will get better?" His voice was pleading and frail. It sounded hollow and dejected yet resigned to the fact that there was nothing he could do.

"I wish with all my heart, that I could tell you differently, but I can't. Even with all I know from my time, I can't change this. Do you want to hold him? If you want some time alone with him, I will leave."

He loved his wife for caring so much, even willing to let him be alone with their son, hurting as she must be. Tori was thinking of him, putting aside her own grief, and he could never allow that. "No, I don't need time alone with him. Let's lay him between us. Let us both be with him. We all need each other."

She had not thought of that, and seeing it was the only solution for them, she agreed. Gently the mother placed the baby on the bed between them. His burning body lay limp, his glassy eyes looking into space without seeing. The only movement was his sunken stomach rising up and down as his little lungs struggled to bring in the life-giving air.

"My son, my little man, your father loves you. I have always wanted a son, and no child will ever take your place. You know it's your father's voice, don't you? Look, see how he turned his head?" Jean moved so his child might get a better look at him, but the baby turned his head away and looked toward his mother. This did not upset Jean; rather, it pleased him. "See, I told you, we should be together. He knows we are both here. Oh Tori, how can I let him suffer? I feel so helpless. I am his father."

"And I am his mother. I can't do anything either. I should have known better. I blame myself. I should not have been around him after I exposed myself to the fever. I am to blame. Can you ever forgive me?"

"Tori don't. It is not your fault or mine. We love him. Neither of us would hurt this child. He knows we love him."

The baby's eyes closed and opened slowly. His breathing seemed to be easing somewhat, and Tori reached gently and stroked his cheek. His little eyes seemed to be full of tears, as he looked beyond them both, and it was then, Tori started humming 'Tommy's Song.'

It slipped forth, and she found that it came out soothingly, as Christopher closed his eyes to sleep.

"He hears you, my love. You are soothing him, and he feels your love." Tori did not look at Jean or even acknowledge that she had heard his whispered words. Instead, she reached for her son's little hand and stroked his arm with her finger. "This is your song, son. I hummed it to you when you were in me, hummed it to you when you were born, and now I hum it to you as you leave us."

Jean reached out to his son and took hold of his other hand. The father watched the little lifeless hand; it seemed so very small and helpless next to his own. The little fingers did not take hold of his own as they had the day he was born, and Jean knew they would never do so again. It was then that Jean's heart broke into a thousand pieces, each piece burning with a pain far beyond anything physical. He knew his child would not open his eyes again, and he shuddered. Then, as Jean looked at the baby's small face, he felt a part of himself, slowly dying along with his son, and he did not fight it because he understood it was a battle that could not be won.

Before Tori finished the tune, Christopher's breathing ceased, and he peacefully slipped away. Jean and Tori stared at him for some time. Both knew he had gone, but neither moved, because they needed to spend a little more time with their child.

ACROSS town in a dark room, a wind came up from nowhere and blew out a candle that stood beside a statue of the Blessed Virgin Mary. The instant the flame extinguished, one could hear the crying of a young woman somewhere in the darkness. A tall man walked toward the sobbing sound, to comfort and console. He said nothing. Instead, he allowed the grief to spill through the painful words that filled the silence.

"He is gone. The little one has passed on. If only I knew more, maybe I could have saved him. Marie Laveau knows nothing, but on that child's memory, I swear to you, that I will learn all that you can teach me. You must teach me more, all that you know, I must, and I will master it, no matter the cost or the time it takes. I would sell my soul to know all you do. Never again will I laugh at you, or walk away, thinking I have what I need. I have nothing without you, and I understand that now…more than ever." Marie walked to her alter and picked up the white feather that lay in the light of a moonbeam. "Christopher flies with the angels, his spirit will be with them always, and one day I shall see to it that this little white feather, and he, will guide his mother home.

JEAN and Tori stood supporting each other while looking down upon a small wooden coffin. Each was silent, drawn inside themselves with the painful awareness that on this day, as they buried their child, they would be burying a part of themselves.

Tori looked at Jean. He stood, slouching as if his love of life had drained from his soul. The sadness, which hung about him like a halo, touched all those who looked upon this grieving man. Since the child's death, he had put a grip on his emotions and placed a mask on his face. His expression had a hollow look about it, and unless one read the agony deep within his eyes, they would never know the true depth of his sorrow. Nothing Tori said or did seemed to reach him. He had loved their child far greater than she had realized, and now he was dealing with his grief by pushing her away. Jean was a beaten man, the illness had taken what physical strength he had, and now with his son's death, Tori feared for his sanity.

So, it was, in the year 1811, on a sunny September day, in a country cemetery far from the city's sickness and death, they had come to lay to rest, a much-loved child. Jean had insisted that his son not be buried in a cold place, surrounded by people he did not know. He wanted Christopher to be placed in a green and peaceful surrounding. Somewhere that felt like a garden instead of the cold marble city of the dead.

Laffite did not hear the words spoken over his son. He looked beyond the grave and out over the slow-moving river in the distance. What would happen now? He had hoped that the child would have kept his life full, that his son would have grown up, to share everything he'd been denied with his own father. The loss of a friend or even a parent had been hard, but this loss was beyond anything he had ever faced. Laffite felt that he would never be able to put behind him, the emptiness that ate at his heart.

Standing next to Tori and leaning on her like he was, seemed so unfair to him. Jean knew he should be the one supporting her. His wife needed to lean on him, but with his legs growing tired and his head still hurting, it was all he could muster to remain upright. His illness had left him weak, something he deplored, and if he had his way, he would never give in to. The pirate sadly looked back toward the small wooden coffin and then into the face of his wife. Damn the fever and damn New Orleans. He hated it all, and if he could, he would take her and board his ship and leave, never to return.

Tori knew Jean needed her right then. His whole body had begun to shake, and she understood that it was a massive effort for him to be standing by her side. It was so soon after he had been at death's door, and she admired him for his dedication and endurance. Her arm went around his waist, and gently she pulled him toward her. He did not resist; instead, her husband leaned closer and looked at her face, his eyes brimming with unshed tears.

Tori began to cry. She cried for her son, for his father, and most of all, for herself. The grieving mother needed Jean to share this with her and not shut her out. Grief-ridden Tori leaned against her husband as a flood of tears continued to flow down her ashen face.

The sight of his lady slumped against his chest, with such an agonizing look of grief, struck him. It was then that Jean realized how much Tori needed him, that they needed each other. Without uttering a word, he took her in his arms, and the two of them clung to each other, slowly rocking back and forth until the service ended.

Then it was over, the words and prayers had stopped, and the only sound that filled the heavens was a bird's call. Looking at Pierre and his wife, then toward Dominique and the Destrehans, Jean asked if everyone would leave them alone for a while. They needed to say goodbye to their child by themselves. They wanted to be with their son and no one else. There was not a soul there who did not understand. Without a word, the few friends and family moved slowly away from the graveside. J.D. and his wife, understanding only too well, the sorrow their friends were suffering, hurried the small gathering along.

IN moments, the grieving parents were standing by themselves at last. Neither wanted to leave, both stood looking at the small wooden coffin. It was then that Tori realized the tremendous toll the death of her son was taking. "I can't; I just can't face this. Jean, this is the second child I have lost, for I fear that Linni is lost to me too. Both my children are out of reach, and I want them back. I need my baby; you need your son. What are we going to do? How will we go on?"

Jean looked again into Tori's face, lifting her chin up with his trembling hand, and then gently, he brushed the tears from her cheeks. "We will get over this together. Starting now, my love. I know we must share this grief or lose what we have. For Christopher, we will go on." His voice was cracking, but the strength and determination behind it was as powerful as ever. Tori was no longer alone. It seemed Jean had stopped pushing her away and was ready to deal with the death and what life would be like, without their son. "Let me hold you close for a while, let us both in our own way tell our son he will forever remain in our hearts."

The day was still, and only the bird calls broke the silence of the surrounding countryside. The spot was peaceful and quite beautiful, with large old oaks shading the ground here and there. It was the kind of place where a young boy would have loved to play, to explore and climb the giant trees, and run in the cane fields beyond. "Dominique chose well when he found this special place for Christopher. I want a tree planted here, so it will grow and shade this spot, where the boy is to lay." Jean was talking to himself, yet the two black slaves waiting to bury the small coffin overheard him and nodded their sad faces.

"Yez, sur. We's see's ta it. We's be a plantin' da tree right away, Massa."

Jean looked over at the two and saw the shovels in their hands. He knew what they were about to do, and he could not stand it, so without hesitation, he took Tori by her hand and walked away from the graveside. "We will be back soon. You can start now," he snapped, "and be quick. Get the job done."

Tori tripped over her feet as if his words had physically pushed her. She stood still once her balance was restored and softly spoke to the man at her side. "Oh, Jean, please let's walk. I can't take this. My heart is breaking," she whispered, as she pulled him still further away from the gravesite, fearing the sound of dirt hitting the coffin. "I can't stand to watch, and I also can't put up with your anger toward the world. It is not their fault that we are here today. Do try to understand that anger, your anger, is not what is needed or wanted. I need you to be strong for me, not turn into an individual lashing out at everyone, because if you start that, you will end up lashing out at me."

Jean placed his arm around Tori's waist and began to walk. "Never will that happen, and you are right. I must not allow my grief to turn to anger. That is not how I want to remember our son. It stops now." The couple strolled, by themselves to the riverbank, and once they reached the top of the levee, they sat together on the grass and watched the muddy water flow. Jean lay back and looked up at the clouds and just stared, not speaking or moving. He seemed lost in thought and frozen in time.

Tori lay her head on his chest. She could hear his heart beating. His breathing was heavy and slow, and its rhythm helped soothe her ragged breaths, as she choked back still more tears of grief. His hand came up and stroked her head, like a father comforting a child.

"I can't cry anymore, Jean. I feel empty and numb. He just can't be gone. We had him such a short time."

"Ah, but my love, that's just it, isn't it? We did have him, and I will always have him with me. You gave me a son and I will always be thankful. We shared something that no one can ever take away from us. He will always bind us together, no matter what happens from this day on." Jean spoke no more; he just lay there looking up at the sky.

Tori watched him and then turned her head and looked out over the river. What more could she say? His silence spoke for itself.

IT was late in the afternoon when the pair walked back to the gravesite, and there they stood, looking at the little mound of dirt. Someone had covered it with flowers, most likely Marie Destrehan, and a small tree had been planted close by.

Jean broke the silence between them and squeezed her hand tightly as he spoke. "He needs a headstone, but a simple one. I shall talk to my brother and have one made up. One day, people will walk by here and look down on this tiny grave and wonder who he was. Let's leave it like that. Let him rest under his tree in peace. You say in history, there was no mention of me ever having a son. Well, let us make sure that it stays that way. For some reason, it seems right. He is ours and ours alone."

"I said I did not know Jean. I do not know everything about you or your life. It is possible that you may have another son or sons in the years ahead, but I can't pretend he did not exist. He was our son, so how can we walk away and forget him?"

"We won't, not ever. But my son is just that. He's my son, our child. He does not belong to history or the future. He belongs to us and now to God, and I want to keep it that way. The headstone will read only his first name, simple and full of love."

Tori saw some wisdom in what he was saying and understood; it meant so much to him to have it that way. She nodded her head in agreement. "Jean, I believe that he would have wanted that. It is true the stone only marks his remains. His spirit is free, and only our love for him…nothing else, is what he has taken." Tori was trying hard to get the words out without breaking down again. "It's perfect." She took in a long slow breath and pictured Christopher in her mind. Her smile was soft, and her expression was filled with love. It was that expression which brought a calm atmosphere that slowly filled the air around them.

The wind blew harder, and off in the distance, the sound of a horse coming down the road broke their solitary moment. Jean looked up and recognized the rider. It was Dominique, and as he pulled the carriage to a halt outside the small graveyard, Jean knew it was time to go. Taking the mother of their child by her arm, he began to walk slowly away.

Ever the gentleman, Jean pulled himself up and took in a deep breath. Some of his old swagger was coming back to his stride as they made their way toward Dominique. He was determined to remain strong and fulfill the role required of him. He was the man, the husband, and her strength. He Jean Laffite would take care of the mother of his child; he would be her rock.

"I will take his memory with me, my lady. Always he will be in my heart, but I will never again come here, not until I am ready to die. One day, I will lay by my son's side, that I promise you. No matter what happens, I will see to it that he will have me with him."

"Jean, I love you, I always will. For now, let's go. We can talk about this later," she said somberly.

"We don't need to talk about it. I will never speak of it again. I have made up my mind. Now, let us depart. We have a life to live. We have to heal and my love; we will heal together." They reached the small iron-gate, and as Jean opened it, he spoke with confidence to his second-in-command. "Dominique, have you arranged all I asked for?"

"Yes, Boss. Your boat awaits less than a mile from here. Pierre will take care of the work in the city, and I will join you both if you don't mind. I also need some time to heal and can't think of a better place than the sea."

Tori was beginning to worry. What plans had Jean set in motion without talking to her? "Jean, what boat? Where are we going?"

"I asked Dominique to arrange transportation to Grand Terre. It seemed the right choice to make. Going back to the townhouse now, well, the pain and the memories are too fresh. Let's take time and live by the sea. I can work there, and we will be left alone to come to terms with our loss."

(In French) "I agree, Boss. We don't need no nosey people coming around, even if they mean well."

Tori squeezed Jean's hand and continued speaking in French, sensing that it would somehow give both men a little peace of mind. "Jean, I agree. I think it is the perfect idea for now."

"It is, and I am pleased you agree."

"It's just we are going to be so far away from him." She turned and looked back at the small grave they were leaving behind.

"No, Tori, he will never be that far away. As long as we carry him in here," he tapped his chest, "then he will always be close by."

THEY boarded the riverboat and gradually made their way downstream. It was several miles after they passed by the Destrehan Plantation that the craft pulled over to the bank on the Mississippi's east side. Until that moment, Tori had thought they would be sailing the whole way to Grand Terre, down the river, so this turn of events took her by surprise.

"Jean, are we stopping for the night?"

"We are not, why do you ask?"

"Because we are no longer traveling along the river. I don't understand."

"Ah, I have forgotten for a second that my wife keeps watch on her surroundings. Here, let me guide you to our next mode of transportation. It is but a short distance this way." Jean helped his wife disembark the riverboat, and together with Dominique following close behind, they walked beyond the small levee toward a canal, where a medium-sized barge was waiting for them. "This Madame is not the river as you see, it is in fact known as the Destrehan Canal, built by J.D.'s father in 1739, or around about there. J.D. keeps it in order now. It connects us to Barataria Bay, and by using it, we will cut our trip home by many hours."

"So this is the famous canal you have eluded to many times. It's the one that you said you use often. Do others use this shortcut?" Tori just wanted to take her mind off her sorrow and maybe get Jean to join her. Asking questions could do the trick. "So, do others use it?"

"Some do. It is a way to the Gulf, but not many are willing to face the rough terrain, should they find themselves without a boat, something that has been known to happen. After all, these waters are filled with pirates." Jean chuckled for the first time since before he got sick. "Should one not have a boat, they would be forced to make their way across swamps, past shark palms, like those over there." He pointed the palms out to Tori and continued to explain. "If you get close enough to those nasty things, you will learn why they have been called such. They dig deep into your flesh and cut like a razor-sharp knife. Also, I may add, they are known to harbor snakes; rattlesnakes love them. If you manage to avoid them, there are the tangled mangroves, like you have seen, and the high tides. The water takes what little land there is and floods it. None, like the idea of swimming in these waters, let alone walking."

"I can see that, and no, I would not like either walking or swimming here, but what of others not so wise?"

"They are foolish to think to try either endeavor. Those who do not choose to ask permission, to travel among our waterways and get caught, may be invited to do so," he chuckled again. "I shall point out if it does not get too dark, a place where some of my men stand guard. Even the governor has people who watch these waterways. Not that they have any control…maybe a little once in a while, and they have never ventured off a barge or boat. They are like bothersome flies that one wants to swat away. Instead, we allow them to remain and let them think they are doing their job. My men, they have fires to light as signals, and a few have small cannons to fire. A warning system that works."

"Cannons?"

Dominique, who had been listening, joined in the conversation. "Yes, tizz true. We have taken a few from the revenue men, and we use them for our signals. It confuses the whole area. One does not know who is warning who." He chuckled before continuing. "When we hear that there is a vessel that we might want, we take it."

"And J.D., he is okay with this? I can't see him liking the fact that pirates take people's boats from them."

Jean laughed out loud. "Dominique, what are we to do with this woman?"

"Trust, her Boss. Trust and love her; that is all."

"Wise words, my friend and Tori, J.D. lets me handle those that sail my waterways, and so try to remember; I am not a pirate! I am a privateer. I have papers, as you well know, and that my dear makes everything legal. You see, J.D. has nothing to worry over."

It was Tori's turn to laugh. "I shall ask him about that when next we meet. As for now, just take me home, Jean, and by barge, please, I don't think walking the swamps is something I would enjoy, and you are in no state to carry me."

"She has you there, Boss," frowned Dominique. The past few days had worried the older man, but seeing Jean and Tori now beginning to heal, he knew in his heart that all would be right in time. Going back to Grand Terre was precisely, what they needed, what they all needed.

Tori had settled into Jean's arms, and as the exhausted pirate slept, she watched the star-filled sky above her. It all seemed surreal, her child was dead and buried, and they had talked about anything other than Christopher. What was going to happen now? How long would it be before they returned to New Orleans this time? The small grave's image left so far away, filled her mind, and she cried softly until she too fell asleep.

Dominique sat and watched the waterway. It was a shame that Tori was asleep because if she had stayed awake just a little longer, Jean's wife would have seen the lit fires along the way. Signals from the Boss's men that they were being watched. There would be no cannons going off this night, just friendly fires, showing their respect for their Boss's loss.

ONCE back in Grand Terre, things settled into a routine that fit everyone's schedule. Jean was kept busy and even sailed out into the Gulf every few weeks. The sea was his way of healing and coming to terms with how things were now. Tori began her fencing lessons again and worked harder than ever. On the days that Jean was at sea, she had Dominique instruct her inside the house because winter had brought with it the bite of a cold wind and some sad news that shook Tori and frightened her.

Once again, something she'd had no knowledge of struck the area. The catastrophic event occurred, and by its size, Tori knew it had to be recorded in history, yet, somehow it had slipped by unknown to her. She guessed many others in the modern world had no idea about the event either. For her, it was proof that history held far more than one could know, and much could slip by unnoticed.

News came by way of the traders who traveled up and down the river, and the stories were wild. Many tales seemed impossible, but in the end, most were confirmed. From the first earthquake until the last, Grand Terre heard reports about the terrible events each week. The first came less than a week after the night of December 16th, 1811. That was the beginning and the first of many powerful earthquakes along the Mississippi. By the time the strongest ended on February 7th, 1812 all that traveled from North of Baton Rouge were talking about their harrowing experiences.

Many homes were destroyed, and worse, many boats on the Mississippi experienced the impossible. The river, they told, had changed its southerly flow at one point and run northward. Great waves had sunk many smaller craft, and the flooding was extensive. Many aftershocks kept people on edge for weeks and weeks, and Tori was loathed to even think about moving back into New Orleans. The idea of the buildings being demolished by a quake had her determined to remain in Grand Terre, where they had not felt one tremor.

Dominique agreed with her and feeling somewhat shaken by the tragic events; he decided to make a change to his routine. The faithful second-in-command gave up the sea for a few months, as did Jean, to make sure Tori remained safe. Laffite worked even harder running his empire, and Dominique spent more and more time with Jean's wife as they nervously awaited further news of destructive earthquakes.

NEITHER Jean, his wife, nor anyone at Grand Terre felt any aftershocks, and not one had been reported in the city, so after talking about it for many weeks, Tori decided that the event was a one-time happening. She reasoned that it had not occurred often, or she would have learned about it, and she had not known that such a massive quake had hit along the Mississippi Delta. California, Tori told Jean, was known to have large earthquakes, but the Midwest and East coast, not so much. Also, after picking her brain, Tori decided she had never read of any earthquake hitting New Orleans. By the end of February, the aftershocks were smaller and less frequent, leaving her to surmise the danger had indeed passed.

New Orleans was spared, and all was normal, with no damage reported, until one traveled well past Baton Rouge, indicating to all that it was safe to resume life as they knew it with no trepidations. Life in Grand Terre resumed, and soon, just like all other catastrophes, talk of the river, the earthquakes, and damage were forgotten. Tori would tell Jean; New Orleans would let the good times roll, no matter what came their way.

ONCE things had settled down, Jean and Tori realized staying in Grand Terre would not happen. Both knew their time among the pirates would have to end, and that the time had arrived. Dominique had made it known that they were being unfair to Pierre, who was in no condition to keep up such a hectic pace. His workload had increased due to Jean's absence, and his health was a worry.

By March, Dominique took command of his ship Padoure and sailed out, claiming he, like Boss, also found the need to feel the Gulf's waters beneath him. It was Tori who received word, a few weeks later that the pirates had nicknamed Dominique, the 'Terror of the Gulf.' Her friend may have had his papers declaring him a privateer, but the man was acting more like a pirate, and Tori was glad that she would not remain in Grand Terre, to witness this side of him. To her, he was a grandfather image, the teacher, and the mild-mannered French hero. She wished, only to remain knowing him in that light, so any further mention of him and his actions at sea was not spoken about in her presence.

# Eight

Spring of 1812 came to the city of New Orleans, and with it, warmer days. The horrors of 1811 and its plague filled summer slipped, or rather, were pushed from everyone's minds. To dwell on something so bleak was not the nature of these people, who seemed to be forever pursuing the art of pleasure in Tori's opinion. Her life was full of mixed emotions. Ever since Christopher's death, she had been consumed with such grief that it had left her utterly confused and hurt. Adding to her anxiety was the fact that she had, in no way, expected to remain this long in the past, and she'd certainly had no intention of becoming so entangled emotionally. Asking Jean to help her find the lake and let her go was a huge stumbling block for her now. What would happen to the gentleman pirate if she left, and what would happen to his role in history? Tori still had not told him about what lay ahead for him and was torn between telling or not. What she wanted was to go home, away from all the sorrow and burdens of knowing too little, or too much.

Laffite's wife often wondered why it seemed that something was always happening to keep her from that one crucial goal of going back to the lake and home? From the very beginning of her arrival, she had been taken further and further away. When she had arrived at Grand Terre the first time, Jean had given his word to take her to the lake, and for Tori, back then, home seemed to be within reach at last. Then the baby's birth, their son...Leone's death, Christopher's death, and she could never forget the missing will. That damn will, it had given Edward power over her, more than he understood or guessed. At Leone's funeral, the threat that Edward had made forbidding Jean or herself to ever step on the Duval plantation haunted her. By his proclamation, the lake had been placed permanently off-limits. This was the biggest of all roadblocks. Edward did not have a clue about the lake and what it could mean for her, and Tori was sure that if he ever learned about her desire to reach that location, he'd place guards around it or use it to lure her into a deadly trap.

All of that aside, the worst was, she'd begun to think that maybe she was not meant to go back or even have the chance to try. That perhaps she was expected to tell Jean and J.D. all she knew of the coming years. Tori was more torn now than ever before, and she would not talk about her fears with her husband until she was confident, the knowledge she had to divulge would cause no harm.

JEAN had arrived home in time for dinner, for five nights in a row, and even begun to talk about social events rather than business. Tonight, he had even dressed for dinner and hinted at a special surprise he'd arranged. Then to Tori's utter shock, Marie Laveau had turned up to style her hair. It was a surprise from Jean that was meant to lift her spirits and to put behind them the awkward situation of seeing each other again. Neither of them had seen Marie since the day they lost their son, and Jean wanted more than anything to put the first meeting with the voodoo queen behind them. She was the best New Orleans had to offer, and he would always want the best for Tori, so avoiding her was impossible. Besides, he intended to let Marie know how grateful they were for all she had done.

Jean was sitting on the edge of the bed, watching the girl work her magic and was pleased to see Tori smile at what would be a stunning look for her, and he hoped that the rest of the evening he had planned would bring her even more joy. So far, Jean had avoided talking directly to Marie and hoped that Tori would broach the subject of thanking her first. Ever the careful individual, Jean spoke to his wife in a matter of fact sort of way. His voice lacked enthusiasm, but it was not altogether off-putting. "I think maybe that it is time we ventured out more. I have spoken to my brother, and he has suggested that I, that we, visit him at the cottage. What do you think?"

Often Jean spent long hours with his brother at what would be called Laffite's Blacksmith Shop in the future. This building was never a blacksmith shop; that was located on the lot behind it. The building Laffite referred to was the home of Pierre's mistress and owned by one of Laffite's captains.

Rene Beluche was the captain of a vessel called Spy, and called Barataria his home. He gladly leased the cottage, for a tidy sum to Pierre, something that Tori had not known in her time. She had met Rene many times and liked the man and hoped that maybe he would visit them in the city because after she had paid a visit to the cottage, she could ask him more questions about it without a problem or explanation. Not that she'd ask questions about what they did with the place, besides house Pierre's love. No, she'd ask how old the place was, and who had owned it before, or if he and his father had always owned it. Those were the questions on her mind that maybe one day she would be glad to have answers to.

Tori forced a smile and answered his question. "I think I would like that if you are finally ready to introduce me to Pierre's love and his children. Yes, I would like that very much. I do think it is about time, don't you?"

"I do, and, as soon as a break comes with my work, we shall go. I can't say when, but soon, I think. I do agree it is time."

Knowing how busy the smuggling had become, Tori knew she would not hold her breath for a visit happening anytime soon. Jean's men took more British ships each month. The cargos these ships carried were abundant with spoils, far more than one could imagine. If other vessels of different nationalities, other than British or Spanish were taken, which Tori knew was the case, it was kept under wraps, and she never asked.

Marie Laveau watched the two as she worked on Tori's hair and saw the toll the child's death was taking on the couple and decided to try and help. She waited until they were about to depart the room, to go downstairs when she spoke her mind. To Tori's amazement, Jean stopped and listened. He held Tori's hand tightly and nodded his agreement to what the young woman had to say.

Marie spoke in a calm tone, but one that denoted the couple pay attention. "I know this has not been easy, seeing me again. I have learned much being here, and I do not agree with what I see. I will not stand here and hold my words, for they need to be spoken. You both speak, but you don't talk. You listen without hearing, and you avoid the one subject that you need to be open about. Forgive me, but Bessy has answered my questions and informed me that no one mentions the child. This is not good. You must talk of him. He needs to be remembered. Not talking is destroying you both. The pain of not doing so is like a wound. A wound to the soul heals faster in the open rather than covered and left to fester. For surely, a festering wound, of any kind, will, in the end, kill. It can kill the body, or it may choose to kill your love. It is your choice, but what you have is worth fighting for. It is what your son would want. He would want to be remembered, talked about, kept alive in that way, and always. Now, I shall take my leave and pray that I am called for again soon and will see that my words have been heeded."

She did not remain in the room but quickly departed, knowing by both Laffites' expressions that she had indeed reached them. Things were going to change and for the better.

Christopher could rest in peace at last, and his parents could begin living again.

AFTER hugging and a few tears from Tori, Jean and his lady went downstairs to dine. When they entered the living room and found Jean's surprise, Tori realized he had been more than ready to hear Marie's wise words. Laffite was now genuinely willing to move ahead and leave the past behind. He had already begun to do so, all on his own, it seemed, for waiting to join them were her two dear friends, J.D. and Marie Destrehan.

"Oh, Marie, J.D., I can't believe it. You are really here." Tori raced across the room to hug the woman and then embraced J.D. before looking back at a very pleased Jean. "This is why you had me dress up and got my hair styled, and oh, how did you keep this from me? Did Bessy know? She had too, right?" Jean and their guests were laughing, and Tori joined them before she could calm down.

"My love, my Tori, I have for some days now, thought that we needed our friends. Not only for their wisdom but because I have been such a fool. J.D. was the one behind this meeting; I can't take credit, but I do agree with him; it was long overdue."

Tori swung around and smiled brightly at their guests. "I thank you both. It is just what the doctor ordered."

"Well, it is what J.D. ordered," laughed Marie. "I also know that he has much to talk over with Jean, some of it quite beyond me, but then I detest politics. You and I will chat about more pleasant things, I'm sure. I have news of Kristen and David. They married, as you know, and I was lucky to attend the wedding. You would have loved it. Kristen sends her love and hopes to visit soon. I rather doubt that though; what with the building of their home. Kristen's insisting on helping in all sorts of manner. I hear tell; she is even helping with the actual building. That girl is quite beyond my comprehension. She does have a heart of gold; there is no denying that. My husband and I had a wagon full of items loaded, for those who lost so much during the earthquake. Ours was joined by two more that Pierre sent from here, and once they reached Baton Rouge, still, other wagons full of goods joined them. Kristen and David traveled North to some of the worst-hit areas and helped distribute the much-needed merchandise. Not the way I would have chosen to begin my married life. She insisted, though, and you know that girl, once she puts her mind to something, no one can stop her."

Tori giggled and looked at Jean, who was grinning. "Yes, we do understand how headstrong she can be."

Marie smiled brightly and took Tori's hand in hers as she

continued. "The best part was, they came back downriver with two orphans, a small girl, and boy. Brother and sister, I think, not sure, but then Kristen's letters do tend to ramble. The children are now under her and David's care and will be raised by them. The children's parents were swept away. Such a sad situation, but then all turned out by the Lord's will. The children will be loved and have a good home, and in time, I feel they will look upon Kristen and David as their parents and not just guardians or adoptive parents. They are young enough."

"Kristen is happy then? I am glad for her. You are right, she does have a good heart and might I add, she is quite the card player." Tori laughed at the look on Marie's face. "Oh, just don't tell her father," she giggled. "He would be mortified that his daughter taught me how to play. We do have so much to catch up on, don't we? Gentlemen, let us go into the dining room and eat because I am starving, and for the first time in months, I know this is one meal I shall enjoy very much. Jean, you and J.D. can discuss whatever you wish, Marie and I will do the same."

AFTER the Destrehans left, Tori and Jean remained in the living room talking. The conversation during dinner had been informative, and for Jean also worrying. He had seen the look on Tori's face change several times and watched as she struggled to hide her emotions. She knew more about the politics he and J.D. had discussed than she let on, and Jean wanted her to share with him what it was.

"I should like to toast our new beginning and you, my beautiful wife."

"Jean, what are you up too? I see that look and the way you play with your goatee. What's on your mind?"

"Ah, my love, you know me so well. It is that I wish to discuss with you about matters that only you understand. I saw the look on your face as J.D. again spoke of statehood and his fear that we will no longer maintain our French connection. You can't deny it."

"I do not, and you know, I have told you that statehood will happen. I just don't know when. Trust me, it will, and Claiborne will be the first state governor. This I do know for sure. I do wish I could tell J.D., but I can't, and neither can you. Promise me; you won't say a word."

"I have given my word, but from the way J.D. was talking, you could be wrong. I tend to believe, what many are saying, is not what you think you remember. The outcome could be far different."

"Well then, only time will tell, won't it? And Jean, when it happens, you will have to eat your words."

"Another new term to add to my ever-growing vocabulary from your time," he laughed. "I think Madame; I shall stop my hounding of you for now, as you are not inclined to share more on the subject of history, are you?"

"I am not. Not yet, and maybe not ever. I don't know."

"Well, I know one thing and this you will like. It is time we went to bed, and by that, I do not mean sleep." He was grinning as he took her in his arms and kissed her gently. "I have missed this, missed you. I long for us to return to the way we were, to the passionate life, and I no longer wish to wait."

"Neither do I, Jean. I have missed you, and for once in a long time, we agree on something. Let's make a fresh start." She reached up and pulled his head down to hers and placed a long and deep probing kiss full of desire and longing on his parted lips.

Jean pushed her gently back and looked into her eyes. There was a sparkle to his gaze, and a hint of a smile tugged at his lips. "I thought I might have given up our lovemaking nights for Lent, but I see now that it would be impossible."

"You did not. You give up on sex? You better watch out, or I will have you go to confession for your lies."

"And make the priest blush."

"Better we go upstairs then, and you make me blush."

"That is the best thing you have said all night."

"Then, may I suggest you take me up on it before I cool down."

"Another term, but one, I understand better. You are hot for the cot, as you have explained before. My, you are blushing already, and I have yet to begin." His laughter continued as they made their way upstairs.

Not far away in the kitchen, sat a tearful but happy Bessy. Laughter had filled the house and, in so doing, confirmed to her that she had her family back, and they were happy again. Now, they were happy; maybe there would be another baby for them soon. Bessy would pray on it because she missed the little one, and the house needed the sound of a child; every home required the sound of a child.

TORI and Jean celebrated with the Destrehans, the fact that Louisiana was now a state. "I raise my glass to the new state, the 18th state, of The United States," declared J.D. proudly. It is the way of the future, and we all must change with the times. With a bit of luck, Jacques Villere, or myself, will win the vote for governor. In so doing, we will settle some of the hostilities between the Creoles and Americans. What say you, Jean?

"Only time will tell my friend," Jean answered, with a grin that Tori alone understood.

Laffite's wife turned away from the pirate and faced everyone. "J.D., I raise my glass and agree, we all have to change with the times." She sipped her drink and turned and winked at Jean. "If Clairborne should win, then we will need to give him our support. American or not, he would deserve no less. She smiled at the frowning plantation owner and knew that he would abide by the election results even though he would not like the outcome.

Even Jean was now leaning toward supporting the governor-elect. After all, Tori had told him all about the outcome, thus allowing him time to prepare. Tori had predicted the fact that Louisiana would become a state, despite Jean's optimism. He thought her logic and her memory of history was wrong until it had happened.

With the stroke of a pen, on April 6th, 1812, Louisiana had joined the USA, and Jean told himself that everything Tori said to him would be taken as the golden truth from then on. Now, he stood alongside his dear friend J.D. Destrehan, already knowing that Clairborne, not Villere or J.D., would win the election. What else could he learn, or should he know, he wondered?

Tori did not want to talk too much about the years that lay ahead for the city she had come to call home. Besides, thanks to not paying closer attention in history class, she was not too clear on the dates and times. As a child in Texas and California, she had not been taught Louisiana's history, only American, and most exact dates and times continued to elude her. Jean often pushed her and asked for more details, and she would deflect his curiosity, with descriptions of items and tales of geography, which were not yet known to anyone but herself. Her tactic worked more often than not, but even she knew the time might come when she should tell the pirate more of what she knew lay ahead.

The beginning of June brought with it a somber feeling. No one spoke of the approaching anniversary of Christopher's death, which was still a few months away. It was his birthday, or what should have been his first birthday, that pulled at their hearts. Jean had wanted to make the day a time to recall the happy times they had with their child, but he did not know how to approach Tori, who was becoming more withdrawn. It was through his need to help the woman he loved that the idea came to him. Without her knowing, Jean had a unique piece of jewelry commissioned. It was to be a gift that would in his mind soften one of the saddest days of the year, but the man who was designing and creating the necklace, was not about to be rushed and so a frustrated Laffite knew it would have to be after Christopher's birthday, that he present her with it.

On the anniversary of their son's birth, Tori rose early, and Jean joined her in the garden. He, too, was feeling the heavy burden of sadness, and knowing how much they needed to spend this day alone, the pirate had made plans without Tori's knowledge. While holding his wife in his arms, he softly spoke. "I think my love that today we shall ride. We will spend the day together, and we will talk or not talk if that is what you wish."

"I like that. Can we stay someplace other than here tonight also?"

"I have seen to it already. Already a few of my people have arranged a 'campout' as you call it. Maybe, we can lay under the night sky and pick out a star for Christopher?"

"I would love that. Just you and me?"

"Yes, just you, me, and the memory of our child. Then, when we return to the city, we will have much to do. I believe if we stay busy, we will manage to come through this difficult time. The first year of loss is the hardest. For us, our first year has yet to pass, but it will, and we will survive."

"I know we will. As long as I have you by my side, I can face anything."

"And I also. You are my life, and without you, this anniversary would be... let's not think about such things. Are you ready to depart?"

"I am because Bessy let it slip, your plan that is. Nothing actually slipped and fell. Just another saying, but you know that. The campout is a surprise and a welcome one. I would never have gotten out of bed today, if not for you."

Jean stepped back and offered his arm. "Shall we depart before any good-intentioned visitor comes to offer their support to us on this sad occasion, which we will now make a happier one."

"Let's go. I don't want to see anyone I know, not even family. I only need and want you, and Jean, thank you for this. Maybe we could do the same on, on... you know. But, I don't think I need to talk about that day yet. Let's just take this year one step at a time."

SHORTLY after June 18th, word reached the citizens of New Orleans that America had declared war against the British by an over-whelming vote. Claiborne was able to use this news to bolster his standing among the populace. He used the information about the ongoing battles, in his speeches, to try and win support from all citizens of Louisiana. Villere, no matter how hard he worked, could not muster the kind of dedication from his supporters that Claiborne was able to do, and so, the at first unpopular American, began to make inroads with those who had refused to accept change, when they had become a state.

For two months before the elections, Edward and Simone campaigned endlessly for Claiborne, and for the time being, Laffite and Tori were forgotten. Cayetana was at William's side for all his events, and between the four of them, it soon became apparent, the Creole population was being won over, just as Edward had told William they would be.

THE elections were over, and Jean sat looking at the final count with J.D. and Villere. On the first Monday in July, eligible voters had gone to the polls. The votes were taken and counted by the Louisiana State Senate. William Claiborne had won the popular vote with 2,757, followed by Jacques Villere with 946. J.D. had only managed to garnish 168 popular votes and was no longer in the running. On the second day of the session, the Louisiana House of Representatives and the Senate met in joint session and voted between the top two candidates. In the end, on July 6th, it was Claiborne who won and was duly elected the first governor of Louisiana. After going over the tally themselves, Jean watched as Destrehan and Villere accepted the outcome, and Villere conceded and acknowledged the new governor. However, he was not content to just let the American do as he saw fit, so Villere and J.D. began immediately to draw up plans to see at least one, if not both of them, seated in the new governor's government.

Now, more than ever, with the beginning of the war and the

election results turning out as they had, Jean had solid proof that what Tori told him would indeed come to pass. The war of 1812 had begun, and with it, he had gained a small amount of knowledge of what lay ahead. When and how future events would unfold remained a quandary, and frustrated him, for Tori was still not so forthcoming. She had explained that she was aware of the war of 1812 but had not known when or where it would begin. Beyond that, she had refused to talk about New Orleans or American history, and the rolls both would play. The one small fact she did let slip was that America would eventually win, and a treaty would be signed. However, she explained to Jean that she did not know when or where this would take place. Tori had felt a twinge of guilt about keeping what she knew to herself, about Jean's role and the Battle of New Orleans, but was convinced that it was the only way to keep history on track. Knowing his wife was keeping something from him, he had not pushed her for more information. In the end, however, Jean trusted that if Tori felt it important enough, she would divulge more facts, but until that time, all he could do was wait, be ready to listen, and no matter how he felt, believe.

Ever the privateer he was, he endeavored to keep busy and enjoyed sending his fleet out to engage and plunder as many British and Spanish vessels as they could find. Each time his men took a British ship, he was a hero, and because of the blockades the British had on American ports of call, the merchandise taken was more than welcome. The war had caused a shortage of many items until the gentleman pirate's booty began to flow into the city and beyond. As this happened, the Laffite's popularity rapidly grew; however, not all were happy.

MARIE Laveau had just left the Laffites; she was the only person that Tori ever allowed to style her hair, and this night, she had been informed, was to be an exceptional evening. At first, neither Jean nor Tori wanted to attend the ball held by the newly elected

Governor Claiborne, and his soon to be wife. In the end, they changed their minds because Grimes insisted that it would be to their advantage, and not the other way around. To not show up and support the American would be seen as a slight. This action, in return, could then be used against Jean and his men.

The whole house seemed to bulge with the crowd, which had shown up for the grand celebration. Even the vast expanse of gardens teamed with a mixture of the curious and the celebratory. Cayetana's idea was to open the house and grounds to all so that they could meet and see their governor, who had only their best interests at heart. Even though he had been elected, less than a month after Louisiana became a state, he still had a lot of work ahead of him to gain the trust of both the Creoles and Cajun population. His wife to be was the one who told him such an event would undoubtedly, go far to improve his standing within the community. Initially, Claiborne had wanted only the top echelon attending the affair. Still, Edward and Simone had agreed with Cayetana that it would behoove the American to incorporate all. What the devious couple did not whisper his way, was they had their own agenda as to why all should feel free to attend. Simone had bet Edward that if the gala were open to most of the citizens, Laffite would never be able to stay away. Thus, the event would offer the perfect opportunity to begin in earnest their degradation of the much-endeared pirate and his wife.

From the beginning of the evening, many Creoles acted as though the American's had an offensive odor about them. They often refused to converse in English, and those that would kept their conversations curt and often sarcastic. All knew that the American governor did not speak Creole, allowing them the opportunity to speak freely in front of the man without fear. Often their comments were cynical in nature, and many smirked while conversing. It seemed that the only time the man was safe from ridicule was when his Cayetana was standing by his side. To allow her to hear or observe such degrading behavior was to risk being called out, or worse, arrested for treasonous actions.

Tori and Jean arrived at the mansion with the Destrehans and joining their small gathering of friends, was none other than the man who had run against Clairborne and lost. Jacques Villere intended to obtain a position within the American's cabinet so he could maintain a watch over all that was being proposed. Many changes were coming, and Jacques, unlike Destrehan, was not so willing to change, if at all. He was more than willing to place road-blocks; in front of any plans the American may present because he believed the governor had to bring more of the Creole politics into the way of doing things and not the other way around. Supporting Jacques was Bernard de Marigny, who also was determined to put the government back into French hands.

Tori was amazed by the turnout and even more amazed at the undercurrent she felt while walking around. "Jean, I had no idea so many people were going to be here, and to be honest, I don't have that feeling of unity that Clairborne promised."

"I agree, but in time I am sure many will come around. That or the man will be voted out, and a Creole will take his place. My guess would be, Jacques would replace him, but that is not what is set to happen, is it?"

"I am afraid not. Claiborne will remain, governor, that is if history remains the same."

"And why would it change? You have no plans to unseat the man." Jean grinned and winked at her, trying to make light of the conversation.

"I have no plans, but I think maybe Edward and Simone might, and by me being here and having made them the enemy, well, things could change."

"So Villere could become governor, you think?"

Destrehan had just joined them and overheard Jean's last remark and not knowing the full conversation, put in his two words worth. (In French) "I doubt that my friend," J.D. chuckled. "As an

American, we need him more than Villere or the citizens of this city understand. We are, after all, at war with the British. Who, I might remind you, is an enemy of France. Many Creoles may voice their opinions that we should support France, but they can, as of now, do nothing to gain support to do much more than grumble. It is my opinion, with Villere in charge, they may have sought to support the French. Though not my first choice, our new governor is a strong man, with connections that go all the way to President Madison. As our leader, we will remain safe, and our beloved New Orleans will survive, grow, and incorporate all cultures, Creoles, Cajun, and Americans alike. However, I did not come here to talk of nothing else but politics. If I did so, my wife would make my life exceedingly difficult," he smiled broadly at Marie.

His wife giggled. "I most certainly would. So, Jean, listen to my husband and enjoy the evening. May I suggest that you begin by allowing my husband the honor of dancing with your wife; I would dance, but my feet are not so happy this evening, and I know that my husband has been waiting for the opportunity to ask…"

Tori laughed and stepped forward. "J.D., it would be my pleasure to dance with you. Jean can fetch Marie and I a glass of wine while we are occupied, and Marie, you can sit here and rest your feet."

"Wonderful idea Tori." Marie was all smiles. "Jean, if you wouldn't mind, a drink would be refreshing. I shall remain here and watch the most handsome man," she lovingly patted his arm, "escort your wife onto the floor." Madame Destrehan was genuinely happy and most relived to sit for a short time. "Take good care of him, Tori."

"You can be assured of that, Marie. We will be right back for that drink, so keep an eye on my Jean for me. No getting into trouble, Jean." Tori had winked at her husband as she took J.D.'s arm and walked toward the dance floor.

In seconds, Tori found herself in the arms of the man Jean called family. J.D. and Laffite went back a long way, he had told Tori once, but he had not elaborated on that subject. For her, it was enough that Laffite felt the Destrehans were family because she felt the same way. If her husband's secret history with the plantation owner was the reason for his closeness, then so be it. Tori would not demand to know more, and she knew this pleased Jean. The couple happily swired around the room, and Tori was far too involved to notice that they were under close scrutiny by the governor and his friends, who stood not too far away.

Simone watched as the pair slipped gracefully by, admired by all. Inwardly she fumed and decided to use the moment to her advantage. Stepping slightly aside from Clairborne, she spoke in French with the Creoles that were close at hand. "It would seem that Laffite's wife is quite taken by the statesman. Unusual, as he is of French heritage. After all, I do hear tell that she has been making more American acquaintances than not. Poor choice if you ask me. She will soon learn that the uncivilized Americans can offer New Orleans and its people nothing. Louisiana may be part of America now, but New Orleans will never become American. Such a thought is absurd. Is it not?"

There was agreement all around with this statement. Emboldened, Simone carried on. "The Americans I have met are all barbaric, with no class at all. They lack an understanding of any proper etiquette, let alone protocol. Few, if any, speak French, and they seem to have no want in learning. Even Laffite's wife continues to speak English much of the time, and I find myself wondering if it is not deliberately done so, because of her love of the upstarts." Hearing more agreement spoken around her, Simone felt even empowered to continue. The ever-cunning woman moved to Claiborne's side and continued in English. "Why, it is almost a slap in your face governor, that statesman Destrehan, should be dancing with a pirate's wife when it is evident to all that his duty should be, for him to oblige his hostess with the honor."

Edward loved her. She was stoking the fire on both sides, once again for him. The governor's dislike of Laffite was growing, and the Creole's love of the Americans was slowing down, but he cared not about anything else other than the downfall of Jean, his brother Pierre, and their whole operation. Soon, he would have the governor so full of hate toward pirate that the man would be willing to do anything to get rid of him.

The dandy realized that Simone might have wounded Claiborne's pride by speaking in French to those gathered around her when it was well known that the man did not utter a word of the language himself. The young Cayetana had been translating for him, and as Edward could not overhear what she told William, and he worried. Simone had, after all, not been so kindly in her words toward the Americans.

Edward could never allow the governor to feel anything but a friendship between them. It would be better if he changed the subject and steered clear of such truths, as Simone had spoken, which would not serve them in their ambitious goals. That was after he had added his little jab. "I agree, Simone, my dear. Just how much longer are we citizens of this city going to allow Jean Laffite and his bunch of cutthroat thieves to get away with walking our streets as if they own them? Their very appearance here this evening is a slap to our esteemed governor's face, indeed to us all. We must be the very laughingstock of all Americans here this night."

The small crowd was beginning to get worked up, a little too much for Edward, who realized that the time had not presented itself yet, for Jean's demise. He had to appease both the governor and the Creoles right then and tone things down a little. Edward needed to keep the flame of hate low, for just a while longer; it had to smolder before it could consume. "Let us not jump and hastily make the wrong move. We are, after all, Southern gentlemen, are we not? The Laffites will make a mistake soon enough, and when they do, we will be there to catch them. The city has many eyes, William, and you have many friends. I, for one, will not rest until you have the respect you so deserve. Now, let us not ruin this evening with anger. Let us show these Americans, genuine southern hospitality, shall we?"

There was agreement all around. Edward Duval was not only a

fine and upstanding gentleman, but he had become a valued friend and a great citizen of their beloved city. With such high regard, he was listened to and admired, primarily by those surrounding Claiborne.

Edward had achieved his goal for the evening and satisfied with himself; he asked Simone if she would care to dance. Snapping her fan closed, she looked at the dance floor and grinned one of her sheepish smiles. He knew that expression of hers and suspected an ulterior motive was at hand, and he was correct.

Quickly, the young plantation owner swept Simone onto the floor, maneuvering her into the dance's flow, and then subtly, he allowed his lover to guide them close to J.D. and Tori. It was just enough for Edward to see her plan, and he grinned. Pulling Simone close to him, the dandy swiftly spoke his message, leaving no doubt that she should follow his lead. "Just do as I suggest, and for goodness sake, no scenes, please." Before she had a chance to ask what he meant by no scenes, they bumped right into Destrehan and Tori.

Duval had made his move look like an accident and followed it with all the charm and manners that protocol required. He spoke in French, totally ignoring Laffite's wife. "Please do excuse me. It was so very clumsy of me to lead my lovely lady into your path, as I did. I was just overcome by her beauty. Don't you agree, Sir, is she not a real belle?"

Angry at first by this intrusion, J.D.'s temper quickly melted, as he was a softhearted man when it came to the matters of love, and love was obviously what this young couple was all about. "I do indeed agree, and your apology is duly accepted."

"Why thank you, and might I add, that you are a true gentleman to be so kind, as to excuse such a blunder. If I may be so bold, as to offer you the hand, of my lovely lady for the remainder of this dance. I would be honored and feel truly vindicated, should you accept."

It all happened so quickly that Tori did not have a chance to object. One second, she was with J.D. and the next, she was in Edward's arms. Simone, on the other hand, found the whole maneuver a delight, as she was now the center of attention and loving it.

Destrehan was soon under her spell and forgot entirely about Tori, who at that moment would have slapped Edward's face and walked away had he not reminded her that to cause a scene at such a time would indeed be in poor taste. "Just relax and enjoy the dance. I have waited a long time to have you where you are right now, and I can assure you that this is only the beginning, my dear."

Undaunted Tori, spit back from behind a sarcastic smile. "You can say whatever you want, but I can tell you this, if Jean sees you dancing with me, your measly, little life might very well be in danger of being challenged to a duel. Have you thought of that?"

His body stiffened slightly, then just as quickly relaxed. Still speaking in English, Edward pulled her a little closer and whispered in her ear. "Your pirate's days are numbered, and then you will come running to me, begging on your hands and knees, for no one else in this city will have you. I will see to that."

Tori smirked and responded using perfect French. "I would not come to you if you were the last man on earth, let alone beg on my hands and knees. You disgust me, you overdressed, pompous pig."

Edward's face twisted in anger. Not only had she proven she mastered his language, the bitch seemed unafraid or undaunted by him. Tori always seemed so sure of herself, and he hated that. The dandy also knew he would rather die than let her know how he felt at that moment. Hiding his anger, he smoothly added his next jab in French. "Let me assure you; you will pay for your harsh treatment of me. You will learn your lesson, and if you would care to observe, let us begin, shall we? Your downfall has begun, my dear. As you can see for yourself, your husband watches us and does nothing. I fear he is a coward, after all."

Tori's gaze toward Jean was aided as Edward swung her around so that she could have an unobstructed view. She would have laughed out loud when Jean winked and gave her a slight nod, a signal to her that he knew she could handle her situation. Smiling, she then confidently leaned closer and hissed into Edward's ear, still using French. "No, Edward, he's just a gentleman, who knows his lady can handle swine like you. Now, if you would please excuse me, the very stench of you has me in need of fresh air. May I suggest you leave and take a cold shower? You need to cool off. Even a randy dog has more manners, something you seem to lack a great deal of." With that, she pushed herself free and walked over to Jean, who smiled and proudly took her by the arm and walked past Edward, toward an open doorway.

Laffite was chuckling. "Whatever did you say to him, my love? The man looks as if he's about to explode. His face is positively the color of Simone's gown, a horrid shade of red. The woman never did look good in that color." His laughter could be heard clear across the room because the music had stopped. The dance was over, and the widow in J.D.'s arms left the dance floor to join Edward.

Simone could not wait for that horrible Laffite to fall from grace. "She is utterly deplorable, like her husband. To leave you standing there, it's the height of rudeness. No true lady would have dared to offend a gentleman with such a display. Edward, my love, I declare that woman is no lady at all."

Everyone had witnessed how Tori had left Edward before the dance ended, an open act of defiance, and a shameful one at that, one that Simone could not let slip by without using it to her advantage. When she was confident, she had Claiborne and his entourage's full attention, she lowered her voice and spoke from behind her open fan. "And now they have the audacity, to act with no decorum. Why, both the Laffites laugh openly at my dear friend here. Poor Edward, to have to endure such rudeness, is a complete disgrace. I, however, admire your self-control, my dear. Not many could endure such a blatant snub, without insisting on an apology or even calling the culprit out to demand satisfaction. If I had not been in the statesman's arms, I would have joined you immediately."

Edward was so angry that he completely missed the quick maneuvering of her lace-trimmed fan, something she did to hide the enjoyment she was experiencing at his expense. Adding to his anger was the fact that his lover had pointed out the awkward situation to all. Tori had left him in the middle of the dance. If that wasn't embarrassing enough, Simone had purposely brought to everyone's attention how stunned he'd been by the insult. That he'd simply remained standing there until the music stopped, granted, it had ended soon enough, but that was not the point. His lover had made him look more the fool than a hero in his eyes, and then to insinuate that he should call the man out! Demand satisfaction from the pirate? Was the woman stupid? He doubted she was; more likely, Simone was having fun belittling him in front of the crowd. Yes, that was more like it. His rage simmered as he watched her lower her fan to smile at him. The bitch would pay for her insolence later, he told himself. Right then, he had to make things look as if he was indeed more than just in control of his emotions. "True, my dear, it was an insult such as you yourself would never commit. I suggest it is because the woman simply does not know any better. I pity her; the manners of her pirate are influencing her in more ways than one. Come, let us put them out of our minds. I shall dance with you and then with our governor's soon to be wife. I trust neither will dare leave me standing alone!" Edward laughed, and the small entourage joined in.

BACK at the townhouse, in the living room, later that night, Tori and Jean once again reminded themselves that Edward and his hatred would always be around. However, they felt that his threats were empty and no more than just a lot of hot air. He would never call Jean out or do anything to disgrace himself. Therefore, they had no real worries, and as far as Simone was concerned, she was nothing more than an annoyance, and a rude one at that.

"Jean, I believe if we steer clear of those two, they will soon find other entertainment that does not include us. I hear that Simone is close to Cayetana and helping plan the wedding that is to be held in November. Knowing how busy that will keep her, I think it is safe to assume she and Edward's attention will be elsewhere."

There was a knock on the door, and Bessy entered carrying a small box. "This here came just now, and the man, he said you was to have it right away." She handed the item over her master and turned to leave.

Jean looked delighted, but no explanation was given as to why, "Thank you, Bessy, and you are right to bring it to me. I have other plans now, rather than talk about annoying people with your Mistress. You can take the rest of the night off. We are not to be disturbed, and I mean by no one."

"I sure do thank you, Massa. I shall have me some tea, an, then sleep. Deese old bones sure could use some. Night Miss Tori."

"Night, Bessy." Tori gave her a questioning look.

"Now, don't you go lookin' at me wid that face. I aint got a clue as to what he be up too. Must be somethin' real nice like, cause whenever he tells me, I ain't needed no more, that tells me, more'n you knows." She was laughing as she walked away, and even after she was out of sight, Tori could still hear her.

"Tori, could you come here and sit with me for a moment? Forget about Bessy. She is happy, and that's what we want. Please join me," he patted the space next to him. His voice was soft but demanding. Whatever it was, he was most earnest about it.

This worried Tori, and she found herself a little more anxious than curious. Jean was not watching her; he was looking at the box in his hands, with a slight smile. "Jean, what is it?"

The pirate looked up with an intense stare. The light was shining on his hair that curled around the base of his neck. To Tori, he looked as if he had a halo, a thought that tickled her funny bone. 'How can a rogue have a halo? And dear God, will you look at him, talk about good looking.'

His shirt was open, exposing his chest. The soft linen, so pale, always made his tanned skin seem darker. The way the breeches molded to his thighs she could almost see the outline of his calf muscles. The sight of him like this always excited her, and Tori wondered if she'd ever seen the man look bad? His very manner was a turn on. How was it possible that she should always find herself, desiring his touch? He might have something to show her, but Tori had other ideas on her mind.

"Is something wrong, Tori? You look as if your mind is elsewhere?"

"No! No, nothing is wrong. What is it you want, or should I ask?" she said, moistening her lips seductively.

"Why, my love, you shock me. Do you think that is all I have on my mind? Come, sit here by me." He again patted the seat of the sofa. "I have a gift for you. It is something that I have been waiting for. It took so much time to get it right, but now it is ready."

She watched as he lifted a small velvet box out of a larger wooden one, and she noticed that as he held the velvet one out to her, his hands trembled. "What's this?"

"Go on, open it. It's something that you can keep with you. Something that will always be close to your heart, from mine."

Tori did not speak. The curious woman took the box and sat next to him as she lifted the top to reveal its contents. Inside, lying on the blue velvet interior was an intricately designed gold heart-shaped locket. It was so delicate and beautifully designed that to Tori it was far more appealing than the diamonds she wore at that moment.

"Open it," he said, placing his hand on her shoulder. "Go on."

Carefully she held the gold heart in her hand and turned it to release the catch. It snapped easily, and like a miniature book, the locket folded open. Holding it toward the lamp, to see the contents more clearly, a small gasp of surprise left her parted lips. Tori's body went limp, and her eyes brimmed with tears as she gazed upon the little lock of hair. The solitary baby-soft curl formed a tiny circle, as it lay in place, protected under glass. Opposite it was inscribed one solitary word, Christopher. "Oh, Jean, it's lovely." Then words failed her as tears of love and joy began to tumble down her face. Her hands trembled as she held the necklace to her lips and kissed it.

Crying was not what he had wanted. It was supposed to have

made Tori happy, but as he took her face in his hands and looked deeply into her eyes, he saw that they were not all tears of sadness. His voice was filled with emotion, as he tried hard to explain himself. "I know it's been hard for you. It's been hard for me also, my love. I miss him, but then at least I did have a son for a while. Tori, you gave me that. Now, I give a part of him back to you. You can have him with you always. Here, let me put it on. But, before I do, there is more. Here, read the other side? I had it written in Italian," he smiled. "A private understanding between us?"

She turned the locket over and looked at the back, and there scrolled into the gold were words. 'Amore passa Tempo. Pass ail tempo con amore.'

"They say what? Or do I have to learn Italian to find out?"

"It says. Love passes time. Time passes with love. So much meaning behind so few words, don't you agree?"

"But why in Italian?"

"Just part of the romantic in me. I think that Italian has passion and so…"

"It's beautiful, and it will be an Italian phrase I will be able to speak with ease. The only Italian, I plan to learn, though." Tori turned her back to him and lifted her hair to make it easier for the gold chain to be fastened. In seconds, he had removed the diamond choker and replaced it with the locket. The cold metal warmed next to her skin, and instantly, she felt as if it had always been with her; just as she knew, it always would be.

Jean did not speak or move away. His fingers trailed downward, from the base of her neck to the top of her shoulders and lower. His lips brushed the side of her face, and Tori heard the words "sealed with a kiss," spoken in a deep husky voice. She let her hair cascade down as shivers of passion began to arouse her. Jean's body was so close, his face brushing hers as he bent to kiss the top of her bare shoulder again. His hot breath against her skin made the muscles in her stomach tightened in anticipation. Ever the master of seduction, he was applying his skills slowly and gently till Tori knew her body was once again his to command. "I love you, Tori, and I need you, right now, here, this moment."

Those words whispered into her ear were more than she could take. She turned to face Laffite, knowing already what she would find. His desire was pure and very evident. The way his voice had lowered to a soft but demanding whisper caused her heart to skip a beat in its racing rhythm. He was sitting there, looking at every curve, while mentally undressing her. His eyes wandered slowly up and down, stopping only to bore deeper still into hers, with their hypnotic power. Words were not needed, actions would speak a thousand times louder, and both knew what it was they desired.

Reaching out, she took hold of his hands and placed them on the top of her breasts, an action that caused her nipples to harden under his touch. Not once did she look away from his gaze. Not once did she utter a single word. Jean took hold of the material, unfastened the back of her gown, and quickly slipped the garment down toward her waist. Lightly his fingers traced the valley between her breasts where the locket lay. It was a gold heart, shining in the firelight, next to the heart of the one he would love forever. Her erect nipples caught his attention then, drawing him to them like a magnet. He lowered his head toward her breasts, placing his mouth tenderly upon one and then the other, teasingly holding each of them firmly but gently between his lips. Each time he took hold of her in this manner, it brought forth the same soft moan of delight, and when he stopped to cradle his head between the soft fleshy mounds, he could hear her pounding heart. She entangled her fingers in his hair, deliberately guiding his head up toward her lips.

Fully aroused and not willing to delay her desire, to have him inside of her, she passionately begged him to take her. Then it was his turn to groan as her hands brushed against the throbbing bulge in his breeches. Tori was expertly and successfully unfastening his pants' buttons, ready to release its prisoner when he stopped her.

Quickly he took hold of her hands. "Not so fast, my little minx. I intend to enjoy you slowly, like a good wine, to taste and sample the delight of each sensation at my leisure. I will savor every inch of your body; all night if I want. I will not be made to hurry."

Then, like the fire burning hot, its embers aglow with a life of its own, so was their lovemaking. Many times, that night, he took her, and each time together, they rode a wave of sexual intoxication into oblivion, until in the end, sheer exhaustion sent them both into a deep and contented sleep.

The next morning Jean had another surprise in store. He began to make plans to visit the Destrehans for a few weeks and had Bessy pack all they needed for the trip, in secret. He arranged for Pierre and Dominique to run the now busy trade while they were to be away. Dominique had returned from his adventures at the end of July. His takings had earned him some time off, and he stood ready down in Grand Terre to run the operation, something he considered child's play when compared to commandeering ships and their cargos. So, just before the middle of August 1812. Jean and Tori were once again with the family that they adored.

THE wind started to pick up, and the clouds raced across the sky. Marie and J.D. had ordered that everything be battened down. Jean was well aware that a storm was heading their way, and in his experience, the approaching storm could be a big one by the looks of things. He had studied the sky day and night and concluded that it would be far better to be prepared for the worst, than be caught unguarded.

Tori had watched him and his reactions to the changing weather. Laffite's wife had seen how he took J.D. aside and talked in a low whisper. Something was going on, and she, for one, intended to find out what it was. When she saw Jean walk toward the river, Tori took a chance to catch him alone. "Jean, you look worried, and if you keep on looking at the sky like you are, I am going to worry. What is it? You need to explain, or I shall ask J.D.?"

"You should not be out here. The wind could snap one of the

branches, and you could be hurt. Look, there is no point in hiding anything from you, but please do not talk of the storm when the children are around."

"Do you think it's going to be that bad?"

"I do. That is why I told J.D. to secure the plantation. He is there now. The man agrees with me; it's better to be prepared than not."

"Is it a hurricane, is that what has you worried? I mean, it could just be a small squall passing with a front, right? You can't know what's heading our way for sure. It could be a line of thunderstorms, like those that hit the night that…the night Christopher was born."

"I too remember that night and no, my love; what heads our way is nothing like that. I do not wish to make you worry more. But, Tori, every bone in my body is telling me we are in for far worse. It is, in my opinion, a tempest of the strongest sort heads our way. Where she comes on land that will determine how bad it will be for us."

"I thought as much. Look, I am not one to panic when it comes to hurricanes, but I do know it's the water, the flooding that kills. Are we safe this close to the river?"

"J.D. assures me we are, as long as we all stay on the upper floor of the house."

"But the wind?"

"As you said, it's the water we have to concern ourselves about. The winds have yet to harm the house. It is sturdy, and we had best head inside now. I have seen all I need to, and the hour is fast approaching when we shall find ourselves to be in the thick of it. You can help Marie, and I will go and help J.D., but we all need to be inside before nightfall, or sooner if the winds pick up."

On August 18th, 1812, Destrehan plantation was ready as it could be. By nightfall, the winds had indeed begun to pick up, and bands of rain pelted the house sporadically. On J.D.'s orders, no one was to go down to the ground floors, due to the possibility of flooding. If the river did burst its banks and come as far as the home, it would be next to impossible to detect in the dark. He had spoken in a grave tone to make his point but not harsh enough to alarm his children or wife.

Tori looked out the last set of unshuttered doors toward the river. The Mississippi was just across the road, and the bank that held the river at bay was not exceedingly high. Chances of the waters flooding the plantation grounds were good in her estimation, and she thanked God that the house's second story was as high up as it was.

"Trying to see the river?" Jean had joined her to look outside.

"You might say that. It's impossible, though, isn't it? I mean, even when the rain lets up, the visibility is zero. It is just so darn dark out there. Do you think the bank will hold?"

"I do. If not, we are safe up here. Now, step away from the doors, and join us. We have time yet before the storm is upon us."

"You are kidding, right? I mean, it sounds awful already. How much worse can it get?"

"We shall have to wait to see. Please, try not to worry and maybe help Marie with the children. A story would be nice to calm them, don't you think?" He placed his arm around her waist and walked with her toward the center of the room. Jean had done all he could to help the Destrehans prepare and even sent word to his brother Pierre early that same day, to take Marie and leave the city for higher ground. He told the messenger, a young black man, to then travel to his townhouse, where he would ride out the storm with Bessy and the other slaves. Jean instructed the lad to tell Bessy she should send word to them when they could return safely. The young slave had looked a bit worried, but upon learning, he would be staying at Laffite's home until he could bring back a message from Laffite's housekeeper, he was much relieved.

By daybreak on August 19th, Laffite knew he'd been right, and there was nothing left to do but hope all had taken heed. He knew his captains at Grand Terre would have sailed out into the Gulf, to ride the waves of the storm and avoid their vessels being pushed ashore with the high tides and winds. These men knew how to read the sky and, most likely, felt the change long before the city's citizens.

Dominique would be well at sea by now; on his ship Pandoure, and Jean knew that as captain, the vessel and all who sailed on her were in good hands. As for all those on Grand Isle, and on his side of the inlet, at Grand Terre, there was nothing to do but worry and pray. If the village was lucky, the storm would not be a direct hit. If it passed them by, coming ashore East of them, many would be saved. The surge would be a big worry, but things could change, and the wind could become a huge factor if the course of the storm took it closer to the mouth of the Mississippi or over Barataria Bay. Carlotta would be safe, as long as she remained in one of the rooms upstairs in his home. He had constructed it with just such storms in mind. The walls were thick, and the bricks sturdy. The height would survive a twenty-foot surge if it had too, and Jean prayed it would not come to that.

It was just past five in the afternoon, and the winds had continued gaining in strength. They steadily howled outside, and stronger gusts roared and tore across the land. Twice Jean and J.D. had braved the fierce gale force to view the river. They had left the upstairs rooms and taken a short walk between the addition and the main building. This was the safest route, as the space between the two structures protected them from any flying debris. It did not stop the wind's force, though, and after the last adventure out, both agreed it was too dangerous for them to attempt it again.

When they returned to the living room's safety, they fastened the door behind them and made certain all other entries were secure. Jean took Tori aside to tell her what he thought. "I estimate that we are to be hit by the brunt of this storm. As a matter of fact, I think we are close to hearing the worst of it now."

"I don't have to look to see how bad it is, Jean. I can hear it, we all can. It is no longer gusting, the winds seem steady, and they sound vicious, howling like they are."

"Aye, they are strong, but what I witnessed just now, I have never seen, or hope to see again. Two large ships were moving upriver. Not one had a man at the helm, as far as I could tell. The surge is so strong from the Gulf that they have literally been swept along on the strong current that forces the water upriver."

"My God! You are sure? Maybe they were trying to outrun the storm and go up to Baton Rouge for safety."

"No, I am certain. Neither had a sail up, and no person could be seen on deck. Besides, twice, the larger of the two rammed the other. I fear this storm is far worse than we thought. Let's pray the levees hold and the storm passes quickly. The hours we have witnessed with such fury shows its size, which must be considerable. That, or she is a slow-moving beast."

"I don't think it's slow-moving. The clouds were racing by yesterday, ahead of it. Surely that indicates the speed of the storm itself."

"I cannot tell you that. If I were at sea, I know only that I would be sailing away from this monster and my love, you would be green as the emeralds you won. The Gulf will be tossing all vessels like you can't imagine, and those crews will have to fight to stay afloat."

"Jean, I am sure they are far away from the danger, and as you told me earlier, they are all seasoned men. It's those onshore I worry about."

"That is so. For those in its path, the night will be long. I fear, and I pray that those in the city escape harm."

By early that night, Tori sat with the family, listening to the gale-force howl, as the rain pounded steadily on the building Several times, either J.D. or Jean had to resecure the large wooden shutters over the verandah's doors. The rain, which had been blown away from those doors, now seemed to have a mind of its own, regardless of the storms, direction. Several times, branches from the surrounding trees slammed into the shutters, causing the children to cry out in fear.

Going out to either of the wings to see that the window coverings were still intact was impossible and far too dangerous. All they could do was hope the shutters held fast. There would be no sleeping in those quarters for the children until the weather calmed down, and even then, it would be Jean's call. He was the one who could judge best if the calm were merely the eye of the storm or not, and the Destrehans trusted his judgment.

Oil lamps had been lit, and Marie had seen that they would have food and wine while they rode out the weather. The whole day before they settled in the living room, Marie had Nelly had the house slaves bringing up food and water along with many bottles of wine and brandy. The marble tub had been cleaned and filled with drinking water, on Tori's advice, and Marie, who had never thought of doing that in the past, praised Tori for her clever idea.

Both Jean and Tori helped keep the children away from the doors and windows, while J.D. sat at a small desk, writing and looking at his pocket watch constantly. Marie had one or two of the youngest Destrehan's sit with two slaves, who entertained them and helped keep them occupied. Nelly kept close to her Mistress, yet, she also seemed to appear at the right spot when one of the children acted up or was frightened. Under the circumstances, Tori had to admit to herself that the small group was holding it together quite admirably.

The house and its property were now on the other side of the storm's rotation, and the winds began bombarding from a different direction, driving sheets of rain and pelting the shutters that wobbled and shook precariously. Now that the hurricane's eye had passed, the new onslaught struck the front of the home. With full force, heavy rain and debris smashed loudly against the building.

At least coming from this direction, these strong hurricane-force winds would push the Mississippi's waters back out into the river and off the plantation's land. They would also push the river itself, in the right direction, and back toward the Gulf. Tori wondered if the ships Jean and J.D. had seen moving upriver would now float back down towards the city, or if they had met a worse fate and now lay at the bottom of the muddy water?

WITH the hurricane once again raging outside, Tori sat with Marie, who held the youngest in her arms. The mother kept her eyes on the others, who were trying to sleep. They lay all around her on the floor, from the youngest to the oldest. Her face showed the fear she felt, and rather than have her friend sit in such a terrible state, Tori decided to take her mind off the weather. "Marie, what do the slaves do, where do they go? Does the overseer keep them gathered in a safe place?"

"Overseer? Oh, I see, you don't know about my husband's ways, and why would you? It's not like we talk of such matters, is it? J.D.'s ways are not what many, call normal. They are different than most. You see, he has no overseer, my dear."

"Really? I thought all the plantations had them."

"Most do, but a few like ours do not."

Tori frowned. "Forgive me, but who then is in charge and sees that the work is down and that the slaves don't run away? Forgive me if I am overstepping, I just don't understand."

"My husband pioneered the system he now uses, and a few have followed. He blends the harsher overseer ways with a more lenient task system. We use head slaves called drivers to allot the tasks and inspect the work. Many prefer to have a white overseer, but J.D. does not. He does have a few white men help when harvest time comes around, but that's it. So far, it has worked out. Only once have we had trouble. We had two of our head slaves join an uprising, but they were dealt with, and I doubt anything like that will happen again."

Tori was reminded about the bloody story of the uprising, and images of heads on spikes flashed in her mind. Surely the Destrehans did not place their slave's heads on spikes as others had? She did not want to talk about any of it, let alone ask if J.D. condoned the action, so she decided to change the subject. "I am impressed that J.D. should think so differently about the way to run a plantation. He is a fine man. Even now, he works at his desk; you are blessed to have him."

"I am, and likewise, you are blessed to have Jean. We are lucky to have you here with us. Jean was the one who told the drivers to move inland and return when the storm passes. He was wise to do so by the sounds of the gale outside. So now you know where our slaves are." She smiled and then looked down at the youngster in her arms. "Would you mind checking on the children for me? If I move now, this little one will wake up, and the last thing we need, on top of the howling wind, is a howling child." She laughed at her own words, and Tori found herself joining in.

"Oh, Marie, you can make me laugh. I will check on the children for you. Then, I will be back, and we can chat some more. Maybe about more pleasant subjects, though?"

BY around two-thirty in the morning, the winds had started to weaken. They came in strong gusts now and then, but the worst seemed to have passed. Knowing everyone was safe, Jean and Tori left the family and went to their bedroom, which this time was in one of the wings. The shutters to the windows in the room had held fast and would remain so until the following day. The roof was intact, and the roaring noise of the hurricane had greatly weakened.

"It was pretty bad, wasn't it, Jean? I mean, that was a strong hurricane that just hit us, right?"

"It was, and we won't know how bad, until a few days from now. I am sure the river has flooded her banks in many places. The levees downstream would have taken the brunt of the force. South of the city, had it far worse than we. I fear, many will have to rebuild, and I pray that my men were able to ride it out onboard their ships. Now, let us rest up; there is nothing we can do."

"You are worried about Dominique, aren't you?"

"I can't lie to you, but he is a good captain and knows the gulf. His ship is strong, and his crew are all seasoned. I shall choose to think he will sail into port, unscathed, in the coming days. Now, come here and lie next to me. I, for one, am too tired to change, and holding you in my arms will help me forget that there will be much too do in the coming weeks."

Tori was worried, how would New Orleans have stood up, and then all the families down at Grand Terre. The plantations along the river South of the city; how would they have dealt with the surge? Jean had said the levees South of them would have born, the brunt of the storm. First, they would have faced the surge from the Gulf waters and then the flooding waters that returned after, but Grand Terre worried her. The small huts and flimsy cottages all would be devastated, and the children and families, how would they survive? Where could they have gone for safety? Most of the islands were only a few feet above sea level. Would Carlotta have taken in any of the children, whose parents were at sea? She hoped so. Laffite's wife fell asleep worried and praying that the storm had missed the island settlements and that most of those who lived there, lived still.

WORD came to them three days later. The worst that they feared had come to pass. The stories of flooding and damage being nasty did nothing to calm them. The young black slave told them that he had seen the flood. That as bad as that was, the wind had done as much damage in his eyes. He did have a letter for them, and this he handed over to Laffite, saying that it had been given to Bessy and she knew he would want it.

He began his story speaking in English, and he looked only at Laffite as he spoke. "She tol me, that I was to git it to you, and that be why I left so soon. I would had come faster like, but the road was gone, and Bessy said, I must wait. She said the house has some roof gone, but it is still standing, that be your house, that be standing. Anyways, that there, letter, I think has the telling of what happened."

The boy looked around the room proudly. He had accomplished his mission, and he had done so while seeing all the damage along the way. "I kin tell you that there was not's a house standin' for over an hour's ride after I left the house and Bessy, and all. Most places that still stand, they be closer to here, and even them has roofs missin' and some wid walls down, but they be there. Some places I know'd for my whole life's be just gone. Nothin' left, not a person, not a stick or stone. Them, trees a-tween here an there, they lost all their leaves, and in places, many be snapped in halfs like. Like a kid does to a stick. Yez um, that what they looks like. It be like someones just snapped um. The canes be gone too. Them fields be all laid flat, an most under waters. There be a mess out that way. I sees wid my own eyes, folks that was sure enuf deads, an I was sure affeard of them."

Tori was distraught now. If things were as bad as she was hearing, then there would be a large loss of life, and she found herself praying that all her friends had ridden the storm out safely. "Jean, does it say who it's from? The letter?"

Jean frowned and glanced at the letter in his hand. Then he looked toward Tori and spoke in French. "I am sure once I open it, that will be clear." Jean looked at the young lad that had been brave enough to bring it to him. He looked at J.D and placed his hand on the young black slave's shoulder. Speaking in French, he addressed his friend. "I think this young man deserves a long rest and some hot food. Maybe we can arrange that? Then I will read the letter, as it is written. I see it is addressed to me in French, which is good for all. The lad's English is fair, but I feel yours has a long way to go, J.D., my friend."

"You are right; I missed much that he said and understood even less. I will arrange his food right away. He had a long journey to return to us, and I am grateful." J.D. smiled and signaled for his slave to follow. Laffite watched them leave, and then he sat down to read the letter, which upon opening, he saw was from none other than Beluche.

Tori watched his expression as he read the contents of the two pages, and as much as she wanted to ask what it said, she decided to wait. Jean's lips pressed together, and the furrows in his brow deepened, indicating that the news was grave indeed.

Finally, he folded the sheets and looked at the adults, who were all waiting for him to talk. "It is from Beluche. It seems he had not gotten his ship downriver and into the Gulf before the storm."

"Oh, Jean, that can't be good."

"I shall reread his letter slowly and share what it contains." Tori sat down and watched him. His face was awash with sadness as he read each section.

"A great deal of the buildings in the city have been damaged, and many totally. It is estimated that more are gone or damaged than remain at all. The marketplace near the river has been blown down and scattered to the wind. Most of the ships sustained much damage. Those that were torn from their moorings, which by all accounts, was all but a few, now sit in water that is very shallow. It is estimated fifty-five ships in total are lost.

Most will not be salvageable. All small craft and barges are at the bottom of the river, none of those survived."

The room was quiet, as Jean looked back at the letter and read more of what it contained. He did so for a few minutes before looking back at Tori. "The military barracks and hospital need rebuilding, and the convent lost its roof and one wall. Many lives were lost to the river and its flood of the surrounding area. The government storage buildings are destroyed, and the contents are scattered. Trunks and boxes of all sorts of merchandise are floating down the river or are stranded on the now muddy banks. Many of these items sit in fields, which flooded where the levees broke. Where the water is receding, the merchandise is left behind, along with, forgive me, many bodies of those who were swept away."

"Oh, Jean. I can't imagine the horror of seeing such a sight."

"Not one lamp post in the city escaped the wrath of the wind, and all are down or bent beyond repair. The vicinity and much of the city will need to be rebuilt."

"And they will, Jean. New Orleans will rebuild." Tori had reached out and taken Jean's hand, hoping to reinforce this fact.

Jean just nodded his head before saying more. "Beluche did say that Gambi and a few others are already selling slaves for high prices. People do want to rebuild quickly and are in need of labor with which to do so. He tells that merchandise from Grand Terre is being unloaded from Gambi's ship also. The man raided the warehouses before the storm and filled his ship, along with others. All sailed out to wait until the worst passed."

"Jean...I know the merchandise is good, but you told me you would not deal in slaves, remember?"

"I do recall, and I am not. But do not expect me to stop my men from such at this time. They have lost much I fear, and if supplying the needs of the city will help them, then so be it." Jean looked at her, and then he smiled slightly. His voice did not sound quite as firm as it had. "Tori, my love. This is what I do. I supply what the city needs and at a fair price, might I add. I will gain enormous profits from all that I can sell, but in no way will I charge beyond the means of those I sell too. My men can help the supply and demand, so who am I to stop them. Even the citizens of New Orleans are thankful, so shouldn't we be also? Good, will come of this, and we will see to that. Without me, my men, and what we can supply, this city would be in a dire situation. There is little merchandise that comes our way, due to the war, and the British blockades, as it is. Now, come, look on the bright side. Your pirate," he winked, "can do good and win over many, who, until now, have fought against what I do." He was grinning, but it did not fool her. Tori knew he was gravely worried and trying to make light of the situation.

"If you put it that way, I suppose I see the need, but I still don't agree with slavery," she snapped, "and I won't change my mind on that, and you know it. Sorry, Marie. J.D., if I offend you. It's just how I feel, and I won't change my mind."

Tori's way of life was hundreds of years away, and she just needed to remind herself of that because everyone was looking at her strangely. Laffite's wife walked up to Jean and put her arms around him. "I'm sorry. I shouldn't have snapped at you." Tori felt him hug her back and knew he understood. Wanting to change the subject, she stepped back and asked the one question that needed answering. "Jean, when can we go back to the city ourselves?"

"That will depend on the next letter I get. Until then, let us help J.D. and his family see to their plantation. They have been lucky but not unscathed. The crop may be a total loss, and the slave cabins need work. It is the least we can do for now."

"Jean, there was no news of Grand Terre, of the ships that went out into the Gulf other than Gambi?"

"That will come soon. Let us not worry over something that is out of our control."

J.D. saw no reason for them to return to the city until they had news that it was safe to do so. Jean had readily agreed but told the Destrehans that it would be to Grand Terre he would travel to first. He fully intended to use the backwaters and would leave as soon as a vessel was sent for him. Tori did not question if she was to join him or not. She knew already Jean would deem it unsafe. She would return to their home in the city and await what news he would bring with him on his return.

THE trip back to New Orleans was long and filled with sadness. Many homes, which she had often seen on her journeys along the river, were no more. Fields of cane and crops were swept away or lay flattened on the soggy earth. Many magnificent old trees had been uprooted, and she could see where more than one had been pulled clear of the road. The outskirts of the city itself were no better for wear. The damage was everyplace she looked, but so was rebuilding. Streets had been cleared, and wagonloads of building materials moved from one location to another. Even after many weeks, though, some of the roads were still strewn with debris, and her driver had to find alternate routes to Laffite's house. One good thing came of this rerouting because they passed by Pierre's cottage and the blacksmith shop. Tori saw that both were still standing and in good shape. Not that she was worried really, as she had known the cottage would withstand everything, be it fires or storms. The building would remain, and many would enjoy visiting it in her time, as she had done with Dan.

BESSY was beside herself upon Tori's return and talked nonstop for hours about the horrors of the storm and the aftermath. "Miss Tori, they say many folks got themselves washed clean away. Paper tells hundreds of peoples, chillen too. Bless um, small babies had no chance, none. I plum sent two our peoples out ta collect thin's dat be washed up and had um clean up some thins and hands them out. Peoples, black peoples, needs help to eat, more then work. Lord, one old slave, sold ta work, dun dropped down, too tired ta stand no more. But he and others got all them lamps up an workin' like, so you can walk at night and not fall down no hole, that you can't see in the dark. They worked hard an got it done, so's they be safe too."

Tori listened without interrupting the woman because she realized how upset her housekeeper was. It was evident in the way she spoke without realizing it. Her dialect had altered, and her speech sounded like that of an uneducated slave. Bessy had learned much and tried hard to improve her ways since Tori had come to live there. She had done so well, and Tori was proud of her grammar, that was until now. After a while though, as Bessy calmed down, Laffite's lady was able to understand her rambling better. The woman's English improved, and her descriptions of the goings-on began to be more reliable and less inflated. Regardless of her many accounts, one fact remained evident, and sadly true. Tori realized that many lives had been lost and, most likely, far more than they would ever know.

One bit of good news had reached her since Jean departed for Grand Terre. He had sent word that Dominique's ship had limped into port and that her captain, although wounded, would heal in time. His ship had not sailed out to sea instead, he had chosen to dock his vessel at port Plaquemine not far from the mouth of the Mississippi. Jean had added that Dominique had spent some time on top of a friend's roof and that the water had risen ten feet or better. The fact that the Pandoure and her crew had survived was a miracle and one that the captain would forever be grateful for.

Tori looked at a piece of paper and saw it was a letter addressed to Mayor McRea. It was dated 23 August 1812. A note in Jean's hand said: keep this for me. It is important that we maintain this should we have need of it. Curious about what the document was and why it was important, Tori's eyes scanned the parchment. The Pandoure had weathered the storm, with the loss of her masts, and the captain had nearly been killed. Her hands shook, and her eyes filled with tears. She looked to the heavens and spoke softly. "Dear God, we could have lost him. Thank you for keeping him safe for me." Wanting to know more, she read on, the ship had made an application to obtain permission to pass the fort and come to town to undergo repairs. It also mentioned they needed a doctor to attend to Dominique, something Jean had not mentioned in his letter. Tori read no more, she only wanted to know that her dear friend was alright, and she knew, Jean would advise her as soon as he himself received word.

SUPPLIES were in short supply until ships began docking and unloading their cargo. Many of these vessels were from Laffite's fleet, and what could have been a blessing soon became a curse. The taxman was there, and prices began to rise beyond what most felt were fair. Even though it was a month since the storm, Dominique supplied the revenue men with his inventory. It detailed the prizes Captain You had taken with his fellow pirates before the storm. This included two English vessels and five Spanish ships. Dominique's share came to $743.02. The ships and their cargo were valued at \$36,921 and sold for \$20,721. It would be the last time old Dominique would deal with the revenue and taxmen on their terms. All his months at sea had gained him little in return.

Whispers about Jean and his men, rebuilding their large barges, to smuggle goods into town were everyplace, and the demand for the pirate's merchandise was high. The law of supply and demand was making the Laffite brothers richer with each passing day, and as they profited, others envied them to the point of hate.

THE middle of October had found things pretty much the same with the Laffites, with two exceptions. Pierre's health had suffered from overwork, and Tori explained to Jean that he would be sure to suffer another stroke if he did not change his lifestyle. "Next time he might not be so lucky," she had explained, and Jean had taken her warning seriously. Pierre also had listened and told his brother that he would take things slower, but just until he regained his strength, something Tori thought he never would do.

The second change was that Dominique's letter of Marque expired on October 15th, and on that date, he sold Le Pandoure. The document of sale was signed Frederic Youx. This spelling caused Tori to wonder again about the man's identity. Tori had been witness to the signing of the bill of sale after all, Grymes had handled the matter. What surprised her was seeing her old friend's name changed. Dominique was never referred to as Frederic, and his last name had always seemed to favor the 'You' spelling. If this was planned, she never knew the reason.

From then on, the older man was often seen with the Laffite brothers strolling the streets of the French Quarter or sitting in a café.

On a happier note, by the time November rolled around, Dominique had become aware that his favorite couple had once again regained their former passion. It was plainly obvious to all because of the way they looked at each other. It was like watching lovesick children, not two grown adults, Jean's second-in-command had declared. The older man was beyond pleased with this development, but it did not mean he stopped his teasing of the lovesick pup as he called Jean. Nor did he stop supporting Tori's point of view and sided with her against both brothers on all matters.

As to worrying over the governor and his ever-growing need to put the Laffites out of business, well, the American had a wedding to keep his mind occupied, so both Laffite's were left to do as they pleased.

November 8th was the big day, and even though both Pierre and Jean had been snubbed and not invited, Tori had seen it as a blessing. It had been no surprise to her that the event was closed to them, but upon receiving a dinner invite a few weeks later, she wondered if she'd been wrong about how Claiborne and his wife felt about Jean.

BOTH Laffite brothers and Dominique had agreed to meet at the cottage. This was so they could go over matters that dealt with all the goods they had at their disposal. Tori had insisted on joining her husband, using the excuse she wanted to see Marie and her younger sister, Catherine Villard. The younger sister lived just across the street, in a cottage remarkably like Marie and Pierre's. It stood on the corner, where, in Tori's time, Lafitte's Guest House bed and breakfast stood. She recalled her visit to the place but did not dwell on it. Nor did she disclose the changes that would happen over the years, to the area she had grown to love.

Once the meeting began, it became clear Tori had no intention of leaving Jean's side. This action was not acceptable to Jean's partners in crime. Pierre was tempted to send Tori out shopping, to keep Jean's mind on what was going on with the books and ledgers before them. Love was one thing, but work was another, and right then, he needed his brother's full attention.

Dominique's gruff attitude and looks of thunder toward Jean's direction caused Tori to chuckle inside. She knew only too well that the older pirate's bark was far worse than his bite, where she was concerned, but not so with Laffite. After making how he felt clear to Jean, he proceeded with his news. The pirate announced that he was now the proud owner of a new ship called le Tigre, a schooner who flew Cartagena's colors and that he had also gained his papers from the fledgling nation's new government. It was at this point that the old man stopped talking and shot Tori another frustrated look. Jean may have paid attention to his news, but the lady had not. Knowing Dominique was trying hard to finish the day's orders and do so without further interruption, Tori made up her mind to give the man a break for once. Winking in his direction and smiling slyly, she walked away, to let the men have their meeting in peace.

Instead of chatting with Marie, Tori wandered outside the cottage toward the blacksmith's lean-to and his fire. Turning to look at the small Creole cottage, Tori frowned. When she had seen it with Dan, people claimed it was the oldest continuous bar in America. They always said it was Laffite's Blacksmith Shop, and in a way, they got it right. She turned back to look at the black man working in the lean-to, who didn't seem to be paying any attention to her.

Behind the lean-to was another small cottage, and attached to it was a sizable shed structure. She assumed this was the real blacksmith abode, not the one she had just left. The noise of bellows and clanking of metal on metal drew her attention back to the man. She'd seen him many times, but always his conversation had been with Jean. The blacksmith had never so much as uttered a word her way.

During the warmer days, he worked outside, and in the winter, on colder days, he would work inside the building attached to his cottage. By the condition of the narrow path, between Pierre's cottage and the blacksmith, Tori rightfully assumed it was used quite often. Knowingly she smiled to herself. This was how they ran the business and got away with it. They would meet at Marie's cottage to do the books, and this blacksmith shop was the cover.

History had that much right, at least. The front worked for all involved, and it was ingenious. They were hiding their true occupation right out in the open, and no one seemed to care.

While thinking about all she knew, Tori stood watching the smithy, as the colossal man hammered out a piece of red-hot iron. He was shaping it slowly into what she assumed would end up as part of a wrought-iron grill on someone's balcony. The man, known only as Thiac, was a person of few words and undying loyalty toward the Laffite brothers, especially Jean. He owed his freedom to him, and it was a debt that Tori would come to realize he took as seriously as life itself.

Watching him work, his body naked from the waist up, Tori could see the strength that rippled his muscles, with each swing of the hammer. The strip of metal he had been pounding was placed back into the inferno, and hot as the fire was, Thiac took up the bellows to urge the flames higher still. Small sparks escaped from within the amber coals and briefly flew up toward the sky. Like fireflies, they danced about, lighting their way in a glorious pattern, not unlike miniature fireworks on the Fourth of July.

Undaunted by the heat of the licking yellow flames that shot out toward him, Thiac reached in with the tongs and removed the now white-hot metal. He then resumed his hammering and bending. Once he seemed happy with the shape, he stopped to dip it into a bucket of water. As he did this, a white cloud of steam rose into the air, temporarily blocking her view of his sweat-covered face.

Tori did not see him turn her way, and when the steam cleared, it was a surprise to see him just standing there, looking at her, tongs in one hand, and the wrought iron in the other. For a few seconds, things seemed awkward, but as soon as Tori spoke, Thiac relaxed.

"Thiac, I'm Tori, Tori Laffite."

"Yez, I know who you be."

"Stupid me, I should have known that. Jean would have told you about me, right? You have seen me with him, but we have never talked, have we?"

"No Mistress, we have not spoken, and as to what I know, well now, most of the people, in this here town, they know'd who you are. Sides, it was Dominique who told me about you. There something you need? Cause I have work to do here. Can't stand around talking all day."

"No, I guess you wouldn't want to do that. I was wondering, though, if you would be able to make something for me? I mean, if I were to describe it to you, maybe even draw it out. As crazy as it might seem, could you try? It would mean a lot to me. Just an idea that I have, about a new shape razor."

"Mizz Tori, I can try, but why you'd want a new shape for a razor when the old one do the job just fine?" Thiac was shaking his head slowly from side to side and scratching the back of his neck. It was as if the action would help him puzzle out just why it was that womenfolk, especially white ones, came up with some ridiculous ideas. There again, it was not his place to question, only do, and by the way Boss's wife was walking toward him, she meant every word of her inquiry.

"Oh, you, wonderful man," she said, taking his hand and shaking it as if they had a deal. "I know you won't understand. I don't know why I didn't think of this before. Here, let me show you what it is I want." Tori led him over to a clear patch of dirt and squatting down, she looked up into his face and indicated that he should join her.

Now, Thiac had seen things in his life. He knew only too well that ladies, white ladies, would never deem it proper, to carry on the way Mizz Tori did. But then, Mizz Tori was special. It was not that she was not a lady, oh no. It was just that the lady did not seem to see anything wrong in her actions or how she was treating him. Her small soft hand was holding his firmly and with no hint of disgust, as she was pulling him down beside her. Then, without hesitation, Boss's wife asked him to look at her idea, as her finger drew something in the dirt.

She spoke to him and showed him what it was she wanted while making him feel like he was essential and needed. Her words were not an order; it was a request, and that made him even more determined to deliver up whatever shape or size razor her little mind could conjure up.

WHEN at last Tori and Jean left the shop, it was apparent to all that she was pleased with herself. When Jean commented that she looked a little too smug about something, she replied without giving away a thing. "Well, you will have to just wait and see. It's an idea from my time, one that I miss. Your wonderful blacksmith, that big gorgeous hunk of a running back, has agreed to make it for me. This little invention, I can tell you, will drive you wild."

Jean could hardly contain her. It was as if she were walking on air. Tori was laughing and spinning around him as they made their way slowly down the street. His wife was at it again. Didn't she know that just being near her, watching her walk and carry on like she did, was more than enough to drive him wild? Who cared that people were stopping to stare at the spectacle she was making of herself, and maybe overhearing her talking about things that made no sense at all? He would not stop her unless he deemed it necessary.

Exactly what a 'hunk running back' was, he'd have to ask her later? As for now, her joy was his also. Damn anyone who did not accept it. His lady made him happy. Tori was his wild and uncontrollable love. However, reality hit him when he saw a couple across the street point their way. Things were getting out of control. They were talking about his wife; he was certain. The way she was carrying on was going to draw far too much attention, and it did seem prudent that she conduct herself more like the ladies of the day. He took her arm and kept her firmly by his side and walked at a slower pace to rein her actions in. His wife did not seem to mind or even notice his attempt at controlling her. Tori was not paying attention to Jean's actions or looks of disapproval.

She was just so excited about her invention. It wasn't exactly her invention, was it, she thought? However, in a way, it could be. What if by her coming to this time, she managed to introduce a few odds and ends. A razor here, a hot dog there, then the idea of pizza popped into her mind.

Jean was watching her closely. "You seem to be miles away with your thoughts. Did you hear what I said?"

"No, sorry, Jean. I did not. It was something about the dinner tonight, wasn't it?"

"Yes, dinner. I feel as though it is something that we cannot avoid. It's just that I won't be able to escort you there. Something has come up with one of our shipments, and I will be a little late. Only a little late, I remind you." He looked at her and saw her puzzled expression. "You don't mind, do you? I wouldn't ask you to go without me. It can't be helped, and it is also imperative that we attend the event."

A concerned expression, with a touch of pleading, was written across his face. Whatever it was that he needed to do, meant a great deal to him. He would never ask her to go unescorted to any function otherwise, and the dinner was apparently just as important as whatever it was, that would delay him.

Jean was torn, and she knew she could help and had no qualms about doing so. Tori understood he would show up and join her, just as soon as he had seen to his other task, whatever that was. If she had to bet on it, he would most likely be at the gathering before her anyway. Besides, it might be fun to go alone and see what everyone would do—what a scandalous idea, arriving by herself. A mischievous grin turned up the corners of her lips as she looked sideways at the man who was scrutinizing her every move.

"Now, don't you go getting yourself into trouble. You can be a little too adventurous when you want. As my wife, you will be expected to act appropriately. Carrying on like the minx I know you can be, is a no go, as you say, especially at this affair."

"Isn't that what you like about me?" She said, pinching his rear as they walked. "The minx in me is always ready to play, and you love it. Don't say you don't."

Jean immediately shot her his how-dare-you look. "Madame, may I remind you that I do not care how you act in the house, but you will conduct yourself as a lady out here in public."

Much to his dismay, his words only seemed to add fuel to the fire. Tori was in a very playful mood and tossing her head; she mockingly answered his reprimand in a teasing reply of her own. "Why, Sir, would that be a lady of your time or mine? I can assure you that mine would be more to your liking, but then if it's a lady of today that you want, I think I can accommodate you." She batted her eyelids and, within seconds, had outwardly assumed the image of a lady of the era. She was mimicking the women a little over the top, but it was working. Tori knew that she would burst out in laughter at any second, especially if Jean kept that dumbfounded expression on his face.

Jean's expression was on the verge of losing its seriousness. He tried to sound firm, but the slight grin gave him away. "All right, you win. You know what I mean. So, stop acting, so infuriatingly..." he stumbled, searching for the right word.

"Proper? Is that the word you are looking for?" she laughed.

This was getting him nowhere, and if he kept playing this game with her, he knew that the day's work ahead of him would never be finished, let alone begun.

"Madame, you are impossible. I know when it is better to retreat from a battle, I cannot hope to win." He bowed before her, then took her hand to his lips and brushed it with a light kiss. "I have decided it would be better if I were to leave you now and see to the pressing matters at hand, concerning work. So put that idea out of your mind."

"And what idea would that be?"

"You know precisely what I mean. Now, if you don't have any objection, I shall be on my way." He slipped his arm around her waist and began once again, heading toward the waiting carriage. "I shall, of course, drop you safely on our doorstep, just to keep you out of trouble." It was his turn to laugh then. "Don't look so sad. Take this opportunity to rest up for the evening ahead of us. I should be able to finish my work early if I start now, and then who knows? I might escort you myself if you still wish?"

She knew that it was very seldom, if ever, that Jean Laffite did not get his way. Another round won for the pirate, Tori thought, but then who was counting anyway? The woman bit her lip, she was counting, of course, and damn, the pirate was way ahead of her this week as far as getting his way, but not for much longer. She still had a few tricks up her sleeve to even the score.

TORI had taken his advice and rested most of the afternoon. For a while, she sat by the fire in the study reading. The house had been quiet, and the chilly day had kept people, like herself, inside.

The invitation to the night's dinner sat on the table next to her chair. She picked it up to read again the details that were exquisitely scrawled across the paper. The invite was dated November 16th, 1812, and it was to be a celebration for the city's rebuilding. Also, it was the first time since their marriage, that Governor Claiborne and his young bride would be seen in public.

The limited number of guests included the governor, the upper Creole echelon, and a few until now, ignored Americans. The upcoming evening was the talk of the town, and knowing that many of the influential merchants and government employees would be attending, Tori thought she understood at last why it was so crucial for Jean to attend. She smiled as she read the details. The fact that they had received an invitation to such a dinner spoke volumes. It showed how far the Laffite brothers had come. Apparently, they were no longer considered pirates but rather wealthy merchants, who had made it possible for so many to rebuild in such a short span of time.

Tori felt proud to think that the city was at long last, recognizing Jean's accomplishments. The time had come to show Claiborne and his cronies that Jean was no pirate. He was a privateer and businessman of the highest degree. Claiborne would have to acknowledge, that like Jean's brother, he was respected and held in high standing by most of the population. Could this dinner be the turning point and why Jean would choose to fight with Andrew Jackson against the British? It was a puzzle in her own time, why he chose the American side, versus the British, and the question had remained unsolved throughout history. Again, for the thousandth time, Tori wished she knew more history than she did. The important thing she had to remember though, was that he had fought, and she needed to make sure that history repeated itself. Then for the first time, Tori wondered if she would be around for the battle.

The lake still called to her, and always, she was trying to figure a way around Edward's banning of the Laffites. If Tori could return to the lake, then she might cross back, and if that happened, she would no longer be here to guide Jean. This thought perplexed her, and like always, she struggled with what to do? Each day she remained in this century with Laffite was a day longer than she'd intended, and each day she knew it was making it harder to leave. Leaving him would be the hardest thing she'd ever have to do, but not trying would be harder. If she failed to attempt going back, she'd never learn the truth, never find out if there was a way back at all. Besides, she had a promise to keep and Linni. Tori still had a daughter who needed her and who she missed more than she would allow herself to admit. Her son was gone forever, but her daughter could still be united with her mother. This was always in the back of her mind, and she knew it always would be.

It was early evening, and the time had come to dress. The gown that lay waiting for Tori was like nothing she had worn before, at least in this day and age. She'd had it made without Jean knowing, and this night's affair seemed like the right occasion to wear it. The design was something that had not been seen anywhere in New Orleans, she was sure. The color was black, which was a highly unusual choice for the day. Black was only for mourning; pastel colors were the fashion of the day.

Jean's wife grinned as she held the garment before her. The ladies would be horrified by the idea of having a black dress, for any other reason but mourning, and Tori laughed while picturing the shocked faces of a few old fuddy-duddies, who had always held something against her. Those females needed a comeuppance as far as she was concerned. For too long now, she had put up with their glaring looks and unwanted opinions that were always barbed and nasty.

Her hand stroked the material after she put the gown on, and Tori stood still thinking about her decision. 'I think maybe tonight I will put an end to their incessant criticism, which in my mind is solely based on jealousy. Once those old biddies are put in their place, Jean can continue to move up in their small so-called elite world. I intend to open doors tonight, not slam them shut, and this little number will help me.'

Tori looked in the full mirror at her image. 'Was this to be one more thing she was to introduce to this era, the black formal?' Fleetingly, she remembered her long-ago promise of not changing history. 'Surely a small item, such as a formal black dress, was not changing history, it was simply enhancing it.'

Her nerves twitched. It was bound to cause a stir, maybe more than she was willing to admit. Still, with Jean on her arm, what did she care? However, there it was, the nerve-gripping reality, slapping her in the face. Jean might not be on her arm, at least not right away, and this thought made her question, could she do it? Tori knew it was a knockout dress. One that would drive Laffite crazy, something she loved doing. However, a small voice in the back of her mind kept asking if this wasn't going just a bit too far? It was a little voice, and as she stared at the gown, it faded. Nothing was going to stop her from having some fun and make a bit of history at the same time.

The dress had been constructed, with seduction in mind. In this day and time, the very sight would send a message that was sure to ring loud and clear and drive many to gasp. The garment outlined her figure and clung seductively to her hourglass shape, and strangely Tori felt a surge of confidence, mixed with just a touch of rebellion now that she had it on. Laffite's wife felt sexy and sultry, not feminine and demure.

She knew many more would gossip before flocking to their own seamstress to copy the latest fashion as that worn by Madame Laffite. That task would not be so easily obtained because of the material used to construct it. Jean had acquired a roll of the exquisite sample on one of his raids against the British, and as far as Tori knew, no other rolls were to be found anywhere in New Orleans.

The fabric was almost gauze-like, constructed of the highest cotton blend. The small puffy sleeves rested on her shoulders and attached to the dress's low neckline, which ran straight across her chest. Just under her bustline was a wide silk ribbon that encircled her body. Artfully attached to this in a pleasing design were many small matching white feathers. The bodice fit like a glove, and the ribbon which fit snuggly held her breasts in place. The material below the feathered ribbon fell smoothly to her feet. It was not quite form-fitting but close. There was just enough material to give her freedom of movement, yet tight enough to show every curve.

Tori pulled gently at the tops of her long black silk gloves. Once in place, they reached well above her elbows. She'd placed a thick gold bracelet on each to secure the tight-fitting gloves in place. The gold bands were designed to look like many small flying birds. The idea was that they should look as if they were holding up the gloves. Once in place, the effect was stunning. Around her neck and resting just above her cleavage was the gold locket that held Christopher's hair. It was simple and elegant at the same time.

As always, Marie Leveau styled her hair. The choice this night was not so elaborate. Tori's long hair was swept up on each side and held in place by small golden combs on which Marie had placed several white feathers. A few strands of hair curled and hung down each side of her face, while the rest flowed long and wavy down her back. This style was very unorthodox for a woman of her age, as most chose to continue to follow the fashion and style their hair by piling it up and off the neck. It always amazed Tori that such styles maintained their position without the aid of hairspray.

The voodoo-practicing stylist sprinkled her client's hair with Gardenia's sweet smell and strategically wove in a few thin threads of a delicate gold chain. These chains reflected the light when Tori walked, causing an illusion of intricate golden flashes, which danced the hair's full length. All in all, the vision was precisely as Tori had planned it.

Laffite's wife was ready but still had a few minutes before her carriage would arrive. Standing looking out the window, she found herself thinking of Marie Leveau and how the two had spoken more than any other time. Tori looked at the golden bands on her arms and frowned. Marie had told her how feathers symbolized air, flight, and travel. While all three were easily connected to birds and feathers, those three words had caused Laffite's wife to shiver. Planes and time travel came to Tori's mind creating an uncomfortable feeling. Their conversation had continued, which was unusual, and even more so, was the fact that Jean's wife had joined in.

"Miss Tori, when I attended your husband, during his sickness, you may recall I placed a white feather by his bed. I did so to ask his guardian angel to watch over him and also so he could find his way home. Your husband was on death's path, but my spell worked as did the herbs." The girl smiled. "It pleases me to see you also feel a connection to feathers. Your choice of design indicates so."

Tori frowned, "I don't know that. I would say I had a little connection, more like an idea, that's all."

Marie shook her head, no. "Forgive me, but I have always felt that the element air rules you and your husband. I am ruled by earth."

Tori grinned and couldn't help responding. "Air, earth, fire, and water. I am familiar, read about such at one time. I would have thought Jean's element would be water. He is a pirate, after all." She laughed, and Marie joined her.

"Miss Tori, you and I will talk more one day about this. For now, know I have placed three white feathers in your hair, blessed they are, and they will guide and guard you this evening."

She had left after that, and Tori had not thought much about it till right then. Guide and guard her! Just made up spells and hocus pocus; that was all it could be. Marie was an enigma, a person who, at times, seemed wise and at others, more like a con-artist.

Bessy announced the carriage had arrived, and without another thought about Marie and her strange ways, Tori placed the cloak around her shoulders and prepared to depart. Jean had not made it home on time to escort her, so like she'd promised, Tori set out to meet him at the dinner.

ACROSS town, down by the river, the dock area had grown quiet. At this time of the evening, most of the people had either gone home or remained inside. The few souls left walking the streets hurried along, wrapping themselves up against the cold wind that continued to pick up. Night fell early this time of the year, and the dampness of the evening had caused Edward to pull his cape up closer around his face.

The dandy had been standing there for nearly an hour, and his impatience was showing. He lit a long thin cigar and was about to give up waiting when out of the dark shadows, a figure approached him. Edward took in a slow breath and stood his ground; after all, he had the upper hand and knew just how to deal with the low life. He'd used this man before, and lucky for him, the man knew how to pick locks and keep his mouth shut. After breaking into Grymes office and retrieving his brother's will, the drunkard, who had remained outside, had re-locked the door and left with a sum of money he was happy with. Edward had never received another word from the bastard; that was until today. A note had been

508

delivered, and in it was written a blunt statement, 'bring money, if you want the information I'm in possession of. Dockside, like before.' This request had both offended and intrigued Duval.

"You got my money," the raspy voice asked? The man came closer and repeated his question. He was obviously in a hurry, and the way he kept close to the wall and its darkness indicated that he did not want to be seen meeting with Edward.

The dandy flipped his cigar away and faced him. "If you have any information that I can use, I assure you that you will have your money. Now, what is it that you had to drag me down here for, and at this time of night, in this damn cold? Keeping me waiting for over an hour, I might add, is not a desirable way to begin business. It had better be good."

"Oh, it's good all right, and I've been thinking that it's worth a bit more'n we agreed on. As I be sticking my neck out like I am. If they found out it was me who told, I'd be dead quick like." He motioned his hand across his throat.

Edward looked at the individual who stood before him. He looked like a weasel, a dirty little rat. The broken down, ugly wretch of a man was nothing more than a low-life, ready to sell his soul to the devil and those of his friends. Edward's attitude was simple if this scum was so hell-bent on going to purgatory, who was he to stop him?

Red-rimmed eyes, sunken in black hollows, surrounded by tallow skin, spoke of heavy drinking and the reason behind his need for the money perhaps? His appearance must have been handsome once, Edward thought. His younger years would have presented a body of healthy muscles and dashing good looks. However, all that was left before him now was a broken shell of a man and a very frightened one at that. "Of course, if the information is good, I will see to it that you get more. Now, come on, out with it, before someone sees us. I assume you don't wish for that to occur, now do you?"

The sailor looked around, and then, making up his mind to

go ahead, he pulled Edward further into the shadows, where he revealed his secrets through a toothless grin.

Edward could not believe what he was hearing. At last, his chance had come. Indeed, this was exactly what he had been hoping for and more, much more. Reaching into his pocket, he gladly pulled out a small leather pouch of coins and placed it into the dirty outstretched hand.

It was greedily snatched away. Trembling fingers with broken, bitten nails tore it open, and then the sailor looked inside, as anger filled his face. "This ain't enough. I done told you, I risked my life telling you what I just did. You owe me more. You agreed!" His free hand grabbed Edward's shoulder and was firmly gripping it, with a strength that somehow seemed too strong for such a frail-looking individual.

"What I think is that you would sell your own mother's soul if it suited you. If you think you are in danger of being found out, then my advice to you is to leave town." Edward shook himself free and brushed at the place where the dirty hand had been. "Now get out of my way. You have all I intend to give you." The dandy was pushing past the grimy individual when he felt his arm once again being grabbed, followed by something pushing into his side. He froze, as the face of the sailor came close to his. The man's foul breath, comprised of tobacco, and rotten food, almost made him gag.

"I ain't about to leave here, and I ain't about to risk my neck for this paltry sum," he shook the small bag in Edward's face. "Now, you best empty your pockets, or say hello to my friend that's knocking at your side door, if you get what I mean?"

Rage, not fear, surged through Edward; no one threatened him anymore, nor would they ever again. He struggled to control his emotions, knowing that his brain, not brawn, was needed in a situation such as this. "Indeed, I do know what you mean. Point well taken, my good man," he chuckled. "And maybe I was a little hasty in asking you to leave with so little. After all, you might once again have some more information for me, might you not?"

The unshaven face looked into Edward's eyes as if trying to read what was there. He squinted and pushed closer toward the fancy-dressed gentleman. Then, as if he had answered a difficult question and come up with a satisfying solution, he grinned. "Aye that I might. I can see you're a real smart business bloke and all." He released his grip on Edward and placed his knife back in the folds of his jacket. The sailor reached up and pulled the collar around his neck, much like Edward had done only moments before. The difference being, his coat was worn through in places, and the material was far thinner. He was thirsty, cold, and in a rush to end the transaction. "How's about it then? Where's the rest of my money? Words are cheap. I need to know that our continued agreement like, is going to be worth my while."

Edward reached into his inside pocket and slowly withdrew another pouch. The sound of coins jingling from within made the sailor grin. The dandy tossed the bag in the air several times, catching it each time with the same hand. It was as if he were trying to decide just how much of the contents should go and how much should stay. Suspense and anticipation were building.

The sailor thought he had hit it big at last. He licked his dry lips, which curled in a smirk as he anxiously wiped them with the back of his hand. This action was intended to erase the spittle that covered his chin and one side of his lower lip. However, he ended up making matters worse by breaking open one of the many fever blisters that clustered around the corners of his mouth. When this happened, the man's tongue licked at the small raw blister, stopping any blood flow. The grimy sailor continued to stare at the pouch in Edward's hand. Finally, Edward tossed it toward him, and as quick as lightning, the old sailor's hand snapped out and caught it.

"You take what you think is fair, and we will call it even." Edward leaned against the wall, tucking one leg behind the other.

The greedy man just nodded his head stupidly and turned his attention to the contents of the purse. He was so busy counting out the pieces of gold that he did not see Edward casually reach inside his cape and pull out a small derringer. Once the dandy had the gun in hand, his actions were fast; Edward struck with deadly intent and with no hesitation. Holding the small weapon right up against the man's chest, he pulled the trigger. A muffled shot rang out in the still night air and was still echoing, as the fatal bullet came to rest deep in the man's chest. Only then did the sailor stop what he was doing and raise his eyes to those of his assailant. The look of horror registered as a white-hot pain seared through his body. His heart quivered, then raced, and shuddered again, fighting to keep the regular rhythm it had known for so long. Slowly, the sailor slipped down to the ground, his one hand reaching for the point of entry, where the slug had attacked its target. He could not understand why, nor did he want to believe that the man had shot him. His hand came away, covered in warm blood that streamed in the night air.

"Bastard," he uttered as Edward turned his head away. "You filthy bastard. I'll see you pay for this, you son-of-a-bitch." The sailor coughed as his mouth filled with still more blood. On its deadly journey, the bullet had passed into his lung and caused a strange bubbling sound in his throat. The realization that he was going to die had not yet set in.

Edward sneered. "Oh, I very much doubt that I will pay for ridding society of the likes of you. No one will even care when they find you; I am quite certain of that." He grabbed the pouch out of the man's hand and hit him, hard in the face with it as he spoke.

Not expecting such an act, the sailor's head snapped back and hit the wall with an audible thump. He was now barely conscious plus very weak and no longer a threat in his attacker's opinion. Edward and the sailor stared at each other as the dandy reloaded his gun. Once this action was completed, Edward Duval knelt and reached into the sailor's pocket to retrieve the first pouch he had given the man. Slowly the dandy stood up and placed the pouch into his pocket. During this whole time, neither had looked away from the other and briefly, the wounded man thought he would now be left alone. He was wrong. Very slowly, Edward looked around to make sure they were alone in the dark alley. The place was ideal; it was dark and deserted. Only the noise from a nearby tavern drifted briefly down their way, whenever the door was opened and closed. "I don't think you will talk to anyone. It's far better that you don't. Can't have the likes of you linked with me in any way, can we?" He placed the gun for the second time close to his victim, only this time it was up against the man's temple. Realizing what was about to happen, the sailor's eyes bulged, but before he could utter a sound, the dandy looked away and pulled the trigger.

Funny, the sound of a shot to the head made, he thought. Just a dull sort of snap and no echoing either. He also found himself thanking God it was dark, so he could not see the results of his work, for surely he would pass out if he did. The man's brains were most assuredly splattered all over the wall behind him. He even thought there was a good chance that some of the swine's filth may have splattered onto his hand and gun. Edward, however, had no intention of remaining a second longer to verify either of these circumstances. Time was of the essence, so he turned and quickly ran from the crime scene with one destination in mind. He was headed for the safety of his own lodging to change and eradicate any sign of his gruesome deed, before moving on to his next location.

Duval still had so much to do before the evening's activities. He had to tell the governor about this new information for one, and then meet up with what he was sure would be a furious Simone for another. Still, he mused, she would not be angry with him for long when he explained why he was so late. If ever a man looked pleased with himself, it was Edward at that moment. Caution, however, caused him to hesitate. He would not celebrate this time. Not until he knew the results of his actions were all completed, as he planned.

THE governor met with Edward in his study, making it clear that he had done so, only because he had been informed that it was a matter of utmost importance. Trusting Edward's judgment on such issues, Claiborne felt it would be prudent to hear the man out. He also decided he would listen to what Edward had to say without the chance of being overheard as the circumstances were highly unusual, to say the least. The governor did not need a scandal of any sort, at this point in his career, and even though the young Duval was a valued friend, his enthusiasm could, at times, override his judgment. Just why Edward would call at such an inconvenient time when they would have seen each other in a few hours, intrigued him, though. This was the time that a person would usually spend attending to one's attire and be preparing for the evening's festivities, not paying social calls.

Entering his study, he found Edward pacing like a caged animal. Excitement was written all over the man's face. Whatever was going on with him was not something deplorable, just the opposite; it looked as if it might be something he was going to enjoy. "Edward, what brings you to my home at this most inconvenient hour? You look as though you have lost total control of your senses. I do so hope; this has nothing to do with this evening's festivities." The governor took the younger man by his shoulders and, after giving him a hearty slap on the back, guided him to a seat, and pushed him down into it. "I would have thought that you would be picking up Simone about now. You do realize that women tend to be a little overly sensitive in the area of promptness. That is when it is ours, and not theirs." William chuckled to himself as he continued, not letting Edward get a word in edgewise. "Women hate to be late to these darned affairs. For instance, my wife, God bless her, goes on and on about the importance of us always being prompt. Our job is to set a fine example; that is what she is always going on about. Must say, she seems right on that subject. What do you think?"

Edward was back on his feet, springing up so fast, it would seem, that the chair itself had propelled him forward. He was all but spluttering, trying hard to get the words out of his mouth. "Yes, yes, of course, I agree, but I think when you hear what I have to tell you, Sir, you might not mind being a little late this evening yourself."

The dandy walked to the sideboard, and the glass decanter, then without thinking, helped himself to the contents, an act that caused Claiborne to raise his eyebrow. He was just about to remark on the audacity of just such an action, when Edward calmly turned and continued speaking, oblivious to the fact that he had in any way conducted himself rudely.

"You see, governor, it has come to my fortunate attention that a one Jean Laffite and his band of no-good pirates will be moving a large and very illegal shipment of goods this very evening. Right as we speak, this very second, I suspect they are hard at work, confidently going about their business, right under your nose. No offense intended I assure you. It is just that tonight they are in New Orleans herself, at the old warehouses, down from the new market area. All those goods, coming right into port and smuggled right past the law and no duty paid. It is an outrage!" he shouted. "A slap not only to yourself but to all the fine merchants of this city."

Claiborne had taken a seat. If what Edward was telling him was correct, and he had no doubt that it wasn't, then this could be the chance he'd been waiting for. He could finally capture the so-called gentleman and expose him for what he was. Furthermore, the governor could use the contraband to prove his point, and there would be no escaping such damning evidence. A smile crossed his lips at the thought of Jean being caught red-handed. Of proving once and for all, that the much-loved man was far more than a mere privateer. It would be enough to put him in jail for a long time indeed. There again, if he could prove that Laffite was really nothing more than a pirate, why then he could even hang him. He'd be the American hero, a governor who upheld the law for all citizens of New Orleans. Then a sudden thought of failing once again and being the laughingstock sent a chilling sensation through him, causing him to stiffen and look sternly at the grinning Edward, who stood awaiting his response. "How did you acquire this information, and are you certain you have the details, correct? I mean, for both our sakes, I would hate to act hastily, only later to find out it was a mere rumor, so to speak."

"I can assure you, William, that the information is valid. I would place my life on it. The individual, who supplied me with the facts, did so at great personal risk. He told me he knew I could take the knowledge of such a transaction to the right people. I am sure he meant for you to know. It is, after all, widely known that we are friends and do frequently entertain together. The whole city knows that Simone and I were at your wedding for Christ's sake. Yes, he knew I would bring this information to you. The man wanted the Laffites brought to justice, is how he put it to me. Before you ask me, I must tell you that he made me give my word of honor, as a gentleman, that I would not reveal his identity, and I intend to keep my word. I can tell you that he is a man of high integrity who wants to have no part in the glory of Laffite's fall from grace. The glory of Jean Laffite's dishonor and capture will be yours alone."

Edward could see the governor's emotions starting to rise. The color in his cheeks had brightened, their redness burning against the sickly white of his fingers that rubbed his chin as he listened. The man, however, was not won over to act yet. He still had to be convinced that now was the time to move. Seeing the man hesitate, the dandy spoke slowly and deliberately lowered his tone of voice, so as not to sound hysterical but knowledgeable. "I think, no, let me restate, I know William, that this is just what you have been waiting for, and if I might add, to hesitate any longer might let the damn pirate slip through your fingers once again. Time is critical. We do not know how long it will be before he leaves the area of activity. He is invited to this evening's affair after all, and we both know that he and his wife will show, and they are prompt, which means he will have to leave the docks soon. William, listen, please. Should you arrive after he has gone, he will simply deny any connection with the goods. No, you must catch him in the very act, and that time is now!" Edward slammed his fist into the tabletop beside him, reaffirming his conviction in the matter.

The governor's stomach lurched, at the thought of losing his chance, after being so close. He could not take that risk, and Edward was plainly convinced that right then was the time. Now, it was his turn to stand abruptly. His strides were full of determination and self-assuredness, as he came toward his young Creole friend. "All right, Edward. I will trust your judgment on this. We will act immediately. This should not take us much time if all your facts come to bare. The evening does not, however, have to be spoiled. I will have my wife escort Simone to the dinner. We will meet them together later, with what I hope will be very pleasing news. News, I might add, that should get us out of the deplorable situation of arriving late." With that said, both of them laughed and set about to ruin the untouchable Laffites once and for all.

JEAN had finished unloading one of the large barges, but there were still a half dozen or so smaller boats pulling close to shore, and one more sizeable flat bottom barge had just tied up. The unloading had been slow, hampered by the wind. The crafts constantly moved, making their already precarious situation worse. If the barge moved unexpectedly, heaving its mass against its moorings, the unwary man could lose his footing and find himself in the murky waters or worse, crushed between the bank and barge. Several of the men had already succumbed to the treacherous conditions and slipped overboard. Lucky for them, they had scrambled to dry land, where they were reassigned duties inside the warehouse. It was the only option open to Laffite, as every man was needed. The soaking wet sailors would trade positions with those inside and keep on working without freezing.

All worked in the dark with low light from their lanterns. This was done to avoid alerting the authorities or anyone else who might have been in the area. So far, the beehive of activity that was well underway had remained undetected, and the lookouts, feeling secure, had left their posts to help hurry up the process of moving the goods from boat to shore.

Jean had planned to take only two or three hours but saw it was going to take far longer due to the windy conditions, so the extra hands were welcomed. The goods were numerous and easily moved once on dry land, but getting them from point to point, was frustratingly slow. Standing there in his seafaring outfit, his head wrapped in a bandanna to keep his hair out of his ever-watchful gaze, Laffite looked the part of the smuggling pirate. He stood impatiently, ensuring that his goods were safely moved and stored. "Hurry it along, men; we can't take all night. Dominique, what is taking them so long with that barge? Old women could work faster than they are." The pirate's worry over the amount of time already spent in the open caused him to bark his question at his second-in-command, something that hardly ever happened.

Dominique found himself wanting to box Jean's ears, to bring him around. They had smuggled cargos like this many times, and always things ran like clockwork. So, they ran a little slow this evening. Was this cause for Jean to speak to him, no better than he would a stranger, who angered him? "Old women, you say? Seems to me that the men are working as fast as they can. With one barge unloading and the other already finished, we are just about caught up, if not a little ahead, considering the conditions. You will arrive for your dinner on time. Have no fear of that little pup. This old sea dog will see that you do," he said sarcastically. Dominique's muffled laughter could be heard across the water, and still, others found themselves chuckling, having overheard the remark made to their Boss. This was far better than boxing his ears, Dominique thought. The look on Jean's face alone, at being called a pup, was astounding.

"You think that funny. Calling me a pup? It is you who is funny, and if I told you what I thought you looked like right now, you would not be so amused, I think. On second thought, it is only fair that I tell you that you look like a pufferfish, with your cheeks all blown up and your eyes bulging."

Pierre hushed Dominique's gasp, with a punch to his shoulder and a drop-dead look that sobered the moment. Jean's brother turned and faced him. "I tell you, Jean, for some reason, I do not like it. There is no one on the docks tonight, have you not noticed? My Marie Louise, she had a bad feeling about this evening, and somehow, I wish I had listened to her. Merde, (shit) the hairs on my skin are standing on end." He rubbed the back of his neck and turned to look up and down the empty stretch of dockside. "I tell you, I see no one, and that is not right, is it?"

Dominique chuckled, and in a not so serious voice, he answered the worried man, "Pierre, think with reason. Would you be out in weather like this if you did not have to? Why, this is the type of evening that one should be inside, preferably with a woman, a bottle, and a cozy night of lovemaking. Not taking a balmy walk, seeing the sights. Who would want to watch a bunch of pirates unload their wares anyway?"

Jean shot him a glaring look as he growled. "How many times do I have to tell you, we are privateers and not pirates!" Having made his point, he turned his back on the two and stood to face the river mumbling.

Dominique was not affected by Jean's outburst and went on goading Pierre. "I think you would rather be in the arms of your lover Marie, or have you grown tired of this one also? Is no woman ever going to be enough for you, I ask? You have a wife that you seldom see. Her name, in case you forget, is Adelaide. Then there was the woman, the one who gave you Pierre, who is growing up under the care of the Sauvants, but no, you take yourself a mere child-woman, shipping poor Adelaide off with her daughter. When will you stop thinking like a pirate and start thinking with your brain and not your little head?"

Jean had been watching his brother as Dominique teased him. He could not help but smile. Privateer was just another name for a pirate, any which way you looked at it. After all, they were moving the goods under the very nose of the harbormaster and the duty collector. He twisted his mustache and grinned. Pirate or not, he did not want to debate the definition; for tonight, they were something completely different; they were just everyday smugglers. "It seems to me that you two have everything going along as it should. Gentlemen, if you don't mind, I shall leave you to your debate, and to the remainder of the evening's endeavors. One can't keep a lady waiting, nor can one escort her dressed like I am. Why most people would claim that I was dressed like a pirate if I were obliged to do so. Wouldn't you agree, Dominique?"

Dominique found it difficult to contain himself, but answered in a severe tone, nonetheless. "I would indeed, Boss. Don't know why you can't escort her in such attire, though. Seems to me she likes you like that. All the way to the islands and back if I remember correctly. Or has the lady tamed you some and turned you into a land-lover after all?"

"You may be able to bait my older brother with your sharp tongue, but not so with me," kidded Jean. "Now, off with you both. Finish that last load. I, for one, will be on my way." Jean was still smiling when the first shot rang out, followed closely by another. The sharp echo was still ringing in the night air when the sound of marching boots joined it. At first, no one was sure what was happening; then, before they had time to act, the whole area seemed to explode into a war zone. Soldiers swarmed around them from all directions, shouting as they ran toward them. Every avenue of escape was cut off, even the river offered no respite, for moving up the waterway, were two small boats. Each vessel had six men aboard, and all were ready to fire their weapons if needed. Cornered as they were, the men tried to fight back, pistols and rifles were fired into the darkness, but the soldiers shot with deadly accuracy.

Seeing two of their comrades go down, Laffite's men moved swiftly. Several of the empty skiffs were pulled up onto the shoreline and turned over, giving a few of his men some cover, while they reloaded their weapons and prepared for the next onslaught.

Jean had taken aim with his weapon and watched a soldier fall, as his bullet hit the man in his shoulder. Once his gun had been discharged, and with no time to reload, he drew his sword ready to fight, but glancing around and assessing their situation, he concluded it was beyond grim. Jean was not about to die or let his men meet the same fate. He could see they were outnumbered, so he decided to call out the order to retreat.

The men understood their situation's gravity and not wanting to be caught and charged with smuggling; they attempted to escape. While Jean stood his ground, watching his men trying to follow his orders, it quickly became apparent to him that the fight had been over as soon as it had begun. One of his men had been shot in the back while running, and a few more had been wounded. There was no way out, and to stop the ambush from becoming a bloodbath, he knew he had to act fast. Realizing he had no other choice if they wanted to live. His words rang loud and clear in the night, "Halt and put down your arms. Do so or die," and then he waited for the inevitable arrests.

The soldiers came out of darkness, bringing with them lanterns that had been shuttered until the last possible moment. Now, in the eerie light, Jean stood in horror as the realization of what had just occurred sunk in. The soldiers ordered them all to disarm, as they cautiously moved forward. Jean lowered his sword, as a very pleased-with-himself governor sauntered up to him. "I highly recommend you drop that weapon before one of my men think you are intent on using it. They will shoot you, have no doubt of that."

Laffite watched as Claiborne casually lit a cigar from the lantern he carried. Though his face was a mask of his true feelings, his voice could not hide the pleasure of his success. "Seems I have caught you at last," he said, holding his lantern higher, casting the light to fall on the scene of a half-loaded barge. He watched for a few seconds more as the pirogues and skiffs were sized. Then he turned his attention toward the space between the river and the warehouse. "My, my…this should keep you and your men in prison and out of my hair for quite some time, don't you think? That is if you don't swing for it."

Jean just looked at him and said nothing.

"Soldier, please relieve the man of his weapon." William's eyes stayed fixed on the pirate, as the man handed over his sword and gun. Once he was disarmed, the governor felt empowered and let a smile pass over his expression. He moved forward and whispered into Laffite's ear. "Nothing to say for yourself? No? I doubt that there is."

Captain Holmes joined them to announce his findings. "No one seriously hurt, sir. Two of theirs are dead; a few took hits, but nothing life-threatening; the rest are in custody. We await your orders."

"Excellent Holmes. Job well-done, I would say." He turned to face the group of pirates, who now stood under guard. Then in a louder voice, Clairborne sarcastically spoke so all could hear his triumphant speech. "Because of your men's brave actions here tonight, Captain Holmes, we will rid our town of the likes of these scum. As for you, Laffite, and your men, you won't be able to talk your way out of this one. You and your people are finished once and for all, in New Orleans. Take them away." He turned to look Holmes directly in the eyes so there would be no misunderstanding. "Toss them all in the calaboose, and no special treatment for their so-called Boss either. See to it, that he goes in the same cell, as some of the other hooligans. No nice solitary cells for any of them."

Claiborne inhaled deeply on his cigar and turned to face Jean again. He blew out a long wisp of smoke, taking his time before speaking. He was enjoying the sounds around him, the sounds of soldiers rounding up pirates and none too gently. "Oh, but, before I forget myself being the gentleman that I am, I will, of course, do you one small favor this evening. You may not concern yourself with the worry of the shock of your arrest; pertaining to your lovely wife, that is. I will, of course, take it upon myself to have someone gently inform Mrs. Laffite of your arrest."

The governor turned triumphantly, and giving no chance for Jean to reply, he sauntered away, shouting orders as he went. "See to it that they are under guard at all times and no special treatment, if they try to escape, shoot them. That includes the so-called gentlemen, both the Laffite brothers. Put the scoundrels under lock and key quickly. No visitors, either." His voice was crisp and his stride fast, as if he had other matters to deal with now that Jean's capture was complete. Not once did he look back toward his victory as he walked away, and as soon as he was out of sight, he was met with a pleased Edward.

"It was as I had said. My information has won you a victory, and the arrests are all yours. The glory all goes to you, and the people of New Orleans will honor you for it. As for my small role, well, we can keep that between us. Let us join our wives and celebrate."

"I agree, Edward, we will celebrate at long last, and I will not forget what you have done for me tonight. I am in your debt, sir. Now, as you said, let us join our wives."

JEAN cursed himself for having been so stupid. He should have listened to Pierre. The docks had been too quiet. So quiet that they screamed a warning. Now, with his brother, his first lieutenant, and himself in jail, there was little he could do. Laffite could not see any way out that night, if indeed at all. It looked as if the governor and the law had caught up with him. The evidence would weigh heavy, maybe too heavy. It was evident that the goods came from many different ships and nations. Worse yet, some of the articles came from an American ship thanks to one of the Italians. Those items would be the most damning. John Grymes would have his work cut out for himself, and as good as he was, Jean doubted he was a miracle worker.

# ❧ Nine ❦

Tori took a deep breath as the carriage pulled to a stop in front of her destination. The sound of a large crowd filtered out from inside, as the front door to the home opened and closed. The servant had just let the couple who arrived ahead of her enter. Music also drifted softly on the crisp night air; its melody momentarily surrounding her as if to greet her arrival.

The doorman left his position and approached her carriage. Once at her side, he extended his white-gloved hand. This was one guest he was genuinely fond of, and thereby, he offered her the extra attention. Over the past few years, she had often briefly stopped and talked with him, never treating him as if he were below her, yet always maintaining her standing. He was just a servant, true, but that was no reason for people to act as they usually did. Unlike all the others, he knew this guest was a real lady and a good human being, with a heart of gold. "And a good evening to you, Mrs. Laffite," he said in his Irish accent, his face beaming and his lips turning upward in a full smile, as he touched his cap. "By yourself, this evening, are you then?" He took hold of her hand, steadying her as she descended from within the carriage.

Her voice caught in her throat and temporally rendered her speechless. Tori was not as confident as she had felt earlier. The house was going to be full of friends, and just as many people, she did not know so well. Out of those, many were hostile toward her and Jean. However, it was too late to turn back now, so she just forced a smile and hoped the doorman could not tell how nervous she was.

"Begging your pardon, Ma'am," he whispered, bending his head in her direction, "but, if I had a Missus that looked as fetching as you, I'd not be letting her out of my sight. That be God's truth and no blarney." His comment was softly spoken, so only she could hear it. He smiled brightly and winked. "You look right, wonderful, sure'n you do. Be hitting them away with sticks, you will." He had felt her trembling hand the moment he'd grasped it. Never would he have thought she had anything to be frightened of, especially with notorious Jean Laffite as her husband. She had arrived without her husband, though, and he deduced that was the reason behind her hesitation. Lord knows, looking like she did this evening, many of those hotheaded Creoles would act no better than drunken sailors, sniffing after a whore. That had to be it, he told himself. She was missing the protective arm of her husband, no doubt, and he felt for her.

"My husband should be joining me very soon, I hope. Maybe, I should just wait until he arrives?"

He did not know if she was asking him or herself that question. One thing was for sure, she was afraid of something, standing there staring straight ahead, with her hand glued to his. Now, he felt genuinely sorry for her and partly to blame. His Missus was always telling him he blabbered on too much. What had he been thinking? Chattering on and on about her being alone, looking so fetching, and all? He had to put it right and quick. The man had to say something to boost her courage and get her moving because another carriage had pulled up behind hers, and they would not like being held up. "Still, a lady like yourself with a husband like you have, maybe you won't have no trouble," he squeezed her hand, tipping his head slightly. "You just go on about your evening and have a good time. I'll be telling the Mister that you're here when he arrives."

"Thank you, Sean, I mean that." Now, it was her time to nod her head and smile. Tori bet no one else visiting that night would be calling him by his given name. Laffite's wife hesitated only a second more, then released his gloved hand and took a deep breath. "Here goes nothing, and Sean, thank you."

"You are most welcome, always." He tipped his hat again and

turned to close the carriage door.

Tori started up the walkway toward the entrance, wondering why she had ever decided to go alone this evening. Would she ever learn? Time and time again, she had put herself into compromising situations. Was it for the attention or the challenge, she wondered? Again, she reminded herself, she would know many of the guests, and under normal circumstances, she would not have been so nervous, but then under normal conditions, she would not be dressed in an outfit such as the one she now wore. It would, no doubt, be the scandal of the evening. That was a sure bet if the doorman's reaction was any indication. Sean had only glimpsed the outfit under her cape and acted surprised. Dressing like she was, with Jean at her side, was one thing, but this was sheer madness.

The door to the grand home opened just as she reached it. "Good evening," she said as she presented her invitation to the gray-haired black man, who took it without even reading it. Not that he could have read it, even if he wanted to. His job was to take the card and place it on the silver tray, nod his head and admit those whose card he received. The task was straightforward on purpose. Too complicated, and the old black man could mess it up, but keeping it simple, was an assurance that things ran smoothly. Rules were easily met, and this rule was plain as could be. Anyone without a card was to be denied entrance at all costs.

How simple to crash one of these affairs, she thought, as a sly smile slipped across her scowling face. Tori imagined handing in a card at the next event to which she was uninvited, that said, 'bullshit, I'm coming anyway.' This thought made her chuckle to herself.

"I will be joined by my husband, Monsieur Laffite in a while. You do know my husband?"

"Yez', um," his head nodded. "Everyone done knows who he be. Don't you worrys none. I know'd I got his card." The frail old body turned, as he pointed his bony old hand toward the silver dish. "It be right here, safe like, where I done put it. I be a letting him in da second he gits, here. Sure'n I will." His stern old face was beaming with pride. However, Tori couldn't help but notice that his gaze was wandering all about the hallway. He was looking at anything and everything but her.

A young black girl had come to her side and helped her remove her cape and without comment, curtseyed and disappeared, taking the garment with her. Tori turned back to the grinning black man whose eyes were wide open as if he had just been shocked with a thousand bolts of electricity. "Thank you," she said, watching as his face slipped quickly back into its somber mode. He did not utter another word, only nodded his head and looked beyond her, to the way she was supposed to go.

The old man's eyes followed Tori as she turned and began to walk toward the gathering. Now that her back was toward him, he had a chance to study her carefully as she progressed down the hallway. If that was what these white folks was goin' to be callin' a gown, then Lord God, he was thankful his girls, was all black. He had seen some thin's in his days. The goin's on dat white folks did, well they just made him wonder sometimes. Now, a fine white lady, dressin' like dat. It just didn't seem right. Nice to look at though, he had to admit, real nice to look at. A slim smile crossed the old man's lips, "Dis job might be a gittin' better, ah huh, ah huh. Hours is long. Legs is old, but these nigger eyes, sure'n goin' to be enjoyin' demselves," he mumbled. "Best not let on none, though. Da Massa, he might go an git him a blind nigger for da job," he said shaking his head. His old face grew stern, as he took control of himself. "No sur. I be careful now, real, careful. Come on face, git dat look, of don't know'd nothin' planted on you. And nigger, you best stop yabbin' like, cause more folks is a comin' your way."

It was only a matter of seconds before every face turned toward her. The ladies, some of whom raised their fans to conceal their shocked expressions and whisper among themselves, stepped back. It was not only about the way Tori was dressed that caused such a stir, but the fact that she had arrived, obviously unescorted, and to many, that was just beyond scandalous behavior, it was darn right preposterous.

Tori could no more turn and flee than she could move forward. Her feet had become immobile, frozen to the spot. It was as if she were physically held in place by a pair of invisible hands. Hands that not only gripped her body but had somehow taken hold of her mind as well. Laffite's wife knew she had gotten herself into this predicament, but what she was going to do about it at that present moment, she had no idea.

It was her dear friend who, undaunted, came to her rescue. Once again, Mrs. Destrehan arrived out of nowhere, it seemed, proclaiming in a voice of authority her warm greeting. She made sure all around could hear and thereby pass on what was to become Tori's lifeline. "Tori, it is so excellent to see you, my dear. We were not too sure you would take our advice and join us ahead of that darling husband of yours. Now, do tell me about your gown. It is most unusual. I can't say that it would suit me at my age, but then, if that's the latest fashion in Paris, younger women such as yourself, will look simply ravishing in the coming season." She placed a loving kiss on each of Tori's cheeks and then slowly moved the two of them toward her husband, J.D. and his friends.

Like being released from a nightmare, Tori was able to hide her amazement at what had just occurred. "Just how did you know about Jean?" Tori quickly whispered Marie's way.

"I didn't my dear, but, seeing you standing there, looking as if you were about to turn around and run, or worse yet, never move at all," she giggled, "well, I told myself, and that husband of mine, I positively had to do something. It's like old times, I fear. You have not forgotten the first affair you attended with Jean, and how I managed to keep the hordes at bay. I do hope I have not stepped over my bounds. It's just those silly fools, carrying on like they were. Frankly, dear, it got me quite angry. You do look ravishing.

Something, however, tells me it's not quite the style from Paris."

Tori bit her lower lip at this statement, and Marie grinned.

"No, I thought not, but that little lie will give them all something to carry on about and less time to gossip about other matters."

Marie was enjoying every moment and had no intention of stopping. As for Tori, it was so good to see her friend having fun. Jean's wife was thankful that Marie, in her wisdom and with her lies, had given her what she needed to get on with the evening.

Quickly, like a buzz of bees swarming in a flower-filled meadow, the ladies mingled, spreading the latest gossip. The gown was from Paris, and was it not the most exquisite creation they had ever seen? Just look at how it moved when she walked, and how it hugged her form, causing a silhouette-like vision. The more they looked and talked, the more they increased their desire to obtain such a garment. The last thing on their minds was to question the validity of its origin. After all, had it not been deemed the latest design from France, by none other than Madame Destrehan, and she would know, having strong family ties in that direction. Many made mental notes to find out just who Tori's seamstress was. They had to have a gown like it; they told each other, or something close to it. Just look at the way the men flocked to her side. Already she was the hit of the party, but, then, wasn't she always of late? It was said that almost everything Laffite's wife did, was emulated by the women of New Orleans, all except for a small few that was. One such lady, filled with jealousy, was overheard saying that if Tori were to cut her hair off like a man, most of the women would follow, except for herself. Then with an air of arrogance, she announced she thought them all fools. While talking, Simone sauntered across the room with Cayetana; her eyes, looking at everyone they passed, but her expression did not give the slightest hint of her true feelings. She was maneuvering to join a small group, who stood openly, appraising Tori Laffite.

Simone was sickened by the admiration unjustly thrust upon the so-called beauty. She hated Laffite's wife with such vengeance that

Tori would have most certainly dropped dead if the emotion could have physically killed. "I can tell you," Simone said to the governor's wife, "I, for one, would not be caught dead in such a gown. If, that's what you can call it. Such a flimsy fabric, surely better to use for undergarments or better nightgowns. It's just not proper. Fashion or not, I find it in deplorable taste, and this time, I think she has gone too far. Black too. What was the woman thinking? The very way she has our men running to her like that. It's like she is a common street...well, you know...nothing more than a lady of lesser means, shall we say?"

The small group, some of whom secretly would have loved the chance to be in Tori's place and looking half as good, lied in jealous agreement. Simone, tired of the spectacle, turned her back and walked away. She was followed closely by those around her. These women took comfort in the fact that Simone carried on as she did, for not one of her entourage would dare to speak so, even if they wanted.

While these simpering, sniggering belles continued to divulge ugly accusations amongst themselves, hoping to impress the prestigious governor's wife, Simone turned her dwindling attention elsewhere.

Off to one side of the dance floor stood a gentleman that had caught her eye. He was tall, dark, very well attired, and had an air about him that intrigued her. His prominent Spanish features would have typically affected Simone in the exact opposite way than they were at present. However, something about his eyes had held her captivated. They were the kind of eyes that had a way of stripping one naked, slowly and deliberately, as they traveled the length of your body, and she found herself wanting nothing more at that moment than to make the stranger's acquaintance. Thoughts darted around in her mind as she continued to stare at him. Edward's lover came to a quick conclusion; this stranger was the type of man who made love with deep passion and no commitment. Simone told herself to wait a bit longer before making a move to introduce herself. After all, she didn't need her lover to find her acting like her old self.

EDWARD was not only late; he'd dared to send her ahead, escorted by William's wife. Simone looked around the room and frowned. The governor was late as well, and that made three men if one counted Laffite as a gentleman, all late, and no sign as to indicate why. Something was amiss, she understood that, and knowing Edward, she'd guess it was a card game. He'd have some answering to do when he arrived. Until then, though, she was bored, so she continued to observe the handsome stranger and his actions.

The way his eyes scrutinized each woman he gazed upon, as if he was visualizing bedding them, stirred her emotions. She knew that look well enough, having been on the end of such scrutiny herself many times. Here, before her, stood a man whose passion was as raw as her own. True, Edward could satisfy her as a lover, but she had become somewhat bored with him. The thrill of seducing a new lover, though, was like no other thrill she could imagine. It was the very spark; she felt she missed and required. The thought of it squeezed at her insides, sending undeniable messages up and down her spine. Simone understood that she could run the risk of losing Duval by pursuing a relationship with whoever the Spanish gentleman was. However, to be found out, and possibly caught, that was the exciting part of just such an illicit endeavor. "If you will excuse me, ladies. I see an old friend of Edward's that I feel I must go and say hello too. It would not be polite of me to do otherwise, and Edward would never forgive me if I neglected one of his associates. You do understand, do you not?"

They all understood very well. The admiring and sultry expressions that had been passing between the stranger and Simone had not gone unnoticed. The widow had always had a reputation of being rather forward and flirtatious, and apparently, she'd not changed her ways in that department, but then a little innocent flirting could hurt no one. The small group told each other, why should that Laffite woman have all the fun, after all?

The gentleman in question was not new to these gatherings. Instead, he chose to attend, only those affairs that he felt would not bore him to death. It was all the stupid women and their silly games that infuriated him. Why the females had to be so coy, he could not understand. Too often, he would seduce one of the so-called virginal beauties, only to learn that he was not the first to lay with them and that disappointed him.

Standing by himself, looking the part of a wealthy, well-dressed gentleman, he could bet that tonight would be no different. It would be only a matter of time before his sordid little game would commence, initiated by someone other than himself, of course. He never had to begin his antics, for sooner or later, one of the ladies would approach him. The gentleman was so sure of himself; he began to try and guess which female would be the first to attempt an introduction.

He sipped his glass of wine and looked around the room once more. His gaze had fallen several times upon the small group of ladies, at whose center stood a ravishing creature, and by the way, she was observing him, the game; would, in his estimation, initiate very soon. Another sip of wine slipped passed his lips as he continued to let his thoughts wander. The manner in which the women went about meeting him often amused. He would give them points on just how well they used their minds to come up with an original idea. An original idea, however, was something that, as, of yet, seemed beyond any of them. Being original in anything was a rare characteristic with these so-called ladies. He found nothing real about any of them. Instead, they were all like sheep to him. They all talked alike, dressed alike, and God help him, acted almost identically. Those few he did give high scores to were those who refused to fall victim to his charms. Now, they were to be admired, and he found he would not toy with them for long. Most times, he would leave those ladies alone, respecting their wishes, but not always. It was the pursuit that drove his passion, not the conquest.

His name was Senor Francisco Armando y de la Garcia de Vega. To his close friends, he was merely Cisco. He was of definite Spanish heritage; there was no doubt in that. It was told that he came to New Orleans, from Spain, to start fresh in the land he'd fallen in love with and how he made his living was not common knowledge. Some claimed that he came from a very wealthy family and did not have to support himself by any means. This was, however, a mere rumor started by himself. After all, it was a necessity to have a high standing, to obtain invitations, to events such as this one. What amused him was that most of the invites came from anxious mothers, looking to make a good match for their eligible daughters. Those mothers who were blinded by what they thought they knew; that being, he was wealthy, single, and available, were many. Recently though, he had learned it was whispered that he was often seen at John Davis's house of gambling, and some assumed he made his money that way. For the prominent families, this unsavory distinction was a black mark, and therefore, he was not suitable for their daughters.

Cisco could not allow such suggestions to take hold, and therefore, he had decided his attendance was required to set in place a new persona and up the gaming field. The man took another sip of his wine as he reflected how already the new rumors had taken root as far as his reputation was concerned. The Spaniard had let it slip on purpose, early in the evening that he was at this time residing in a suite of rooms, at the largest of hotels, and his business dealings, which he never divulged, kept him away weeks at a time. So it was, the new persona he'd hopped to cultivate had soon been accepted and whispered among the guests. It was said he was buying vast tracks of land and intended to build only the most elegant home. After that rumor spread to the few doubters, he was once again a mysterious gentleman and an honorable citizen, something he intended to remain so. Having accomplished the resumption of his upstanding reputation, Cisco could now turn his attention to the real reason for his attendance.

The Spaniard had come here tonight to meet a certain woman, one he had been watching from a distance for some time, and he was not disappointed. Her entrance had been spectacular. The way she dressed for the evening had everyone abuzz, ladies and gentlemen, alike. The female in question was quite unlike all others he had met since coming to New Orleans. Instead, she invented it. Like a queen bee, with all the little workers swarming around her, she was far different from the rest of the 'hive.' She did not follow the day's trend, for that alone, he admired her. Like himself, she seemed to enjoy shocking people, but then something about her fascinated him, drawing him to her, like a moth to a flame. Cisco had become so caught up in observing her every move that he did not notice Simone approaching him, nor did he see the frustration that flashed in her eyes and expression.

As Simone neared the stranger, it was not hard to see what held his attention. Goddamn, that bitch thought Simone. She even had this one panting after her like a hound in heat. "Not this time," she mumbled under her breath. Duval's lover told herself, this was one fire she intended to put out, and reignite for herself, to enjoy later that evening. "I see, you are shocked by the gown that our dear Tori has chosen to wear this evening. It is shameful; is it not? Not to mention the color. A slap to widows such as myself."

Cisco looked at Simone through his deep chestnut-colored eyes, carefully hiding his emotions behind a cool mask of unreadable dimensions. He quickly sensed the jealousy and hatred behind her remark, despite the smile on her cold, porcelain face. He could have some fun here with this vixen, for undoubtedly, she was just that. "Did you say shameful? Why, Madame, I myself find it exciting that she should dare to be the first to expose such a fabulous new fashion." Crushing jab. Now, bring her hopes up, he told himself. "One, I might add, that I'm sure would look more ravishing on you, but do excuse me. I do not believe we have been introduced."

"Simone Claudette La Combe, Monsieur, and you are?" Was that her usually calm sultry voice that was quivering so, she wondered?

"My pleasure, I'm sure. I am Senor Francisco Armando y de la Garcia de Vega, at your service." He bowed low, taking her hand in his. Cisco's lips brushed lightly across the back of her knuckles as his fingers suggestively stroked the palm of her hand.

He openly smiled. The way his name rolled off his tongue never did cease to amaze him. Nor did the obvious reaction it had, on those so easily impressed, by what they assumed to be the name of nobility. "Tell me, did you say that you know that ravishing creature? I should very much like to make her acquaintance, to pay my compliments, of course." Just a little fuel on the fire of jealousy, he thought. Let's see what you will do with it.

Simone was seething on the inside yet smiling sweetly on the outside. Coyly Edward's woman maneuvered her damning blows toward Tori. "It is true she is an acquaintance of mine. I would be honored to introduce you to her." She placed her hand on his arm and leaned in to whisper her next remark. "I feel it only fair that I should warn such a fine gentleman as yourself; she is not the lady she pretends to be."

Cisco almost burst with laughter. He was really having fun now, but to laugh would only give away that he was merely toying with the stunning widow. No, instead, he took a step backward, and with a concerned look on his face, he questioned her. "You mean to inform me that a lady of your obvious standing has such a friend? I am shocked, or maybe I misunderstood you? She, like yourself, is a woman of status, is she not?" He could tell Simone was fuming and thoroughly confused, yet she played the game far better than most of her contemporaries. Her next move, he imagined, would be the old turn tail and run.

Simone was panicked a little, but turning around and leaving was the furthermost thought from her mind. She had to say something to the arrogant idiot, who was smitten by Tori. Simone had to ruin Laffite's bitch, without touching her own integrity in this man's eyes. A different tactic was needed here if she were to succeed. "You did indeed misunderstand me, Monsieur. On two counts, I might add. I did not claim her as my friend. Also, I did not mean her character is in question. It is just that the gown she wears…it was made to conceal, shall we say, flaws in her appearance. The woman had a child not long ago, and it is hard for a lady to maintain her youthful appearance once that has happened. You see before you a vain individual, I fear. She has herself so tightly pulled in by her undergarments; why I declare, she can hardly walk. The very act of breathing is strenuous for her, and she might very well burst the seams of her gown, were she to sit down. The desperate woman has nearly pushed out of it already."

Simone knew she was not making any sense and was babbling, but at least she had his attention, something that only spurred her on. "I have spoken out of turn, and surely you must think me terrible and brazen. Talking of such manner of things, to a gentleman such as yourself, but then I seem to sense that such talk does not shock you. I am correct in that assumption, am I not?" She traded her coy expression for her sexiest. Without needing words, she relayed her message quite clearly. 'I'm yours, and I want you now.'

If Cisco had not been so involved with his intention of meeting Tori, he would have taken this Simone up on such an open invite. After all, this was a new approach from a lady of her standing, and he gave her a high score. She had a fire in her that would be all-consuming and, if utilized to his advantage, could produce a night of pure pleasure. He would have to remember her for the future, but right then, he was interested in only one woman, and it was not Simone.

At first, he had no attention of angering the beauty standing by his side, but the devil be damned side of him took hold. His eyes ran slowly down Simone's body in an appreciative way. She was a beautiful vixen, and Cisco was sure he would be missing a good time in her bed, by what he was about to say, but he could not resist it. "You mean to say, Senora, that her figure is held in place, by a corset pulled so tightly, that it gives her the illusion of a youthful appearance? If so, then vain indeed." He seemed to ponder what he said, as if in doubt.

"That is so, I'm afraid. Victoria, known now as Tori to her inner circle, another vain act to gain attention. To change one's name has such vanity; she cannot let herself age as a woman should." Simone had him; she was certain. After all, he had begun doubting Tori's overall appearance. A smug smile curled the corners of her mouth ever so slightly.

"Then please explain to me how it is done? For, I do not see. I think it is you who is mistaken. Look at her gown closely, my dear. If it is a corset, such as you say, it would have to be invisible. For even the finest undergarments, such as the one you have on yourself, are visible to the well-trained eye, are they not? The material of her gown is such that even the smallest flaws would stand out."

Simone turned to look at Tori to see what he was talking about. Invisible indeed, she thought. Yet, the spectacle before her spoke for itself. For the first time, she saw the back of Tori's gown. The material seamlessly draped her body. It was stunning and formfitting. So fine was the design that the construction would never allow for an undergarment. Cisco's eye had detected the truth. If Laffite's wife did have a corset on, it would most definitely leave an outline and be visible to all.

The widow's mouth dropped open when she realized the stranger had pointed out the obvious and done so while enjoying himself.

The Spaniard bowed slightly, and with a slight grin playing on his lips, he made his intentions known. "If you will excuse me, I shall join her other admirers and introduce myself. Somehow I feel that you are suddenly in no frame of mind to have me meet the lady in question." With that, he left Simone standing alone and quite stunned by his actions. The man was chuckling to himself, as he sauntered away as if to add to her humiliation. Never had Simone been so publicly put in her place, and she was not happy.

Cisco told himself what happened had been entertaining and to think that he'd nearly passed this party up tonight for a game of cards. What a mistake that would have been, he thought. This night was positively more fun than he'd had in a long time, and it

538

was only beginning. His enthusiasm did not wain as he pondered a future when he would have the chance to see just how smooth he could be. Winning back Simone was going to prove interesting and challenging, after what he had done.

The Spanish gentleman had intended to introduce himself right away, but before he could join the woman in question, dinner was announced, and all moved toward the dining room.

Tori had no choice but to make her way toward the adjoining room and hope to find a seat next to someone friendly and maybe even a person she and Jean knew. Without Jean, the last thing she wanted to happen was to be seated anywhere close to Simone and or Edward. With that as her focus, she spotted a place by a dear friend of the Destrehans. It was to this seat, Tori made her way, pleased that it would place her close to the door and out of earshot of Simone, Edward, and their friends.

The older gentleman did not hesitate when Tori joined him. "Allow me, my dear," he said as he pulled her chair away from the table.

"That is very kind of you, Frederick. I was hoping to sit close enough to Marie or J.D. as we have much catching up to do."

"Oh, my dear, that won't happen tonight. Both of them left quite suddenly, I fear. Something to do with a family matter, I do believe. I hope my company is not a disappointment." Frederick smiled kindly, and seeing that all the ladies, including the hostess, were now seated, he gladly joined Tori.

Jean's wife was surprised as she had not seen the Destrehans depart. "I do hope it is nothing serious."

"I believe they were in a hurry but not overly upset. With a family as large as theirs, one can only assume it has something to do with the children. Do not worry, Madame; let us enjoy our meal."

"If you say so. I will inquire later as to their reason for departing so early."

"A most prudent action, my dear."

Tori looked around the room and had to admire the setting. As always, and like most homes, the lighting was subdued. Two sixteen-foot-long tables sparkled with the crystal glasses and silverware, and every seat was occupied. The stemware did not sit empty long, and for that, she was thankful, because she was now becoming concerned over Jean's continued absence and needed to fortify her nerves.

Laffite's wife had seen the governor and Edward arrive late and found that they looked too pleased with themselves about something. Also, Tori could hardly miss that they kept looking toward her during the meal. To her, it seemed as if she herself somehow was the source of their continued enjoyment. How that could be, she did not have a clue? Unless it was her attire that held their attention. Tori decided to look the other way and talk with Frederick, but before she had a chance to do so, the evening's calm atmosphere was interrupted.

Simone burst out with laughter so loud that the dinner party stopped talking briefly to look her way. She blushed politely and put her napkin to her lips, trying to hide her continued mirth. With her outburst under control, the meal continued, and people went back to their polite conversations. The food was served, and thankfully, Frederick chatted about the rebuilding of New Orleans. Tori could listen to him without paying much attention. Her worry was Simone and her odd actions. Edward's lover had been content to sit sipping her wine, picking at her meal, and looking toward Tori with a look of triumph on her face.

WHEN dinner ended, everyone made their way back into the grand living room where they gathered in small groups, and rather than stand there, wondering what to do; Tori excused herself. She had noticed that the atmosphere in the house felt almost hostile. The reason behind such a sudden change among the guests evaded her, but it did leave her feeling most unwelcome.

Tori anxiously stepped outside onto the verandah for some air to sort out what was going on. She'd let the women gather, and the men smoke while making up her mind as to what her next course of action should be. What she wanted most of all was Jean, but he was not with her, so second best was to be alone right where she was. The worried female took in a deep breath, and as she exhaled, her mind began to put things into perspective. The whole evening had changed right after dinner. Somehow it had turned ugly, and it was obvious how both friends and enemies alike were watching her and whispering amongst themselves. That was the one thing that upset her; that they should be openly gossiping as they were, without even trying to hide that she was the subject of whatever was happening. The puzzled female looked back inside through the glass doors to confirm her suspicions. Maybe she had just imagined everything, but what she witnessed right then both surprised and shocked her. The men had forgone their traditional smoke and had joined the women instead.

UPON seeing Tori looking into the house from outside, a few of the guests looked away uncomfortably, confirming whatever was going on was not her imagination, after all. People, whom she knew well, were turning their backs to her? If only Marie and J.D. had not left so soon, because if they were inside, Tori would have an answer, or at least, allies. Her eyes locked with her dinner partner Fredrick and even he snubbed her, but not before shooting her what could only be described as an ugly glare.

At that moment, Tori did not have a clue what to do about any of it. Just standing there looking inside was not about to solve anything, plus she did not like feeling she was on display. No one had stepped outside to join her, and none looked like they would, so there would be no friends and no answers forthcoming. Her gut twisted in a knot, and rather than continue to stand where she could be scrutinized, Tori turned and walked to the edge of the open area and looked up at the night sky and whispered. "What am I supposed to do now, tell me that?"

The air was crisp and felt good. It was just what she needed to clear her mind. The new moon was shining down on her, and somewhere, Jean was on his way to join her. Damn, she hoped he would get there soon or she would have to leave. Being there without him by her side was just no fun, not any longer anyway.

The sound of the glass doors opening broke the night's silence, and the noise from within escaped the interior to flood over the patio. The tranquility and her solitude had been interrupted just as her thoughts had. Somewhat upset by the distraction, the lonely female turned to see who the intruder might be and was met by the icy expression of Simone's frosty glare. The two of them silently stood facing each other for what seemed to be forever in Tori's mind. Both women were trying to judge the other's intent and wait to see who would break the awkward silence first.

In the end, it was Tori who spoke. "Really, Simone, we had better stop meeting on verandahs. You do remember our first meeting, no doubt? I don't think that Jean would like it much. The idea of you following me out here that is. He might think you like me or something."

"I don't give a damn what he thinks, or you for that matter," Simone snapped back. Then she walked right up to Tori and stood grinning at her.

Tori was not going to let her intimidate her, so she shot right back with another quip. "My, my, such language. Do you kiss your mother with that mouth? Oh, of course not. She doesn't even talk to you. Wonder why?" At least that wiped the grin off her face, Tori told herself. She was thinking, 'see how you like them apples, lady,' when Simone made her move.

"Bitch," she hissed loudly, followed quickly by slapping Tori's cheek.

The blow was hard enough to cause Tori to take a step backward. The slap had stung and left her dumbfounded.

Seizing the moment, Simone continued. "Let me tell you, Miss high and mighty, if you think having your family not talk to you is bad, I can't imagine having no one in New Orleans talk to you, and that's what's about to happen to you. Your Jean can't help you either, as it's his fault everyone will turn against you."

Simone was almost laughing as she tried to contain her excitement, but Tori would be damned if she'd show how much her face was hurting or how worried this woman had her. The woman's slap had not only stunned her; it had left a burning sensation that almost made her cry. However, right then, her worries seemed to fade, as fury and rage took over. 'She is a real see you next Tuesday', Tori thought. 'One that has asked for it now, no holds barred, I am going to shrink her down to size and without stooping to anything physical either.'

Taking a step toward Simone, Tori spoke in a lowered voice. "Just what in the hell are you talking about? I think you have gone over the edge, my dear. Someone had better take you home before you stumble and hurt yourself. You have the ravings of a drunk, Simone. Don't think I did not notice how much you consumed and how little you ate. Dangerous combination. Better be careful, or you might find what little you did eat, tossing up all over the place." Seeing the smile fade from Simone's face, as she swayed a little, Tori continued. "See, I am right; a person in your condition does not know what they are talking about, let alone remain standing for long."

Words or actions would not deter Edward's lover. She was too fired up, and she'd be damned if she would stop before exposing the events surrounding Laffite's demise. "I'll tell you what I'm talking about, and they are not drunk ravings either. No one, who is anyone, will talk to the likes of you after tonight." She took in a deep breath and then spoke very slowly. "That is when the news of Jean's arrest for smuggling stolen goods is talked about all around town. Not the only one arrested either. He, along with his brother and many of his men sit in jail right now, and when this is common knowledge… when it becomes public, you will be shunned. Shunned like you already are by those inside in case you didn't notice."

Tori could not believe her, and yet, why would she lie? This information could be the answer as to why everyone was acting strangely. Her face had gone pale, and her expression was grave as she mulled over the bad news.

Simone's face had done the direct opposite. Sheer joy emanated in her voice, and her face flushed with excitement. "Yes, you heard, right. The whole load of them are sitting in the calaboose as we speak. Caught red-handed, with their stolen goods I hear. Oh, what a shame, such a waste. I hear they hang pirates, but what would I know. Oh, one more little fact, there is not a damn thing you or your husband can do about that. It's said that Claiborne himself was witness to the entire ordeal; he was the one who apprehended them all." Simone forced a laugh of sorts from between her smirking lips, as she continued almost hysterically and out of control. She was filled with a vengeance that fed her wicked amusement. Nothing was about to stop her or her cruel intentions. "You can do one little itty-bitty thing, when and if, you get to see him…Jean that is. You can tell him that Edward finally got even with him, and my poor dear, you can be sure he's not finished with you yet. He, for some strange reason, beyond my comprehension, seems to feel he is owed something. I wonder what that could be?"

With nothing left to say and feeling victorious, Simone turned and walked inside. She was looking for Edward to let him know that she'd spoken to Laffite's bitch. He would get an enormous amount of enjoyment out of her actions. They both could watch Tori try to pull herself together. Watch how she'd have to walk back inside, in front of everyone, in total shame, knowing her husband was in chains for piracy. There was no doubt about it; that task was sure to be difficult for her.

Tori was left alone and in shock. She had no reason not to believe what Edward's lover had just told her. It explained everything from Jean's absence, to the way people had been acting, ever since the governor and he had arrived. That was why the pair had looked so smug and pleased with themselves. There was no doubt that they had slowly and deliberately spread the news, to further their own pleasure, and humiliate her more. Then more clarity hit, as instantly the reason behind Simone's outburst at the dinner table was explained. It had to be due to the bitch learning about the arrest from Edward. That's why she had laughed out loud. Why the black widow had sat and smirked at her throughout dinner.

Tori's world was collapsing around her. Turning and looking up at the sky once more, her emotions raged inside her. They were emotions from anger to panic, to sadness, and finally to the utter loneliness of the moment. Had she done this, caused all this by being in the wrong time? Once again, she found herself troubled by the old familiar idea that she could indeed be changing history, and if so, how could she stop? What about the Battle of New Orleans? Would it happen now? Could her being there change that outcome too? The frightened woman hugged herself and shook her head from side to side. One truth was painfully evident. She could not go back inside and face what by now, would be a very unforgiving crowd. Even those who sided with her and Jean would not do so in public for fear of reprisals. Like Simone had told her, there was nothing she could do. There was no way to avoid the ridicule and hostilities that would greet her once she stepped inside. At least it would be brief because there would be no way she'd stay and try to reason with those who were so quick to judge and take sides against her and her husband. All she needed was a bit of time to get up the courage to face them, and face them she would.

Tori continued to look upward to the heavens as if to gain strength from its sheer vastness. Instead, the night sky, so full of stars, made her feel small and helpless. The moon, which had looked friendly just a short while ago, now looked as if it too were laughing. What in the hell was she going to do, she asked herself repeatedly? How could she make things right?

A shooting star shot across the night sky, falling to earth in a fireball of silent splendor, and Tori spoke out loud in a voice filled with despair. "How I wish you were a 747 that I could board and get the hell out of here. I don't belong, and we both know it." Her eyes were filling with unspent tears as her frustration grew. Tori needed someone, anyone to be there for her, but she had no one, and at that moment, her mind began to imagine all sorts of outcomes for the scenario she now found herself caught in. Then before she had time to wonder, even more, a stranger's voice spoke to her from among the shadows.

"If a person could afford one, don't you think a private jet would be better?"

Her heart skipped a beat. Had she heard, right? It was impossible; it had to be. Her rational mind told her she had to have been imagining the voice. Yet, knowing this was not so, her eyes scanned the darkness for where the stranger, whoever he was, surely stood. At first, she saw nothing, and again, she began to wonder if her mind had played tricks on her. Then while trying to accept that fact, she told herself if there was one thing she desperately needed to do right then, it was to keep a grip on her emotions and thoughts and not go crazy.

"I repeat, myself, don't you think a private jet would be better?" The stranger stepped out from the shadows and stood looking at her. He tried to smile while watching her tormented face. All the man wanted to do right then was offer his help to this lovely lady from his time. "I can assure you I am quite real, and no, you are not going nuts. I, on the other hand, almost lost it when that bitch slapped you. Maybe you will forgive me for not stepping forward, but then, you handled her quite nicely yourself."

Tori took a step backward. This was real; he was real, and if so, how was he here?

"Look, I know what she told you is a shock, and it is truthful, I am sad to say, but then you know that."

Tori answered him in a shaky voice that even to her ears didn't sound convincing. "I do not know that for certain. She could be playing a cruel joke. That would be right up her alley."

"I am afraid, not this time. Look, the rumor about the news began to spread shortly after the governor and his friend joined the party. Nasty piece of work he is, the man who sat next to the governor. He was bragging openly. They quite enjoyed themselves at dinner, didn't they? One would have thought that at least Claiborne would have had the decency to take you aside to inform you."

Tori ignored this statement. She didn't give a damn about anything or anyone else right then. All she cared about was the man who stood before her. By what he had declared, he was more than just another ordinary stranger; he was like her. "I don't understand. Who are you? How are you here?"

"I am your new friend, and by the looks of it, my arrival is just in time. No, pun, I assure you." He stood still and let her process this last statement. Her expression still held pain and worry, but there was also a look of bewilderment. The red mark from Simone's slap was fading, but Tori's loneliness and confusion was not.

The stranger understood only too well how she was feeling at this moment. He had felt the same way until he'd adjusted to his circumstances. That had been a difficult time, but nothing like what she was facing right then. Plus, he'd had help, someone to cover his back, and that's what she would be in desperate need of now. Tori needed a friend, someone who really understood her. No one inside the house could offer her that. Time and fate had brought them together, and none too soon it seemed.

The stranger stepped forward slowly. It would not take much to convince her that he, like her, came from the future. That was the easy part; the dodgy part was going to be convincing her that he intended no harm. He had to get her to accept his friendship and help, but would Tori Laffite let him do either?

# END OF BOOK THREE

Watch for the conclusion of the
Legends of NOLA series:

*Enemies and Allies*

# Acknowledgements

I WISH TO thank my family, who visited New Orleans countless times over the years with me. Long before the internet was available, I had to do hours upon hours of research in and around the French Quarter. I want to thank all three of my children and offer my apology to them for all the times our family vacations involved plantations and battle sites. Somehow you endured the endless road trips with laughter and understanding.

I want to thank the Louisiana Historical Association and the Research Center on Charter Street. The personnel there never let me down or ceased to amaze me. One of my proudest moments came when they accepted a copy of my book for their archives.

The Destrehan Plantation was not open to the public when Daniel, my husband, and I first came upon it. They were battening down for an approaching hurricane when we pulled onto the grounds. Mr. Joseph Maddox listened to my husband's plea and was gracious enough to give us a personal tour and history of the place. We have since returned to visit Destrehan many times, and though our paths have never crossed with Mr. Maddox again, I wanted him to know that I did try my best to keep the historical facts correct as promised. From the shell of a neglected building all those years ago, now stands a proud and fine example of a historic plantation home. It is open for tours, and I highly recommend a visit.

To my friend, MaryChris Bradley, there are no words that can express my deep gratitude for all your help and wisdom. Without you, this book would still be sitting on my computer.

I would also like to thank the fine people I met at Lafitte's Blacksmith Shop, located on Bourbon Street. It was because they were always willing to talk about the building and its history that I was shown "the writing on the wall." May I suggest if you are ever in New Orleans, that you visit this bar, and be sure to tell them I sent you.

Ask to see the writing and the Lovers in Stone. I won't put a spoiler here; let us just say you will understand when you read the story. It is guaranteed to give you goose bumps.

Finally, with all my heart, thank you to Jean Laffite and Tori, for letting me tell their story and for never letting me give up. Together, we somehow always found a way to validate the historical events that unfolded in your epic adventure. I shall always miss your voices, your laughter, and you. It was hard saying good-bye, and it was not until I found myself typing Jean's good-bye that I could finally let go.

"Tommy's Song" by Goldillox, is available at: Spotify, Amazon, Google Play, eMusic, Simfy, Deezer, Rhapsody, X-Box Live, MixRadio, MUVE Music, and other music sites.

# About the Author

**D.S. Elliston** currently lives in Florida. Most days will find her in her office, accompanied by her two cats who love to play in her numerous piles of notes. She admits she loves the long hours of compiling research material and historical facts for her projects.

*Legends of NOLA* is a multi-book saga. Her writing goal is to thoroughly entrance the reader to such a point, that they don't realize they are receiving a history lesson.

All her books are fiction based on fact and leave many wondering if the adventure they read actually happened or not.

Made in the USA
Middletown, DE
26 November 2023

43499570R00315